PRAISE FOR HOLLY LISLE AND *TALYN*

"[A] stern and stirring treatise on the dangers of enforced peace and the virtues of paranoid preparation for the worst."

—*Publishers Weekly*

"Lisle has crafted an original plot, and its world and characters are very convincing." —*Booklist*

"Yet again, Holly Lisle creates a world and society that completely absorbs the reader. A lot of fantasy has been written about the destructive effects of war. I think this is the first tale I've ever read that admits that peace, too, can bring a devastation of its own. The Tonks are a well-realized culture, and the warrior class in particular is painted with a detail that brings the characters to life. Lisle presents an unflinching examination of relationships amidst this clash of societies. This is not your average fat fantasy book. This will be worth more than one read."

—Robin Hobb

"It's always a delight to read [Lisle's] books." —S. L. Viehl

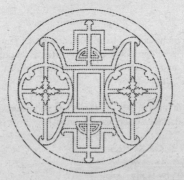

Talyn

A NOVEL OF KORRE

Holly Lisle

TOR®
fantasy

A TOM DOHERTY ASSOCIATES BOOK
NEW YORK

This is a work of fiction. All the characters and events portrayed in this novel are either fictitious or are used fictitiously.

TALYN: A NOVEL OF KORRE

Edited by Anna Genoese

Maps by Ellisa Mitchell

A Tor Book
Published by Tom Doherty Associates, LLC
175 Fifth Avenue
New York, NY 10010

www.tor.com

Tor® is a registered trademark of Tom Doherty Associates, LLC.

ISBN-13: 978-0-765-34873-9
ISBN-10: 0-765-34873-X

First Edition: August 2005
First Mass Market Edition: December 2006

Printed in the United States of America

0 9 8 7 6 5 4 3 2 1

For Sheila Kelly,
Who liked this one best.

Good friends are blessings.
Thank you.

Acknowledgments

Deepest appreciation and heartfelt thanks to:

Matthew, for being wonderful and supportive and encouraging and inspirational, and for having faith . . . and for telling me, "Do something, dammit," when it mattered most;

Jean Schara, Scott Bryan, Jim Woosley, and Sheila Kelly, for the first draft read-through and comments;

the folks at the Forward Motion Writers Community (http://fmwriters.com), for all the years of encouragement and support, and for understanding the importance of cold water and the sword when it was time for me to go;

Robin Rue, for finding this book a wonderful home and a wonderful editor;

Anna Genoese, for being that wonderful editor.

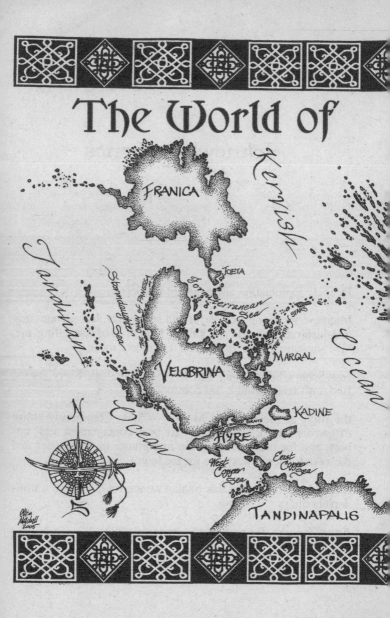

The World of

FRANICA

Kerrish

Tandinian

Stormdaughter Sea

THE HAND OF PANESSA

JOETA

Formediterranean Sea

Ocean

THE PATH OF STARS

MARQAL

VELOBRINA

KADINE

N

Ocean

STRAITS

HYRE

West Copper Sea

East Copper Sea

S

TANDINAPALIS

Olivia
Midwell
2005

Korre

BAEKI

SINALI

Sinalian Sea

ISLANDS of the FALLEN SUN

Tandinian Ocean

Brindle Sea

Spalli Sea

Sea of Somor

GRETON

Gold Channel

TANDINAPALIS

BANIKA

VELOBRINA

PINDAS

Brittlebreak

JOETAAK

ERYESTAAK

ONTAAK

MATTAAK

West Bay

BEYLTAAK

SAVISTAAK

INJTAAK

CONFEDERACY

MEAK MOUNTAINS

JOONTAAK CHAAVTAAK

BIRCHTAAK

KRAATA MOUNTA

LODESTAAK

WESTERN

NIITAAK

of

HYRE

RIVER

MIRTAARY

HAVARTAAK

FDING RIVERS

DINTTAAK

RIVER

RIVER

KOPATAAK

GOATAAK

HWEESTAAK

BONDESSTAAK

STITAAK

GALETAAK

Harsh Bay

West

AKLINTAAK

HARSH

Copper

HARSH
POINT

Sea

FISHTAAK

DRAVITAAK

STONELA

Ellisa Mitchell 2005

STONELA

Rules of Pronunciation

Tonk
All letters are pronounced.

Doubled vowels
Vowels are pronounced first vowel long and stressed, second vowel short and unstressed.

Doubled consonants
Consonants are "bounced"—pronounced once and then lightly pronounced again.

Following these examples:
haddar : HA-duh-DAY-ar
Tiirsha (one of Talyn's surnames) : TIE-ir-shuh
taak : TAY-ack

More information on the language, costuming, and customs of the world of Korre can be found at http://www.hollylisle.com.

Pada and I stepped out of the Shields Building at twenty past the Dog on the last day of Madrigas to find shreds of the moon peering out from behind scattered clouds offering the only light on the dock. The air bit into me—my light uniform had been enough when I went in, but while I worked, early spring had given way to tenacious winter, and I was not more than three steps away from the warmth of Shields when I wished I had my cloak.

"Lamplighters are late again," Pada said. Pada has a great gift for stating the obvious. Conversations with her ever include such statements as "Ah, the tide is high" and "Well, the streets are certainly crowded today," which makes her wearing company to keep.

The whores who clustered by the front door late at night, hoping for safer custom than from sailors in port, gave us good even, and we nodded acknowledgment. We in Shields guard all the taak, and the lands beyond, and we thus represent all.

Beneath our feet, the ancient boards of the dock creaked and shuddered. Beyltaak has no money for renovation, but I wonder every time I step out the door of Shields, if this will be the time the boards concede defeat and dump me into the icy bay. To our right lay the warehouses—looming hulks of black against black, since the lamplighters had not been through. To our left, the ships—and I couldn't help but notice how few rose and fell against the wharf, their wooden hulls bumping softly at their moorings, their furled sails flapping in the wind off the bay. Poor business, and in spite of that, the inescapable stink of fish.

When we were past the whores, Pada picked up the thread of her previous narrative in midsentence. ". . . and then he said, 'I would that you would, with me, just once, for I dream even when waking of knowing the pleasure of you.'" Pada rolled her eyes. "And *then* he offered me whole bolts of fine ribbed velvet in red and purple, as if I was some street tart who'd flop on my back for his bedamned rags."

I watched Pada from the corner of my eye. Even in the dark, I could see her fury. She's prettier than me—delicate and blond and fair, with huge blue eyes and the features that gather men's glances like flowers attract bees. She takes all such adulation as her birthright—as her due. But she thinks men should just admire her from afar, and give her things. "If you don't want him to make such offers, stop leading him around by the nose."

Pada stopped dead on the dock and stared at me as if I'd slapped her. I was watching the whores behind us, and the dark cluster of bones players before us, and movement at the mouth of the alley just beyond that, and I thought perhaps, whether we were in uniform or not, we might keep moving. None of those on the dock at that moment were the best of company. But no, Pada *would* have her dramatic piece.

"I?! Leading him around by his nose?! He clings to me like a motherless calf. And for this, I should take his cloth and bed him?!"

I decided to get moving again; unlike Pada, I do not trust the Shielder uniform to keep away all evil, any more than I trust my looks to turn all men to pudding. I'm tall, with nice eyes and features that people call either strong or angular—or sometimes handsome. My mother was a great beauty in her day, but all I got from her was good thick auburn hair. The rest of me is a female version of my father. It's a look that works much better for my brothers.

"Talyn, do *not* walk off and leave me when I'm speaking with you," Pada shouted from behind me.

I kept walking, and after a moment heard her clipped steps

hurrying to catch up. Good. I wanted to get off the dock and into the safer, already-lighted part of Beyltaak.

Pada caught up with me as we passed the gamblers. They paused to touch fingers to forehead, and again we nodded acknowledgment, and kept moving.

Under her breath, Pada hissed, "Think you I should bed him for his cloth? That I should let him value me so lightly?"

"Not what I was saying at all," I told her. "I think you should have pogged him months ago, without any gifts or bribes." I kept watching her from the corner of my eye. "Had it been me, I would have dragged him into a closet, ripped his fine velvet off him, and ridden him until he screamed." She turned horrified eyes to me, and I had to hide my smile. Shielders live under Ethebet's Law, but to the best of my knowing, Pada has never once availed herself of her privileges. Instead, she guards her dusty virginity like the least privileged of Mindan taakswomen. I added, "If you have a fine bull in your corral, don't cry ruin when he won't pretend he's a steer for you."

She dared not respond to that, so she returned to her original rant. "Ribbed velvet!" she said. "It's insulting. Some of the Shielders get gold and diamonds and bolts of Drabadi silk and apartments on the bay from their lovers."

I'd been hearing this part of the refrain for at least two months now—so often I think I could have done it word for word in tandem with her. I knew what was coming next—and indeed, it came.

"He could sell his bedamned ribbed velvet and get me that little place on Short Street if he *really* loved me."

I have the patience of the Five Saints—mostly—and have learned the art of keeping my tongue still in my head when around Pada, who has all the discretion of the wind. But at that moment a long day fighting heavy attacks while waiting for replacements who arrived late, and dealing with a new commander brought in from Havartaak who must have been sent to us to keep his previous command from killing themselves—added to sheer weariness at Pada's endless complaining—overcame me, and I said what I really thought.

"And then the difference between you and the working girls waiting back at the Shields door would be . . . ?"

In most instances, I've found it a poor idea to tell a friend what you really think, if what you think is not what your friend thinks—and I have generally found this out by doing it, and living to regret it. This time was no different. I heard the words hit the night, and cringed, and Pada leapt into me.

"How *dare* you?! How *dare*?! To suggest that I could be compared in any way to a . . . a *whore* . . ."

In for the whisper, in for the shout. "Because it's true," I said. "You are offended not because he tried to bribe you to bed him, but because you didn't think his bribe was good enough. You say if he loved you, he would give you something bigger and better—but if you loved him, you would not want silks or diamonds or apartments. You would want only him. As you set this up, Pada, your virtue is no issue—only your price."

I think had she carried a blade, she would have run me through in that instant, the murder in her eyes shone so clear. But she had her tongue with her, and in a pinch that always seems to serve. "You're a fine one to talk of virtue," she snarled. "You'd bed a man because you liked the color of his eyes."

I smiled a little. "I *have* pogged a man because I liked the color of his eyes. And enjoyed every minute of it, too. And got nothing from it but the pleasure of the business and a wonderful week with him a year later, when he took his week's leave in Beyltaak just so we could be together."

"And you haven't heard from him again, have you?"

"I have not."

"Because no man can respect a woman who does not guard her virtue."

"Because he got killed in the mountains when the northern line moved and the Shielders in his unit got separated from the Senders."

This set Pada still for a moment. I hoped it might embarrass her enough that she would put her nattering to bed for the night, but I do not have this sort of good fortune. She started back quick enough—but at least on a subject other than poor nose-ringed Dosil the velvet merchant.

"What happened with you and that broaching spell today? I thought sure you'd missed it entirely, and I was moving to intercept it when at the last instant you blocked it."

So our new topic was to be my inadequacy. Joy. Friends from

work rarely become friends in the true sense—in all the years I'd been in the Shielders, I had yet to make a friend I thought I would want to see if ever the war ended and the Joint Forces released me from duty. Proximity, danger, and the fact that our lives depend on each other all meld us into a unit, but many of us are of metals that do not blend well.

But, ah—the war. We will not soon see the end of that. For three hundred years and a score, we of the Confederacy of Hyre, who hold the western half of Hyre, have been locked in battle with those king-pimping bastards from the Eastil Republic; we fight for independent home rule for each taak, and for the democratic voice of the citizenry, for moderate taxation and the right of all capable citizens to use magic. The Eastils fight to force their king and his government by representation on us, and with it heavy taxes, endless restrictions, and both votes and magic in the hands of only those whom that shit-gobbling, child-devouring King Trimus deems worthy. We also dispute ownership of a couple of prime pieces of land and one tremendous bay, but ours is no mere squabble over real estate. We Confederates are almost exclusively descended from the proud, free, nomadic Tonks who once roamed the steppes of southern Tandinapalis. Some of us can trace our lineage a thousand years. Those Eastils are a mixed and grubby lot, most of them descendants of prisoners sentenced to the colony on eastern Hyre before the war began; criminals drawn from cesspools and prisons and brothels in Velobrina, Kadine, Marqal, and even Franica and the Path of Stars. Some of them, or their ancestors, fled there voluntarily hoping to practice their weird religions and weirder predilections. And there they all remain . . . and scum, as everyone knows, breeds nothing but more scum. So until we defeat them and force them to either see reason or flee, our war will go on.

"The Eastils threw a unit of a different sort of Senders against our detail," I said. "They've a new twist on their shield-broacher spell that hides anything coming head-on. I could not see the one you mention when it first came at the shield; only a slight sideways turn in its arc put it back into my sights. It could well have come through on me."

"I thought perhaps you were not concentrating," Pada said.

The thought that I could shove her off the dock and into the bay crossed my mind, and evidently my eyes, because she immediately backtracked. "But you said . . . a new spell?"

Changing the subject is as close to an apology as Pada will go. I didn't pursue her slur—I just said, "They've come up with something subtle. I suspect if we cannot backtrail their Senders and have our Senders destroy them, they're going to be trouble."

"Not for me." Pada looked smug.

"Oh? You learn some new magic I need to know about?" I kept my voice even. It has been a rough day for everyone, I reminded myself. Don't shove her in the bay. Don't shove her in the bay.

We came even with that alley I'd been watching—and out of the shadows stepped two men, both big, both armed with long knives, both staring at the two of us unblinking. They reeked of cheap wine and salban smoke, and they wove from side to side as they stood.

I braced myself and ran personal defense and attack spells through my head and tried to remember who had last been court-martialed for use of magic against civilians, and how that had gone.

The bigger of the two—Mountain Left, I thought—said, "You're . . . shuh . . . shuh . . . Shielders, aren't you?"

"We are," I said, praying under my breath that those two would suddenly get scared and run away. If I remembered correctly, that last court-martial had ended in a permanent placement in eternally frozen Gavas Base.

"We juh . . . juh . . . jusht wanted to thank you. Good work." They raised their daggers to their foreheads and bowed, and I could envision sliced foreheads or one of them losing his balance and sprawling forward and running me through by accident. But they survived the salute and so did we. They faded into the shadows, we hurried on our way, and my heart moved out of the back of my mouth and down into my chest where it belonged.

I am daily grateful for the Shielders uniform, and for the men and women who have fought so long and hard to make it a symbol of good.

As uniforms go, it's rather ordinary. Emerald swordsman's shirt, front-lacing vest and pants, both in black camlet cloth, low-heeled soft leather boots, and the beret. The Shielder beret is black, too, and the pin on the front is the sword and star. Unit insignia, ribbons, and ranks go on the vest and the shirt's dropped shoulders, just above the sleeve gathers. But all Shielders wear the same beret, and that beret is, many times, more magic than we would dare cast. It can be a symbol of fear—for each wearer is a warrior and a master of magic, and if pressed we can link into the web of active Shielders to channel the power with which we can defend ourselves or protect others—but it is also a symbol of respect and devotion and love. We hold the line for everything we love—and everything our fellow citizens in the Confederacy and its many taaks love.

Only Senders, who wear a variant of the same uniform, differing in nothing but the color of shirts and berets—garnet—and two crossed lightning bolts as their beret pin, receive the same respect as Shielders. The Conventionals—cavalry, foot, artillery, engineers, and miners—see us as doing the least work and getting the most glory. But they cannot do what we do. They volunteer—joining at nineteen or twenty, and serving a six-year enlistment, after which they can choose to stay or choose to return to civilian life.

We in Magics—Senders, Shielders, and even Intelligence—wake up one morning, shortly after reaching adolescence, to find our mothers crying over our beds up in the eaves and men in uniform down in the kitchen waiting to tell us that we have magical talent that has manifested and that we will be going with them. Intelligence knows before we know. And their people get to us the instant they discover us. I was thirteen when they came for me. Pada was twelve. Some of my comrades have started as young as ten.

The first thing they tell us is that we will be in the service of the Confederacy until we break or die. Not an easy thing to find out as a child. They train us, they hurt us, they take everything we have and everything we love away from us . . . and then, gradually, they give us power, and skill, and privilege. We pay for it with our lives and futures, but we are in turn well paid. With respect. With love. With some freedoms beyond those enjoyed by other citizens.

And yet, I cared little for magic and would have given away even Ethebet's Law for a chance to pursue my own loves and dreams.

We stepped off the dock onto the reassuringly solid bricks of Sheep Street, and around a corner onto Market Street, and Pada said, "And there's the Star's Rest," breaking the silence with another of her startling observations.

"And the sky is, miracle of miracles, still dark at night," I muttered too softly for her to hear me. She would not have appreciated my sarcasm.

The Star's Rest is Magics' place—Shielders, Senders, Intelligence, and those few we choose to bring with us. The doormen know us by name, as we know them: old Shielders and Senders introduce the new; old doormen stand watch alongside new to make sure each knows the people he should. Magics owns the Star, just as Conventional owns the Rowdy Bosom over on Hasty Street, and within the Star's walls we have our own tiny kingdom. We pay our doormen well, both in tips and favors, and in return they keep the world away when we would spend a little time among our own, private and—because we are in private—able to behave or misbehave without censure, and without bringing shame on the uniform.

Mardoc greeted Pada and me with a bow and a faint, sad smile. "Is all well with you?" I asked him, and he nodded, but added, "How well it is with the rest of the world remains to be seen." He ushered us through, and closed the door quickly behind us.

Pada and I tucked our berets into the cap loop on the left side of our pants, walked through the foyer, and moved to the West Dining Room; but even before we saw inside, we both felt the wrongness in the Star. From the gathering rooms to the front and the recreation rooms in back and even the bedrooms upstairs, quiet bore down on us—the murmurs of voices kept low like the slow roll of breakers along the shore, an absence of laughter, and whispers everywhere, when anything short of shouts inside the Star's Rest usually proved futile. Our annoyance with each other put aside, Pada and I exchanged worried glances and hurried into the dining room.

From a back table, a familiar voice. "Heya! Talyn, Pada! We've seats and news."

My friend Karl. He and I, sent together to an emplacement near the front lines just prior to what our intelligence assured us was going to be a hellish combination attack, had spent the eve before the battle taking what comfort we could find from each other, so certain were we that we would die on the morrow. We did not, and our familiarities with each other have been a source of some discomfort to each of us in the intervening years. We remain friends, but suffer awkwardness in each other's company when alone. In spite of the fact that Karl is as square jawed and broad shouldered as the hero of any saga, with gleaming black hair and eyes like anthracite, neither he nor I ever made any pretence of love in our brief, desperate union. Whatever we've been looking for, it isn't each other.

Beside him sat short, pert, chirpy Dardie, his current lover and one of the Shielders on his watch, who did *not* know of Karl's and my indiscretion; and beside Dardie sat her runner, Jass—Intelligence's newest find, and a nice little boy. I put him at twelve. He still suffered from homesickness and yearned to go back to the life he'd imagined before his magic interfered. When they took him away from home, Dardie gathered him in like a lost hatchling, and he followed her around everywhere. It breaks your heart to see it—we all started there, but we never realize how pathetic we were until we watch the new ones wandering around all lost and scared.

I took a seat beside Jass while Pada scooted into the booth next to Karl.

One of the serving girls came by, and I ordered black lager and a thick steak—rare—and steamed greens. Pada got herself brown stew and one of those weak little horse-piss beers she claims to like—she thinks she's too delicate for a real drink. But what do I know; maybe she is.

When the serving girl left, I leaned forward and said, "What of the news, then? Has a city fallen to the Eastils? The front line moved closer? New magic against us?"

"Rumors of a cease-fire," Karl said, and sat back.

"Where?" Pada asked.

Karl shook his head. "Not a *local* cease-fire. A real cease-fire—the whole line, negotiations on both sides with the *Feegash* standing in the middle to arbitrate, and the possibility of an actual stand-down for all of us."

The girl came back with the drinks—mine and Pada's, and

refreshers for Karl and Dardie and Jass, who drank his lager black as mine. Good lad. I nodded to him, and he caught my glance, grinned a little, and took a sip. Didn't choke, either.

The serving girl left again, and I said, "Pig balls. Not even the Feegash could untangle our war, nor would they try."

Pada agreed. "The disputed High Valleys and all the riches they contain remain disputed, and Whayre Harbor sits idle, with the richest fishing and the best trade routes blocked and under attack."

I nodded. "And how do we reach settlement, when *we* are free, while the Eastils have their pissless agglomeration of a republic where the few speak for the many and not a city or town can raise its own army or mint its own coin or field its own defenses, and where the money flows to king and court and damned little flows back? Are the Eastils suddenly come to reason, to disband their republic and their monarchy? Or are we expected to bow, who have not bowed to man or god in our lives?"

Karl said, "I don't know how it's to be done. I don't know what they're saying, or what they're planning, but I know at least some of the rumors are true. My brother Borin came in from the front lines today, and told me the Feegash observers are supposed to be arriving on the morrow, with the first light. They're to be on both sides of the line. They will offer themselves hostage to the cease-fire while their negotiators work out the details."

My food came—a slab of meat thick as my wrist, charred black on the outside, good and bloody on the inside, and with it, some of the Star's fire-sauce, and red-top and root-greens so lightly steamed they still crunched when I ate them. Perfect. But I didn't have as much appetite as I had when I walked through the door. The idea of a cease-fire, of peace obtained not by a clean win but through the negotiation of strangers who would not have to live under the peace they decreed, made me sick.

"It will come to nothing," I said, hoping my words would be true. I hate the war—but I believe in all that we fight for. And though I was not a volunteer and would not have my freedom until the Confederacy found its way to peace—if then—still I knew I would rather fight than become a voiceless part of the Eastil Republic.

"This time," Dardie said, "I think it might come to something." She sipped her own drink and shrugged. Even she didn't look her usual optimistic self. "Racel from headquarters told me the full-wings have been running in circles for two days, putting together disarmament plans for each of the taaks in the Confederacy." She kept her voice low—I knew anything she got from headquarters was supposed to stop with her, but this mattered to all of us.

"*Disarmament—*"

I think Pada and I whispered the word together. I know her expression of horror reflected how I felt.

"The Eastils would never give up weapons or shields," Pada said.

I agreed. "They'll say they have—and then when we sit here helpless, they'll come pouring over our borders and murder the lot of us before we can raise a shield, or even a cry."

Jass, who'd been sitting and listening to all of this while sipping his lager, finally spoke. "My da says the Eastils couldn't get a straight word out of their mouths with a drop-line and a sharp knife."

We all laughed at that, but it was muted laughter, burdened by the weight of unfunny truth. We suspected that peace unearned would come with a later, bitterer price—and after three hundred years of war, we wanted our peace free of strings.

Hell, we wanted to win—and if the rumors had any real truth to them, our leaders and our enemies were conspiring to take our win away from us.

We wouldn't stand for that. Would we?

Bellies down, faces in the dirt, nine men worked their way along the mountain ridge under cover of darkness; they braved the cold and the reality of potential death at any instant, knowing that if they got through and if they succeeded, their actions could win the war for the Eastils.

Captain Gair Farhallan signaled his men to stop with a quick wave of one hand. Behind him down the line, everyone froze.

Below and beneath him, far north and east of where intelligence had reported the closest enemy position, a cavalry unit worked its way along the very trail Gair had mapped out for his own use. Worse, the unit traveled north—the same direction Gair wanted to go.

Mounted on small, rugged mountain ponies, heavily armed, the unit looked to be making good time. But where? Where had they been, and where were they going? The path, about half a league on, split, with the eastern branch going through a narrow pass and into Eastil territory. The western branch, the one Gair had wanted, dropped quickly down the mountains and into an uninhabited, heavily wooded valley that led eventually to populated Confederate lands.

Gair and his men were supposed to head into enemy territory, assume their cover as Confederate civilians, and make their way as far west as Injtaak, the Confederate taak, or city-state, that sat closest to the mountains and the Eastils. Republic spies had reported Injtaak to be the locale for the Confederate half of the peace talks, and the likely presence of most of the major taaklords made the gathering an opportunity to throw the whole of the Confederacy into disarray. The mission held incredible potential for the Republic, but also the potential for a terrible public debacle if the Confederates caught Gair and his men either before or after they completed their mission.

Gair and his men had trained for years to blend in with the Confederates—language and customs lessons, map studies, political briefings. He knew the Republic had trained other squads in the same fashion, but none of the squads knew each other. Each small company would be attached to a fighting unit, like Gair's company had been—kept close to the front lines, available to send across the border at a moment's notice. This seventh mission marked a turning point for Gair—this time, he and his men would be doing more than acquiring information. This time they had a chance to take home the big prize.

But as he watched the enemy pass and wondered where they were headed and what they planned to do, he wished he dared have his mage-communicator send information back to the Republic's forces gathered on the eastern slope of Mount Terfa. Further, he wished he knew—or had time to find out—whether they would turn east or west at Saryann Pass.

But he had neither the time nor the manpower to go after the troops to be sure of their movement. He only had the men he needed for his mission—no extras—and he had no more time to spare than he had men. And he dared not have his communicator open a speech-line to the unit communicator—some Magic on the other side might be listening in, and the open line would signal his squad's position as clearly as a cookfire or shouts.

So Gair waited, resenting the length of the line of horses and men and weapons, and the fact that he would have to take his squad down the mountain by the harder, riskier alternate route to avoid scouts and outriders, and resenting every moment that he lost waiting. If anything else slowed them down, they might have to move in daylight in order to make up the time.

The cold of the rock beneath Gair seeped into him and chilled him, flesh and blood and bone, and he suppressed a hard shudder. Slowly and cautiously, he pulled his cloak tighter around him. He felt for his men, stuck behind him, none of them any warmer than he was as they hugged the ridgeline on top of this mountain, in this cold, beneath the pale hard eye of the moon and the unforgiving stars. He would be glad when they could move again. Movement gave warmth and purpose and a feeling of security even if that security was false.

Two days, he thought. At the outside, three. In that time, they could end a war, destroy the barbarians' governments and their resolve, and open the door for the Eastil Republic to come in and bring civilization and order to these lands. He buoyed himself with those thoughts as he waited to take his men down the mountains.

I woke with my seven-year-old brother sitting on the foot of my bed in the eaves like some demented gargoyle. He wore my beret on his head and my cloak around his shoulders.

"Stand and be recognized," he said.

I threw my pillow at him, but not hard. I did not want to knock him from the bedstead and cause him any hurt. He laughed at me, and said, "So, then . . . what gifts did you bring me?"

"I brought you nothing, you beggar. My company isn't enough for you?"

"I want a beret and boots and a cloak like yours, and sugar-strings and . . ."

"If you're lucky, you won't get what you think you want," I told him. "Except maybe the sugar-strings." Of my parents' fourteen children, eight of us are in the service, six of us drafted into Magics. Which has to have been a source of delight for the Forces, since my father took an early option to participate in the Breeder program. I love my taak, I love my countrymen, I love the Confederacy and all it stands for . . . but I do not want to see Riknir follow in his brothers' and sisters' paths. If he has no talent for magic, and no taste for war, I will be the happiest big sister in Beyltaak.

I rolled out of my narrow bed, keeping my head down—years of sleeping under the eaves had honed in the lot of us a habitual half crouch on waking that returned instantly whenever we came home. I could stand straight in the center of the loft, and did. My parents kept all our beds up there still—even though four of my older siblings have married and we could never manage to all be home at the same time. Those beds stood as a mark of my parents' faith in us, I think—that we would survive service, that we would come home as we could—or perhaps they were a way of warding off disaster, a superstitious talisman. As long as the beds remained in their places so we could have our own when we came home, then we would stay safe.

I cannot say, but I know I found it a wonderful comfort to come home, always knowing that I had a place to stay, and that the place was mine.

Rik said, "So you really didn't bring me anything?"

I rubbed the sleep from my eyes and yawned. "If I had, I would not give you a thing. You vex me."

He pointed at me and grinned. "You're lying. You *did* bring me something."

"If I give it to you, will you leave me in peace long enough that I might wash and dress?"

He nodded.

From my kit, I produced first the bag of sugar-strings, and handed it to him, and acted as if I would close my kit. He thanked me, but I saw his face fall. He is as transparent as only a child can be. I winked at him then, and opened the kit back up, and from it pulled a black beret on which I'd embroidered the silver sword and the gold star, though inside a red circle that marked it as play clothing instead of the green shield that would mean it was a true uniform—the embroidery would have to do, because he could not have an actual pin. And I took out also a cloak like our uniform cloaks, heavy lanolin-rich wool on the outside, fine green silk on the inside, with a bit of gold piping all along the edge, and a solid silver cloak-brooch nothing like the official one. I did not want anyone mistaking Rik for a Sender, nor did I want him getting in trouble for impersonating one.

He didn't care. His eyes shone. "Tally, they're beautiful." He held the gifts reverently, and touched the sword and star on the beret, and ran a finger along the piping on the cloak. Then he put them carefully on the foot of one of the narrow cots, and ran over to me and hugged me, squeezing as hard as he could. "Thank you."

I pulled him close and ruffled his hair. "I'm glad you like them." I hoped I would never see him in the real uniform. If the peace came, it would at least spare him that.

He took his gifts down the ladder and gave me my few minutes with washbasin and brush. I tugged on work pants and shirt, pulled my hair back—though not in the braid mandated when I wore the uniform—and went down the ladder after him.

The smells that had been tugging at me up in the loft now hit me full-on: a pie cooling on the pie rack in the kitchen, bread baking in the oven, bacon strips and potatoes frying on the griddle, and fragrant tea on the boil. My mother hugged me. "I did not hear you come in last night, but your father did."

I returned the embrace with one of my own. "Edrig let me in—he stayed up late tinkering with a design in the workshop."

"That child. He and the boys in the smithy have some idea for a new war engine that has had them up all hours. I have been by once or twice, just to see what they're about." She shook her head. "They will put their days into it, and their nights, and will use materials and effort that might better be spent on something practical, and in the end they'll make a tangle of it."

I sighed. "Aw, Ma, you never think he will do anything—but he's a good boy."

She turned away from me to the griddle, and flipped bacon

and potatoes. "All he hears are his dreams, and all he sees are his dreams, and dreams will not buy land or win a war."

My mother, Five Saints bless her, hated the impractical with a passion that most mothers reserve for dirty children and a messy house. After fourteen children, though, I suppose she had to focus on a war she thought she might win.

And yet, in spite of my mother, most of my siblings and I harbored secret dreams—little shards and scraps of fantasy that we held tight to our hearts and cherished while we imagined what life might be if we could do what we wanted.

My own personal bit of madness did not provoke quite the level of dismay from my mother as some of the whimsies of my siblings. I had long yearned to set myself up as a jeweler, working with gold and silver, electrum, bronze and copper and fine stones; I had a workbench down in the long hall behind the house, and there, next to my father's kilns and smithing fires, I kept my table and peg, my apron and soldering irons, my mandrel and files and saws and drills and hide mallet. I'd accumulated the tools over the years and learned to use them gradually in the same period of time, and in the past few years made more than a coin or two from my work. My mother respected anything that paid, and when I spread a bag of gold rhengis on our table before her and told her it was the price I got for a granulated gold ring with a fine bezel-mounted clear ruby—a piece she had only the day before declared gaudy and lumpish—she spoke not another word against my pursuit of nonsense in time that might be better spent, and even let me start showing Rik how to do some of the simpler tasks.

So my visits home became near-unalloyed pleasure. During the day I spent time with Rik and worked on my jewelry; in the evenings I sat with my parents and whichever other siblings managed to find their way home for a day or two, as well as the ones who still lived there, and I told tales and listened to tales and spent time with the wives and husbands of my various sibs and played with my growing collection of nieces and nephews—and only rarely did I have to fend off questions of when I would marry and take deferral for Breeder rights. In spite of the war, our lives were good. The house purely burst at the seams sometimes, but always my parents made room for an extra place at the table and extra sleeping space in the loft.

"And what will you be working on this time?" she asked me, putting crisp bacon and a pile of crunchy brown potatoes in front of me.

I dug into the food with glee—my mother's cooking is the stuff of legend, and even simple things have her magic touch. "I have a commission from the Beyls for a silver brooch, a complicated bit of cut-metal work with granulation, and with a handful of opals to shape and set. I expect it to take me all of this visit and much of my next one."

But I do not think she heard anything past "the Beyls." They are the first family of Beyltaak—not the original founding family, certainly, but the latest ones who managed to grab the power and the name and hang on to them.

"The *Beyls*," she whispered. "Why, you could become famous doing work for them. Perhaps they could even do a few favors for you . . ." Unsaid were the words, "and get you out of the military."

I grinned. First, jewelers don't become famous. They are simply workers, even if they are workers who do what they love. Second, the Beyl son in my unit liked my work enough to buy some of it from me, but a direct connection to the great family had not even been enough to keep *him* out of the Shielders. It certainly would not garner me my much-dreamed-about freedom. I did not, however, voice these objections to my mother. Wonderful woman though she is, once she makes up her mind that a thing might happen, no reality can shake her.

My father finds this quality about her charming and amusing. He says her eccentricities come from the fact that she came from Dravitaak, down south against the underbelly of the world, where children were born with their brains already frozen solid. He humors her and loves her and loudly agrees with some of her more outlandish notions, all the while nodding at us behind her back, so that we might know when she has once again taken the bit of fancy between her teeth and run with it.

He does not, however, tolerate the same flights of fancy from any of us. I remember from my earliest days hearing him tell one older sibling or another, "There is no known fact that cannot be shattered by one clear-eyed observation. So keep your eyes open and your mouth closed, and do not think you *know* anything. Theories are your friends; facts can get you killed."

We stepped out into the world a dubious, watchful lot, my brothers and sisters and I; but in spite of our huge representation within the military, all of us are still alive, and I do not credit that to luck. Neither does my father. Each time one of us walks out the door, he hugs us and whispers, "Watch your back." He seems to think my mother does not know of this piece of advice he gives us. He whispers, always, perhaps thinking that he'll upset her with his worries. But once I had to take my leave when he was not at home to give me his usual benediction, and my mother walked me to the door, hugged me, and pushed food into my pack, and as I was getting ready to step out the door, said, "He is right, you know."

I remember turning back to her, puzzled.

"Your father," she said. "He is right. Watch your back."

Up in the loft, a few visits later, the older ones of us who were home for a few days lay talking in the darkness after both parents, down in their room, had started to serenade us with their snores. We discussed them, as we often did, and I mentioned Ma's warning.

My oldest brother, Tyrig, laughed. "She knows all about him," he said. "She knows he thinks her theories are silly, and she knows he tells us about them behind her back. Much of what she does when she is with him is for his amusement, and perhaps for ours. She plays the fool, but she is no fool." He chuckled. "Before the two of them received their Breeder program deferrals, she was a spy for Dravitaak—that was how she met Da." And he said something next that I'll never forget. "In a fight, she'd be as good with a blade as she is with her whisks and spoons. If ever she tells you something in seriousness, heed her—I trust her cautious view of the world more even than Da's."

So this was the woman who made me my breakfast that morning—a woman awed by celebrity, opinionated about everything, overtly silly and stubborn, and underneath all of that, wary and perhaps even dangerous. After twenty-one years, I knew her only somewhat. She drove me to distraction with her worries that I would not marry, or would not marry well, that I would fall under bad influences in the service of my taak, that I would eat too little and grow thin and scrawny and sickly—and she loved me, as I loved her.

"Why breakfast this morning?" I asked. I will take my mother's cooking whenever I can get it, but usually she subscribes to the old adage "He who wakes last eats little."

"I wanted to talk with you." She served up a plate for herself—much smaller than the monstrous serving she had put before me—and sat across from me at our long, narrow plank table.

Something about her voice rang alarms inside of me. "What has happened?"

She smiled a little. "More than all the others, you are your father's daughter. Wary every step you take. I'm grateful for it, truly. I worry less about you than the remaining thirteen combined."

I speared one of the potatoes with the point of my knife, ate it, then took a sip of the bitter spring water she paid to have hauled from her home taak—stuff that she claimed had restorative properties. She watched me.

"And . . . ?" I asked.

"He has been recalled to active duty."

I put down my knife. "Da?"

She nodded.

"They can't recall him! He far exceeded the quota he needed in order to fulfill his Breeder requirements. And he has been doing Shielder training all along."

She sighed. "He did, and he has. But he could not make the Forces not need him. He is to travel to Injtaak, to participate in a meeting of all the major taaklords. I do not know what his duty will be."

"When is he to leave?"

"They came for him well before dawn this morning. He has already gone."

I stared at her. "*Already* gone?"

"They gave him only enough time to pack a single bag. They promised that he would not be gone long—that this is a temporary assignment."

I sat there disbelieving. "You have no idea why they wanted him?"

"None. They told me nothing, and him nothing except that his taak needed him and his skills for a little while."

"In Injtaak."

She looked at me.

I did not say anything.

She asked me, "I want to know . . . what have you heard?"

And that was the question she was not supposed to ask, and I was not supposed to answer. She'd been in the Forces, she knew the rules, and I still wore the uniform and would owe my oath to my taak for the rest of my life. Yet men had come for my father, had taken him away, and my mother, like most mothers, excelled at worry.

I said, "This goes no further than you."

"I know that. And you know I shall say nothing. Only tell me that he is safe."

"The Feegash are gathering the taaklords from every taak in the Confederacy to Injtaak. Across the mountains, the leaders of the Republic will meet in a town called West Strovin. From what I was able to gather before I came home last night, the Feegash will begin negotiating a peace between the Eastils and us."

She looked thoughtful. She moved her potatoes around her plate with the point of her knife and stared off at nothing for a long time. Then she looked at me, looked at my plate, and said, "Eat. Your food will get cold."

I took another bite of the potatoes, a bite of bacon, more of her tonic water.

She held her silence for a long time, until finally she sighed. "The Feegash," she said. "I could be no more surprised had the Saints themselves decided to step down and involve themselves in the war."

"Nor I," I agreed.

Nor, perhaps, even the Saints themselves. The Feegash came from Ba'afeegash, a small, rich mountain kingdom in the heart of the ferocious Great Heart Mountains in southern Tandinapalis. In recorded history, Ba'afeegash had never been overrun, conquered, or under the rule of any but the Feegash. It was the most ferociously—even violently—neutral country in the world. It called no one enemy, but tolerated no threat. No one—*no* one—crossed into its borders with a weapon and lived to tell the tale. It lay in such an inhospitable region, with its borders so well laid out and planned, it was said that two lads with peashooters could hold off an invading army, so long as they did not run out of peas.

Ba'afeegash's army was small, but it contained what most Conventionals insisted were the most vicious fighters anywhere. If ever the Eastils resorted to the utter cowardice of mercenaries and hired the Feegash, we would have to do the same or acknowledge defeat. Thank the Saints that in this the Eastil bastards had always agreed with us—that this was *our* war, and no place for outsiders.

Second to their mercenaries, the Feegash were famous for their negotiators. But whereas any who chose to pay the coin could acquire Feegash mercenaries, Feegash negotiators charged nothing, but went only where they thought they could help. They were held to be the fairest, the most reasonable, and the most resolute negotiators in the world.

Which begged the question: After more than three hundred years of unending war, why had they come to Hyre? I told my mother, "Yet my sources are good—and that Da has been taken off to Injtaak seems to add another layer of proof."

"Well, I can understand why the Beyls would want your father on hand. He has a touch with magic no one else can match. I can think of a hundred ways he could help to guarantee the safety and success of the mission, and I daresay the Forces can think of a hundred that have not crossed my mind. And peace would be a good thing, could the Republic be held to its end of it. I suspect, though, that not even the Feegash can give us that."

I dug into the rest of my breakfast, certain she was right.

Gair, asleep beneath dense undergrowth at the base of the mountain, woke to his communications man shaking him by the shoulder.

"Trouble," Lorak said. "I got a coded send from base. Meeting is moved up a day—if we keep to our current pace, we'll arrive too late."

Gair swore, and forced himself to wakefulness. "From this instant on, we *are* Tonks. We speak only their language—" He caught himself in midsentence and switched to Tonkin. "Damn . . . we're going to have to buy horses and race to Injtaak."

While Lorak roused the sleeping squad, Gair crouched over the dirt, stick in hand, sketching out the lay of the land before him, placing every landmark and digging furiously through his memory for someplace close where they could get the horses they needed. And he tried to figure out his story—because a bad story might let them get all the way into Injtaak and the meeting, but would surely not let them get back out. And he wondered who had changed the date of the meeting, the crafty Tonks or the wary Feegash. Bastards, all of them.

By the time his men gathered round him, he had a plan that would get them the horses they needed, and get them to their destination on time and without raising the countryside against them. He sketched it in the dirt quickly, and then he and his squad moved out.

2

"I'm afraid I'm going to ruin it," Riknir told me.

I looked over to see what he was doing. He'd finished bending the plain copper band he was working on into a circle, and he had the edges lined up perfectly. And he was staring at the little dish of copper solder pallions and the flux and the soldering irons heating in our work fire as if he were trapped in the midst of a nest of snakes.

I laughed at him and ruffled his hair. "If you destroy the piece, we can melt it down to use for something else. That's why you're starting with a copper ring." I hugged him. "And when you finish it, you get to wear the ring."

"Maybe I should just help you some more." He frowned at the unfinished ring in his hand.

"How about if this time I help you? I think you'll not have such a fear of it once you've done it alone, so I'll stand by and watch you, and you can ask for my help as you need it."

He nodded, and nervously reached for the brush and the flux bowl, then glanced at me, checking. I nodded.

He painted his flux, going a little wide with it, which would make a messy bead, but it was his first solo piece and his hands were shaking; I wasn't about to make him rub the flux off and start over.

He finished painting, and sat on the stool breathing hard, brow furrowed with concentration. Then he smiled, and nodded a little to himself, and used the tweezers to place tiny solder pallions on the flux right down the seam line—he used about twice as many as I would have used, but no matter. He'd have to do a bit of extra filing, but it would be good for him. Mistakes are, after all, the finest teacher.

Then he took a deep breath and turned to the dozens of different-sized soldering rods heating in the fire. He tossed two more charcoal bricks in the bottom, started pumping the foot bellows the way I'd taught him, and got the rod handle ready. He was doing well, and I was proud of him. He waited until the tips of the rods were exactly the right color, and I grinned. I hadn't thought he had paid such fine attention to that bit of the process. Then he clamped the handle around the base of a rod with a point two times too big for his project. This time I did say something. "Smaller, Riknir. You'll have a hard time keeping that one on the work and off your fingers."

"Oh." He released the rod and chose another, considerably smaller. That one would do.

As he started applying the tip of the rod to the pallions, one at a time, and watching the tiny squares of metal turn liquid and flow along the flux he'd painted on the seam, I realized that he and I were no longer alone.

Landsman Breega, my unit's newest messenger, who was only a few years older than Riknir and who wore the real Shields uniform that Rik so coveted, stood in the workshop doorway watching us. Breega was still so taken with all the lovely formality of military life that, though he had lived down the street from my family all his life and knew me personally, since being taken into Magics he had yet to call me by name. He even referred to himself by his rank. He'd grow out of it soon, I hoped.

"I'm sent with news, Shieldsergeant," he said, and I sighed. So this was not to be the day he did.

"They need me back."

He nodded. "Increased incoming from the Eastils. Everyone has been pulled off leave and the major is having ducks."

I kept a straight face. The major wasn't too bad most of the time, for an officer, anyway, but when things got tick-tight, he was well known for, as Breega put it, having ducks. But that didn't mean that Breega should be announcing the fact in front of civilians, and children at that. Things in Shields we keep in Shields.

"Do I have time to pack?"

"We have a packer with your mother right now, Shield-sergeant."

Maybe he'd stop it if I hit him. No. Probably not. And anyway, if I did hit the child, I'd end up having a long talk with Major Damis about clobbering a fellow soldier, and I could get to watch the major have ducks at me. "Thank you, *Landsman*," I said, giving him a hard look, and watched Breega race off to ruin someone else's leave.

"Well then." I looked at Riknir, who wore his disappointment from head top to toe tip. "If I leave my tools with you, will you see to it that you put them away when you're done with them?"

His eyes got wide—I'd never left him in charge of them before. "I promise," he said. "They'll be perfect."

I hugged him and said, "I know they will. You can use everything to finish your ring, and you can show it to me when I come home again. Does that suit you?"

"I can use everything without you here?"

"Just for this project. Nothing else with the soldering irons—you know Ma will have me strung up if you set yourself afire or burn yourself full of holes."

Rik laughed. He knew.

Ma came out just then, my kit in one hand, and in the other a bag that I knew contained a lunch for me. "You're off too, then."

I hugged her. "Riknir has my permission to finish his ring with my tools," I said. "He's going to care for them for me until I get back."

She is good, is Ma. That right eyebrow of hers only rose the tiniest fraction before she got it under control. "He'll do a good job of it, I'm sure," she said.

And then I was gone, Shielders pack slung over my shoulder and Ma's lunch in hand, moving down the streets toward the wharf at the steady dogtrot you learn when they teach you to march at speed and that you can never after forget.

I met a handful of colleagues coming from other directions, so Breega wasn't the only one doing the summoning. All of them were moving at the same speed as I, so I had to guess that I hadn't overreacted to Breega's implied urgency.

We didn't speculate on the situation we were heading into; we were on the street and already sure to be causing enough worry among the civilians just from the sight of all of us streaming back to Shields. Were we to begin bandying speculation about the attack Beyltaak faced while we ran, someone would be sure to overhear us, and the rumors would fly.

Out of habit, we fell into formation as we joined up, until by the time we reached the wharf and ran along the dock toward the Shields Building, a good twenty of us jogged along the boards two by two, our feet thundering to an uncalled cadence.

Major Damis, my unit commander, met us at the arch and rushed us through long, dimly lit corridors back toward the heart of Shields, the Shielders' Active Defense Center, shortened over time to SADC. And he clearly *was* having ducks. His eyebrows, which are black as moonless midnight and thick as caterpillars, bounced up and down his forehead as if danced on strings by a mad puppeteer, and he shifted from foot to foot. "SADC quick as you can go, people," he urged.

We passed through the arches into the SADC to find the hub full already, every bench taken, every on-duty Shielder already masked and on the bar. All of us who had come at a run stared at each other, bewildered.

"Into uniforms only if you have them, and onto benches—any bench, any bar. We don't have time to put you with your partners. You'll be doubling up back to back, two to a bench, for the duration of this, and you'll be trading off in half days. If this gets any worse, we're going to have to add benches and trade you off in three-quarter days."

I hadn't done back-to-back with anyone since training, and we'd done it then only because the training hub was so small. I had to wonder what exactly we had coming in on us.

Those of us with uniforms in our kits stripped out of our civilian gear where we stood and threw on whichever uniform we'd been wearing when we took leave. We weren't in the dress of the day, most of us, but Damis's urgency was contagious.

And when I took my partner's back, not even getting time for a greeting to identify who had *my* back, I found out why. I slipped on the mask, an eyeless cloth head covering with heavy padded earpieces; the mask renders me blind and deaf to everything outside of my head. I got as comfortable as I could with only half of the padded bench available to me, with my partner's spine jammed against mine and my knees hitting those of the masked Shielder facing me. And I gripped the metal link bar that leads, like one spoke in a wheel, to the metal hub in the center of the SADC. There's nothing magical about that metal hub with its twenty long iron spokes. It serves no more purpose than to let all the on-watch Shielders share a physical contact with each other. We could do the same thing by holding hands or hanging on to the same rope, and when we're out in the field that's what we frequently end up doing. Some of us do not even require a physical contact every time; without bragging too much about it, I number myself among them. But over the hundreds of years the Shielders have been at this, that big metal hub has been the one form of connecting device that has reliably survived direct physical attacks from the Eastils. And we all need that contact sometimes, most of all when things get bad.

And things were bad. I slid into the View, and got my first look at the sky over Beyltaak from those who were already lobbing barriers. The Eastils were raining hell in on us; I had never seen anything like it in my life.

The View is a thing I think none of us will ever clearly describe to those who have not the senses to see it. But how I wish we could. It is a realm with no fixed walls or firm landmarks; everything within the View is fluid—every single thing in Beyltaak, from the weeds along the back paths to the paths themselves, to the houses, to the cats and dogs and horses, to the silverware on tables and the tables on floors, to the people eating their dinners and the dinners they eat, are living, breathing, moving, and radiant with the energy that fills them. They expand or contract as their relationships to other objects change; they repel the unfamiliar and embrace the familiar, so that when two friends meet upon an oft-traveled road, the road embraces them joyously and the friends meld together into one shimmering, dancing form, and their houses, no matter how far apart they are in the physical world, slide together in a gentle glow of attraction. Fresh enemies blaze red as they see each other or even think about each other, old enemies dull to gray with the hatreds that devour their energies and their lives.

I see my town more clearly than any but the others who share my gift, and the beauty that exists within this place of mine has filled me with such love that I cannot imagine living anywhere else by choice. And yet I know that every other place holds this same secret beauty, and I am filled with wonder.

Because we can see this energy, Shielders can work with it—some more effectively than others, but all of us to some degree. Civilians imagine us casting a big, shiny bubble over our taak that keeps the foul magic of the Eastils at bay. They imagine that our job is to prevent this giant, lovely bubble—this "shield"—from breaking or developing holes that will let in the bad magic. The way they see it, our work is passive; build a wall, then hold it in place.

Nothing could be further from the truth. There is no wall. There is no bright shiny bubble. There is only them, and us. We sit, blind and deaf, surrounded by the fires of life, watching for the incoming attacks of the Eastils, which are designed to attract themselves to specific energies and so can look like almost anything—like the people or places or things they are designed to destroy—and in the very few moments between the time the attack is launched and the time it would hit its target, we have to identify the force coming at us and throw an energy that will repel it between it and its target, either scattering its force or sending it back where it came from.

The example we get when we start Shielder basic is of holding a magnet in our hands, and having magnets thrown at us. We're to look at the magnets coming, identify their attracting force, and ward them off by turning our own magnet so that it will repel what is coming at us rather than attracting it. What they do not tell us until much later is that there are thousands of kinds of magnets, and each can be repelled only by another magnet of the same sort.

So that is the job for which I was taken away from my family at such a young age: to watch over a flowing, glowing, ever-changing landscape; to identify as hostile the energies that are launched at that landscape with sometimes blinding speed and that have been designed to look as much as possible like the things they are sent to destroy; to determine the precise type of attack that is coming; to shape from Beyltaak's available ground energy a force that will repel it; and to do it over and over again, without making a mistake. Using the hub and bars, we Shielders slip far enough behind each other's eyes that we can share the View, and by doing so, we are able to see things others miss.

Usually we can handle Eastil attacks with Shielders on ten of the twenty link bars. An average Shielder can handle five or six attacks in an hour if they aren't spaced too closely. A really talented Shielder can handle a dozen, or even more. I've handled as many as ten during one awful hour, but I'd never had to deal with that many hour after hour.

The one thing Shielders have in our favor is that magical attacks are not like arrows; there is no way for the enemy to create them in advance and store them up and send them out in a barrage. Every attack has to be created and shaped and sent by someone very much like us on the other side—and it's up to the enemy Sender to identify his own targets and disguise what he is sending and form it to hit his designated targets, because random attacks, without the attraction of design, are unlikely to hit anything.

Senders are as talented at what they do as we are, but each of us has different weaknesses, and those are the reason magic makes an effective weapon at all. The Senders' weaknesses are entirely creative: coming up with attacks that we cannot recognize from long experience, or hiding those attacks until they are too close to permit us an effective response, or building and launching attacks fast enough to overwhelm our defenses. Our weaknesses are that they always have a good idea where we are and where the targets we protect are, and that timing is usually in their favor—given sufficient time, we *will* recognize enemy attacks and determine how to repel them, but *sufficient* time is hard to come by. We all, Shielders and Senders, share two weaknesses. First, working with magic is draining; we cannot stay inside the View for an unlimited amount of time, and we cannot work with the energies of the universe except in short bursts. We all have to recuperate after each volley.

Second, the View is seductive. It embraces us, caresses us, *loves* us. It is unutterably beautiful, endlessly deep, and full of mysteries. It vibrates with a music that sings in our ears and our eyes, on our taste buds and in our bones. We are never more alive than when we are within the View.

Leaving after a long, slow shift is hard. Leaving after a battle, when the world outside is harsh and the reality of pain and death and loss await, is almost impossible.

Sometimes Shielders *don't* leave. Which is why we never go in alone—never with fewer than ten. Nine can pull one back from . . . well, wandering. Eight can pull two back. And six can hold three in place while one goes back to the physical world for reinforcements.

When we fail to bring them back . . .

Ah, Jostfar. The price of failure is watching our comrades' bodies die over days or sometimes weeks, without ever seeing from them reaction or recognition, without seeing on them any sign of injury. Watching their families plead with them to come back, though we know our friends have gone too far to hear, and will not find their way home.

We swear to each other that we will not wander away. And we swear to keep each other from wandering.

But sometimes we fail.

In any case, those of us Magics Forces in taaks like Beyltaak, which are near but not right on the border, spend most of our time floating in the liquid universe of the View trying to figure out where the enemy is and what he's doing. As best we can, we watch the other side. And our enemies watch us. And when they think they've located a flaw in our defenses, or when they come up with a new sort of attack, they launch whatever they have against it, and either we stop it or we don't. And at the same time, our Sender units, guarded by the small mobile teams of Shielders who watch over them, are out in the field launching against their targets.

Both sides avoid targeting civilians, and also avoid destroying land, crops, livestock, and buildings. Both sides have rules worked out over long centuries, both sides abide by them. We Tonks intend to claim and rule the Eastil lands when we win. No doubt the Eastils intend the same for us. It's acknowledged on both sides of the border that no good can come from destroying the wealth we hope to claim and the people we hope to rule. Or in our case when we finally can deal with the Eastils directly, that we plan to put onto ships and send back to whatever dreary land originally spawned them.

All of these things made the attack I found under way when I grabbed the linking bar almost incomprehensible. My mind focused on the View, and suddenly I was in the midst of dozens of simultaneous attacks, attacks following on attacks as quickly as we could fend them off. Not only were there too many launches coming in at us, but they were Large Random Common, a class we rarely saw. It was as if our enemy had decided it didn't matter which targets he hit so long as he hit something and hit it hard. Large Random Common attacks run counter to a hundred rules and a dozen treaties and agreements, and yet, there they were.

We could identify the launches because they were common, but they were so powerful that we had to drain ourselves casting the shields that would hold each one off. And once we successfully turned a broaching spell, we had to sit there shivering while we waited to refill our own life energy; we're a bit like cups beneath a pouring spout. Each time we empty, we must be refilled again before we're any good to anyone.

The Eastils had either found a way to avoid being emptied, or brought so many people in against us for this attack that they were able to work at their regular speed but still overwhelm us by sheer numbers. They weren't going for cleverness or accuracy or deception; they were just pounding us with size and fury, and I realized that in this instance, size and fury were all they needed. We were in trouble.

I turned launches so vast I could not conceive an enemy Sender creating such a thing without sucking the life out of himself in the process; just turning them was sucking the life out of me. There were forty of us on the link bars, and I could feel a secondary hub being brought into service and linked to our hub to bring onboard the handful of late-arriving duty-ready Shielders not already doubled up on the prime hub.

I felt a couple of officers link up, too, as the enemy hell kept pouring in on us, and that scared me. Officers are Shielders who took injuries that bent them but didn't snap them while within the View; who got torn by the View but who survived, and who know what it takes to be in there. Officers are not supposed to go into the View; they've served, they're particularly vulnerable to the call of wandering, but their experience on the bar makes them priceless, and dying in the View would, most times, be spending—for no gain—knowledge we could not get back.

Yet we were failing to hold back the tide; I felt the broachers slipping past us, hot inside my skin and painfully bright behind my eyes. Some did no hurt—they could not find their targets, so they scattered unspent, losing their force and their intent. Some, however . . .

When a broacher gets by us, we Shielders feel the pain. All of us. We feel the fires burning us. We feel the magic ripping us apart. We cannot withdraw, because the damned Eastils up the barrage if they feel us pulling back. We have to stay with the horror of our failures burning beneath our own skins, knowing that while we suffer in our minds, people we know and love suffer in the flesh.

Five years on the bar, they tell us. That's all most of us will be good for. In that time, a few of us will break completely, losing ourselves inside the View for the rest of our short lives, dwindling away to nothing because we can no longer eat or drink, because we can longer speak or hear or taste or feel or see anything in the physical world. Some of us will watch our comrades tumble into oblivion, see the writing on the wall, and seek Breeder deferrals, praying to the gods that we're fertile while trying hard to ignore the fact that we're passing our own pain on to our children by our actions. Some of us will stand fast, growing stranger and stranger, until at last we're taken off the bar, sent for a month's Recuperation and Retraining, and returned to the battle as junior line officers.

Senders last no longer than Shielders. They have to be in the View to use it; they have to merge with their targets, at least briefly, to hit them. It is all very personal inside the View, and no one feels like an enemy. Everyone becomes family—and beloved—for the moments that we touch them. Even the Eastils.

I had a bad moment, when the fighting was at its fiercest, when I nearly lost my hold on the physical world. A broacher slid by me while I was holding back another one, and though I saw it, I could not reach it. It tore past me and latched onto someone I knew, a neighbor woman I had loved since I was old enough to walk. She was—aside from my father—my mother's dearest friend, a smart, courageous woman who had raised a houseful of children after her husband died, never complaining, never doubting herself where any of us could see. She always had a kind word, always had a laugh, and I knew her as I knew my own family.

I felt her death, felt her see me as her life slipped away from her and she found the View for just an instant, felt her lift her chin and say, as she had said so many times before when the Fates cast against her, "It is meant to be."

Her death was too much for me, and I faltered and let go of the bar and the rest of my unit, and began to drift away from the hub, trying to hide, wanting to die.

And I felt a touch: a stranger pulling me back, saying, "Bad as this is and weary as we all are, if you don't hang on, you'll take a dozen of us with you. Be brave." She caught me and would not let go, sharing her own strength and melding with me until I regained my courage and could return to the bar and take up the fight again. And then she faded away, and I realized that she was one of them. She was an Eastil Shielder, but tied as tightly to the View as the rest of us. And she was right. In that battle, any one of us who fell would take down both friend and foe.

We would be enemies in the physical world, she and I. But we were sisters in the View.

I fought, and my comrades fought. Then, without warning, the barrage ceased. It didn't thin first. It simply stopped.

I sat within the View, trembling, feeling the pockets of terror and grief, and the Eastils were gone. Simply gone.

And suddenly I realized that I had something that I'd not had before.

I signaled to the major, who came and pulled me off the bar.

I tugged the mask up and squinted a little as my eyes adjusted to the light in the room. "I have news," I told Damis. "I need to speak to the commander."

He looked at me. "You look hell-ragged, Talyn. I'll give you a moment to make yourself presentable if you wish."

I felt tears drying on my cheeks and knew my face would be

pale and tear-streaked, my eyes swollen. I had no idea how long I'd fought, but my uniform was sweat-soaked. "No, sir," I told him. "This cannot wait."

"As you wish. What do you have?"

"I almost fell," I told him. "One of the broachers that got through . . . it hit a friend who has known me since I was born. I almost lost my way back out."

"But you didn't." He was not the most patient of men, our major, but he listened well enough when it mattered.

"One of the Eastils pulled me back."

He nodded. It happened—to save half of our own, we'd been known to keep one of the enemy from falling, too. War within the View is a funny thing, if you can call anything so terrible funny.

"She had to link me pretty tightly. I caught what she knew about this attack."

We were walking back through the ancient Shields Building, through a stone hall lit by the arrow slits that punctuated it, and at the moment kept unpleasantly cold by the same. Come summer, of course, those slits would make the place pleasant; sea breezes would keep it cool and smelling of salt air and week-dead fish. Coastal taaks have their disadvantages.

The major said, "You sure what she knows is true knowledge?"

"I'm sure she believes it, sir," I said. "How true it is I cannot say. If they fed her lies, what I have could destroy us."

"Tell me what you found. Intelligence will make of it what they will."

I nodded. "This attack and one like it in Havartaak were designed as diversions, to hide the movement of a very small, elite fighting force. The girl knows one of the members of that force; the two of them are lovers."

"That would be hard information to plant falsely."

"Yes, sir. For that alone I thought it worth a moment in your ears and the commander's."

"What do you know of this fighting force?"

"A little. Destination and purpose. They're heading to Injtaak for the peace conference, and they intend to disrupt it."

The major frowned. "Then I think they fight on our side,

whether they mean to or not. I like not at all the idea of this bargained peace brokered by busybodies, unless the bastard-humping Eastils intend to give it to us by a surrender."

"I think as you do."

Major Damis sighed and stopped in the hallway before the commander's huge double doors. "Yet we cannot let them succeed in their plans; we cannot permit them to shame us. Our taaklords will not sell out the Confederacy; there will be no unearned peace." He clapped me on the shoulder, looking me in the eye from a bit below level, and said, "Well done to extract such a tidbit while under such duress. Well done indeed."

He said nothing about my near fall other than that, though he could have. So he did not think me compromised; he did not think me near breaking. Just by that smallest of details—that thinnest demonstration of his faith in me—I got some better hold on myself; if my major was not sending me to the unit healers, this battling of grief and shame that warred inside me must be nothing others had not felt and survived. If they had survived, I would too. The Confederacy needed me; my taak needed me; my people needed me. I would hold on for them.

He was watching my eyes; after a moment he nodded. "Come, then," he told me. "It's time we talk with the commander."

Gair signaled a halt at the edge of the forest. Before him lay the fields that surrounded Injtaak.

"We stop here. Wipe the horses down," he said. "Then we're going to walk them and groom them until they don't look like we've been running them."

All six of his men stripped the blankets off the stocky, shaggy mountain ponies they'd managed to acquire, and started rubbing them down. Gair hated to spare any time, but if his team rode into town looking ragged and unkempt they were going to arouse at least some curiosity. Under usual circumstances, strangers in a tight little community like Injtaak would be subject to scrutiny and suspicion anyway, but not today. He could see tents pitched in the fields looking like a harlot's festival; the brightly colored waxed-felt shaddas, or pack-houses, were a vestige of the Tonks heritage. Their violent, barbaric, nomadic heritage. Gair thought the Tonks should be happy to put their history of living in tents and hunting their neighbors for sport behind them; he could not see it as any source of pride. He thought the Tonks ought to be able to see the benefits of civilization and representative government, too, though, and if three hundred years of fighting had shown anything, it had shown that the Tonks were as blind to progress as they were tough and determined. Most of their number lived in houses most of the time now, but it wouldn't have surprised him a bit to discover that they'd started wearing their enemies' bones as jewelry again.

Wellam, who had enough of a knack with horses that Gair secretly thought him half Tonk, finished first and approached Gair. "Shall I ride in and scout?" he asked. "I'm clean, my horse is presentable; I should be able to find out where we can spend the night, and take the time to locate the building where they'll meet tomorrow."

Gair shook his head. "We aren't going to assemble again until after we have done what we came to do; just wait. I want to give everyone final instructions together."

The rest of his men finished quickly enough, and Gair, watching in all directions to be sure they had not yet been observed, gathered them together.

"You'll each enter Injtaak from a different direction, and find such lodging as you can. Most of the important people will be staying in their shaddas, so we should be able to find rooms at one of the three hostels. If you need to reach me, you'll find me in the tavern named Black Hodd's, which is supposed to be on the corner of Fox Lane and Butter Street. Unless it's an emergency, though, don't come anywhere near me, or acknowledge me in any way. Before the sun rises tomorrow, you must be in your position at the Faverhend, but don't think to sneak in tonight; they will have soldiers sweep the building before the hend starts tomorrow. We aren't going to assemble again until after we have done this. If you have questions, ask them now."

"The hend will start at daybreak?"

"This is the best intelligence we have; the meeting between the Republic and the Tonks will not take place until midday, but at sunrise tomorrow—the hour of the Sparrow to locals— everyone who is of any importance among the Tonks will file into the Faverhend and discuss the issues they'll be working on prior to the actual meeting. I cannot tell you what an opportunity this is for us; we have no record of any meeting of this sort occurring among the taaklords for more than a hundred years. We missed our chance on the last one, and people on both sides have kept on dying because of it."

For just an instant, he dropped his voice and spoke in Hyerti, the official language of the Eastil Republic. "God and King Trimus bless us all, and find favor in our mission." He and his men clasped hands, and all of his men whispered, "God hear us."

"May we meet safely on this side, or triumphantly on the other," he added, speaking again in Tonk.

Then they mounted up and scattered.

Gair held them all in his heart. They had been his best friends and closest comrades for all the years the team had worked together, learning and waiting and praying that they would have an opportunity to act.

This moment—this day—was their gift, their chance to bring civilization to this land, and peace, real peace, to his own.

The commander wasn't a madman. Imagine that. I didn't like the little bastard even so. He has the coldest eyes I have ever seen in a human being, and I think if he ever had an emotion in him, it died of loneliness long ago. But he listened to me as I stood before him, and he didn't doubt what I'd said. He'd once spent his time on the bar, too, of course; there is no way to become an officer without having survived time on the bar, for how could one command Shielders who has never faced what we have faced? So he knew what the bar could be.

When I finished, he said, "At least we didn't lose all those citizens today for nothing."

Thoughtless bastard. I *felt* the citizens we'd lost—every one of them. And he knew it. Then I realized that Havartaak had been the other taak today that had taken massive bombardment, and that had suffered civilian casualties; the man might be suffering losses of his own.

So I tried my best not to think him a reptile, to be generous in interpreting him.

I stood and awaited dismissal. He watched me. And said,

"You're one of the av Tiirshas. Radavan av Tiirsha is your father?"

"Yes, sir."

A look of faint amusement crossed his face. "I served with him back when he was on *active* duty."

"He's on active duty *now*," I said, and immediately wished I hadn't. It was not that I was betraying any confidence—most Magics who take a Breeder deferral end up active for brief periods at one point or another, and I had not blurted out where he was or what he was doing, at least. Breeder deferral can buy back most of a life, but with so few Magics, it cannot buy back all of it.

But as I spoke, I could hear irritation in my voice at the commander's assertion of his own superiority, that he had remained active duty throughout his career and had not taken a Breeder deferral; many Magics saw that deferral as the easier path. None of those, of course, have raised fourteen children—but that truth lives neither in the field nor in the barn, as the saying goes.

Worse, I could not swear the commander had truly been smug in his speech; my mind is quite capable of assuming the worst when I must deal with people I don't like. And though most times I have the self-control of the Five Saints, I've been known to speak out of turn once or twice in defense of my family.

The commander noticed my tone. His eyebrows rose, and his eyes turned icier, and I could see myself pulling extra duty at some menial task after my shifts for my insubordination. And then Major Damis, bless him, said, "I'm alternating the Hawkshanks and the Red Watch on doubled-up three-and-two shift for the next three days, until we've had a chance to get through these peace talks with the Eastils and the Feegash."

My unit was the Hawkshanks, and usually I would have welcomed a three-and-two schedule with as much grace as I would have welcomed being clubbed over the head by an Eastil. A three-and-two means working three quarters of a day—twelve of the day's sixteen faces—followed by being off eight faces, then coming back and working twelve more. It's a brutal, disorienting schedule to work—it offers no regular time for sleep and no way to adjust, for if you begin your first shift on the Sparrow and leave it on the Fox, you'll begin your next work period on the Bull and leave on the Ram, and on and on, never stepping out the door to the same light two days in a row.

But working three-and-two would keep me in a state of exhaustion during my little free time and keep me from thinking too much.

The commander looked surprised. "If Talyn's information is correct, it seems unlikely to me that we will see another barrage like the last one."

"We may not," the major agreed. "But we could, if the bastards want to draw us off whatever it was they put so much trouble into placing. If we have the people already on the line to get on top of another such attack from the first volley, we should be able to prevent most, if not all, losses."

The commander's lips thinned into a mean little line as he looked past the major to me. But he said, "We're here to protect our people, Major. Go ahead with your plan."

I was tired, but not tired enough to go to my quarters to sleep yet. Under normal circumstances, I would have gone to the Star's Rest for a meal and some entertainment, or perhaps out on the town with a few friends, before I returned to my room in the Shielders' barracks.

But these were nothing like normal circumstances. My father was away and out of touch with my mother, my mother's best friend had just died, and though we in Magics may not be permitted to make family our first priority, we may make it our second. I took leave of Major Damis and notified the duty sergeant of my intended whereabouts.

It was no happy thing walking through the streets of Beyltaak. The taak had suffered from the Eastils' barrage. The Zatavars' bakery on Fishbinder Street was burning; people fought the flames, but it looked to me to be damage to property only. I saw both Mother and Father Zatavar manning buckets in the fire line, and no one weeping as they would over a lost child. Two blocks away, though, crossing Wide Lane, rescuers pulled bodies out of Lorlina's brothel; like others passing by, I quickly checked the faces of those lying beneath the sheets on the walkway to make sure that one of my own people was not numbered among the dead. Lorlina had welcomed her last customer, I discovered, though I did not know any of the rest; her place had served mostly the better-off sailors from the docks and travelers passing through. The brothel was undamaged, though, and no doubt Lorlina had left it to some family member or one of her girls.

This is the way of attacks through the View. Conventionals send missiles that can be seen by the eyes, heard by the ears, felt by the flesh; their surprise is only in the instant before their impact. They never leave horrors unannounced for the unsuspecting after they have done their work; they have no way of threading a needle and leaving a building standing but everyone inside it dead, undiscovered until someone back home misses a family member and starts a search.

Many of us hate Magics for that; compared to the fighting done by the Conventionals, our work is dirty and ugly and it wears on the soul.

Walking through the street in the aftermath of the attack, I could not find my pride in my uniform or my service. Though I knew how many attacks my comrades and I had turned away, I could see with my eyes and feel with my heart those that I had failed to protect. The dead speak louder than the living in the ears of the guilty, and I heard them clearly, whispering to me as I made my way home.

I thought of my father, away in Injtaak, and I wondered if perhaps the time had come to settle for peace instead of victory. If perhaps, after three hundred years, no victory was possible.

When the innocent dead speak, it's hard to hold on to our certainties, and I am not so strong that I have never had doubts. I had them then, and for just an instant hoped that we might have peace even if it was the weak peace of diplomats and not the strong peace of soldiers.

When I got home, I could tell that my news would come as no surprise to my mother. Ma sat on one of the benches at the long table in our strangely silent house, with her head buried in her arms. She made no noise, and for a moment a new horror overcame me—that if I touched her she would not move, and that I had come home to find one last place filled with the victims of the Eastils, and my own world destroyed.

But at the sound of my step on the floor she raised her head and looked at me with eyes red from much crying, but now dry.

"I'll fix you something to eat," she said by way of greeting, "and we'll talk."

"I can't stay long," I told her. I shrugged. "I have no appetite."

"You knew about Shakan."

"I was there when it happened," I told her. "I came to tell you, had you not heard."

My mother clasped her hands in her lap and took a deep breath. "These are hard times."

"They've been hard times longer than anyone can remember."

Ma stood. "Just a few slices of roast and some pan potatoes, Talyn. You're too thin."

If I were wide as a spider house, she'd think me too thin. I'm a good, sturdy woman.

But her hands needed work to give her mind some peace.

So I held my tongue and watched her start dicing potatoes. And the silence of the house struck me again. "Where's Riknir?"

"Your brother went over to help Shakan's family. Her last two littles will be going to live with their oldest sister, and Rik is helping them pack a few things."

She was making a pile of potatoes that would feed my whole unit. I suppose once a woman has cooked for fourteen children, it becomes hard to judge how much only one will eat.

"I really can't stay for long, Ma," I told her. "My unit is going on three-and-twos until after this business that Da is involved with is done."

"You'll eat," she said in that voice that mothers teach to future generals. "And you'll tell me . . . how are you?"

She looked me in the eye and I flinched.

"I thought so," she said, and slid a bit of fat off the tip of her knife into the cast-iron skillet she'd been using since long before my birth. The fat hissed, and Ma used the back of her paring knife to scrape the potatoes from the cutting board into the fat. "Your father used to carry that same guilt with him after something got through. He thought that he could be infallible, too; he would never admit it, but I could see it in his eyes. He believed that if he were only a little more perfect, he could stem the tide of destruction, and that no one else would ever die."

I settled into my seat at the long table and looked at my hands. "Maybe he was right, Ma. Maybe he could have stopped the dying if he had just been a little better at what he did."

"Really? And how would you have stopped the dying today?

What magic would you have used to hold back the Eastils and what has to have been one of the worst barrages you've ever been through?"

"How would you know that?"

"Everyone in the taak knows that, Talyn. We did not see you and the rest of the Shielders running through the streets back to Shields and think that you were going to a party. Everyone sees you; everyone knows who you are, whether you wear your uniforms or not. And how often have we seen all of you called back at once? Almost never is how often," she said, her Dravitaak accent suddenly noticeable in her speech.

"I—"

She put a finger to her lips and glared at me, then turned to press the potatoes into the fat with her spatula. "Almost never. And we go months—sometimes years—without any attacks getting through at all, and today they rain out of the sky and burst up through the earth. And no one—no one—thinks it was because you and your comrades were not doing your jobs."

She turned the potatoes with sharp, angry movements. "But you will persist in blaming yourself, just as your father did. You will carry the deaths in your heart until you have about killed yourself from the worry of it, when I would swear on the souls of the Five Saints themselves that knowing you, there is not another thing you could have done besides what you did to keep those attacks from getting through. I *know* you. You would not let yourself do less than your best."

I closed my eyes to keep tears from leaking from them. I would not do less than my best; she was right about that. But my best wasn't good enough, and I had not been able to save people I loved.

How could I think I had done enough? I could not.

My mother watched me, eyes narrowed. "You're just like him."

"Who?"

She turned back to cooking, and started slicing slabs off of a cooked roast into the skillet with the potatoes. "Your father. You're just like him. He would never listen to me either; but I'll tell you what I told him. You do what you can, but you cannot save the world. People die. People are always going to die, no matter what you do, no matter how hard you fight it." She chopped an onion, silent for a moment. The smells in the kitchen finally beat out my despair, and I heard my stomach growl. "Because with you or without, that's what people do," she added after a moment.

I listened to the onions sizzle, and accepted the plate she presented to me a moment later, and dug in.

She was right, of course. I'm sure she was right when she tried to talk sense into my father, too. And I'm sure he sat in front of her, digging into an enormous plate of potatoes and roast or something equally filling, and knew in his heart that she was right, and wished to all hell that he could make what she said make the slightest difference inside him.

Guilt is a good friend, isn't it? It will stand at your back when every other friend has abandoned you, and in the face of all reason it will stay by your side, and even when you tell it, "I am moving on now," it will say, "I shall never leave you; never."

If only I could find a lover as faithful as guilt.

Gair sat with his back to the fireplace, far into the shadowed back corner of the tavern, where he could pour his beers into the sawdust without the serving girl noticing.

She brought him drinks regularly, and recited the short list of meals offered at Black Hodd's with a charming cheerfulness when he asked, and without hesitation recommended the roast pheasant as being the best meal on the menu when he expressed uncertainty. She did not look twice at his silver, and she had a bright smile and round, full breasts that he got to admire every time she set a drink down for him or took an empty mug away; she wore her outer tunic open to the waist, while the cloth of the inner tunic was so gauzy it provided nothing more than a few faint, lacy patterns across those fine, ripe peaks.

At one point, while the evening was still young, she settled into the bench across from him and said, "You're all alone. Have you no friends to come and keep you company?"

"I'm traveling," he said. "All my friends are in Lodestaak."

"You are a long way from home, then. You must be here for the Alltaak Hend."

"No." He sighed. "Merely inconvenienced by it."

It took her an instant to work her way through that. "You had a hard time finding a room, then."

"I bought myself space on the floor under the eaves here, tucked in with half a dozen men who will no doubt snore and kick," he said, laughing a little, "and when I wake I fear it will be to find my face in some stranger's unwashed armpit. Meanwhile, my horse is roofless in the common corral, left to fend for himself; but I think, looking around at my probable floormates here, that I would trade places with him."

She nodded wisely. "I *thought* you neither old enough nor fat enough to be a taaklord." She touched his shoulder and whispered in his ear, "Nor rude enough; you have not once pinched me or offered to pay me for my services." She frowned at that, and he realized that she was not a whore; the serving girls in the Republic usually were. "I have a room and a bed at the boardinghouse. We're not actually permitted to have guests at night, but if you were very quiet and left after the housemistress left for market in the morning, you could share with me. Some of your would-be roommates are very drunk already and have been mixing their beer with house wine; I do not envy you their company. Besides, I don't think I snore, and I *do* wash my armpits." She gave him a little wink and had the grace to blush.

His regret was genuine when he said, "If I did not have to be on the road before the sun rose in the morning, I could not say no. In my whole journey, no one so pretty has been so kind."

She smiled as she rose and cleared away his meal. "If you change your mind, only let me know before I leave."

So she would not be making the same offer to anyone else.

He was sorely tempted. He was not certain if she was offering her bed alone, or if she had included her body in her invitation, but even if it was just the former, he had not enjoyed the pleasure of a woman in his bed in long months. For that matter, he had not enjoyed a bed in that same time. Mostly he'd had his camp cot and his bedroll, and sometimes naught but the hard ground.

And she was so round, and so sweet.

He bit the inside of his lip; letting his mind wander over the imagined hills and valleys of her sleek young body would not help him get through the night, and taking his mind off of his mission would not let him get back to the Republic, to women who were equally succulent but not enemies to his nation and his cause.

He sighed, welcoming the distraction of a group of five men who strolled into Black Hodd's as if it and everyone in it belonged to them.

They wore black. Black silk, black linen, black embroidered wool, black round-domed hats and black cloaks, black overshirts and full pantaloons, shiny black riding boots with tall heels and silver-capped toes.

Feegash diplomats.

Gair's lip curled in loathing, an involuntary reaction that he saw echoed on the faces of many in the bar.

He would say this for the barbarian Tonks; they were good enemies. They had no more liking for a soft, easy solution than his people had. He had not heard one soul speak in favor of negotiated peace since he arrived in Injtaak. Not one.

Well, the serving girl's fat, rude taaklords and the meddling Feegash would die in the morning, and Republic troops, massing on the border to enter Tonk lands the instant his communications man sent word of his unit's success, would bring civilization and real peace to this place after centuries of war.

Maybe he would find the serving girl again once his work was done.

Maybe she wouldn't hate him too much.

He sat, watching the Feegash, despising them along with everyone else in the big, crowded room, awash in an unexpected feeling of kinship and sympathy toward the Tonks.

3

The Ram's hour was only half passed, with the new day and Sparrow's first kiss of the sun waiting. But military life is no respecter of hours or beds; I dropped the mask over my eyes with a grumble about the time and a lie to Pada about the dream I'd had to abandon—for in truth I'd not been able to sleep at all—

and settled my hands in place on the linking bar. We were doubling on the benches again; this time Pada and I shared. We would be teaming in the View, too; the major had regular teammates working with each other as often as he could to ease some of the stress of our longer shifts. Shielding goes better when you pair up with your regular partner, I've found, though it is a more pleasant business if you have a whole bench to yourself.

I hurt inside and out. But as I soared into the View, my lack of sleep fell away from me, and my worries and guilt tumbled into silence.

For just a moment I let myself rest within the familiar flow of Beyltaak. Then, however, Pada and I pushed our focus away from home and the main unit. We were assigned to provide backup for the Injtaak Shielders, who had most of the taaklords in the Confederacy under their care.

My intelligence to the commander had come to this: The heads of the Confederate Forces believed the Eastils would launch an attack against the Alltaak Hend either before or during the planned conference; they also believed the most likely form of attack, because it would be the most precise and effective, would be magical.

So every Shielder who could be pared away from regular duty without leaving the taaks unprotected would be on watch over Injtaak and those in it—especially those inside the Injtaak Faverhend.

Ontaak, Maattstaak, Beyltaak, Havartaak, Mirtaak, and Joontaak—the closest taaks with available units—would all be contributing Shielders.

Pada and I connected with the other units as the first taaklords began entering the Faverhend. We identified ourselves, brushing against the other Shielders long enough to tell them who we were and what unit had sent us. The Shielders gathered into a huddle; those of us on the same hub can talk comfortably to each other at any time, though when we're working we talk little. But only by touching could those of us from different units and on different hubs hear each other.

Civilians have odd ideas about us; one of the most common is that we're mind readers. We aren't, but I find it easy to guess which people I meet on the streets of Beyltaak believe this rumor about us, for they squinch up their faces and refuse to look me in the eye, and I can see them thinking very hard about all the things they do not care if I find out, while trying with all their might not to think about the one or two things they wish to hide. And as we part and they believe they have kept their secrets safe, I see triumph on their faces. Those less sure look worried. And those with much to hide cross the streets to avoid me and my kind altogether.

We cannot read minds in the physical world. Not at all, no matter how loudly the guilty might worry, though rumors of some secret unit of Magics that does read minds crops up from time to time even in our ranks. My father laughs about our gullibility every time it pops up again. He says we of all people should know better. Within the View the situation is a little different, but it isn't anything like what the civilians think. If we do not have a tangible connection in the physical world—such as the linking bar and its hub, or holding hands—we can communicate with each other only by brushing our View forms against each other. That method gives us a form of speech and a little more: directed speech comes to us clearly enough, but thoughts are opaque even within the View; we cannot read them unless we flow into each other, and then we give up exactly as much as we receive. And even when we merge, we can see what the one we've merged with has seen. We can hear what he has heard, feel what he has felt. But what he thinks about these things but never says aloud—that we can never know.

But most people carry the bits of their day that most please or distress them on their skins like dust from the road, so that if we brush over them, these surface bits cling to us: that a man has found a young woman to replace his wife of many years and feels guilt at his betrayal and worry at possible discovery; that an old woman recognizes the twist of a sickness that will kill her deep within her belly and pretends she does not know the shadow walking in her footsteps; that a child lies about some small sin and dreads his father's wrath and his mother's disappointment.

They will wear the betrayal, the pain, the lie the way that in the world of the flesh they wear a coat.

And we can touch the coat, and look at it, and know its fabric and the manner of its making.

These things we see on almost everyone, for life's road is a dusty place, and few travel it without wearing its grit. And it is from our knowledge of these things that we get the reputation for reading minds. The sins of those who feel no guilt or shame are as invisible to us as to any civilian who has never touched the View.

Our first few moments in Injtaak, then, we huddled against each other so that we could talk with those not on our hubs. We quickly divided the taak, the Faverhend, and the people within the Faverhend among the many teams present. And then we settled in to watch.

Nothing was going on. The taak glowed with healthy light, Pada's and my sector flowed and shimmered, our people turned bright with excitement or dull with fury. But, Saint Ethebet preserve me, the whole thing was as exciting as watching a bowl of water.

We watched nothing for a long time, and then Pada told me, "I followed your advice," and the feel of her voice was so dark and sharp when it burst in my head it startled me.

No sound carries within the View. So the voices we "hear" appear inside our heads, missing loudness and softness and tone. Instead they are bright or dark, bland or colorful, rounded or angled. Getting the mood of the speaker is an acquired skill, and while there are many commonalities, not all speakers come across in the same way, so we have to learn each other's voices individually.

Pada's usual pointless nattering is round and dull and it flows like an unending river. When she is excited, her View-speech is bright—sometimes painfully so. Pada's anger is sharp and hard, her bewilderment is dark.

So.

"What advice?" I asked her.

"To bed Dosil without requiring better gifts first."

Oh, Saints. After holding on to her virginity forever, Pada had experienced sex for the first time because of something I had said. And her thoughts were still sharp and dark. My heart sank.

"What went wrong?"

"It was boring, and it was messy, and it hurt. And he is already talking about the next time, as if there is going to be a next time."

"The first time hurts," I told her. "But the second time usually doesn't. And . . . why did what I told you convince you to bed him?" My conscience was going to nag me about this. I could already feel it starting up.

"You said there was no difference between a whore and a woman who wanted gifts before she would bed a man."

Well, I did not see a difference, but clearly I should not have made this assertion to Pada. Dosil might be thanking me, but Pada was not. Still, having told the truth, I could not deny it with a lie. "It all looks the same to me."

"It sounded the same to me, too," Pada told me. "When *you* said it, anyway." This was the first time I could prove that she had listened to a thing I said. Maybe when I wanted to get her attention on *any* issue, I needed to tell her she was acting like a whore. That ought to make our friendship, such as it was, even more interesting. Pada might wear Ethebet's braid, but she still thinks like one of Saint Minda's.

"I am sorry, truly, that you did not enjoy yourself," I said, and I meant it. Because now I was going to hear about how this was my fault for as long as Pada and I worked together.

But for the moment, at least, Pada was not inclined to lay blame. She was taking a different tack. "I cannot understand how you could enjoy such a . . . such a *beastly* thing. I know you do; you are not just pretending. When you talk about it, your words are bright and colorful and they dance inside my head. While I felt like an animal," she added.

"You're supposed to feel like an animal; pogging is an animal thing," I told her. "To get the fun out of it, you simply have to learn to be an animal that you like."

I got no words from her for that—just a dark cloud of bewilderment.

Below and around us, the taaklords were up and moving, heading for the Faverhend. They faded and brightened, connecting and reconnecting as they greeted each other and moved forward. Beyond the Faverhend, Injtaak lay quiet, placid, soothing beyond words. I could afford the time to give Pada an example.

"Take me," I told her. "I don't want everything always the same. Pogging can be sweet and gentle, and once in a while that is well enough, but I want to know that my partner is there with me. I want to be sure I am all he can think about. Sweet and gentle does little to make that happen. So I see myself as a mountain cat, all teeth and strong muscles and sharp claws. And I do not worry myself with thinking too much. Thinking gets in the way; feeling doesn't. And telling them you bite does much to separate the men from the boys."

"I was thinking," Pada admitted. "I was wishing that Dosil would finish and get off me," Pada said. "He had the stupidest expression on his face, and he just went on and on and on."

"You take what you want," I told her, "or you'll not get it. Next time, flip him on his back, jump on top of him, ride him like a good horse. Take him at your pace—canter, gallop, and jump."

"Me lead him?" Pada was scandalized; her reply was bright orange, sharp as hedgehog quills.

I should have been ashamed of myself for using her upbringing against her; she'd come from a family who had never lived under Ethebet's Law. Both her mother and her father were civilians, as was her only sibling, an older sister. Pada had been raised to think that the woman waited for the man, that virginity was a sacred state and sex was a duty to be endured and got through and not mentioned. Saint Minda was known to have said, "Be quiet, be still, do your duty, but hold chastity in your heart."

Which would tell me only that Minda had either never gotten herself bedded or had done a piss-poor job of it if she had.

But Minda was hugely popular with civilians. Pada's father had likely never seen Pada's mother naked; Pada's mother had likely never pogged Pada's father outside their marriage bed, and equally likely had never enjoyed herself while she was in it. With her body rigid, her thoughts pure, and her mouth pressed tight so that she might be a good, silent chaste wife. Which had to be a real romp for Pada's father, too, come to think of it.

And every time Pada went home, her parents reminded her of where she came from, and because she was a dutiful daughter, she had held to their ways even when she had the freedom to find and follow her own.

Ethebet's Law frees the men and women who live under it from the burden of virginity at marriage. It permits us to select and abandon partners, even those who do not live under the same law, with complete freedom, though we and we alone must bear full responsibility for any children who are our issue. Nevertheless, we can skip marriage entirely if we so choose, even if we bear—or father—children. If we marry we may divorce, and—man and woman—we hold our assets as our own instead of jointly.

These freedoms can be good or bad—children suffer without both parents, and most Ethebettans settle down and marry when they start a family. Most families stay together. After all, Jostfar expects honor and moderation from all of us, and though he has given us endless freedoms, he expects us to use them wisely and in good faith.

However, the freedom to do otherwise is always there.

While they are with us, our partners live under Ethebet's Law. And that situation leads more than a few of us to find our mates and partners from within the service; not everyone finds Ethebet's freedom of choice a comfortable fit.

The resistance comes from shopkeepers and other business-people, who follow Saint Minda for her economic blessing and who have miscalled perpetual virginity, prudery, and fanatical fastidiousness "chastity," and have labeled these flaws virtues.

Pada's parents are Mindans, and they will not be happy that their younger daughter will no longer be able to marry on Saint Minda's Street under her porphyry arch.

I should have regretted shocking Pada. But I did not.

"You lead," I told her. "And while you're about it, keep away from the bed. Walls, floors, tables, chairs, the grass outside . . ."

Her orange grew brighter, her spikiness more pronounced. She stood out in the muted terrain of the View at that moment like a fire in a dark room. Others around us were beginning to notice her; their attention was beginning to drift.

Which meant I had just become an obstacle to our mission.

Then in the physical world the bells began to ring; within the View ringing bells are like tiny sparkling stars, silent but beautiful, their energy bursting in white light and then shivering away to darkness. With the bells announcing the coming of day, the Alltaak Hend would start for real.

Pada noticed the attention she was getting, and to her credit she got herself under control. She is not worthless; she's truly a good Shielder. Hard to tolerate, difficult to like many times, but she knows her work, and she does not put anything before her duty.

We dropped our discussion and put ourselves into our work.

His men were in place. Gair had walked the circuit around the Faverhend, unobtrusively checking to be sure that the side doors all the way around were closed and guarded, and that for this special meeting only the vast front doors stood open. The taaklords, male and female, headed through the doors as the sun rose over the horizon and the bells throughout the taak rang in the Sparrow, the Tonks' first station of the sun and first hour of the day.

As the bells stopped ringing, every Tonk in sight turned—more or less as one—to face the sun, and murmured, "Haabudaf aveerzak."

Gair turned with them and repeated the phrase, which was a greeting to the new day and which meant "Blessing upon us all" or "We bless ourselves," depending upon how one chose to translate it. That simple prayer completed, the Tonks turned back to their business. But Gair paused, momentarily unnerved. He was uncomfortable with public displays of piety, and unsettled by the uniformity displayed in that fleeting instant. In the Republic, temples to a hundred different gods jostled shoulder to shoulder in the bigger towns and cities, and at all hours of the day and night, men and boys gathered in the public places to argue the merits of their gods and their religions, sometimes with words and sometimes with fists. They'd brought their gods with them from all corners of the world, and the Republic had proven a fertile breeding ground for their followers.

That wasn't the way of things in Tonk lands. The Tonks were a uniform people with a single history; they were born into different clans, but all those clans had worked together and traded together across Tandinapalis for thousands of years. The Tonks still held all of southern Tandinapalis, but perhaps two or three thousand years earlier, a handful of clans had packed up their ponies and their shaddas and trekked across the frozen wastelands of southern Tandinapalis, across the island chain that traversed the Copper Sea, and up the peninsula into Hyre. Those clans had settled heavily across western Hyre and lightly in eastern Hyre, from whence the Republic, which came later, had suffered mightily getting rid of them. The Tonks shared a handful of closely related dialects of a single language, a single history, and five flavors of their single religion, Jostfarianism.

It wasn't even much of a religion. Their god was a distant, grandfatherly one who didn't have a great deal to say about obedience or disobedience, and whose whole role, as far as Gair could see, seemed to be to let the Tonks know that as long as they were Tonks and didn't hurt each other, they were all right with him. Jostfarians embraced five saints: apocryphal figures whose actions embodied the things Tonks considered virtuous as well as the things they thought were vices. Their saints weren't saintly at all; they had flaws. And the flavors of Jostfarianism centered on convenience rather than differences of opinion or philosophy. Each patron saint had followers, but the followers chose their saint when they chose their career. No one seemed to get excited about which of the saints was the best—except perhaps the Mindans, whom Gair could almost understand—no one seemed to care which saint anyone else followed, and the Tonks didn't show any interest in introducing Jostfar, their god, to anyone who wasn't Tonk. It was all very polite and all very dull.

And, from Gair's point of view as someone who could end up administering a taak and civilizing the people after the war, it was also terrifying. Because the whole Tonk culture seemed to present a shell smooth and hard as the surface of an egg, with no crannies that could be penetrated, with no way to win the people over to a new and better way of life.

They were Tonk. Everyone who was not Tonk could never be Tonk, and that was fine with them. That was the basis of their society, their culture, and their philosophy.

And it was going to have to change.

He took a deep breath and walked up to the front doors of the Faverhend. He realized that every taak in the Confederacy— every little independent city-state in western Hyre—had a building like this one, where the men and women of the taak gathered to speak their minds and vote. He knew that this was, by Tonk standards, a small Faverhend, because Injtaak was a middle-sized taak, and in theory, the building had to be large enough to accommodate all voting citizens of the taak at the same time. In the case of Injtaak, it had to hold about three thousand standing people at once.

This mission had been put together in haste when the first mention of peace talks and the possibility of a meeting of all the taaklords arose. Gair and his men, already attached to a unit stationed up in the mountains, and in place to be used for any opportunity, had been in the right place at the right time for this.

According to Lorak, Magics had sacrificed most of its Sender units' fighting capabilities for the better part of the next month in order to create diversionary cover for Gair and his men as they made their last push for Injtaak. Conventionals waited just behind the border at a dozen spots, prepared to move at the first word of success. Everything hinged on Gair's mission.

And he and his men had position, and the requisite skills to do the job, and they had access.

They could end this war, after three hundred years of struggle. They could destroy the fat old men who from positions of comfort ordered strong young men into places of danger and death. They could put an end to the barbaric excesses of the Tonks and bring them true civilization and turn Hyre into one strong, rich, peaceful nation.

But he worried that they were underarmed for what they had to do. The Faverhend looked like it held a thousand people, and though the vast space and the forestlike pillars made it difficult to count accurately, Gair thought that number was not too far off.

The bells stopped ringing, but the taaklords lingered outside the Faverhend, talking. Talking. Godsall, were they not going to get inside and close the last of the doors?

Gair was ready to give the signal. But he had it on the best authority that all the delegates would be present before the Hend actually started, and that when they were all present, the doors would close.

He knew his men would hold. They would hold until the end of the world if they did not get their signal. But this was the Republic's great opportunity, and a handful of old windbags on the steps of the Faverhend were interfering with it.

He wished each and every one of them a quick death, and prayed that he would be the one who would deliver it to them.

* * *

"Ready to bump?" I asked Pada. Our task, and the task of all the Shielders assigned to temporary duty in Injtaak, was to wander among the spirit-forms of not just the thousand or so participants of the Alltaak Hend, but also the six thousand citizens of Injtaak—men, women, and children—the unknown number of camp followers, hangers-on, support personnel, traveling troops, and people just passing through, brushing against them and hoping to find, in the dust of worries and guilt that they carried at the surface, a sign that they were enemies—Eastil troops, or spies and saboteurs from one of the Republic's allies, or mercenaries hired to cause trouble. We were looking for single pebbles in a big, fast-moving stream, and we knew it.

If we found them, we would signal what we found, and pray that Conventionals in Injtaak could use our information, or if not them, then the Shielders and Senders assigned to arms.

"Pick a direction," Pada told me. "I'll start from the opposite corner of our quad and we'll meet in the middle."

Movement within the View takes almost no time; if you know where you want to be, you are there. Its ease can make physical travel an unbearable burden; those of us who have ridden the heavens can find the back of a horse's best pace suddenly a plodding one.

We chose our starting points and reached them in the same thought; I moved at an easy pace, making a point of brushing against every human I passed. I caught irritation, boredom, amusement, frustration, fear . . . that stopped me, but then I realized that a wife faced off against her angry husband with her children tucked behind her skirts and a frying pan clenched in her hand. Bad. But outside of my mission. I prayed she would get through her ordeal, and moved on. Boredom, boredom, more boredom, an intent to lie about a mistress to another mistress *and* a wife. That one was a taaklord. Right. Back to boredom.

And then something unexpected. I touched silence.

The person I touched—male? female?—carried none of the detritus of life on his or her surface. I felt like I had been running through a muddy field and had just fallen into a pure, cold spring.

Who *was* this person?

A mystic? A saint undiscovered?

I tried to dig deeper, to push myself into the smooth, cool surface of this stranger. I felt something almost like a bubble surround me, but the stranger I wanted to read remained as much a mystery as before. This was a person beyond my ken, beyond my experience.

And then, to my shock and embarrassment, this person turned his attention on me.

"I'm male," he said. "I'm a Feegash diplomat—one of those here to negotiate this necessary peace between your people, who do not want peace, and the Eastils, who also do not want peace, though the world around you wants you to make peace because your fighting affects those beyond your borders." He touched me, lightly but with focused intent, and in that touch I felt the spark of connection. A tiny, palpable sting. "And you are . . . gods . . . you are remarkable. But this is neither a time nor a place for talk. You have a duty, as do I. I do hope that someday we shall meet again."

And his attention turned away from me, and I found myself back in the mud and the dirt, the cool spring having moved on and left me far behind.

But that little buzz of connection between us continued to vibrate for a moment. The Feegash had been . . . lovely.

I moved back to my duties, feeling small and grimy and chastened, and I covered myself in the boredom of the comfortable and annoyed, in the nervousness of the pettily dishonest.

The odd thrill of the Feegash diplomat's touch still echoed inside me, distracting—a faint reverberation that seemed to call me away from my hunt. I pushed it away. Forced myself to focus.

Nothing. I could find nothing, but I knew my chances of finding something were poor. I wished, as I had before on occasion, that some way existed to control the lay of the land within the View—to map it and everyone in it so that we could search the Faverhend and the surrounding streets in some sort of order.

We could check only those whose attention focused on the Faverhend; those taaklords whose attention wandered all the way back home, to crops or livestock problems or ships late back from foreign ports, or to lovers waiting far away, disappeared from our view entirely, only to pop back in when something caught their attention. Here then gone then back then gone then here . . . They made my search nearly impossible, and I found myself hating them for their lack of focus.

That sleek-as-polished-stone Feegash diplomat, though—he was always right there. He did not waver, did not drift.

I tried not to be enchanted by him; he was, after all, the enemy in many ways. He wanted for us something we did not want for ourselves, and wanted to force it past us because of the opinions of the world outside our borders. How could I not hate him?

But I did not.

Brushing my way through the crowd, my attention only half on what I was doing, I tripped over my target. Or at least I found one of them. He crouched between two steep roofs at the back of the Faverhend. He was one of several men who had traveled to Injtaak over the mountains from the Eastil Republic; he ached from a night spent someplace cold and hard, and was nervous about the wooden shakes of the roof on which he hid because he was deeply afraid of . . . fire.

Fire. When the doors of the Faverhend closed and locked with the taaklords inside it. *Fire* was their plan?

I pulled back from him so that we were not touching and screamed my discovery, shaking myself loose from the View for just an instant with my vehemence. "Here!" I was screaming, and I was for a moment back on the padded bench with Pada's shoulder blades digging into my back and my hands locked around the linking bar like claws. "Here!" I shouted, and dove back into the View. "One of them is here!"

I passed on what I knew—location, intention, armament—to the first Injtaaker to brush against me. And the Injtaaker dropped out of the View immediately and passed on what I had found.

Brilliant red flashes in another quadrant, as another of our hunters found another of their agents within the View.

But the doors to the Faverhend closed, because while things in the View happen instantly, translating them to the physical realm takes time. Distance has to be covered, communications made.

The physical world is never so simple and logical as the world of the View.

* * *

Gair watched the doors close, and heard the crossbars inside drop into place. Quickly and loudly, he whistled a tune into the chill morning air: "The Madman's Reel," which was an uncommon bit of music, and one unlikely to be mistaken for anything else. As he whistled, he pulled a miniature crossbow from beneath his cloak, and with gloved hands slid a bolt into the groove, cocked and aimed and fired in one smooth motion, and dropped one of the two door guards with a bolt into the chest. Gair reloaded, fired again, and his second shot hit the other guard, the one running toward him, in the face. The second guard, too, fell to the ground, twitching.

Gair turned away for an instant, wincing. He did not let himself think about the guards' deaths right then, because he had a mission; he had to carry out his mission. Three hundred years of war and horror and senseless death on both sides of the border would end if he could succeed.

But, oh, gods, he hated killing. Hated knowing that every life he ended came bound to a family, a past, a future cut short. That most of those who died were men like him, decent people in hard circumstances. The soldiers in the Republic Conventional forces never knew their enemy; they had not spent years learning their language, studying their philosophy, discovering their achievements, and memorizing their history. They could believe the tales of Tonks eating babies and sacrificing virgins on lusty altars.

But Gair knew better; he knew that the enemy could in many ways have been him, and that the Tonks had done much that was good and even some things that were magnificent.

And though they no doubt had villains among them, he could not fool himself into believing those two guards had been villains. He would carry their deaths with him for the rest of his life, however long it might be. And the next horror—which he prayed would be the last horror—would be even worse.

Gair then pulled the first of three vials of Greton fire he carried from their straw padding and hard casing, and threw it with all his might against the huge twin front doors of the Faverhend. Greton fire required no spark to ignite; neither did it need tinder to keep it burning. The vial hit the doors and shattered, and the liquid sprayed out, erupting into flames as the ingredients within the two chambers of the glass mixed for the first time with each other and touched air.

Only the Gretons knew how to make Greton fire—what they put in the vials or how they got it in there without disaster remained a mystery to the rest of the world. His people maintained friendly trade with the Gretons as much because of their production of weapons as for any shared philosophy.

The door exploded in flames. Gair heard running and shouts from the other side of the Faverhend; he also thought he heard the shout of one of his men. At the same time, he saw flames begin licking their way around the corner from the side door nearest him to his right. So some of his people were succeeding, even if one was in trouble. He ran to his left, clutching the crossbow in one hand, loading it as he ran, determined to save his men if he could, and to guarantee the success of the mission.

He ran left; that door was not ablaze. Which meant that Wellam hadn't been able to set his fire, which meant, most likely, that he had fallen into the hands of the enemy. Gair threw his second vial against that door, and heard the *whump* as the Greton fire ignited. It burned hot and spread fast; evidently some of the taaklords had run to that door and pulled the bar out of the brackets, but by the time they got the door open it burned like a Franican's hell. The taaklords opened the door, and the fire sucked inward, and Gair heard screams.

Gods.

Three hundred years of war coming to an end, he told himself. No more friends dead in battle, no more families torn apart by sons or daughters lost in the front lines. A few had to die so that many could live. And this time those who died were those who kept the war going, and not those they sent to fight it. Still . . . gods! The sounds, the smells, the sights . . .

The streets were filling; people shouting and running, throwing together bucket lines from public wells to the flames with a speed that could come only from long practice. But these were people who lived in wooden houses; fires would be something they knew far too well.

Water would spread Greton fire, not put it out—but they wouldn't know what they were dealing with until it was too late.

He started to back away; the building burned hard and fast,

and none of the doors stood open. None of the taaklords or the Feegash had stepped free. A thousand lives would be the final price of peace—but now real peace could come at last. Gair moved in front of Lorak's hiding place and gave the signal for Lorak to send his message to the waiting Republic. A simple hand gesture: a clenched fist raised high and pulled down to chest height.

And then he saw Lorak, with his hands bound behind him and a spear at his back, being marched away from the blaze, right past Gair. He did not look up—did not in any way signal that he recognized Gair.

But a tall man with pale eyes and a lean, hawk-featured face was suddenly standing beside Gair, and he laid a hand on Gair's shoulder.

"And this one," he said, and Gair couldn't move. Couldn't speak, couldn't run, couldn't fight. Something about the man's touch froze him, held him pinned to the ground while soldiers walked up to him and bound his hands and hobbled his ankles.

"No," he wanted to say. "Not me."

But his tongue was as frozen as his muscles. The man looked into his eyes and said, "This one is the officer in charge. Keep him separate from the rest of them." The Tonk's hand was still on Gair's shoulder. The two of them stood staring at each other, and Gair felt . . . something . . . moving inside of him. And the man said, "The roofs of that house . . . and . . . that one," pointing to the places where Arrige and Bokkam hid. "There are only seven of them. Keep the others alive if you can."

The building burned. The taaklords and the Feegash diplomats would die—were perhaps dead already, since Gair no longer heard the screams. But no message would go to the troops massed on the borders at the key points. No word that Gair and his men had succeeded, and that the way was clear for them to move.

The Tonk broke eye contact and moved his hand, and Gair felt life flowing back into his limbs and his tongue. But he no longer had anyplace to go or anything to say. He felt the spear at his back, and heard the rough Tonk voice say, "Move, then, you shitbag."

* * *

I had never before seen my father at work. Nor, in truth, could I say that I had *seen* him now; what he did was not a thing that eyes could follow. However, I recalled again those rumors of mind readers in our midst, rumors of that secret unit. And in that moment I could not see any practical difference between what my father had somehow done and what he said—and all of us had mostly believed—could *not* be done.

Because he stood both within the View—linked briefly to our hub and us by nothing but the force of his mind—and without, and from his position merged with the enemy leader and dragged out of him the hiding places of the other Eastil bastards, and at the same time told the Conventionals with him how to find them.

Four of the enemy died during capture, but we took the leader and two others. We would get good information from them. Then they would wait in cells for their ransom—the exchange of some of our prisoners for some of theirs. The Confederates long ago worked out rules for the treatment of prisoners of war and for prisoner exchanges, and over time got whichever scum-licking king who held the throne at the time and his degenerate rabble who ran the Eastil Republic to respect them; the heathen horde eventually came to see that getting their people back in one piece and untortured was worth treating our people well.

My unit and I stayed briefly to check for any who had not escaped the Faverhend through the tunnels. The Eastils hadn't succeeded in destroying the standing leadership of the Confederacy, but they had succeeded brilliantly in infuriating the taaklords. This stunt alone would probably be worth another thousand years of war. Out of the thousand-plus taaklords, seconds, scribes, and Feegash diplomats and their attendants who had been in the Faverhend, fourteen were dead: eleven Feegash, who had not known of the presence of the tunnels, of course, and three scribes who had tried to drag the Feegash away from the doors and down to safety, and who had given their lives for their altruism. Had the Eastils known us better, they would not have tried fire. And we could have lost most of our taaklords in a single stroke.

Yet had we lost every single taaklord and every second, the Tonks and the Confederacy would have gone on; we would have kept fighting. This attack only proved again that the East-ils did not understand who we are. We are not sheep that follow a shepherd. We have no king who tells us what to do. We stand together, a hundred packs of wolves in western Hyre alone, un-counted clans spread across the whole of the world—where each pack accepts the temporary leadership of one of its num-ber. If those who lead fall, others always step forward, ready to take their places.

We are Tonk. We know who we are, and who we are does not change, and it will not change. We cannot be conquered in our hearts, so we cannot be conquered in our lands. And this is something that fool king of the Eastils will never comprehend until the day we march into Fairpoint, which is his capital city, and take his throne away from him.

I dropped out of the View when the word passed that our shift was done, and pulled off my mask and stretched. My body ached from tension, but my mind was at rest. We'd beaten the Eastils—beaten them well this time.

The major was waiting for us as we shook off the lingering tendrils of the View. "Bonus pay for all of you," he said. "Pick it up as you go out the door. You did good work today—you saved a lot of lives."

Not all of them, of course. It is ever painful to admit that we cannot save all of them.

He'd not been jesting about the bonus. The paymaster by the door gave me my regular pay in coin, and as my bonus, a stack of horse cash as thick as my thumb. I checked the amount and signed on my line, then waited for Pada by the door; when she got through the line, I held up my wad of horse cash—tan paper printed with brown ink flecked with gold that pictured a gallop-ing horse on the front and the House of Aklintaak on the back. "Are you thinking what I'm thinking?"

She grinned. "We can at least go look."

"We'll know by the crowd when we're a block away, if it's true."

I was right and I was wrong. We knew it was true when we were still *two* blocks from the horse market, because clusters and knots of citizens were hurrying there with pockets jangling. The Aklintaak traders had come to town, bringing with them the finest horses from the Aklintaak fjords, and from the Tonk breeders in far-off Tandinapalis. When they came to town, they frequently stopped by the post money changer and traded their horse cash for gold, since gold is a bit easier to spend locally unless you're in the service. Taakfolk are used to taking strange currency from us. Horse cash is as good as gold, though. It's backed by Tonk horses, and those, frankly, are better than gold.

We were tired from a long shift, dark had fallen long ago, and bed would be the only sensible destination, and even so, the horses called to us. I've heard all the jokes about how a horse is as good as a man to a Tonk girl; but if you remove the innuendo from that statement, it is not far from true. Even Tonks born in taaks instead of among the nomadic clans learn to ride when they learn to walk, and spend as many hours in the saddle as they can arrange from then on. Horse masters are on an equal social standing with those of us in Magics, and just a step below the taaklords. A *good* horse breeder can afford to be picky when deciding whether to include the local taaklord on his dinner invitation list.

Pada and I wore our uniforms, having not taken even the little time we would have needed to go to the barracks to change. So the crowd opened up for us, and we found ourselves hanging off the paddock fence like children, watching as the handlers trotted the new arrivals past us to the stables.

They would not be for sale until the morrow, after they'd been fed and rested and groomed, but if we saw a horse we liked, we could put a marker and a sealed bid on it.

I wanted many of them. I could not in truth say that I *needed* a new saddle horse, but having one would give me a second that I could alternate. I saw a fine dappled gray gelding that I fancied—he had a smooth gait and a good solid back, and he carried his head up and danced a bit as he trotted. Beautiful.

And then there was the bay. Ah, Saints. She came from the Tand steppes, I would bet my life on it. Not a spot of white on her. Her coat gleamed like dark rubies beneath the torches, with the black of her muzzle, mane, tail, and legs sheened like good silk. She had the light bones, the quickness, the fire, the delicate stature of a pureblood Tand, and I'd bet her pedigree was twice as long as mine. Those Tand horses always look like they will blow away in the first hard wind, but there is no horse tougher. And rarely one faster. If I wanted to drop half a year's pay in a day, I might have her. But if I had her and didn't breed her, I'd be criminally remiss, and I couldn't afford to start breeding horses and still work with my jewelry.

She would no doubt go to a taaklord. No doubt. And he would rejoice in her, or be a fool.

But in my heart, I lusted after her, and promised myself that someday I would have a horse that fine.

Pada, too, watched her with yearning. "By Jostfar's blessing, I'd even bed Dosil again if he bought her for me," she said, and then looked at me sidelong and winced. "That *is* tawdry, isn't it?"

"You're getting better." I shook my head. "But for that horse, *I* might even bed Dosil, though he sounded like a dreadful lay."

Pada, bless her, got the joke of that and laughed. We shared a companionable moment watching a parade of good horses— palominos and duns and the oddly blocky spotted horses of the Velobrinan north, whose thin necks and heavy heads always bother me. The Velobrinans breed for the coat, and they end up with some hellish conformation because of it. But we have a few in Beyltaak who like to play with the breed, doing crosses with good Tonk horses to see if they can get animals that have the Tonk soundness *and* the pretty spots. Those Velos were probably a special order.

"Going to put a bid on anything?" Pada asked.

"Maybe that first gray I saw," I told her. "I'm tired of using the unit's horses as backup for mine when we do long trips."

Pada nodded. "He had good legs. Nice flex in the pastern, good solid rump, hocks and fetlocks well put together."

Pada *can* be interesting when she's talking about an interesting subject. "How about you?" I asked her.

"I'll put a bid on that bay mare," she said. "Might as well give everyone something to laugh about when they unseal it. But I already have two saddle horses, so I won't be doing a serious bid."

I swung down from the paddock and turned, and almost ran into a man dressed all in gray, in flowing silk breeches and a smocked velvet doublet studded with gray pearls.

A Feegash of some sort, though not a diplomat . . . and in Beyltaak. And he had been standing there watching Pada and me. I hated him on sight, wished him gone, and could not find anywhere within me the momentary peace I'd held when speaking to that Feegash in the View. But *that* man had been a Feegash in someone else's taak. This one was polluting mine. He looked me up and down, and with his face expressionless and his voice neutral, said, "Pleasant even to you, soldier," and moved away from me.

"A dagger through the ribs would be a sweet solution to that problem, wouldn't it?" Pada muttered.

Sometimes I know why I like her.

We went into the stables and I looked over the gray. Felt his joints, checked his teeth, looked at his legs and hooves. He was all over sound, as sweet up close as he'd looked from a distance, and he was five years old, from a breed known for horses that lived into their midtwenties and sometimes crept up on thirty. He was a big, solid lad, his withers chin-height to me— and I'm a tall woman. I prefer a big horse, to keep my stirrups up and my boots out of the weeds. Conventionals and Magics ride where there are no roads.

"He's sired by Braakwa's Ranger," the stable hand said, and I added an extra fifty horse cash to the price I could expect to pay for him. Well, I always could pick the good ones. "You looking, or bidding? Stablemaster will show you the papers if you're bidding."

"Bidding," I said. The gray wasn't the Tand mare, but he was superb.

I went to the stablemaster and looked over the horse's papers. Nice lines on both sides, but that Braakwa's Ranger had sired him—that promised only good things. When I said, "I'll bid," the stablemaster took out his bid sheet and wrote my name and contact information on it. Then he gave me a numbered envelope. I got a low number, which was good; it meant if my bid was high bid, but matched another bid, I would probably win by virtue of being first to bid that amount. On the bid sheet, I wrote the bloodline name and tag number of the horse I wanted, and my bid—and I went a little high because I decided I really wanted that horse.

I closed the envelope and wrote my horse's tag number on the outside of it, the stablemaster sealed it with wax, I stamped the seal with my Shielder ring, and he dropped my envelope into the bid barrel.

And there *he* was again. The gray-clad Feegash.

"I want to put my bid on the horse in stall eight," he said, speaking too loudly.

The stablemaster looked at him with distaste. "This is a closed market, sir," he said.

"I just saw you take *her* bid," the Feegash told him, pointing to me.

The stablemaster was patient, if cool. "I did not say this market was closed. I said it is a closed market. You're not Tonk, and you're not of this taak. Therefore, if you hope to buy a horse, you will have to go to the public market, which will be held a week Cladmusday in the public arena."

"Will the horse in stall eight be available then?"

The stablemaster didn't even have to look at his roster, though I ventured a peek out of the corner of my eye to see which horse he wanted. In eight stood the bay Tand mare, described by the gray lump of a Feegash as nothing more than "the horse." "No," the stablemaster said. "She's proscribed."

Which meant that her breeder had marked her for sale and ownership only to other Tonks. The best of our horses we keep to ourselves.

But the Feegash didn't know what a proscribed horse was, and the stablemaster explained it to him. He got an odd look on his face then; he stood very still, lost in thought. And then, without another word, he turned and walked away.

The stablemaster and I exchanged glances, and he said, "Foreigners."

I laughed.

Pada, true to her word, put her bid on the bay, and we headed back to our barracks. We would have to forgo the Star's Rest; we would have to forgo much of anything save a quick meal of the jerky and traveler's bread that we kept in our lockers for such days as these.

"I do not suppose the major will put us back on regular hours yet," Pada said as we walked back to the post.

So *she* was back. Pada, stater of the obvious.

I was in too good a mood to be annoyed. "I imagine you're right," I told her.

We passed the Feegash just a little way from the stables. He had his hand on the arm of one of the richest importers in Beyltaak, and the two of them were staring into each other's eyes like lovers about to fall into bed, only from their expressions, I would guess they weren't going to make it to a bed, or even to a horizontal surface.

I elbowed Pada, and glanced over at the two of them, and she followed the direction of my gaze and shook her head. "Well, importers. What do you expect?" she said, and shrugged. "I heard DuSyttar was haatuuf. Never saw him with anyone—man or woman—before this, though."

Jostfar's Word permits all adult relationships equally. Saint Ethebet herself mentioned women loving women not as sisters and men loving men not as brothers in one of her Examples, and if my ever-tedious, fanatically Ethebettan colleague Vanim had been with me, he could have quoted her word for word. A handful of warriors in Magics take lovers of the same sex at one time or another, and a few do so exclusively, though it is something most of us have no interest in.

"I'd think he'd have better taste than some foreigner, though—even if he is an importer," I told her. "Doesn't truly fit what I've heard of him, either. And all I've ever heard of DuSyttar is that he's a stingy bastard who likes his gold better than life itself."

And then the two of them, not speaking, turned and walked back to the stables, and I frowned.

"Which might have been wrong. Guess who thinks he just figured out a way to get himself a proscribed mare," I said.

"You don't think DuSyttar will really buy the horse, do you? Good Saint Minda, the Feegash could have a house on Short Street and silk curtains at every window for the price that horse will go for!" Her fists balled tight, and she said, "And that Feegash bastard could *own* the house. He will be able to do nothing but ride the mare—that horse and her issue will belong to DuSyttar no matter how often the Feegash beds him."

A thought occurred to me. "Perhaps DuSyttar hasn't told the Feegash that a Tonk cannot even give a proscribed horse as a gift to one of the moriiad." I laughed suddenly. "Or maybe DuSyttar has done the numbers and decided that buying a good horse and getting Feegash ass for free until the Feegash finds out the truth of the bargain is an equation he can get behind. So to speak."

Pada rolled her eyes and said, "By Jostfar, but you can be crude sometimes."

I laughed again, and we put the couple out of our minds.

4

Gair sat in a cage, his hands chained in front of him, his ankles chained together, and both chains linked by running rings that kept feet and hands close together, but that would let him reach up to scratch his nose with one hand so long as he held the other one all the way down to his ankle.

He wasn't going anywhere. The Tonks had taken his boots, stripped him to his stockings, pants, and undertunic, and searched him for hidden weapons with a thoroughness that guaranteed he was carrying nothing more lethal than hair anywhere on his body.

They had not been brutal to him. But they would not; the Tonk were respecters of rules, and the prisoner-of-war rules were sacred between the two nations.

So Gair would eat decent food. He would have safe shelter, a place to sleep, room to move, a place to piss. They would not beat him or torture him. They might trade him. Or they might keep him until he died. Prisoner exchange was not one of the guaranteed rights; negotiators tried to get the most for the least, and he was a minor officer without any invaluable knowledge within the Republic. All of his special skills had been honed to make him look like a Tonk, and to let him be invisible to Tonks.

And now that the Tonks knew him, and had no doubt marked him magically so that he could not move in Tonk lands without setting off alarms, his value to the Republic was nil. He had to face the possibility that his failure meant that he would never know life without walls again.

Hale had the cage next to Gair's on the back of one wagon,

and Bokkam's cage had been placed on the back of a second. The Tonks were transporting the prisoners; Gair had heard Beyltaak mentioned as their destination.

Hale had some bruises and a cut under one eye. Gair leaned his head as close to Hale's cage as the bars would allow, and in Hyerti whispered, "What happened?"

"I was running, and I fought when they cut me off."

Gair nodded. "They go over the line with you? Beating? Torture?"

"Rutting Tonks—of course they didn't. They're so upright they carry their spears up their asses. They were polite as all shit while they pinned me down and chained me and shoved me in this box with bars for transport. They aren't going to do anything to jeopardize getting their own people back, even though the Republic is *never* going to trade for us."

Gair sighed. "Miracles happen."

Hale looked at him sidelong and gave him a wry half smile. "Want to take bets on when they'll happen for us?"

Gair didn't. He didn't want to think that this was going to be his life: that the only language he was ever going to hear again except in surreptitious whispers was Tonk, that he was then and forevermore the captive of barbarians, even if they were honorable barbarians.

So he changed the subject. "You have any idea what happened to the others?"

Hale's face twisted with bitterness. "Arrige took two arrows in the back when he didn't stop on command. Lorak killed the man who came after him first, but fell to the second and the third, according to Bokkam, who ran in the same direction. I'm almost certain that Wellam is dead, too. I think I saw him go down, but I'm not sure. He might be with some healer right now. Neither Bokkam nor I know about Snow Grell. He might be dead, but he might have escaped on foot, too. Or stolen a horse. Shit—or sprouted wings and flown away. You know Snow Grell."

Snow Grell Warrior Born to the Hell Hill Woman would have a better chance than any of the rest of the team of crossing hostile terrain alone and getting home alive; he'd immigrated to the Republic from the Hva Hwa, a primitive nomadic tribe that roamed central Franica, when he was seventeen and had already passed his manhood tests among his people. Snow Grell was the shortest name he would answer to; the Snow Grell was, he said, the name of the creature he'd killed with his bare hands and claimed as his spirit. If the scars on his chest and belly and arms and face and back were any indication, it had been one hell of a fight.

The Hva Hwa followed one of those nature religions that spent a lot of energy on the business of spirits—plant, animal, and otherwise. Gair figured they were simply tapping into the same View Magics were always going on about, but that they had a different angle on how they used it.

No one knew why Snow Grell had left his home and his people, or why he'd traveled the dangerous route from the Franican tribal lands to Hyre. No one knew why he'd offered himself in service to the Republic Conventionals. Gair knew that he was dedicated and loyal, and not much else about his life before he came to the Republic. But if Snow Grell was a fair representative of the Hva Hwa, the primitives might have a few twists on magic that the Magics ought to be exploring. Snow Grell had a nasty tendency to be right where people were sure he wasn't when they were talking about him, and he could be impossible to find whenever he wanted to avoid camp chores. Gair had always suspected that he was using a bit of his religion-magic on them, but had never been able to prove this.

"I hope he got away," Gair said. "I hope he runs like hell and gets back to the Republic in one piece, because of all of us, I think he'd be least likely to survive imprisonment. He wasn't made for cages."

"None of us were," Hale said. He leaned his head against the bars and closed his eyes. "The Tonk who took my name and my ring-mark said we'll be in prison until they receive official acknowledgment of our military status from the Republic, and then we'll be moved to prisoner-of-war barracks."

"They told me the same thing. Apparently if our boys are bad about the records, we'll be in trouble. Without uniforms, without anything from the Republic on us, and with only the say-so of their people in Magics that we're Republic agents and not Tonk malcontents, our prisoner-of-war status is shaky. And though I have heard the barracks aren't bad, rumor has it that the prison is pure hell." He closed his eyes. "I wonder what happened after we failed."

"So do I," Hale said. "Did they send the troops over the border anyway? Did they launch Magics again? Or did it all fall apart because we couldn't get everyone?"

"We got a lot," Gair said softly. "They stopped screaming pretty early on." He'd been removed from the site before the Tonks could start pulling charred bodies from the rubble. He suspected they didn't want to give him an opportunity to gloat over the destruction he'd caused. He wouldn't have, though.

He would have linked the sounds of screaming to the twisted bodies. And his thousand ghosts would have had faces. Burned faces.

Had the Tonks wanted to torture him, they would have made him watch the price others had paid so that he could do his duty. The articles of war in the Confederate-Republic Prisoner Exchange Treaty had no specific prohibitions against making soldiers look at the results of what they had done.

The wagons started rolling with a lurch, and because of the way he'd been sitting in his cage, his head slammed against the bars. It hurt. He deserved the pain, he thought. Still, he moved around so that he could lie down. He had a pillow and a blanket in his cage, and they would serve. He managed, with much rattling and clanking, to get himself rolled into the blanket with his head on the pillow, and he closed his eyes and prayed for dreamless sleep. He prayed for leniency from the dead—from the thousand or so men he had killed while trying to do his duty, and for those men, women, and children who would die, and keep right on dying for all the many years to come, because he had failed at the charge he had been given.

I could say the next shift was a hard one—it was busy, after all, and Pada had received a rest day because she was sick with something minor but draining and the healers did not want her to spread her sickness to the whole unit, so I worked back to back with Vanim av Khom, who is a good man and a dedicated Shielder, but dull as mud. I cannot even be annoyed with Vanim, as he is so earnest. So very, very earnest. He means well, he idolizes my father, and he is never sullen or snappish, which Pada sometimes is, especially when she's sick. But he likes to talk about the philosophy of Saint Ethebet while he works. Ethebet's history. Ethebet's strengths and weaknesses. And her Examples—the long, long list of her sayings that most of us read once when we choose our patron saint and then never look at again, but which Vanim has memorized.

All. Of. Them.

Five preserve us all, the Saints have given us direction and example, but none of them were wits.

So I walked out into darkest night, went straight to my quarters, instructed a runner to have me up early or suffer the consequences, and fell into a sleep in which I do not think I even moved.

And what felt like a moment later, the runner came pounding at the door and poked her head in, and I was going to snap at her and tell her to let me finish my sleep. But daylight was pouring in my window.

"The horsemaster at the market sent word you won your bid," she told me. "And that you're to go pick up your horses."

Pass that through two more runners and a stable hand and I would have received word that I'd run my lid on whores and I was to go kick them. I decided that I needed to start insisting on receiving my messages in writing, the way officers did.

I gathered up my horse cash and my gold on hand and stopped by the post bank on my way to the stables to pick up the rest of the money I'd need to cover my bid. The gray made an impressive dent in my savings, but he was young, and he was a good mover, and my unit was due for a rotation to the mountains soon; this time I would have two saddle horses and would only have to use unit beasts for pack.

I walked into the stables, and someone said, "That's her," and suddenly all the stable hands and a handful of taaksmen who had been loitering and admiring the horseflesh were staring at me with expressions that I could not begin to decipher.

The stablemaster kept looking at me and shaking his head as I paid my money and signed the papers that made the gray mine. There was a sheaf of them, for in Tonk lands a horse's owner must be able to prove provenance; we do not treat horse thieves well. I received the gray's pedigree, and my copies of all the provenance papers—the House of Law would receive copies as well, and the stable would keep a copy. And I received my pocket license for him, which is a small card done on special horse cash paper, written out with the gold-flecked ink of the Aklintaak traders, noting the horse's brand and his tattoos. They give each horse a unique tattoo on the inside of his lip, and how they do this I do not want to think. Horses have sensitive lips; I suspect there are a lot of Aklintaak tattooists with hoof-shaped dents in their skulls. But they do it somehow, and those of us who purchase from them receive this card, which receives our name and signature and seal and the stable stamp and is finished off with a coat of sealer so that it can't be tampered with. For if the Tonks as a whole are cautious about their horses, the Aklintaak traders are fanatics.

The stablemaster painted the sealer over the card in front of me, and I said, "I'll go get him now . . . or is someone already bringing him up?" Because he gave me a strange look.

"You still have the other stack to go through," he said.

I said, "There are *more* papers now? Who else could possibly need a copy?"

And he said, "For the other horse."

"There is no other horse. I put a bid on the gray."

"The horse your admirer bought for you."

He and I stood looking at each other for a long, awkward moment while he waited for me to acknowledge that I knew something about this and while I waited for him to start talking sense.

"By the Saints, man," I said at last, "what are you talking about?"

"I'm talking about the anonymous admirer who paid fifty thousand round in horse cash to buy you that Tand bay."

I felt the floor begin to sway underneath me, and I leaned forward and braced my hands on the stablemaster's worktable until the room steadied itself.

"You didn't know," he said, and he sounded amazed.

"Fifty . . . thousand . . . on a *horse*?" Pada could have owned most of Short Street for that.

"You truly had no idea."

I stopped staring at the desk and looked up at him. "Master Kahdra, I could not accept such a gift. Had I known, I would have told the madman who paid . . . all that money . . ." Fifty thousand *horse cash*? Saints on sticks. ". . . to keep it. I could not own such a horse."

"And yet you do."

"No." I closed my eyes and clenched my teeth; turning down the finest horse I had ever seen was harder than anything I had ever had to do before. "Please return my anonymous admirer's money to him, and tell him that while I appreciate the gesture"—I looked into the stablemaster's eyes and mouthed the words "fifty thousand?"—"I cannot accept such a gift. Cannot."

The stablemaster smiled at me. It was a genuine smile. "You're a hell of a woman. I don't know many who would have turned that gift down." Then the smile went away. "But I cannot return the money."

"Why not?"

"The person who paid for the horse is not the person who acted as purchasing agent."

Suddenly I remembered DuSyttar and the gray Feegash in the street together, and how the Feegash had been watching Pada and me. How he had been staring.

Him?

"The Feegash man?" I whispered to the stablemaster, since we had more of an audience than I cared for.

"No," he said. "He had hoped to act as a purchasing agent for someone else—the actual purchaser—and had we known he intended to buy the horse for a Tonk, we would probably have permitted him to place a bid. But he somehow talked DuSyttar into placing the bid in his stead."

"Then . . . when this started, a Tonk was trying to use a Feegash as a purchasing agent in a closed auction?" That sounded impossible.

The stablemaster shrugged broadly. "I do not know, Shielder. A dog might have been trying to use the Feegash as a purchasing agent. Who paid for the horse does not matter. Who owns it does. You're Tonk, and you are the horse's owner. I cannot give the money back to the person who handed the money to me, because DuSyttar did not pay with his own money and the Feegash made DuSyttar sign papers saying that he could not claim the money in case of failure of the sale. I cannot give the money to the Feegash because I have no provenance that it came from him. The actual money came from a silent account at the docks, with a note that you were sole party in the transaction, and that you were to receive the horse. The silent account was to be closed as soon as the money was paid through."

I tried to get my thoughts around this.

"Someone wanted you to have that horse," the stablemaster said.

"I see that." I looked at him. "Why don't *you* keep the money?"

"The money has already passed from my hands to those of the Aklintaak traders, minus my percentage for brokering the deal, and the sale is final."

"You could keep the horse and resell it."

"I could not. Because if I did not carry out this transaction in the manner in which it was entrusted to me, I would find myself a man without taak or trundle," he said softly. "And my name would be stricken from the Beyltaak records. This is *horses*, Shielder."

And we Tonks take our horses seriously, by Jostfar.

He added, "I do apologize for the disruption that this is causing you, and for the disturbances it will no doubt create in your life. But this involves a sum of money so great that I must ensure the sale goes as required. If you care about my reputation and my future at all, you will be leaving here today with two horses."

And there I had it. I would take the horse or ruin the career of a man I respected tremendously.

"Pass me the papers," I said.

I could always sell the horse later.

After I found out who had bought her for me, and for such an outlandish sum of money. And after I found out why.

I rode the gray out of the stables, and led the bay, and I felt the people of the taak watching me as I passed. They knew horses, too, and they could see me on my lovely three-hundred-cash gelding leading a mare that made him invisible.

Going on post was a misery. Word had spread before I crossed the checkpoint, and I had a turnout that would have embarrassed anyone. I cringed and cantered past everyone to the post stables, and the stable hands clustered around me as I dismounted, petting the nose of my gray, for whom I needed to find a name, and eyeing the bay as lustfully as Pada and I had two nights before.

"Ooooh, Talyn, she's marvelous," they murmured, and "Who gets to exercise her?"

I'd need to pay double what I'd anticipated in exercise fees, and food, and the stable fee. Pasturing is free on post, but privately owned horses take up space and supplies that could be housing unit horses, so we pay for everything else. The fees are not exorbitant, but they were going to be twice what I'd anticipated, at least until I figured out what other arrangements I could make for the mare.

Jostfar's heart, but she was a pretty thing. A sweet nature and a soul of pure fire—and if I ever rode her, I knew I would have to cut off the hand that held the lead rope to make myself give her away. So I dared not ride her. What fate is it that gives a woman the horse she would have given almost anything to own, in circumstances that will not let her keep the horse, or name her, or ride her, or even stand in the stall stroking her nose and giving her bits of sweet feed from the palm of that woman's hand?

And who, who, who had done this? And why? Why? Why?

I paid Lachlin, who cared for Flight, my only horse until this mess, to be my primary stable hand for both new horses as well, making sure she knew that the mare was only temporary. Lachlin rode, she groomed, she cleaned and fed, and she was good at all of it. I did not have to worry about the horses while they were in her care. And I gave the boy Nodder, whose real name I do not think anyone knew, a small stipend to cover for Lachlin on any day in which she might not be able to do her work.

Then I hiked back to my quarters, doing a good imitation of being lost in thought so that I could ignore the catcalls of some of my less restrained colleagues, who as I walked by loudly applauded the sexual prowess that could get a woman a fifty-thousand-cash horse.

The damned Tonks couldn't build a smooth road to save themselves, and the ones the wagons rode over felt like they'd been made of logs laid sideways. They were dirt—nothing but packed dirt—and he supposed he could be grateful that they had dry weather for the trip, since the only thing worse than a hard dirt road was a muddy one. However, Gair had spent three full days with his head bouncing up and down on the thin pillow, or getting slammed into the bars of his cage when the wagons went through holes, and he couldn't find much gratitude in himself.

And then, after passing outlying farms dotted between big swaths of forest, they rolled through the massive gates of a high-walled city, and he got his first look at Beyltaak. It looked worn. He could see the grace notes of an earlier age in the buildings on either side of the cobblestone streets: real glass windows and fine woodwork along the tall peaked roofs and over the narrow arched doors, little flourishes like window boxes that in season would be filled with flowers. But he didn't see anything that looked new. And everything old looked like it could use fresh paint, and maybe some repointing. And of course there were the holes, where buildings had been hit by the Eastils and where the ground had been cleared, or mostly cleared, but where nothing new was going up.

Beyltaak was one of the major taaks of the Confederacy, but it was as poor as most of the Eastil cities, and as battered. And all he could think was, No one is winning this war. After three hundred years, it's time to end it.

But he had failed.

And then a handful of urchins caught wind of what the wagons held, and gathered up pebbles and rubble and started pelting the cages. Word would have spread, of course. The Tonks might not be rich, but their communication system was as good as the Eastils'. Everyone knew what he and his men had tried to do. And though the military might be bound by the prisoner-of-war agreements, private citizens had a bit more leeway.

Many of the rocks hit the bars. Many more did not. Gair did not cry out, though some of the boys had strong arms and good aim. He covered his head with his arms, but he sat upright. He would not let them make him cower.

This was the start of his new life, such as it was, and the only control he had was control over how he faced it.

The boys shouted curses as they ran behind the wagons, and

their shouts drew the attention of others—adults. Adults who caught what was going on, and whose response was to pick up rocks of their own. Or to spit.

Maybe I'll die, he thought. It won't be as honorable as death in battle, but it will keep me from spending a lifetime in a prisoner-of-war camp. Death would be preferable to a life of imprisonment, he thought.

The rain of stones and spit got harder, and the crowd got bigger. This was the way it was going to end, then. He was going to die in a cage.

He put his arms down at his sides. Better it went fast than slow, if that was to be the case. Better he died with his eyes open.

And then a woman on a big gray horse pushed her way through the crowd. She was in uniform—he recognized her as one of the Shielders. Green and black uniform and Shielder's pin on her beret. She was shouting something, but he could not hear her over the roar of the crowd until it started to quiet, and the rain of stones stopped.

I confess it. I wanted to ride right on by when the citizens started to attack the surviving prisoners from the Alltaak Hend attack as our Conventionals brought them into Beyltaak. I watched those three animals roll past, and thought they would have killed a thousand of us in a single blow if they had but known a little more about us. They were chained in their cages and already bleeding, and it was only the fact that I was in uniform that kept me from throwing stones or spitting right along with the taaksmen and taakswomen who trotted after the carts.

We all understand the exigencies of war. We know the price we pay for demanding our right to live our lives our way, and we acknowledge that the Republic has the right to defend itself from attacks we might make. But I'm like most of my countrymen and taaksmen; I respect the uniformed enemy, but despise the spy.

And these three soldiers had been acting like spies, all of them. They looked like us, they spoke like us, they'd been dressed like us. They had come among us in the guise of friends, and had used our generosity against us. They had been treated with kindness, and had repaid that kindness with attempted slaughter.

No one could call the taaklords civilians—as leaders of their taaks, they are by default prime military targets, and they know this when they accept the mantle and privilege of the taaklord. They had at the time been engaged in matters of enormous military significance, so none of us could criticize the damned Eastils for the time of attack, either. We might very well have had people of our own trying to do exactly what these three had tried to do. But to civilians, these three looked like spies. And everyone despises a spy.

I was in uniform, though, and my father had identified these three men as active-duty Eastil soldiers performing their duty by direct order when they were captured. Which meant they were protected by the prisoner-of-war agreements. I was mounted—on my gray, whom I'd decided to name Toghedd, which means "thundercloud"—and I *was* in uniform, and we have duties in this life that may not be pleasant, but that are duties nonetheless.

So I rode into the mob, and my uniform stopped the shouting, and my bellowed order to "Cease and desist!" stopped the stoning. People were still spitting at the prisoners, but a little spit never killed anyone, and my people had a right to be angry.

"They're not spies. They're soldiers. Prisoners of war," I shouted. "We do not treat prisoners of war this way, because so long as we do not, our own people will not be treated this way if taken captive. Someday the person in the cage could be your son or daughter, your brother or sister, your mother or father. Is this what you want for them?"

They hung their heads then, and broke away in little clumps to go home, so that by the time we arrived at the House of Law, no one followed the wagons but me.

One of the prisoners in the front wagon, the one who had been sitting there with his arms at his sides letting the stones hit him, told me, "Thank you, and Saints' blessings upon you."

"I didn't do it for you," I told him. "I did it for my fellows, who may someday be in your situation." And then, though I am usually careful with my words, I said, "I hope *you* rot and suffer and die for what you did."

And I rode away.

Not far—only to the front of the building, where I tied Toghedd to one of the hitching posts. I pulled the sheaf of papers from the saddlebag and carried them up the steps.

People tapped foreheads as I passed, and I nodded to them, but I heard whispers behind my back as I made my way through the long hallway to the records room.

"I have a problem, Maro," I told the records clerk.

"You, Talyn? I would have thought you problem free, after your sudden windfall."

I sighed. Even in the hall of records, the word had spread. Well, of course it had. Maro had gotten copies the day the whole thing happened. "That *is* my problem. I cannot keep that horse. I do not wish to sell her and profit by the gift. I have no idea who gave her to me, and I do not know why, and I cannot be beholden to anyone in that manner; it risks my integrity as a Shielder. What if someone should tell me, 'I gave you that horse, and now I want you to do just one little thing for me?' " I sighed. "If I accept her, I put myself into that position."

Maro frowned. "You truly do not know who gave her to you?"

"I truly do not."

"None of us thought that to be the case. We all had guesses about who might have given her to you, though none of us have seen you anywhere around the Heights of late."

The Heights is the richest neighborhood in Beyltaak. The Beyls live there, along with importers like DuSyttar and horse breeders like the Norns and the av Driiaks, and Lad Faaraks, who owns the Beyltaak fishing fleet except for the independent boats. Because of my uniform, I can go there as I please. But I am not a part of that group, and though they treat me respectfully, it is respect for the uniform. That respect does not make the leap to me as a person. In an ideal world, someday I would get regular commissions for jewelry from the Heights, and I would be welcomed into the houses as a craftsman—but even an ideal world does not have me taking a lover from the Heights. Nor does it have anyone from the Heights buying me a horse at ridiculously inflated prices.

"What is the most anyone ever paid for a horse in the market before this?" I asked him.

He did not even have to look for the record, which told me

this subject had been a matter of serious interest. "Twelve thousand two hundred ninety horse cash," he told me. "About fourteen thousand gold at the time the sale was made."

"Gold and cash trade one to one."

"They didn't at the time. Cash was trading higher because the stud Markhold's Heresy was rumored to be coming to market."

"And that price was his sale to the av Driiaks. About five years ago."

Maro nodded.

"I remember it now. Good Saint Hetterik, I knew whoever bought the mare had overpaid, but I honestly didn't know by how much."

"Appraisal on the mare was posted as seven thousand gold. After all, the best anyone can hope from her is maybe a dozen good foals. Maybe half again that if she has a long life and a busy stud card. And she might give birth to the next Markhold's Heresy, but she'll never have the value of a prime stud."

"I know." I shook my head. The gift of the mare made even less sense to me; she had clearly been purchased by someone who didn't know horses, didn't understand the horse market, and had no idea what he was getting—or giving, in this case—for his money. Which meant, first and foremost, that the giver was not Tonk.

And I did not actually know anyone who was not Tonk. I had spoken in passing to sailors and fishermen and traders from other places; I did, after all, have to traverse the docks every time I wanted to leave my quarters or the Shielders Building to go into Beyltaak proper.

But I did not know any foreigners well enough to receive from them a horse the price of a small city.

"No one will ever be able to get that money back out of her," I said.

"No," Maro agreed. "Maybe one of her offspring, if she drops colts instead of fillies."

"Maybe."

"So," Maro said, straightening his shoulders and tapping his pen nib on his record book. "You have come to me to have me help you with a problem about your horse."

"I want to give her and her offspring to Beyltaak."

Maro and I did catechism together long ago. And his eyebrows used to crawl up his forehead in exactly the same fashion when he was called upon to recite one of the Saints' creeds. We had to know them all, and memorizing them was a misery for him.

"You want to give the taak a horse. The whole taak."

"I do. I thought that the best use of her would be to breed her and let the profits from the sale of her offspring go into the taak coffers. Jostfar knows the docks are a sagging mess, and parts of the town are falling to pieces, and then there is all the damage from the recent attacks."

He smiled at me. It was a kind smile, but also had about it that little bit of condescension I get from my father (albeit increasingly rarely) when I have managed to completely miss the point of something he said.

"Did you think about this?"

"I've thought about little else since the day I got her."

"No. Not the idea of giving her to the taak, which is enormously generous of you in spirit. But have you thought about the details? The taak will have to pay for her housing. Her pasture. Her care and feeding and her training. For her stud fees. For the care and housing and training of her offspring to the point that they will be ready to sell, which, if anyone hopes for a big return on the cost of all of this, will have to be after they have demonstrated the spectacular qualities that would make them good breeders. Say when they are four or five years old. So the taak would have to spend money for four or five years before having the first hope of realizing a profit, and that profit is at the moment speculative at best. If bred, will she catch, if she catches, will she deliver, if she delivers will the foal be valuable, if it is valuable will someone care to pay what it is worth?"

I propped my elbows on his table and hung my head. Clearly in this case I *had* missed the point. Badly. "Ah, shit," I muttered, and Maro patted my shoulder.

"You meant well."

"That plus actions will clearly see me into some barbarian hell."

Maro laughed. "Keep the horse. Enjoy her. A seven-thousand-horse-cash mare is not going to be either the salvation or the ruination of Beyltaak, and for all that someone paid Jostfar's own ransom plus a patch for her, she is still a seven-thousand-horse-cash mare. If you still want to do something more for the taak than what you already do by serving in Shields, sell one of her foals and give the money to the taak, earmarked for restoration. But you need not feel guilty, Talyn. I think it clear that you did not court this gift, and you are not beholden for it. No one begrudges you the gift, truly. Though we have had more than a little entertainment speculating about the madman who bought her for you. And now, knowing that you are a complete innocent in this, we can have even more."

And that is how I came at last to own the horse that was given me.

"Name?"

"Captain Gair Farhallan of Karvis, Bretonstate, Eastil Republic."

"Lineage?"

"Sir?"

"Your lineage, son. Your people. Who are your people?" The old man at the records desk looked up from his writing and studied Gair for a long, quiet moment.

"My father is Mawon Farhallan of Season's Change. His father was Sturm Farhallan, but I don't know beyond that."

The old man gave him a look made up of equal parts pity and disgust. "Who are your *people,* boy? Not your family. Your . . . clan . . . tribe . . . your forebears of your original land?"

"I'm an Eastil, sir. I don't know what my original land before that might have been. My father mentioned some of our ancestors coming from Joeta and the Kingdom of Shreehaven in northern Velobrina."

"And there you have it," said one of the Tonks behind him, who had a hand on Hale. "They do not know who they are. They do not know where they come from. They have no people. You almost cannot blame them for being a bunch of dirty savages."

Savages? Gair thought. *We're* savages? We have paved roads, you ignorant ape. We have a representative government that makes sure everyone receives equal treatment under the law, and that gets funds to poor outlying regions so that no town has to stand on its own during hard times. We have a logical national system of taxation, not some piecemeal robbery by individual taaklords. We have public education, and we have a single national currency. Our mayors don't get to mint their own money.

But he said nothing. He was not in a position to say anything.

The old man said, "Lineage: none. And your plea on the charges?"

"I'm a prisoner of war," Gair said. "Under the rules of the prisoner-of-war agreement, if I was acting under orders and faithfully carrying out my duty as a soldier and an officer, I may not be charged with a crime or tried for a crime by any member of my nation's enemy nation or allies for those acts which were my orders until such time as the war is won or lost; until then I may only be placed within an approved and inspected prisoner-of-war facility to be held until returned to my nation either by provision of prisoner exchange or by free release by my captor nation, though my actions while serving my country can be presented by my enemy to my commander that I may be tried if they were not carried out with the exercise of my duty." Every soldier stationed at the front lines had to memorize the articles of the prisoner-of-war agreement. Gair had never thought he would have to use them, though, and certainly not that particular one.

The old man tapped his chin with his pen and said, "Well . . . you know the rules well enough, I'll grant you. But there's a problem with your place in them."

In Gair's belly, something cold and sharp twisted. "Sir?"

"We have provisional identification of you and your men from our folks in Magics. They vouch for you that you're soldiers, not spies. But your identification papers have not come through, and we have no confirmation from ERMiCCS that you belong to them." The old man looked at the papers in front of him, frowned, then turned and called into a room behind him, "You got anything yet on those three captives in the Injtaak case?"

"They're apparently still running short staffed over in the Republic," a woman shouted back. "I got a single 'We'll look into it' message from ERMiCCS yesterday, but they aren't even answering today." ERMiCCS was the Eastil Republic Military Command Communications Senders, who made up about one-fifth of all Senders in the Republic. Usually they sent nothing but messages, but in that massive assault on Beyltaak and Havartaak that had been Gair's unit's cover, he knew, a lot of them had been pulled off their usual duty and thrown into the lines as fighting Senders. "Current theory is that they wiped out so much of their Sender capacity with that attack before the All-taak Hend that they're going to be limiting all nonessential Sends for the next month, until their full staff is recuperated and back on force."

That, Gair thought, was probably about right. And essential sends would be confined to direct military purposes; the fate of three prisoners of war who had failed spectacularly in their mission, and who had cost their Republic the majority of its Sender capacity for a month—with nothing to show for it—was going to be down at the very bottom of the list of things to do last, when everything else was up and running.

Gair sighed.

"Here is what we'll do," the old man said. "You're clearly Eastil, clearly a genuine prisoner of war. I can't put you into the camp until I have your paperwork, but I won't put you into the prison to await trial, either. I would not want your people to treat our soldiers that way because communications were down. So. We have a few jail cells in the back here—they don't have much in the way of amenities that prisoners of war have, but they're better than the prison. You'll stay there for the next month, or less than that if we establish regular communications with your ERMiCCS before then. Once we have your clearance, you will join your people. You'll receive prisoner-of-war treatment from me and my people."

Gair nodded. Under the circumstances, he could not ask for better.

The two soldiers who had escorted him into the building walked him back through a long, straight hallway to a series of cells farther back. Each cell was separated from the one next to it by a wall of bars and metal mesh, which he supposed kept prisoners from passing anything to one another. The cells were made for two people, and each held a single bunk bed, a slop bucket, a washbasin and pitcher, and two small metal cups. Each cell had, as well, a little walking space and a tiny window set high in the stone walls and heavily barred—but Gair would not complain that the window had no view. After all, it was a window, and it brought a cheerful ray of light into the small space. And the cells were clean and smelled of rush mattresses and soap.

A month at worst, he thought. He could tolerate this place for a month. He would at least be able to talk to Bokkam and Hale, and they would not be murdered in their sleep by angry Tonks; the cells were empty when the old man chose one for him and unlocked it.

Hale came back second, and got a cell of his own. And when they led Bokkam back, he too received an individual cell. "We don't have much use for these," the old man told him. "So unless we get busy you can each have a place of your own. I'll put you in together if we fill up, but that is not too likely. Folks don't have much of a taste for crime at the moment. Leastwise not of the sort that would send them into my keeping." And he added, "You'll get three meals a day and one hour in the yard to walk about or run if you choose. And my wife does the cooking for anyone we hold in here, so if you don't find it to your taste, you'll want to keep your opinions to yourselves."

And he turned and walked away, leaving Gair and Hale and Bokkam alone.

"Separated each of our cells by a whole cell," Bokkam said.

"Smart man," Hale said. "Put us together and we could have joined forces on an escape. This way anything we do is going to have to be in the yard, and I'm betting we'll be closely watched there."

Gair didn't say anything. He washed the blood and spit off his face and hands, climbed into the top bunk, and lay down with the sunlight falling across his face. For a time, he had morning light, which he loved, and the steady rise and fall of voices of men he held as friends, and a place where he could, if he was lucky, avoid thinking too much about anything. For a time. He would face his obligations to his country and his men soon enough, but for just a little while, perhaps he could sleep, and if the mattress was not soft, neither was it the ground. And if the place was not freedom, neither were people stoning him or spitting at him. He still lived, when he had been sure he would die, and where life remained, hope was handmaiden.

He closed his eyes and let himself slide into the darkness of sleep.

He dreamed of a woman on a tall gray horse, and dreamed that he rode at her side, and that she smiled at him. And he took odd comfort in that dream.

I took the mare home next day, and presented her to my parents, who had already heard plenty about her, and all the wrong things at that. They were not amused.

"I did not sleep with anyone to get her, Ma," I said. She and my father had dragged me into Da's office and closed the door, and they were talking with their voices low enough that any of my siblings who were lurking on the other side would not be able to hear them.

"Fifty thousand horse cash," Da repeated for the fifth time. Or maybe the tenth. I was wearing down, and I had lost count. He chewed on his bottom lip—never a sign that things are well in Da's world. "You had to have done *something*."

"I did nothing. I swear it. I have no idea who paid for her. *No one* has any idea who paid for her. And I tried to give her to the taak, but she would be more a burden than a financial gift, I found out. So I want to keep her and breed her, and sell her offspring and donate the profits to the taak for rebuilding."

My father said, "First, we are not horse breeders. Second, I do not want that horse here, because a horse that any fool paid that much money for is going to be a temptation for thieves, and the way things have been lately, I don't want to bring that sort of attention on my family or my house."

My mother nodded. "And Rik has been asking us questions about her, and about you, and I just do not know, Talyn—you have never given us cause to be anything but proud of you, but this business with foreigners . . ."

The urge to beat my head against the first hard surface got stronger. Yes, we all three agreed that the person who had bought the damned horse had to be a foreigner. That was acknowledged fact—no Tonk could ever be so stupid. But he—or, let me be broad-minded here, *she*—was no one I knew. I had told them repeatedly that I did not know any Saints-preserve-me pogging foreigners more than to give polite greeting on the docks on my way to and from the post, and I certainly on-my-Tonk-soul had not bedded one either before or after receiving the damned horse, and I did not intend to.

Where we were running into trouble was that my parents could not understand what could motivate some foreigner to buy me a horse if not the privilege of bedding me. And that they thought some foreigner would find their daughter worth fifty thousand horse cash for a romp on horizontal surfaces says things about what my parents think of me that I would, Jostfar's truth, rather not know.

So we had circled round, again, to what I ought to do with the horse, and I had come to the conclusion that nothing I could say was going to get them to board her for me, even if I paid the breeder fees and hired someone to care for her and train her offspring. My da had a point, truly. My family lives in a good-enough neighborhood, but they don't have a house on the Heights, and I would not want them to be a target for thieves because of something I had done.

Or *not* done, damnall, because for the life of me I could not see what I had done to bring this embarrassment down upon my head.

"I'll take her back," I said. "I can't breed her on post. We haven't the facilities to deal with foaling."

"You might as well ride her," my mother said. "Maybe in the future you'll end up in a post where you can spend some time for yourself." Which referred obliquely and without actually putting it in words to that point in the future when the View finally got to me and I took an officer's commission. Or when I did what my brothers and sisters were ever after me to do, which was to take a Breeder deferral for myself. And *that* I could not do, though I had been careful that neither they nor my parents ever knew the truth behind why I did not marry or bear children.

"Right, Ma," I said.

Some of life's biggest moments drop on you when you are not looking, and stick to you, and brand you, and change you in ways you cannot understand and would never expect, and when they first happen they look like nothing so terribly important and then they gather mass and speed and momentum and when you finally realize what has happened it has become far too late to move to safety. If only when they happened bells rang and eagles dropped from the sky carrying notes from the Saints in their beaks saying *"Run!"*

But they don't.

I rode the little Tand mare back to post—the first time I'd permitted myself to ride her—and she was as perfect as I had thought she would be. I acknowledged that short of giving her away, which would do no one any good, I was going to have to take responsibility for her. And if good was to come of the whole business, it was good I was going to have to take responsibility for personally. I named her Dakaat, which means "fireball," and promised myself that I would think of her as just a horse and not as the most publicly humiliating experience of my life.

And then the Fox team was ordered back from the front lines for regular rotation, and our unit received travel orders to the Ontaak front to cover the Wirewings of the Seventh Senders and the Hedgehogs of the Thirty-fourth Conventional in retaliatory strikes, and I didn't have time to think about much of anything else for two long weeks.

5

Hethdas was a hard month for me personally, what with the Eastil attacks and the long hours and the horse fiasco and finishing the month on the front lines under heavy fire. But then the fighting let up. The Hedgehogs got a pullback order, and the Wirewings were put on direct-response-only status, which meant that they could Send only one for one in reply to incoming Sends from the Eastils. But there were no incoming Sends, which meant they sat there.

And on the first day of Kroviidas, which happened to be Ethebetsday, a post-based Shielder unit took over coverage for them, which is not at all the way to arrange protective coverage for mobile units, but no one was asking me, and the Hawkshanks received orders to return to post, so we went.

That's military life. You go where they tell you, and you do what they tell you, and you serve with your life and your heart and your soul because that is what you have to give to the cause you believe in and the land you love, and when you see those in charge make blunders you think could rival Haamishat's at the Battle of Water Line you still go where they tell you and do what they tell you, because you are sworn to serve. And you hope and pray they know something you do not that will make it all come out right.

Most times they do—we draw our officers from the enlisted pool, so they are steeped in reality before they get their first dose of theory, and this tempers them. The Eastils, on the other hand, send officer candidates to fancy schools from the time they're boys; and the Eastils permit themselves to draw only from male candidates—even for Magics, where we have men and women serving equally. Worse, by good account the wealthy can buy their sons commissions to guarantee them officer status. And while a small handful of Eastil officers have risen through the ranks, most Eastil lieutenants have never seen action when they receive their first posting. Eastil lieutenants redefine the word "green."

There is a story of one Eastil squadron, led by an officer of high family and astounding ignorance matched only by his breathtaking arrogance who was, after the latest of a series of unforgivable blunders, waylaid by his men, put in a box wrapped with ribbon, and left along a known Tonk patrol line for our people to find. On the outside of the box was the list of the officer's blunders, and a plea from the Eastil enlisted for us to take him.

The story goes on that our boys in Conventionals wanted to decorate the officer for outstanding service to the Tonk cause, then turn him loose so that he could go back to doing what he did best, which was clearly sabotaging his own side. But Headquarters wouldn't let them, because Headquarters insisted he would be a valuable trade.

Except once he was a prisoner and enrolled on the prisoner-of-war lists, we could not get anyone to trade anything for him. Ever. Someone claims we even tried to trade him for one of our mules.

That's the story, anyway, and I don't know how much of it is true. From what we have seen of the Eastil High Command, most of us think it is *exactly* true, including the bit about the mule.

How the Eastil enlisted refrain from committing wholesale slaughter of their officers is beyond me. And yet they have managed to put units into the field for as long as we have. This, I think, speaks only of the quality of their regulars.

I rode into Beyltaak at the tail end of the procession, tired and dirty and desperately longing for a good hot soak and a good hot meal and maybe even a good hot man at the Star's Rest, and the first thing I saw was a handful of Feegash diplomats, and by this I mean perhaps three and perhaps a dozen because the bastards all dress in black and when they're all moving they look as alike as ants. And these were running into and out of a house on Blackfalcon Street like ants at a nest that has been stirred with a stick, and a passel of Feegash servants, who dress in a sort of baby-shit brown—because the Feegash may be wonderful diplomats and soldiers and even servants and all, but they're clearly color-blind and have no one who has learned a damned thing about dying fibers to create attractive colors—were carrying boxes into the house, and not carrying boxes out.

Which I took to be a bad sign, for clearly these Feegash were planning on staying. They had a lot of boxes.

We signed ourselves in at Command and Control, and if people had their lips stuck together any tighter their mouths would have fused. The air in the place was tense, and no one had a word to say about anything.

Paalin had the door of the Star's Rest when I got there, and he gave me the sort of worried look that you never want to get when you're just back from the front and two weeks behind on anything that might be called news.

I tucked my beret into my belt as I crossed the door and decided to go with meal first and bath second, ignoring the comfort of my comrades' noses in favor of the latest talk.

And there was talk. Sweet Jostfar—the wall of sound that greeted me as I stepped across the threshold only got louder as I made my way to the tables back and left.

And some of my folks were there, sitting along one of the big tables with the Blackblades of the Nineteenth Shielders from down in the Raw Hills. Pada waved me over and made a place for me, and one of the serving girls put black ale in a big tankard in front of me without being asked, and when I looked up at her said, "On the house. Master's orders."

The master of the Star's Rest had never, in my knowledge, given away so much as a copper-cup tipple to a customer; he loved us dearly, but he loved us the way a farmer loves a good-growing crop. And you don't give money to the corn, do you?

I stared at the tankard and muttered, "Now all it will take is for the moon to start bleeding, and I'll throw myself into the sea."

"Close enough," one of the Blackblades said. Her tag said av Biijaam, and her stripes made her a shieldsmaster, one grade up from me. "You saw the Feegash."

I nodded. Our whole unit had ridden past them; she would have heard from someone who rode unit horses and who, consequently, didn't feel bad about handing the horses off to the stable hands and going for the fast drink. I'd rubbed down both Toghedd and Dakaat, cleaned their hooves, put fresh straw in their stalls, and fed and watered them before I headed for the Star's Rest. If you do it right, that's no quick thing.

"You hear anything about them?"

"Not a damned word."

"They're in all the big taaks right now, and scheduled to bring more of their people over to set up camp in the smaller taaks over the next year. They're in no hurry now; have all the futtering time in the world, they do."

"The Eastil king and all seven of the core taaks have agreed to a complete cease-fire and the withdrawal of all troops from the front lines for the duration," Pada said. "And to negotiations for peace, and probably for disarmament, and probably also for the placement of peacekeeping forces and observers from Ba'afeegash in every taak that agrees."

"The Beyl did *not* agree to a cease-fire, when the Eastils have never held up their end of one," I said, but all the Blackblades shook their heads.

"He did. At first he wouldn't even meet with the Feegash. His oldest son died in Injtaak—one of the scribes who went to help the pogging Feegash find their way out of the Faverhend—when we should have let them all die, clearly. And he held the

Feegash and the sticking of their noses in our war responsible
for Haamer's death. But the taaklords of the other six core taaks
all signed the cease-fire agreement, and every single one of
their taaklords sent communiqués to the Beyl, requesting that
he at least meet with the negotiators. So he really didn't have
much choice, if he was to keep the taak alliance strong."

I nodded. Each taak is an independent city-state, but for us
to have any strength, we have to act together on some issues.
Where war with the Eastils is concerned, we have always
acted with one clear voice. And the core taaks—that is, Beyltaak, Niitaak, Havartaak, Mirtaak, Dravitaak, Ereystaak, and
Aklintaak—between them hold most of the taak-affiliated
Tonks in the Confederacy. No one counts the nomadic Tonks,
because no one can. The roaming clans migrate with the herds
and the seasons, and swear allegiance only to each other. They
make up, we guess, about a third of the population of western
Hyre, but they pay no taxes and live within no walls. They send
individuals into the taaks to join units, but they field no units of
their own. They breed wonderful horses, and goats that are
damned fleet of foot, and herding dogs of breathtaking skill and
obedience.

But the taaks hold all the government anyone recognizes; the
nomads have no voice in taak policies because they inhabit the
free lands. And the taaks can't speak for the nomads, which
means that even if all the taaks agreed to a cease-fire, no one
could guarantee that it would hold, because the nomads could
decide it made for a good time to go raiding across the border.

The fact that six of the seven core taaks requested that the
taaklord of the seventh take this meeting was not something
that even the Beyl could ignore. But it damned well should have
been a meeting he could walk away from without signing a
cease-fire agreement.

"What about a Hend? Has anyone stood in the Faverhend and
spoken to this cease-fire issue? I know I have not, and I cannot
see where the Beyl can decide this on his own."

"He brought the issue before the Hend two days ago. And he
convinced everyone that this is necessary—that in order to explore the possibility of peace fairly, we must have a true cease-
fire. And that we owe it to our dead to seek peace."

I was dumbfounded. "The taaksmen *accepted* that? They

agreed to look anew at negotiated peace, and probably at disarmament, because people have *died*? *Everyone* dies. It's how you live while you live that matters, and what you die for when you die."

I saw nods along the table. But the senior shieldsergeant from the Blackblades said, "We know that. But we aren't civilians. In any Hend, the civilians who have never served outnumber those who serve or have served about six to one. And clearly a good majority of them believe if everyone would just stop fighting, no one would ever die again."

"So the civilians voted in favor of the cease-fire."

The Blackblade sighed. "It is one of those times when representative government might have served us better. Because had we given the Beyl the power to speak for us, he might have stood with the military. He served."

"Six years in Conventionals," I said. "And no reenlistment. His father served for twenty before becoming Beyl."

"I'm sympathetic enough with your woes, but I'm from Pittaak," the Blackblade said. "You'll at least have a say in this. Our taak is not even held in consideration for this first round of talks, and if your taak and the six other core taaks vote in favor of disarmament, we'll have Eastil hell to pay if we decide not to go along.

"The negotiators came here last week and met with him for the better part of a day. The Beyl, his chief aide, and two damned Feegash met behind closed doors for the whole thing. When the Beyl walked into the room he swore that he would die before he would agree to go further with the Feegash and their peace, and when he came out, it was to get his secretary and the scribes on duty to copy the notice of a Hend for posting around the taak."

I closed my eyes. "So we're committed to pursuing peace."

"Looks like we're going to be committed to catching it. The Feegash have already won over a handful of the folk on the Heights with talk of markets opening up in Velobrina and the Path of Stars, and even in the Fallen Suns. And you know how much our merchants would love to get their hands on some of Fallen Suns' minerals, and woven goods—especially their laces—and some of their exotic woods."

I knew. I had simply never considered the possibility that a true Tonk would sell out freedom for rocks, cloth, and wood. The Fallen Suns, uncounted thousands of islands that lie in the northern Kervish Ocean, have been refusing to trade with either side of Hyre for about a hundred years. Maybe more. Members of their trade alliance lost several fleets of trading ships to Hyre's pirates, and no one is certain whether they were Confederate pirates or Republic pirates, but the Sunnas have proven remarkably adept at holding a grudge ever since.

Most of the world has, in truth. Confederate pirates keep foreign goods from reaching Eastil ports, and Republic pirates keep foreign goods from reaching Tonk ports, and somewhere in the middle of all that, the foreign merchants have decided that sending things here is a bad risk. We manage to get our own goods from port to port by virtue of armadas, and so that nobody starves, the Tonks and the Eastils signed a waiver so that no one, including our pirates, bothers fishing fleets so long as they have their flags up and stay in their own waters. We can be unpleasant to drifters, of course, unless there has been a storm.

The few foreigners who come here cannot understand how we can maintain agreements with each other, like the prisoner-of-war agreement and the fishing fleet agreement and the mutual agreement to police but not use the High Valleys, and still not make peace between our two nations. But they're foreigners—even more foreign than those king worshippers in the Eastil Republic. Most of them have no more concept of freedom than does a cow in the barn, who is fed and watered and put daily out to pasture, and slaughtered at the convenience of her keeper. They are primarily chattels of their owners, their emperors or chieftains or queens or whatever the lord in the castle looking down on their hovel gets himself called these days.

I ate my food without another word, letting the flow of talk wash over me. It was bad talk, about the disbanding of the military forces, about rumors of an occupying peacekeeping force, about the end of Magics and Conventionals and the end of a chance for victory, about a bitter peace lived under the watchful eye of foreigners. Talk was of the end of our world, the end of our way of life. About abject failure. About the death of hope.

When I was done with my meal—and I had not the stomach

for much of it—I got myself a hot bath in one of the upstairs public tubs, letting the lavender-water seep into my skin and chase away all thought with its pungent scent. When one of the men from the Blackblades slipped into the big tub with me, we did not waste time with talk. The aura of fear, of the end of everything we cherished, bore down on us, and we found such comfort as we could in the flesh. Out of consideration for others who might want a soak, we moved to one of the private rooms and spent an hour or two of screaming, clawing, lip-biting mindlessness. When we had exhausted every possibility, and ourselves into the bargain, and our demons lay quiet for a time, we rose, still wordless, and rinsed off in the showers—icy water in those, straight from the mains, and unscented, but not much else will clear the mind like a torrent of cold water.

Neither of us offered a name, neither of us gave good wishes or thanks. There'd been little enough pleasure in what had passed between us, and no solace. No peace of mind followed.

I wished I had just gone to bed and gone to sleep.

We went our separate ways—he to his unit's travel lodgings and me along a street lit by the soft glow of the streetlamps, through the taak's roughest taaksmen and taakswomen, to my quarters. To the only life I had known since I was a child. To an uncertain future.

Men came and went from the other cells, passing through in an hour, or a day. The monthday from their entry into the Beyltaak jail came and went, and a new month started, and at last their jailer came back to the cells.

He looked tired, and gray, and much older than he had just a month before. He coughed wretchedly, and leaned against the bars when he spoke to them.

"I cannot keep you here any longer, no matter that I believe you, no matter how I would want my boys treated in your jail. My wife is sick, and she cannot cook for you, and I'm so sick I cannot do it either. Your people are still not answering our communications, and your papers have not come through. Without your papers or at least something that proves you're Eastil soldiers, I cannot send you to the prisoner-of-war camp. I've made arrangements with Parver over at the prison—he will put the three of you in a cell away from the regular prisoners, and he'll have one of the boys there make sure you get good food and clean water, though I do not think they'll be able to let you into the prison yard. We're keeping you there unofficially so that you do not have to be charged with crimes or put into the queue for sentencing and justice. Don't want to see you executed when you could be the key to bringing some of our folks back home."

The old man coughed so hard Gair thought he would collapse right there, and he would have reached through and steadied the jailer if the mesh had not been in the way.

"I and mine will keep sending for your papers. But even if your folks don't get their communications back up soon, you will not be in the prison for long," he added. "The Feegash are halfway to negotiating a peace between the Eastils and us. No one is quite sure what they're saying, because they have not had a single public meeting, but they must be some smooth-talking bastards; they have won over the people with influence from one end of the country to the other, and now all those folks are talking peace like it was the true path of Jostfar's desire. And your king has already agreed to their proposal, so from your end of things I would say the deal is done. My guess is you will all be home this time next month."

Gair swore softly, and behind him Hale erupted with a string of Hyerti profanity so heated it needed no translation for the old man to catch its drift. The old man laughed, and the laughing dragged him into another string of racking coughs. "Ah, you're real-enough soldiers. None of our lads or lasses look at this Feegash peace with any joy, either. But the votes keep going against those of us with a little sense, and before long looks to be all of us will find ourselves living in a new world."

Sweat popped out on his forehead, and he took a couple of deep, wheezing breaths. "Lot of the spring sickness going around this year," he said. "Not pretty, is it?"

"I hope you get better quickly," Gair said. The old man had been kind to Gair and his men when he had no reason to be. When he had plenty of reasons not to be. Gair liked him.

"My thanks," the man said. "I hope I do as well. And Saints watch over the three of you while you're in these lands."

The old man let the three of them bathe and shave and made

sure their clothes were clean before the prison wagon came to take them away. Gair thanked the old man for his kindness, and stepped into the wagon, cringing at the sound of the chains clamped to his ankles. Another month.

And then what? Who would he be if he was not Captain Gair Farhallan? If he was Gair the civilian, whose military skills consisted of looking and acting and talking like a Tonk, and crawling around the countryside unseen, and fighting. Those were not going to be skills with much worth to an Eastil civilian.

He closed his eyes as the wagon took him and his men away.

Oddly, as she had every night since she had stepped between him and the mob throwing stones, the woman on the tall gray horse came with him, riding behind his closed eyelids in the quiet places of his mind.

I woke to someone running down the corridor through quarters, pounding on doors and shouting, "Assemble, assemble, assemble, assemble!"

I scrambled—out of the shirt and shorts I sleep in and into the posted uniform of the day. My hair already hung in a braid down my back, and I put it into some sort of order with water from my washbasin. Did a quick brush over my teeth, fought to get the boots up over socks that inexplicably chose this morning to ball up at the heels, and ran like hell through pouring rain to the assembly hall where we meet during bad weather.

I wasn't the first one there, but I was a long way from the last, so I had the chance to watch the people up on the podium. Officers in full-dress uniform, the Beyl himself in the regalia of his office with his second at his side, equally dressed, and one Feegash diplomat, wearing black from the top of his pretty head to the toes of his feet. Have I mentioned how much the Feegash color palette annoys me?

The officers stood at ease, talking to each other in low tones. The Beyl and his second son, who had now ascended to the rank of Beyl-second within the Beyl family, both sat in the chairs of office provided for them; neither of them talked, neither showed any animation or interest in what was going on around them. They seemed defeated. The Feegash stood off to one side, quiet in a way that caught the eye. He reminded me of herons on the shorelines of standing water, who when they are hunting freeze to such stillness you would not think they were alive, until a fish swims too close to their feet and they strike.

I watched him, frankly interested in who or what he was hunting, and saw that he was slowly scanning the crowd.

He would have caught my eye anyway. He was tall, sharp-featured, hair the color of good, clear amber ale and eyes to match. His skin was pale against the black he wore, but it wasn't an unhealthy sort of pallor. He stood well—strong and confident and alert. And I liked his legs. He wore the Feegash style of leggings, which cling to the legs and manage to make most of the Feegash men I've seen look like scurrying little plovers, with their round bellies and their little stick legs. But for this man, those leggings worked.

Except for his eyes, he was so still he seemed not even to breathe. He seemed oddly familiar to me. Even the fact of his stillness seemed familiar. And then his gaze caught mine, and he clearly realized I had been staring at him. He smiled at me, and that smile knocked me back on my heels.

I hadn't intended to, but I returned the smile and felt my cheeks grow hot. Nor am I one of those blushing virgins who giggle and simper before the glances of any good-looking man. I'm a combat veteran; I believe I was sixteen the last time I blushed.

So I stood there, with my hands clasped behind my back, my cheeks burning, feeling that surely the floor could do me one small kindness and open up and swallow me, and the Feegash broke eye contact and glanced over at the Beyl, and raised an eyebrow.

The Beyl looked out at all of us, clearly decided that any of us who had not yet arrived would have to get the news at second hand, and rose. He stepped to the front of the dais and said, "I will not dither with this, or try to make it seem something it is not. The seven core taaks have signed the Feegash peace agreement with the Eastils of the Republic of Hyre. For us, at least, the war is over."

There were no cheers in the assembly hall. Not one. The Beyl did not smile, either. He was announcing the fact that we had, in truth, lost—and he knew it, and we knew it, and while at some point in the future we might find things to cheer about, at that moment our lives changed, and the future as we knew it fell away, and we saw the cause for which we had given some of the best years of our lives, and in some cases our whole lives, reduced to executive fiat and diplomatic maneuvering that looked for its direction and its purpose not to justice and not to freedom, but to the profits of merchants and the fears of little men.

"Well . . . ," I whispered.

The sergeant beside me said, "Those who refuse to fight for freedom do not deserve to have it."

I could only nod and hope that things were not as dire as that.

Our post commander took the place of the Beyl, and began explaining our role for the next few months. Shielders were to serve as peacekeepers—we would all be taking border watches to make sure that taaks who had not yet signed the agreement could not break the cease-fire the seven core taaks had chosen to uphold.

Some of us had questions. We could not understand how we could be placed in the position of shielding against our own people—after all, those taaks which had not yet signed either the cease-fire agreement or the peace treaty certainly had the right to wage war.

And I could see from the look in our commander's eyes that he agreed with us. However, we were told that one of the provisions of the treaty was that all signatories would enforce it against all nonsignatories as well as signatories who might try to break its provisions.

Which meant that, for at least a while, we were allied with the damned Eastils against some of our own people.

The next bit of news was no better. Following adoption of the treaty by a majority of greater than fifty-one percent of the taaks, Beyltaak would begin observed disarmament, with Feegash inspectors watching as we destroyed our war matériel. The other six core taaks would be following the same program, and the Republic of Eastil would disarm along with us, major cities and border emplacements first, and smaller cities and towns as the inspectors got to them.

The time frame given to us for the total disarmament of Hyre was one year. To do it in that time, I thought, they were going to have to bring in an awful lot of Feegash observers.

Ethebet's Law and taak Common Law would be replaced

by something else, but the details of that were still being worked out.

Some military members would be released from duty immediately.

We listened in stunned silence as the details of this treaty unrolled over us. All Magics and Conventionals units would be broken up, and those people not released from duty in the next six months would be retained on a temporary basis, and moved into peacekeeping and inspection teams. None of these teams would retain any sort of military capability—not even a defensive capability. The Ba'afeegash mercenaries, operating under the joint command of the Beyl and a Feegash liaison, would be brought in as our defensive force until we demonstrated a satisfactory adherence to the provisions of the treaty. I was not the only one in the audience who noticed that the commander did not mention *who* had to find our adherence satisfactory.

It went on and on, and it was worse than we could ever have imagined. We could not comprehend who had found such a treaty acceptable. Nor could we understand how our taaks had signed away even their defense without consulting us.

Yes, the commander told us in the short question-and-answer session afterward, there had been a Hend in which this treaty had been discussed and the articles gone over one by one, and our fellow citizens had voted it in. We had been away on maneuvers at the time, and so had missed our opportunity to voice any objections we might have, but in a democracy, the majority ruled anyway, and had we all voted against it, we were told, Beyltaak would still have ratified the thing.

To us this had the feel of conspiracy—I could see in the eyes of my comrades in arms the same dull fury I knew showed in mine. Those who offer their lives in service to their taaksmen deserve better from their taaksmen than political maneuverings that rob them of their right to speak, simply because what the warriors have to say is not what those in power want to hear.

I vaguely remember walking out the door of the assembly hall after the meeting was over. I do not recall a single step of my walk to the Star's Rest, though those who do remember it say the skies had opened up and the rain poured like rivers on all of us.

I remember sitting at one of the long tables in the Star's

Rest's common room, vaguely. I remember, equally vaguely, the anger in the air, and brief spates of loose talk—suggestions of a coup, followed by some voice of reason noting that we did not serve the individual taaklord, or individual members of the taak who may have set us up by making sure we would be unavailable during the Hend; we served the office of the taaklord, and our taaksmen as a whole, and the laws of Tonk and Jostfar, and none of these had changed. That which we served still existed, and we would serve to our last day with honor, bearing the oaths by which we lived our lives the dignity, reverence, honor, and duty they demanded. We would not revolt.

Instead, we got very, very drunk. And at some point, as I lay alone in bed with the room spinning round me, a man in a cage smiled at me. And I smiled back.

As I said, I was very, very drunk.

For Gair and his men, the single cell all three shared in a mostly unused part of the prison was acceptable. It was not much bigger than the cells each had occupied alone in the jail, with four bunks instead of two; it had a fixed trap-cleaning toilet instead of the slop bucket the jail cell had used, which was an improvement, and running water from a small tap instead of a basin and a jug brought by the warden. It had two tiny windows up toward the ceiling, and even though they couldn't see out of them, Gair and his men appreciated them. The windows were not glassed over, so the spring breezes blew into the stone-walled cell, carrying the scents of early-blooming sweetbush and fragrant spring sea heather, and the sounds of birds building their nests under the eaves. In the winter, Gair imagined prisoners appreciated those windows less.

But that wasn't going to be an issue for them.

Still, Gair was growing anxious. A month had passed since they'd reached the prison, and as yet no word had come from the Republic confirming their prisoner-of-war status. He'd heard from the guard on duty when he came in that the old man over at the jail had died—the spring sickness had taken both him and his wife. Gair felt the pang of their loss; the old man had treated them well, and the old woman had cooked the sort of meals for them that she would have wanted a Tonk prisoner of war to receive. They had been good people, and Gair and Hale and Bokkam said a prayer for them when they got the news, and by so doing startled the guard who told them.

Gair was ready to go to the prisoner-of-war camp. He was equally ready to go straight home, if someone would just offer that as an option. He'd heard about the peace treaty from the guards—there wasn't much talk of anything else, in truth. People being discharged en masse on both sides of the border, and talk of disarmament though that hadn't started yet, and a lot of unhappiness from most of the common folk, from what he heard, though he heard more than one muttered tirade against the merchants who evidently had worked hard to get the peace vote through.

Well, he would live with it if it got him home, he supposed. And he would figure out what else he might do with his life, though he had never thought much past service before. He'd never had the time.

Their papers would come soon, and he and Bokkam and Hale would move on.

Soon.

Those of us whom the Beyltaak military kept on past the massive cuts of the first three months—cuts which sliced our forces by near two-thirds and dumped hundreds of unprepared military folk into an unprepared civilian world in Beyltaak alone— were kept because we knew how things went together, and so knew how to take them apart. For the Conventionals, this meant destroying weapons—from armor for men and horses to swords and catapults and crossbows to shields and caltrops and spring traps, as well as disposing of things like tents, uniforms, field kits, cavalry mounts and tack, and the thousands upon thousands of other things it takes to field an army of combined foot soldiers and cavalry.

For us, it primarily meant disassembling Shields one piece at a time, though we, too, had a fair amount of matériel to get rid of. We burned the masks, sold and eventually gave away our benches to anyone who would take them, and hauled the metal from linking rods to the suddenly busy blacksmiths and the lads over at the forge, one heavy rod at a time.

The forgemasters and their crews had never been so busy. Along with all the armor and swords and shields and linking bars and Saints know what else from Magics and Conventionals, they still had regular work, which had been steady enough. The war metals ended up graded and sorted according to quality and type, then melted down into ten-stone pigs for storage.

But the Feegash didn't want either us or the Eastils to hang on to the varying grades of iron and copper and brass and all the rest, because that would make rearming too easy. So as my few remaining comrades at arms and I worked, a handful of official Feegash observers, who always dressed in black, would come with their Eastil representatives in tow and with the Beyl or one of his sons or daughters along to make sure that everyone observed the rules. They would also bring purchasers, who would negotiate the price of the metals with the Beyl, and would arrange shipping on the spot.

I watched this process over and over, and I saw the gold that poured into Beyltaak—gold being very pretty and very nice for spending and goddamned useless for making weapons, so we could have all of that we cared to hang on to. And I saw our hard metals leaving for foreign hands in foreign shores—metals our people had dug out of our earth and forged in our foundries, metal with which three hundred years of Tonks had hung on to our borders and our freedom.

Magics is an essential part of any military, but as with all armies everywhere, the ground troops are the ones who determine whether the war will be won or lost. I saw us bleeding three hundred years' worth of iron into the vast lands beyond our shores, and I realized that we might never again be able to put together an army with sufficient strength to defend our own borders. If we did, it would be because our miners found new veins of ore, and new ways to get to it faster and better.

Pada and I spent our free time riding; we went out in the hills when we could get away from Beyltaak, or rode over the military trails on post when we could not. If we left the post, we took our strings out. I'd take all three of mine—my exquisite Tand mare and my fine gray and Flight, my sturdy dun steppe horse, another gelding, who had been my only personal mount before things got odd for me at the horse market. Pada used her two horses—a gorgeous black gelding and an old bay that she'd been riding since she was a child—and in contravention of the regular rules of the unit, she also snagged one of the unit horses as a packhorse. The rules had all fallen into the dirt by the time we started looking for ways to escape, though, and we were far from the only ones who fled Shields at every opportunity.

When we were in Shields, we felt like we had come to our mother's funeral and had been forced to stay and dismember her and sell off her remains and her belongings piece by piece to strangers. Those who didn't escape physically like Pada and me took to living in the wine casks at the Star's Rest.

I went home as infrequently as possible during those months. My father could not speak to me without ending up weeping, my mother took out her anger over this stripping of our taak, her adopted home, by forcing those of my brothers and sisters who still lived under her roof to practice, endlessly, the un-armed combat techniques of Dravitaak, where a shortage of natural resources had left people with a desperate need for such means of fighting.

Ma had trained all of us while we lived at home, of course, but since the peace process started, she'd clearly become impossible. Rik sent me a message once begging me to come home because Ma had him on the practice floor so often his bruises were getting bruises, and he was more afraid of her than of any surprise invasion by the Eastils.

Thinking about Riknir was my only bright spot in all of this. He would not spend his life in Magics even if he developed the talents for it.

And it did look like we would have markets for his budding jeweler's talents. For the first time in living memory, Beyltaak harbors groaned with the trade goods brought in from foreign ships. The Feegash had been as good as their word, negotiating trade routes so that we were once again on them. The ships came, the buyers came, and the money came. One day I stepped out of Shields to find workmen on the docks replacing the old boards with new. Another day, more workmen added new, brighter lamps to the docks.

The whores were the first to benefit from the new trade, and several of them suddenly started wearing silk and lace on the docks. But they were not the last. Empty lots within the taak started to fill up with new houses—lots on the hills and with a clear view of the bay sold first, but less choice land started moving quickly, too. The price of land became dear, while the price of common foodstuffs fell to the point that farmers started threatening to stop farming if the Beyl did not add a tax to the cheap foods coming in from across the seas.

"I got Stavinassi lace at the market yesterday," Pada told me a week before she and I were to be released from duty. We were on our way to temple, a duty we had neglected of late, though whether out of a sense of fear that Ethebet had abandoned us or a dread that we had failed her, I cannot say.

Ours was the last surviving group of the Beyltaak armed forces who would not move over into permanent peacekeeping or inspecting duties. Pada had made some sort of peace with the idea of binding herself to Dosil, and Dosil—the poor fool—had at last bought her a house on the bay, and had paid a taaklord's ransom for it. She would be moving into some semblance of domestic bliss as a merchant's wife, where she would keep the house and raise the children and do all those things that society matrons do, and she was happy. Happy to be almost done with the funereal atmosphere of Shields, happy to have a future of her choosing ahead of her. She still did not think much of Dosil, but she had learned discretion with astonishing speed, and now complained about him only to me, and only in lowered tones. "I only paid two shadris per span. It is ordinary lace—nothing like Tonk lace. It is both thin and plain. But I thought I could use it as curtain edging." She grinned at me. "Imagine lace on curtains."

"Imagine," I said, trying to keep the sarcastic edge in my thoughts out of my speech. I am not a lace-on-curtains kind of woman, and I think once Pada has lived the life of a goodwife for a year or three, with her wings clipped and her tongue curbed, she will discover that she is not, either.

And yet we may all find that we are to become lace-curtain men and women, we warriors. For who will win the continuation of Ethebet's Law and honor the Meditations of Saint Ethebet when the merchants have silenced us and stand atop us shouting the pronouncements of Saint Minda? Only Minda ever sought to speak for all the Saints, and the Mindan followers of Jostfar are the only ones who hold their path above all the rest, and would seek to press its strictures upon those who follow the other Saints.

Saints Hetterik and Cladmus and Rogvar offer little of value to those of us who would follow Ethebet; Hetterik championed lifelong celibacy, and while he is the saint of lawyers and mystics, the mystics are too far into their own worlds to offer their support, and the lawyers have argued more against Ethebet than for her.

Rogvar has ever been the favored saint of nomads, hunters, and farmers, those who sanctify the hunt and bless the fields and consecrate the herds with naked parties in open fields. Rogvar's folk are good people, and they hold their precepts sacred—they value life and death in equal measure, and take neither for granted; they embrace the ebb and flow of seasons and the richness of the earth. But they are not, as a rule, great talkers, and they live far from the Mindan horde, so are not often inconvenienced by them. And pressing the points of someone else's philosophy out of a great love of justice would not be their field, anyway; they bend to let the weight of the world wash over them, which is a good path. But it is not, and cannot be, the warrior's path.

Cladmus led artisans and all those who created from raw materials, and had little to say about the lives of his people except where they spun reality out of their dreams and visions. I could decree my path for Cladmus in the temple and turn away from Ethebet. I had served with honor, and my service was now, to all appearances, come to an end. Many of my comrades on their day of separation had gone as their first act and at the temple committed themselves to a new life under the hand of a new saint.

But many had not.

Pada and I had chosen the Great Temple, which sits in the heart of Beyltaak, for our ritual. We were agreed that we would seek the voice of Jostfar there, because the keepers of that temple were best versed in all five Saints and all six paths—they dedicate their lives to Jostfar alone, and serve the words as their sacred duty. Because they must serve all the words of all the paths, they are bound to favor none. They and they alone wear the mark of Jostfar singly, and live without choosing the path of one of the Saints. The keeper of the post temple is an Ethebettan; she could not offer us the broader guidance we sought.

Pada and I entered through the tall carved doors of the Great

Temple, and the silence of the place rolled over us. The temple was busy—it ever is, for Jostfar speaks most clearly when the air is still and the mind is listening, and the words are always at hand there.

We made obeisance at the well. All wells and springs are the symbols of Jostfar, and sacred, for water is life. Each of us drew up a dipper of water and drank slowly. We wished each other luck, and parted company. Two people cannot seek a path in the company of each other; communion between god and man is a private thing, and brooks no third voice.

I went first to the shrine of Ethebet, which in the Great Temple is a sword half sheathed in an uncarved stone. Uncounted soldiers before me have stood there, and rested a hand on the sword's oversized hilt, and searched for guidance. My search would be whether I would follow Ethebet's path at all; it was no easy question. I rested both hands on the hilt with my wrists supported by the crosspieces, and in my mind told both Jostfar and Ethebet, "I have sworn to serve my taak, to defend with my life or by my death my taaksmen and the Confederacy and those who dwell within it, and to defend the paths of the Saints and the justice of Jostfar against enemies from without and from within, and I do not seek now to end my oath. I seek only to know how I may best serve in this new peace."

I sought my own silence then, and let my gaze drift over the Meditations of Saint Ethebet written on the wall before the sword in stone, not seeking favored sections or familiar passages, but only waiting for something to fall beneath my eye that spoke to the moment and the place in which I found myself.

And Meditation 397 stood out for me. "In peacetime, the path of the warrior remains hard, for the gratitude of the masses falls away, and those who value peace above all call for the warrior to put away the sword. But the enemies of peace never sleep, and the warrior who lays down his sword offers his throat at the altar of sacrifice, and gives to the enemy the lives of all those he swore to protect."

I closed my eyes for a moment and thought on Ethebet's words; that Meditation would have been all many of my comrades needed to decide them on their path. But I have never looked at the Meditations on the shrine walls as an oracle; if I did I could as well buy one of the scribe's copies from market and pin it to a wall in my quarters and throw darts at the list when I was uncertain about the direction of my life.

I wished rather to choose my path with the seriousness it deserved; I wanted to honor the sacredness of my life, and the random toss of a dart would not serve that.

Instead, with the Meditation in mind, I sought the assistance of one of the keepers.

He smiled at me. "We've seen a lot of Ethebet's brood through these doors of late."

"I'm in the last unseparated group," I told him. "We'll likely become scarce again soon enough."

"No hurry," he said. "Ethebet's scholars have penned some fine works. Which do you need?"

"I'm looking for glosses on Meditation 397," I told him. "And"—I took a deep breath—"those works by Cladmus's scholars that offer direct counterpoint."

His eyebrows rose. "You've some work ahead of you. Cladmus and Ethebet run at crosscurrents on the issue of path and duty. Cladmus champions the vision of the one as the paramount duty of the pathseeker to his path; Ethebet's focus is on the duty of the one to the protection of the many, even if the price of that duty is the cost of the one. If you're getting into Meditation 397, I have everything from parables and treatises to histories that are offered in support. And"—he looked up at the ceiling, thoughtful, and then at the aisles of books and scrolls and bound manuscripts that filled the temple from front to back and side to side—"first a quick visit to Cladmus's shrine. You will have to tell me which of two of Cladmus's Meditations speaks more to your question."

He led me through the stacks at a goodly pace, and we rounded the corner to find the interlocking ring that is one of Cladmus's symbols, and his wall of Meditations.

The keeper frowned and peered at the wall, and finally said, "Top left, second column, number 117, or middle of the next column, number 351."

I read the words of Cladmus in Meditation 117. "The voice of Jostfar is immanent in the pathfinder, and makes itself known in the path, only when the pathfinder walks alone. This need, the need for the pathfinder to follow his own vision, is therefore also his highest duty, that the full beauty of his life may be laid bare and Jostfar's blessing may be shared by all."

I located 351, and read it next. "The way of the man of vision is heaped with the scorn of the masses, for the price of the vision may be the sacrifice of love, of friendship, of honor, of charity, of family, of home, of everything but the single truth of that vision. Yet the worth of the vision cannot be known until it is brought forth, so it is the duty of the visionary to suffer the loss of all else if that is the price his vision demands to allow itself to be born."

I sighed, for a moment envying Pada, whose big decision was whether or not she should agree to Mindan law when marrying Dosil, or whether she should fight for the right to retain Ethebet's Law and bring Dosil in under that, so that she would retain her property and her name and the right to divorce him if she decided he did not suit her. Her family was pushing for Mindan law, and for her to return to Minda's path, and she remained undecided.

For me, the question looked like it was going to be whether I preferred to be scorned as a soldier without an army, or as an artist without a patron. Either way, it looked like my days of being respected by the masses were about to come to an end.

I looked at the keeper, and I do not know what he saw on my face, but he laughed softly.

"If you ask a hard question, you must prepare yourself for a hard answer," he told me. "And yet, it may not be as bad as all that."

"You have recommendations?"

"I think so. I would suggest a mere two books to you. Neither is a scholarly gloss or a treatise; nor is either a collection of stories or parables. Both are histories after a sort—they are biographies. One is quite old. It is the biography of Helmath of Boldrintaak, and I have it both in the original High Speech and in a later Middle Speech adaptation. The High Speech version is better if you're comfortable reading it. The second is a recent writing on the life of Loteran the Philosopher, who was an eminent Cladmian. Died in Kopataak four years ago."

"Why those?"

"Because Helmath was a warrior in peacetime. And Loteran

was a visionary in wartime. Both were unswervingly true to their paths, both lived lives that exemplify the Meditation you wish to know better and its obverse, and both dealt with issues that may help you answer your question and determine your path."

I took both books, thinking that war is a hard religion to follow, but that peace looked to be just as hard and twice as confusing, and left a hefty offering in the offering box. The keepers need to eat, after all, and they need to be able to commission more books. And then I went to the little eatery where Pada and I agreed we would meet when we had finished our rituals.

In truth, from the size of the two biographies I carried under my arm, I thought I would be lucky to complete my own path-seeking ritual in a week, and *that* only if I spent every spare moment in its diligent pursuit, but I also thought Pada would loose her sharp tongue at me if I did not show up at our meeting place for a week. And we had been getting on well enough— two souls adrift together in a stormy sea—that I did not wish to cause a rift.

She waved me over to the little table with a broad smile. "It's to be Ethebet, not Minda, for me," she said. "I went first to Minda's shrine and closed my eyes and turned thrice before the wall, and with my left hand on the arch I put my right hand out, and when I opened my eyes I'd gotten 62."

Which would be at about shoulder height for Pada. Apparently, in Pada's search for her path, the Saints needed to be sure that they had nothing important to say that lay toward either the ceiling or the floor, or she would render them mute.

"And 62 is . . . ?" I asked.

"Veer not from your chosen path, neither left nor right, nor question where your path may lead, for that to which you have bound yourself may not be unbound."

Which if you ask me is a fine Meditation for a sheep, but a dreadful one for a human. Nevertheless, Minda herself had cost herself a follower. And had done it by permitting that particular bit of thought to fall in the middle of a column. See what I mean about some who would do as well to throw darts at the wall? Religion should be a course of sober reflection and study and thought, but quite some few see it as nothing more than a lottery, and will happily base the course of their lives on a single throw of the dice.

"Very good. Of course, if Dosil gets that same Meditation, you may have difficulty getting him to convert to Ethebet's Law." Assuming we would be permitted to remain under Ethebet's Law—something I kept trying very hard to avoid considering.

Pada frowned, her eyebrows drawing in and her nose wrinkling. At the tables around us, I saw the men who had been surreptitiously watching her begin to gather themselves to come to her aid should she just give a sign what had disturbed her. I could be bleeding with a knife between my ribs and not draw such instant concern. It may seem that I speak from envy about this.

Well, I do.

"I think if he would not permit himself to live under Ethebet's ruling, even if he still followed Minda in his heart, I would put him aside and find another."

I could *see* the men at table around us, who were listening in on our conversation with less and less success at hiding the fact, thinking, Yes, oh, yes, put him aside, take me, take me, I'll lie in a puddle on the ground and you can walk on top of me to keep your shoes clean if you'll just take me, and I swear on all the Saints the temptation to tell Pada "If you would only stop pogging your horse, you would have an easier time with Dosil" almost got the better of me. If nothing else, I could have had a fine laugh watching that thought working its way through their brains—but then one of them would have run over and begged her to let him watch, and I do not know that I would have been able to keep from killing him.

So I kept my mouth shut and let them all live, and Pada and I had a pleasant enough lunch. Envy makes an interesting spice for steak and greens.

As we were leaving, we brushed past the Feegash diplomat who had been at the assembly where we first received news that Beyltaak had signed the peace treaty. He looked at me, that same intent gaze I'd seen at the assembly, and he cocked his head to one side and smiled the tiniest bit, and nodded to me as we passed.

And the strange thing was, he never noticed Pada at all.

"Feegash *and* haatuuf," she muttered after we had passed him, and I raised an eyebrow.

"How do you know he prefers men to women?" I asked, wondering if perhaps the Feegash had some way of marking this in their attire or hair fashions.

"He did not even notice me," she said.

I tried not to laugh. I did. I failed, but I tried.

6

The last of us said our good-byes in a small ceremony presided over by our commander and our remaining officers. We received our last commendation pip—a small gray bar with an emerald green stripe running diagonally from left to right that signified we had served to our unit's end. It was not a pip that most of us would bother sewing on; the uniforms that we had worn with such pride would go into our trunks, folded with reverence and more than a little pain and put away as a part of our lives that would never come again. When it was over, we stood in the common hall for the last time, gathered into little clusters, talking with people who had been second family to us for most of our lives.

People, it became increasingly clear, we were unlikely to ever see again. Our skills had more value abroad than at home, apparently.

I'd been offered work across the sea in Greton, training and breeding horses for taaklord wages. Had, too, been offered a position in the Sinali principality of Hivu as a magical watcher. The Hivusi were trying to get a dozen Tonk Shielders to keep track of their borders for them, and the money for that work was almost obscene, it was so much.

"I have an offer to travel to North Point Isle up on the Path of Stars," Pada said. "I'd work as a Magics communicator and stormwatcher for the city, the island, and surrounding region," she said.

"That's up on the equator, isn't it?"

She nodded. "Right above Marqal. It never snows there."

I didn't feign surprise—I hadn't the heart to make fun of Pada any longer. "But you're going to marry Dosil, aren't you?"

"He was happy enough to bed me under Ethebet's Law," she said with a dark look, "but he wanted to bind me under Minda's law, which would have given him control over my money, my property, and my actions, and which would have forbade us the option of divorce. If I did not return to Minda, he said, he would disown me." She smiled a small, pointed smile. "So I sent him into the street right then and found a buyer for my house on Short Street the next day."

Pada valued property. She valued money. She had been putting aside the majority of her earnings as a Shielder for as long as I had known her. She probably had more gold than Dosil; and he had tried to claim control of it. Fool. I was not the least bit surprised that she had rid herself of Dosil. But that she had sold the house on Short Street that he had bought for her—*that* astonished me.

Her smile grew broader. "And then I went to the Star's Rest and bedded the first three men whose paths I crossed."

Apparently it took peacetime to bring out the warrior spirit in Pada. I laughed, and thinking to be funny, I said, "All at once, or one at a time?"

She looked at me through narrowed eyes and said, "I'll never tell," and I honestly did not know how to respond, except to say, "Well, then . . ." And, out beyond my depth in a conversation with Pada for the first time ever, I changed the subject back to the work offer she had received.

"Are you going to take the offer?"

"I'd be insane not to. I'll have one of the apartments within the weather tower itself, and they are fine and well appointed. The North Pointers are willing to pay me in either gold or horse cash, and they have offered to start me at four hundred horse cash the month."

The amount staggered me. "Whose calendar?" I asked, suddenly suspicious. Our calendar has thirteen months, six weeks to the month, more or less, and six days to the week. But some folks use the solstice calendar, which has only four months, and some use religious calendars which have varying numbers of months, some with as few as six, some with as many as twenty. Nor is my knowledge of the subject all that vast; I discovered there were different calendars when I started taking commissions for my jewelry from foreigners and found out that figuring a due date for a piece was not the simplest thing in the world.

"They use a twelve-month calendar," she said.

"That's still a lot of money, then."

She nodded. "And they'd pay my passage and ship my belongings, and give me a month each year—by their calendar—in which I could come home to visit with my family. It has to be during the calm season, and I would not also receive my wages while I traveled, but it seems a reasonable offer."

Pada was not as close to her family as I was to mine. A month probably seemed more than adequate for visiting them; I doubted that she saw them much more while she was still living in the same taak.

"What about you?" she asked.

"I've received offers," I said. "I'm not leaving, though. My family is here, and I'm going to stay and make my jewelry."

"Then you chose the path of Cladmus?"

"No," I said, lowering my voice. "I'll keep my braid and follow Ethebet." I did not know why that was such an uncomfortable admission for me to make. Already, in Beyltaak, we warriors felt ourselves unnecessary, and got the first taste of knowing that others saw us the same way. The taaksmen would ask us how the disarmament was coming, and we would pass on what we knew—but no longer did anyone look at us as essential to their survival.

Beyltaak was the fourth of the core taaks to complete disarmament. Many of the smaller taaks had not even signed the treaty, but as the larger taaks fell under the interim measures of the treaty, more and more signed.

And the process of peace moved smoothly. Our communicators, who alone of Magics would stay in their current locations and positions, though as civilians, received regular reports from Tonk disarmament inspectors in Eastil towns that they were complying fully.

Eastil inspectors sent the same reports about us. They'd watched us closely, and I confess that at last I realized that this thing was going to happen as the Feegash had negotiated it—

that the Eastils would not sneak vast caches of weapons past the inspectors, that they would not come pouring over the mountains after us or sail into our ports one day with ballistae aimed at our homes.

The Confederacy and the Republic were two dogs leashed and muzzled within sight of each other, but with a new owner who had no intention of letting them fight.

The peace was real.

When I walked out the door of Shields, I was going to be free. My life would be my own, and I would be able to teach Rik how to work with gems and metal without having to worry that someday three men from Magics Intelligence would show up and take him away and put him into service to his taak for the rest of his life.

My other brothers and sisters would be safe, too, and my growing horde of nieces and nephews. My parents had done the near impossible—raised fourteen children in wartime, seen many of them go to war as soldiers, and had every one of us survive to see peace.

And if some of us didn't know how to deal with peace—well, we would have to learn.

"When will you be leaving if you take this work?" I asked Pada.

"The ship is in port now, and will sail on Rogvarsday."

"That's four days."

She nodded. "I sold my house and received full payment for it. My belongings are already boxed—it will be as simple to have them loaded onboard the ship as to have them carried to my parents' house or to a new one I buy for myself. I'd still be working in the View, but no one would be trying to kill me anymore." She frowned a little. "I think it will be hard to learn to live in a new place, and learn a new language, but it will not be forever. It will be for a while." She shrugged. "I have to do something, Talyn. And unlike you, I have no second work for which I trained myself. I thought I would be a soldier forever, and I acted accordingly. This would let me do what I know how to do, and provide for myself—since I have discovered I don't want to pay the price of having someone else provide for me."

"You're going to do it."

She looked a bit surprised. "I suppose I am."

"I'll miss you," I told her. And I, too, was surprised, because I discovered that I meant it.

Pada's story wasn't unique. Apparently the rest of the world had a great hunger for magic-talented people, but had not been selectively breeding for them for the past three hundred years. All of my comrades had received the same sorts of offers I had received. Most of them were going to take those offers. Most of the Shielders who had separated out before us were, in fact, already gone—scattered across the face of the world like seeds blown from a dandelion in a particularly hard wind.

We think of the people in our taak as people we will know for the rest of our lives. People are born, live out their entire lives, and die within its walls, simply because their taak is the only place in the world that will ever truly be their home. We expect that we will know everyone we know for as long as we both live.

This scattering was unprecedented; I stood in the vaulted meeting hall of Shields and looked at faces I had known all my life, and should have been able to see any time because they were my people—*my* people—and I realized that most of them I would never see again.

In that moment, I felt a huge hole rip in the fabric of my life. And it was one I could not fix.

"Stand for inspection!" someone shouted from down the long corridor, and Gair and Hale and Bokkam all stood, and lined up before the bars.

A short, balding, fat man in exquisite clothes followed two guards Gair didn't know, who wore unfamiliar uniforms. Men from the prisoner-of-war camp? His heart leapt. He and his men had been kept in this cell so long he had begun to lose hope.

He heard the man in the only other occupied cell on their corridor say his name when asked, and heard the list of his offenses read off. Gair was sickened. The man was scheduled for execution within two days, he discovered.

"Make that today," the fat man said after the sentence was read to him. "I see no reason to keep an animal like that in these walls another day." He had a strong Greton accent, and Gair realized he was a foreign speculator who'd bought the prison as a profit maker. Gretons owned some of the prisons in the Republic—Gair had never been in one, but he had not heard good things.

So. Not from the prisoner-of-war camp.

The man and the guards started to turn back, and Gair felt a moment of panic. "What about us?" he shouted, and all three men stopped and turned, surprised.

"There's someone else on this wing?"

"There are three of us, sir," Gair called. If he hadn't shouted, it might have been days before someone came their way again. He suppressed a shudder.

The three men walked down the corridor again and stopped before Gair.

"Records," the little fat man snapped at the one who carried the sheaf of papers in his hand.

"I swear, Master Woodfinder, there are no other prisoners listed on this wing."

The little man glared at his assistant and said, "Find their damned records. This—this is the reason these holes need to be inspected when you buy them. You see that now? Do you?"

"There will be no prison records on us, sir," Gair said, knowing that he was speaking out of turn, but knowing, too, that his situation had no chance of improving if he waited for these people to find records that did not exist.

The little man glared at him. "And why is that, you?"

"Because we are prisoners of war, sir. We were being kept here while our records were sent from the Republic."

The little man erupted with laughter. "What a fine, fine story. You give us a tale we cannot check, but that runs counter to every system and rule that has ever been put into place for the treatment of prisoners of war, and you think we'll believe it because we're new and special forms of fools? Is that it?"

"It's true, sir. We were taken prisoner during the Eastil communications outage. There has been some problem with reaching them to get our records, but surely someone should be available now."

"Surely, eh?" The little man looked up at Gair with cold eyes ringed by rolls of fat that gave him a piggish air. "From the lengths of your beards, you may have been in here a while, son, so I'll give you the news. The war is over, the armies on both sides of the border have been disbanded, all the prisoners of war have gone home, and if ever there *was* someone who could prove that you were telling the truth, that someone is long gone. But if you *were* telling the truth, you would have been able to prove you were soldiers when you were taken prisoner. You would have had your tags, your ring, and your tattoo—and even if someone took your tags and your ring from you, the tattoo would still be there." He smiled a slow, mean smile. "So let's see it."

"Only the regulars had tattoos, sir," Gair said. "Special units did not, and did not carry identification of other sorts on sorties. Our job was to infiltrate the Tonk population; Eastil identification could have betrayed our mission."

"Which is a bit convenient, isn't it?"

"Not if it keeps us from going home, sir," Bokkam said. "We had rings and cards, but those, and our uniforms, and anything else that could link us to the Eastil Republic we buried in a cache not too far from Injtaak," Bokkam said. "We could find the cache, sir. We marked it well."

"Necessitating a trip to Injtaak for you and your friends— and a chance to escape in the process, no doubt? I don't think we'll be traveling to Injtaak together, you and me."

"We could prove who we are by talking to an Eastil representative, if one can be found," Gair said. "The Tonk Senders and Shielders could use their magic to identify us—that's how they caught us in the first place. And the guards here know why we're here."

"Oh, I'm sure they *did*," the man said. "*Did* being the important word. If you paid them to lose your records, you did yourself no favors, son. That's part of the reason they're all gone—that they were willing to lose records for a bit of gold. I bought this place from the previous owner because he was tired of dealing with guards who didn't follow the rules, who didn't keep proper paperwork, who sold prisoners their freedom and sometimes even safe passage out of the taak to go with it. The corruption in here started to stain his name. I'm a bit tougher. I'm Greton. I don't run any of my businesses from the top of the Heights, so people in my businesses don't have the opportunity to become corrupt. I don't mind getting in and checking on people to be sure they are following rules and staying honest. I started a poor man, and I know how to work."

Gair looked at the new owner of the prison with dismay. "How, then, can I prove to you that the three of us are legitimate prisoners of war?"

"That's your problem. But you're not going to occupy one of the best cells in a wing that I'm opening back up while you solve it. You three can go into basement holding until we find out who you are. Might give you incentive to be more forthcoming about who you really are, and why you're really here. Because until you present me proof of who you are and why you're here, not a one of you will see the sun again."

And he turned and walked away, his men following him like two leashed dogs.

Later that day, a squad of guards who were strangers to all three came and put Gair, Bokkam, and Hale into shackles—though not without a struggle—and hauled them into the cold, damp, moldering darkness of the cellar holds.

How odd that my nightmares were about a man in a cage calling out to me, pleading with me to save him, and about a woman all in white sitting on a hill far away, watching me but neither saying nor doing anything. It was not odd that I was *having* nightmares—only that the subject should be so far from reality. For we last Shielders were no more than out of Shields than two units of the Ba'afeegash Light Horse Mercenaries and three units of the Ba'afeegash Heavy Foot offloaded their horses and arms and equipment and set up camp within the empty buildings.

I would have thought my nightmares could find enough fodder in that hell's image to keep them churning for years.

I cringed watching the moriiad moving into our world. We were under occupation—we Tonks who had never tolerated the presence of an occupying army on our sacred soil since the Tand Wars in the North Taaks of Tandinapalis twelve hundred years earlier. We were an occupied territory, and if our occupiers were not conquerors, but simply a peacekeeping force to ensure that we did not return to war against the Eastils, and if they brought little in the way of weapons, and if they were civil in ways both large and small, and if they put their backs into repaving roads within Beyltaak and building new roads outside of it, and digging new wells, and if they did not interfere with our self-government, none of that mattered. They lived on our land, in our buildings, within our walls, and the simple fact of their presence chafed.

I sat at the long table with my father and mother, and with those of my siblings who remained in the house on Fallwater Street, and listened to my father make dark predictions, and watched my mother chopping vegetables as if they were Feegash mercenaries.

"This peace cannot hold," he said, and the muscles in his jaw bulged and twitched. "It's no true peace. It's a ploy of the damned Eastils, and I'll wager house and hearth against a stone in the road they have vast caches of weapons set by against the day that the last of our warriors have sailed to the Dragon Sea and the last of our steel pigs has been pounded into wheel cladding and horseshoes in Franica and Sinali. We'll sit here naked as the day we were born and watch them pour over us like birds to an orchard when the fruit is ripe, and watch them peck us to bits, and install their king as our king, and tax the lifeblood from us and turn our children and our children's children into mindless little Eastil sheep that jump at the crack of their whip."

Which were wind-horse words and he knew it. But still, in these times, he'd earned the right to a bit of exaggeration.

My mother said nothing.

I bought myself a little house out by the East Grounds, where I would have good pasturage for my horses and a workroom for my jewelry, and I tried not to think about what the Confederacy was come to, and what our future was. Like my father, I could not see any good in it, but like my mother, I could not find it within myself to utter the fears that filled me, and in any case I had no one to talk to. Rik, perhaps, but he was still a child, and filled with childish fury that the Shielders were gone without him having once worn the uniform. He did not yet see the larger picture—of everything else that was gone. He rode my old horse, Flight, which I had given him, daily through the streets to see me, and we made jewelry together, and trotted through the wild lands outside the taak as we found time, and we did not talk about the Tonk, or freedom, or the paths.

Each morning I rebraided my warrior's braid, and each morning went first to the small shrine I'd built to honor Ethebet, and there I practiced the karaadda, the unarmed dance of war that I'd learned at my mother's knee, because I had sworn myself to do so. Each day I renewed my path, but my path lay barren. The peace did not need me. And if I found that fact bitter, still I prospered under it. My taaksmen, made wealthy by new trade and treasuries no longer drained by war, spent their money like new-made princes, and part of what they spent it on was jewelry.

Each night I spent in sweat-drenched nightmares, and if most of the features of them changed nightly, two things remained. One was the man in the cage pleading for my help. The other was the distant woman in white, who vanished each time I approached her, though I swear each night she was a little closer to me when I first saw her than she had been the night before.

The nightmares left me dry-mouthed with fear, trembling without knowing why, and feeling both helpless and stupid for not knowing what they meant.

I would have paid all my new-made wealth to be rid of those dreams.

I had just finished my day's karaadda and, sweating and flushed and a little short of breath, had stepped into my workshop to start my fire so that it would be ready for me when I had finished my shower, when a Feegash diplomat stepped through the door. *The* Feegash diplomat, in truth—the one who had stood on the dais that day that the commander announced peace, the one I had seen in the streets who never failed to catch my eye.

"You have been recommended to me for a special commission," he said, and studied me with a smile far too warm for my comfort.

Business is business. This has become the catchphrase of the merchants in the taak, and on the way to making my living as a craftsman, I had become a merchant, too. So I did not tell him, "Go die in the street like the dog you are." I said, "I will be happy to discuss a commission with you, but I would be grate-

ful if you would come back at the ringing of the Chicken; I'll
have the doors open and will be presentable."

"You could be nothing less than presentable," he told me.
"Still—I'll be happy to return later. The Chicken, though . . . I
still have not become comfortable with your hours—they shift
and shrink and stretch with the seasons, and I—"

I interrupted him. "The next ringing of all the bells," I said.

"Ah," he said, and caught either a whiff of me or perhaps
heard the edge in my voice. "I shall absent myself until then."
He stepped backward out the door, pulling it shut behind him.

I dropped the door bar into its brackets behind him, something I am not wont to do under most circumstances. My taaksmen knock before entering, and there is little cause for locks.
But dealing with foreigners, well, foreign means incomprehensible, doesn't it?

I took my shower, a quick step-in-soap-off-step-out process,
since the spring water that feeds the public waterworks is just
this side of ice even hard into summer. Muscles pushed hard as
I'd pushed mine little liked the shock of ice water when they
were still hot, yet I did not wish to take the time to heat the
buckets of water on my stove that would take the edge of cold
off a bath.

I deeply missed the baths of the Star's Rest, which were deep
and perpetually hot and fresh. But most of the Shielders were
gone, and to even survive, the Star's Rest had opened its doors
to the public, and stepping once through the doorway to find it
full of strangers and foreigners and empty of the comrades with
whom I had shared my life had nearly broken my heart. I had
not been back since.

So, cold and soggy but clean, with my hair back in its braid
and dripping down my back, and in a work shirt, leather apron,
and leather breeches, I opened the door just before the bells
rang in the Chicken, and the bells had not finished echoing
through the street than the Feegash was back, with his bright
cornsilk hair and eyes pale as new beer but ringed with black,
like those of the mountain cats that had sometimes crossed our
paths when we were in the field, and with his broad, friendly
smile that did not make me forgive him for being Feegash.

I added fuel to my work fire, then offered him one of my
work stools across the table from my peg. "You have already

seen some of my work?" I asked. "Or shall I show you what I have on hand?" I'd created a few pieces for myself that were not for sale—they were pieces that I had created to demonstrate my facility with various finishes like oxidizing and scratching, polishing and matting, as well as with the core techniques of jewelry crafting, which included stone cutting, stone setting, chain crafting, doming, enameling, beadworking, wireworking, and more.

"I've seen two of your pieces. I'm quite certain that I want you to create the piece I have in mind—but I would still like to see what you have on hand."

"May I ask what you've seen?"

"An opal cloak brooch worn by Aaral Beyl. And a jewel-hilted dagger—cabochon rubies and inlaid onyx in fine silver, I believe—that Aaral had you do for his mistress."

Aaral was the youngest brother of the Beyl with whom I had served in Shields, and he had become quite a patron of my work. I'd done a round half dozen of those daggers for him, and he had, if the rumors circulating had the right of it, given one to each of his mistresses as a token of his esteem. Some of us speculated—crassly—that he hoped to see them find out about each other and use the daggers on each other; he was fond of blood sport, was Aaral, and my least favorite of the Beyl brothers, for all that he paid both well and on time. We speculators also wondered if he was not more likely to wear at least one matched pair of the daggers between his ribs before too long.

What sort of man gives his lovers knives? Especially when he also keeps secrets from them.

"I recall both pieces," I told the Feegash. He was looking for something showy, then. I pulled out my work case and opened it for him. It is a plain, polished wood box, lined inside with black velvet, and it shows off what I have done without detracting from it.

And the Feegash was impressed. "I especially like that," he said, lifting a gold chain made of overlapping links that wove through each other in a pattern that looked more complex than it was. It was an elegant piece, and nothing like the gaudier jeweled pieces I would have expected him to favor.

I waited until he put the chain back in the box, then closed it. "So. Tell me what you wish to commission."

"I'm going to need a few things to start—but in the long run, I daresay I could employ your skills full-time and take you away from the uncertainty of commission work."

He was offering to be my patron?

"We should concentrate on this first commission first, I think," I told him.

He tilted his head a little and gave me that smile again. "You don't like me much."

"I don't know you," I said. "But you are Feegash, and I was a Shielder before this peace."

"And the peace does not suit you."

I don't dissemble well. "No."

"Even though you are free now to pursue a craft other than war."

"Still no."

He laughed, and it was the sort of laugh that catches a woman low in the belly and sends fire through her blood. My mind was doing a fine job of recognizing him as the enemy, but my body had other suggestions to make. "Nor do you make long speeches about it. Well enough. If you'll agree to it, I'll hire you for this first commission and see if in that time I can convince you to see me as something other than the enemy."

"I'll be happy to take your commission, but I have to tell you that I'll see you as the enemy until you send the mercenaries back home and gather up the rest of your people and follow them."

"Words I have heard from every Tonk since I arrived, in one form or another. And yet I have not heard them said with such deep conviction, I think, as just now and coming from your mouth." He sighed. "I want five gold wristbands," he said. "One is to be a gift for the head of our delegation—my thanks for his permitting a diplomat of my junior status to accompany the rest of the negotiators on this trip. The others are to be for my fellow diplomats, for tolerating my presence."

"There are only six of you here?"

"Diplomats? Yes, though we brought staff and support people with us. And there *were* to have been only five diplomats. I was fortunate to cajole my way into this assignment."

I did not want to be curious, but he said that with such enthusiasm that I could not help myself. I sighed and asked, "Why?

Why would you want to come here, where you had to know you would not be welcome?"

He leaned his elbows on the table and stared into my eyes, and his voice was suddenly conspiratorial. "You want my official reason, or the real one?"

"If you mean would I prefer you lied to me or told me the truth, I'd rather have the truth," I said.

He stared at me for just an instant with an expression of disbelief. And then he burst out laughing. "Well, *you* are certainly no diplomat." He shook his head and stared at the floor, chuckling, and I was startled by what a wonderful laugh he had, and how very charming he looked at that moment. Some men have faces that look strained when they laugh, as if they have not had much practice at it. This Feegash had a face used to laughter, and better yet, his was the kind of warm, friendly laughter that invites the listener to join him. I found myself smiling at him. He took a breath and said, "I have spent years with people who would rather die than phrase things as you just did. Your words felt like—like a Tonk shower. Shockingly cold, but clean and refreshing once you catch your breath. The truth, then. I was working as one of the diplomatic envoys in Injtaak during what was to have been the peace discussion between the Tonks and the Eastils. You remember that?"

I nodded, noncommittal, but suddenly my heart was racing.

"Things went wrong, but just before they did, there was this woman . . ." He stared off at nothing, his eyes unfocused. "This may not make much sense to you—it doesn't even make much sense to me when I say it out loud. She was one of the Shielders who were guarding the conference."

"It's called a Hend," I corrected.

"Yes. She was not there physically, and I would not even have known of her presence or the presence of the other Shielders but that we were told they would be keeping guard during the confer—the Hend. But while she was searching for enemies, she touched my mind." His voice grew soft. "I don't know what she looks like. I don't know what she sounds like, or how old she is. She could be a toothless crone. She could be married with a dozen children and a bad-tempered husband. It might be that I have no chance with her, and that this thing I have done is chasing after dreams and nonsense. But whoever she was, she had the most perfect mind I could have imagined. She was beautiful beyond compare on the inside." He looked at me, and gave me an embarrassed smile. "So I have come here to find her, because I fell in love with her mind and I must meet her and see if I can win her."

I laughed to hide the emotions that were churning inside me. "Even if she is a toothless crone? Or a woman with a dozen children and a bad-tempered husband?"

He shrugged. "If she already has a love and a family and a life, I will wish her the best of luck and take my grief away quietly—I will not stand between her and any happiness she already has. If she is old, or ugly, I don't care. Her mind is beautiful. She is a goddess on the inside, and I cannot but believe that sort of radiance will show through in her eyes, and that no matter what she looks like, I will still see her as beautiful."

I looked into his eyes, into those beautiful eyes, and finally knew why he had seemed familiar to me from the first time I saw him. He was the mystic, the undiscovered saint, the spring of cool, clear water I had touched. The one who had carried none of the grime of life in his thoughts. And he had come to Beyltaak in search of me, because he had fallen in love with my mind.

The air in my workshop felt thin, as if I had suddenly been transported high into the mountains.

"Tonks keep to our own kind, you know," I told him. "If you find her, the chances stand that she will want nothing to do with you—that you would be a betrayal to her path and her beliefs and that your presence in her life would bring shame to her family and perhaps even cost her them."

"One obstacle at a time," he said. "First I have to find her."

"And how will you know her?"

"I don't know," he admitted. "She touched my mind. I do not have the magic that would let me search for her." He sighed. "Please do not take offense at this, but when I first saw you, I hoped you were her. You were in the crowd at the announcement of peace, where I had been sent to observe, and of all the people in that crowd, you alone stood out. You seemed familiar to me." He smiled sadly. "And you were so beautiful I hoped you were her—though I know this is terrible selfishness on my part, to hope that a woman so beautiful inside could look like a goddess outside as well."

He thought I had the most beautiful mind he could imagine, and that I looked like a goddess. I was still waiting for the part that would offend me.

Yet I could not love him. He was a foreigner, a Feegash. Worse, he was one of those directly responsible for pushing a cheap and unwelcome peace on my people, even if he had held only a minor role.

"Where would you have gone if you had not come here?" I asked, and I know. I know. This is one of those questions women ask when they are looking for excuses to do things they should not do, and I was looking for excuses, but . . . he thought I was beautiful, and yet he didn't care about the way I looked because he had fallen in love with my mind, and he would take an ugly woman with my mind rather than a pretty woman without it.

That is the sort of revelation that will make even a strong woman's resolve waver. And yes. I wavered.

"I was offered the post of second diplomat of the Feegash delegation in Reedisatanis, the capital city of Bheki."

"That would be . . . a promotion?"

"It would have been a huge promotion. It would have been a leap over three full grades in one jump. Second-in-command is no small thing, and second-in-command in a capital city posting would have been a huge honor."

"And you gave that up for a woman you have never seen and have no sure way to find?"

"And you think I'm a fool. That is why my official story is nothing like the truth." He sighed.

My beautiful mind was smacking itself repeatedly against all the hard surfaces the soul can devise, though I hoped none of that would show on the outside.

He had given up a huge promotion that would have taken him to what tales say is one of the most beautiful and exotic cities in the world, for just the chance to meet me.

And I was not even going to tell him that he had found me, because I was a Tonk, and Tonks stick to their own kind. Because if I brought home a Feegash diplomat, I would kill my father and shame my mother. Because the path of the Tonk warrior—Ethebet's hard, narrow road of honor—had no room on it for some outlander with beautiful eyes and the soul of a saint who loved me for my mind.

Because he was not the sort of man I could hide in a closet and only bring out to take to my bed. And he deserved better than that, anyway. He deserved someone who would love him freely and proudly and who would stand before the world unafraid to declare that love. That wasn't any woman he was going to find in Tonk lands.

I took a deep breath. "You set yourself on a fool's mission," I told him. "If you can still get that promotion to Bheki, you should take it. Every obstacle you can imagine and a hundred you cannot stand in your path. You are not Tonk and cannot be Tonk, and because of that, this mission of yours is doomed." I shrugged. "The world is full of women. Find another one—one who isn't Tonk."

But he shook his head. "You don't understand. I would crawl naked over broken glass to reach her if that was the only way I could get to her. If I don't find her, if I don't make her know how she touched me and changed me in that instant, if I don't at least tell her of my love for her, I fear that I will never know a night's peaceful sleep." He looked away from me, down at the floor, and all trace of his wonderful smile was gone. "I know it's a fool's mission. I knew it at the time; even before I came here, I knew that Tonk women would not welcome the attentions of foreign men. All the diplomats who were offered the opportunity to work on the Hyre Peace Agreements were required to do extensive study of the Tonk culture as well as of the many Eastil cultures." He shrugged. "So I knew. But while the world is full of women, they aren't her. So I'll find her. Or I'll die trying."

And what was I to say to that?

I changed the subject back to wristbands, and he and I agreed upon a design and a price and a delivery date, and he gave me his name in signature on a contract—Skirmig. His name was Skirmig. Nothing more. He put half down on the price of the work, with the other half due on delivery, and at last he started for the door.

And I stopped him with as transparent and foolish a ploy as

ever I have used. "How am I to find you if I have questions?" I asked him.

"I am rooming at the Harbor Hall while I try to find her. I'm a fool, I know, but I'm not going to be a fool who buys a house here until I find out whether I'll have reason to stay."

I closed the doors of the workshop behind him, and dropped the bar into the brackets and leaned against the smooth wood. And I wept.

I wept that this chance at love—slender as it might be—was forbidden me by my path and my honor. I wept for a man who dared to pursue a dream that would have brought both of us joy, but who would have only pain from his dream because his god and mine had ordained it so. I wanted love as much as any woman, and because of past pain and grief would never find lasting love with a Tonk man—and what woman would not gladly give up everything for a chance such as this?

Me. I was the fool who would not. I was the fool who would *not* crawl naked across broken glass for something that could be a miracle, that could be the most perfect and wonderful love imaginable.

But I was the fool who *would* carry the pain of my decision with me like a serpent in my belly. I thought that Skirmig would not be alone ever again in suffering his restless, sleepless nights.

I wondered suddenly if Skirmig was the man in the cage in my nightmares. It seemed to make an odd sort of sense.

Bokkam was sick. Gair could hear him coughing in the next cell over, a hellish wet cough that rattled in the back of his throat. At the worst times, Bokkam cried out in the darkness. Sometimes he seemed to think that he was at home with his mother and father, that he was a child who had done something for which he was being punished. At other times, he wandered to the few days when he was lost in the mountains alone, and he prayed for release.

Gair could do nothing to help him.

He had to face the fact that neither he nor his men were likely to survive this ordeal. The new Greton prisonmaster had seen them placed in tiny single cells in what could only be called a dungeon—it had no natural light, no circulating air. The rough-cut stone cell walls stayed damp, grew moss and mushrooms, smelled of plant decay and piss and shit. The guards who now brought them a daily meal and emptied their slop buckets when it suited them had also been instructed to beat them. Gair never knew when they would come for him, or for Bokkam or Hale, either, but the guards always waited until one of them was asleep, entering the cell without waking their target or alerting the other two men—for they kept the cell doors well oiled and in perfect repair so that they opened soundlessly. They dragged their chosen victim, in that horrible helpless bewildered state of half sleep and half waking, to another part of the dungeon, close enough that the other two could hear his screams, but not close enough that they could hear any spoken words.

Usually they confined themselves to three of them taking turns punching and kicking, or else two binding their victim to the wall and the third beating him with a knotted rope.

Sometimes they did other, worse things, and then the stink of blood or burned flesh would hang in the air for days.

The stone back wall resisted Gair. He could not work even a single block loose to start a tunnel. The seams in the stone floor were too close for him to wedge fingers between, to even discover if he might prise one free. And most times he ached too much to move. His enemies kept their beatings close enough together that he knew only the most fleeting moments when pain was not his companion, when breathing was not an agony.

Most times they did not even ask him anything. They just beat him, or beat Hale or Bokkam. All three men understood that if they would confess to crimes and tell the guards names that could be linked to copies of actual prison records at the House of Law, they would be moved into regular prison quarters with the other inmates.

But they did not know any names to offer. And they were all growing weaker.

Gair lay on the straw mat that was his bed and listened to Bokkam in the next cell over hacking and wheezing like an old man on his deathbed. They were all going to die, and Gair's endless prayers to the many gods of the Republic—for his own had done nothing and he hoped to find one who would listen—would come to naught.

Only in sleep did he find peace. In sleep, she came to him—the Tonk woman on the tall horse—she came and sat beside him and held his hand and told him things he could never remember when he woke. Or she stood over him and with bright light burned a path through their enemies. They were always in a meadow when he was with her—a meadow filled with flowers and wild horses. When he was with her, he could feel the sun on his face.

And even if the guards woke him from those dreams with another beating, he longed for more sleep, so that he could see her again.

7

I was riding Dakaat alone outside the walls of the taak, over a path of jumps and obstacles that I'd devised to keep the horses and myself in shape. My doubts rode with me; since my first meeting with Skirmig, I had spoken to him three other times, and each time I became more and more sure that if he had just been Tonk I would have bound my life to his. He was a diplomat with a warrior's eye, a saint's soul, and a man's passions, and the few times his hand had actually brushed mine all I could think was that it wasn't enough. I wanted all of him.

I had not yet confessed that I was the woman he sought, and so I watched him searching, and watched his hope and his desire warring with growing despair.

I'd talked my parents into making room at table for a stranger, and set a date when he and I would visit them—I told them he was a foreign client who had been long away from home and missed the feel of a family, and told him only that I thought my parents would find him and his tales of the rest of the world interesting. I did not know what I hoped to accomplish by taking him to meet them, for even if they liked him as a storyteller, he still would not be Tonk.

But having told my half-truths and committed myself to a course of action that I was sure could end only in unhappiness, I then went into hiding, riding the horses and working constantly and dreading the day when I would have to put my duplicity into action.

The easy canter of the Tand mare beneath me soothed me. She ran with the smoothness of poetry, and we worked well with each other's rhythms. She was a willing creature with a light mouth and a love of speed enhanced by curiosity and keen intelligence; she took the jumps and brush piles and water and bridges eagerly, one ear cocked forward and one swiveling back to catch my voice.

Riding her, I slipped into a place where she and I and the path were all that existed, and the sleepless nights and the nightmares and the day worries all fell away.

But soothing as this state was, it was not wise.

Neither she nor I was prepared for the young man who suddenly appeared in front of us, moving out from behind a brush pile waving his arms and a brightly colored rag.

Her attention shattered and she tried to bolt, and I had to saw the left rein hard and yank her head around, forcing her to move in tighter and tighter circles until she came to a shuddering stop. This kept her from going entirely to pieces and taking me with her, but it was a rude way to treat an animal, and I was furious with the stranger who had made it necessary.

I stared down at him—a thin, tired-looking young man, short, tanned by long exposure to a sun brighter than anything he could find in Hyre, with hair and eyes of nondescript brown. "You could have caused her to break a leg or killed us both jumping up like that."

"I'm sorry," he said. "Truly. If I had not a desperate situation, I would never have done such as this."

He had the odd edges of an accent that I had heard once or twice before, I thought—in sailors far from their home port. I could not place him, though—but I would have staked my life on the truth that he was not Tonk.

"What desperate situation?"

"I'm looking for friends. Three of them—only three. They were taken prisoner and brought here, but then they vanished. When the last of the prisoner-of-war exchanges were made, they still had not so much as shown up on the lists. And yet I know they came here."

"You know."

He nodded. "I ran alongside the caravan that brought them in, keeping out of sight, until they were taken within the walls of your House of Law. Then I ran home, certain that they would be safe and that I would see them when an exchange was made. But they never arrived in Fairpoint, and no one knew anything about what had happened to them. And no one cared. Everyone said no record of them being taken existed, and that ERMiCCS—ah, that is the Eastil Republic Mili—"

"I know what ERMiCCS is," I told him.

"Oh. Of course you do. Well, the petty bureaucrat in charge told me that ERMiCCS had a complete list of everyone taken prisoner, and that my friends were not on that list, and that they had therefore not been taken prisoner, and the fact that I claimed that I had been with them when this happened, and that I seen them taken, meant that I was confused or a seditionist and that he was going to recommend that I spend time with someone who would straighten me out." The young man stared up at me. "I ran," he confessed. "I ran back here, because I knew what I saw, and because the military command there had fallen into disarray, but when I got back, things were just as confused here. And by that time, most of the people who could help me were gone, far out of my reach. But not you. You're still here."

Me. Some ragtag who was a foreigner even by Eastil standards was looking to me for salvation, and I was already neck-deep in problems with foreigners. "Why me?"

"First, you're a Shielder," he said.

"Not anymore. There are no more Shielders. And frankly, your friends are probably dead . . . whatever your name is."

"I am the warrior Snow Grell," he said. "Snow Grell Warrior Born to the Hell Hill Woman, of the Hva Gana tribe of the Hva Hwa."

I dismounted Dakaat and met Snow Grell as close to eye-to-eye as the two of us could manage, for all that he was short and I am not. He knew who he was, and he knew who his people were, and he was a fellow warrior. And if he was not Tonk, still in these times when Eastils with their muddy mess of dialects and their confusion of gods wander through our streets, and when rumors have started to creep into the street that the Beyl himself takes orders from some damned Feegash, I could respect Snow Grell as someone who would understand Ethebet's path, perhaps. Warriors talk on the ground, level. So. "Well met, warrior," I said. "Why did you seek a Shielder? And of all the Shielders who remain in Beyltaak, why me?"

He said, "I seek a Shielder because Shielders can see where others cannot."

"You want someone to go into the View to look for them."

He nodded. "And I seek you because you are the one who stopped the crowd from stoning them when they were taken through the streets in cages. So you, too, know that they existed once, even if they do not now. And I must know if they are alive, and if they are, then I must find a way to bring them home." He stared into my eyes, looking for something. "I took an oath when I joined the Eastil army, but before and more important than that, I swore myself to the god of war of the Hva Hwa. The god teaches that we are brothers in blood, that we protect our own."

Yes. I understood that. I remembered the men he sought—the two who had tried to protect themselves from the stones, and the one who had sat straight with his arms at his sides and let them hit him. I remembered their faces, and their haunted eyes, and I remembered wishing them dead. They had been warriors who acted like spies, and I did not respect their methods. They were Eastils, and I loathed Eastils now more than I had hated them before we had peace shoved down our throats.

But warriors did not abandon their comrades. I had seen those three; I knew they were real. I could not imagine a Tonk commander hearing of the presence of unreported prisoners of war in enemy hands who would then threaten the man who brought him the report—but Tonks aren't Eastils. And these were not normal times in any case.

I took a deep breath. Under the peace agreement, Shielders were forbidden to go into the View anywhere in Hyre, and all the tools we had used to make the transition easy were gone. But the View remained, and we could reach it while sitting in a circle holding hands if we had to. And I knew my own comrades. They would understand the importance of this.

I had sworn myself to the warrior's path in peacetime. To me, this looked very much like that path.

"I'll look for you," I told him. "It will take me a few days to locate enough other Shielders to act as my backup, and we will have to keep this secret, but when I have enough of my comrades on hand to make the journey safe, I'll go." Dakaat leaned against me, bored. I leaned back, and she sighed and shifted on her feet and flicked her tail, swatting me more than could have been by accident. "You must realize that they are most likely dead—that disease or mischance befell them before they could be entered onto the rolls and that whoever was responsible for entering them could find no identification on them—"

"They would not have carried any identification," he told me. "My unit operated behind your lines."

"As I said, the odds are that they are dead. But I will search. And if they are still alive and still in Beyltaak, I will find them. And if I find them, I will let you know. A lot of ifs and no guarantees. And if I find them for you, their fate is in your hands alone. My help ends with giving you the information."

"I understand. Thank you. You have done more than most would."

"I have done what a warrior would."

He bowed deeply. "When you need to locate me, you will find me here."

"Here?" I asked. "Here on the path, or right here in front of the jump and the bridge?"

"Where we stand at this moment. If ever you need me, or when you have news for me, wait here for me. I will come to you as swiftly as I can."

"You would rather live out here than inside the taak? The inns would not even question your presence in these days, and I could leave a message for you."

"I prefer the sky above me at night. Walls can protect, but they can also cage, and my belly tells me to avoid the cage."

I accepted that. "I'll return as quickly as I can—but it may be days."

He shrugged. "If it is weeks or months, I will still be here. You are my last avenue of hope, and theirs as well, if they still live."

I took leave of him, and could feel Dakaat's relief as we can-

tered away; she loves to run, and loves the challenge of the
path, but she is a creature of habit, too, and grows impatient
with anything that interrupts her routines.

I was most of the way home—already on Fatham Road, in
fact—when I realized that if nothing else, Snow Grell had given
me something solid and clear to work at. My mind found real
peace for the first time since the day Skirmig walked into my
workshop and shook the ground beneath my feet.

"I've missed you," my mother told me as I stepped through our
front door, towing Skirmig in my wake. She gave me a solid
hug and in my ear whispered, "Your father is in a state. You'd
best go talk to him while I entertain your client."

I'd spent three days searching for other Shielders within
Beyltaak, and after what I'd found I had an edge to me that
could have sliced through steel like butter. I was not the person
to go calm my father. But I am the dutiful daughter, so I went.

Da was out in the workroom, with what had been my corner
now full of Rik's metalworking equipment. Da was cutting
dovetail joints into one edge of a cherry board with a tiny jig-
saw, and he seemed calm enough, at least until he looked over
and saw me.

"I need to ask a favor of you later," I told him. "But Ma said
something was wrong."

"Beyltaak has eliminated all service pensions," he said. "A
Hend vote of the merchants and citizens who did not want to
pay into the taxes that paid pensions anymore reversed in a day
a promise honored by every Tonk in Hyre since Tonks came to
this land—that the taak would take care of those who took care
of it. Those of us who spent our entire lives in service have now
been put aside with a comment that since there is no longer a
Beyltaak military, no entity exists that can pay the promised
pensions. But it is not about that, because the government always paid pensions. And it isn't that the taak is poor in these
days. It's richer than it has ever been. This is about the merchants on the hill having for free the protection of the Feegash
mercenaries. One day, and our future is erased."

"Did you have anything put aside?" I asked, hoping that this was a rant about the principle of what was done and not brought on by a future of genuine hardship.

"We *had* a lot put by. Most of our savings we used to make sure that your brothers and sisters who accepted assignments in other parts of the world would have passage home no matter what happened."

That had to have been enormously expensive. Of their fourteen children, eight of us had developed the skills to be taken into Magics—my parents were one of the tremendous successes of the Breeder program. And six of my eligible siblings had accepted jobs in faraway places after the war. The money was hard to turn away from, and most of them had no skills outside of their military skills, which were suddenly unwelcome anywhere in Hyre. They had scattered across the face of the world, and if Ma and Da had given each of them the funds to purchase single-direction passage on a good ship from someplace like Bheki or the northern Fallen Suns for themselves and their families, they had spent ten thousand gold rhengis if they had spent a single bronze leeyd. Ensuring safe return passage for six offspring would strain even the life savings of two high-ranked Magics officers.

"I can help," I said.

His face went a dull, dark red. "I don't want to be a burden to my children," he said. "I never wanted that."

"Da, this is not you and Ma being a burden. This is fat bastard merchants and ungrateful taaksmen changing the rules." I frowned. I actually had brought to table someone who might have some sway over the fat bastard merchants on the Heights who were no doubt behind this—or if he was too minor a diplomat, who certainly had connections to those who did.

And if he did something to help my parents, perhaps they would look at him in a different light. Perhaps I would look at him in a different light.

I bit my lip. "My guest is here," I said, "and it smells like Ma has a feast already on the table."

My father put down his saw and his board and sighed. "Let us go in, then, and see what sort of man this Feegash diplomat is when he sits at table."

Skirmig and my mother were laughing about something

when Da and I walked through the door, and he was helping her carry platters from the sideboard to the table. My older sister Eriiya; her husband, Cadan; and their four children, who range in age from the babe at breast to the six-year-old terror, would be joining us, as would my sibs who still lived at home: Rik; Sitraan and Lodraan, the boy twins; Edrig; and Kada and Fada, the girl twins. We were actually going to be light at table for a Jostfarday gathering.

Ma shouted that the meal was ready as soon as Da followed me through the door, and the noise from all other parts of the house suddenly compressed itself into the long, narrow kitchen. Adults and older children sat elbow to elbow at the benches on either side of the long table; smaller children sat cross-legged on the floor behind parents where they could be watched and reprimanded. My father had one of the two chairs, seated at the north end of the table. My mother had the other chair, at the south end closest to the stove. Sixteen of us all told, and this was the least crowded a Jostfarday meal had been for us since my sibs and I were young enough that the family was just us, without husbands or wives or prospective lovers or growing broods of grandchildren.

Da stood, put his hands behind his back, and looked up toward the ceiling. "Thank you that I was born Tonk. Thank you that I was blessed with family. Watch over those of my children who cannot be with us this day, and their children; watch over those who can as well. And over Lett and me—hard times being what they are, look kindly on us. For the breath we take, and the bonds we share, we give thanks."

"We give thanks," we all said.

That was about usual for Da's prayers. Short, to the point, mentioning only what mattered to him. I have sat at table in families where the prayer became an opportunity for the head of house to chastise the young or berate an errant spouse or sib before Jostfar and the Saints, bring out a long list of grievances against Jostfar himself, ask for gifts and favors like a spoiled child, mention politics or personal slights, or tell Jostfar in painful detail about the events of the day, when, if we acknowledge Jostfar's presence, he already saw, and if we don't, what point the prayer? I have noticed it is never the cook who makes these prayers, though, for while such prayers wind on, the cook chafes and the food grows cold.

I have come to loathe sitting at other folks' tables, for it is impossible to guess beforehand when one of these long-winded talkers-to-God is hiding in wait to ruin the meal.

It always makes me appreciate coming home, though. And it gives an extra layer of meaning to my father's adage, "Thank Jostfar for your blessings and handle the rest yourself."

After the prayer, everyone talked while my mother directed the passing of the bowls and we loaded our plates. To me the talk sounded subdued—we had a stranger in our midst, but more than that, for the first time in my family's memory, we sat at table with someone not Tonk. Skirmig's black-on-black clothes in the midst of our brilliant jewel-toned visiting garb made him look like a shadow in a garden. He was not us, and I tried to imagine bringing him every Jostfarday to sit among my sibs while we argued over who would get the drumsticks or the breast meat and debated the probable sex of one of my sisters' next babies, and the specter of telling him I was the woman he had come looking for took on weight. No matter how much my family might come to like him over time—assuming they would not turn me out and never let me through the door again for taking him as a lover—he would never be one of us.

And then, oh Saints, he opened his mouth.

"Forgive me if this question is . . . indelicate," he said to my father, and I bit the inside of my cheek and prayed it wouldn't be. "But why, in your prayer, did you thank God for being Tonk?"

In the stunned silence that followed that amazing question, sweet Jostfar, half of everyone in the room turned to stare at me for bringing such a fool into our midst, and the other half turned to my father in expectation of seeing him unlace the idiot from top to bottom with words, for my father has a tongue in his head that can drip honey or razors, and for a foreigner—a moriiad—to question the content of my father's talk with his god seemed to call for at least the razors of the tongue. If not the real thing.

But Da merely raised an eyebrow and said, "Because I am thankful to be who and what I am. Are you not?"

I was tempted to leap up and tell everyone, "Unfortunately,

my guest and I must leave now," but I had not the time, because Skirmig chased that question with another even worse.

"Of course I am. But do you not think that thanking God that you were born Tonk suggests that you think it is better to be Tonk than . . . anything else?"

Da was going to kill him if my brothers didn't do it first, and my parents were going to disown me anyway for bringing this rude idiot into their home.

But Da laughed. "I *do* think that. Why in Jostfar's name should I not thank him for it?"

"Skirmig, perhaps we ought to be leaving," I said. "I believe you said you had something else to do come the bells of Nightingale, and listen, there are the bells," I said, but my father waved me off.

"He came to table; let him sit, girl. Whatever else he must do can bide a bit." And that said, he returned his attention to Skirmig. "You're Feegash, and a diplomat as well, and because of that you've spent your life trying to find all the ways that people are the same, so that you can use these ways to get them all to talk to each other without killing each other. This is your work, but more than that, it's a part of who you are. Am I right?"

Skirmig nodded.

I ate potatoes and lentils and paper-thin slices of my mother's roast beef soaked in her thick gravy and couldn't taste a thing.

"That's one way of looking at the world, and it has its uses, but survival over the long term isn't one of its uses."

Skirmig seemed unaware of the silence around him, or that he had caused it. He was oblivious to my horror, to my siblings' disbelief, and to the looks my mother was throwing my way like little poisoned daggers. He said, "Acceptance is always in the best interests of everyone."

My father laughed again. "Nothing is always. The Tonk have been a people since time began," he said. "We can trace our ancestors back a thousand years on either side; we know our own kind; we speak a common tongue and worship a single god. We bear the marks of our paths on our skins and in our hearts and lives, and we bear the stewardship of our taak with our fellow taaksmen all the days of our lives. We know who we are. We do not welcome outsiders within our walls, we do not welcome them within our families. The reason is that if we did this, we would before long lose our place in the world. Would our children worship Jostfar, or, say . . . your god, whatever his name may be?"

"All gods are aspects of the same universal mind that is God," Skirmig said, and I wished my mother had put me directly across the table from him so I could kick him.

At least my father was having some fun from all of this, though. He chuckled and said, "Aye, that mongrel rabble over the border puts that forth as their reason for making room for temples to every two-bit tree god and hearth goddess and mad hermit with a vision. But that rabble has only been in existence for a few hundred years, and in that time has changed its official language twice, its official religion half a dozen times, and its form of government at least three times that I know of. And your folk, who have been in place as long as mine have and still have the language and the religion you started out with, are no warmer to outsiders than we are. And for the same reason."

"I think my people until now have been wrong in that," Skirmig said. "But I would be grateful for your insights into the benefits such closed societies might have."

"There's one benefit, and one benefit alone," Da said. "It's about survival. If you know your own, you can recognize the stranger in your midst. If you are wary of the stranger in your midst, you can identify those who would mean you harm."

"And you would never meet the strangers who mean you well."

"I cannot swear that I've met any of *those* yet."

"*I* mean you no harm."

"And yet you and your people have brought nothing but. Because of the Feegash, this taak and others across the Confederacy—more every day, from what I hear—are for the first time occupied by foreign mercenaries; our streets are filled with strangers speaking in languages we do not know about things that may or may not be dangerous to us and all we hold dear; some of our children are scattered across the world where we cannot see them or talk to them or share their lives; the children who remain are confronted by gods and philosophies that are not ours, and tempted by people who are not ours; and the government that we Tonks built and fed with our lives and our faith is fallen into petty clans that work for their own gain against the good of all, and that toss away honor and duty in favor of profit." He speared one of my mother's potatoes with too much enthusiasm and said, "If there is good in that, I cannot see it."

"You have peace. Your children are not dying on the battlefields. The Feegash mercenaries are building you good roads between the taaks, and digging new wells and clearing lands for new farming and new building."

"The only armies I know that worry about the state of the roads in territory not their own are those who plan to invade over them," my da said, and I saw Skirmig flush.

"I would love to have the chance to show you the whole of the Feegash plan for peace," Skirmig said. "You're perceptive and you know history, but you have not seen the inside of everything that we have so far accomplished, and I think you would feel better if you could just see how this will all work out." He smiled—that warm, beautiful smile that managed to take my breath away even as I was sitting there hating him and hating myself for having brought him to dinner—and added, "Change is hard. But sometimes good things can come from change."

"You'll have a time convincing me," my father said. "But I'll certainly listen while you try."

Skirmig, who apparently did not understand the challenge implicit in my father's words, smiled as if he had won a point. My mother saw the break in their conversation as the perfect opportunity to end it, though, and sent bowls round the table bearing seconds while saying, "I had a letter from Gannan that he and Clavii reached Long Forshend safely, and have found a house, and that Clavii is expecting again."

Gannan is my brother, who was Senders, and who after the war took service up north in the Fallen Suns, and Clavii is his wife, and the babe she is expecting will make six for them, which puts Gannan at the top of the dutifully-producing-grandchildren-for-my-mother list.

And this started what I think of as the Roster: which of my brothers and sisters have news of which other brothers and sisters, which of any of these are expecting children, which babes have learned to walk or speak or ride a horse or feed themselves, who has been accepted into apprenticeship or taken on an apprentice or received a commission or bought a new horse—and if horses are involved, all the particulars of that, since a new horse is almost as good as a new grandchild (so long as it didn't cost some fool fifty thousand horse cash).

The Roster silenced Skirmig as neatly as any cork would have, and better, I could watch his amusement shade gradually into bewilderment and then into a sort of astonished horror as he began to get the feel for the real size of my family. There are, at the moment and in my immediate family alone, thirty-five of us, including wives or husbands of sibs, and children. Thirty-six when Clavii has this next one. We don't even count my father's sibs or their families, or my mother's sibs and their families. They wouldn't fit within the walls.

On occasion, all my sibs and all their children and my parents and I have been together at the same time. When we are, we have ended up in the kitchen. And when we are all together in the kitchen, we are all talking.

It can be a lot to take. Pada came to table with me once and swore she would never do so again, for all that the food was the best she had ever tasted—and I did tell my mother what she'd said about the food. Meals at Pada's are like sitting through a funeral, and frankly, I think everyone there is mourning the death of the meal. I would have to think Pada's mother has never eaten food, she cooks so badly.

A regular Jostfarday dinner for Skirmig and his two brothers, one married with one child, could not be anything like the breathtaking babble we swim through at table. Though of course they don't have a Jostfarday in Ba'afeegash, but they must have *some* day for family.

I could see Skirmig starting to drown in the family ocean. And apparently, so could Riknir, for out of nowhere he leaned over, just turned eight years old but with some sympathy in his eye, and solemnly told Skirmig, "Tally is teaching me jeweling. I'm her apprentice. After table I'll show you my pieces if you'd like, since Tally says you like that sort of thing. My workroom is quiet; these lot"—and he nodded at the rest of my sibs—"don't go in there. It's my place and Da's."

In Skirmig's eyes, gratitude. "I'd love to see your work," he said. "Maybe I could commission a piece or two from you."

In Riknir's smile I could see that Skirmig had just grown wings and hooves and galloped straight into the heavens.

While Riknir showed Skirmig his work, and my mother and the rest of the horde did dishes or crowded the kitchen, talking, I pulled my father aside.

"Da, there's a problem. Big. I need to get one safe set of Shielders together—don't ask why. I have been to everyone I know, and asked everyone I know, and I can find only six Shielders in all of Beyltaak. And you're one of those."

He paled. "Four besides the two of us? Or five?"

"Four. I counted myself."

"Jostfar help us. How could anyone have let that happen?"

"It can't have been an accident, Da. It can't even have been the agreements. To be sitting here without enough Shielders for a single safe circle, the Eastils almost have to be involved. I would bet they have been paying their old allies to hire our Shielders away, and probably our Senders and Communicators, too, so that we will be even more disarmed than they are. So that as soon as the Feegash declare Hyre at peace and pull out their mercenaries and move on to their next project, the Eastils can use their troops and their allies' equipment and overrun us all."

"And the damned merchants have played right into their hands, being willing to sell anything for gold, including their freedom. And ours."

We looked at each other. "We have to do something."

"I'll send messages to your sibs that they're needed at home, and tell them why. I'll put them in the family code—we can't assume the mail won't be read aboard ship."

We developed the family code because in wartime there are occasions when messages between family members need to look innocuous to pass through inspections. Our family code is simple enough, and devised by Ma. We use her pale blue Dravitaak paper instead of regular white Beyltaak paper to let each other know to check for a coded message, though if we end up someplace without our supply of her paper at hand, we have gotten creative, staining big blue "I love yous" with berries or "accidentally" dropping a bit of grape wine onto the page as we write, and letting it stain a bit before wiping it off. Da uses blue wax to seal the envelope instead of the deep green he prefers. Anything different will do—all we have to know is that we should check for a "blue letter."

The code itself is a pin code—not very sophisticated, but home mail doesn't receive the same sort of scrutiny as the letters of heads of state. Or diplomats. We place as many sheets as we think we'll need atop each other, and jam a pin through all the sheets in five or six different places. Each place where there's a pinhole, we write one of the words in the message. We number the pages, write a letter around the hidden words—and we've found that more than five or six code words on a page can be very hard to cover up while still being coherent—and send the thing off.

But they're still letters, and letters take time. Especially when sent around the world.

"We may be able to get them back in one or two years, depending on the ships, the winds, and the amount of trade that comes through here," I said. "So what do we do in the meantime?"

"I've stayed in touch with some of my people," Da said. "I'll have them together to discuss this. You bring every Shielder you can convince to come to temple on Hetteriksday, first bell of Nightingale. I'll have one of the Keepers watching for you to show you where to go."

"Two days." I considered that. "Fine. I'll be there, as will everyone I can convince to come."

Da said, "Go back to your guest." He frowned at me. "He's too smart for his own good."

I sighed. "I was hoping he would have better manners. You would think a diplomat would."

"Had he been here as a diplomat, I'm sure he would have been the perfect guest. He was looking at us as future family, though, and that seems to have brought more of the real man to the front."

"What?!" I looked at my father, shocked and embarrassed at the same time. "No, Da, he's here looking for someone he hasn't yet been able to find."

"That might be what he tells you, Tally, but when he looks at you, his eyes say he found the person he was looking for in you." He have me a quick, hard hug, and said, "Watch your back. And watch your heart. He's not Tonk, and I think he could hurt you."

And with that warning, Da hurried into the noise of the kitchen. And I went out to the workroom to see how Rik and Skirmig were getting on, and found Rik patiently showing Skirmig how to choose soldering irons and how to apply solder, and I heard my words, repeated in my tone, coming out of his mouth.

They both looked up when I shut the door behind me, and both gave me smiles that put the sun to shame.

"He liked the brooch I did as a present for you, Tally," Rik said. "He wanted me to do one like it, but I designed yours just for you. No one else can have one like it. So I'm going to design a different one for him." He held up a gold piece that looked suspiciously like a Mendu—a Beyltaak minting worth ten gold or ten horse cash. I nearly choked, and looked closer, and the galloping horse on the front of the coin was, indeed, Mendu, one of the finest stallions ever to come out of Beyltaak stables. "I got half in advance, just like you do."

"That's a lot of money." I stared at Skirmig, and said, "May I have a word with you, please?"

Skirmig looked startled, but said, "Excuse me, Riknir—I'll have to get my next lesson another time."

Rik looked worried. "I have to give you your present before you go, Tally."

"I won't leave without saying good-bye," I told him, and hugged him, and over his head glared at Skirmig.

We went out of the workroom, avoiding the kitchen, where several of my brothers had fallen into an animated discussion of the last tiiva match and were moving coins and Ma's spice jars around the table to represent the horses and riders, and getting louder by the moment. Two of my brothers ride for rival teams, and sometimes tiiva discussions in the kitchen can turn into rematches—without the horses or the tiiva sticks or the ball, but with twice as much shoving and shouting.

I ended up leading him into Ma's herb garden in the back.

"What did I do?"

"You're going to pay a child who has just turned eight twenty rhengis for a piece of apprentice work? Are you insane? Or is overpaying something that all Feegash do?" Suddenly an awful thought came over me, and I said, "What do *you* know about a fifty-thousand-horse-cash Tand mare?"

Skirmig looked shocked. "Fifty thousand horse cash? For a *mare*? God, a quality Tand stallion might go for half that or maybe a bit more in Ba'afeegash, and I think we end up paying more for our horses than anyone else in the world. It's so hard to get them to us, you see. But a mare? What idiot paid that?"

I breathed a little easier. He understood the difference between a mare and a stallion in deciding the price of a horse, which is more than many foreigners do. You would think that people who buy horses and ride horses would understand horses, but mostly they don't. They feed them, ride them, and maybe remember to clean their hooves, and cannot understand when things go wrong *why* they go wrong.

I told Skirmig, "That's what I'm trying to find out. Some anonymous foreigner paid that exorbitant sum to give me a mare that is—without argument—a very, very fine mare, and that was without a doubt the finest horse appearing at the horse market here in the last several years, but that was not worth the ransom of a taak. And I have not been able to find out who gave me the horse, or why. It has caused me no end of embarrassment, and it gave my comrades in Magics a great deal of fun at my expense and has handed the whole taak tangible reason to wonder about me."

He thought about that. "I have access to diplomatic . . . resources. Perhaps I could find out who bought it for you."

"The fuss has died down about that now," I said. "And I wanted to talk to you about Rik, anyway. You intend to pay twenty rhengis for a piece that he's making at the age of eight, and he is unlikely to see that kind of money for his work again until he is an adult and a full craftsman, and even then it will be hard to come by. If the first one is too easy, it's almost impossible to stick with what you're doing when it is never that easy again."

"You haven't seen the brooch he made you, Talyn," Skirmig said. "Hold judgment until you've seen what he's done."

Skirmig was right. I hadn't seen my little brother's work.

I went back into the workroom to find Rik diligently drawing out designs on paper. The designs were rough—he has a decent hand for eight, but he is still eight. He put them aside when I came in, and fished out a small, polished wooden box. "Da made the box for me," he said, but he didn't need to. I would have recognized Da's work anywhere. Rik looked anxious. "I hope you like it, Tally."

I took it, and opened the hinged lid, and stared in astonishment at the piece that Rik had made.

It was an odd five-sided piece of slightly domed hammered silver, as big as the palm of my hand, and he had painstakingly sweat-soldered hammered silver wire onto the surface in a complex tangle of spirals that seemed, when I stared at them, to have some hidden meaning if only I were clever enough to puzzle it out. Off center and at an angle, he'd bezel-mounted an interesting piece of polished amber, and when I looked at it closely, I realized that it held a bug. I grinned at that—the amber was for me because I love it, but the bug in the amber was pure Rik.

I turned it over. He'd spent hours on the finish work. He'd made a beautiful pin and as solid a clasp as I'd ever seen. The back was as smooth and neat as the front. It glowed. It was beautiful. It was easily worth twenty rhengis. It was as fine as anything I'd ever done.

I stared at him. "You did this . . ."

He laughed, delighted by my reaction. "You should have seen Ma's face when I showed her. And when I showed Da, he said anything that good needed a special box to keep it in."

I hugged him. "It is the best present anyone has ever given me," I told him, and I meant it.

"Better than the horse?" he asked.

"A thousand times better than the horse," I assured him.

"You could wear it on your Shielder's cloak," he said. "And that way you wouldn't have to keep it in a box." He looked so hopeful I got a lump in my throat. He'd wanted so much to be a Shielder, and now that was gone. Gone—and shattered.

"I'll wear it with the cloak," I told him. "That way I won't actually be wearing the uniform, but I will be a little, too."

"I made one for mine, too. A lot like yours. It was my practice piece for doing yours—it isn't anywhere near as good. But I can wear it with the cloak you made me, and you can wear yours, and it can be *our* uniform."

I hugged him too tight, but I couldn't let myself cry in front of him. I hurried out of the room as fast as I could after that. The death of a child's dream is no small thing.

We rejoined the family, and the time passed too quickly for me, as it always does on Jostfarday, though I could tell that my big, ferocious brothers arguing about Paviic and whether he and his horse had cheated in one of their long runs last match was boring Skirmig mindless. Of course, he hadn't seen the match. Personally, I thought Paviic had fouled, and said so. And when I looked over, I saw that my mother had Skirmig backed against a wall. I could see both their faces, and suddenly I realized what she was doing. She was giving him her "mother speech," which a few boys I'd fancied in my youth had repeated to me after they suddenly decided to take an interest in other girls; it consisted of my mother explaining, in a reasonable voice, that if the male in question ever hurt her daughter, she would hunt him down and kill him, after first castrating him like an undesirable colt.

Ma never quite got around to defining what she meant by "hurt," apparently, and from the look in her eyes, the lads I'd fancied had gone for a broad definition, and cleared the field for men made of sterner stuff. It's a wonder and a miracle any of Ma's daughters found husbands.

I went to rescue Skirmig, embarrassed and hoping that she hadn't gotten to the anatomical references yet, and overheard her say, "That you love her does not mean that she is right for you, or that you should have her."

Love? Had he brought that up, or had she? Perhaps they weren't talking about what I'd thought they were talking about. I turned in midstep, gracelessly colliding with the table, and to cover the misstep, made a show of taking one of the pastries that had survived my horde of family.

"I'm her client—," Skirmig protested.

Well enough, then. It had not been him claiming love.

To which Ma said, "And I'm her mother. And not blind. She's already survived enough wounds. If you hurt her, too, I'll kill you."

Which was my cue.

"I have some commissioned work I need to finish today," I said rather too loudly, stepping up to the two of them. "We really must be leaving."

One of my brothers yelled to me from across the room, "I thought you were going to come out and watch me take Vargaa through his paces on the south field, and maybe do setups for me."

I turned to him and grinned. "And you thought this because I so love doing setups?"

All my brothers laughed. I *hate* doing setups and make no secret of it. Chasing the ball when it goes out of bounds and bringing it back and tossing it for the rider . . . Yes. That was what I wanted to do with the rest of this Jostfarday.

We made our retreat, my father giving me his usual admonition, my mother whispering, "Think, Talyn," in my ear as we left.

We walked in silence for some time, back toward my house. "Your family is very protective of you," Skirmig said at last.

I shrugged. "All families are protective of their daughters."

Skirmig laughed a little. "You should not think that. You are . . . lucky." And then he frowned. "Your mother said you had survived . . . wounds?"

"I was a soldier. Soldiers get hurt. It was, nonetheless, an odd thing to tell you. I think she misunderstood our relationship."

"She read me right enough," he said, and my heart skipped a beat and I swallowed hard. He didn't know what I had overheard my mother say.

At which point I realized that we had reached my house.

"I have to tend to the horses," I said.

8

I needed to send him out of my life. Finish his commissions and then not accept any more, or return his money on those still unfinished and tell him that I was having trouble working with him because of his being Feegash, and when he followed me into the barn, my first inclination was to tell him to go away. Really, I swear on Saint Ethebet's grave, it was. But my second thought was Why? After all, I could pog him so long as I kept him under wraps and did not make any plans for a shared future. Pogging him didn't mean I had to keep him. It could be as easy and casual and meaningless as sex in the baths at the Star's Rest had been; friends working off a little tension after a long day of hard work. The lads in Shields had known the way of things with me—that handful of them that I liked enough to bed, anyway—and had not tried to turn sex into love. They were . . . trainable. I thought Skirmig would be trainable too.

And then I turned to tell him that I would be only a few minutes with the horses, and he kissed me. No warning. There should, sweet Jostfar, have been a warning, for if I thought anything at all during the explosion inside me that followed, it was, ah, Saints, what have you done to me? . . .

Because even if he proved to be trainable, that still left me to deal with me. And I might not be so easy to keep in the corral this time.

Up close, in the flesh, Skirmig was a big, lovely animal, and I tried to blame the fire in my blood on that. He smelled of quality soap and something lightly spicy and foreign, and underlying that, he smelled of man—good smells all. His arms around me were hard with muscle, and the question of why a diplomat would have the muscles of a farm boy, and how he managed to have them without getting calluses on his hands, flickered briefly before drowning in an exploration of lips and tongue that took the bone out of my knees. Beneath his dreary black clothes, his cock pressed up against my leg hard and urgent and ready.

And suddenly I was ready, too.

It's a kiss, I wanted to scream. It's just a kiss.

But it wasn't.

It was the first step to the end of the world, and I felt it when I took it—felt the firmament shift beneath my feet and ghosts sliding up behind the edges of my eyes—and Ethebet preserve me, I took that first step and kept right on walking.

He was like an ice-cold pond on a hot day—he jolted me awake inside and out, made me feel alive, made me hungry.

By Jostfar, he made me hungry. And I hadn't been hungry— truly hungry—since Adjii and his beautiful blue eyes died at the front and took the one man who didn't care about my scars away from me. That first time had been for the color of his eyes, and because I'd liked his crooked grin and the gap between his two front teeth. Every time after that, though I never dared tell him, it had been because I was in love.

Love.

I couldn't feel anything like that for Skirmig. I didn't dare. He was Feegash. He was the cause of my taak's sorrow, its shame.

But even had he been Tonk, I didn't know him. I didn't know who he was, I didn't know his people, I had not walked his land or eaten at his mother's table or sat up all night trading stories with his brothers.

And he wasn't Adjii, either, to overlook the scars. He had talked about finding the woman whose mind had touched his, and how he didn't care if she was old or ugly. But then he had talked dreamily about a future with a perfect woman who would share a house and a life with him, raise a family, make him meals, sit and talk at hearthside, be his one best friend.

And that woman was not—could not be—me.

I had every reason to push away from him. I had every reason. And I, who had never ignored reason before, ignored every sane thought in my head and kissed him back with everything I had in me, every yearning and every hunger and every wish I had pushed aside and refused to let myself look at again.

I once saw lightning strike a wagon loaded with Greton fire our raiders stole from the Eastils in a prebattle sortie. There was the lightning itself, which was impressive. The crack, the crash, the rip of thunder through the air. But with the crack, every single vial of Greton fire exploded at once, spraying the pass and everything and everyone in it—and everything went up in flames at once.

It was horrible. Terrifying. Unstoppable. We lost the sortie team and their prisoners, the horses and wagons, every bit of plant cover in that stretch of the pass—all in less time than it takes me to tell it.

When I kissed Skirmig back, it was lightning to Greton's fire.

I wanted him. All of him. Right then, right there.

I stared into his eyes—eyes gone dark with hunger, centers black and huge—and my heart galloped in my chest like a wild thing. His upper lip trembled, his breath came fast, his body against mine was hard in all the best places.

"I bite," I said around the sudden constriction in my throat.

"Good." He growled, and his grin was wolf-sharp. "If you treat me right, so do I."

"Beds are boring," I said.

"Anyplace that won't give me splinters is fine with me," he answered.

I looked around the inside of the barn. "I cannot guarantee no splinters."

"Then I'll take my chances." He shoved me against one of the barn beams, old wood, ax-planed but with the roughest edges worn smooth by hundreds of years of people and horses brushing against it as they moved by, his hands on my breasts through my clothes, lips against mine hard and demanding.

I grabbed the laces of his black breeches and ripped them from their hooks, tearing hooks and breeches as I did, but they slid down his legs and he had some other damned thing on, some black thin silk knit thing that I had never seen on a man and that got in the way of me and him, so I yanked that down, too, and grasped the length of him in two hands, and felt him hot and hard and sleek and heavy between my palms. I heard him groan, felt the rumble of it in his chest, and pulled my mouth free from his suddenly frantic kiss and bit the skin on the side of his neck, lightly at first and then harder, and felt him shudder, felt his breath against my skin in short hard puffs. I bit harder, and tightened my grip on him, and my belly tightened in anticipation of mounting him, of him entering me.

His hands worked their way beneath my long skirt—fancy dress for the family meal, when I generally preferred my own breeches, and just for an instant I wondered if in wearing that skirt, with its easier access, I had already been planning this moment. But like my other thoughts, that one died fast beneath the onslaught of sensation; Skirmig worked my cottons out of his way, and slid one hand deftly between my legs and plunged his fingers deep into me, and the madness inside me burned hotter. I arched against him, managed to work one leg free of the cottons, and felt them slide to the floor around my other ankle.

For one little eternity I shuddered beneath his touch, crying out, taken over the edge of control again and again, as he played my body the way a pipes player coaxes the fiercest, richest sounds from his pipes.

Panting, trembling, my tunic and underblouse soaked with sweat, I at last hooked the leg that wasn't tangled in cottons around his waist, shoving his arm and hand and the fingers driving into me out of my way. Everything to that point had been too much, but also not enough. I guided him into me, welcoming his hardness and his ferocity, growling as he filled me, digging my fingers into his buttocks to pull him deeper.

I lost myself. A rift opened up inside of me, a hunger with a thousand eyes and a single voice, and that voice howled, *Yes,* whispered *Yes,* clamored *Yes.*

I levered myself off of the beam against my back, flipped him into the haystack, and locked my knees to his hips and grabbed his thighs with my hands and impaled myself on him, driving him into me harder and harder, until his breath sobbed from him and his whole body locked and he cried out, "Wait!" and he fought his way free of me, caught me around the waist, tossed me facedown into the hay, sheathed himself in me with hands clutching my hips, fingers digging to the point of pain, his whole body tight as a drawn bow.

Plunge, thrust, buck, scream, with the thousand eyes inside my head devouring it all and pleading for more, and I rolled again, shifted, knocking him into a saddle rack, and he bent me over the saddle tree—and, more, more, again, fighting like cats, biting and scratching and clawing, it all falling into tight little images still and sharp against a blur of tangled arms and legs, breasts and cock and aching desire—him with his back against a stall and the horses wild-eyed and panicking on the other side, me hanging on to a beam and him biting the point where my neck joined my shoulder, us lying on something flat, face to face, staring into each other's eyes as we crashed against each other, him slamming down into me and me rising up to meet him, and at last, at last, at insane last, him standing and me with legs wrapped around him, not moving at all, trembling together, locked in a union that held us at the edge of an abyss, with certain annihilation a finger's breadth away.

"Now," he said, one last time, and somehow got down on his knees without dropping me, without us pulling apart, and he took me one last time over the cliff but this time he fell too, and with those eyes inside my head finally blinded and with the voices finally silenced we toppled down and down and down into oblivion.

I woke up first, to discover half my clothes still on, and half gone missing in various parts of the barn, and not a single muscle in my body that didn't ache.

I know pogging. It's an entertaining way to spend an otherwise dull afternoon, getting sweaty and shivery and having a good ale together after it's over, with the universe still rolling smoothly in its appointed course when you've finished.

And I know futtering, for which empires are lost or won or bartered away and souls are sold to a world's pantheon of devils, which leaves the ground scorched where it passes and topples cities and drops the moon into the sea with a tidal-wave splash that sinks guilty and innocent alike.

But this . . . this was something else yet again.

Never, never, never had I passed out from sex—though I had crept close enough once or twice to suspect it might be possible—but this hadn't been just sex. This had been sex that had somehow gotten tangled up in that strange place where Skirmig kept his stillness, or perhaps in the place where he shoved the demons the rest of us wore on our skins. This—this whatever it had been—had jumped on me as if I were a horse strong-bitted and it a rider stirruped and with a whip, and had ridden me at a gallop over dangerous cliffs. This thing we had shared fell sideways through the fact that as a Shielder I live ever on the edge of the View, no matter how carefully I keep myself away from it when it could hurt me. It detoured into the reality that neither one of us had been touched other than accidentally in long months, and came slamming through my guilt at wanting him and the desire I had felt and pushed aside, and felt and pushed aside again.

We had damn near killed each other. I wore bruises from neck to knees, and to his matching bruises he added bite marks and the long scratches of my short nails furrowed across his chest and limned out with tiny beads of blood. He lay there, breeches gone, shirt ripped open and hanging from his shoulders in tatters, breathing deeply and steadily, oblivious of everything.

I leaned against the wall for a moment and stared at him and tried to make sense of what had happened.

I am no delicate virgin to shrink at the first good poke from a nice cock. I like some spice to my pogging, a little sharpness along with the sweet.

But I'd never left a man looking like he'd been mauled by mountain cats. Had it not been for the fact that his chest rose and fell so steadily, I could have looked at him lying there and believed him dead.

I looked down at my hands, and the blood under my nails. Saw that my clothes, too, would never serve as anything but rags again. Saw bite marks on my breasts that I did not remember getting, moved around the pain in my joints, studied my bloodied knees and elbows and sucked thoughtfully at a split in my lower lip, and carefully explored its swelling with one finger.

I could be grateful for the bitter cold of Beyltaak winter, I thought. It would be some time before I would dare to show any bit of my skin from neck to wrists to ankles.

Skirmig stirred, and I looked around until I found the remains of my skirt and wrapped them around me. I pulled the shreds of my tunic over my breasts. I still had on my riding boots and my stockings, though I could not even see what had become of Skirmig's shoes or those thick black woolen hose he'd worn beneath his breeches.

For that matter, I could see no sign of his breeches.

He opened his eyes, saw me staring down at him, and gave me a weary smile. "By the gods, Talyn, you've slain me. And if I were not lying here wondering how I might get you to treat me so again, I would flee for my very life."

"What *was* that?" I asked him.

He chuckled—a raw, raspy sound dragged from vocal cords worn ragged by shouts and howls and growls. "You mean you? Me?" He made a gesture with one fist, back and forth, that I think must be near universal. "*That?*"

I nodded.

"That . . . my God. That was two eagles mating in flight. That was . . ." He closed his eyes. "That was . . ."

I walked over to him, feeling every step, and sat down beside him, and in spite of every ache outside of me and every one inside, I wanted only to grab him, stir him to rigid life, take him again.

"That was madness," I said.

He opened his eyes, and his brow furrowed with sudden concern. "Ah, gods. It was. I did not have any lambskins with me, I did not think to check if you drank that Tonk tea one of your people told me about. There was no thinking to that at all."

I shrugged that off. "That wasn't what worried me."

"You are one of the tea drinkers?" he asked, and I saw a tiny spark of relief flicker in his eyes.

"It is not something I have to bother myself about," I said, and tried to keep the tightness from my voice. I got back to what had worried me. "No—I simply have never been . . . like that . . . before. I have never done things without knowing that I intended them. I have never actually done anyone real hurt." I ran one finger along a bite mark on his chest next to his nipple that went deep enough into his flesh to have drawn blood. Already it bruised black all around the edges, and he was going to have to see a healer or he would have infection in the wound. I suspected I wore a mark or two like it on my own hide, and I found myself wondering exactly how I would explain them to Master Idrann, my preferred healer of the taak's several.

"You never lost yourself so completely before?"

"No."

He sighed—one of those smug male "I came, I claimed, I conquered" sighs that does make a woman want to find a good stout horsewhip, and he grinned at me, clearly proud of himself.

"Has it ever been like that for you?" I asked. Perhaps, for all my experience, I had missed something that was actually common.

"No." He arched an eyebrow. "But I always hoped it might be."

"Why?" I asked. "You have worse than splinters now. You have actual holes."

"And when my dressers see them on the morrow, they will gnash their teeth in envy. My God, woman—you think I'll weep at a few little holes when I got them during the most amazing experience in my entire life?"

I discovered right then that I am as capable of smugness as any man.

But I was not yet . . . appeased, I suppose, for lack of a word closer to my need. "I felt as if we were being watched," I told him.

And he laughed. "We were. The horses couldn't take their eyes off us."

"That isn't what I mean." I sat there for a moment with my arms around myself as much for comfort as to keep my rags from falling off, and thought about those eyes inside my head opening up, those screams, that feeling of someone else's hunger tearing through me like a starving man through honey bread. And I thought about trying to put that odd sensation into words, because the eyes were not really eyes, the screams not really screams. Not when I thought about it. Not when I stood back from the whole business and looked at it and tried to draw a line around the part of what I had done that had not been me. There were no clear lines. There was nothing I could push a pin through and say *There, that! That was clearly nothing I would ever do. Ever.*

In spite of my embarrassment at seeing what I had done to him, in spite of equal discomfort at what I had allowed to be done to me, I had to admit that it *had* all been me. That I was capable of doing things with a man that I would have sworn I would never do.

But I felt at that moment like a stranger in my own skin. I didn't know what other surprises this new me might have in store, and I discovered that I was afraid to find out.

Skirmig seemed to realize that I was not completely at ease with what had happened, for he rose, wincing as he moved, and came over to me. He stood behind me and wrapped his arms around me, and he was warm and he felt strong, and somehow safe.

"I don't know how things got so out of control," he admitted. "I don't know where that madman inside of me came from. Next time we'll go slow," he said, and nuzzled the side of my neck, and I felt my heart begin to race again. His hands stroked from my rib cage down to my navel, and I could feel his cock hardening against my buttocks. "Or at least slower," he amended, and his fingers slid under the band of my skirt, and over my belly. And over the ridged scars.

He stopped all movement except for the one finger that slid over the scar on the right.

"What's that?" he said, and his voice sounded tight.

"War wound," I told him.

The left hand explored the scar on the left. Both hands moved in and explored the bigger scar in the middle. He turned me around, lifted my skirt, and looked at my belly with the same scrutiny I got from any new healer I went to see.

"What in the hells . . . ?"

"Those were the wounds I got that night the Eastils broke through our lines. I got off easy compared to most of those in the View with me at the time. They cut the balls off the men. Did the same to me as to the other women, cut us up inside, but all of the other women died."

"Why? Why did they do *this*?"

"Because the ability to move within the View—to use the magics of the universe—is a trait that passes with some regularity from parent to child. The Eastils could have killed us as easily as do this, but they decided instead not to kill us directly, but to send us back to our people to be childless. We were a warning—to parents whose children were being taken for Magics, to others in Magics. Or maybe we were simply someone's revenge for something one of our people did. I have no way of knowing. But to a Tonk, childlessness is worse than death. This was punishment and warning and taunt all rolled into one."

He frowned. "But . . . But while we sat at table I heard your sibs make some comment to you about bringing home a lad with whom you could have big, strong babies—"

And I interrupted him. "My family does not know what my injuries were. Not my mother, nor my father, nor my sibs. And they will *not* know. They know I nearly died and nothing more. I swore my healer and my comrades to secrecy, and I swear you to secrecy, too. You will never tell a single one of them about this."

"But it must kill you every time one of your family says a thing like that."

"Right now, I am a disappointment to them—the daughter and the sister who got so caught up in Shielding that she has not taken the time to bring home the right man or to start making babies. If they find out the truth, I will become, instead, an object of pity, and every time we sit at table I will have to see everyone cringe and look sideways at me when one of my sisters or sisters-in-law announces that she has caught again. I will have to hear the hitch in their voices when they announce that one of my sibs is marrying. That one of my nieces or nephews has learned to walk or talk or ride or any other thing that children do. I will have to live with their pity. And though I have found my own path to living though I must do it childless, I will die rather than live with their pity."

I felt something hot and wet drip onto my shoulder and roll down my chest and into the cleavage between my breasts. "If I can find who did this to you, I will kill him," Skirmig said, and his voice shook. "Slowly and terribly, one little piece at a time."

It shocked me that he was crying for me. "He's long gone, whoever he was. Faded back into Eastil territory. He might even be dead. Our Conventionals tore the Eastils apart in the battle that followed this happening. We lost twenty men. They lost over a thousand." I shrugged it off. "Such a thing never happened before or since. Most of us think it was a single Eastil team gone renegade, following a team leader with a special grudge against Shielders." I pulled away from him and said, "It was war, Skirmig. People die. People who don't die bear scars for the rest of their lives. You want to see the price some of us paid, watch the folk in the streets at dusk, when the day's work is done. The ex-Conventionals who have no legs or no arms, who are blind or missing their faces, who are scarred so horribly children weep when they see them. You won't see so many among my comrades; most of the ex-Magics who fell lay for a little while in the chambers of the fallen, lost in the madness of the View with no way back. For the most part, those in Magics suffered wounds of the mind, not the body, and they died in a few days. Or a week. At the outside, a month. I was an exception, in that my injuries were physical." I turned to look at him, and saw him standing there bruised and bitten and naked and shivering and covered in gooseflesh, with his cheeks shiny with tears.

"I don't know if you care to hear this, but your wounds do not matter to me, except for the pain they cause you," he said. "I grieve for you that this happened, but it does not change the way I feel about you."

I laughed. "That I'm just the person to jump in a barn? Good. I wouldn't want to change that. And when you find the woman whose mind matches yours so perfectly, you can cherish this odd memory without any tinge of regret." I turned away from him. "I'm going into the house to shower. You are welcome to use the shower too, if you would like."

"That isn't what I meant," he said, and I turned back to look at him, suddenly wary.

"What did you mean, then?"

"That I love you, Talyn."

"That's bite marks speaking."

He laughed a little, but shook his head. "I love you. I've known it for quite some time now, but . . . I can't be silent anymore. I know I'm not Tonk, but I love you."

"And when you finally do find the woman whose mind so perfectly fits yours, what will happen to that love?"

He gave me the oddest smile, and for a moment I thought, *He knows,* and then he said, "Will I find her? If I find her, will she love me back? In all the time that I've been here, there has been no trace of her, and every day I seek the silence within that would let me feel her if she came to me. She does not come to me, Talyn. I think she knows I am here, and this is her way of telling me that she does not want me."

"But if you found her, you would still want her?"

He looked down at his hands, with their scraped knuckles. "She was perfect."

"While I am present."

"No." He looked exasperated. "You're perfect too. I can't explain it. It seems as if I found what I sought with her, but in you." He shrugged. "I don't know what to tell you. I rearranged my world to find her and I haven't. I cannot lie to you and tell you that if I found her I would not want to find out more about her. I cannot swear that I would no longer want her. I don't *know* what would happen. All I can say is that everything I ever wanted in a woman I have found in you, even if you weren't the woman I came seeking."

But I was, so it was hard to be offended, thinking that he might pass me over for . . . me.

Not that I could tell him that. Not that I would.

"I have to go shower and find intact clothes," I said instead.

He gave me that pitiful look men use when they're pretending they're little boys. "I have no clothes I can wear home."

Which was true. And were I him, I would not care to walk home in the rags he had left, and in his current condition.

And I had some men's clothing he could wear. An old shirt and breeches of Adjii's lay folded away in a trunk in my sleeping chamber. The clothes were casual wear—the tunic loose and worn, plain—just something Adjii had worn and forgotten to take with him. The woolen breeches had patches at the knees. Sometimes I took the shirt out and held it close and sniffed it because it smelled like Adjii, though the smell grew fainter over time, and I dreaded the day when I would pull it out and it would be just a bit of cloth again.

"I don't have anything you could wear," I told him. "But once I've dressed, I'll hire a child to run a message to your house, and one of your servants can bring you fresh clothing."

"Which means I'll be naked until my servant arrives?" he asked, but his eyes gleamed and his mouth curled at the corners in a wicked smile.

"No," I said, and I could see that my abrupt, sharp response wounded him. "I have a good warm robe you may borrow. And when I have showered, you can use the shower, and while you do, I'll make us a meal."

I fed the horses, something that I hadn't managed to accomplish the first time I tried it, and hurried from the barn through the short covered passageway into my workroom, and then into my house. I could feel Skirmig following me. I pointed him to a place by the stove where he could sit and stay warm, and then I hurried into my icy shower and stood there until my body went numb and my nail beds turned purple.

In Bokkam's cell, Gair heard another desperate, strangled breath, and then a long pause. He clenched his hands so tightly his fingernails bit into his palms. Bokkam sounded like he was trying to breathe underwater—his lungs gurgled and bubbled. Gair guessed by the changing of the guards that a full day had passed since the last time Bokk had said anything, and nothing he'd said in the last few days had been to anyone but the ghosts that hovered around him. He'd talked to the sister who had died as a small child, and to an uncle who had died in battle, and to his mother, who had died of causes unknown while Bokk was at the front. He hadn't answered Gair or Hale for days.

Gair prayed, though he no longer knew if he was praying for Bokk to live or to die. He might have been praying for himself: that he might die quickly and be spared the horrors Bokk endured.

Another dreadful, rattling gasp.

A horrible long stop. Gair was sure Bokk was done for. Gone. And then the breathing started back again, but now speeding up, getting faster and shallow-sounding. And still wet.

Gair laid his face against the stone of the cell wall, feeling the dampness, lost in the flickering darkness. Out in the passageway two guards taking a break from rounds had a bottle of ale and a woman, and they were taking turns with each. From time to time all three would listen to the sounds of Bokkam's breathing and revise their wagers on when his last breath would be.

If he could have killed the three of them right then, Gair would have.

Bokkam's breathing slowed again. Long awful inhalation, followed by worse exhalation, followed by nothing for so long that Gair would be sure it was over, followed by one more breath. And one more.

And then, nothing.

Gair waited.

Still nothing.

And waited.

Still nothing.

"Has he done for then, do you think?" the whore asked. "For if he has, that would be my mark on the candle that wins it."

"And if you win, what do you want? Both of us at once?" one of the guards asked, and they both laughed, and the whore said, "Tell me if I've won and then I'll tell you what I want."

One of the guards heaved himself up from the mattress the three of them shared and picked up a long stick, and came over to the cell beside Gair's, and jabbed the stick through once, and then again, and then a third time.

"He's dead enough for the knacker," the guard said, and laughed. "The whore won it."

Gair clenched his teeth and squeezed his eyes shut against

Bokkam's death, and against the callous indifference of those who had witnessed it. Bokkam was a veteran of fierce battles and a hero; he had risked his life for his people and his country, had offered himself as a sacrifice for their safety and their way of life. He should have had mourners, a parade of veterans who had served with him marching through the streets behind his bier. He should have had honors. Speeches. The wreath of heather at his brow, the sword in his hand. Instead, he had shit-soaked straw and the laughter of his enemies.

"What do you want, then, Lurdy?" the other guard asked, and the whore said, "I want to watch you bugger each other."

Both guards burst out laughing. "If we wanted to do that, we'd have had no need to pay you, would we?" one said. The other said, "We're best off to throw that thing in a sack and haul it up to the refuse pits before it stinks any worse."

In Gair's heart, Bokkam rode on a fine oak pallet, with beautiful women weeping as the bearers carried him past, with heather at his brow and sword in his grip and sunlight on his face, to the pyre where his soul would be set free to ride the heavens with his fellows.

Gair had long doubted the reality of heaven, but the pomp and glory of military funerals made him hope sometimes that it was true.

He opened his eyes, and stared out at the guards and the whore on the mattress, cursing them and swearing their deaths if ever he could reach them. But he wouldn't. He knew now that Bokkam had been the first, but that he and Hale would be following, whether soon or late. No matter what he dreamed each night, no one would be coming to right the wrongs done them. No one cared any longer for the promises made to the soldiers who had offered their lives for their countries. Aboveground, the sun shone down on not one, but two, nations of oathbreakers. And though Gair still breathed, he was already buried in his grave.

Hetteriksday came, and the bells rang Nightingale, and I stepped into the temple dressed in clothes that hid everything but my face and my fingertips. My bruised lip I had disguised as best I could with reddened bear fat, so that I looked like I hoped to seduce a man, but not so much like I'd just battered myself with one. A bit of powder bought from the mistress of Whispering House made the bruise on my left cheek less obvious.

The healer's salve that worked its way into the bite wounds burned almost constantly, and my muscles had stiffened so that not even my morning dance of the karaadda could save me from a bit of gingerness in my steps. And any shreds of my self-regard that might still have survived my mad encounter with Skirmig had died horribly in the hands of Master Idrann, whose scathing remarks as he cleaned up the wounds still hung in my head. Saint Cladmus, who inspires the hands of healers, clearly never got carried away in a barn, and would not think highly of those who did.

As Da had promised, the keeper was waiting for me, and hurried me to a back staircase, and sent me up stairs I'd never had reason to use with a murmur of "Red door. Be sure to knock and identify yourself."

And when I did, I found my father, and some of the old warriors of the taak, and my few remaining comrades, and two near strangers, spread out along both sides of a long, narrow table. The room they occupied was big, without any windows, airless, smelling of smoke from the cheap fat that burned in the lamps that hung along the walls. The flickering light cast odd shadows across the faces of those present, so that one moment they looked the part of saints, and the next, devils.

Dim though it was, the light wasn't dim enough to blind my father, and more the pity for me. He gave me a shocked look that he hid quickly enough, but clearly the powder and the bear grease had not concealed as much as I would have hoped.

"What happened to you?" he asked me. Never one for dancing in the thunderstorm when the door stands open, my Da.

"Fell off my roof while fixing a leak," I said.

He raised an eyebrow that told me he didn't believe a word of it. But I had at least not shamed him in front of anyone else with my response. We'd acted as father and daughter to ward off further public discussion of my bruises. When we were alone I knew he would pursue the truth of what had happened with painful tenacity, until I gave in from sheer exhaustion and told him. But that would come later, and if I could avoid being alone with him for a few weeks . . . or mayhaps a handful of months . . . he might drop the issue. But probably not.

"All of yours here?" he asked me, and I looked at the few Shielders I'd been able to gather.

I nodded.

"All of mine are here, too," he said. "So this is every Shielder in or around Beyltaak who still holds oath with Ethebet."

We looked at each other with dismay. Eleven men and women sat at table with Ethebet's braids down our backs, with swords in our hearts and the love of our people branded on our souls, but we were not eleven strong to take into the View. While Da had somehow managed to reach two nomadic Tonks whom I had seen in and out of Shields, both still active Shielders at the end of the war, his other finds had been officers; they'd stepped away from active Shielding to preserve their sanity at the point where they started to break. They would be able to offer limited backup and support for those of us who were going in, but they couldn't actually go in with us.

Assuming my father could go all the way into the View and stay there—and I wasn't sure that he could, since the rules for who could be offered a Breeder deferral had changed about as often as pay rates in the Forces—we had eight active-duty Shielders, and three experienced officers who could sit at the edge and watch us and warn us if they saw us heading into trouble. But we were two short of a minimal safe entry team, and far short of comfort. No sane person would head into the View with only seven teammates.

And if we had any sane people sitting at table with us right then, those of us who were going in anyway were going to be in even bigger trouble.

"How did you come to discover Beyltaak had been stripped so bare?" my father asked, and everyone looked at me.

"A Hva Hwa warrior approached me to tell me that we had three prisoners of war somewhere in Beyltaak that had not been returned to the Eastils. He knew them. I knew of them, since I was present the day they were taken to the House of Law, and stopped a crowd from attacking them. Da, you knew of them, since you helped capture them."

My father looked puzzled. "I did little in active duty these last years."

"Injtaak," I said, and the confusion vanished from his face.

"Oh." He held silence a long moment, then sighed heavily. "Those three should have gone right into the prisoner-of-war system," he said.

I nodded. "But they didn't. The Hva Hwa, who served with them as a volunteer, went through their ERMiCCS and was told they hadn't even been taken prisoner, since they had not been reported."

"But they were," my father said. "I had to sign their in-processing papers, since I was the one who identified them."

I nodded. "But what *was* done is useless to us—ERMiCCS is gone, and our Council for Prisoners of War is gone, and the Hva Hwa just wants to know if the three of them are even still alive. If they aren't he would like to know what became of them, but that is not something we could tell him."

"You think to go into the View to look for them?"

"I do."

Around the table, the other men and women present sat quietly, considering the situation. They would have to decide how much the honor of their taak meant, and how much the presence of wrongfully held enemy prisoners of war within the taak meant, and what they as ex-Shielders would want the enemy to do with our people in a similar situation. And they would have to weigh all of this against the risk to their lives, which was real and, with so few of us, substantial.

Pordrit, whom I knew from Shields, said, "You know they were here?"

"Yes." I took a deep breath. "They went into the House of Law, and all record of them vanished. The man who would have processed them in died during the spring sickness. No one else at Law recalls them."

"There are too few of us," one of the officers said, but he didn't sound to me like he was making an excuse, just stating the obvious for those of us who might have missed it. I thought I might have introduced him to Pada, if only she were still around.

"I know," I said.

They were all looking at me. One of the nomads said, "If we decline, what do you intend to do?"

I'd spent time thinking about that. What I did would not depend on whether I had help or not; unsafe did not mean impossible, after all, and who I was and how I lived my life meant more to me than personal safety. It always had.

"I'll go in anyway," I said.

The male nomad nodded. "I would do the same."

Around the table, an odd, ragged laugh. "As would I," others agreed, and we all looked at each other. "What I feared most was that I would have to go in alone," the female nomad said, and I could only nod my agreement. That was what I, too, had feared.

None of those who had come refused to participate.

But the same man who had first questioned me said, "Once we have searched for these three, what do you plan to do with what you find?"

"I will give the information to the Hva Hwa. He has chosen to make the Eastils his people; he can bear the burden of retrieving them if they still live. By going into the View, we break the treaty; we cannot then stand before anyone publicly and declare that we have located forgotten prisoners of war unless we are able to provide proof, because our only proof comes from our having broken the treaty. If we make our findings public, even though we do it for the benefit of their people, the Eastils can use our actions to hurt our taak. And we cannot admit what we have done to our own people, either. Sympathizers for anything that ever belonged to or was used by the military are hard to find these days."

Everyone nodded.

My friend Pordrit said, "That's acceptable to me."

"Do we go now, then?" my father asked, deferring to me. I had brought this thing upon us and made it a matter of duty and honor; had I been silent, everyone else would have been safe. So I would bear the weight of the decisions.

"Yes," I said. "We get it over with."

All of us looked at the officers. "My call name is Talyn," I said. These were not officers with whom I had ever worked.

My father looked at the three of them. "You know mine." They nodded.

The male nomad said, "Call me Betraa."

"Pordrit," my old teammate said. Pordy and I could have been good friends, but she and I almost never ended up on the same rotation.

"Ordran." This the girl from Silver Shields.

"Matta." Another of my teammates. He and I had always gotten along well enough, though we'd never had much in common.

"Ravii." The female nomad.

"Uudmar." The last of my teammates who wasn't far away, and the one I liked least. He was hardheaded.

The officers had all our call names—essential in reaching us to warn us if the View started to take us. They gave us their names as a matter of courtesy, and in case some awful disaster should call for one of them to enter the View with us.

My father's old friend rose. He's a widower whose children and grandchildren are all still in his wife's taak, so that he only sees them when he rides cross-country or when they descend on him for holidays. He has shared so many dinners at my parents' table that I'm surprised Ma doesn't set him a place every night in self-defense. He smiled at me, and raised one eyebrow, and I though, Oh, Jostfar, he doesn't believe the roof story either. "I'm Volann."

Another of my father's old cronies stood when Volann sat and said, "I'm Yarel."

The third was an older woman, solid muscled and tired around the eyes. I didn't know her, not even her name, though I had seen her in Shields. She had been important. Very important. I suspected she ranked all of us, my father included, by several grades—but we sat at table in a new and rankless world, and unless we wanted to compound our crimes, she was still just one of us. She looked us over and said, "I'm Heldryn," and sat down.

And they all looked at me. "Since I know the men we're looking for, I'll take point," I said. "Spread out a little behind me, feel for 'Eastil' and 'prisoner of war' in the surface worries, and on our first pass, only target the sick, the dying, and the frightened. If our three people are still here, that's what we're likely to find. Sick. Dying. Scared. Well, angry too—but if we brush everyone who is angry in the taak right now, we'll be forever getting through this."

My father cleared his throat. "Don't get distracted," he added. "Don't be seduced. We've all been away for a while—some of us longer than others, but all of us too long. We're going to feel far too good, and be more vulnerable than usual, and this would be risky even if we were fielding a complete team."

"I'm going to make a suggestion that you may not like," Heldryn said. "Let Talyn take on the search alone since she is the only one who can recognize our targets. The rest of you act as checks for her; keep her focused, keep her present, and keep an eye on each other. It may take us longer to find these people if they're still here—but you should all make it out again."

And that made sense. I hated to look at us as such weaklings that we could not all search at the same time and still hang on to each other, the way we would have if we were in there with twenty people, but it *had* been a long time. And in a lot of ways, the View is like having intense sex—seductive, passionate, rich and compelling, physical, exciting, and very, very strange. And I hadn't done so well in my last encounter with intense sex, either.

I didn't need any bite marks on my brain.

The eight of us that would be going all the way in climbed on top of the table and sat in a squashed circle, holding hands. The View, always very close for me, started to billow behind my eyes like a ship's sail catching its first breeze. It tugged me forward, upward, inward, pulling hard. I could feel the rest of us sliding in, too. My hunger for this frightened me; staying always carefully outside the View, I had known how much I missed it, but when it caught hold of me completely and dragged me all the way in, I would no more have resisted it than the air I breathed.

I was soaring again, in the company of others who were just as drugged with the glory of the moment as I was.

Careful, a voice said in my head. *You've taken off too fast. You're breathing quickly, your pulse is racing. Slow it down, back out a bit.*

One of the officers, who to be able to reach me had to have a hand on my shoulder and perhaps one still on the pulse point at my throat, and who would be standing right behind me. But I couldn't feel my physical body at all. It was gone, and I realized with a start how easy it would be to misplace my own skin and never find my way back to it again—to just cast it off like a used husk and be done with it.

I willed myself to slow my breathing down, though I could no more feel myself breathe than I could feel the officer touching me. Still, as long as I didn't completely lose the connection between my body and my spirit, I could control what my body was doing. And clearly the connection still held, for after a moment I became vaguely aware of my weight again, of being seated cross-legged, of having hands locked in mine. I was grounded, yet still within the View.

I felt the others linked to me being warned, pulling themselves back down.

Sheepish, we exchanged apologies when we had all reached safe places inside our heads. None of us had been ready for that first glorious burst of freedom. Of magic.

Start looking, my father told me. *We'll watch your back.*

When had Beyltaak become such a hedonist's playground? I started moving above the shifting terrain of people and places, watching them flow together and apart, and the colors of the world I had once known so well were different, and the shapes were different. And everything was oddly scattered. We had been tight-knit, and now the fabric of our world as laid out against the flow of the View was tattered and loose and unfocused.

The glory of the moment for me shifted into something that nosed around fear. These had been my people, and they'd fought together and bound their lives and their futures to one another, and now they had pulled into themselves, seeking the amusements of sex and wealth and power . . . and they had become strangers.

How had this happened? How had they changed so completely, and so badly, in such a short time? Had war been all that tied us each to the others?

We need to get out of here, one of my comrades within the View said. *This place is making me sick.*

I understood.

I'll hurry, I said, and moved down toward the forms that radiated sickness, fear, pain.

I felt my comrades with me, holding on to me, and I was

grateful to Heldryn for suggesting that I alone seek while the rest guarded. I felt fragile inside the View as I never had before. I felt like a stranger in my own land. *Away* called to me with a powerful voice—away from the wrongness among my people, away from the foreigners who added their alienness and tore at our sturdy fabric, away to the bright, painless places within the View where responsibility and duty and honor were nothing but random sounds.

I chose the darkest, most hurt, most frightened forms, and flowed against them, brushing them for ties to the Eastil lands and acknowledgment that they thought themselves prisoners of war.

It took me less time than I would have supposed.

I found the first of the prisoners of war. The second huddled close by. Both of them wore, in dark scars on the very outermost surfaces of their pain, the recent and awful death of their third.

I flowed into the one who considered himself the leader of the failed team, and found his name—Gair—and his anguish, and many details of how he had come to be trapped and forgotten, and, after a bit of digging, his location.

Gair lay deep inside the dungeons of Beyltaak's lone prison. He was sure he would die there. What little hope he still clung to was only that it would be soon.

I found in the hellhole in which he was captive two things I had not expected to find. The first was pity.

Gair had followed his orders, as soldiers do, but he had not followed them blindly or unquestioningly. He believed that he had been fighting for something that would improve the lives of his people, but that would also improve the lives of mine. He had given everything he had to this belief—and if it was a wrongheaded belief, it was one that had been trained into him from an early age. He thought he was bringing the Tonks peace and civilization, and I discovered that I could not hate him.

And his people, and mine, had betrayed him. Betrayed his comrades. I understood the feelings of betrayal and bitterness he wore so close to the surface; I shared them. My people had sold our freedom for peace, and had turned their backs on the soldiers who had fought to defend them during our time of war, breaking the promises that they had made to them. My parents faced hardship that they should never have faced because of that kindred betrayal.

Along with pity, I discovered an odd sort of admiration. He held honor dear. He bled for his men, for those who had died as well as for the one who remained and suffered along with him. He had fought in many battles, had carried himself well, had dared to question his place in the world, and had found a purpose that he had risked everything to bring to fruition. He had failed, but first he had fought. He was the sort of man with whom I would have gladly served. My enemy. But a worthy enemy.

I pushed for a connection to his thoughts; I wanted some way to tell him to hang on, I wanted to give him a little raft on which to weather the last bit of the ocean that was drowning him. I wanted to let him know that land was close, if only he didn't give up.

But he had turned too far inward; he was lost in his own pain and sickness and dread for his last surviving comrade—who was sicker even than he was—to realize that for a moment at least he was not alone.

When I realized that I could not reach him, I finally pulled back. I hurt for him, and the temptations of the View ran strong inside of me—to escape from all pain, to soar forever, to put aside worry and need and fear and simply exist in a place free from all burdens and all cares.

Get out of there, my father said inside my head.

The easy way is not the best way, I reminded myself, and grabbed on to my father and the rest of the team. I fought to keep the pain and the despair I felt clear from my own surface—it is when we go too far down into that darkness that we pull others in behind us, and with our too-small team, I could destroy us all.

We won our way back; I found my path back to my flesh. I was, for a moment, grateful for the pain in my body. It made a clear, bright marker, and let me come back to ground.

We stepped out of the View together, all eight of us, and quickly hugged the officers, and then each other. None of us discounted our flirtation with disaster. We all could have been lost, and we knew it.

Da looked at me. "You found them, then."

"Yes. The two who still live. The third died not long ago."

"And the two who live?"

"Both prisoners of war. Honorable men wrongly held and badly treated. Both of them ill, weak, despairing."

"Where are they?"

"In the prison. In the dungeons."

"We cannot leave them there," Heldryn said. "Honor demands that they be set free."

My father turned to her, and I saw pain in his eyes. "We must first give the Hva Hwa the chance to mount a rescue. If there is any other path to freeing them that does not lead to our betraying what we have done, we must take that path. I discovered other problems while we were in the View, and I thinks others did as well. Something is terribly wrong beneath the surface in Beyltaak, and if we are imprisoned or executed, we will not be able to find out what that something is."

Betraa said, "I felt it."

All of us who had been in there nodded.

Da leaned against the wall of our meeting room, standing between two lanterns, looking far too much like the ghosts and demons of tales. "We have to keep meeting," he said. "We have to start Shielding again. We need to get more of our people back." He sighed. "We can't be that easily seduced by the View again. This was a small observation-only mission—go in, locate someone, get out. And we all nearly fell anyway. Had our taak needed us to fight, to keep it safe, had we been under fire, we would have been lost."

Heldryn frowned. "You're suggesting we . . . step outside the treaty permanently?"

Da nodded.

"It's death if we do and we're caught," she said. "I don't say that to convince any of you not to take the step, but only so that none of us pretends this is some little thing you are suggesting."

The nomad Ravii said, "There are worse things than death, and whatever has gone wrong in this taak stinks of them. This wrongness had the air of poison to it. Something wicked in our midst, something evil sitting at table wearing a false smile."

Da said, "I have already sent letters to my children who took work far away that they are needed at home. I would suggest that those of you who have friends or family who were in Magics or Conventionals call them back. Quickly."

"There is no quickly," Pordrit said. "The passages will be clogged with ice soon, the winter storms will be upon us in full fury, and the next ships will not come here until spring. Whatever we need now, we will have to get on our own."

I said, "We need to send riders to the lesser taaks to warn them not to sign the treaty, or if they already have, to keep all their people close to home no matter what offers they might receive. We need to see if we can find some Communications people in Beyltaak who are Tonk first, and who would work with us instead of the Feegash no matter what the treaty says. We might be able to reach those of our people who are doing Communications and View work elsewhere and let them know what has happened here before any ships with letters could reach them."

But my father pushed away from the wall and stepped over to the long table and leaned on it, palms flat, staring at each of us in turn. "To whom do we entrust these tasks? For whomever we hand this information, we also hand the truth of our actions. We can reach family and friends and feel somewhat sure that they will not betray us. But the taak messengers? The Beyls? Those who might actually be able to do something to correct this problem we sensed are not, overall, people who will cast a kind eye on our actions. And when we find those we can trust and who can help us, what do we tell them? We cannot describe clearly even to ourselves what we found in the View. We say wickedness, and wrongness—but how does it work? Where is it hiding? What is it doing? We must have facts that people who cannot touch the View can see, and we must get them in a fashion that we can claim publicly."

"We need to buy the ear of a Feegash diplomat," Heldryn said. "Someone who won't ask how we came across our information when we bring it; someone who will be willing to pursue the Eastils who are sneaking in here and working their poison and who will have the influence—and the integrity—to expose them when we track down what it is they're doing." She rested her face in her hand. "But you can't buy them. To my knowing, *no one* has ever successfully bought one. By Ethebet, we can't even subvert one with sex. The taak crawls with Feegash now, and not a one has visited a whorehouse, nor found a lover we might pump for information. Either they're the most devout celibates I've ever seen, or they only futter each other."

"You've been trying to get one into bed?" Ordran asked, looking startled.

"No. But I've been offering the whores a bonus on their regular fees if they could get close enough to one to give me information I could use." Heldryn gave us a sour grin. "I have grown hungry for information since the Beyls allowed the Forces to be taken apart."

My heart sank. I watched my father out of the corner of my eye, and I saw the moment when he stopped being my father and donned once again the role of Shielder. His lips thinned, his eyes narrowed, and his shoulders went back. He sighed with resignation; he didn't look at me at all. "I believe I know of a diplomat who has not been so . . . circumspect. We might be able to win his ear."

I could see the hope in their eyes. And I could feel the weight of the bond we shared as Shielders, as taaksmen, and as Tonks settle onto my shoulders. I was no longer private taakswoman Talyn, that daughter of Radavan with the overpriced horse and the little jewelry business. I had somehow put on Senior Shieldsergeant Talyn Wyran av Tiirsha dryn Straad, Hawkshanks Shielder, and what that woman with the overpriced horse would balk at, the senior shieldsergeant would do with regret but determination, and for the good of her taak.

Da wouldn't have to say a word to me about this. I had received my orders, and I knew how to carry them out.

9

The next day I rode Toghedd out the taak's gates, and through the forests along the paths; I went at dusk, when horses are skittish and most folk prefer not to ride, for I hoped to avoid passing any others on the paths back to the place where Snow Grell and I had agreed to meet. The bitter cold bit into me; I did not envy the Hva Hwa his outdoor accommodations in such weather. In fact, I wondered if he would even be there.

Toghedd wanted his head. He fought the bit, urging me to let him gallop, for sensible horse though he is, he longed to run. The freezing weather filled him with a friskiness that sent him skittering sideways with every snap of the wind, and at the sound of my voice he bucked and bounced like a jackrabbit. I hadn't ridden him much the last few weeks because of the cold. He seemed determined to get the most from the outing.

In the twilight, a woods looks different. We went around the jumps rather than over, and Toghedd shied at the bridges like he thought wolves lurked beneath them; I patted his neck and clucked reassurances, but in the long shadows I felt a little skittish, too.

We came to the deadfall, and I looked around. Toghedd shifted beneath me, uneasy; he snorted and his ears flicked back to fore and side to side ceaselessly, busy as a gossip's tongue with a new tale to spread.

And at the deadfall I sat, tense in the saddle, turning Toghedd from side to side to look for the Hva Hwa. He had said just to wait for him—that when I arrived, he would know. But if he was out hunting, if he had given up and gone home, if he had frozen to death in the bitter cold . . .

And then Toghedd whickered, and I heard a soft cough not too far away. In front of me, in the deep shadows.

And Snow Grell seemed to materialize out of nowhere.

"You have news?"

"Two of them still live."

He winced. "Two?"

I nodded. "The team leader. Gair. And the one named Hale. Both are sick, both are weak, both have given up and want only to die."

"You know where they are?"

I nodded and told him.

He stared down at his feet and I heard a soft sigh. "A prison. And a dungeon. Ah, gods, and I am but one man. Are there any in Beyltaak who would listen to me if I told them of my friends and the wrong being done them?"

I almost said, "No." Beyltaak was not the same place it had

been less than a year before, when men and women knew that prisoners of war mattered. But then I thought of Skirmig, and of how I intended to use him anyway. I could hardly claim to be too good to take this thing to him, when I intended to take advantage of his passion for me for things far less honorable.

"I know of one man who might help you. He is a foreigner to both of us, but I have his ear." I paused, considering that. It might be that I was being presumptuous. Having gone one round with me—and no small round at that—he might have decided he'd had enough, and that the wise thing to do would be to find another woman. Or take up the life of a celibate. "I think I have his ear," I added.

The Hva Hwa breathed out heavily, the steam curling in a heavy cloud in front of his face. "Will you take this problem to him and see if he can get the two of them released? Or will you take *me* to him, that I might petition him in my own words."

"You cannot mention my part in this."

"I know."

"If you take this to him, you lose any element of surprise. You cannot bribe your way into the prison and steal a key and hurry them out in the dark of night; once everyone knows about their presence, they will be watched. And if my . . . this man I know . . . if he then decides that he must study the problem, or that he cannot make a decision on his own but must take it to his superiors—and he is not the man in charge, though I think he has a great deal of power on his own—you may lose them both. Neither of them will live much longer, I think."

"Can they travel if I find a way to sneak into the prison? Will they be able to run across the countryside with me in this weather, sleeping under logs and half buried in snow, eating their meat raw when we cannot dare a fire and some days eating not at all?"

I didn't need time to consider that. "No. Living as you are living now, they will be dead in a day."

"Then I have no choice but to throw myself on your mercy and ask you to win me an audience with this man of power."

He was right.

I sighed. "Come into the taak tomorrow, and ask for me. Tell people you have heard a woman jeweler might have found a ring a friend of yours lost, and mention that you are looking for both the ring and the friend."

"A ring?"

"I have one I made that I think looks foreign. I can claim to have found it and shown it to friends, who then left Beyltaak and told you about it. It gives you an excuse to bring your tale to me, and me an excuse to take what you know to him."

"Very well, then. I will do that."

"Then I will see you on the morrow." I said nothing else. I turned Toghedd around and rode him carefully along the dark paths, back to the gate, where I had to explain to the gatekeeper why I had been riding so late before he would let me in.

I lied.

I seemed to be lying a lot all of a sudden, I realized.

A rap at my window the next morning woke me not much past the break of dawn, and I opened one eye to see my neighbor Algra's beak of a nose poking out of the hood of her wolf-ruffed shuu as she peered into my window. She frowned when I opened both eyes and gestured to my front door. I crawled reluctantly out from under my covers, looked at the dead embers of the fire, and watched my own breath puff in front of me as I found my robe and sheepskin slippers with the wool still on and dragged myself to my front door.

"Some man has been all over the town since before the sun rose asking for you," she said, clearly happy that once again I was going to be the source of an interesting tale to tell her friends over the night's ale.

"Some man?" I blinked stupidly at her and turned to gather kindling to feed the fire in my central stove.

"A *foreigner*," she whispered.

"Not like we don't have plenty of those around now." I refused to be baited.

"None of us have told him how to find you until I could come to you and see if you *wanted* him to find you."

"Depends," I said. I could have used more sleep, and I did not have to feign either testiness or the wobbly exhaustion that I displayed. "What does he want?"

"He thinks you found his friend's ring."

I pretended to give that serious thought. "I might have. The last time my unit went on away duty, I did find a ring just outside the gates of the taak as we were coming back." I frowned. "It's a foreign-looking thing." I went over to the cupboard where I'd planted the ring the night before and pulled it down. I showed it to her. It was heavy and silver, had a black stone polished to a high sheen set in the dead center and angled. I'd carved the silver into patterns. I liked the piece, but it wasn't a Tonk piece. It had no traditional elements to it; I had just been playing with some extra materials. No Tonk would have wanted it, so I'd simply kept it.

Algra studied it. "Foreigners wear some strange things." She asked me, "So should we then tell him how to find your house?"

I sighed. The Hva Hwa could have waited until midday to come searching for me, couldn't he? Might I not have had at least time for more sleep, and a shower, and a hearty breakfast? But he had been sleeping in the snow under a tree in the hopes of being able to rescue his comrades, and his comrades were trapped in a situation that gave me nightmares. So I supposed I could not complain too much about the disruption of my comfort.

"Bring him over. I'll see him."

She scurried out the door, hoping to get some story that would be worth a round with her friends, and I trudged off to throw on day clothes.

I had little to say to Snow Grell when he arrived, other than "Keep the fire going; I'll be back as soon as I can." I saddled and bridled Dakaat, also made frisky by the weather and lack of regular exercise, and rode through town to Harbor Hall, and then to the Heights, where Skirmig had newly rented a house according to the Harbor Hall manager. I felt awkward going to him; I had not seen him or had word from him since our adventure in the barn, and as the days passed, it seemed more likely that I would not. Some part of me was relieved by the idea of that; another part grieved. And part of me was embarrassed, too, that I had raced headlong away from things that I held sacred and things that I had believed to be true about myself to become a stranger in my own skin, and one that I didn't much like, at that.

But I would face Skirmig and the possibility of his rejection because whatever shreds of myself I still held about me were bound to my honor as a Tonk, and to oaths I had sworn to uphold in the exercise of my duties as a warrior.

On the Heights, I asked about and found someone who knew which house Skirmig had taken, and with my heart in my throat, I knocked on the door.

A stranger answered—a thin, small man dressed from head to toe in dun brown. A servant, then.

"I have come to speak with Skirmig on a matter of great urgency," I said.

The little man looked at me, and at my horse standing by my side, and he said, "Your name?"

"Talyn," I said.

"Your *full* name."

"He knows me," I said.

"Your business?"

"It's private."

"Then I'll tell him you're here," he said, and closed the door in my face with more enthusiasm than the exchange warranted.

In the space of a breath, Skirmig was at the door, red-faced and apologetic. "He did not let you in? God forgive! I thought— I had the impression—after our . . . ah . . . I didn't think you wanted to see me again. That you were angry with me. Please, wait and I'll have one of the servants take your horse to the stable, and then you must come in—"

"I cannot," I told him. "I've come to ask if you will agree to accompany me back to *my* house. I have someone who desperately needs your help, and the matter is urgent."

I could see his disappointment that I had not come because I wanted him. But he nodded. "I'll be a moment. I must get a coat and"—he gave Dakaat a wary look—"a horse."

I mounted up and waited. He was longer than a moment, but not by much. His own mount was merely adequate—a bit knock-kneed, rough gaited, and weak through the withers. It was a Tonk-bred beast, but a scrub, the sort of animal we would gladly sell to foreigners.

He rode beside me, and I noted that he sat on the horse as if he were a bag of flour strapped in the saddle. He plow-reined the animal, and his toes in the stirrups pointed down and out. I cringed.

Foreigners.

"I had hoped you had come to see *me*," he said. "I'm glad you came at all, but . . ."

I discovered that in his presence, my embarrassment at my behavior faded, replaced by a return of the fierce hunger I had felt the first time we touched. Looking over at him, all I wanted was to touch him again. To move against him, wrap my legs around him, feel him deep within me.

"I was ashamed of myself for doing you such damage," I said.

He laughed a little. "I was a hero. The other men at the baths begged to know who you were."

"My healer gave me a lecture," I said. "And my father didn't believe for an instant that I hurt myself falling off a roof. I've been uncomfortable going outside until the bruises faded."

Skirmig winced. "I am sorry about that."

I shrugged. "We could be more careful next time."

Such hope in a man's eyes is a thing of beauty. "Next time?" he said.

I tried not to think about my fellow conspirators, and the fact that I was basically obligated to a next time. I wanted him, and for a while, at least, I could have him with my father's blessing, if not for any reason I could publicly confess. I tried to concentrate on that. "I would be happy about a next time."

Jostfar, that smile of his was addictive as salban smoke.

He went into my house while I put Dakaat back in her stall; he was deep in conversation with Snow Grell by the time I joined the two of them.

Skirmig turned to me. "You can confirm that these men were here?"

I nodded. "I kept a crowd from stoning them as they were being taken to the House of Law."

"And you believe what his sources have told him is possible? That through error or malice they were not returned to the Eastils with the other prisoners of war?"

"I think it possible. I hope it isn't true, but humans are prone to error."

Skirmig rose and paced from one side of the room to the other, head down and hands behind his back. "Their presence here will cause problems with the peace. No doubt their presence was forgotten when the units disbanded." Back and forth he went. "The peace itself will be blamed, and the Eastils will demand reparations, and the Tonks will demand proof that none of their people have been locked away by accident. . . . The whole business will get ugly." Back and forth. Back and forth. "We cannot leave them in the dungeon, though. In good conscience they must be freed." Back and forth. "But their presence here must be secret. Must be. For the good of everyone." Back and forth. "What to do, then?"

Snow Grell and I looked from Skirmig to each other, and back to Skirmig again. I'd seen wolves in cages who looked no different.

Skirmig stopped suddenly, and turned to Snow Grell. "If we get them out, have you a place and a way to care for them until they are well enough to travel?"

"I'm sleeping in the open air," Snow Grell said. "I have neither money nor shelter."

"Damnall," Skirmig said, and began pacing again. "I'd rather none but the three of us knew they were here. Ever." Back and forth. "Though I can guarantee the silence of my servants, I cannot provide these men with shelter, or allow them to be connected to me."

We are responsible for the lives we would save, Saint Ethebet says. We are responsible for the state of our honor. I sighed. "If you can get them here without them being seen, I can give them shelter. And food. And take care of them until they are well enough to travel."

"Two men? And your enemies, at that? I couldn't consider it," Skirmig said.

"I could. This house has a goodly loft that I have thus far left unused. Snow Grell could stay here and care for the two of them, all three could keep out of sight, and when they can travel, they can leave with none the wiser."

Snow Grell stared at me. "You would do this?"

I nodded.

Skirmig said, "May I speak with you privately for a moment?" I rose and joined him in the corner.

"What of your reputation?" he asked me.

I should not have laughed, but I did. "You mean the one I'm going to destroy anyway the first time I appear in public with you at my side?" Then I added, "No one will know they're here, remember?"

"Are you not worried that they will . . . take advantage of you . . . while you sleep?"

"No. I sleep with my door barred. Besides, they are men of honor. Men of honor do not repay kindness with rape."

"You speak as if you know them."

I had, in fact. Careless of me. I could not say *I have looked inside one of them and seen someone worthy of my admiration.* I was stuck with generalities and platitudes to defend my position, but those I had in plenty. "They are men whose friend risked his own life to save them; to receive such loyalty, they must be men who warrant it. And they are warriors. Eastil warriors, but the Eastils, too, know honor."

Skirmig rested a hand on my belly and looked into my eyes. "Like the ones who did *that* to you?"

I didn't flinch, though I began to understand why he was so against the idea. "Doing the right thing entails risk," I said. "If it did not, everyone would do it."

"Very well. I can bring them here tonight. I will lie to remove them from the prison—I'll dress some of my servants in official robes, and go into the prison with them accompanying me, and tell the prisonmaster that I have the order for the execution of these two—Gair Farhallan and Hale Son of the Wede? I have those names correct? I will demand that they be hooded, and I will have my people carry them out on pallets, and will make it appear that I have put them on the back of a wagon, but I'll switch them with a couple of my servants, and bring them here in my private carriage." He rubbed his temples and gave me a beseeching look. "You don't really want to do this, do you?"

"I do."

He sighed. "Of course you do. If you did not care for such things, you would not be the woman I love."

My heart missed a beat.

Ah, Ethebet, I thought, and swallowed against the sudden racing of my pulse and the quickening of my breath. "I'll be here," I said. "I'll be here, and I will have the loft ready for them."

And I turned away. I was not ready to question his love for

me, or whether I wanted him to love me, nor was I prepared to consider how I planned already to misuse him.

He is a foreigner, I reminded myself. Not Tonk. You cannot have a true future with anyone who is not Tonk.

Snow Grell had been watching us. "I will go with you to help you get them," he said. "I will be able to identify both of them for sure."

"Yes," Skirmig said. "You'll come with me."

Fear skittered down my spine, and I had a sudden premonition, and without thinking, I acted on it. "No," I said. "I need you to stay here and help me. You gave Skirmig very clear information on both prisoners; he'll be able to find them."

I could not say what it was in Skirmig's voice that caused my gut to knot, but in truth the only genuine link between the two embarrassing, inconvenient prisoners of war locked in the dungeon of the Beyltaak prison and a duty Skirmig clearly wished to avoid was Snow Grell.

I could not say that I had heard *anything* in Skirmig's voice. But that premonition—of Snow Grell riding off with Skirmig and meeting his doom—stayed with me.

He says he loves me, I thought. But I don't know him.

Men in hoods and black robes marched into the dungeon, silent as ash falling on snow, and the guards, whoreless for the moment and fully dressed, came to attention, looking scared. Gair lay against the wall at the back of his cell, too weak to do more than lift his head to watch. Behind the phalanx of hooded men came a man richly dressed in the garb of the Feegash diplomat, a man tall and powerfully built with one of those pretty-boy faces that women so loved and men so loathed, and Gair thought, He's far too important to be here. Important people did not come into dungeons; they sent lackeys and received reports.

In Hyerti, Hale wheezed, "Ah, gods, what new pile of pig shit is this?"

And then the handsome man said, "I've come for the two nameless prisoners. They're to be executed tonight."

"Which at least answers the question of which of us will have to suffer through listening to the other die," Gair said. And he thought, Fine. Well enough. At least execution will be quicker than rotting in a dark hole in hell. He was past caring. He was almost grateful.

The guards opened the heavy doors, and the hooded men carried in two stretchers and two black sheets, and Gair thought—What? They're going to do it here and carry out our bodies when they're done. But they placed him onto the stretcher with surprising gentleness and covered him, even his face, with the black sheet. Hale said, "I was honored to serve under you, Captain."

Gair said, "You were a good man, Corporal."

It was funny, he thought, that though they had been simply Hale and Gair to each other since it became clear that their capture would not end in transfer back to Eastil hands, at the end of their lives they chose to say good-bye through their rank and their record of service. At some level, Gair thought, what they had done and what they had hoped to do were more important than who they were.

He could feel the stretcher being carried up long winding stairways. Through busier parts of the prison, though all were oddly quiet.

And outside. Into bitter cold, and darkness.

Gair almost wept. Just once more, even if it was on the way to his own execution, he would have liked to see the sun and feel its warmth on his skin.

The silent hooded men loaded him onto what felt like an open-air wagon, and a moment later Hale lay beside him.

Hale was coughing. When he caught his breath, though, he muttered in Hyerti, "We have darkness to cover us. So let's kill the driver, steal the horses, and ride off into freedom."

Gair laughed—the first laugh he'd had in longer than he could remember, and sure to be the last. Since Bokkam's death, he had become too starved and weak even to drag himself to the pisspot; he'd been lying in his own shit for some unknown, unthinkable time. Death hovered over him like a vulture impatiently waiting its next meal.

"I thought you'd like that," Hale said.

"Thanks, friend. One last laugh is a thing to cherish."

The wagon rolled over cobblestone roads, while behind it another horse-drawn cart followed. They did not travel far. Then the carts stopped, and Gair fumbled through the darkness, found Hale's hand, and gave it a quick squeeze. Hale squeezed back.

"For Eastil honor, then," Gair said. "We'll go as men."

Two black-dressed men, hoods thrown back, pulled the black cover off Gair and lifted him and hurried with him, saying, "No sound." There was something surreptitious in their actions.

And then, instead of being taken to a gallows, Gair was shoved to the floor of a richly appointed carriage where the too-pretty Feegash diplomat sat, and the diplomat stared down at him and wrinkled his nose and muttered, "God in heaven, you stink too much to live. I'll have to torch this carriage when this is done." An instant later, the same two men shoved Hale down on the floor beside him.

"Get on with you, then," the diplomat said to the hooded men. "Get those bodies to the burial pits, and make sure you make record of the executions."

The inside of the carriage was warm—heated in some fashion unfamiliar to Gair, and the delicious warmth and dryness flowed into him.

"Make no movement and no sound," the diplomat said. "I cannot imagine why we would be stopped, but your lives depend on your silence from now until you are hidden away in the place I have found for you." He coughed, and opened a window, and the bitter cold of the night rushed back in again. "God in heaven," the diplomat said again, and leaned his head into the cold to breathe.

Gair supposed he and Hale did stink, though his own sense of smell had died out of self-defense some time ago. He felt bad about that, but not bad enough for it to ruin the odd realization that he and Hale had just been rescued. That, gods willing, the two of them might survive to see the sun again, and might someday return to the Eastil Republic and live the lives he was sure they had lost.

"Thank you," Gair whispered.

The diplomat moved his eyes and turned his head just enough to look down at Gair. "Don't thank me. By my hand you would be dead—your presence is an embarrassment and an awkwardness that could cause me no end of problems, and your deaths, as well as the death of that little troublemaker who came looking for you, would have been a fine solution to my problems. You live only because the woman I love asked for your lives."

And he turned his face away again.

Gair closed his eyes, wondering. Who knew where to look for him, and how? What troublemaker did the diplomat mention? And what Feegash woman would ask for his life . . . and why? What woman at all?

I had Snow Grell beside me when I ran out my door to greet Skirmig's carriage. Not like the neighbors wouldn't notice a carriage; its wheels rattled no end on the cobblestones. I could only hope that at such a late hour, and in such foul weather—for bitter cold had given way to an ugly wet cold, and to sleet and snow coming down so hard I could barely see from my front door to the street—my neighbors would not bother to come out to see *why* I had a visitor at such a late hour.

"You're going to want to put them in the barn," Skirmig said. "They stink like nothing I've ever smelled. God, you might want to bring the horses into the house." He leaned over and whispered in my ear, "You don't have to do this. Truly. They aren't going to live, either of them. And when they die we're going to have to sneak them back out of your house and haul them away and get a boat and drop them out at sea at night so no one will wonder what you've been doing." He caught a finger under my chin and turned my face so he could look in my eyes. "Say the word."

How much did I have to do to satisfy honor? How much of my life did I have to give up to make things right to my enemies? Was it enough that because of me they were no longer trapped in a dungeon?

No, I decided. It wasn't. Not if I told Skirmig to take them away and find some other place for them. If I did that, he might find someone else to care for them in their last days. But he might also shove them out of his carriage into an alley on his way home and let the taak deal with the frozen bodies as soon as someone discovered them.

I looked at him with that realization clear in my mind, and I decided I didn't trust him.

"We'll bring them into the house," I said without enthusiasm. "You and Snow Grell carry them in. I'll start bathwater heating on the stove. And build the fire up so that we can burn the rags they're wearing."

And he smiled at me—that impossible, beautiful smile—and he said, "That's what I love about you, Talyn. You are truly good." He kissed me, and my knees went weak, and all I could think of was that if I had those two men in my house, it would make ripping Skirmig's clothes off and throwing him to the floor in front of the stove and having my way with him an awkward proposition.

I told myself, Don't think about it. I was the one who broke off the kiss, and when I did I felt the sleet and the snow again, soaking through my clothes to my skin.

"Get them inside quickly," I said, and hurried into the house to fill pots with water to heat on the stove. I dumped some of my dried lavender into each pot, hoping it would help cut the smell.

Skirmig hadn't been joking about that. Within moments of bringing them into the house, the air was nearly unbreathable, and I wondered how much worse it would get. After all, their filthy rags had to be keeping at least some of the stench in. And looking at the two men lying on pallets in front of my stove, I couldn't help but think that Skirmig was right about their chances of survival, too. They were nothing but skeletons with the skin still on. They were going to die no matter what I did for them.

But they might as well die clean, on clean beds, in clean clothes. They were warriors and honorable men, and they deserved at least that much.

I wrapped a rag over my face to cut the smell, and when that didn't help, rubbed the rag with a block of perfumed soap. The lavender starting to heat up in the pots didn't help. The rag over my face didn't help much—I needed stronger soap, but I didn't have any. And as bad as the smell in the room started out, it got worse as the two men warmed up.

I tried not to breathe.

Skirmig watched me, shaking his head. "I'm going home," he said. "I don't know how you're going to stand this, but I already can't." He stared at my three houseguests, and his distaste

for them showed. "I'll come by tomorrow to see how you're doing. And . . . to help you with any . . . big . . . problems." He
pulled his cloak up over his nose and mouth, and hurried out
into the cold and the dark, slamming the door behind him.

I got a sharp knife, and started cutting the clothes off the man
who lay nearest me. His name, Snow Grell told me, was Hale—
I had known the name from being briefly inside Gair's spirit,
but I would not have been able to attach either name to the battered wrecks of bodies that lay before me. Hale groaned, and
the Hva Hwa hissed as I peeled the rags away from his flesh.
Hale had open sores, seeping wounds from multiple beatings,
rope scars and burn scars and other marks of torture. I had
known all this, but knowing was not *seeing*. Seeing was far
worse. I felt tears well in my eyes and blinked them back.

The man who owned the prison might be Greton, but the
guards were Tonks. My people. *My* people had done this.
Tonks. Men born into a long tradition of honor.

I cut away all of Hale's clothes, trying not to look at his pitiful sticklike arms and legs, his ribs that poked out so sharply
they looked like they would rip through his skin. I wanted not to
see. I wanted not to feel.

"Burn his clothes," I told the Hva Hwa, and he nodded, and
picked them up without any sign of reluctance.

"I'll burn them outside. You do not want the smoke from
them in here."

No. I didn't. "Very well. I'm going to bathe this one, and
then start on the other."

"Hale." I looked at Hale, who looked back at me with anguished eyes, and said, "I'm going to get you cleaned up, and
put you in a clean bed, and then your friend and I are going to
get you something to eat."

He moved his head slightly, a little nod of acquiescence. And
tears rolled down his cheeks.

That was more than I could take. I turned to the stack of old
cleaning rags, and grabbed one and soaked it in the lavender-
scented water boiling on the stove. I kept my face turned away
from him, pretending to wait for the rag to cool, and got myself
under control.

I started washing him. He whimpered, and twitched away

from me at each touch. Not that he could move far enough to do him any good. But he tried.

The other one—Gair—turned his head enough that he could look straight at me. "Why did you save us?"

And when he looked at me, recognition sparked in his eyes and mine. We knew each other. His were the calm gray eyes that had watched me from inside his cage—he was the one who had put his arms down to let the stones hit him, so that he could die with some dignity and some control. He was the one whose honor and courage had so spoken to me when I was inside the View. He was a man I'd found worthy of respect.

But that quick spark was more than that.

I knew him. He had called to me in my dreams. I had the oddest conviction that he was the man in the cage in those dreams and nightmares—that his was the voice calling out to me ever more urgently for the past year.

And even more than that. More, much more.

In my gut, something insisted that in another place and time, he and I had fought battles side by side, that we had sat together at table, that we were comrades in arms.

And yet more. Impossibly more, insanely more.

I looked in those eyes and I saw . . .

. . . babies. And tots, and sturdy boys and dark-haired girls. A life I had once dreamed of—a life I knew I could never have.

That flash of deep knowing, of cut-to-the-bone conviction, stood as one of the most bewildering moments of my life.

After all, his were the people who had stolen from me my chance for those selfsame babies. For a family of my own—that thing I never let myself think about anymore. He was my enemy. I was acting to care for him because it was the right thing to do. The honorable thing to do. Not because he would ever be anything but my enemy.

So what had birthed that mad feeling? Not any sense of attraction, Ethebet knows. Gair was grotesque—a broken, stinking, scarred living skeleton, his beard and hair tangled and matted and so terribly blood and filth-encrusted that Snow Grell and I were going to have to shave everything off. He stank. He oozed.

"I didn't. I only helped your friend find you. Then I asked my friend to use his connections. He saved you."

"The man who brought us to you said that were it not for you, he would have had us killed just to keep us from becoming a problem. An . . . embarrassment. That our being here was a threat . . . to the peace. But that he loved you. That he saved us because you asked him to."

Skirmig had said that?

He told these men that he loved me? And at the same time told them he would have preferred to kill them? I took a deep breath—a mistake, that—and reminded myself that I didn't know Skirmig. I didn't love him. I didn't. I listed off in my head all the things about him that I could never accept: that he was a foreigner, that he was part of the cause of this pathetic peace under which we now lived, that if he understood honor he had not yet chosen to show it. I reminded myself that I was charged with the task of using him, that I intended to spy on him and betray him for my people's ends, and that he would certainly never love me if he knew the truth about me.

Logic is a fine thing; it makes choosing horses and houses and campsites and battlefields easier. Possible.

It is worthless when choosing men, because the head can shout logic to the end of all days, but the heart listens to another set of words entirely. My heart was deaf to all the sensibilities of my head. It knew its own logic, which had nothing to do with reason.

And even if I could have brought myself to do it, I did not have the choice to embrace sensibility and push Skirmig out of my life, any more than I had the choice to shove my Eastil guests out into the snow. To the first I was bound by expediency and duty—no matter my wishes—and to the second I was bound by honor. And duty. I had to stay close to Skirmig because my people needed to know what he knew. We needed to find out what the Eastils planned. We needed to find out how Beyltaak had so completely broken away from what it had once been.

And I needed to not pretend, at least to myself, that I would be with Skirmig only out of duty. I wanted to be naked with Skirmig again. I wanted to have him kiss me; I wanted my knees to go weak again; I wanted to make him writhe and shout.

In the midst of awfulness, the mind wanders far away. My body was scrubbing filthy, stinking, wounded, dying men, but my mind retreated to the barn to indulge in a rematch with Skirmig. And then, watching myself do things I had sworn I'd never do, my mind came back to the house.

I wasn't having too much luck looking at myself in a mirror right then, either.

I kept scrubbing, and told Gair, "I was a soldier. In the war. We don't treat prisoners of war the way you were treated. It's a matter of honor—and honor didn't die when the war ended."

"Not entirely . . . perhaps."

It hurt me to hear him speak. His voice creaked and rasped. "Rest," I said. "Don't talk. I'm about finished with your friend, and Snow Grell should be back soon, and we'll get you both some food, and something to drink, and . . . we'll help you."

We're going to watch you die, I thought, and I averted my eyes so that he would not see that thought on my face. If he was as bad off as his friend, they would be lucky to live through another day.

"I wanted to thank you," he said. "Perhaps I'll see the sun again before I die."

If you last until morning, I thought, I'll be willing to guarantee it. But I didn't say anything. I had a lump in my throat that was hard to breathe around.

Hale's injuries were hard to for me to take; I had a few scars of my own, and the memories to go with them, and I could almost feel where he had been.

Snow Grell came back in, bringing a gust of icy air with him. "Done," he said. He looked at his friend Hale and turned away. "Damned cowards, to do such things," he muttered.

He helped me, though. Together we finished cleaning Hale, and we washed Gair, whose scars and wounds were, if anything, worse. We wrapped both of them in clean blankets because I had no clothes for them, and at that moment finding clothes for them seemed like wasted effort. We got them both onto cots in the loft, which, open to the central room and just above the stove, was the warmest place in the house.

They coughed a lot. Their breathing sounded bad. I was going to have to bring the healer into this if they were to have any chance of surviving—and Skirmig, who had hoped not to involve anyone else in this rescue, was going to have to accept that. My healer would be discreet. But I would not leave those two men to my own pathetic ministrations. Assuming, always, that they survived long enough for me to get to the healer.

Once they were in their cots, Snow Grell took Gair's rags and the rags we'd cleaned them with outside and burned them. We'd been careful always to pour the hot water on the cleaning rags, and never to dip used rags in the water, but even so, after I showered—and the water was so cold it hurt, but I didn't care—I set Snow Grell the task of scrubbing the pots.

Meanwhile, I made tea and broth for the men and fed them. Just a little, and slowly; I had seen what solid food or even too much liquid would do to someone who had been without for too long.

When Snow Grell finished, I could smell only lavender downstairs. He came up the stairs and said, "It's clean as if none of this had ever happened." And I believed him. In the military we learned to clean. And I had to guess the Eastil military had been no different in its focus on order and cleanliness.

The Hva Hwa looked at me. "You need to sleep," he said. "You're gray." He pointed to a roll of blankets in the corner that I hadn't noticed. "I'll sleep up here. If they need anything, I'll make sure they have it."

I nodded. "I'll be up to check on them when I wake," I said, and dragged myself downstairs and dropped into my bed, and fell into a sleep filled with hellish nightmares of torture and horror. I probably would have done better to stay awake until daylight.

Gair lay beneath warm blankets on a clean cot, bathed, fed, cared for, and in the darkness, where no one could see him, he wept. He did not think he would live. He had actually seen his body for the first time in this horrible new shape it had taken on, and he did not see how he *could* live. His knees were bigger around than his thighs, his elbows were bigger than his upper arms, his flesh fell away between his ribs so tightly that he could see the pulsing of his heart within his chest. His wounds seeped and smelled—and now, in a place with clean air, he could smell them.

He would not survive. But he didn't care. He had at the end of his life known the kind face and gentle touch of a good woman, and if she was his enemy, he didn't care about that, either. He would not die in shit and darkness. No one would ever beat him again, or burn him, or cut him, or any of the other things they had done to him before he became too weak and sick and scrawny to make an amusing victim.

He really did want to feel the sun on his face one more time; had it not been for that, he would have gladly let go and embraced death that minute.

Soon, though. Death would take him, and it wouldn't be so bad, he thought. Not now.

10

The Hva Hwa was thumping on my locked and barred bedroom door, shouting to me that some woman had come to see me and was standing out in the middle of a snowstorm and could I tell him what I wanted him to tell her. I crawled—not yet ready for the daylight—out of the little death of sleep, with a headache and the aftertaste of nightmares. I wrapped my robe around me and went to the door; the woman standing on the other side of it wore an exquisite coat and breeches and boots in the Feegash style, but in lovely colors. Until that moment I hadn't seen a single Feegash woman, nor had I seen any proof that the Feegash knew what colors were, and I wondered where the ones who didn't know had been hiding the ones who did.

"Come in," I said, and closed the door behind her. I wasn't dressed to go outside and stand to talk with her, and if I left the door standing open cold air would eventually reach the loft.

She smiled at me. Bright, pretty smile, something I was in no mood to see at that moment. "You have done for some the wonderful jewelry," she said, in an almost impenetrable accent. I had to guess it was a Feegash accent, but the only Feegash I had heard speaking until that moment spoke Tonk as well as I did, and with only the faintest traces of accent. "For myself I much want. To buy, yes? You create for me these wonderful thing?"

Business. Usually I would be delighted, but usually I wasn't hiding two prisoners in my loft and having my door answered by Hva Hwa barbarians. I rubbed my eyes and yawned, and said, "I had a terrible night. Sick friend. Usually I'm already at work by this time." I didn't turn her away; I wanted to be able to give my parents money if they needed it, or other things if they wouldn't accept money, which meant that I wasn't in a position to be turning away business. "Come in, follow me. We'll go into my workroom and I'll show you some samples and you can describe what you would like."

She was looking at me oddly. "You like change different clothes? I wait you."

She had a point. The fire in the stove had died down during the night and the main room was chilly. The workroom, closed off from the rest of the house, would be bitterly cold. If I didn't put on warmer clothes, I would have to wait until the work fire heated the room, and that would take time. In just my robe I would freeze. But the longer I delayed in the main room, the more likely one of the men in the loft just above us would cough. But . . . with a Feegash who would not talk with my neighbors, what could it matter? "I'll be with you in a moment," I told her, and hurried in, and threw on a pair of warm woolen breeches and my warmest sweater and thick stockings and boots, and hurried out to join her. "Come," I said, and heard movement in the loft, and coughed to cover the noise.

I built a work fire while we talked—she seemed oddly uninterested in the details of the jewelry I made, but she kept watching me, almost as if she were a potential buyer sizing up a horse at auction. I turned once to find her staring at my arse, and when I showed her the pieces I kept for display, her gaze kept drifting to my bosom. I began to get the idea that she had sought me out for something other than jewelry—but why in fierce Ethebet's name had she done it on a dreadful dark, sleeting day, and in particular on this day, when I hadn't had nearly enough sleep to graciously fend off an unwelcome approach?

And why me?

She was Feegash, and I only knew one other.

"You aren't here to buy jewelry. Why did Skirmig send you?"

She paled and her eyes met mine. "No. I came for gift for husband."

"I don't think so."

She bit her lip and averted her gaze.

"I want the truth. Count of three, and then you're out in the cold again."

I couldn't begin to follow the flurry of expressions that crawled across her face, but the final one I recognized well enough. Cunning.

She licked her lips and smiled at me and said, "You very beautiful. I . . . no have husband. I want woman. Take off your clothes for me I can see you," she said. "I give you money."

I was so shocked I laughed. "Out. Now."

"I look at you, I promise I no touch."

I took her by the upper arm, hard, and started to march her toward my front door.

And she twisted around to look up at me, and I saw something that shook me. She was scared. She was scared pissless, and a tiny bit of that might have been that she was afraid of me, but most of it wasn't.

I wanted to throw her out, but I hesitated. Something about this was important. It was wrong, it was strange, and I was almost certain it had something to do with Skirmig, and if I kicked this woman out into the snowstorm, I wasn't going to find out why she was so frightened, and if she truly was frightened of Skirmig. And if I had any reason to be afraid.

The View hung at the back of my mind, tempting me. If I went in, I could brush her, with her fear thick as dust on a summer road, and find out the truth. Except I was alone, and I was no fool. One person going into the View alone could be a quick path to a slow death. I could wait until the next time the other rebels and I met at temple. But bad fear often comes from things that won't wait for weeks, or days. Or even hours.

"And if I take my clothes off, then what?"

"Then I look at you. And then I leave."

"You'll . . . look at me."

"I promise. I do nothing more."

I stared at her.

"You no do this for me, will you?" Little beads of sweat shimmered on her upper lip. I could see white all the way around the irises of her eyes. She was smiling, trying hard to make this seem like something she could walk away from. But her eyes said it wasn't.

I'm not shy. Years of public baths quelled that. "You tell me why, I'll take off my clothes."

"I tell you. You beautiful, I want to see you. I in love with you."

"You've never seen me before. And you didn't come out in this weather on this day to look at my naked arse."

"You must . . ."

"The truth."

Her upper lip trembled. Her skin was pale; she was sweating. "Already you know too much. For the truth, I die."

And that, Jostfar help us both, sounded like the truth—at least as much of it as I was going to get. I would like to think of myself that I would not send some innocent woman to her death if I could prevent it, for something so minor. Ethebet seemed determined that I carry responsibility for the lives of moriiad— foreigners—on my shoulders. Having accepted the burden twice in the persons of Gair and Hale, could I then refuse it a third time? I thought not. So I stripped off my sweater and turned in a circle once. The workroom was freezing. I looked her in the eyes and said, "Did you get what you need, or do I need to drop the breeches, too?"

"Enough," she said. She bit her lip, and a tear slid down her cheek. I could see her shaking. "You no tell no one about this, yes?"

I nodded. "I won't tell. If you can ever come to me with the truth about this, I want you to."

She said, "No. I never tell." But she was nodding yes at the same time. Vigorously.

And that made my skin crawl.

Who did she think could hear her while she was hidden away safely in my house, in the middle of one of the worst storms of the season? And hear her . . . but not see her? What sort of magic did she dread?

"Did Skirmig send you?" I asked her.

"No!" She turned and ran from the room.

I hurried after her, but the various obstacles in my workroom got in the way, and I was not fast enough stop her. The door was standing open when I ran into the main room. All I caught was the fluttering of her coat, like some bright bird flapping away through the storm, as she raced down the road.

I don't doubt I could have caught her had I wanted to enough. She was short, with short legs. I'm tall and a good runner, and I'd had years of conditioning in the Forces. I hadn't grown soft and fat yet.

But I could not get over her aura of trapped-wild-animal dread. I would let her go simply because I could not help but think that if I pursued her, I might end up costing her her life. I shut the door against the storm and leaned against the log wall and closed my eyes. What had that been about? It seemed— mad. A frightening madness that made no sense.

The Hva Hwa leaned over the edge of the loft. "She is gone?"

"Yes. How are your friends doing?"

He shrugged. "They are still breathing. They are not prisoners. So they are better. But still they are not good."

I went up the narrow stairs. He was right. They were not good. I was reminded again of Skirmig—specifically, of Skirmig's prediction that I would have to find a way to get rid of their bodies before too long. Clean, shaved barefaced and bareheaded, and covered in clean blankets, they somehow looked even more pitiful than they had the night before. Perhaps it was the fact that dirt no longer hid their pallor or the way their skin, stretched tight, clung to their faces.

"Make them some more broth, wake them up, help them drink it," I told the Hva Hwa. "Do you by any chance have skill as a healer?"

"Not even a little bit."

"Nor do I. While you're making them some broth, then, I'm going to go fetch my healer. He's a good man, and he will not turn away from them because they are not our people."

I ached for every minute of sleep that I had not had. But some things take precedence over sleep. I'd gotten good at ignoring my body's needs when I served in Shields.

I pulled on boots and my heaviest coat, hooded it, and set out for Master Idrann's house. I went on foot; the horses would both have had a hard time in the storm, and I didn't want to risk them.

I jogged along the street, wondering at my life. The only time I could remember feeling as uncertain about my future was when Master Idrann told me the Shielder medic was right, and that I would never have children. My loft was full of foreigners, I'd pogged a foreigner and probably would again, I was involved in a secret cabal that had met illegally once and would again against the strictest of orders from the Beyls but in the best interests of the taak. The part of my life that I could acknowledge had no importance to anyone; I loved creating jewelry, but once upon a time I had done things that saved lives and protected my home and my people. I had become . . . irrelevant.

I went around to the back of Master Idrann's little house and tapped on the window. After a moment he opened the door and hurried me inside.

Idrann left his nomadic clan on the steppes in Tandinapalis on the day he became a man, found passage to Hyre somehow, and claimed family within Beyltaak; he had chosen a healer's path, but followed Ethebet and wore a warrior's braid. His face and hands bore the tattoos of that Tandinapalis clan, and even though his hair was starting to gray at the temples, he had a warrior's bearing.

I trusted him.

"More bites I must protect from infection?" He smiled when he asked, but I winced anyway.

"Worse."

"Mmm. Worse. Shall I get my needles and threads?"

"Bring your whole bag. I have something at my house that I need your help with—but I'm invoking Healer's Secret."

He closed his eyes. "Ethebet, tell me she doesn't have the one who bites there."

Ethebet wasn't telling, but I said, "No."

Idrann is a good man. He tugged on coat and boots and gloves, pulled up his hood, grabbed his healer's pack, and followed me into a storm that had, if anything, gotten worse. Street cleaners were out shoveling and swearing, keeping paths open, but they were fighting a losing battle. In places the drifts were to my waist, and in others the falling temperature was hardening slush into ice, and layering snow on top of that.

Beyltaak lies far, far south of the equator. We get a long line of bad storms every winter, and the tail of the last bumps the nose of the next more often than not. But even for Beyltaak, this was ugly, ugly weather. Snow and ice drove into our faces like needles, and the wind devoured all attempts at normal conversation in its own banshee wail.

Idrann, trudging along beside me, leaning hard into the wind with his head down to keep his face from getting cut by tiny ice shards, shouted, "You couldn't have brought your problem to me, eh?"

"I have two problems. And no," I shouted back.

"Two. Damnall."

We didn't say anything after that. It was too much work, and we had to save our breath for fighting our way up the hill to my house against snow and ice and wind.

We fell in through the door when the wind let go of us, and Master Idrann kicked the door shut behind him. "It's a hell of a day, Talyn, and if this was minor I'd have your hide—but it's you came to see me and not some others I could mention. So I've no doubt you have a real need for me. Where's your problem?"

"Loft," I said, and nodded toward the stairs. "Leave your coat and boots and gloves, and I'll hang them by the stove for you so they dry out and warm up."

He shrugged out of his sodden coat and handed it to me. He favored the traditionally tanned nomad-style fur coat instead of the oilcloth with down-filled liner that those of us in the Forces got used to. Which meant the house would stink of wet animal and tanning piss as the damned thing warmed up. But I owed him for coming out in such dreadful weather, and I wouldn't leave his coat wet—that is a breach of etiquette not even a Tonk so far fallen from grace as I could consider.

He slung his pack over his shoulder and climbed up the steep stairs. I heard the mutter of his voice talking in low tones to Snow Grell, and the sounds of him moving around up there, and then an inarticulate exclamation.

He swung over the side of the loft and dropped to the floor beside me an instant later, his face twisted with rage. "What happened up there?"

"They were prisoners of war," I said. "I just found them, with the help of the Hva Hwa up there, and . . . a friend . . . of mine rescued them from the place where they'd been kept. He brought them here. Snow Grell and I cleaned them up and started feeding them."

"Godforsaken Eastil whoremongering treacherous bastards," he snarled.

I turned to stare at him, shocked. "What!?"

"The monsters who did that to them—they ought to be skinned alive and then boiled in a pot."

"Oh." I reran my explanation to Idrann and realized that I had managed to leave out a couple of important points. "Those are *Eastil* prisoners of war up there," I told him. "And the men that did that to them were Tonks."

Idrann stared at me. "No. No Tonk would do such things to prisoners of war."

"And yet they did."

"Who?"

"I don't know. Some of the guards in the prison's dungeon."

"Here? Right here in Beyltaak? The people who did this could be people I treat?"

"Yes."

He looked sick. "How was this allowed to happen? And how did you find them?"

"I don't know how it happened, Master Idrann. And if I tell you how I found them, you'll be involved. And I don't think you want to be involved."

His voice dropped and his eyes narrowed and he said, "Please tell me that not everyone is taking this peace the Feegash have shoved down our throats lying down. Please tell me someone is working for *our* people."

"If I tell you that," I said, "you're still going to be involved."

"Involve me. By Ethebet and Jostfar and all that is sacred, *please* involve me."

I nodded. "The remaining Shields in the taak have gathered secretly. We'll gather again. We are looking for ways to protect the taak against invasion from the Eastils; when searching for those two up there and a comrade of theirs who died in the dungeon, I found out that something is wrong."

"What's wrong?"

"I don't know. I cannot figure it out; it's an oddness in the View, a way that people are acting with each other that is unlike anything I've ever seen."

Idrann said, "Come to me to request any help that I can offer. You shall have it."

"My thanks." I nodded to the loft above our heads. "About them?"

"I'll treat them. They've traveled far toward death—I cannot promise you I can turn them back, either of them. But I am not without skill, and while life remains, so does hope. Both of them are young enough that they might have the reserves and the will to survive. I would think the fact that both are still alive right now proves they do."

"No one can know that they're here, or that you are treating them," I told him. "One of the conditions of their rescue is that their presence in Beyltaak remains secret. The person who rescued them stands to lose much if this secret gets out."

"Then my walking to and from your house every day for the next three or four months to treat them will cause problems?"

"Three or four months!"

"They might heal up faster than that. But it could also take longer. They both have filled lungs, infections, wasting of the muscles that is going to have to be treated daily with stretching and weights if they are to regain their strength. They have broken bones that, because of their poor condition, have not healed. They have open sores and other wounds. That they live at all is testament only to the strength of their wills, for their bodies have gone far past the point where any reasonable man would have let go of life in favor of whatever peace lies beyond."

I closed my eyes and clenched my teeth. Three or four months of daily visits from Master Idrann. Three or four months of hiding them in the loft and dreading anything that might give their presence away to my neighbors. Three or four months of three men occupying my home, eating my food . . . preventing me from seeing Skirmig in privacy.

That should not be an issue, I reminded myself.

But it was.

"I should probably give over my patients to Master Detta for a while and simply be on hand all the time to get them through the worst of this," he said. "I have a cot, and you have enough space in your loft for one more."

"And you think that you'll not be missed in three or four months? Or question your absence?"

"In these days? With every third man, woman, and child gone to far-off places? I think they'll believe the lie I tell Detta."

I had space in my loft for half a dozen men if they were friendly. That didn't mean I wanted to use that space. But Idrann's suggestion would at least solve the problem of how to move him from his home to mine every day without causing questions. I could hide *him*, too.

Oh, fortunate me.

"I have the space," I said.

I could have left the Eastils to die, I reminded myself. I was the one who insisted that they be saved. And when I looked at it that way, when I considered the value of the lives of two honorable men against my own inconvenience, how much could inconvenience be permitted to matter?

All day long I cleaned and carried. All day long, while outside the storm raged, I kept the fire in the oven burning and prepared broths and mixed poultices to Idrann's instructions. I listened to Idrann's patients screaming in pain as he did things to heal them—lancing boils and applying the hot poultices that I had prepared and setting broken bones so that they might heal.

Healing is no gentle art. It draws as much from the arts of the torturer as from those of the saint. I hurt for Gair and Hale. And hearing them, my body remembered its own encounter with the healer's touch, and tightened in sympathy with every one of the Eastils' cries.

I needed to get out of the house. Out of *my* house. I tried to imagine the next few months, which would be filled with terrible smells and awful sounds; with brave men reduced to tears, whether shed or unshed, from pain they would have to endure if they hoped ever to live as free men again. I already felt in my gut the gnawings of dread that in spite of everything, I would wake some morning to find one of them dead. I did not want to care what happened to them; they were my enemies, and in a different time, if they had been ordered to kill me, they would have. I would have killed them, too, and neither respect nor regret would have entered into it.

But these were not those times, and I did care, Five Saints help me. I hurt for them even though I would have done anything not to. I wanted them to survive, and have the chance to go home again to their wives or their lovers.

But I did not want to have to share their pain.

And on the tenth day of listening to them screaming as Master Idrann forced their arms and legs and wrists and ankles and fingers and toes to bend so that their joints would not lock stiff, and listening to them sob as Master Idrann pulled packing out of their wounds and swabbed them clean and forced new packing back in, opportunity and temptation and the promise of damnation opened my door and walked in.

I'd done a good job of not thinking too much about Skirmig. I knew I was going to have to contact him again, but nearly two weeks without his presence had had a calming effect on me. I could think about him clearly. I could see clearly what I had to do where he was concerned.

The neighbors all went out after the last of the storm passed and cleared the section of street in front of their own house or business, and pitched in with each other to dig out those sections that fronted the homes of the old and the sick or weak. I'd spent a blissful two days out in the cold and the silence, chipping away at ice and snow with a sharp-nosed shovel, wishing that I could revert to childhood and go running home to live with my parents, and knowing that I could not. When I ran out of street that needed cleaning, I wanted to weep.

And at that moment Skirmig arrived on my doorstep with his coachmen and his servants and his fine carriage, and stepped into the house to the smells of poultice and sickness and the sounds of the torture chamber. He said, "They have a healer here to take care of them now, have they not?"

"Yes."

"Then come for a ride with me. I have a proposition for you."

He did not touch me. Did not smile at me. He simply stared up at the loft with narrowed eyes and thinned lips and fists balled tight, and when I said, "Give me a moment to get my coat," he stood that way, still staring, until I rejoined him, and we stepped outside.

When we were seated in the carriage and the horses started down the street, he said, "I don't know how you stand that."

"Not well," I admitted. "It's giving me new and different nightmares to replace the old familiar ones. But I have to be there for them, to bring food in and run errands for Master Idrann, who is staying with them until they are better, and who is hiding so he does not give them . . . and you . . . away by being seen going to and from the house several times each day."

He looked into my eyes and took both my hands in his, and said, "I have servants who can do what you are doing, Talyn. Who can run and fetch, bring things to your healer, make sure no one goes up to the windows and peers inside. You do not need to be there, in that hell. Are you having time to work on your jewelry? Your commissions? Are you having the time to get out so that you might meet with new patrons for your art?"

"No."

"No. You are giving up your life and your art to save the lives of two of your enemies, and while this makes me think with all my heart that you are an angel, still I must protest that you are being seriously misused."

We stopped in front of his house. "Come with me, please," he said, and led me into his home, keeping a careful distance from me all the while.

I followed him through the building—it was a good house, though modest by the standards of the street or when compared to the houses bought or rented by the rest of the Feegash diplomats in Beyltaak. I did not know if it was smaller and less glorious because he was the junior diplomat, or because he was not as rich as the other diplomats, or if he had simpler tastes. But it was by no means a hovel. It had floors of black twistwood from the great hardwood forests in southern Velobrina, floors rubbed and oiled but not polished, which were warm and worn by the passage of hundreds of years of feet. They gleamed but did not shine. The house's walls were fine plaster, painted in the style of an earlier age with scenes of Tonk nomads and with the beautiful geometrics of Tonk border work running along the baseboards and the ceilings. The old-style Tonk floor plan featured a central room with a central stove, offshoot rooms to the sides, and a loft overhead; this traditional building style comes from the shadda, and though it is not so common in the newer sections of the taak, it is the main home style in the fine old neighborhoods.

The front door led into a little entryway that kept the cold from getting into the main room, and the main room, round like mine but four times as large, had doors leading off in six directions. Skirmig's was a beetle-house, then—so called for its six "legs"—the rooms or series of rooms that shoot out from the main room. Mine is a rabbit-house, because it only has four legs and they're short. My parents also have a four-legged house, but theirs has long legs; it's a fox-house. There are a few four-legged houses on the Heights that have whole corridors with rooms on either side of each leg. Those are horse-houses, and the people who live in them are supposed to be especially lucky. Beetle-houses with their six legs, and spider-houses, which have eight, confer different kinds of luck. At least they do if you listen to the old people. Those of us who are younger know the traditions, but we usually don't put much faith in them. Some traditions, after all, are simply silly.

Skirmig's house was one of the long-legged beetle variety, furnished with foreigner chairs and tables that didn't fit in the traditional Tonk rooms. The dining table was small and had all separate chairs, not benches. The rugs on the floor were in muted browns and grays and beiges, and though the patterns were very pretty, they seemed drab and lifeless to me. The tapestry hooks on the walls were empty—which would help to explain why the house felt drafty. The built-in bookshelves were nearly empty, and the only things they did hold were little silver statuettes and miniature paintings. No books. Not a book anywhere.

I followed Skirmig down one of the legs and into a room that I realized, after an instant, was a workroom. If the rest of the house seemed drab and alien to me, the workroom was a tiny slice of heaven. Light poured through huge windows, and worktables circled the work fire in the most thoughtful design I'd ever seen. The tools were good, and there were a lot of them. And all of them were jeweler's tools. I owned some of the same equipment I saw, but not most of it, and none of mine was so finely made. Skirmig had spent a fortune putting this room together.

I wanted it.

"Here's my proposition," he said. "I would like for you to move into this house, where you can work in peace, and let me become your main patron; I'll make sure that you have enough supplies for anything you should care to design as independent commissions, and I'll see that you have some time to work on them when you aren't working on the pieces that I wish to commission from you. And I have an interesting idea that I would like to see you pursue."

He was not touching me. I cannot say why this seemed so obvious, but it was the main point that I was concentrating on while I was trying to listen to him offer me work.

He said, "I will, as your patron, provide you with a place to live convenient to the studio here. I will take care, as well, to make sure that you don't have to worry about other obligations. I will have my servants watch your house and make sure that your healer has all the supplies he needs, and that all four men there have good food and whatever else *they* need. Two of my servants will move into the house when you move out so that there is a plausible excuse for activity there, which will hide the Eastils until they can be sent back to the Eastil Republic."

He was looking into my eyes. He wasn't touching me. And his words were wind in my ears, barely loud enough to get my attention over the roar of my thoughts.

For days, apart from Skirmig, I had been at peace with myself, quiet inside. I had managed to convince myself that I did not want him, did not need him, would live quite happily without him—that I was able to be a respectable Tonk woman and that when we were together again I would do what I had to do to help my people but that I would not allow myself to involve my heart.

But standing there with him, in his presence again for the half of an hour, or perhaps even less, I wanted . . . Jostfar forgive me for what I wanted. And what I wanted, I desired with a burning, bone-biting, trembling desire that left me breathing hard and afraid to move.

"What about us?" I asked, and the words were thick in my throat and my voice was a rasp.

He never took his eyes from mine, but he was silent for a long time. "That is up to you. I understand the problems that my love of you causes for you, and may continue to cause for you with your family and your . . . friends." His voice cracked, and he swallowed hard, and took a deep breath, and continued. "So if you decide that you wish to pretend that . . . other thing . . . never happened, I will respect your wishes and I will not so much as touch you. I will be your patron and I will respect your work and further your career as best I can in exchange for your best work, and that will be the whole of it."

I considered that. Considered the possibility of living in the same house with him and never touching him and pretending that we had never been naked and wild with each other. I would be able to look myself in the mirror if I chose that path. I would not be betraying my people or my beliefs; I would still be close enough to Skirmig to do what I had to do for my father and our conspiracy. I would have everything I needed.

And nothing I wanted. Looking into his eyes, I knew that if I stayed, I would be his lover. There was no other way for me. I had to have him. He was like salban smoke to me—an addiction, a compulsion—and I could not be so close to him, close enough to feel the warmth of his skin through his clothes, close enough to smell the faint whisper of soap in the scent of him, and not want him inside me, on top of me, beneath me, behind me.

I touched him then, a hand to his chest, palm flat against his shirt, and I know I meant to say something but on the graves of the Saints I swear that whatever words were in me fled me in that instant and the air rushed out of my lungs in a sob. I could feel him trembling beneath my hand, but he did not move, and I began unlacing his overtunic. And still he did not move, but the hunger in his eyes was raw, and fierce, and deep as an ocean.

Slowly. I made myself move slowly, did not rip did not tear did not toss, when I wanted only to throw him to the floor and mount him and ride him until we were both out of our minds.

I slid the overtunic off his shoulders, and began on the dozens of tiny buttons that closed the front of his undertunic.

"If you undo them one at a time, Talyn, I swear I'll die," he said. Still he had not touched me.

"I'm trying to take my time," I said. "Trying to prove to myself that every time with us will not be like that first time. I . . . need the control."

He nodded carefully, staring into my eyes, and whispered, "Yes. Perhaps you do," and I undid the third of what looked at that moment to be a hundred buttons, and I remember thinking, Maybe if I just rip the tunic open slowly, that will be good enough.

I heard the buttons hitting the floor like a hailstorm, but far away. Far away. I was staring into Skirmig's eyes and my mouth was moving closer and closer to his mouth, and the instant our lips touched, those uncountable watching eyes opened up inside of me again, and that ocean swell of hunger, like a thousand starving men presented with a feast, and I lost control.

But Skirmig didn't, and for the first time, if from very far away, I realized that he was honestly stronger than me, not just physically but in other ways.

"No," he whispered in my ear as I started to bite him. His lips brushed against my neck, gently, gently. "Hold it in. Want it, but don't give in to it."

I wanted. Jostfar forgive me, I wanted everything.

He lowered me to the floor and began to undress me. He moved as slowly as I had, until I wanted to scream, and the watching eyes inside of me cried out for wildness, for biting and clawing and thrusting and thrashing and screaming, for hot sweat and teeth on the nape of my neck.

He kissed me all the while, his tongue moving against mine, his lips pressing hard, sliding firmly. And when I lay naked beneath him, he held himself over me, hard and ready, and I arched up to meet him.

And he broke away from our kiss and, laughing, leaned down and licked along one breast and mouthed the nipple, sucking it slowly and deeply.

"Don't tease me," I groaned.

In answer, he pinned my wrists to the floor with his hands and lowered himself against me. I could feel his cock sliding between my legs, but each time I tried to sheathe him, he lifted away from me.

"Patience," he whispered. "Control will be its own reward."

I gritted my teeth. "I do not want to be patient anymore."

And he laughed.

I'm a sturdy woman, and I have been riding since before I walked. I suspect my thighs could snap a man in half; they were certainly strong enough to get me what I wanted. I wrapped my legs around his back, locked my ankles together, and tightened my thighs, pulling him inexorably into me.

Skirmig's eyes went wide and his mouth stretched into an animal grin, and he said, "You're a bad girl."

"Not as bad as I intend to be."

He laughed. And held himself in complete stillness within me, and stared into my eyes.

I tightened myself around him. Relaxed. Tightened again, and he shook his head. "Be still. Hold me tightly, but be still."

It should have been nothing. It should have been dull, or simply ridiculous, this motionlessness. But it was not. I stilled, too, and we held ourselves like bow drawn and arrow aimed, with the release that would come quivering between us like a promise. His smallest movements from breathing, from little shifts of his weight to keep his balance, and from the pulse of his length inside me, resonated through my body; through his exquisite stillness, holding himself poised so, he brought me once, and again, and yet again to shuddering lip-biting silent release, where my back arched and my legs locked and my fingers dug into the floor and it was everything I could do to keep from screaming aloud.

Still he did not move, and I lost myself again, quicker. And then again. And again.

Those watching eyes within me wanted more, but only when I lay trembling and weak, when the merest brush of Skirmig's breath on my skin pushed me over the edge again, did he begin to move inside of me. He stayed right with me, right there, eyes locked with mine, and withdrew himself from me in one achingly slow, silken glide, all the way out of me. And then, so slowly, even more slowly, back in. Pushing farther. Deeper.

That simplest movement undid me. My eyes shut, my head whipped back and forth, and I screamed and bucked against him, unable to maintain my own stillness any longer. My breath sobbed as if I had run from Beyltaak to Savistaak, and I heard myself begging him something that could have been either "more" or "no more"—not even I could have said for sure. I was mindless want, screaming need.

He thrust again.

I thrashed, I growled. I screamed and whimpered and writhed, and he brought me, over and over and again until I ached in every muscle and my skin felt flayed from my flesh and then—only then—when I was sure I could take no more, when I was convinced that if he did not stop I would die of too much sensation, did he begin driving into me, hard, pounding down against me, and the mad watching hunger within me took me and I rose up to meet him one last time, and we came together, with him crying out my name and me so far beyond words that I only barely comprehended what he said.

And when, spent, he lay still within me and atop me, he whispered in my ear, "Control."

Tears streamed from my eyes. I trembled and shuddered at the slight drafts that brushed against my skin. When he pulled out of me I cried out, and he laughed softly, and rolled to one side on the floor, and closed his eyes, and fell asleep.

I crawled across the floor and found my clothes and pulled on undertunic and breeches—just enough to keep off the chill. And then I curled against him and looked at his lovely naked body, and at the easy way he breathed in sleep. I had never felt so raw, so helpless, so utterly under someone else's control, and the sensation had not been entirely pleasant, though I could honestly say I had never had such complete and mind-shattering sex before in my life. I thought perhaps something might be said for the pleasures of pogging on a mattress, with a good cold shower after. At least that didn't leave you weeping and stupid on a wood floor, too weak to stand and too sore to want to.

The light crawled across the floor from the tall windows, and as I was finally falling asleep, too, it slid across him.

And I saw for the first time a cobwebbing of delicate, silvered scars that traced across his chest, belly, and thighs. The hair of his body hid them, but as I looked closer, I could see that they formed patterns. Pictures. I sat up and studied them closer. Something about them made me uneasy. There was some artistry to them, but it was crude and piecemeal; the images together formed neither a story nor a theme. I found knives and naked women, animals (wolves and eagles mostly), swords and chains, fanciful monsters with scales and wings and huge eyes and long teeth. Geometric shapes, triangles inside of squares inside of circles. Spirals and waves of various sorts that started nowhere in particular, and ended nowhere in particular.

Had the light in the room been less bright, I would not have seen these. I certainly hadn't seen them in the barn. They were old and had faded.

Perhaps it was my scrutiny that woke him, or maybe the floor had become too uncomfortable or the sun through the window too warm. His eyes opened, and he saw me looking down at him and he smiled. "You're amazing."

"I can't walk," I said. "I wouldn't even care to try. I never thought I would say these words, but you were too much for me."

He laughed, and I traced one of the patterns on his chest. "What are these?"

He looked down at himself, lay back again, and shrugged. "I did those. When I was younger."

"Some sort of ritual?" I asked. Some of the Tonk clans did tattooing to mark the coming of age, especially among those who still rode with the herds.

He lay there looking at me, his eyes heavy-lidded and sated. "No. It just . . . felt good," he said. "It was the first time I'd found out how to reach the point where pain becomes pleasure. It was . . ." He shrugged and sat up and started looking for his clothes. He located his pants, and pulled them on. "It was childish. There are other, better ways to do that."

"Find pleasure?"

"Pain." He turned to me. Shrugged again. "Pleasure, too, of course. But you felt it between the two of us—I know you did. Both times. We reached the point both times where pleasure becomes pain, and went past that, through that, to the point where it hurts so much it stops hurting and becomes pleasure again. Nothing else so satisfies as that moment when pain breaks and pleasure takes wing again."

I wasn't sure that I agreed. In fact, I was almost certain that I didn't. And yet, Skirmig smiled at me and pulled me to my feet and kissed me, and bit my lower lip, and my bottomless hunger for him stirred to life within me again, that starving, insatiable thing that coiled within me demanding more and ever more, and I knew that whether my mind would follow me willingly or not, my body was only an instant away from yanking his pants down and shoving him to the floor and riding him until he begged mercy. Or trying, if my knees would hold.

He was the one who broke off the kiss, and he grinned at me and said, "If I did not have something I wanted to show you, I would pursue that. I see it in your eyes; you protest, but you would take me again in an instant."

He saw me too clearly right then.

He wrapped an arm around my waist and led me from the beautiful studio he had created, down the corridor to the heart of the house, and then down another of the legs to a room empty of all devices, the walls white, the floor—of blackest nightwood—polished to a liquid shine.

"This is *my* workroom. I am going to teach you Silent Magic," he said.

"Silent Magic?"

"It is the magic of the Feegash. None but a few select men of my people have ever learned it. It is forbidden to outlanders, and forbidden to women as well. This room is the center of my practice."

I stopped.

Among the Tonk, there are secrets that women hold, and men's secrets as well. Traditions. Places where we give each other the necessary space to be who and what we are without the tempering influences of each other.

And there are clan rituals which never go outside of the clan.

And there are Tonk rituals. In truth, most of being Tonk is one vast series of rituals only the Tonk know. Or may know. And I would no more offer to teach Skirmig a woman's ritual that I would a clan ritual, or a Tonk ritual.

And yet, he was bringing me to a place where he performed a secret magic of Feegash men, and offering to teach me— neither Feegash, nor male—this magic.

Were he of our people and behaved so, we would name him oathbreaker and cast him out, then execute him as a man without a name or a people. The honor of the Tonk and the wholeness of the Tonk way of life would demand it.

Had his people so little regard for honor and tradition, for their place in the world, that they would not care about the betrayal of ancient secrets and traditions to someone not of their kind? Or was Skirmig the only one without honor?

And what did he hope to gain by his treachery? How might this vast betrayal benefit him? Did he hope to impress me with his skill? Or in some strange fashion did he think to win my trust by sharing such things with me—as if a betrayal of trust could ever create trust.

Or did he hope to use me in some way? To teach me something forbidden so that he could claim I owed him something in return? That seemed to me the most likely outcome. There was some Tonk secret I knew that he wanted to learn, and he thought by doing this he could maneuver me into telling him what he wanted.

Which would not happen.

But I'd be happy to learn anything he wanted to teach me. By doing so, I could earn my father's trust in me, and ease my troubled conscience where Skirmig was concerned.

He pulled me into the room and assumed a cross-legged pose on the floor, and gestured that I should do the same.

We sat in the very center of the room, and suddenly he had paints in his hands, and a brush, though I did not see where he got them. He painted a circle on the floor between us using blue paint. I had a foolish urge to ask him how he made the circle so round without a compass, and to ask, too, if that roundness was important. I cannot draw a straight line with a builder's edge. But I held my tongue and watched.

Inside the circle, in red paint, he painted a square standing on its points.

In pale yellow, he painted a triangle that began in the left corner of the square, extended all the way through the square at its second point to the edge of the blue circle, and then stopped within the square on its third point. He did an identical triangle from the right point of the square, this one in brighter yellow. The final design looked lopsided to me, and I wanted to fix it— to extend the triangles through the squares to the circles on their small sides.

"This is the Hagedwar," he said. "It means 'Eye of the World' in Feegashi. It is the magical path of the mind through the physical plane to magic. It is the greatest and most powerful secret of the Feegash people."

"Why are you sharing it now?" I asked.

"Because I love you," he said simply.

Yes. Well. A man who broke his oaths and called it love. This I would remember—*this* was the measure of this man.

I was buying trouble with him, and I knew it. He said he loved me. He had a disturbing fascination with pain. Every time he touched me I felt as if he laid me bare in front of a screaming horde of watchers. And when we were done, I felt dirty and ill-used, as I never had with anyone else.

And yet I still wanted him. At that moment, I would have had him on me without question, as if I were some mindless rutting beast. And from my mouth came words I swear I did not put there; words I knew I could not mean.

"I love you, too," I told him.

His smile was so sweet my heart doubled its pace, in spite of my reservations, my doubts, my distrust and distaste.

He said, "Then let me teach you this, and see if you can learn the secrets that have eluded my people since we first discovered the Hagedwar. And if you can find them, you can teach them to me."

"If it is in my power to do so, I will," I said. I did not add that anything I found out beyond what he taught me would also have to be knowledge not proscribed to the moriiad before I would pass it on.

Skirmig traced his finger just above the diagram. "So. I will teach, you will learn. And then we will share what you discover. Here is the Hagedwar. The circle is the world and everything beyond the world in the physical realm, the realm of thought, and the realm of magic—it represents all that we can see and touch, all that we can know, all that moves through us unseen. The circle is Banjgran—the Infinite Eye of God. It is the realm of potential magic, and it includes everything, because everything can be reached by magic, though the Feegash philosophers have not yet cleared all the tograms."

"Tograms?"

"Each segment where the planes cross is a togram, and each has its own power and its own voice. Their powers are hemtu, their voices are shedvu."

Oh, Jostfar, how I hated the tedium of new terms and wordy definitions. And he had a lot of them. The red square was Hunatrumit—Flesh and Thought of Man; the light yellow left-pointing triangle was Sugritnaj—the Will of Soul; and the dark yellow right-pointing triangle, Grandolfitnaj—the Will of God. Tograms, those were the little triangles and circle-slices and polygons formed between each of the lines of the shape. Each of those damned things had a name, too, and he wanted me to learn them all. Because they all stood for different ways that the world, man, the soul, and God interacted. They were, he said, all different keys that opened different doors. It was a lot of talk. A lot of theory, and theory, frankly, puts me to sleep.

I'm a doer. I like to be out riding, or cleaning stalls, or practicing blade work with a friend. I am happy digging up dirt in my yard to put in new plants. I can sit still going into the View, but that's only because the part of me that is aware of what is going on is still doing things. Sitting on the floor listening to Skirmig go on and on and on about how this little bit of that diagram affected this part of magic, and how you could do these things with that part, and how no one could even figure out how to get into that third part—no. I might as well have been listening to him speaking to me in his native language.

I stifled a yawn for the third or fourth time, and fought to get what he was telling me, but finally I could not abide all the words any longer.

"Show me," I said.

He stopped what he was saying, and looked at me like this was some concept he had never heard of before. "You have to have the framework first. Once you have the theory—"

I shook my head. "If I can see you do it, I'll be able to copy what you're doing, and then I'll get the theory. I can see how things fit together by watching you do them and by doing them myself. I've never been one to look at a diagram and hear a lecture and make use of that."

"But this can be dangerous if done wrong."

I nodded. "The View is dangerous, too. But our instructors started taking us in from the first, going in with us, a group of them with one of us, and then a group of them with a couple of us, until at last we could go in with just each other. Show me. I'll risk the danger."

So he told me how he built the Wall of Will—sitting, breathing, focusing, a couple of tricks he did of holding an image in his mind and then changing it. I did as he said, and he watched me, and when he thought I might have created a decent Wall of Will around myself, he started describing how, holding our Wall of Will in place, we were going to aim straight for the middle portion of the diagram, and he must have seen the expression on my face go mulish, because he dropped his reference to the diagram, and instead, step by step, he just led me into a light

trance that put us both on the border of the View, the place Tonk
Magics call the Edge. I kept my silence, though I felt guilty
about it. He was standing on the edge of my magic, and though
I had said I would help him find out what I could about his
magic, I had made no such promise about mine. Some part of
me felt as if I was betraying him for not telling him I knew
where we were, but I simply could not tell him. My love for my
people, and the oaths I had taken to serve them above all else
save Jostfar, held me.

In this light trance, I could still hear Skirmig's voice in the
physical world. I could still speak to him. In the Edge, I could
see his middle form—the one between the body we wear in the
physical world and the ever-changing bit of light we are in the
world that is purely spirit. At the Edge, we are beings of light,
though we retain our human forms and human genders. We are
beautiful creatures in the Edge, and somehow heartbreaking—
for in the Edge we ever retain the form and shape of youth.

From where we stood, with Skirmig close to me and the odd
eternal lightlessness that defines the Edge spun around us both,
I could easily have pushed that little bit further and stepped
straight into the View. But that was a madness I did not choose
to embrace.

"We never go any deeper than this," he said. I'd thought him
beautiful in the flesh. As a creature of light, though, he was
breathtaking. "Beyond this point, light fades into darkness very
quickly, and the realm that lies before you becomes all-
devouring and deadly. There is a way in, but no way out, for the
darkness spread before you is the very mind of God, and not
even the greatest Feegash masters dare tread there. None who
have ever entered live to tell what they found there, and none
now enter."

The darkness he referred to was the View. What he saw as
darkness and terrifying void, I saw as light warmer and brighter
than the sun, glittering with rainbow hues, alive with the very
stuff of life itself.

In that instant, I learned three things, and had Skirmig been
my enemy, they would have been useful things. First, he had no
comprehension of how Shielders and Senders did what we did;
second, I had magic available to me that was stronger than anything he might throw against me; and third, he and his people

had discovered ways to manipulate the weak energies that lay on the Edge that lies between the physical world and the greater world of the View . . . and the Edge was a realm the Tonk had never even bothered to explore. Enough of us were born with something inside us that let us go all the way into the View that we didn't need half measures. Or at least we'd never thought we did.

But now what we needed most was half measures, since the Shielders and the Senders were scattered across the face of the world. Whatever Skirmig might be able to do with magic, he didn't need to bring nine of his best friends along to accomplish. The two of us were not risking death where we stood.

The Eastils would come against us, I felt sure. Probably at the first of spring, when the harbors thawed and the passes cleared. For the survival—and even the triumph—of my people, I needed to know what Skirmig knew. Had he been my enemy, I would have rejoiced in my advantage.

But Skirmig was not my enemy. Not trustworthy. I had to remember that. But not my enemy.

So I looked about me and said, "Now what do we do?"

Skirmig raised a finger and drew against the drear lightlessness of the Edge the same diagram he had drawn on the floor, only this time he drew it in glowing light and three dimensions and as big as the two of us with some extra space thrown in. The figure glowed in the same colors, but now it was gemlike, as if spun of light cast through rubies and sapphires and amber. The triangles became triangles in all directions; the square became a cube, the circle a sphere. I could see in three dimensions the way the shapes connected, the places where flat lines had become solid bars and bands through which I could feel energy moving. In different directions, different speeds, different patterns. I could *feel* the power in this thing, and taste the different flavors in it. It drew some of the fire of the View into it, and filtered it. As a whole it did not have the power of the View, but it did not have its danger, either.

"You must learn to spin the Hagedwar before you can use the magic of this place."

"Why this pattern?" I asked. "Why these colors, these shapes, this form? Would other shapes and colors and forms do the same thing? Or different things? Or nothing?"

"The Hagedwar is the magic of the Feegash. I do not know where it was born, or how it grew to be what it is—there are stories, but the truth of them is lost in the depths of time. But I do know that only this form will work for the magic I can teach you, and what I have learned of this magic has cost the lives of hundreds of great scholars and philosophers over thousands of years, and even now there are parts of the Hagedwar we cannot decipher and cannot use. Other forms are possible, but they are wild, unexplored, and because they are unexplored, deadly. From time to time one of our young scholars will open a new form to see what will happen with it, and he will bring back an interesting result or two. And then, without fail, it will devour him, and he will serve as the cautionary tale for his generation."

So the form before me was simply one template out of an unknown number of possibilities. I said, "Cast the form again."

"I'm not finished showing you this yet."

"But I think I saw how you cast it, and I want to see you do it again to be sure."

"You . . . *saw* . . . how I did it? *Saw?!* How could you see this?"

"I watched the energy move from you into the patterns you willed. Was I not supposed to do this?"

He sat silent for a very long time, and I could feel a sudden unnerving wariness about him. In spite of my attempt to be circumspect, I'd revealed something of my abilities that I should, perhaps, have kept secret; I had demonstrated a greater facility with his people's hereditary magic than he could hold comfortably alongside whatever plans he had.

The silence he wore around himself, that amazing and beautiful calm that had first drawn me to him, might cover secrets, I realized. Perhaps they were secrets he feared I would strip from him in spite of the layers he kept tight wrapped around himself. And if he held his people's secrets in low regard, he might yet value his own.

I thought of the pictures he had cut into his own skin, and of his confessed desire for pain, and I thought I might guess the sort of things that could shame him, and the sort of things he might wish to hide.

I would not spy on him, I promised myself. Even if I discovered that I could. He deserved his privacy as much as I deserved mine.

"Seeing the movement of magic is part of the process . . . eventually," he said at last. "I simply had not expected you to see so quickly. If you truly have, of course. *That* we will have to discover by trial." He erased the Hagedwar with a single swift thought, and said, "Watch. And when I have finished, you will repeat what I do."

He spun out the shapes before me, and the blue sphere came first. The red cube second. The right-facing four-faced triangle, which the Tonks call the josthaddaar—God's Looking Glass— was next, and finally the left josthaddaar, which Skirmig twisted so that the points of each triangle poked through the face of the other triangle. "The tetrahedrons can never line up along any face," Skirmig said, "or the doors into the magics will lead into the wrong places."

Tetrahedrons had to be josthaddaar. Fine. I could work with his terms. And having everything lined up correctly mattered. I had over the years grown capable of following rules, though rule following had not been a part of my nature as a child.

When Skirmig built his Hagedwar the second time, and I could see where the points touched and how they worked, I had to consider whether or not I should successfully build a copy in front of him. His response to the possibility that I might be able to see the magic that he had learned with great difficulty made me think he might feel better if I could not work with it—at least not at first. But I did not want to work actively to deceive him; that was a very different thing from withholding information that was not mine to give. I decided to cast the Hagedwar as best I could.

I spun out the energy as I would have to form a Shield, and got only a tiny glow, a little worm trickle of blue that fed into a flickering, sputtering sphere that pulsed and faded for just an instant, then popped out.

I felt a fool for thinking I would easily duplicate what he had done; I had been so certain that my years of experience using the energies of the universe would allow me to replicate what I saw Skirmig do. I could see exactly how he had done it, after all, and I had worked with the vast raw energies of the universe for years, with the very forces of life and death.

But Skirmig was ecstatic.

"Oh, my God, my God, my GOD!" he crowed. "That's brilliant, my love! Brilliant! You're wonderful! I cannot tell you how long I labored to get even the merest flickering of light. You had shape and color—when you develop strength, you'll have the whole thing." So he was not hurt that I had accomplished something already. I warmed to his happiness; his effusive, unalloyed joy was infectious. I could feel his pride in my accomplishment, and it was a broad and generous thing. He was happy with me, and happy for me.

I felt something very close to love for him at that moment. A little flickering thing.

He said when I developed strength, I'd have the whole thing.

The first thing we learned as Shielders, though, was not brute force, but control. We learned to channel everything we did through the magical equivalent of narrow pipes, so that we did not destroy ourselves with the energies we handled. We learned a mind-set that concentrated on the highest results for the least possible costs.

But at the edge of the View, power had already been channeled and narrowed.

I'd channeled it further.

I needed to let go of my filters, and use everything that was available.

"I'm going to try again," I said.

"Marvelous. Do what you did before, but think 'more—bigger' and you'll have it."

I thought more. Bigger.

Saints help me, I nearly roasted us both.

The second blue sphere erupted from nothing like an azure fireball; it started no bigger than my hands but in the span of an instant expanded out in all directions to swallow us and everything around us and bathe the whole of the Edge within vision in its brilliant blue fire, and then it exploded.

The explosion threw both of us out of the place I thought of as the Edge.

I lay sprawled on the hardwood floor, my head throbbing, my eyes blinded by the afterimages of that light, my ears deafened by the noise of the explosion.

Neither my physical eyes nor my physical ears had been anywhere near the explosion . . . but the aftereffects still lingered.

This, then, was not such a benign form of magic after all. And, clearly, using *no* channels and filters was a very bad idea.

I lay there until I could see something besides pulsing light. And I heard Skirmig say, "Ouch."

I sat up. He lay on the other side of the painted Hagedwar, clutching his head, but grinning nonetheless.

"Skirmig? Are you hurt?"

"You're a wonder," he said. "I'm slain, I believe," and he chuckled to let me know that this was not literally true, "but I have lived to see the miracle all Feegash philosophers have claimed was possible in theory but impossible in fact. And at the hands of a woman, no less. You will be goddess of us all, beloved."

He sat up, rubbing his temples, and winced, and looked at me with admiration plain on his face. "My fair princess, you will astonish the world." He shook his head, bemused. "I wonder what power the Feegash lost by denying the Hagedwar to women all these centuries. I wonder if other women through time might have done what you did, or if you are unique." Then he smiled at me so tenderly, and said, "I suspect the latter."

"I made a dreadful mess of it," I said. "How could that be wonderful?"

"You pushed enough power into the sphere that it could no longer hold—the mathematical philosophers have long said such a thing might be done within the confines of the Siraband, but until this moment no one has ever done it, and the practical philosophers—those who work directly with the energies of the Siraband—have held it to be a mathematical anomaly, and all the maths related to the break-point event simply a philosopher's game played by old men with too much time."

I held out my hands, palms up, and shrugged. "What? That was in Tonk . . . mostly. But by Ethebet's sword, I have no idea what you just said."

His smile was secretive. "The Siraband is the place where we were. Those men among the Feegash philosophers who play with numbers instead of energies have calculated the ambient energy of the Siraband, and have declared that in theory energy greater than that ambient energy could be held within the forms of the Hagedwar, but that if they were, magic would begin to exhibit some . . . anomalies. And some of these anomalies would be very *useful* . . ."

His voice trailed off, and he stared off at nothing for a moment. Then his brow furrowed and he turned back to me. "It's unlikely you'll ever be able to repeat such an occurrence; the combination of random events that brought it about had to add up to a miracle. But it happened, and that is the important thing. And if it happened once, it could happen again. Men skilled in the arts could act on the knowledge that the break-point event is real."

He pushed to his feet and offered me a hand. "We've done enough for one day. I must do some reading, and after accomplishing all you have you are going to need to rest."

I nodded and stood on my own power, not taking his hand. I staggered a little as I stood, but not so much that he would need to catch me.

"Will you stay with me, then?" he asked. "Will you let me be your patron and introduce you to people who will cherish your work?" He took both of my hands in his own. "Will you stay with me?"

I nodded. "I will. How could I not?" The yearning for him was there, along with all the darkness. My people's need was there, too. Both commanded me to stay. So, at least for a time, I would stay. And that stranger's voice inside my head moved my mouth and I heard myself saying, "I love you."

He hugged me tightly, and said, "I've prepared a room for you, in the hopes that you would say yes. Later we can send for your things, but for now let me take you there, so you may wash and rest and then perhaps change into one of the lovely gowns I got for you."

Gowns? I have never been a gown sort of woman. I'd never known any women who were. Unless the Feegash had gowns made with horseback riding in mind.

He showed me to my room.

Skirmig had spared no expense. It was the only room in the house that fit, too; the furniture was Tonk, as were the decorations. The massive carved four-post bed was a clan chieftain piece—certainly hundreds of years old at the very least, and equally certainly something that a nomad chieftain had used in his concubine quarters. The posts wore the colors of the Geraddii clan, which had gradually—over the last century—given up its nomadic ways for the pleasures of the taak. Very few of the Geraddiis still rode the herds, but there were enough of them in Beyltaak alone to make a horseclan again if they chose. They were a prolific lot.

The armoires were of much later origin—clan chieftains were more than happy to make someone haul a giant bed around the countryside for them because you could do fun things with a bed and a half dozen nubile concubines. But no Tonk with full possession of his faculties would haul around a giant, heavy box the sole purpose of which was to keep clothes from wrinkling.

The room had good light, a view of what, come thaw, would certainly be a lovely garden, several chairs in different styles, a long, padded wooden bench with metal rings at both ends that looked odd to me, and some large renditions of Tonk geometric art done on canvas that matched the borders on the plaster.

The room had its own bath, too, with shower, washbasin, and sitter, which was luxury enough, but as Skirmig showed me around, he demonstrated that the shower had both hot and cold water on tap that could be adjusted to preference. And that was unthinkable luxury. We had hot water in Shields, too, brought up from a hot spring beneath the earth. But it ran into the baths. The showers were cold. And at home, both my parents' house and then my own, we had only cold, and had to heat water for a bath on the stovetop.

Skirmig showed me the shelves where soaps and shampoos and perfumes of every sort crowded in mad profusion, and beneath, towels of a fine, fluffy material made of soft cloth covered on both sides with tiny, almost carpetlike loops. They bore no resemblance to the coarse, flat rag-weave towels I'd used all my life.

The Feegash seemed to view bathing as an art as well as a necessity.

He kissed me, and said, "Rest. I'll send a girl in to help you get ready for dinner, and then we'll discuss how we are to move your things, and which of them you want to have with you here."

He left and I showered, delighting in the wonderful warmth of the water for far longer than I had any reason to. I dried off, wrapped myself in several of those amazing, soft towels, and lay on the bed—*my* bed—feigning sleep. With eyes closed and breathing deep, I did not fall into the realm of unknowing, but returned with purpose to the Edge. And there I stood, alone and unguarded, and endlessly repeated the movement of power from me into the forms of the Hagedwar, until at last I could cast the thing correctly, and hold it.

And when it sat before me in its beauty, I began to study it, to try to decipher its worth on my own.

I did not come to any astonishing revelations, other than to define for myself a bit of truth about its nature. The Hagedwar is to magic what a fine crystal prism is to light: both break up an energy that seems to be all the same into parts that are very different. The prism breaks white light into colors, which makes it a charming amusement, though no use can be made of the different colors of light—or at least the Tonk have found no such uses. The Hagedwar breaks raw magic into a multitude of different refined energies. Looking at it, without Skirmig's words to distract me or prejudice my view of it, I could see how those energies flowed and how they differed. I caught faint hints of how I might use them, but I did not touch. For that, I would wait for a demonstration from Skirmig, to see which energies he used and which he did not. After the explosion, I was wary. The Hagedwar was no more a child's plaything than the View. It deserved respect.

In his fever dream, Gair lay beside Talyn, comforting her. She was crying, which he somehow knew was not a thing she did, and as he whispered to her she turned her back to him and would not look at him. He held her tight against his chest and rocked her and said, "You're safe now. You're safe. You're with me and I'll never let anyone hurt you again, I swear it."

She was hurt. Bloody. Scarred. Someone had done terrible things to her, and in the dream Gair knew who had done them, and thought he could get past the bastard's defenses and kill her torturer before the bastard could do her any more harm.

And then Talyn turned her face to him and stared into his

eyes, and she transformed into a demon, beautiful and terrible in the same breath, with wings black as midnight and claws sharp as needles and hard as iron that dug into his chest all the way through the skin and past his ribs to slice into his heart. Her voice was deep and rich and terrible, like the low notes of an earthquake. "She is not for you. She is *mine*. If you pursue her, I will devour you," the demon said, and ripped his heart out through the wall of his chest and shoved it, still beating, into its mouth, and tore into it with teeth like daggers.

Gair screamed from the pain, and woke sweating with the pain still eating him so that for a moment he was not sure if he still dreamed, or if through some nightmare of magic the dream had become reality, and that was why he couldn't breathe.

Then Snow Grell was leaning over Gair, shouting for the healer to come quick, and the healer looked at Gair and poked and prodded him with his fingers and swore. When Idrann came back, running, it was with knives and tubes and a suction apparatus attached to a bellows, and the next instant the healer had shoved a sharp metal tube between two of Gair's ribs and the moment after that, started pumping on the bellows, sucking fluid and pus and blood into the cow-bladder bag that hung below it.

The metal tube in Gair's side hurt beyond description. But a flood of foul stuff poured out of him, and when it stopped and the healer couldn't get his bellows to draw out anything else, Gair realized that he could breathe again.

"Silver, now, to clean the wound," the healer said, and told Snow Grell, "Hold him down. This will hurt worse than the tube did."

The Hva Hwa bit his lip and averted his eyes in sympathy, but he grabbed one of Gair's upper arms with each hand and leaned on him, pinning Gair against any weak flailing he might manage. And the accursed healer pulled out the metal tube and jammed a silver rod thick as Gair's thumb and twice as long and shaped like beads stacked one atop the other into the hole left by the tube. Every bead on the rod forced Gair's ribs apart and then let them move back together so they could be forced apart once more, so that Gair felt like his chest was ripping apart. He screamed and tried to pull free of Snow Grell's grip. And then, because the pain was so terrible, he puked, and Snow

Grell and Master Idrann had to roll him over on one side so he didn't drown in his own vomitus.

"Let me die," he begged. "Please just let me die."

"You're not going to die," Snow Grell said. "You're going to live, and you're going to be glad of this someday. I swear it. You're not done yet."

"All I want is just to feel the sun on my face one more time, Snow Grell. That will be enough. Please. Take me out and let me see the sun and leave me there to freeze to death in peace."

But then he thought of the nightmare. Of Talyn, the Tonk woman who had saved his life. The woman who had found a way to pull him out of hell. He'd dreamed that she was in trouble, and he knew it was just a dream, but when she came up to see him again, he would make sure. Just in case.

Not that he could do anything to help her if she was in trouble. He couldn't even help himself—had to have the healer or Snow Grell or Talyn feed him, bathe him, clean his ass after he shit. He had become nothing but a burden.

He would reassure himself that his nightmare had been nothing but his own sickness and pain playing games with his mind. And then he could die in peace.

11

A servant stood over me, staring down at me, her eyes curiously expressionless and her face a smooth mask. I realized that somewhere in my explorations of the Edge and the Hagedwar, I'd fallen asleep after all.

And that I had kicked off my towels and lay naked atop the Tonk concubine bed.

How awkward. For both of us.

"My name is Haithe. I'll be your dresser," she told me. "Master Skirmig has stepped out on business, and bade me have you dressed appropriately for the meal and such guests as he will be bringing with him."

She wore the dun brown of the Feegash serving class, but

hers was the face and carriage of an aristocrat. And looking at her, I could only think that she seemed almost not even in the same room with me. Did she consider me so far below her? Or, because I was Tonk, was I not worthy of consideration at all?

No matter, I decided. No matter how I might look from her point of view, from my point of view she was not Tonk.

"I've been dressing myself since I was a child," I said. "And I don't have any other clothes here but those—" I wrapped myself in one of the towels again, and pointed to my little pile of things stacked on the chair.

She pulled the doors of the armoire open as I was talking, effectively silencing me. It was full of clothes. Dresses. Just dresses. The gowns Skirmig had mentioned—nor had he been joking when he called them gowns. They were lavish creations. Baldachin gleaming with gold and silver threads, dark opalescent silk, light watered silk, astrakhan bodices, angora insets, duvetyn, Norchenn crepe, velvet. Every imaginable color, various styles.

I pulled one out and stared at it. "This is never going to fit me," I told the girl. Haithe. Her name was Haithe. "This dress was made for someone half as big around the middle as I am."

Haithe didn't smile. She said, "There are undergarments for that," and opened the other armoire. She had understated the case. There were, indeed, undergarments, but they had nothing in common with my cottons or my light breastbinder. These things had hooks and laces and wires and straps. I'd seen yokes and harnesses for plow horses less complicated.

The idea of a dresser to help me into these things suddenly seemed less ludicrous.

But the dresses still wouldn't fit.

"You should be able to wear any of the dresses hung to the far left to start with," she told me.

I pulled one out. The waist on it looked less ridiculously tiny, but still nothing that I could wear.

She handed me tiny pantlets of black silk covered back and front with rows of black lace and red ribbons. I put them on, thinking them ludicrous. But they *were* clean. And then I stood there, in silly silk pantlets and nothing else, while she eyed me critically. "Mmmmph," she said at last, and while I had not much liked her before, I began to truly dislike her with that cold dismissal. She turned back to the armoire that held the under-things. "We'll have to wax you. But not now; there is no time."

Wax me? I didn't know what she was talking about, but I knew I didn't like the sound of it.

"Waister first," Haithe said, and got out a black silk square with half a dozen straps and buckles on it and hooks and eyes, and two little half-moon shelves at the top, and said, "You'll want to lean against the wall for this, with your back to me. It will give us a bit more leverage."

She wrapped the thing around my waist, and the two shelves shoved my breasts up toward my chin. I felt the steady click, click as she worked her way down a row of hooks, and the thing tightened around me. It felt constricting and I didn't like it. Then she said, "Now we have to do the tightener," and started hooking the little metal rings attached to the straps onto a big wooden lever, and she said, "Exhale as hard as you can," and like a fool I did as she told me, and the next thing I knew, she was pulling on the lever and the waister was crushing me and I couldn't breathe. "Not enough," she said, and braced her knee on my tailbone and pulled harder. Then I heard three sharp metallic clicks, and she moved away from me and turned me around, shaking her head. "You have a long way to go. That's just barely good enough—but we should at least be able to get you into the green charmeuse."

I leaned my back against the wall, sipping air in tiny gasps, and said, "This thing is . . . awful. Get it . . . off me."

"You'll get used to it," she said. "Once you've been wearing it for a while we should be able to get your waist down to half the size it is now."

"My waist . . . isn't meant to be . . . half the size it is," I told her.

"It's going to have to be if you're going to wear the dresses the master acquired for you."

"He should have . . . learned my size—" *before he had them made*, I was going to say, but then I realized that he had. The Feegash woman at my door had been, if not the dressmaker—for these dresses represented hundreds of hours of combined work each—then at least a dressmaker who had also acted as a buyer. She did not need so much to see my size from the waist down, for the dresses before me had full, floor-length skirts, and so long as she could get a general estimation of my hip size and my height, she would be able to adjust their hang. But she had needed some very specific measurements of me above the waist.

Haithe next helped me into silky stockings of the sort I had torn off Skirmig that time in the barn. These clipped to the waister. After that, she helped me into the dress, and considering the amount of trouble I was having just breathing, I was grateful for the help.

She put my feet into odd boots—these angled sharply forward with the heel raised much higher than the toe, and like the waister, they laced on. I couldn't bend forward far enough to reach my feet. By Ethebet's sword, I couldn't lean forward far enough to *see* my feet.

With Haithe kneeling before me, lifting my left leg and putting my foot into the boot, tugging and straining, and then doing the same with the right foot, I felt like a horse being shod. And when she was finished, I stood there wobbling, hobbled by the uncomfortable shoes, and by the breath-stopping waister, and she led me in front of a mirror in the room and I saw myself.

"Who dresses like this?" I blurted, staring at myself in disbelief.

"Feegash women of position," Haithe said, studying me with those flat, uncaring eyes.

My waist had been squeezed ridiculously small, and my face was flushed from pain and lack of air. My breasts poked out the top of the neckline so far that I could see pink silvers of my nipples above the cloth, and the breasts themselves had been shoved close to my collarbones. I lifted the skirt and studied my feet, which were no longer shaped like feet, but like sharp pointed things on the ends of my legs.

Feegash women of position, I decided, were insane.

Haithe did not think herself finished with me yet, though, for she said, "We'll have to do something about your hair. That braid just won't do."

"Don't . . . touch . . . the braid," I growled.

"It doesn't match the style of the dress, and it looks hideous," she said. "Barbaric."

"It's religious."

"One of your pagan affectations." She shrugged. "We'll leave

it. For tonight, anyway. The master will want us to do something different with it when he sees it, but we can leave it in
place for one night, I suppose. He'll know that I tried to get you
to let me fix it."

My warrior's braid wasn't going anywhere. If Skirmig
thought to change me so much, I would simply leave.

I thought about my obligation to my people. And, Jostfar forgive me, I thought about how beautiful he was, about the feel of
his hands on me. . . .

Well, I probably wouldn't leave. But I wouldn't let him
change me, either. I was not some child's doll to be dressed and
preened and paraded around in foreign garb.

"Get me out of . . . this mess and let me get . . . back into my
own clothes . . . before I die," I said through clenched teeth.

"The master bade me dress you for dinner and guests, and I
have done so," she said, and must have seen in my eyes that my
next move was going to be to attempt to kill her, even if then I
would have had no one to help me get out of the awful clothing.

"I'm not wearing . . . this dress . . . to dinner," I said. "I
won't be able to eat a thing."

"Women of position eat little," Haithe said. "And you're far
too thick through the middle already." She shook her head.

She started to leave, and I grabbed her upper arm, hard.
"Where are *you* going?"

"I have other duties to attend to before the master returns.
You may do as you like until the meal. I'll come for you then."

I could do as I liked? I would *like* to be able to breathe. To be
able to *walk*. I could not believe than any woman would permit
herself to be squeezed into such uncomfortable, bizarre clothing. I knew I didn't intend to be again. I could go pick up my
own clean clothes from my house; they were comfortable and
practical, and I had one set of very fine traditional clothing suitable for presentation and events of state. Special beads for my
braid, embroidered breeches and overtunic, good-quality paints
for my forehead, wonderful jewelry of beads and bone that told
my rank and my place within my clan. If they weren't made of
silk and lace, that mattered not even a little to me. But being
able to run—that mattered. Being able to fight, to sit down comfortably, to touch my toes . . . "Help me out of this damned
dress before you go anywhere."

She slipped free of my grip, and I lost my balance. I staggered and caught myself, but she was already halfway across the room. "The master told me to help you dress. He did not give me permission to help you undress. He does not look favorably on that sort of . . . initiative." And with that she turned and hurried away.

The bitch.

I took a few tottering, hobbled steps after her and realized I couldn't even hope to catch her. I considered my situation. Run? Hah. I couldn't even walk. My feet hurt already, but I couldn't reach them to do anything about the pain. I couldn't sit comfortably—the waister cut into my breathing so much worse when I tried to sit that I thought I would die. I tried to imagine myself wearing this fool's garb while sitting at table with a meal spread before me, making conversation and eating, and if I could have breathed, I would have laughed.

I could not undo the dress on my own because it laced and tied and buttoned all in the back, could not remove the tightly laced boots until I could get out of the dress, and couldn't breathe normally or move normally until I'd shed the whole ridiculous outfit.

I rummaged through the twin armoires looking for a single reasonable gown to substitute for that dreadful outfit. Every single dress, and there were eleven of them besides the one I wore, were as bad as the current monstrosity, or worse. I studied the waists of the dresses to the far right, and if I touched my thumbs together and encircled the dress waist, my fingers came close to touching in the front.

Feegash women had apparently learned to exist without eating, breathing, or shitting, but I wasn't Feegash. I was Tonk, and Tonk women ride horses and toss hay and lug produce and water, and on the home front wield swords and fight like wildcats to defend their children and themselves. And they don't do it while wearing brutal dresses or painful shoes.

I could find nothing among the dresses any better than the ridiculous thing I already wore, so I checked the other armoire. It held bizarre lace and silk and leather breastbinders designed not to bind the breasts at all but to make the damned things stick out like spears, and stacks of pantlets of filmy silk and tanned fur and loose-woven lace and a dozen other things, all of them so tiny I could see no purpose in wearing them at all.

In my entire search, what I found was nothing—not a single useful item.

I gathered up my own day wear, which no one would consider suitable for greeting guests of high rank. I had nothing else, though, so it would have to do. I could barely reach it. I couldn't get to my boots at all—that would require bending over, and I didn't bend anymore.

No matter. The floors in Skirmig's home were warmer than mine ever got this time of year, warmer than the ones in my parents drafty loft when all fourteen of us children dragged ourselves out of bed to my mother's call. I would manage shoeless for a bit.

I hobbled out of the room Skirmig had given me, and made my way past Skirmig's servants, and to a one the bastards scuttled out of my way like sand crabs fleeing a stick before I reached them. Perhaps Haithe had told them they were not to help me, or perhaps Skirmig had instructed them to leave me alone. Either way, however, they made it clear I would get no help from them. So I found my workshop. And closed the door.

And then I looked over the very fine selection of tools Skirmig had placed in the room.

I found metal-cutting shears and good knives. I looked at the wonderful material in the dress I wore, and sighed. It wouldn't go to waste; I'd make sure of that. I could rip the seams and turn it into wonderful Tonk dress clothing, and salvage the beadwork and the embroidered bits as well. But it had just lived its last day as a gown.

I started slicing—from the too-low neck downward through all that beautiful silk. When I'd cut the thing off and shed it, I still couldn't breathe, but I felt lighter. I hadn't realized how heavy all that fine silk was. I disposed of the uncomfortable layered underskirts that hung beneath the dress and made the skirt stick out at the sides and back. One quick flick of the knife through the waistband turned that into a puddle of cloth on the floor, and when it hit the ground I lost an even heavier burden. I hadn't paid much attention to that thing when Haithe tied it around my waist—I was still in shock from having the waister levered onto me.

And then I was down to the waister itself. I couldn't hack

away at it with the shears—it was too tight against my skin. I couldn't slide the edge of the knife under the fabric and cut away from me, either. If I tried that, I would just succeed in stabbing myself. I didn't like dragging the blade down the front of the waister when I had no idea how much pressure would take the blade through the waister, and how much extra pressure would go through both the waister and me. But the waister was going. And I was never putting one on again. I ran the knife down the front of the material once, just hard enough that I could see threads on the surface layer popping apart.

On the second pass, a couple of rips opened. Oh, sweet sound, the tearing of fabric under pressure. I got a couple of nicks, too, but I didn't care. I was light-headed from the exertion, but breathing was in sight.

On the third pass, I sawed at the heavy top, where all the fabric had been reinforced and stitched through multiple times. I went slowly because I was pressing hard and I didn't want to run myself through when the band gave way.

When it snapped, I sliced myself one more time anyway; in spite of everything, it took me by surprise when it popped. But when it snapped, it did so with such force that the tear in the material ripped straight down through the rest of the waister and it fell apart like rotten fruit. And I could breathe again.

I stood there gasping for a moment, dizzy and in pain, with blood running down my breastbone and my belly and anger boiling in my heart. But I had my small victory over Haithe and the rest of the cowardly servants.

I sheared through the reinforced bottom, but that wasn't such a chore. It had flared to make room for my hips, and it was no tighter than normal clothing would be. I bent down and untied the vile boots. Stood barefoot on the floor in the middle of a pile of ruined clothes, naked except for the silly silk pantlets, and reveled in the unalloyed pleasures of being able to breathe freely and move freely.

And Haithe walked in. I was going to have to get a lock for that door if I was to work here.

Her hands flew to her face and her mouth opened wide, but no sound came out.

I yanked on breeches and tunic, and stood staring at her.

Other servants came racing into the workroom as if summoned, and I wondered if she was making some sound that I could not hear.

They all stared at me, and then the rest of the servants froze in place and their eyes unfocused, and their mouths went wide in that same silent scream.

The hair on the back of my neck stood up, and my skin crawled.

"What in Ethebet's name—," I muttered, but I reached behind me and grabbed the knife I'd been using off the table, and felt around until I came up with one of the metalworking mallets. The servants outnumbered me badly—five or six were in the workroom with me, including several big men. And that count did not include the ones I could hear shuffling about out in the hall. I had no idea what these people were doing, but I was going to be as well armed for whatever was coming as I could manage.

And then they stopped doing . . . whatever it was they were doing.

No. That doesn't quite convey the awfulness of that simple act. Let me try again. Their mouths all closed at precisely the same instant, as if they were a choir of exceptional talent led by a choirmaster of tremendous skill, and they had received their cue.

Only there was no choirmaster.

I shivered in the warm air. All of them save Haithe turned away without a word, and left. Haithe said, "My name is Haithe. I'll be your dresser. Master Skirmig has stepped out on business, and bade me have you dressed appropriately for the meal and such guests as he will be bringing with him."

I stared at her. "Are you mad? I'm not letting you put me into another of those fool's suits when I had to go through so much trouble to get out of the last one."

"The master will be upset if you are not appropriately dressed for dinner," she said, as if that were a reasonable explanation, and walked across the workroom and put a hand on my arm as if to lead me back to my own room.

I caught her chin in one hand and tipped her face up so that she was looking directly into my eyes, and I said, "If you do not remove every piece of that awful clothing from my room immediately and send it back to wherever it came from, I am going to burn it. I will never put on another piece of that dreadful stuff. Never. Do you understand me?"

A flicker of *something* showed in her eyes for the first time. She stared up at me and said, "But the master wants you to wear those dresses," and for the briefest of instants, I felt as I felt when Skirmig touched me. Or kissed me. I felt eyes opening up inside of me, and hungry mouths crying to be fed—and I wanted, in that instant, what they wanted, and I thought, Well, fine, then, I suppose I can put up with the discomfort for Skirmig, if it will make him happy.

And then I shoved Haithe away from me and caught hold of my emotions.

"Get rid of them. Now," I growled, using the same voice I used during fight training in Shields.

She stared past my left shoulder, and then with a nod she turned away and hurried off. I looked behind me. No one was there.

I wasn't enjoying Skirmig's house and hospitality very much. He cared little for honor. His servants were strange and frightening. I didn't like them. My father had given me the order to make use of Skirmig, but he had not told me how I ought to do it.

Perhaps I ought to reconsider Skirmig's request that I move in with him. He could come visit me when he wanted me.

Of course, my house was full of dying Eastils and the barbarian and the healer I'd talked into caring for them, and so occupied, my tiny house wouldn't offer much privacy for the two of us, either for work or for sex.

No matter. I needed space to think, and I needed a clearer plan. I left the workroom and hurried to the room Skirmig had prepared for me. I wanted my boots.

Even if he and I managed to work something out, I could at least go home again until the two of us had a chance to talk about the dresses. And the servants. And those silent screams. I sat on the edge of the bed and pulled them on.

And Skirmig walked into the room, and every rational thought I had fled.

"I can't stay here," I told him. "There's something wrong with your servants."

He leaned over and kissed me, and when he finished I was as breathless as I'd been from the waister. Only without the pain. "I hear you got into a fight with a dress," he said, and his eyes were full of laughter.

"I will never believe that women wear such clothes as those," I told him.

"You'll be meeting half a dozen of them at next bell; they've come to meet you and see your work. And I had hoped to introduce you as their equal, my beloved, so that they would be kind to you."

Their equal? My eyebrows rose of their own accord and I said, "These women . . . can any one of them ride a horse bareback across an enemy-littered field at a gallop? Can a single one of them fight in Shields, or cast your Hagedwar, or wield a sword, or kill a man with a neat twist of arm over neck?"

"Well, no," he admitted.

"Then they *aren't* my equal, and perhaps they had best dress as I do and hope *I* will be kind to *them*."

Skirmig burst out laughing, picked me up, spun me around as if I were a child, and then kissed me in ways that made it clear that I was not. Inside me, the eyes stared, the mouths begged, and something—something painful—washed away. "Good God, I love you, woman," he said. "For all that you are hell on gifts."

"I am? How?" I asked.

And he said, "That dress cost as much as the—"

And he stopped, and his eyes widened just the tiniest bit, and he said, "—the house you live in." But that was not what he had been intending to say.

And my mind said, *The horse*—but he had *sworn* he was not responsible for the Dakaat debacle. And then I thought, His oath? And of what value is that?

"Now . . . what was it about my servants that bothered you?" he asked.

I thought about it. There had been something . . . something . . . It had slipped my mind, it lay right at the tip of my tongue. . . . Oh, of course. "Haithe refused to help me when I asked her to get me back out of the dress," I said. "Had she helped me, the dress would have been spared."

Skirmig nodded. "She's obedient. But I'll explain to her that you are to be the mistress of the house, and that she is to obey you as she obeys me. You won't have any further disobedience from her."

I was to be the mistress of the house? Was I? When had we decided that? I'd thought, somehow, that I had planned something different, but if I had, it must not have been an important plan, because I had forgotten it.

"Thank you," I said. I had a brief, aching feeling that there was something else about the servants that had bothered me—perhaps even that had bothered me a great deal—but whatever it might have been, it eluded me, and I finally realized that, whatever it was, it could not have been important.

Skirmig told me, "I'll send a servant to your house to bring your clothes. I'm guessing you have something suitable for meeting important people."

I grinned at him. "Certainly."

"I'll be back shortly, then," he said. "And if necessary I'll keep the guests occupied until you are ready to meet them."

Gair heard a knock at the door, and heard the healer answer it.

"No, I won't let you in," he said to mutters on the other side. "I don't care who you say sent you. Go away."

He slammed the door.

Someone knocked again. The healer opened it again. "I told you to go away."

And a pause.

"No. If Talyn wants her clothes, she's going to have to come get them herself. I don't know you, and for all I know, you've thought of a clever way to rob her with my help."

He slammed the door again.

The people on the other side were persistent, but the third time they started pounding and yelling, the healer did not open the door, and after a short while, the strangers went away.

To be replaced, only a moment later, by someone kicking in the door.

No muttering this time—Gair heard the diplomat bastard's voice clear and loud.

"Talyn has agreed to move in with me," the bastard said. "I

have come to pick up her clothing, and the Feegash troops are here with me to make sure she gets what she wants."

"She wouldn't just leave," the healer said. "She wouldn't send us notice of this instead of coming herself. What have you done with her?"

Gair would have given anything to be able to sit up on his own and to see what was going on below. He would have given more for the strength to go down there and fight them, pursue them . . . to bring Talyn safely back to her home. He turned his head and saw Hale looking at him, and saw the fear he felt reflected in Hale's eyes.

The bastard's voice was cool and amused. "I think you must know her very little, witch doctor. When she makes up her mind, Talyn does it quickly, and she doesn't look back. You and your dying charges up there would be, for her, looking back on a pathetic scale." The bastard sighed, and Gair could hear men with heavy boots stomping through the house, drawers opening and slamming shut, voices speaking softly. "I need not be either gentle or kind about this, though," the bastard added. "If you're a good, polite little savage, I'll send two of my servants to stay with you and make sure you don't damage or steal anything that belongs to my love. If you're a bad little witch doctor—and you'll be bad if you stand in my way, or interfere in my business here—you and the filthy stickmen upstairs can die today."

In the silence that followed, Gair remembered his nightmare—of Talyn hurt, held captive by the bastard, and tortured as he had been tortured when the Tonks held him in their dungeon.

It had been a dream, and he had never in his memory dreamed true dreams before. Except of course he had dreamed each night he was imprisoned that Talyn was with him, and she had been the one who had saved him at last. So that had been a true dream, after a fashion. Perhaps this was a true dream, in the manner of his other dreams about her. Perhaps Talyn was honestly in trouble.

She was a warrior, and like him, she served a code of honor that would have required her to assure the safety of those for whom she had taken responsibility. Idrann was right; she would not have run off one night and not come back—at least to say good-bye and make arrangements with Idrann—unless something was amiss.

So change that "perhaps" to "certainly."

Talyn was in trouble, and she had only a graying healer, a Hva Hwa hunter, and two starved, near-death warriors to rescue her.

Gair realized that he couldn't satisfy himself by seeing the sun, then dying. He had to live. Talyn, the woman who had given him and Hale their lives back, needed him.

I was grateful to see Skirmig when he came around the corner carrying a stack of my clothes, including the fine Tonk dress garb. It took me only moments to put on everything, and not much longer to paint the clan marks on my forehead, work the beads into my braid, and stand before him fully dressed.

"You look . . . beautiful," he said. "Fierce, but beautiful."

I hugged him. "I hadn't asked you before, but when did you want me to move in here?"

"I thought you already had," he told me, smiling. "What could you possibly need from your little house that I cannot provide for you here?"

"My horses," I said. "The rest of my clothes. My stock in my workroom. Some personal belongings that I'd like to have here. And I'll need to make some sort of arrangements for Idrann and the Eastils. Idrann is hiding in my house so that he can care for the Eastils without everyone in the taak knowing they're there. For *your* protection, remember."

"I remember," he said, and his mouth kept smiling but his eyes didn't. "I'll, ah . . ." He looked away from me for a moment, and chewed on the knuckle of one thumb. "Here's what I'll do. I'll have two of my servants go stay in the house permanently. They can take in food, bring you progress reports, live there and make sure your neighbors know that they're responsible for watching your home for you while you decide what to do with it."

Something about this plan seemed oddly familiar, as if I had heard it all before. Except, of course, that I had not. "What to *do* with it? My house? Why would I want to do anything with it?"

"You're going to live with me. Here. Why would you still need your house?"

"Because I'm Tonk and you're Feegash and I prefer to leave my options open."

"I love you."

"I love you as well," I told him. "But I'll still leave my options open. You and I have decided nothing long-term yet, nor am I ready to consider such decisions." I studied him for a long moment. I did love him. Did I? Yes, I did, though uncertainty marked my memories of this, as well. I loved him. But I did not trust my new circumstances, and I did not trust my friend and the three Eastils to the care of any of Skirmig's servants, though I wasn't sure why.

"I'll check on the Eastils myself," I said. "I'd rather be able to see how they're doing every day."

"But if you go to your house every day, in spite of the fact that you aren't living there, and if you carry food and supplies to the three of them, your neighbors are going to become suspicious. And rightfully so. My way makes the whole situation . . . plausible. And my servants will take excellent care of your property, and make sure your . . . guests . . . have everything they need." He looked into my eyes. And gently touched my cheek. And smiled.

I got lost in his eyes. In his sweet smile. And suddenly I didn't want to go check on Idrann and Gair and Hale every day. Skirmig's servants would do everything that needed to be done. Of course they would. Skirmig was right. Obviously. I couldn't understand why I hadn't seen it before.

With my foolish worries dispelled, we went out to greet Skirmig's guests. They clustered in the center room of the house; four men dressed all in black silks and velvets and lace, like Skirmig, which would, I supposed, make them his diplomatic superiors, and three men dressed in fine brocades and watered silk and linen of dullest drab gray—and I had never seen Feegash men so dressed, so had no idea what those three might do. The men were crows and gray falcons. And at their sides, like the shiny baubles crows love, or the little songbirds gray falcons hunt, stood the women who *did* wear the clothes I had so narrowly escaped—seven ladies dressed in gorgeous gowns in all the colors still hanging in my armoire.

And, Jostfar save me, they had waists so tiny no food could possibly get through their guts, and breasts lifted and shaped and pointed until they nearly leapt from the tops of those low-cut dresses, and these women minced about in tiny steps that would have shamed a Tonk toddler. Could they have children? If they did, would the babies come out squashed and deformed? Or had they made themselves as sterile as me with their foolish clothing? I could not stop staring at them. Their heavy skirts weighed them down, their white-painted faces made them look half dead, and their hair had been fixed in complex, horrible piles that had to have taken hours and that made them, to a one, unable to move their heads freely. They were all thin and frail; they leaned on the arms of their men as they walked, although all were younger than me. Each of them was easily half the age of the man she accompanied. Sometimes only a third the age.

And I thought, How threatened by their women are these Feegash men, that they have to take child brides and then cripple them like this before they take them out? How fearsome must these women—or perhaps their great-great-grandmothers—have once been to warrant such imprisonment? No *wonder* I had never seen any women of Feegash society before. They'd risk death just stepping out the front door dressed as they were; a badly placed cobblestone in the street would pitch one forward and crack her skull or, top-heavy as she was, break her neck. And I was betting that even barring serious injury from the fall, once down, a Feegash woman wouldn't be able to get back up under her own power.

Poor things.

What had Skirmig been thinking? I could never have pretended to be one of these women, no matter what I did. My only hope of dealing with them lay in my being as foreign to them as they were to me; people excuse the grossest slips in etiquette from foreigners, but excuse nothing from those who make a pretense of being like them. Tonks have a saying: Don't play the game if you don't know the rules. I didn't want to know their rules, and I could clearly see that I didn't want to play their game.

If I was going to win this day, I was going to have to play my game, and by my rules. I needed to be the Tonk warrior to the hilt.

So we sat at table, me and Skirmig's companions and their
ives—a little section of Ba'afeegash's elite who were trying to
bring Ba'afeegash society to Beyltaak—and the men told stories of sailing and debating and fighting in far-off places—for
the men in gray were the masters of the Ba'afeegash mercenary
corps living at that very moment in Shields—and I told stories
about *our* war, and about horse riding and hard drinking and
Magics battles and one field excursion that led to hand-to-hand
fighting even for those of us who generally lived well behind
the buffers of Conventional forces; that was the terribly off-
color tale of a group of us Shielders and Conventionals at a
bawdy house on the border after a rough battle who decided to
blow off a little craziness, and who after much merriment and
pogging found ourselves fighting our way out of the place
naked with our uniforms tucked under our arms, and the men at
the table laughed until they choked and their faces turned bright
red and they couldn't breathe. It's a good story and I tell it well,
if I say so myself, with lots of good detail . . . and most of it
true. And this was an audience who had never heard the tale before, so I got full benefit. But while the men and I told our tales
and drank ale and cleared our plates and asked for seconds, the
women sat in silence, and picked at their food, and glanced at
me from time to time with expressions that I simply could not
read.

I could understand that. If they didn't know what to make of
me, neither did I know what to make of them.

After the meal, Skirmig brought out my display pieces from
my studio, which I had not realized he'd already retrieved, and
the men passed them around, and the women looked at them
without touching them.

And I heard sounds from them for the first time. Little
"ooh"s and "ahh"s. Whispered, though. And they did not look
anywhere but at their husbands when they whispered.

Still, their reactions were gratifying.

When we finished, the men rose from table, helped their
women to stand, and led them down one of the house-legs.

"Go with them," Skirmig told me. "Take your work. The men
will come to the men's parlor with me, and then the women will
be permitted to speak publicly, and they'll be able to talk with
you. I'm *sure* they'll want to. And since to a one the women

control the money in their households and will decide whether or not you sell any of your work to Feegash society, you'll have to win them over." He looked at me again and grinned and shook his head. "Based on your performance here, I'm guessing you may have a rough sale before you, but I have faith in you."

Bemused, I tucked my work, each piece in its own velvet wrapper, into the bag I wore at my waist, and followed the tottering line of women and their escorts into a sitting room, and watched their men help them sit down.

So the women, who couldn't even walk without some assistance, and who weren't allowed to speak in the presence of men, controlled the household finances.

In Tonk society, the one who looks like he holds power does.

Feegash society was making my head ache.

I strolled in with Skirmig beside me. He kissed me, and I kissed him back, and heard a few indrawn breaths from the people behind me. And I could only think that it was a good thing I'd gone to this party as a true Tonk, and not an imitation Feegash; I would have been nothing but an embarrassment to Skirmig. This way, I was simply . . . well . . . exotic.

The men left, with Skirmig last. He closed the door behind him.

And the click of the latch against the strike plate was the magic key that opened the women's mouths. All at once and at full volume, they wanted to know if it was all true—that I had been a soldier; that I knew how to kill a man with my bare hands; that I had been to bawdy houses and amused myself with the male concubines in them; that I had sat at table with men and women where anyone could speak at any time; that I walked the streets unchaperoned; that I and other Tonk women could pog any man we pleased, and people could know about it, and we wouldn't be executed for our behavior.

So then I had to explain about Ethebet and the other saints, and how Tonks chose the set of rules that they lived by, and that we each tolerated other Saints' rules even if we didn't think much of them. But that all rules had equal legal protection, and that Jostfar looked at all of us as acceptable. So long as we were Tonk. I explained that only the Tonk could follow Jostfar, and that only the children of two Tonk parents were Tonk. That we did not execute people for having sex unless they were rapists or molesters of children. That sex was not equally free for all Tonks, but that the amount of freedom we had was our own personal choice, dictated by our choice of Saints and path.

Which led to them talking about their lives, and how they were legally their husband's property, and how the Feegash accepted foreign brides and made them Feegash, but that brides then lived under Feegash law.

Which meant that—no matter what—I wasn't marrying Skirmig. That was fine. I knew I was barren, so I was not eligible for marriage in Jostfar's eyes anyway. And I had no wish to marry an outlander, and become as an outlander myself. Skirmig and I could be together, and love each other, and perhaps grow old together, without me becoming his property. Or wearing those awful dresses.

I asked if those dresses didn't hurt.

And the women laughed, and started comparing the dresses to things that did hurt. And that was how I came to discover a truly dark and horrible side of the peace-loving Feegash that had been invisible until then.

The men were perverts. The women talked openly about being beaten, branded, passed around by their husbands among their husbands' friends in gatherings of the men in which they were a sort of dessert to top off the evening. At these gatherings they were bound and displayed and tortured for the amusement of all the men present, and then all the men took turns on them, often repeatedly. The mistress of the house in which one of these gatherings was held knew that this would be her fate at the end of the evening; she would be the night's entertainment. Feegash men, these young wives told me, had a lot of their wives die on them. All of the women with me were third or fourth or fifth wives. They all had a horrible sadness surrounding them as they spoke of this. They all knew that they would end as their predecessors had—dead from torture or rape at the hands of the man who should have protected them, and his friends, who should have honored them. And yet these pitiful wives didn't flee, because fleeing would make them criminals, and change an eventual deferred death into an instant one.

"How can you live like that?" I asked them, stunned and horrified by their plight.

One of them said, "Well, you need not pity us so much. I swear to you the men will be out there right now discussing when Skirmig will marry you so that they might have their turn on you."

"I'm not eligible to marry," I said, sickened, trying to imagine Skirmig thinking that he might treat me in such a way, or survive if he tried. Surely he was not such a fool as that. But he had spoken of his love of pain. "It wouldn't matter, because if those men tried such a thing with me, I'd kill as many of the bastards as I could before they took me down."

And they sighed. And shook their heads.

"You don't understand. It wasn't like this in the old country. There it was awful, but you knew it wasn't your fault. Here . . . it isn't as easy as all that here. When your husband and his friends have you, a terrible hunger fills you—a madness like watching eyes opening inside you and watching mouths screaming to be fed. And you will do anything—*anything*—to give them what they want. It is a secret power of the Feegash men, that they can make you want them to hurt you, and make you beg for more."

Another nodded. "When they're done with you, you wish you were dead. But not while it's going on."

A third said, "It doesn't start so bad. Sex, a little roughness." The others were nodding. "And then it gets worse. Instead of biting and scratching, there are ropes and whips. And then brands. And knives."

One of the women pulled up one of the long, full sleeves on her gown to reveal her arm. It had designs cut into it, like the designs I had seen on Skirmig's arms and legs and belly.

They were, I realized, the same designs. Wolves and falcons, knives and ropes and whips and shackles. Women naked, bound and gagged.

The other women looked at her arms and tugged up their own sleeves. "Our bellies are like that, too," one said. "Thighs, backs, anyplace that doesn't show in public."

"Sooner or later, they get carried away. And the hostess for the evening dies from their excess. Her husband holds a little funeral for his late wife, and the next day brings in a virgin he's been keeping in his concubine apartments for just such a situation, and the whole thing begins again."

"We all started out living with the concubines, being trained to please."

They nodded carefully, their high-piled hair making such gestures precarious.

"All of us know of the little girls who are there now, too, waiting to take our places when we're gone."

I could say nothing. I rose and fled to the privacy room and vomited into the sitter. And then I stood in there with the door shut, trembling and terrified not just of the fate of the women with whom I was talking, but of my own fate. Who *were* these men that I could have a pleasant meal with them, talk to them as equals, and discover that at that moment they were likely seeking an opportunity to rape me? To torture me? With Skirmig's consent and participation?

I had found out early enough to save myself. I would leave. That night, immediately. I would not say good-bye to Skirmig, I would not offer him explanation or apology. I would simply leave and never look back.

None of these women spoke of love—of ever loving their husbands. How could they? They were slaves of the worst and most terrible sort. Love, though, had nothing to do with this situation. Because Skirmig had sought to make me their equal. His words, and at the time that had seemed innocent enough. But he already knew the truth—he knew of these women and their eventual fate. He had most certainly participated in some of the degrading sessions the women described. Had he helped kill some of these helpless creatures as well?

He was a monster. I had fallen in love with a monster.

As a Tonk bound by Ethebet's dictates, and knowing what I knew, I had justification to slaughter every one of the men in the other room as enemies of the taak, for engaging in slavery, torture, rape, and serial murder within the city walls.

My empty sheath hung in my room in my own little house, symbol of my compliance with the peace. Of course, I had offered up a secondary sword as my actual sacrifice to compliance; my best sword lay wrapped in oiled rags and hidden within the secret heart of Beyltaak, where no one but I would find it.

I could have all eight of those monster's heads before the next bell tolled, and lay them out on the steps of Law, and carry their pathetic slaves before the Beyl and his taaksmen to have them tell their tales and show their scars after the fact. I could have them produce the concubines and the virgin girls kept captive.

No Beyl and no taaksmen would do anything but commend me for my actions.

I leaned against the wall of the privacy room, closed my eyes, and considered my route. The fastest and easiest would be back into the room with the Feegash women, then out the window, into one of the hidden drops, and through the tunnels to my home. If luck was with me, I could have my sword and be back before anyone noticed my absence.

The less obvious way, of course, would be to head through Skirmig's house and find the hidden drop here.

It was a big house and might have several, though, and because it was a home built long ago by wealthy folks, I had no guarantee that the drop would be a simple push-through in the basement like the one in my house. Drops could be hidden in walls or behind pictures or bookshelves or in other equally clever places. I knew of false walls in the backs of closets, under carpets, behind mirrors. . . .

I could not waste the time on finding a drop here. One lay in a little copse of trees not far from Skirmig's house. That one would have to serve.

I took a deep breath, clenched my fists, and thought about the criminals. I considered their victims, all of whom still lived but would surely die if I did not intervene.

I would not think about Skirmig as a person I had cared about. That I had loved. Any love I could ever have felt for him was over. Dead. I would do what had to be done, what no one else but I *could* do.

I was Tonk, but even more and deeper than that, I followed Ethebet and served Jostfar. With all my heart and soul and strength and breath, I loved and served. And I would act, for my people and for justice.

I stepped out of the privacy room into the gathering room to discover the room almost empty. All Skirmig's guests were gone.

Skirmig, though, leaned against a table by the door, an expression of worry on his face.

"One of our guests told me you were sick," he said. "It happens sometimes with those who aren't familiar with Feegash-style cooking. It's much richer than traditional Tonk cooking. A day or two of rest and you'll be fine."

"I will, I'm sure," I said, agreeing with him and walking toward him. If I had to deal with only one man at a time, I didn't need the sword. "So where *are* our guests?"

"I sent them home. They loved your work, and I have no doubt many of them will buy from you. Perhaps even all of them, though little Jervigga mentioned it all seemed rather large and bold to her. I think you'll end up having to do more delicate variations of your patterns for some of the women."

"No doubt," I said. "Some of those women seemed terribly fragile to me." I was within arm's reach of Skirmig. Another step, a single quick move, and I could snap his neck, drag him into the privacy room, lock the door from the inside, and lie to the servants about his whereabouts. That would give me the time I needed to head out and hunt down the other men who had been present, kill them, and round up their wives to take to Law.

He touched me, and in my mind I could see myself making the moves needed to kill him. But my body didn't move. Skirmig stood staring deep into my eyes, worry clear and deeply graven on his face. "You look distraught and weary," he said. He stroked my hair and played with my warrior's braid. "My beloved, you are to be the queen of a vast and glorious kingdom—the kingdom of my heart, and so much more. No queen should ever wear such an unhappy expression on her beautiful face. No queen should ever be as clearly upset as you are." He stroked my face with his fingers, and whispered, "Let me kiss away all your sadness, beautiful Talyn."

He kissed me so gently, so tenderly, so beautifully, and a delicious lethargy seeped into my blood and my bones. It was so sweet. I felt my eyes getting heavy. My body weighed almost more than I had the power to move.

"Poor beautiful Talyn," Skirmig whispered, "this sickness has taken so much out of you. Here. I'll help you to bed, and you can sleep in luxury and silence. And when you wake, you'll feel better, I swear it." He hugged me tight. "Let me take care of you. Let me keep you safe, beloved. I'll take care of you. Always."

He scooped me into his arms, and my head fell against his shoulder. And I remembered nothing else.

12

Skirmig stared into Talyn's darkened room where she lay, a coiled shadow-shape beneath the covers. She slept deeply, and if he had done his work well enough, she would sleep for a handful of days, and wake refreshed and remembering only the version of events that he had planted in her mind.

But he was in trouble. She had been ready to kill him. Right then, right there, with no warning and no second chances; she had turned away from their love and dismissed it entirely because of some ragged view of ethics she carried deep inside her, because of some stupidly heroic need to defend a handful of useless little parasites who had been bred for nothing but men's entertainment for centuries. Feegash women of the upper classes were chosen because they were weak and servile and stupid and pretty. Feegash men used them up when they were young and then discarded them because they didn't get any better with age.

It wasn't as if they were real women. Like Talyn, for example.

Skirmig would have been more understanding, really, if Talyn had been ready to kill him over misuse of a Tonk horse; those at least existed for some purpose other than to spread their legs and scream prettily as the occasion dictated.

The edge of fear dulled, and he started getting angry. Who was she to pass judgment on the likes of him? She was a barbarian, a superstitious heathen, a sword-bearing god-ridden moralist in a world that had at last shouldered past the sheer irrelevance of morality without a second glance. *He* was a man of civilization, of refined and cultivated tastes, an appreciator of fine art and great literature and great beauty. He knew languages and philosophy; he held a clear view of the world unmuddied by sentiment or superstition; he had risen above shallow emotion and embraced reason. He knew the true value of life, which was nothing at all—life was the thing that preceded death, a mere blip, an error in the universe's silence, a bit of motion between dust and dust. If some deaths came sooner than they would have naturally, what of it? If some lives were stretched longer than they should have been, what of that? In the end, everything was dust anyway, so what did it matter how he amused himself in whatever span of years he could eke out?

He leaned against the doorframe, staring at her.

He should simply get rid of her. Bind her as she slept, bring over the diplomats and merc masters, wake her and have one last glorious go at her, but through the greddscharf with eight bodies and eight sets of eyes and hands instead of just one. Take her all the way from pleasure to pain and from pain back to pleasure and ride her all the way to the delicious sweet finale of death.

And then just walk away, knowing that he'd made a mistake and that there could never be a queen for his particular kingdom.

He could do that.

He *should* do that, because this last bit of tampering he had done with her was a shoddy bit of work; he was in the position of sweeping dirt under a rug, and watching the pile rise until it all spilled out again. He could not actually remove the memories of what those damned silly twittering whores had said to her without breaking her. All he could do was offer suggestions that nothing those women said had been important or real.

Her judgment, though, would eventually shake loose of his control, and she would return to her original conclusions. Only the next time, she would also know that he had manipulated her.

She would be both determined and angry, and she would be harder to stop.

He closed the door of her room and walked away.

He had the obvious solution before him, he recognized it, he understood its value—and he wasn't going to take it.

Why the hell not?

Because he loved her, more fool he.

He wanted to be with her because she was the other half of himself. She was weak where he was strong, strong where he was weak. She had a beauty born of intelligence and will and fierce conviction that would only grow finer and sweeter as she aged. She could come to appreciate the world as it really was over time; he was sure he could help her shake off her superstitions and her primitive moralism and discover the clarity and the freedom that lay beyond.

He loved her, and if that love was an appalling weakness, perhaps it was a weakness he needed to cherish. It could be the colorful little inclusion in the diamond he was becoming; a thing that added a bit of charm and a touch of humanity to a man on his way to perfection.

When she gained control of the Hagedwar, she would begin to see her own existence—her own place in the order of things, both as it was and as it would be with him—more clearly. She would gain a genuine understanding of who he was, of why he could do the things he did and still be worthy of her love. He did not shade the world with the foolishness of "good" or "bad"—and as she grew, neither would she.

Meanwhile, he would take his little half measures to keep her under control, and he would keep a wary watch on his back, lest she break loose and come after him at some inopportune time.

In his dream, Gair clawed his way toward Talyn, who was trapped in a cage, thrown into the sea, sinking fast. "Get the key!" she was screaming at him. "Get the key."

But he could not see a key, did not know where he might find a key, and he knew that he would not be able to save her, no matter how hard he tried.

He woke, sobbing.

I wandered through long, lovely fields of flowers, the blue skies above me filled with soft white clouds, a stream—heard but not yet seen—burbling nearby. Perhaps behind that little copse of trees.

A herd of wild horses galloped past.

Children shouted and laughed and played nearby, somewhere out of sight.

Ahh. I was back, then. To the place of my dreams and nightmares. The man in the cage was gone, but the woman in white was there. She had not been there at first, but then I'd been looking around. I'd glanced from the hill where she'd stood or sat before, and when I looked back, she was there.

She started walking toward me, something she had never done before. She wore Tonk garb of the old fashion, but all in white. White beads, white embroidery, white paint on her brow, white feathers in her warrior's braid.

She is one of Ethebet's, I thought. Like me. But who are her people? What is her clan? I did not know her tattoos or her paint.

She smiled at me, and I returned the smile; we were, after all, sisters of the sword.

She reached me and without a word dropped her pack, also white, at my feet. From it she pulled out a meal blanket and spread it before me, and then she knelt, and out of her pack drew such a feast as I had never seen. Roast birds of all sorts, great slabs of beef and caribou and moose and whale carved and steaming, gravies and sauces, fishes griddle-fried or baked, heaping plates of potatoes like my mother made, a bounty of vegetables from every corner of Hyre. Fruits of all seasons. Desserts both familiar and fanciful. Ales and wines and juices.

The white blanket grew to accommodate the things she pulled out, and I dropped to my haunches and watched her. In all my life I had never seen such a variety of foods in one place.

And when the blanket groaned with good food and good drink, and when I was sure she must certainly stop, she began to pull other things out of her bag. My jewelry. Grand houses on good high ground—horse-houses and spider-houses in taaks across Hyre, and across the seas in Tandinapalis. Herds of horses. Gems and metals. People who bowed to me and served me and brought me all that I commanded. I was . . . a Beyl? No. More powerful even than that. I stood astride a world, and held the world in my care.

With that much power, I thought, I could do so much good.

When at last she finished, when what seemed to me to be nearly everything in the world lay before me on that white cloth, she pulled one final thing from her bag, and held it in her hand. It was my soldier's flask, marked with the Shielder emblem, filled always with water.

"You stand at the place where your one path becomes two,"

she told me. "On the one path, you will have all of this." Her free hand made a sweeping gesture that encompassed everything that lay on the white blanket before me. "On the other path, you will have this." And she held up my flask.

I looked at the banquet, at the riches, at my work, at the dreams of Tonks made real—vast spaces and good horses and houses on hills. I started looking closer, at first casually, and then with increasing urgency, and when at last I was sure I had seen everything the woman's banquet offered, I said, "I cannot find water here."

She smiled at me. "No. The water is here." And she held up the flask.

I reached out and touched it—the flask felt cool and slightly damp to my fingertips, and I knew the water in it would be fresh and clear and cold.

I looked at the rich feast, at all the wonderful things to eat and drink. At all the wonderful things to have. I reached out a hand, thinking, If I did not have water, I would still have ale. And wine. And all the fresh fruits in season. I would not want. Except for water itself.

What is water? In a physical sense it is life in its simplest form—without it, we die. But the woman in white did not offer me merely physical water, any more than she offered me houses and horses on a blanket.

So what is water when it is more than water? It is purity. Simplicity. It is truth unvarnished and undecorated. It is a promise. It is quiet, and silence.

And she offered it to me in my Shielders flask.

Honor. Promises made. Promises kept. The truth.

She saw me looking at my flask, and then at my jewelry, and the horses, and the wide green hills.

"Neither path holds promises beyond what you see. Know that both may hold grief and hardship. And both hold death at the end, as do all paths. We are mortal, after all."

I nodded.

Reached back and touched my warrior braid.

Like all humans, man and woman, I am many things. But I am, at last, Ethebet's creature. More than everything else that defines me, my choice to follow her dictates and precepts defines me. Ethebet's path is the path of service, of hardship, of honor and silence, of promises made and promises kept. Ethebet's path is water to me. It is my life.

I reached out, and from the woman in white I took my flask. She nodded.

"If you took the flask, I was to give you one other thing." She smiled at me. "By Ethebet's behest, I give you a sword. A good, strong sword that will serve you on the path you take. Wield it wisely and well, knowing that you do so in Ethebet's name, and with her blessing."

And from the white bag, she produced a plain sword in a plain sheath. It bore no ornamentation, nor was it made in the Tonk style. It was flat and dull and lacking in grace, the hilt wire-wrapped, the pommel pyramidal, the crosspieces heavy and serviceable. I pulled it from its sheath, dismayed to find rust on the blade and dried blood in the runnels, and the edges dull and nicked. It had seen service, this blade, and poor care.

Dismayed, I looked at the woman in white.

I saw amusement in her eyes. "It needs a bit of care," she admitted. "But nowhere in all the world is there another blade that will serve you as well."

She swept a hand across the blanket, and the banquet vanished. She rose, and the blanket leapt into her pack, and she slung her pack across her shoulder with the ease of a Conventional on a march.

She offered me her hand, and I took it, and she pulled me to my feet, and then leaned forward and kissed my forehead. "Go with grace, sister," she said. "You are Ethebet's daughter, with whom she is well pleased."

And then she was gone.

I could still hear the children playing. Could still see the horses galloping. The fields were still fragrant, covered with thick grasses and wildflowers.

But the sky grew dark, and the wind turned bitter cold, and suddenly the children's laughter turned to screams that faded into the distance. Fires flickered on the horizons all around me, burning the fields. Burning toward me. Hemming me in. And riders came galloping toward me before the flames, swords raised, screaming for my head.

I woke, clawing at my blanket for the sword Ethebet had given me, and sat up gasping. I had no sword. I had no flask.

I did, however, have a desperate need to use the sitter.

I dragged myself out of the enormous Tonk concubine bed and half crawled to the privacy room attached to my room. And relieved myself, and was sick at the same time.

When I was done, I cleaned up the mess, crawled into the shower and turned the water on, and let the warmth and the wetness sluice over me, cleaning me, bringing me back to the real world from the strange, nonsensical place of my nightmares.

I had no strength. I could not remember ever having felt so weak or so sick. My head throbbed and my belly felt fair to touch my spine, even as the thought of food made me sicker.

I tilted my face into the water and stuck out my tongue, and lapped a little.

It helped. It was soothing.

After a bit I found my way to my feet, and leaned against the shower wall for a few moments longer. At last I turned off the shower and dried off and wrapped a towel around myself and made my way back to the bed, holding on to the wall to keep myself up.

I realized as I was climbing beneath the covers that Skirmig stood in the doorway watching me.

"At last you're awake," he said, and crossed the room and helped me pull the covers up. "Three days, and I had begun to despair of you waking up again."

I lay with my head on soft pillows, with fine-woven sheets against my naked skin, on a mattress that cradled me beneath blankets that warmed me, trying to get his statement to make sense.

"It can't have been three days," I said. "I remember the banquet, and getting sick at the end of it, and you helping me in here—but that can only have been hours ago."

"Three days," he said. "With the morning of the fourth nearly here. You have not moved, have not made a sound, have not opened your eyes once in all that time, and even my healer, who is a calm and sensible man, was growing frantic."

I frowned. "What . . . happened to me?"

"You were poisoned," he told me. "One of my colleague's

wives, acting in the pay of an Eastil agent, put poison into the dark ale. Three of my colleagues are dead, and you nearly were."

I closed my eyes, remembering the dark ale, and two of the diplomats and one of the merc masters trying it at my recommendation, and all of them liking it enough to indulge freely. It was Tonk ale, though, so they were not likely the targets. The ale had been there for me.

But they were dead and I was not.

I'd had more of the ale than any of them. But they were dead . . . and I was not.

That didn't make sense.

I was not a Beyl to drink a bit of poison every day that I might foil attempts to kill me by poison.

They were dead. I was not.

My head throbbed, and I closed my eyes.

Instantly Skirmig was at my side, holding my hand, saying, "Stay with me, beloved. Stay with me. Live." He squeezed my hand. "Let me bring you food. Broth, maybe some flatbread, something gentle for your stomach. You must eat something."

With my eyes still closed, feeling that I was falling into a bottomless well as the room spun madly around me, I said, "Just water. Good spring water." My voice sounded far away to my own ears.

That answer seemed very funny to me, but I wasn't sure why.

I don't know whether he brought the water or not, for I fell down into sleep again.

"You're up already?"

Gair, who had with the greatest of difficulty managed to drag himself down the steep stairs from the loft, stood teetering against a post. He felt like hell. The silver thing the healer had jammed between his ribs had finally come out, and he could feel the dampness of something oozing into the dressing. Maybe pus. Maybe blood. His skin hurt. His muscles hurt. Godsall, even his teeth hurt. He'd waited until the bastard's two spies left to get supplies; he started for the stairs as soon as he heard their voices and Idrann's, and then heard the front door close. He had to talk with the healer.

"I'm up," he said. Speaking provoked a paroxysm of coughing, and he ended up clinging to the pillar to keep from falling to the floor.

"Good Jostfar, man, you need to be lying down," the healer said.

But Gair shook his head. "Have to . . . get my strength back. Fast. Only . . . do that if . . . I start moving."

The healer, who had been boiling bandages, stopped and studied him with eyes both curious and wary. "Why? What's the hurry?"

"I dreamed again that . . . Talyn needed me. That I was . . . too weak . . . to help her."

The wariness went away and Idrann shook his head and laughed. "You've had a fever. You're going to dream strange things. But they don't mean anything. Talyn's fine; you don't know her, but I do. I've known her since she was a child. If ever there was a woman who could take care of herself, that's the woman. That Feegash bastard has more on his hands with her than he'll ever handle, I swear it to you."

"He cheats," Gair said, and started coughing again.

Now Idrann looked interested. "Cheats? What do you mean?"

Gair clung to the pillar, wishing he could be back in the cot with the blanket pulled over him, where he didn't hurt so much and where breathing didn't feel like it was going to kill him. The coughing racked him until at last he sagged to hands and knees and gave himself over to it fully.

He coughed, and yanked off the thin shirt the healer had put on him, and spit into it. And coughed and spit some more.

Idrann came over and watched him. "You did need to be up," he said. "You get that all up and out of your lungs and you'll start breathing better, and start healing better."

Gair, in agony, with every cough feeling like it was taking pieces of his lungs out with it, had a hard time being appreciative.

The spell passed at last, though, and the healer took the shirt, and rolled it into a ball, and found another for him. "I need to change your dressings now, too," he said. "It'll be easier if you're up."

The healer pulled bandages off, washed the wounds with

something that burned like fire, and put new dressings on, and Gair kept from screaming only by forcing himself to remember that Talyn needed him. He could not afford to be weak.

"You're healing fast," Idrann said. "I wish your friend was doing half as well."

"So . . . do I," Gair said. He blinked back tears of pain, and said, "Is his fever . . . any less?"

"No," Idrann said. "There is a poison deep in some of his wounds that I cannot reach with any of my medicines or tools. If he had the will to live, I think he would do better. But he is drifting away."

"You have to . . . save him."

"I'm doing everything I can. But at the last, he has to want to be saved. And nothing has called to him the way these nightmares of yours have called to you."

"She's . . . going to need us . . . both. The . . . bastard has done . . . something to her. Something . . . bad. Hale and Snow Grell and I are going to have to get her out of there."

Idrann said, "I have no wish to make a fool of myself over fever dreams. But I confess I am uneasy with her long absence, and with the bastard's excuses and explanations when he came to gather her things."

Gair nodded.

Idrann sighed. "I have a way of reaching Talyn's father. One that will be hidden from the bastard and his spies. I can send her father to her, and if there is a problem, he can take care of it. But why are you so sure these dreams are not just your sickness?"

"I'm . . . not a dreamer. And the dreams—they're always . . . the same."

"Tell me," the healer said, but Gair heard the voices of the spies coming back with the supplies. "Help me," he said, and started climbing the ladder. Snow Grell appeared at Idrann's side at a word, and he and Idrann pushed Gair up into the loft as quickly as they could; Idrann was covering him with a blanket, and he was coughing like one possessed, when the bastard's spies came in the door.

Neither Gair nor Idrann would give away the fact that Gair had been up. The Tonk and the Eastils were odd allies in this new situation, in which the Feegash were their mutual enemy. The alliance was something they understood, and at the heart of it stood Talyn, who had placed them firmly on the same side. Her side.

Gair lay back and stared at Hale, who slept in silence, waxy and frighteningly still, and Snow Grell, who hovered over them like a ghost.

He wished that Talyn would visit Hale in *his* dreams, so that Hale, too, would wake with a hunger to live, and to fight. For Gair did not see how—even if he got his strength back—just he and Snow Grell could save her against the bastard and all the bastard's servants. And Gair would not see his home again until he knew Talyn was safe in hers.

He had sworn it. So it would be.

I woke, sick as death, to angry pounding on a door, and the sound of my father's voice.

"You have my daughter here. I went to her house to find her, and her servants told me she now lived here. With you. Is this how her own family is to find out about your arrangement? That she does not come to sit at table for three long weeks, and then we discover the news from one of your lackeys?"

I was not in my own house? Where was I?

I heard Skirmig speaking then, and I realized that was where I was. In Skirmig's house. Did I want to be in Skirmig's house?

He said, "I had a party to introduce her to my colleagues and their wives the day she moved in. An Eastil plotted to poison someone at that meeting. Three of my colleagues died. She nearly did."

I'd been poisoned? How did I remember none of that?

"Did you not think her family might wish to know of her near disaster?" I heard my father snarl.

And Skirmig, his voice soothing. "I have not thought at all, in truth. I have been beside myself with worry, and tending to her care myself."

And then my father's angry footsteps in the hall, and Skirmig hurrying behind him, saying, "Wait, let me at least see that she's awake—"

And the door swung open.

I saw my father bending over my bed, asking me if I was well. And heard myself assuring him that I was. But I could barely keep my eyes open, and every time I looked at Skirmig, I got sleepier and sleepier.

I do not know how long after he visited I woke up feeling strong again and hungry as a winter wolf.

But somehow I went from being sick for a long time to being healthy again, with the whole period surrounding that illness an unpleasant, vague memory.

"The ones who hurt you and killed my colleagues are dead," Skirmig told me. "They've been tried, and the conspiracy— which was aimed at both the Feegash and the Tonks—has been crushed, both here and in the Eastil Republic."

Good, I thought; I could stop worrying about what the Eastils were going to do to us and get back to my work.

He fed me, I ate. I shook off the fact that I had been sick for a month—at least I was not dead, as his two colleagues were. I was grateful for his close care, grateful that he had healers who had dealt with the Eastil poisons and who had been able to save my life.

I owed Skirmig a great deal, and felt well enough to show my gratitude.

He was tender with me, and happy to see me up and around again, and he insisted that I wait a day or two before starting in with my work, even though I was eager to start.

And then, when I pushed to get back to my jewelry work, he insisted that we start back in on the magic again, before I lost all the ground I had gained and since I might be able to find a way within the Hagedwar to make sure such a thing as had happened to me never happened again.

Which made sense to me. The jewelry would wait a little longer. The magic, though, called to me. I knew the casting of the Hagedwar as well as I knew the trick of stepping into the View. I could trace the energy that moved through it, from the relatively simple central core to the odd areas at the periphery. I eagerly anticipated working with the magic itself, and when I said so, Skirmig wasted no time; he stood beside me at the Edge and carefully demonstrated three techniques he said were essential to anyone who would shape the world through the Hagedwar.

He was shocked that I could create the Hagedwar as well as he could, but he got over it quickly enough.

We stood on the Edge, and his Hagedwar hung beside mine in the darkness, and they would have been indistinguishable to the casual observer. There are no wandering observers at the Edge, of course. And I could see differences in our castings. Mine had purer colors, and radiated fractionally brighter. Skirmig's played host to slightly muddier energies, and though he didn't seem to notice it, I saw tiny flaws in his geometry, where Will of God and Will of the Soul did not line up precisely opposite each other.

I said nothing. I'm not such a fool that I'll openly criticize a lover on the work he knows best and values most.

Skirmig did not seem to notice any differences at all. He was simply proud of my accomplishment.

He stepped to within a handbreadth of his own Hagedwar and said, "Each of the three skills you must master to effectively cast a spell within the Hagedwar is a form of transportation, and if you remember that, you will not fail at any of them. If ever you think of any of them as anything else—most especially if you think of any of them as an act of creation—your work will shatter before you can reach out and use it."

"I'm ready," I said. "Show me."

He chuckled. "My own teachers would wail and tear their hair at your methods of learning, my love. I had months of lectures and mathematics before I came to this point."

"I learn by doing." I shrugged. "I fear I would never have learned by dry lecturing."

He stepped into the one of the sections of the Hagedwar where the Flesh and Thought of Man intersected only the Eye of the World. I thought of it as one of the red-on-blue bits. He told me, "The first essential skill is the transportation of communication." He took his familiar cross-legged pose within the section, and did something . . .

You can hear my voice inside your head now.

"Yes. Do it again."

Note where I sit within the Hagedwar, and how I align myself to the flow of the magic.

I thought I caught it that time. It was a variation on the method Shielders used to communicate within the View, but actually a bit more convenient. "I see," I said, seeing in fact that Skirmig acted as much out of ritual and superstition as out of need. Which way he faced mattered not at all, any more than the position he took mattered. But I stepped into the same section of my own Hagedwar, settled myself in the same position, and concentrated on using the energy. As always, my first instinct—born of long habit—was to throttle the power available to me down to a trickle, but I caught myself and used it at full strength.

I formed my thoughts upon the stream of power I set in motion, and directed that stream to Skirmig.

Give word if you hear me.

Nothing.

I refined my aim and tried again. *Do you yet hear me?*

I hear you! His excitement reached me in a good approximation of a shout.

So. It was possible to be too "loud" even when no sound was involved. I winced at the echo still inside my head, and Skirmig caught my reaction. "I'm sorry, beloved."

He stepped out of his Hagedwar and waved me out of mine. "You're phenomenal," he told me. "I have never seen anything like you."

"Don't be too impressed," I told him. "The movement of thought is not so different from our means of communication within the View. I found it easy enough to adapt what I already knew to what you showed me."

"That's good. Anything you can do to speed this process along is good."

I studied him for a moment, and had the oddest fleeting feeling that I could not trust him. I shook it off—I suspect everyone has such feelings about their lovers or spouses from time to time—and asked him, "Is there some reason for haste?"

"Only this—that the basics bore me, and I can't teach you the exciting work until you've mastered the basics."

I laughed. In that way, the use of the Hagedwar had nothing in common with work within the View. I had never spent an instant within the View, no matter how mundane my tasks or how repetitive their nature, that I would have described as boring. The View compelled even when it did not enchant.

"I'll be quick as I can learning this, then," I promised him.

But the next task he tried to teach me proved an immediate and forceful stopping point.

It was the movement of matter.

"You can move a physical object from one place to another by the force of your will," Skirmig said. "You can move it unchanged, or you can change its form, though the latter requires an exquisite skill."

"Change its form?" The idea of that stopped me.

"It's a simple enough thing in concept, if not in execution. You can bring heat to the wick of a candle, causing it to burn. You can move the naturions of a bar of gold into the form of a statuette by the force of your intent. But you can do these things only if you have clear vision of both exactly what you are changing and what form you wish it to take."

I stopped him. "Naturions? What are those?"

"The tiniest bits of any object that make it what it is. Gold can be filed into dust, and each filing is still gold, yes?"

"Yes."

"And if you had a small enough file, you could file those filings into smaller filings. And so on. But there must come a point where not even the smallest file could separate into two the filings. What remain are naturions."

"You can change people by moving their . . . naturions . . . around? Animals? Plants?"

"There are problems with that. Altering the forms that life takes may be one of the powers available within the tograms the Feegash cannot yet use. Or it may be that naturions exist only in things that have no life. For it is quite possible to reorder the naturions of a corpse or a piece of well-dried wood. But living wood and living flesh alike resist such change."

"Good," I said. The universe held powers within it that I simply did not want. And I was relieved to know that others did not have them, either.

Still, I tried to imagine taking some of my stock of metal and reshaping it by magic instead of by my hand—and instantly I could think of a dozen things I would do. Forms that I could not create with my hands, I could still see in the eye of my mind, and the whole idea of being able to make them excited me tremendously. I was hungry for this grand chance to try something that might be wonderful.

But when Skirmig demonstrated this skill, I discovered that it had no parallels in the magic I knew. And I discovered, too, that I could not see everything that he did to get the results he got.

I wasn't sure if it was the very concept of naturions that eluded me. Or if I could not clearly see the candle Skirmig wanted me to light. Or if I could not call a hot enough heat to the wick.

"The candle is no simple test," Skirmig said when I had tried two dozen times and had failed by the same number. "It is essential; you must be able to do it to move on. But perhaps you could simply move something small from one hand to the other. Take a ring, perhaps, and hold it in your left hand, get the feel of it, make sure you know its appearance, and then simply transport it into your right hand."

We dropped into the physical world, and Skirmig took off two rings that he wore, and kept one and handed me the other.

"Watch," he said, and we moved back to the Edge. He stepped into his Hagedwar, this time into a togram where the Will of the Soul and the Body and Flesh of Man intersected.

He held up the ring between thumb and forefinger in his left hand. I watched him, watched the ring glow with a brief burst of white light, and then it was in his right hand.

I could not see how he had done it.

"Again," I said.

He demonstrated again.

Still I couldn't see it. "Once more."

He did the trick one more time.

I felt for the movement of energy, tried to comprehend the vast power that lay behind what had not been a particularly effortful action, but it eluded me.

"I'm done for today, I think," I told him. "I need to be able to rest on this for a while and see if I can make sense of it."

Gair woke to a chill in the air, and a feeling that something was wrong. He didn't move anything but his eyes. He looked through the shadows, but could see nothing out of place. "Snow Grell? Hale?" he whispered. "Did you hear anything?"

Over in the corner on the floor, Snow Grell was instantly awake. Out of the corner of his eye, Gair could see him roll silently to hands and feet, and move soundlessly to the edge of the loft. After a moment Snow Grell stood up and whispered, "Nothing moving down there."

Hale, however, didn't answer at all. He'd always been a sound sleeper; not the best of qualities in a field soldier, but he'd made up for that by being brilliant when he was awake. Lately his sleep had been almost normal. And only two days before, his fever had broken at last and Master Idrann had declared the worst of his infections cleared and his chances of survival greatly improved. But suddenly Gair realized he didn't hear Hale breathing.

"Hale," Gair whispered again, for he did not wish to wake light-sleeping spies downstairs. "Wake up, damnall." He reached over and shook Hale's shoulder.

Hale didn't move.

Gair sat up, swung his legs over the edge of the cot with difficulty, and leaned forward, hand just above Hale's nose and mouth.

Snow Grell came over and crouched by Hale's cot.

No air moved. A lump rose in Gair's throat, and he shook his head. Snow Grell laid an ear on Hale's chest and lifted it a long, painful moment later. "His heart does not beat."

Gair clenched his fists at his sides, and the tears rolled down his cheeks unimpeded.

"He should have lived."

Snow Grell said, "He was too tired of fighting to go on, Gair." He went to his bedroll and pulled something from the small pack he kept with him always. He knelt beside Hale again and quickly wove a single long feather through Hale's short hair. "That your spirit may fly free," he whispered, and with clenched fist thumped once upon his own chest. "You were my brother, and I honor your passing."

Gair came from people who had no graceful way to release those they'd lost, and no formal way of saying good-bye that did not include a parade with a train of mourners, drummers, singers, family, and friends. Hale, in enemy lands, would have no parade. No mourners, no drummers, no singers, no family.

But he had two friends.

"I commend your spirit to your god," he said at last, placing his hand on Hale's arm. "And I will remember you forever. You were a good friend, and a good warrior."

They sat in silence with him for a while, and then Gair said, "We have to get him downstairs. Maybe we can move him outside in the cold and bury him in the snow until thaw. We can find a way to get him out in the wilds so we can have a regular pyre for him."

Snow Grell said, "No. You think that diplomat bastard's spies are not waiting like vultures for your bodies? They are. Now Hale has died; he's done with his body and would not resent us using it to our good. Let the vultures have it. They believe you are near death; his death will only help strengthen that belief. Lie still when they come to take him away. Cough and moan, beg for water, cry out at the sights of spirits hanging over your bed, and they will think that you will soon join him. And they will report these things to the bastard."

Gair knew it was true. The thought of Hale thrown to the sea or dumped into a pit and covered with dirt made his heart ache. But Snow Grell was right.

So he crawled beneath his blankets, and pulled them up to his chin, and feigned coughing spells and the visions of the dying, and Snow Grell went down to fetch Idrann and the spies so that they might take Hale's body away.

The spies came up the stairs, and their beady eyes peered from Hale to Gair and back to Hale. "What of the other one?" one of them said. "How much longer do you think he'll last?"

"There's no telling," Idrann said, keeping his voice to a whisper. "Sick as he is, it could be any time."

The spies didn't complain about moving Hale down to the main room. They didn't complain about anything. Ever. They didn't talk with each other much, either, and never spoke conversationally. But they watched everything, so that Gair could only exercise to build his strength by sneaking into the root cellar in Talyn's house well after dark, when at last the two freaks retired to the bedroom and closed the door.

Gair closed his eyes so that he would not have to see the empty space where Hale's cot had stood.

He would repay the Feegash for his men's deaths, for had they not brought their strange, unwelcome peace, he and his men would have been part of a normal prisoner exchange, and all who survived would have lived to see home. And when he was doing his repaying, he would start with that diplomat who had taken Talyn away, and who, Gair's nightmares insisted, was hurting her.

13

"One of your Eastils died last night," Skirmig told me. "I'm sorry to have to bear such sad news." He touched my face and looked into my eyes, and said, "You must not let this distress you; we knew when you took them in that they were not likely to survive. This one lived far longer than I would have thought, seeing him that first time."

I had been near tears, but Skirmig's touch soothed me. "And the other?" I asked.

"Near death. He probably will not survive the week, I'm told."

"Do you know which one died?" I asked.

"No." He gave me an odd look. "Does it matter?"

"It doesn't," I said. But it did matter. I saw gray eyes and thought of cold, clear water, and felt once again the disorienting sense of a shared past, or perhaps a shared future, that I had known for just an instant with Gair, and my flesh prickled from a sudden chill, and I rubbed my arms. And then I lied to Skirmig again, and felt a wash of guilt. "I simply wanted to know which of them I should remember in my prayers."

Skirmig smiled at that. "I did not know you prayed."

"Every night before I sleep," I told him. "Which you would know if you shared my bed with me at night, and not just in the daylight hours."

He laughed a little, his gaze not meeting mine, and took the piece of silver I was working. While he held it up to study it, he said, "I thrash in my sleep, and walk, and talk, I am much plagued by restlessness. So I sleep alone and lock my doors to prevent myself from wandering in my sleep. I do not wish to wake and find myself lost in a snowstorm or stepping off a dock into the sea." He turned the silver over in his hands. "This is remarkable," he said. "Already sold?"

"To your friend Arkil. For his wife."

Skirmig kissed me and said, "I'll let you get back to your

work, then. I'd like to sit with you this evening and practice physical transportation again, though. I am quite certain you almost have it, and perhaps this time we'll find the way to let you grasp the trick of it. Once you have that, we can move on to the third essential, transport of will. But you must have the element of the physical firmly in hand before you venture into the realm of will."

"After dinner," I said, and he turned and went out, shutting my door behind him.

Leaving me to think of the lie I'd told him, and to wonder why I had kept the truth from him. It was such a foolish thing, really.

Since recovering from my illness, though, I'd been having recurring nightmares about the Eastil, Gair. In these nightmares, I was in terrible danger and begging for him to rescue me. I was in pain, bleeding, near death, with a monster hovering over me who was bent on destroying me. I was always fighting, always struggling. But I was losing, slipping away. And each time, Gair would leap to my defense.

I always woke before the Eastil could destroy the monster, but I never doubted in those dreams that he would prevail, and that I would be safe at last.

The dreams embarrassed me, though. I could not understand what was causing them. I had never been happier in my life. Skirmig and I were together, we were in love. We had so much in common—our researches in magic, my art? . . . Well, and each other. Nothing beyond that, really, that I could find, so I suppose we did not have so much in common after all. But what we had seemed to be enough.

We made love with a wildness that grew stronger and more passionate rather than less, and each time we touched was an adventure. If sometimes our lovemaking seemed to get out of hand, and if I still felt that odd sensation of being watched each time, I had learned to push aside my concerns. Because Skirmig loved me, and I knew that as I knew the sun would rise each morning.

I was neglecting my family terribly; I had not been home since I recovered from my illness. But I had been too busy, and I had to hope they would understand. Skirmig and I agreed that once I got caught up on my commissions, we would start making a regular visit to my parents' home each week on Jostfarday, to sit at table with my other siblings and share a meal.

And as I neglected my family, I was also neglecting Ethebet, whose morning exercises I had not done since recovering. I had not pursued the situation with Beyltaak's absent Shielders, though that was certainly in capable hands. Neither had I been faithful in my prayers to Jostfar, or in my visits to Temple. Skirmig was amused by my religion, and though he had not been so foolish as to try to forbid me to go, he had noted on more than one occasion that religions, his own included, did little more than steal an inordinate amount of their worshippers' time, with no apparent benefit to the worshippers. And when I looked into his eyes and he smiled at me, I found myself agreeing with him, even if I was always somewhat surprised that I did.

I was neglecting my horses; I visited them, but I no longer found any time to ride. The stable boys enjoyed them, though, putting Toghedd and Dakaat through their paces in the ring behind the house. I could see them from my window as I made jewelry, and they were both glossy and sleek and well attended.

But I was happy. I had never been happier.

So why was I having nightmares? And when I had them, where was Skirmig that I always had another man rushing to my rescue?

Mine were not the sort of dreams to be shared with a lover, I decided. Skirmig would only be hurt to find that he was not the hero of my dreams. And I loved him, and did not want to hurt him. He kept nothing secret from me; he often told me so. But this secret, trivial as it was, I decided to keep to myself anyway. Besides, I had to admit it likely that Gair was dead; he had been the worse hurt of the two when they arrived. And even if he was not dead, he would be soon.

And that was sad, I thought.

But I did not dare let myself think about gray eyes and deep courage. I did not dare question why, when I saw Gair, I was reminded of my old service canteen filled with icy spring water. Something lay within those slippery images that was too painful to face. I had no place to feel the sadness of others.

My own life was too happy to admit such sorrow or such strangeness, I decided at last, and went back to work.

That night, Skirmig and I sat across from each other in his

workroom, and I held a small cube of pure silver in my right hand.

"You're using that?" he asked.

"I have a feel for metal," I told him. "And I know this piece well. I made it today just for this exercise."

"Well enough," he said. "Let's begin."

I. dropped into the light trance that would take me to the Edge, and when I stood beside Skirmig there, cast my Hagedwar. I almost did not have to think about it anymore. It had become as much a part of me as the View. I stepped into the togram used for physical transport, and held the silver cube up. I knew its shape, its feel, and its weight, and I could see it as clearly in the realm of the Edge as I could see it in the physical world. It gleamed in my hand, reflecting the varied colors of the Hagedwar around me. It rested between thumb and forefinger in my right hand, and I wanted it in my left hand. Wanted the energies sliding past me to pick it up and carry it, right to left, make it disappear from the right . . . reappear in the—

It flared briefly with a brilliant white light, and without warning was in my left hand.

I was so surprised, I dropped it, and it fell completely out of the Edge.

In my head, I heard Skirmig's glee. *You did it. You did it! Now bring it back. You know where it is. It's on the floor of the workroom. You know what it looks like. So get it back without leaving here.*

I knew. I knew.

I wanted it in my hand. Wanted it to ride the current from the world of reality to the realm of the Edge.

A bright flash of light and it was in my right hand again.

I sat cross-legged in the heart of glowing light, passing a silver cube from hand to hand until I felt certain that Skirmig must be heartily sick of watching me do it.

And then I remembered him telling me that I could change the form of objects in this same place, in the same manner.

So in my left hand, I saw it as a cube. In my right hand, I saw it as a tiny statuette of a woman. A Tonk dancer in full regalia, every detail perfect.

And I made it move from hand to hand—and the flash of

light revealed a piece of the most exquisite silverwork I had ever seen.

I dropped out of the Edge and back into reality, wanting to see if this was a thing I had done in my mind only, or if I truly had reshaped the metal.

And in my hand stood a statuette of a Tonk dancer so perfect she might have breathed. Each hair on her head seemed to be separate and real; her clothes draped naturally, and when I held them close I could see the weaves of their different fabrics; her stance was human and lifelike; her lovely face seemed just ready to speak. She looked, I realized, just like Pada. Except she was the size of my thumb.

It was silverwork unlike anything ever done before by anyone in Hyre. It had no rubs, no flaws, no places where the artist had been forced to approximate anything because of limitations of tools or skill. Perhaps the Feegash had works like this, since they were the ones who had created the Hagedwar and studied the magic surrounding it. But if they did, they hadn't sent them to Hyre.

Skirmig slipped out of his trance and said, "Where did you go? I thought you'd lost your focus but would come right back—but you didn't."

I handed him the statuette.

He studied it. And then held it closer.

Then he rose without a word, made a gesture to me that I should wait, and ran from the room.

A moment later, he returned with a viewing glass and held the glass over the statuette for both of us to see.

She did look like Pada—even more so with her face magnified.

"I've never seen anything so perfect," Skirmig said.

Which answered my question about whether the Feegash were using magic to do art.

And then he stood her upon the floor, and stared at her, and after a moment she began to move. The movements were jerky and graceless, and bore no resemblance to a Tonk dance. But that seemed far from the point. She moved.

"How are you doing that?" I whispered, enchanted.

My little figurine spun slowly to the right, took two steps forward, two steps back, spun slowly in the other direction, and re-peated her little dance. Her arms rose and fell, rose and fell.

"Skirmig? How are you doing that?" I looked up at him. Beads of sweat slid from his forehead into his eyes and down his nose and jaw, and he wore the most intense expression I had ever seen on his face, except for when we were making love.

"Skirmig?"

He gasped, and sagged forward, and the figurine stopped dancing.

"That's the third essential," he said. "The transport of will. It's the hardest to master, and cannot be mastered at all save by one who has learned the first two essentials to perfection." He wiped sweat on his sleeve and, breathing hard but grinning, looked up at me. "That was showy. And pointless, except as a demonstration. But you had to see the power of the third essential. Giving inanimate objects the semblance of life is but one of the tasks the mastery of will can accomplish. When you have that, you have the basics of Silent Magic—and I can begin to teach you the applications that will open the world to you."

"Teach me," I said.

He laughed, delighted. "God, I love you," he told me.

"I love you, too."

But for just an instant, as I said that, I saw Gair. And he was running toward me through toppling walls and burning buildings, and he had his sword drawn and was shouting, "Hold on! Just hold on! I'm almost there!"

Outside, another howling blizzard hit, and I was feeling restless and housebound, and had the sudden mad urge to throw on coat and overpants and boots and gloves and hike down to the water-front to take a look at the old Shields Building and the dock.

I like snow, which, living in Hyre, is fortunate. We have a lot of it.

The thaw would be along soon enough, but I had somehow missed most of the winter by being indoors, and suddenly I felt that loss keenly. So while no one was looking, I slipped out the front door and hiked down the hill and through the taak.

Things kept bringing me up short. In the Heights, I found new construction all over; not buildings in the Tonk style, but ugly foreign boxes with sharp edges and narrow slit windows and tall, tall roofs. Unornamented to a one, sporting neither painted roofboards nor carved posts nor grand, wide, welcoming doors marked with the greetings of the Saints. All of them were painted the same shade of dark brown, so they stood out against the natural woods and brightly painted trimmings of *our* buildings.

Lower in the taak, I saw that not one but both of the brothels were gone. In their places were windowless buildings with the same unornamented designs and the same tall roofs. Both were painted gray, and both had signs over the doors in a language I could not read.

I went farther.

The building that had held the Star's Rest still stood, but now in a sign painted in Tonk, Eastil Common, and a third language that I had to guess was Feegashi, it said, "Wayfarerers Inn, Food, Drink, and Pleasure."

The man at the door was a Feegash servant, brown-garbed, and when he looked at me I turned away to keep him from seeing my face. I did not know why I had done such a thing; I had known nothing but kindness from Skirmig's servants, but I found myself frightened by the man in the door.

I made my way to the dock.

It had been completely rebuilt—no more tired old posts and sagging boards. The Feegash had widened it, and replaced the old post-and-beam structure with huge trunk posts and boards interlocked by the sort of joinery I'd seen before on good furniture, but not on docks. The new rails were as heavy as the old substructure had once been. Every board angled slightly down from the center to both ends so that the dock would drain off water. For some reason, it was free of snow and ice.

Salt, maybe? Or another Feegash magic at work?

Two mercenaries stood at the entrance to the docks, pikes in hand. Their flat, unwelcoming expressions slowed me down, but I wanted to see the Shields Building, so I started to go past them anyway.

"Pass?" one of them said.

"Yes," I told him. "I wish to pass."

"No," he said. "I'll need to *see* your pass."

This stopped me. I thought of the docks as they had been

when I knew them—a place for whores and gamblers to try their luck with the sailors in port, and for taaksmen to go in the daytime to watch the ships come in and see what wonders had arrived in Beyltaak.

"I need a *pass*?" How would the merchants get word of the goods they had stored in the warehouses if common folk could not walk down and take a look at it and pass the word along.

The mercenary studied me with visible contempt. "You do."

"I used to work in Shields," I said.

The two of them exchanged glances, and I saw their pike heads dip slightly before moving back to rest position. "Then you probably will not be eligible for a pass."

Always good to know that these bastards had their standards. "Where would I get a pass, assuming I could get one?"

"From either of the Masters of the Merc. You'll have to petition personally, and you'll need a reason to go on the docks. Are you a merchant with your own ships?"

"No. But I have dinner with the Masters of the Merc regularly."

In their eyes I saw nervousness. "When?"

"I'm Skirmig the Diplomat's—" What was I? I was not his wife, nor would I be. I was not affianced to him, either. I did not care to offer up our sex lives as a credential; I cared little who was someone's lover and would not expect the two of them to care, either. "—friend, business partner, and housemate," I said. "My name is Talyn. And your names are . . . ?"

It occurred to me that the rules had changed, and the Shielders were no more, and so I was no longer bound by the conventions and laws of treaties regarding the treatment of soldiers of allied forces. I could use my magic and just knock the two unreasonable fellows off the dock and onto the ice of the bay. "Shame about that big gust of wind," I could say later. "I heard both of those fellows broke both their legs in the fall. Lucky they weren't killed."

But I am my mother's daughter as much as my father's, and I can be persuasive in ways other than direct force. I wanted to see the docks down by Shields, out of my line of sight; I wanted to see what civilians were no longer permitted to see. I wanted to know if the Eastil threat truly had been crushed, or if it was hiding in Tonk warehouses and waiting for better weather.

"Our names," the ranking guard said.

"I want to be able to commend you by name to Skirmig," I said, keeping my voice cold and hard and flat.

They put their heads together, and I could not hear what they said except for the chance phrase ". . . killed the last ones who crossed . . ." when the wind died down for just an instant. They conferred, I waited. Then the senior guard turned to me and said, "What do you want to see?"

"I want to walk on the docks," I told him. "I want to stroll down to the old Shields Building and take a look at the bay."

"In the middle of a blizzard you want to do this?"

"I've lived here all my life," I told them both. "This weather is nothing of note to me."

"Walk with her," the senior guard told the other one. "I have the entry—we're not likely to have anyone else out here in this howling mess."

I walked past the senior guard, and the other one fell in beside me. We said nothing. I had nothing to say to him, and if he had anything to say to me, he had decided it wasn't worth the risk. So I was able to study the once-familiar area in relative silence.

The blizzard played games with me, lifting for just an instant to display a clear picture of one little area, then dropping a curtain over it. I had to catch impressions quickly. But I wasn't liking the ones I caught.

Everything was different. The Feegash had so overbuilt the docks that it verged on the ridiculous. The main docks were wide enough that ten horses could ride abreast. We had kept them three to four horses wide. The finger piers out into the bay offered room for perhaps six riders side by side, and there were twice as many piers as before.

The construction of the docks was heavier than I had supposed, too. The boards beneath my feet neither swayed nor rang at my footsteps. I made only as much noise as I would have made walking on heavy boards built over stone. The harbor is sheltered enough that it misses the brunt of most of the storms we get—it is for this that Beyltaak has ever been one of the choice harbors in Hyre. I could think of no justification for such excessive overbuilding—at least none I liked.

Some of the piers held massive fixed gantries that supported heavy cranes. I could not imagine what anyone could move that would require such enormous machinery; about the biggest things the Tonks ever moved by crane were horses, and they had to be moved one by one. Those cranes looked like they could support the weight of a whole herd.

The warehouses looked about the same to me, though. Still run-down, tired, old, and rather small. I would think that anyone expecting a vast increase in trade would improve the warehouses as well as the docks.

Then, however, we moved within sight of Shields. Or what had been Shields.

Fear crawled beneath my skin and my tongue suddenly felt dry in my mouth. The stone foundations and walls of the old Shields Building still stood, but new construction had easily tripled the size and height of the main building and those portions of the connected secondary buildings that I could see through the snow. I caught glimpses of rows of windows on the upper floors, and they were all of the narrow, slit Feegash sort.

Shields had been headquarters and barracks before. But now it was a fortress.

I did not stare. I turned and headed back. I did not walk out on a pier, which I had thought to do. I wanted to get away from there as quickly as I could.

I found myself afraid—for myself, for my people, for the world that I had known that was slipping away. Or being torn away.

I gave both mercenaries a brief thank-you and walked away as quickly as I could without appearing to be hurrying. I kept my head down, I leaned into the wind and snow, and I walked. No specific direction, nothing in mind.

At least nothing that I was admitting to my waking mind. My feet brought me to the doors of the main temple, and I went in. Breathed in the silence and the smell of books, and felt tears starting at the corners of my eyes.

One of the Keepers hurried up to me. "The rest are already here, but your father left word that if you arrived you were to be shown in."

I stared at him for a moment. "What day is this?"

"Jostfarday, Fiintris first."

I shivered and stared at my feet. Had some part of me known

the day and the hour? Was that part of me working in secret around the rest of me?

I almost turned and fled the temple, but I did not. Instead I followed the Keeper through the corridors of books and back to the stairs and up to the room with the red door. And I went in.

Some of them glanced at me, and Ordran, once of the Silver Shields, made room for me on the bench, but no one said anything. My father was reporting.

". . . we have added hardly at all to our numbers present," he said, "though our numbers in transit are now high. By fall before the harbor closes, we should have more than a hundred of our best people back. Senders and Shielders both, and a handful of Communications folk as well."

"Autumn will be too late," I told him. Them.

Now they all turned to look at me.

"Have any of you been to the docks recently?" I asked.

Universal shakes of the head.

Betraa said, "They let no one pass."

"They let me. Today. I walked onto the dock and down to Shields and back. We're living in peace but the mercs are building for war. The docks will accommodate whole armies of Eastils and any matériel they care to move."

"Then they are in league with the Eastils," Heldryn said.

My father snorted. "They aren't in league with us, Saints know. So if we aren't marching on the Eastils, it would seem the Eastils will soon be marching on us."

"Without Shielders and Senders and Communications, we're helpless against whatever they choose to throw at us," Heldryn said. "We have Conventionals, but not as many of them as we need. We have the tunnel armories yet. But those have ever been kept aside as a last resort, and will not serve to arm the whole of the populace."

It was true, and I knew it. "We are not yet without hope, though. I'm learning a new sort of magic, one that offers some defenses even to those who cannot reach the View. It's based in the Edge, and it works with matter and will. It isn't as directly powerful as the View—when you sit in the Hagedwar, you do not have your hands on life and death as you do when you are in the View. But one person alone can use this magic. And . . .

there are parts of it that connect to the View that the Feegash can't use. Our Shielders and Senders and Communicators will be able to work with those tograms—sections—I think. I'm still finding my way. Another week or two, perhaps . . ."

I faltered to a stop. They were all staring at me.

"This is what you're doing now that you're living with him?" Betraa asked.

"And working on my jewelry." And living a life that does not feel like my own, I thought, but I did not say that.

Away from Skirmig and his grand house and his constantly present servants, I felt like the me I used to know—the one who would never have pursued a moriiad, an outlander. Away from his smile and his gentle voice, I felt light. Free.

I felt so very, very odd. Almost as if Skirmig's house sat within a fog that had dulled my senses and slowed my thoughts. As if I could only see the fog when I was on the outside. I fidgeted with a bit of candle wax that had hardened on the table, scraping it off with a fingernail and kneading it into little shapes, and the words *I don't want to go back there* ran through my mind, and it was only when I looked up from the wax in my hands that I realized that I had spoken those very words aloud.

"But I must," I added, feeling foolish. "I have to find out what I can about the last sections of the Hagedwar. They are the ones we need the most, and I don't yet know what Skirmig can teach me about them."

Da sat there looking at me with narrowed eyes, his head tipped to one side. "You love him," he said. "You want to be with him as he wants to be with you. The two of you belong together, and I want you to reach your fullest potential, and you can do that with him." His voice when he said it lacked emotion.

And everyone in the room, me included, stared at my father as if he had taken leave of his mind.

"He's *moriiad*," Betraa and Heldryn and Da's friend Yarel said all in a breath.

I nodded. "He is. It doesn't seem to matter when I'm with him, but when I'm away from him, it's clear to me how very much that does matter. I could never spend my life with one of the morii. Never."

I've often heard it said that Jostfar laughs when mortals

speak. Even as the words fell out of my mouth, I knew he was laughing at me and my pitiful return to orthodoxy.

"You have an opportunity to observe this high-ranking Feegash at close quarters," Heldryn said. "You're in a fortunate place for us. So before you eke your last shred of magical knowledge out of the diplomat—and I have to wonder how useful such a magic could be if we have not even seen signs that the Feegash *use* magic—give us anything else that might help us."

"Anything else . . . like . . ."

Heldryn gave me a look she must have practiced on raw recruits. Had I not grown up with my mother, I would have been impressed. "When the other Feegash come to the house to consult with him—"

I held up a hand. "They don't. No one comes to the house except hired tradesmen. Once his fellow diplomats and the merc masters came to his house for a dinner party, but . . ."

I suddenly felt lost. I could remember the guests being there—it was the day I'd sliced my way out of that damned dress. I could remember meeting with them for the first time, noticing how helpless the women were, sitting at table and eating and talking with the men. I could remember the women all sitting silent, barely eating, keeping their eyes down. And then, a frightening blank.

Something had been wrong. Terribly wrong. My gut insisted that there had been something strange about the women. Something . . . horrible.

But I couldn't remember what.

One of the women had poisoned me and several of the men. I wanted to think I'd noticed the poisoner acting strangely. Or that perhaps the suggestions of wrongness in my mind came from my first reaction to the poison.

But deep inside me, a tiny voice whispered that there had been something else, something hidden in the shadows, something . . . terrible.

Something about the women.

I realized suddenly that I'd stopped talking, that everyone in the room was staring at me. "I'm sorry," I said. "The day everyone met in Skirmig's home was the day I was poisoned by an Eastil spy, and . . ." I faltered, and shook my head, trying to clear out the odd confusion. "I can't remember everything that happened that day."

But now they weren't staring at me. They were staring at Da.

"She was poisoned?" Heldryn asked in a voice harsh as the blizzard outside. "By Eastils? And you said *nothing* to us?"

My father had the same confusion on his face that I knew I had on mine. He sat at the far end of the table looking at me, frowning like I was a stranger he'd seen somewhere once, and he was trying to remember when and where.

"I went to see her," he said slowly. "At the diplomat's home. She was still very sick, but was starting to get better. She assured me that she was going to live, and the diplomat was giving her the best of care."

He rested his face in one hand. "That can't be right," he said. "I left then. Left her there, and didn't go back to check on her again. I told her mother . . . something. Because Lett was desperate to go see her; to find out why she hadn't been home a single Jostfarday since the diplomat sat at table with us." His other hand joined the first, muffling his voice. "What did I tell Lett? That can't be right, though. I wouldn't have left Talyn there so sick without going back every day to see that she was mending." He put his hands down, looked me in the eye, and said in a soft, shaken voice, "I would never have just left you there. Never. But I did. Why did I do that?"

"I don't know why I haven't been coming home Jostfardays."

"Something foul is going on in the diplomat's home," Heldryn said. She watched me, but said, "While you were at the house, Radavan, did you eat or drink anything?"

"No. He did not offer me so much as a cup of water."

Heldryn, unblinking, stared into my eyes. "You spoke of the Feegash magic. You're learning it. Is it something that could control the mind?"

"I don't know," I told her. "I've seen nothing yet that would work so. But if Skirmig is doing such a thing, he will hardly show me that part of the magic."

"Do you think such a thing might be possible?"

I thought about the Hagedwar, and about the sections I had not explored. The areas beyond the red. And the few areas within the red that Skirmig had simply ignored. He'd said nothing about them, had given no explanation for why we had not moved into them. It wasn't that he'd seemed to be hiding anything; it was as if those areas had not truly mattered.

"I think there are more things I did not know than I thought at first," I told her. "The Hagedwar is a system with tremendous power. The Tonk have always scoffed at the idea of tampering with the thoughts or actions of individuals, because through the View, we would have to slide inside of the person we hoped to control, and while we controlled him, we would be completely outside our own bodies. But with the Hagedwar . . . it's subtle magic. It's delicate in its workings. Its very indirectness, I think, gives it advantages that the View has never had. If tampering with thoughts is one of those advantages, I cannot yet prove it." I sighed. "But something is happening here, and I have no better explanation to offer." I shook my head. "I'll watch Skirmig," I said, "but Skirmig is jealous of me, I think, and my time spent with anyone else. I would not look to him as a source of danger. We must remember who our enemy is. There are far too many Eastils in Beyltaak now, and the Feegash have already uncovered one plot against us. We know who our true enemy is. We have always known."

"Clearly," Heldryn said. She stood and turned away from me. "Find out all you can from him. Learn anything that will let us raise up a new army against Eastil plots and treachery. We'll have trained people come the autumn. But anything we can do in the meantime can only be to our good."

"I need to be getting back," I said. "The servants will miss me, or Skirmig will. And I want to be able to say I did nothing but walk about in the blizzard and visit the docks and the temple. If I am gone too long, I'll have a harder time making that story sound true."

I stood to leave, and it was a somber, thoughtful group of men and women who told me, "Go with Ethebet."

My father, though, rose and walked out the door with me. He rested a hand on my arm to stop me and, when I turned to look at him, said, "I'm sorry, Talyn. I don't know how I managed to fail you so badly when you needed me. I swear by Ethebet's braid that if ever you need me again, I'll be there for you."

"Don't," I told him. "Don't blame yourself for what happened, and don't swear on Ethebet for anything that concerns me. I'll be fine. Take care of Ma and the rest of them. Especially Rik. Tell him I love him and I've missed him, and when I fix whatever it is that is so wrong, I'll come sit with him in his workroom and we'll make jewelry together." I touched the brooch that pinned my cloak. "Tell him I still wear what he made for me."

"I'll tell him," my father said.

"Tell them all I love them."

"I will." He hugged me, and whispered in my ear, "Watch your back."

"Always," I promised. "You, too, Da. We'll win this yet."

14

Gair, who yearned for the sun, came to live only in darkness. At the moment when the spies went off to sleep, Snow Grell woke him, and they crept down to the root cellar of Talyn's house, and they fought hand to hand and lifted heavy things and ran in place, building their strength.

Before the sun rose, and with it the bastard's spies, Master Idrann would tap softly on the trapdoor that led to the root cellar, and both Gair and Snow Grell would return to their places—Snow Grell to go out to clean stables and wash linens, Gair to lie abed and pretend to be dying.

Had the spies not been regular in their habits, Gair was not sure how he would have returned his battered body to health. But they were. They were increasingly like the gear-work automatons the Panessans of northern Velobrina brought each summer to the cities of the Eastil Republic to amuse the masses in the gathering halls and street theaters. They spoke not a word to each other from one hour to the next; they followed a pattern in which the tall one went out each day to the market for fresh foods, and the short one came up and hovered over Gair, staring at him and sniffing at him as if the spy were a dog. Each day the short spy had a harder time negotiating the stairs to the loft; each day the tall spy brought home a slightly lighter load, until at last he carried almost nothing and let one of the market boys do most of the work.

Gair realized one morning, when he was pretending to be in the throes of a fever dementia, and was speaking of ghosts and demons at the foot of his bed, that the spy was dying.

That both of them were dying.

They were young men, and when they had come to Talyn's house they had been strong. Yet now they were gaunt and tottered about like ancient invalids, their once-sharp sight all but blinded, their once-acute hearing dulled.

The deathwatch that had been going on since he arrived in Talyn's house still went on, Gair realized. Only the ones edging ever nearer to death had changed.

Before dawn on the seventh day of the month of Havrigdas, upon which fell the high holy day of Badaag—the day of spring equinox, and which that year came upon Ethebetsday—I dressed not in the Shielders' uniform which I had worn every Badaag since I was a young girl, but in traditional Tonk warrior dress. I braided beads and feathers into my hair, separating out a few thin strands at the front that I wove into a sacrificial braid. A little thicker than most years, that braid, but I had a lot to ask. I painted the pattern of my clan on my forehead in bright blue and deep forest green, and strapped an empty scabbard between my shoulder blades. Then I left the house before anyone else was stirring and walked to temple for the first time since my visit to the docks and temple during the blizzard.

The sun rose over the horizon while I was in the streets, and for the first time in longer than I could remember, I heard the voice of the taak breathe out "Haabudaf aveerzak." I said the blessing, and felt the power of it—that we were in that moment all together, my people and I. That somewhere in the world the sun was always rising, and anywhere that there were Tonks, that blessing would be offered. So that all day every day, and all night every night, we were one people speaking with our god, and we were blessed.

We were Jostfar's people. The long pale light of dawn lay across my face as I walked through the cold to temple, and the ringing of the bells welcoming the Sparrow's hour could not drown out the sound that echoed in my mind of my people in the blessing of the day. I was part of all this, and more at that moment than at any time before in my life, I understood what it meant, and why it mattered. I had been away from the traditions, away from the cadences and the rhythms of the day, away from being part of something bigger than me.

I was a part of the Tonks of Tandinapalis, part of the Tonks in their little colonies in the Islands of Fallen Sun, part of the Bhekian Tonks, part of the taaksmen and the nomads wherever they stayed and wherever they wandered. No matter where we were, my people would this day go to temple and offer our prayers and our sacrifices to Jostfar, and ask for guidance from our saints. We would consult the same sayings looking for guidance, ask for blessings for our people, remember our ancestors and our families.

And in that moment I realized that in doing so, we did not simply reach out to Jostfar. We reached out to each other. We held out our hands to one another—as if we were all standing together within the View—and we affirmed our place in the world to ourselves and to each other.

Our power as a people was everything that we were, and everything that had come before. All that we shared made our fabric strong. And for this, I realized, we did not welcome outsiders. How could we add what was new without breaking what was old? How could we welcome strangers into our number without diluting ourselves—without in the end becoming strangers, to each other and even to ourselves?

I walked up the steps to temple, strengthened by the morning and the walk, and by Jostfar's hand on my shoulder.

Within the temple, the burning bowls were out, sitting in stands on pedestals before the shrines of the saints. Because I went to the main temple, each shrine had three squares of nine bowls (a three of three threes, which is a blessed number to the Tonk), and behind each bowl a lamp burned, and dozens of lighting sticks hung in little buckets from hooks on the pedestals, along with a good horsehair whisk brush and a water flask. We had to bring our own oils, tinders, and incenses, or buy them from the vendors who stood on the steps of the temple this one day of each year and spoke in whispers to all who passed. I bought mine, for Skirmig kept no stock of such things in his home.

Most of the bowls at most of the shrines were in use, and both Minda and Rogvar had long lines stretching from the shrine back to the door. Smoke from incense and wood chips and other things burned my eyes and my lungs as I worked my way back to Ethebet's shrine. Voices in the temple rose and fell, and the sound was like the low roar of the sea with a storm blowing it in.

Ethebet's shrine had no line. In fact, of the twenty-seven burning bowls set before it, only one was in use when I arrived, and the man doing his burning was old and frail, the merest memory of the warrior he had once been.

Before the peace, Ethebet would have had the longest line of all. Tears blurred my vision, and they were not entirely from the smoke. We might be all together in the spirit, Ethebet's folk. But those of us from Beyltaak, at least, had been scattered in the flesh by a malicious hand.

I chose a burning bowl toward the front. I grasped the sacrificial braid I'd made with both hands and yanked it out—for a few moments I could see nothing but stars and a red haze of pain, but I clenched my jaws and shut my eyes against the tears, and made no sound. When the pain subsided, I coiled the braid in the bowl, and sprinkled dry cedar chips into the bowl—cedar being the tree of Ethebet—and then pulled a green cedar branch I'd cut on my way to temple from my waist-bag and laid the edge of my knife against its soft bark.

"In my hands lies a new weapon, Ethebet," I said softly, and carved a thin curl from it. The curl dropped into the bowl. "If I can find the power in it, we who are yours can use it to triumph over our enemies and our oppressors." Slice. "We can win back our freedom." Slice. "We can conquer the Eastils who plot against us." Slice. "But I am still blind, and we are too few." Slice. "Send me a vision of the power of my weapon." Slice. "And send me heroes, Ethebet. Send me warriors of strong will and great heart who, outnumbered, will still fight." Slice. "I consecrate myself to your service, to the freedom of my people, to the triumph of the Tonk over those who plan us ill." Slice. "I will not take my rest until we are triumphant or I am dead." Slice. "Use me as your blade, Ethebet." Slice. "Make me the sword in your scabbard."

I dropped in the last bit of the cedar branch—the tiny twigs and tender greenery—put the tip of one of the lighting sticks to the lamp flame, and lit my little pile.

I stood, breathing the smoke of my offering—hair and a bit of flesh and blood, dry cedar and green cedar—and I let the fire burn down to ash. While it burned, I stared at the smoke, seeking a trance, seeking a vision. But the only vision I got was of the water flask before me, and while that almost seemed like it should mean something, I could make nothing of it. I mixed a bit of water from the altar flask and a few drops of Ethebet's oil, which I'd bought, in the ash, and with my fingers I painted my face, covering all of it. I would not remove the ash. It would come off on its own, and by the time it did, I would have my answer; I would know how Ethebet would use me.

The Tonk are not particularly mystical people, but I had twice before in my life asked something of great import from Ethebet. Each time, she had given me an answer. This was the third time, and this time I asked it on the day of new turning, which fell on her day. Good omens all. I could feel the power of my prayer resonating in the air around me.

Ethebet would answer me.

I knew it.

When I finished with my burning, I walked back to Skirmig's house. I held my resolve close to my heart. Spring would come soon enough, but when it came, my people would be ready.

I had faith.

Skirmig met me at the door, a wary expression on his face. He touched my right temple. "You've hurt yourself. And your face . . . you have—is that ash?—all over it."

He stared into my eyes and smiled at me. "Dearest Talyn, can you not walk through a snowstorm and stay clean?" And he kissed me, and everything faded and grew still within me as the eyes opened, the mouths cried out, and Skirmig's voice whispering "Come, let us get you out of those silly clothes and into a shower and wash that mess away" became the most reasonable voice in all the world.

I smelled spring in the air, though the harbor still gleamed with ice, and snow still covered the ground. A snowdrop pushed its head through the blanket of white on the grounds behind my workroom; once I would have greeted the sight of it joyously, but no more. In a few more weeks the ice in the bay would break up, and not long after that the lower passes through the mountains between the Confederacy and the Eastil Republic would clear, and I still did not have the secret that would give us the Eastils.

Nightmares plagued me. In my dreams I was beset on all sides by monsters, and the Eastil or perhaps his ghost kept fighting them, and fighting them, and fighting them. But they never went away.

My jewelry making slipped away, and I spent most of my time with Skirmig trying to grasp the transport of will, getting metal to move. I sweated and suffered and swore, but the little silver dancer I'd made would not lift a toe for me, no matter what I tried, though Skirmig could get her to walk and clap her hands and stomp her feet. I yearned for the breakthrough Skirmig insisted was coming. And I yearned for the Fheling Point.

"The Fheling Point mixes the Will of God with the Eye of the World," Skirmig told me. "It is untempered by the limitations of the Flesh and Thought of Man. Feegash theoretical philosophers believe it to be the most powerful point in the Hagedwar. It is surely the most dangerous. Over the centuries, a hundred and more of the greatest practicing philosophers have given their lives trying to work within it—all of them masters who held the powers of the Hagedwar as firmly as a man holds a sparrow. God alone knows the number of unprepared fools who have tested themselves against the power of the Fheling Point and lost."

In the Hagedwar, the Fheling Point was one of the two points that poked out of the red square called the Flesh and Thought of Man. It was the dark gold one that was part of the Grandolfitnaj—the Will of God. It terrified Skirmig, and yet it compelled him. When I touched it, I could feel its immense power, and its danger, too.

Skirmig said the Feegash theorists believed it was the key to life and death, the path to the soul itself. He wanted it.

And because I loved him so much, I was running myself into the ground trying to find my way to give it to him.

He said as soon as I could make metal move through the power of the lesser tograms, I would be able to comprehend the method by which I could give metal its own permanent life in the Fheling Point.

"But why do I want to give the little dancer its own life?" I asked. "What purpose will that serve?"

"Giving the statue its own life? No purpose whatsoever, beyond the fact that it is a very small, stable form upon which you can apply your will through the Fheling Point. Think of it as a tiny, visible test."

I could understand that. He wanted the power, not the object. "What will you do with the power when you have it?" I asked. Something inside of me was afraid. I could not give my fear a name or a face, but at that moment I discovered that I was dry-mouthed. And I yearned for cold, clear water.

Skirmig looked into my eyes and said, "I'll bring peace and harmony to the whole of the world." He leaned forward and took my hands in his. "I'll erase war and all the horrors of war, the senseless deaths, the maimings, the oppression, the starvation and plagues that come to peoples whose nations are slaughtering each other wholesale. No longer will men march against each other and die; no longer will warriors cast down death upon whole regions and leave every human being within them lifeless."

I nodded and said, "It is a kind and gentle goal. But sometimes there are good reasons to fight. Will you also eliminate the horrors of bad rule throughout the world? The torture of innocents, the genocides of the different by the powerful, the lawful oppression of peoples by corrupt kings and evil religions?"

He smiled at me as if I were a child, and said, "Ah, Talyn, Talyn, it is this naïveté of yours that makes you so charming. *Evil* religion? Lawful *oppression*? My dearest love, there are no such things. No religion is better or worse than any other religion. No rule of law is better or worse than any other rule of law. Evil is a superstition of the uneducated, a monster drawn of shadow and whispering that when viewed with the clear light of reason vanishes and dies. The Feegash long ago cast out that foolish monster; we found that all men and all actions are the same, neither good nor bad, neither true nor false. All gods are God in the end, and God watches from the high places but does not judge, for there is nothing to judge." He brushed my cheek with a finger and said, "If God does not judge, who are we to judge? Who are we to say that the Brenirs of western Franica are wrong for sacrificing infants; who are we to say the Handumakrath of the Sinali Plains, who sell their daughters to the highest bidder, are more or less good than the Tonk, who worship war and stubborn unreason? We have learned to embrace all cultures and all voices, to open our arms to all mankind, because we are all the same."

I shook my head. "And the people whose god tells them that you and your people are evil, and that all of you must die for the heresy of breathing? Would you not wage a just war against them to protect your own wives and children and your own way of life?"

Again that condescending smile. "Someday you'll see. I'll show you. But for now, simply trust the truth of this: No man who has not been wronged attacks another man; no religion that has not suffered at the hands of unreason declares another its enemy. Were this mythical people of yours to declare the Feegash heretics against their god, it would only be because somehow we had wronged them. It would be our duty to find our crimes, to make reparations, to sit down at table with these good men and work our way to peace."

I laughed. "You people are going to get eaten out there."

"I think not. The Feegash have worked with the truths I tell you for centuries, and our influence—and our peace—spreads daily, and with it, the good we do."

"If the good you do includes turning a blind eye to men who sacrifice infants and sell their own children into slavery while you Feegash stand about declaring them good men, I want nothing of your peace."

"Talyn," he said softly, "you have *never* wanted our peace. Do you think I don't know you work against me—against the Feegash? That even now you seek ways to revive your war? You're Tonk, and as blind and headstrong and addicted to your mad death culture as the rest of your people. As blind as the Eastils, for that matter. I forgive you that—it is your culture and you'll be a long time outgrowing it. Perhaps in fifty years, or a hundred, Tonk children will no longer carry the disease of war in their hearts."

"I don't want your forgiveness," I told him. "I want my people's freedom."

"Your people don't want 'freedom' as you envision it anymore. The riches roll in from the High Valleys over our new roads, and in taaks that have been steeping in poverty and ignorance for centuries, your people hear other languages and see other ways of life for the first time. And they discover that Jostfar and his precious Saints are dull and foolish, and that beyond the little darkness of your superstitious religion lies a world of pleasure you people have never even suspected. Your Beyl owns his own harem of slave girls now, did you know that? He put the money you Tonks used to sink into war toward his own fleet of trading ships, and even now more slaves are on their way to Beyltaak to be sold in your market with your horses. The finest laces of the ancient empires are coming here, and spices to tease the jaded palate, and dream smokes to grant visions to the bored and sad."

I pulled away from Skirmig, and he laughed. "All people are the same," he said. "If you grant them riches, they do the same things with them—they buy jewels to wear and slaves to futter and fine clothes and fine horses, and they turn their backs on the gods they once claimed to love, because they see religion is a hollow sham without merit. Religion is a drug for the poor and weak, and the rules of gods are for sheep; the rich and the strong have no need for any law save their own."

"And yet there are things worth dying for," I said.

Skirmig shook his head. "Not a one. Life is the only currency of value. I will die of nothing but old age." He smiled at me.

"You would live a slave rather than die a free man?"

"Oh, no," he told me. "I'll live a king, and you'll stand at my side as my queen for the rest of your days. As for the slaves of the world"—he waved his hand dismissively—"half of them are criminals who were sold into slavery for their crimes. The other half are weak-minded creatures bred for their lot in life; they would not survive without masters to keep them safe and fed and sheltered. Waste no tears on slaves, my love. Instead, rejoice in the grace and beauty and intelligence that makes you the sister of goddesses, and the most wondrous creature whose feet touch the ground."

I did not choose to be appeased. "We all die, and can control neither when nor how. Our only choice is in how we live our lives. We can live for nothing, or for something. I live for my god, my saints, and my people—my family, my friends, and the Tonks who have given me life and made me who I am. These are the only things in the world that hold true value to me, and it is only in living for them that I can have value to myself. If I must turn my back on who I am to have you, then I cannot have you. If I must turn my back on my beliefs and my people to have you, then I cannot have you."

He looked into my eyes and smiled at me, and the fury that had been growing within me faltered and died, as if it were a flame snuffed out.

"I want you," he whispered, and pushed me to the gleaming black floor of his workroom, and started pulling off my clothes.

I don't want you, some tiny voice in the back of my mind cried out. I don't want anyone who thinks the way you think or wants the things you want anywhere near me. But within me, the hungry eyes opened and the voices of the starving drowned out that desperate protest, and I reached for Skirmig as if I'd been lost in a desert and he were water.

No.

Not water. Never water.

I pulled him to me and ripped his clothes from him and for a while we lost ourselves in frightening passion and rough lust. At some point I realized that some of the servants stood outside the door staring at us, but Skirmig saw my gaze stray from him and said, "Let them watch. They know no pleasure but what we know," and the part of me that scratched and bit and shoved and tore accepted that answer.

It ended at last, and I gathered up my clothes and walked naked through the house and stood in my shower and watched the blood, some of it mine and some of it his, swirl down the drain.

I felt nothing. I could remember the voice within me that had screamed I don't want this, but I could not resurrect it. Something had silenced it, or perhaps killed it. The part of me that was left could not find it in myself to think that what I had done—that what Skirmig and I had done together—was wrong. I could not care about the cuts and bruises on my skin, or the bone-deep pain inside me and out, about the people standing there staring at us without expression or sound as we acted worse than beasts. The eyes inside me had closed, the voices had fallen silent, but the cloud that surrounded me remained.

At the peak of our encounter, Skirmig had said to me, "You and I have a world of adventures before us, my love. This is only our beginning. Someday we'll play at master and slave, and you'll beg me to beat you, to hurt you, to take you through pain and shame back to pleasure. And I will. And you will love me all the more for doing it."

I could not even find it within myself to be horrified by that. I wondered, drying myself off with a towel, dabbing away blood that still oozed, if I could not care what had just happened because there was some part of me that wanted it. If what was wrong in my life was something that was wrong with me.

"I'm happy," I repeated to myself. Happy. Happy, happy. Skirmig loves me, and I am happy.

I could not remember the last time I had stepped outside the doors of his house. I could not remember very many things at all, truth be told. Time seemed to be flowing past me on all sides without brushing against me.

I dressed in comfortable clothes and made myself go back to Skirmig's workroom to sit across from Skirmig because I owed it to my people to learn everything he could teach me. The Tonks deserved weapons against the treachery of the Eastils, no matter what my personal failings might be.

Skirmig smiled at me when I sat down, and said, "I knew you'd find your way back. You'll see the world as it really is eventually, with my help. There is no right. And no wrong. I'll show you: There is only power, and those with the vision to use it."

I did not even have the will left within me to disagree with him.

We moved into trance, and to the Edge, and I spun my Hagedwar, and took the silver statuette that would not move for me, and I cast aside all caution and all fear, and stepped directly into the Fheling Point. I didn't care about anything at that moment. I certainly didn't care about my own safety. If I was thinking at all, my thoughts ran along the lines of wanting to give Skirmig what he wanted and wanting to end the deadness inside of me.

The spark of life that drives the universe—Jostfar's dream

and vision and will—plays music against our skin, trills through our flesh as if we were no more substantial than air, vibrates our bones and touches our minds and our souls and our senses. Most of the time, the music is so subtle we fail to hear it. We might notice a phrase or a stanza echoed in the synchronicity of thinking about a friend long lost and meeting that friend upon the street the next day. We might hum a bar or two of our own when we will events to happen to our liking, and see them do that very thing.

But mostly we are deaf as old bellringers to the songs life plays for us.

So I was deaf, numb, uncaring, and cold as I entered the Fheling Point. I had no expectations, except a numb suspicion that it might kill me. I had no hopes, except perhaps the same thing.

I was unready for what I found there. The universe within the deep gold light poured out its song to me in pure, strong notes. I sat within the heart of the View itself for the first time in far too long—but the shield of the Hagedwar still wrapped around me and protected me. It formed walls around me that anchored me so that my soul would not wander off and leave my body— at least not without extreme carelessness on my part. So long as I stayed within the golden walls of the Fheling Point, the music and the magic of the View could flow through me, and I could use a filtered and gentled version of its power more safely than if I had been with twenty Shielders in the View itself.

I had forgotten the beauty and the glory of the View.

I might as well have stepped unprepared into a room in which Jostfar himself sang the world's breath—and the song ripped the dullness from me. The energy of life itself scaled away my numbness, so that I shook off my pain like so much dust.

I could see a truth I had discovered before on numerous occasions, but had not been able to hold tight in my hands. Skirmig had been twisting my thoughts using the magic that lay in the togram just beneath the Fheling Point, still within the limits of the red. I saw the lines he had cast about me to anchor me. I felt where they had embedded themselves in my soul. I read, as clearly as if he had written it on paper for me, exactly what he had done to me. And exactly when he had done it.

I.
Remembered.
Everything.

I discovered the first hook he'd buried in me, the day that the Eastils tried to wipe out the Tonk leadership during the peace conference. I could see how he'd used that hook to follow me to Beyltaak and to find me. No meeting of ours save that very first one, when we both watched over the business in Injtaak, had ever been by chance. His every word, his every act from the very first, had been false. He knew all along who I was, that I was the woman he had come to Beyltaak to find. I could see later hooks, places where when I turned away from him he used magic to make me turn toward him. Where he used magic to coerce me into having sex with him in that barn the first time, when I had chosen to be true to my upbringing and my faith. Where he had used magic to make me forget what he and the other Feegash men did to Feegash women. Where he had used magic to make me sick and helpless while he tried to decide what to do with me, because he feared me. Where he had tortured me, scarred my flesh, used my body, and had then taken away both the memory of what he had done and the realization that the patterns carved into my arms, my breasts, my belly and back did not belong there. Where this very day he had used magic to dull my resistance to his evils, to turn me away from who I was.

Evils. I could find no other word for his actions.

But even so, some of the weight of what he had done, I had to carry. Because my desire for him, for the smooth opaque mystery of him, was the thing that had let him set his hooks so deep in my soul.

I had allowed myself to be deceived. I had allowed myself to step onto the path that I knew was the wrong path. I had seen something beautiful about him, but the beauty was a lie that covered a hideous truth. He was corrupt, evil, deceitful, vile, cruel; he was everything I detested in any human. And I had allowed myself to be blinded by the serene, impenetrable shell of magic he wore around him. I had thought it reflected him, but in fact it disguised him, and I had chosen to be enchanted by a disguise, rather than to search for the truth that lay beneath.

No more.

I tore free of his hooks, all at once and with a furious finality. He would not know until I stepped out of the Fheling Point that I was—at last—completely free of him. He could not follow me into the Fheling Point. He was not born Tonk. Not of a family bred for Magics. He was blind to the beauty I saw, deaf to the music I heard, numb to the power that was mine to wield. What was for me tapestry and light and song was for him an abyss, an infinite, terrifying void, a black devouring maw. And I would make sure it stayed that way. When I left the Fheling Point, I would wrap around me a shield as impenetrable as the one that Skirmig wore, and take with me the secrets of the magic that he desired above all else.

If I had suffered at Skirmig's hands, if I had been ill-used, still the experience was not without its several valuable points.

Skirmig had, for one, proven to me all my suspicions about the moriiad; Tonks had been right to disown Tonks who bore children by outlanders, to keep the best of what we had to ourselves, to protect our borders, to guard our religion, to stand apart from the rest of the world. The moriiad were everything we had thought them to be, and worse.

I would never again allow myself to make the mistake I'd made with Skirmig. Never.

He had, for two, given me the Hagedwar, and within the Hagedwar, the Fheling Point. Wrapped as I was in its beauty, with the power it offered spread before me, I had the first answer to my prayer to Ethebet. I saw how the Fheling Point could be a weapon. I saw, too, how to bring life to the little figurine I had created; and in the same moment that I saw how I could accomplish that, I realized that I could have a sweet victory over Skirmig, deal him and all the Feegash a vastly deserved humiliation, and walk away to give to my own people the power the Feegash so desperately sought—power with which we could rid ourselves of the moriiad within our borders, and with which we could win, for once and ever, our war with the Eastils.

Within the View, we see all our world and the worlds beyond it as energy without physical form. Nor is this a trick of the mind or a false view. It is the true nature of all things; what we perceive as solid form within the physical world is the real trick. Nothing physical is solid, impermeable, immovable. It is all dancing light and trembling sound that slows for just a moment into something that we can touch and hold and see—and then it moves on. When I looked at the figurine I'd created through the lens of the Fheling Point, I could see it as pure energy, and I could see how I might reach out and grasp the living spark of Jostfar and, by binding it with a tiny bit of my will, breathe it into the energy of the silver figurine. I could make her live, move with a will of her own, become her own creature.

The living statuette's existence would prove the power of the Fheling Point. And her existence would taunt the Feegash, because she would be nothing but an amusing toy, proof that someone else could use the magic they craved—rich, magnificent, glorious magic that they would not attain without me.

Unholy glee filled me. Though I wanted to slaughter Skirmig for what he had done to me, I would not. Rather, I would use him as an example that would let me rally the Tonks around me so that we could get the Feegash out of the Confederacy. So that we could regain our freedom. Our lives.

With what I had discovered about Skirmig, I would be able to prove to my people that the peace under which we lived was nothing but a trick of the Feegash. Not the Eastils after all, but the Feegash alone, whose landlocked nation had become at last too confining. Whose diplomats had seen a way to parlay an unquestioned reputation for integrity into an opportunity to acquire two rich nations without having to shed blood for either of them. Who had built deceit upon deceit until they owned us all.

I thought of all our metals going out, of the High Valleys and their vast treasure mined and harvested to enrich the Feegash; I looked at our fish-rich harbors, our trade access through the Brittlebreak Straits to all the ports in the world. At our horses, at our forests, at our people. And I raged at our blindness. Profit and power had driven the Feegash—power and profit, the end motives of men who have no faith and live for no greater good.

We were a tasty prize, and we had been stupid and careless and had guarded our doors but had ignored our windows—we had looked too near for enemies, and had forgotten to watch the horizons.

But with the Fheling Point, I could see the lies. I could show them to others.

And I could crush Skirmig. Before I finally killed him,

anyway—but I could not kill him yet. I needed him as a display. While I was keeping him alive, though, I could hurt him.

I could prove to him that I had everything he wanted. And that I would not give it to him. I could break his spirit, as I would eventually break his flesh and bones. He was going to hurt for what he had done to me, and for what his people had done to my people. He was going to hurt as no one had ever hurt before.

Starting right then.

I shaped the power around me, and directed it, and poured it through my soul and wove the resulting mix into the metal of the tiny silver figurine. My little trinket would not speak. She would not truly think. But when I was done with her, she would respond to a handful of words, and to a few events in her surroundings, and she would be enough alive to prove her origins were beyond anything the Feegash could hope to attain without the help of Tonk Shielders or Senders.

Or the Eastil equivalent.

At the thought of the Eastils, cold fear ran through my blood and bones.

The Feegash were our enemy—but we had another. If I was studying the Hagedwar, the Feegash would be fools not to have some agent like Skirmig using some Sender or Shielder in the Eastil Republic to do the same thing. His protestations that I was the only non-Feegash ever to be given the secret of the Hagedwar must have been a lie to mollify me and make me feel somehow special. No commander desiring a new weapon would set only one man in one place the task of creating that weapon. He would bring all his resources to bear, perhaps setting up separate groups who would act without knowledge of each other, so that each would approach the problem differently; in that way he would have the best chance of coming up with something truly powerful.

The Eastils had to be working with the Hagedwar.

I could not waste time. The breakup of the ice in the harbor was not far off, the snow would clear out of the high passes not long after, the docks were reinforced and strong, the new Feegash roads led straight to our most critical taaks. And if I had found out how to use the Fheling Point, the Eastils would not be far behind me.

If they were not already ahead of me.

I had little time to amuse myself in revenge against Skirmig, much as I might want it. Much as I might have *earned* it. Ethebet may have answered the first part of my prayer, granting me a weapon against my people's enemies, but she had not handed me an army. I was going to have to create that myself, from the few Ethebettans who remained, and from the Mindans and the Hetterikkans and the Cladmussans and the Rogvarans and Jostfar's own Keepers of the Words. I had only weeks, not months, to create fighters who would be able to stand against not just the seasoned warriors of the Feegash Mercenary Corps, but whatever the Eastils might put together against us.

I could not run fast enough to do everything I had to do in time.

With my figurine in hand, I dropped out of the Fheling Point and shook off the trance of the Edge and faced Skirmig, who sat across from me, still in a trance. Helpless.

I could have killed him right there. Right then. Any love I had felt for him had metamorphosed into a hatred so deep and consuming that it hazed my vision and brought the taste of metal to my tongue. I *wanted* to kill him. But he was my example. My proof of who the Feegash were beneath their veneer. He was the one Feegash who had used me, and who I could *prove* had used me. Without Skirmig, I had no flag to wave in front of the complacent Tonks who had been led to think of the Feegash-forced peace as something benign.

I stood as Skirmig was rousing himself from his own trance, and as his eyes focused on me in the physical world, I kicked him once in his bewildered face and threw the little figurine at him, hard. The silver statuette hit him square in the forehead, opening a gash, and then it bounced to the floor.

I had time to notice that Skirmig was bleeding from nose, mouth, and forehead.

And then my little silver dancer shook herself off, rose with a slow, easy grace, and danced a few steps of a traditional Tonk war dance before coming to a rest.

Skirmig looked from me to the silver dancer and back to me again, and put his hand to his mouth, pulling it away to stare at his own blood. "Why . . . ?" he said, and, "What . . . ?"

He could not find the words he wanted, but I could.

"I found the Fheling Point's magic much to my liking," I snarled. "I also found out how you've been using me. You have no hooks in me anymore, morii, nor will you ever again. My language has no words foul enough to describe you. None. Perhaps I'll create some." I walked to the door, turned, and said, "I would kill you now, but I need you to live for a bit longer. I'll bring death to you someday as my final gift for all you did to me. But meantime, if ever you try to touch me again, I'll shove your testicles down your throat by way of your nose and rip your skin off your still-living body to tan for boots."

I stormed from the room to the accompaniment of an anguished plea of "Talyn! You love me!"

I had the power of the Fheling Point behind me. I had no need to fear for my safety in Skirmig's house. I had no need to fear anything. The shield that surrounded me would protect me from any magic Skirmig might cast at me. It was more powerful than any magic he might hope to cast from within the safety of the red. I could shape the power of the universe as my weapon should he or any of his people try a physical attack. The Fheling Point conferred, truly, a god's power to the hand of man. If I could get it to my people before the Eastils found a use for it, we would wipe the Feegash stain from our land. And then we would at last settle three hundred years of war. And we would do it the Tonk way. With all-out victory.

I had a few things I wanted to take with me when I left, so I went first to my workroom and gathered my jewelry samples. When I left Skirmig's house, I would no longer be a jeweler; I would shed that life and don Ethebet's mantle as her warrior once more. But my work was my work, and I did not wish to leave it behind. I grabbed my display box from the workroom, made the long trek to my room at a run, and threw the few personal articles I cared about into my old Shielder's kit bag. First I thought I would have to leave without Rik's brooch—but it had fallen from the cloak to the wardrobe floor. What I could not find—and what I could not bear to leave without—was my traditional warrior's battle garb, which I suddenly could not remember having seen since singing my prayer in the temple on the high holy day of Badaag. I started to tear the room apart, looking for it, and worrying at the same time about the horses. I had to take Dakaat with me, even though I now knew without question that she had been a gift from Skirmig; she was proscribed, and I would not betray my people by leaving her in the hands of the moriiad. I had to take Toghedd, too, and wondered how much trouble Skirmig and his strange, frightening servants would give me when I went to the stables to get them.

But that was all I needed. The warrior's garb, and then the horses, and then I would be gone.

I had shaken off the magic that had held me in thrall, that had made me doubt not just what I was but who I was, and I would not in my first hours of freedom betray my people and our way on any point.

I gave up searching at last. My warrior's garb was gone. Not in my room, not in Skirmig's room, not in the servants' rooms, not in any of the trunks sitting around. I would leave without it, get my horses, go home. That garb was a creation of years—maybe even decades—a piece of my own history and the history of my people, but what I had yet to do was more important.

I had just returned to my room and slung my kit bag over my shoulder.

"Don't hurry on my account," Skirmig said from the doorway, and I jumped. I hadn't heard him.

"I don't want to be here an instant longer than I have to."

He laughed softly—a chilling sound—and I tasted bile in the back of my mouth.

I turned and stared at him.

"Maybe I can change your mind," he said. And he smiled.

And I could no longer move. Not a foot, not an arm, not a finger. I could not turn my head, I could not blink my eyes; and though I could breathe and in my chest my heart still beat, breathing was hard. And my heart struggled like an old mare pulling a huge plow; it felt like it would burst at any moment.

He walked over to me and ran a hand over my body in a hideously familiar fashion, and I could do nothing about it. I could feel his touch, I could dread it, I could want to hurt him and want to flee and want to scream—but I could do nothing.

"I'd hate to have anything happen to your lovely eyes," he whispered. "Yet. If you don't blink, they'll dry out and you'll be blinded—did you know that?"

I did.

He slid my eyelids down and they stayed. I could no longer see.

"This is better than tying you up," he said thoughtfully. "No ropes to get in the way or slow me down. I can move you however I want you. You can't squirm out of my way, or fight me. Or anyone I might bring in to share the moment with me. It's perfect."

I had to get into the Hagedwar. I had to reach trance and move back into the Fheling Point and find out how he was doing this to me. And I had to stop him.

Something sharp hit me, and his voice said, "You don't get to resort to magic, dear Talyn. I never taught you how to use the Hagedwar without trance; good thing for me, isn't it? I'll keep you from reaching trance, and when I'm not with you, the servants will do the same. You may pass out from the pain or you may fall asleep from exhaustion, but you will not have the opportunity to find stillness or silence. Not at all."

He stroked my hair and began undressing me.

15

Sobbing, bleeding, Talyn cried out to Gair as some monster of a man dragged her away; she lifted her bound arms in supplication, and Gair could see the tears streaming down her cheeks. Her fingernails were bloody, her wrists bleeding from the ropes that tied them. Her captor had slung her over his shoulder, and was running with her toward a dark cloud that spun like a whirlpool in the middle of a hellish dungeon. "Hurry!" she screamed. "Oh, Jostfar! Hurry!" If he couldn't get to her before the monster reached that black vortex, she would be beyond rescue and hope. Lost. Forever.

Gair woke with his heart racing, his skin drenched in a cold sweat. The loft was darkening—evening had come. Gair sat up and looked over the edge of the loft, ready to feign coughing or retching if the spies were out, but the door to their room was already shut. They spent more and more time sleeping as whatever illness they had dug its claws deeper into them.

Gair took a deep, shuddering breath and tried to stop the shaking of his hands. A dream, he told himself. It had only been a dream.

But he knew even as he tried to calm himself that it had been much more than that.

"Get up," he whispered, and Snow Grell was awake in the instant, and on his feet the next.

"What's wrong?"

"We have to go get Talyn. Now."

Silence. "You're still too weak to fight. We don't know where she is. And there are two of us, against a city full of mercs who by this time must be bored out of their minds; they'll like nothing better than to cut us down. You know I'll follow you through hell, but even if we don't plan to survive, we should at least have some hope of saving *her* if we're going in."

"If we don't get her now, she'll be lost. This is our moment. There won't be another." Gair swung his feet off the edge of the bed, wishing he had boots or clothes or a sword. Hell of a rescuer he was going to be.

But he knew the dream had not been just a dream. She needed him. And she needed him right then.

"We'll find her, then," Snow Grell said. "We'll do whatever we must, and we'll save her. Or die trying."

Idrann rolled over and sat up, as wide awake as Gair or Snow Grell. "I know where she is. And I know how to get to her without alerting the mercs or the bastard's spies."

Gair said, "You'll help us?"

"She's Tonk. She's in the hands of the moriiad. She's my friend. Of course I'll help you." He beckoned them to follow him. "Even before the day that you and I first spoke of her, I made preparations, in case this moment came. For I had my worries as well."

Snow Grell picked up his pack. Gair had nothing to take. They followed Idrann down the ladder, through the main room, and into the little back room that led outside. Gair was startled, though, when they did not go out the back door, but instead crept through the hatch and down to Talyn's root cellar, where Gair and Snow Grell had done all their practice fighting. The root cellar was just that—a cellar. A dead end. Why would the healer take them there?

Idrann pulled the hatch shut above them and lit his lamp.

"Clothes," the healer said, and produced tunics, breeches, undergarments, boots, and cloak, all well worn and much mended, all of Tonk make, from a hidden panel in the wall. He closed it, and Gair, who'd thought he'd done a careful search of the room, looked at the place where he now knew a hidden door lay, but he could not see it. He tried to open it, but could not. He could not find any sign of it.

Idrann laughed. "Tonk workmanship. We like wood almost as well as we like horses." He handed the clothes to Gair. "These are old things of mine, so if they don't fit well, I apologize."

Gair put them on. The healer had small feet, but though the boots were uncomfortable, they were better than nothing. Everything else would serve, if only because Gair was not yet back to his fighting weight. The healer was a thin man—but at the moment, so was Gair. "Thanks," he said, and started back for the ladder.

The healer said, "Wait. Both of you. I must have an oath from you."

Gair turned back, and Snow Grell paused and watched the healer with that hunter's stillness of his.

"Swear to me, on your honor as warriors, that what you see you will not reveal to anyone else—ever—and that you will never use it against any Tonk, either for personal gain or in the service of your own people."

Gair and Snow Grell exchanged glances. "It sounds like you're asking me to betray my own people," Gair said.

The healer shook his head. "I am only asking that as the price of my helping you, you promise that you will not use my help to make me betray mine."

Gair said, "I swear it then."

Snow Grell nodded. "I swear."

The healer walked to the back of the root cellar; stopped, pressed a hand flat against the bottom right corner of one wide board that ran from floor to ceiling between two shelves full of dried, smoked, and pickled meats. To Gair's amazement, when Idrann released pressure, the board and the one beside it swung in toward them just enough that the healer could catch onto the edge. Idrann pulled a narrow door open. Behind it lay darkness.

Gair and Snow Grell exchanged disbelieving glances. They'd spent a bit of time in that cellar searching it while they were cooling down from their mock battles. Gair would have been prepared to swear on his honor that the cellar held no secrets. From the expression on his face, Snow Grell would have taken the same oath.

The healer beckoned them after him, and all three stepped into an oddly drafty room, so narrow two men could barely stand side by side in it, but so long that light did not illuminate either of the ends.

It smelled of horse.

It wasn't a room, Gair realized. It was a tunnel.

Idrann's lamp illuminated boarded walls closely braced with ancient-looking planed timbers that vanished into darkness in two directions. The cobbled floor looked ancient and, when Gair examined debris between the cobbles, revealed exactly why the place smelled of horse. Ah, lovely. He supposed he ought to be grateful the Tonks didn't sleep with their horses in their bedrooms. He was certainly grateful he wasn't in his bare feet.

The healer turned and pulled the door closed behind him, and Gair saw a little spring-tensioned latch at the top click back into place. Clever.

"Well enough for a start," Idrann said. "Though we can expect merry hell come morning, when you and Snow Grell and I are gone."

"I hope we'll have merry hell before that," Gair said. Snow Grell laughed.

"To that end . . ." The healer held his lamp low, revealing a long, thin bundle wrapped in oilcloth and bound with tarred string. "Hold this." He handed the lantern to Snow Grell.

Idrann untied the strings, unwrapped the bundle, and revealed four swords in serviceable sheaths. "I had thought when I put these here that when we left, we would have one more."

The healer had planned for quite a lot, Gair realized. And the fact that he'd decided to throw in his lot with foreigners—and enemies at that . . .

"When did you do this?"

"The night after that Feegash bastard came bursting through the door with his mercs and his lies. I was grateful then for Ethebet's Demand."

Gair, whose cover identity as a trader and faithful devotee of the peace-loving Saint Minda had kept him far away from the teachings of Ethebet, had no clue what that was. "And that would be . . . ?"

" 'For every sword you claim, another hide away in secret from all men, against dark days and treachery.' "

Gair considered that for a moment. "And every Ethebettan follows this commandment?"

"Yes. Every *good* Ethebettan, in any case."

"So you people still have an army worth reckoning, just waiting for someone to call it back to life." He thought about the Republic, which owned all weapons, kept them only in the hands of the military, and would never have permitted any soldier to keep a spare hidden away. If everything he had heard was true and the Eastils had disarmed, the Tonks were going to own them come spring, peace or no peace.

But Idrann said, "We would if there were any Ethebettans left. The damned Feegash made sure warriors had no work here, and lured them to far-off lands with promises of good pay and chances to keep their families fed and under roof. So swords we might have in sufficient number, if only we had the trained arms to swing them."

Gair strapped on the buckler and changed the subject.

"How do we get to Talyn?" he asked.

"Follow me."

The tunnel intersected with another, wider one and, as they hurried along it, crossed side passages that snaked away in all directions. It was a warren, Gair realized; well built, well drained, with accesses to a sewer that ran beneath, and little cul-de-sacs hidden in odd corners. And all along it, he passed the back sides of doors and more doors, each with a little marking on it, none of the markings in any way decipherable to Gair.

How far did the tunnels go?

Did every house have one?

Did every taak have such a system of tunnels? And if so, why had his people never known about them?

Gair thought about the fire he and his men had set in Injtaak, and about how the guard who had driven him to Beyltaak after he was captured had claimed that his mission had been a complete failure—that save three Tonk scribes, the only men who had died had been Feegash, and if it hadn't been for those same three scribes, Gair might have found himself a hero. He'd been sure the driver had been lying. He'd heard the screams and the shouts when the fire started, and the spreading silence. He had seen that not a single person had come out of the building. He'd thought that had meant something. He was no longer sure.

"How many people died in the fire my men and I set?" he asked Idrann.

"Aside from your men? Three scribes. A handful of Feegash." The healer fell quiet for a moment, then said, "The Feegash were a good start, anyway."

"Because when the fires started, everyone got out through tunnels like these," Gair said.

The healer said nothing, but he didn't have to.

Gair and his men had been spent carrying out an operation that could never have worked. They had missed a fact about the Tonks so huge it should have been common knowledge to every Eastil soldier.

And he had sworn on his honor never to reveal it.

The Tonks kept the important things in their lives close to them; Gair knew that was the biggest problem the Eastils had with getting good intelligence about the Tonks, because the things their enemies needed to know about them were things they didn't even talk about with each other. They never discussed their families with people they did not know well, and they did not even speak the names of children who had not yet come of age to any they did not consider part of their family already; they did not offer up opinions on their leaders casually, and now that he thought about it, they never asked for or offered directions to those they did not know.

Gair had pretended to be a Tonk, but for all his study, he knew the pretense had been nothing but surface gloss. He had not been born into these people. He did not know their minds. Their culture did not grow outward from his belly and his heart and his blood and his bones—he wore it on his skin and his tongue, and tasted only the plainest and most obvious flavors of it.

He thought of Talyn, who had twice saved him. He could not

imagine a woman of his own people doing what she had done, and he could not imagine why she had done it. He was grateful beyond words. He felt something for her that transcended mere gratitude. But he did not begin to understand her.

Of course, with the attack he'd led on the Injtaak Faverhend a complete failure instead of the complete success he'd thought it was, he could at least understand why she didn't seem to hate him. Why, for that matter, Idrann had been kind in his cautious way.

Gair kept up with Idrann at first, but before long he was falling back to catch his breath. In spite of the nightly sparring with Snow Grell, he did not yet have either his strength or his endurance.

Idrann turned into a narrower passage, and his steps slowed. He began holding up his lantern to every doorway they passed, finally stopping and studying the marks on one.

"Right house, wrong door," he muttered, and moved to the next. "This one will do," he said. "Draw swords, in case we find ourselves in the midst of company."

Gair and Snow Grell, swords in hand, followed the healer through the door. Gair had expected to step into another larder like the one in which the secret door in Talyn's house had been hidden, but instead he was in a tiny room with nothing but built-in ladder stairs, and at the top of them, a small landing and another spring-latched door.

The healer swore softly. "Maybe there will be a peephole up there so that we can at least get an idea of what we're walking into."

But there wasn't.

Now none of them spoke. They were too close to danger, not just for themselves but for Talyn, and all of them felt it.

Gair changed the order of entry by moving in front of the healer and indicating with hand signals that Snow Grell should follow him in and Idrann should put out the light.

He prepared to push into the hidden room, thinking that if anyone knew of their tunnel systems, the Tonks would be sheep for the slaughter to any thieves, pirates, or warriors who came after them. They had a good offense; they were tough people with strong beliefs and a history of good leaders. And they had a good defense, in that every damned one of them could ride a horse and that their religion demanded their warrior class to stay armed even—or maybe especially—when ordered not to. And because of the tunnels, even the weaponless ones could be where the enemy wasn't, so long as the tunnels lay within reach.

But to be able to sneak unseen from house to house within the taak and enter any one of them at will . . .

He pushed open the door, and a loud, shrill bell began to clang.

He jumped back and pushed the door shut behind him.

"The alarm," Idrann whispered. "It will stop in a moment. In a Tonk household, every sword would be in hand by the time you reached anyone, but these are moriiad. They won't know what the alarm is. If we're lucky, it will stop before they can locate the room it came from."

Gair, feeling foolish, murmured, "I would have disarmed it had you told me how. Or if you did not want me to know how, you could have told me not to take the lead until you had prevented it from going off."

And the healer laughed softly. "There's no way to do such a thing. The alarms would be worthless if there were any way to turn them off from the outside. Any time someone comes through one of these doors uninvited, the people in the house have reason to know it." In the darkness, Gair could hear him chuckle. "I would have thought you would expect alarms."

I should have, Gair thought.

The three of them listened with their ears pressed to the boards. On the other side, men and women called to each other in a language Gair didn't know, the voices growing louder and louder, and then fainter and fainter.

And after a while the house fell silent again.

"Will the alarm go off when I open the door this time?" Gair asked.

"No."

"Good. Let's go get her, then."

They slipped into a small round room that was the terminus of one of the house's legs. Gair noticed that the healer took the time to close the hidden door behind them. It would make escape with Talyn more inconvenient, and he almost protested.

But suddenly he realized that this was how the Tonk had kept the damned tunnels secret from their enemies. They *never* left them open.

The Tonk were a people unified in thought and deed, and Gair felt a momentary pang that his people were not so unified.

The round room's many windows let in no light. Gair heard a soft pattering on the glass, and realized the utter blackness outdoors came from storm clouds. Rain—and if it froze, winter would hang on a bit longer. But if it did not freeze, it would push the coming spring closer.

Though he could not give the fear a name, his gut dreaded the coming of spring.

Out in the hall, more silence. The servants were nowhere to be seen. No one patrolled the long corridors. But he did hear one sound, through the center of the house and down another leg—the sound very like leather on flesh.

He gestured, and the other two followed him toward that sound.

The house might as well have been empty. Tonks would have been everywhere, and armed tooth and nail, after a sudden unexplained noise of the magnitude of that bell. Even most Eastils would not have been so trusting as to creep back off to bed. But these Feegash had done a cursory search, and failed to ask the question Why? and had decided not to let an unexplained noise bother them.

No one interfered with the three of them as they hurried toward the unnerving sound.

Gair could not place the sound in any rational context because though the thing it most sounded like was a human being whipped—and he had plenty of experience with that—it shared none of the other sounds. The laughter and mocking of the torturers, the cries of the tortured, sounds of struggle.

And then he and his comrades reached the room from which the sound emanated, and staying out of the light that spilled into the corridor, they peered in.

Talyn lay naked, facedown and unmoving, half on a huge bed and half off. Her eyes were closed, her hands and feet were unbound, and a dozen men surrounded her. One held a whip; others held other instruments of torture. Someone had carved spirals and other designs into her back with a knife, and the cuts had bled freely, and every visible inch of her body bore lash marks and welts and more cuts and bruises. Fresh blood caked over dried blood, and Gair's heart cried out that he had not been quick enough to save her. He didn't know what else the monsters had done to her, but even after she was dead, they were not content to leave her alone.

Bile rose in Gair's throat. "Slaughter them," he growled. "Leave not one breathing."

He led Idrann and Snow Grell through the door, sword slashing, and carved through two of Talyn's killers before they even realized that they were under attack.

The rest turned to face him, a sameness to their movements and their expressions that chilled Gair. But the bastards didn't fight back, though they had weapons in hand. Instead, their eyes went wide and their mouths flew open and they stood, locked in silent screams, while Gair and his comrades chopped them to bits. It was a slaughter in silence, and Gair could not shake the horror of that.

When they lay dead, with the floor pooled in their blood, he made his way to Talyn. "I'll take point and kill anything that moves before us," he said. "Snow Grell, you bring up the rear, and watch our backs. We're going to wipe out everyone in this house before we leave. Healer, you carry Talyn's body. You can make sure she gets a proper Tonk burial, at least."

The healer picked her up, gasped, and put her down again. He felt at her wrist and at her throat, and held a hand before her nose and mouth. "She lives," he whispered, "though I dare not guess how near death she is."

"Then we leave now, and we hurry," Gair said. "Snow Grell and I will find our way back here and kill the bastard who did this to her later."

The healer nodded. "I fear for her," he said. "We *must* hurry." He lifted her onto his back, pulling her arms over his shoulders and bending forward to balance her weight. Gair had carried wounded and dying comrades back from the front lines in the same fashion; the healer wouldn't be able to fight, but he'd still be able to run.

Good man.

Gair led them out the door.

And the healer stopped them. "Wait," he said. "We must remove our boots."

"Here? Now?" Gair whispered. "You're mad."

"In the dark, it would not matter. But when daylight returns, or when they bring out lights to search for us, they will find a trail of blood. And they are moriiad. We dare not let them know of . . . our destination."

By which he meant the secret tunnels, which Gair had sworn he would keep secret. Damn the Tonk; he was right, but he was also inconvenient.

Gair slipped off his own boots and tucked the tops into his belt, then scooped Talyn into his arms and held her while the healer pulled his boots off and Snow Grell guarded them.

She was still as death; heavy, but not in the boneless manner of corpses. She did not flop against him. Instead, she seemed almost frozen, though her skin was still warm. Gair pressed his face against hers, which nestled in the juncture of his neck and shoulder, and willed her to live.

So that he could thank her properly.

Nothing more than that. He owed her much, and he needed to offer his gratitude.

What had the Feegash bastard done to her before he turned his flunkies loose on her to torture her? Had he poisoned her? Spelled her with some grim magic?

It mattered not a whit to Gair. The bastard was going to die.

Maybe even in the next moment. Gair's head came up, and he hissed at the healer to take Talyn back, for as the healer tucked his own boots into his belt, Gair could hear shuffling footsteps coming toward him.

We're going to be caught getting her out of here. The bastard will show up with a dozen well-armed mercs and we'll be lost, and her with us, and all of this will have been for naught.

"Faster," he said, jaws clenched, and gripped his sword tighter.

They hurried.

Not fast enough. As they stepped into the central room a dozen more servants converged on them, and he and Snow Grell wreaked bloody havoc.

These all fought, if not well. They moved like puppets, arms rising and falling in the same rhythm. They weren't much of a challenge for either Snow Grell or Gair, and considering that Gair was nowhere near full health, that was saying something.

With bodies strewn everywhere, the three rescuers ran down the hall, far enough to fade into the darkness, and pulled off their socks and shoved them into their boots. Gair wasn't sure how they would keep from leaving a trail of blood if any more of the diplomat's weird servants came at them.

But, though he heard a door burst open at the front of the house, and running feet and the clank of armor and the shouts of men who certainly were not useless puppets, Gair and Idrann and Snow Grell made it to the secret door, and Snow Grell opened it, and the healer closed it.

And then they made their way back to the tunnels, and Snow Grell took Talyn so the healer could lead, because they weren't going back to Talyn's place.

Idrann stopped at a door not far from the one through which they'd just come. "Her horses," he said. "We'll need them. Wait here."

He vanished into the doorway, and in almost no time at all came back leading a string of five horses.

"Decided while I was there to clear out all the good horses. The bastard is moriiad—stealing his horses wouldn't bring a hanging even if we got caught. Which we won't."

He grinned, pulled a big blanket off one horse, and said, "Wrap her in this. I'll have clothes for her at my house."

"I think they'll look for us there, too," Gair said.

"I think they would. But we aren't going there to stay. We'll just pick up a few things we need, including my horses, which are better than the ragged mounts the diplomat kept, and then we'll go away for a while. I know a safe enough place for us."

They wrapped Talyn in the blanket and draped her over the back of the lead horse. Then, making more noise than Gair felt comfortable with, the three men, the five horses, and the woman they had come to rescue set out at a slow trot.

I could only think that I wanted to die, that a quick death would be a blessing and a kindness. And then I heard Tonk voices—three of them—followed by the cessation of pain and the sweet sound of slaughter.

They carried me away from Skirmig's hell, amid more slaughter. I hoped with everything in me that Skirmig was in the second group to die—but I didn't think he was.

When he'd finished with me and handed me off to his servants, he told me that he'd found his own way into the Fheling Point, and since he had become a god, he was going to go change the world. He'd be back for me in a bit, he said, but meantime, he was going to make very sure I didn't get back to the Fheling Point on my own. His men were extensions of him—the torture and the horror at their hands had been identical to the torture and the horror at his hands. Only with more hands.

I couldn't find my way to trance while my rescuers were carrying me, but when they put me on the back of a horse, I felt I'd found my way home. From the easy gait, I thought the horse was likely my Toghedd, who had a trot smooth as butter. I wanted nothing more than to sleep. Or die. But I feared that if I did not get to the Fheling Point quickly, Skirmig would find his way to me and recapture me. And kill my rescuers.

In trance, I discovered that my Hagedwar was already cast and waiting; I needed do nothing more than slip into the Fheling Point and wrap its sweetness around me. As soon as I did, I was able to break the chains with which Skirmig had bound me.

I could see how he had cast the chains. I would be able to do the same thing—but such chains would be useless against anyone who could cast the Hagedwar and step into the Fheling Point.

I considered that for a moment. Such chains would be useless against only two people in the whole of the world. Skirmig and me. No one else had the necessary links to both forms of magic. Yet.

So even if I could hunt him through the View, I would not be able to hold him until someone could get to him to kill him—and he still had the advantage of me because by his own admission he knew a way to use the Hagedwar without ever stepping into trance.

I would not be his equal until I could do that.

I still had much to learn, and now I had to be my own teacher. I still had to teach everything I knew to the Shielders, so that if anything happened to me, my people would not be without this new weapon.

I still had to find and slaughter Skirmig.

I had so much to do, and no idea how I could accomplish it all in the little time that I feared remained.

My mind kept drifting back to the room that had held me and all Skirmig's men. I kept fighting to stay in the present. It was hard; but by blocking from myself the recent horrors and pretending they had happened to someone else, I could at last focus on the emergencies of the moment.

I studied the world around me through the lens of the Fheling Point. I could reach into the View, buffered from its dangers. I could see the people with me as spheres of light, beautiful and in terrible danger. The mercs were everywhere aboveground looking for them and me, pounding on doors, dragging people from their beds.

So little time, so much danger. And the situation was getting worse with every instant that slipped by. I used magic to heal myself. I didn't worry about my appearance—I simply repaired my cracked and broken ribs and my broken fingers, and stopped myself from bleeding. I would have a few scars, I was sure. But I'd earned them. If ever I decided that I no longer needed to remember what had happened to me in the hands of the moriiad, I would remove them.

I pushed out of the Fheling Point and slipped into the togram that would let me transfer physical objects, and snatched my packed bag from Skirmig's house.

The bag appeared on Dakaat's back, and from my place within the Hagedwar, I arranged it so that it wouldn't fall off. I'd planned to throw it over the back of one of my horses when I went home anyway, so I'd packed with horse travel in mind and balanced the load by instinct.

My three rescuers stopped, and I pushed myself out of the trance, noticing that my Hagedwar, which had always closed as I returned to the physical world, now stayed open behind me. Odd.

I wriggled down from Toghedd's back, hanging on to the blanket, and one of the men called out, "She's slipping!" as he caught me.

He was *touching* me. *Holding* me. I couldn't bear it. I fought, all thought of modesty forgotten, all reason gone, my only goal to get free of his hold. My heart galloped, my mouth went dry as old bone, I could barely breathe, and in that instant his wild-man's face with its bushy hair and enormous beard became the embodiment of all the horrors I was trying to forget. Tonk men do not wear beards—ever—or leave their hair matted and un-bound unless they are mad. He might be mad. No. He was moriiad. He was moriiad. I wanted to kill him. By Ethebet, I tried.

Another man ran back to us, shouting, "Hold! Hold! You're among friends!"

The terrifying morii wild man had made no move against me in my madness save to block my attacks. He did not stop me from backing away from him, either, and I turned, conscious suddenly of my nakedness, and found myself looking at Snow Grell, the Hva Hwa I'd helped. I peered around him to see who was in the lead, and recognized Master Idrann.

Which suggested that no matter what I'd heard from Skirmig about his being close to death, the man who had thought I was falling and who'd leapt to my rescue was the surviving Eastil prisoner.

Definitely another morii.

"I can stand on my own," I said as he offered me his arm. I was shaking so badly I could not be sure I would be standing at all in another moment, but I knew I could not bear to be touched.

The bearded morii picked up the horse blanket that had dropped to the ground when I attacked him, and handed it back to me. I wrapped it around myself and said, "My clothes are in the bag on the Dakaat's back. I need to dress."

He looked startled. "We brought no bag."

"I got it. With magic."

"I thought you were near death," he said. "I feared we would not be able to get you to shelter in time to save you." He paused. "You seem . . . remarkably well."

Idrann came running back. "She's awake?"

"She's standing," the Eastil morii said.

"I'm fine. Now. Though I was near enough to death when you found me. I had to heal myself with magic. But I do need to get my clothes." I looked past the two moriiad to Idrann and said,

"Thank you for coming to get me. I don't know how you knew I needed you, but I'm glad you did."

Idrann shook his head. "Thank Gair. He's the one who insisted you were in trouble and that we could not wait any longer. He wasn't well enough or strong enough to come after you alone, but he said if we waited, we would lose you. So I led him and Snow Grell to you."

So Gair was the man behind the beard. In the dark tunnels, I could not see any detail of his eyes, or I might have hoped to recognize him.

And then the full weight of what Idrann had done hit me. He'd taken Gair and Snow Grell—two moriiad—through the tunnels. *Two Eastil soldiers.* He had led them through the secret Tonk tunnels that every child, on the day he was old enough to use them, swore upon Jostfar and his soul to protect with his own life.

Ah, Ethebet, what future disaster would be the result of my survival? Having survived the treacherous Feegash bastard, what new hells would I yet bring down upon my people just by living?

I turned to Gair. I could not tell whether he looked well or ill—I could not see enough of him past the hair to guess. He'd stood. He'd run. He'd fought. So he was, at least, much better than when I'd left him.

"How did you know?" I asked him. I thought perhaps he and Snow Grell had managed to maintain their ties to the Eastil conspiracy that was likely to come storming over our borders in days. If the conspiracy was tied to the Feegash, which seemed logical, he might have known more than I did about Skirmig's plans for me.

But he said, "I dreamed of you."

He'd dreamed of me. He'd dreamed of me?

Well, I had dreamed of him, hadn't I? I'd dreamed of a damned moriiad coming to my rescue from monsters, and the monsters had turned out to be real, and what's more, had turned out to be more damned moriiad, and the shaking in my legs and arms and hands got so bad just thinking about it that I had to turn away and lean my face on Toghedd's flank for a moment.

I should have been grateful that this Eastil morii had enough of a conscience to consider himself in my debt; otherwise, I was sure, I would have suffered the fate of the Feegash wives, and been dumped one day soon into a pit with dirt shoveled over me. I gathered such strength and composure as I could and turned back to face him.

"Thank you," I told him. "We've exchanged a life for a life."

He nodded. "I am grateful I could repay my debt to you before I left for home."

I dug for the right response to that, through a confusion that almost erased words. "So am I."

I clutched the blanket around me and leaned against Toghedd with my eyes closed. My thoughts were few, popping out of the bloodred storm sea that raged inside me like shipwreck survivors struggling to the surface, then sinking again into the waves. Whips and torture, blood and fire, pain and fear and the insinuating voice of a man who kept saying he was doing what I wanted, that he knew what I wanted, that he was giving me what I wanted . . .

It hadn't happened to me. Didn't happen to me. Happened to some other woman, and I was going to make things right for her.

For everyone.

Going to make things right—and what had Idrann been thinking when he led two of our enemies through our tunnels? How had he planned to deal with men who were planning to go home, and who would without doubt take the information about the tunnels to their commander the instant they were out of our reach? Did Idrann plan to kill them? *That* seemed a faithless way to repay the debt of my life, and a foolish waste of all his work the last months, nursing the Eastil back to health.

I know what you really want.

Pain. Pain. Fear, shame, humiliation, pain and more pain.

Where could I hide. Could I hope for death?

It happened to someone else. Not me. I was strong. I was fine.

Deep breath, stop the shaking, focus on the moment.

There were moriiad in the Tonk tunnels. Two enemies who knew our secret.

Our duty to our people would override any duty to individuals. When we swore our lives to Ethebet, we took oaths that demanded this of us, even at the cost of our personal honor. Yet, Jostfar help me, I could not think of killing the men who had saved me from torture and imprisonment.

Not me, not me. Some other Tonk woman—it happened to her, or I was going to roll up in a ball in the tunnels and never move again.

It happened to her.

And I could not think of seeing them walk free, knowing what they knew. What of duty? What of my oath to Ethebet? And what of what was right? What of men who would risk their lives to save . . . an enemy? That other Tonk woman, the one who had been in such trouble? What did they deserve?

I hoped Idrann had a plan, for I could think of nothing that would serve. I could think of nothing that even made sense. My mind was full of monsters, my ears full of the screaming that still fought inside me for release.

I made my way back to Dakaat, and, holding the blanket around me with one hand, rummaged for clothing with the other. Idrann had taken us to the entrance to his house—I could see his symbol on the passageway door.

He said, "I'm getting my horses and some medicines for you and Gair, and I'll be right back." He vanished into his doorway; while we waited, I found clothes and started to pull them on. And then an ugly thought hit me.

"I should have told him about the mercs," I muttered.

I ran for the door, but Gair's arm shot out and he grabbed me. "Where are you going?"

"I have to warn Idrann about the mercs."

"Mercs?"

"They're everywhere out there. They're going from house to house, and they will certainly search his house. He has to get out of there. Nothing he has up there is worth his life."

Gair stared down at me. "How do you know this is happening?"

"Magic," I said. "I was a Shielder in the war, and I've learned other magic that lets me see into the View without a team to guard me. I've seen the madness going on up above."

"If that is so, why are these tunnels not filled with people hiding from the mercs?"

I closed my eyes. "We have no watch anymore. It's the middle of the night, everyone is asleep. So no one is standing guard to see what is happening and ring the alarm bells, and unless some taaksman manages to wake in time and flee to the bells without being caught, to ring them, no one will ever know until it's too late."

"Are the mercs killing the people they awaken?"

"I don't know. But I have to get Idrann."

Gair said, "No. You cannot go up there. He won't be caught sleeping. He will have a better chance than anyone else of getting what he needs and getting away. He's unlikely to be taken by surprise."

"Unless mercs were hiding in his house, lying in wait for him."

"In which case, if you go up there, you'll be captured too. And I'm betting that the bastard wants you back most of all."

I nodded. "I had . . . something he wanted," I said. I could not admit that I had been the sole possessor of the weapon that would let the Tonks win our war against the Eastils in spite of the interference of the Feegash. Skirmig had that, though— somehow he'd found his own way to use the Fheling Point, or at least some tiny part of it. Enough to hurt m— . . . that other woman.

But Gair was right. I couldn't go up there and chance putting myself into Skirmig's hands again. My blood ran cold at the very thought, and I spiraled down into the darkness of fear, and lost whatever Gair said afterward.

Breathe. Breathe.

For the moment, at least, I was the only one besides Skirmig who had the weapon of the Fheling Point magic. Even if Skirmig had the same magic, so long as my people had it, too, we might still hope to save ourselves, to rid ourselves of the Feegash. For the moment, I *was* the weapon that could set us all free. But only if I stayed free myself.

"I'll go warn him," Snow Grell said. "I'll be careful."

I heard that. I thought of the Hva Hwa's skills at not being seen, and thought it likely that he would be able to walk from one end of Beyltaak to the other in midday with mercs looking for just him alone and reach his destination unseen and untouched.

He went through the door, closing it carefully behind him. And we waited.

And waited.

From in front of us and behind us, I suddenly heard the echoes of hundreds of doors popping open, of distant whispers and whole families fleeing into the tunnels. So someone had reached the bell. Whoever it was would not escape capture; the bell tower was easily surrounded and easily blocked off. Beyltaak had been built with the understanding that our enemies would not breach our walls, nor pass our inner perimeters, nor evade our warships, our Conventionals, our Senders, or our traps.

But we had been betrayed and stripped bare, and the enemy lived within our inner perimeter.

We waited some more.

The door popped open, and Snow Grell slipped through. He was covered with fresh blood. "I killed two of them in silence and secret," he said, "but the other two already had Idrann. They'd bound him and were taking him out the door. I followed them as far as I dared; they're taking Idrann to Skirmig. They've taken a lot of prisoners." He stared at me. "The bastard looks like he will move mountains to get to you."

I thought of my family. The mercs would have gone first to my parents' house. I could be sure my mother, my father, and the few of my brothers and sisters who remained at home were prisoners already.

Likewise those relatives outside my parents' home that Skirmig knew about.

Knowing what he had been willing to do to me, I could well imagine what he would be willing to do to them.

I leaned against the horse, suddenly light-headed with fear. "Oh, Jostfar, what do I do?" I whispered. I had no army to rush in and free them, and I would need one. But I could not leave them in Skirmig's hands.

Gair saw me sag and ran over to me. "Are you too hurt to stand?"

"They'll have my family. You saw what they did to . . ." Don't think about it much, not about what it means, not about where it happened, not about what happened. It was far away. Far away. ". . . to me."

He looked back at Snow Grell. Snow Grell nodded. Gair looked back to me and said, "The three of us will go get them. Where do you think they'll be?"

I said, "We have to check home first. In case they got away. Any of them." I was so scared for all of them. But especially

Rik—Rik who was small even for his age, but had the heart of a mother bear; who would rush in to save his family, and be hurt by men who wouldn't care that he was just a child. Maybe my parents had managed to hide my younger siblings. Maybe they, and Rik, were safe.

But Skirmig would have gone there first if he wanted to find me.

"All right. Lead us."

I thought about what Skirmig could do to Snow Grell or Gair or me if we went in unprotected from his magic.

When I'd undone the last magic he'd used against me, I'd seen how he'd done it. I could form shields against his doing it again.

"We have to wait just a moment," I said, and dropped to a cross-legged position on the cobblestones, and took myself quickly into a trance, and into the already-waiting Hagedwar. I moved into the Fheling Point, and used the power there to wrap Gair, Snow Grell, and me in magic that would stop Skirmig from taking control of us. I stepped out of the Hagedwar, and tried to close it.

It wouldn't close.

I didn't like that change. I didn't trust it. I could vary its size, but I could not shut it down completely. To me, having that open Hagedwar sitting there seemed to create a vulnerability— and I didn't dare permit any of those. I moved back into the Fheling Point and created a shield around the whole of the Hagedwar. It seemed silly and excessive after I'd done it, but I didn't take it down.

My parents had spent many years teaching me that paranoia was a virtue, and that first instincts were often based on things I had noticed but hadn't realized I'd noticed. And that fear was the best friend of the survivor.

Everything I'd ever seen had convinced me my parents were right.

I slipped out of the trance at last and rose. "Let's go."

We hurried through the tunnels, which I knew as well as I knew the streets above, pushing past people who crowded close and silent, waiting, or hid away in the cul-de-sacs, or fled toward the hidden exits beyond the walls. I noticed places where the tunnels were no longer in perfect repair; the Beyltaak Forces had maintained them, and the Forces were disbanded. Some citizens had clearly maintained their own sections after the Feegash brought their "peace"—but many had not.

In a few years, I thought, much of what was once here would collapse, and the careful work of centuries would be lost. If the Feegash had their way, the Tonk as a people would be lost.

I reached the doorway to my family home, and told Gair and Snow Grell, "Stay here with the horses. I'll see if anyone is there."

But Gair gave a cold, thin laugh, and said, "If you don't come back, then we'll have the pleasure of wandering around down here with the horses, or going aboveground and being captured. We need to stay with you."

So we moved all five horses into my family's cul-de-sac and tied them loosely, and I led the Eastils into the root cellar of my family home.

No one was there, but I could hear voices above. They were neither panicked nor angry. It sounded like my mother was cooking, and the family at home was sitting around the table.

I crept to the ladder and listened.

They sounded exactly as they would in normal times. Calm. Unexcited. Unbothered. That in itself was wrong. In a situation like this, with the alarm bell sounded, they should have been hiding.

"Wait here," I whispered to Snow Grell and Gair. "If anything happens to me, you can surely figure out how to get out of here. But it sounds like my family is fine up there. I have to know what's happening with them."

From the look on his face, Gair clearly didn't like this idea. But he waved me on, and I climbed up the ladder, pushed through the cellar door, and crept through the back room to the kitchen. Pressed flat against the wall on the other side, I could hear my mother talking about the ice breakup in the harbor, and my father agreeing with her that it would only be a few more days. I could hear the undercurrent of my brothers and sisters. None of them spoke of the shouting out in the streets, which I could still hear. None seemed in the least disturbed that they were awake at such an unholy hour. My mother was cooking, she and my father were talking, and the rest of our world was spinning in chaos.

I couldn't make sense of it.

I stepped around the corner.

There, at table with my parents and my sibs, sat Skirmig. He smiled at me, the same warm smile I had once loved, until I'd learned to hate it. "And here she is. I told you she'd be along," he said.

My mother turned and smiled at me. "Have a seat, Talyn, dear. Have some breakfast. We've been waiting for you."

"Kill him," I growled. "He tortured me and intends to destroy us all!"

I grabbed a knife from the end of the table and ran at Skirmig, but my brothers stepped into my path, and Corlaa caught my wrist. "He's here as a friend, Talyn," Corlaa told me.

"He doesn't know the meaning of the word. He's an immoral beast, a pervert, a killer. He tortured me—and he's tricked you. He's moriiad of the worst sort." I struggled to free my wrist, but Corlaa, at twenty-two, had height, weight, and strength on me. "He has to die."

My brother pulled the knife from my hand. "You don't need that here," he said.

My father seemed not to notice that I wanted to kill Skirmig. He smiled at me and said, "You've had a wonderful business offer in Sinali. Skirmig came here to tell us about it, and to let us know that you would be leaving with him today."

Cold dread filled me, seeping from my heart out through my blood and bones, chilling everything about me. I stopped fighting Corlaa, and he let go of my wrist. I turned to my mother. "He came at this hour of the morning and told you I was going somewhere with him? And you don't mind this?"

"It's a wonderful opportunity," she said, and gave me a broad, genuine smile. "Skirmig showed us the little dancing figurine you created; apparently the people of Sinali would love to hire your talents to create such trinkets for them. And the money they're offering is beyond generous."

She looked like my mother. And the man in my father's seat looked like my father. But my parents would never have encouraged me to leave Beyltaak and the Confederacy for Sinali, which was as far from Hyre as a country could be—especially knowing what they knew about Beyltaak's situation with Shielders and Senders and Communicators.

I stood there listening to rain outside washing over the cobblestone streets, hearing it hit the roof with sullen steadiness, and my family looked at me, and I looked at them, and I knew that Skirmig had taken them from me. I would get them back—somehow—but he hadn't needed to capture them or torture them. He had done something to them with magic that had made them belong to him.

I was too late.

"You need to go with him," my mother told me, and put a heap of eggs and smoked salmon and onions and pan-fried spiced potatoes on a plate, and put the plate in my place at table, and smiled at me as if she'd just said the most sensible thing in the world. "It will be good for you. The two of you love each other so much."

"You have to leave here, Talyn," Skirmig said. "For many reasons, you have to leave here." He was still smiling, but I caught an edge of fear in his voice. Fear of me?

No. He didn't fear me in the slightest. He was sure that he had me where he wanted me; that with my parents and siblings in his control, I would not resist him.

Fear *for* me, then?

I couldn't imagine why. What he planned for me was worse than anything I could have imagined. He *was* my fear.

And then both of my parents, and all my siblings including Rik, and Skirmig, sighed at the same time.

"The first of the icebreaker ships has reached the docks," my sister said, and the others all just smiled. They smiled Skirmig's smile—and then that horrible shared moment passed and they were themselves again.

"We need to be going now, beloved," Skirmig said. "That ship is here for us."

"You need to die now." I looked for some other weapon, but short of my mother's frying pans, which I would have to go through her to get, there was nothing.

Out in the street, I heard marching in unison.

"They're coming for your friends," Skirmig said. "The two hiding in the next room waiting to rush in here and save you again." He laughed. "Those two fools are the perfect examples of your warrior society and everything that's wrong with it. You people have no idea how ridiculous you are. You've been fighting each other with weapons for a third of a millennium without success. We come in with mere words, and in a year we own all of you. Though you, of course, I'll still make queen. You'll make a good queen, I think, when you learn your place."

He rose, while my family stayed in front of him, protecting him from me. "Come along, Talyn." He stared at me, his smile turned ugly, and I could feel his magic trying to reach me through the shield I'd cast.

But it didn't, and his smile faded. He frowned, and the tramp on the cobblestones grew louder.

I had no sword, but I had the weapon that could fight him.

I *was* the weapon that could fight him.

Gair ran into the room and grabbed my arm. "Retreat," he said. "We cannot win this day, but we must live to win the next."

Skirmig pointed at Gair. "You. Put down your sword and wait for the mercs to get here."

Gair laughed. "I'd cut your head off right now if you weren't using her family as shields, you coward."

I had the satisfaction of seeing the shock on Skirmig's face.

Then Rik said, "Talyn, you have to go with Skirmig. It's the right thing to do."

"Don't talk to me through him," I said to Skirmig. "And remember that I'll be back to kill you."

We fled back through the house and down into the cellar, accompanied by the sound of my family's door bursting in. Snow Grell opened the hidden door, I closed it, we grabbed the horses and jumped on them, and I led Snow Grell and Gair at a trot through tunnels now lit by the lamps of the hundreds of people who hid there.

"Still not safe," I said as I passed each group. "I think we may have lost the taak."

If they believed me, they would flee into the countryside, something Tonks have always been good at, and perhaps join up for a while with the nomads. If they didn't, they would be lost, too. I could feel it.

Beyltaak was falling, and I had nothing with which to fight.

16

Gair waited while Talyn led the horses out into daylight one by one.

"This is one of the military exits. Most of the civilians never knew about it," Talyn said. "And now there's no military to speak of."

They came out into what appeared to be a natural shelf over-hang; it overlooked the walled taak below, and the harbor, still filled with chunks of ice, but now filled with ships, too.

Talyn hadn't said much during their run, and she didn't say anything as they crept to the edge of the cliff and stared down at her home.

"Icebreakers and warships," Snow Grell said behind him, and Gair could see hundreds of men making their way to the docks, and offloading what was clearly war matériel, including more mercs, horses, war wagons, and supplies. The icebreakers were of Eastil design; the warships were of Tonk manufacture—they had the high carved horse prows that all Tonk ships had—but all flew the yellow-and-black flag of the Feegash.

"The Feegash took our ships," he said, crouching beside her as she stared down at the fall of her home. "And yours."

"At the start of their 'peace' and the disarmament, they put advisors on board so that they could help us use our ships to cut down on piracy. So they said." She turned to him, and he could see the tear streaks drying on her cheeks. "But in fact, they had no navy. They're a tiny landlocked nation high in inhospitable mountains. And apparently they decided it was time to get a bigger, richer, better-appointed land."

Gair said, "They were cowards of the worst sort. They used deceit because they were too weak and frightened to use honor. They gave words, and their words meant nothing. They are not men."

"At least we need not mourn them when we wipe them from the face of the earth," Talyn said.

It's such a shame she's a Tonk, Gair thought. I could like her greatly otherwise. "No one will shed tears at their passing," he agreed.

She pointed out a stream of Tonks fleeing along a secret trail. Then she gripped his arm, and he felt her hand dig into his flesh like a vise.

Smoke and flame rose from three locations within the taak.

"The temples," she whispered. "They're burning the temples."

He thought of the Tonk temples, which held hundreds or even thousands of books, and were a center of Tonk life in a way no Eastil temple ever would—or ever could—be. Those temples and the vast libraries they housed were irreplaceable.

People armed with farm implements and clubs fought in the streets, trying to keep the well-armed merc troops from reaching more of the temples—and the mercs were cutting them down. The wind and the steady rain muffled the sounds of battle, but morning had come while they were escaping, and in the thin gray light of dawn, they could see the bodies like scattered, broken toys.

"I'm sorry," Gair whispered, and put an arm around Talyn's shoulder, meaning to offer comfort.

She jerked away away, wordless, and sat on the cold, damp stone, her legs crossed, her hands resting on her knees in an odd attitude, and she closed her eyes.

Gair might have guessed that she was praying, except that was not how Tonks prayed. They prayed standing up, with eyes wide open, looking into their god's face. Sometimes they ripped out chunks of hair and burned hair and wood chips and paper, but they were not, as a rule, people who went to their god as supplicants. He'd heard more than one Tonk quote their proverb "Thank Jostfar for your blessings, but carry your own pack." They seemed to him very much a people determined to carry their own packs, no matter what it might cost them or how damned heavy those packs might be. So he didn't know what she was doing.

Snow Grell tapped his shoulder, and Gair turned and headed deeper into the shelf.

"We need to be on our way," Snow Grell said. "They'll be out here looking for us soon enough, and we should be getting home."

Gair looked at Talyn. He had saved her life. He had served his honor and repaid his debt. He was free to go home. And Snow Grell was right. If the two of them hoped to see the Republic again, they needed to take the horses that didn't belong to Talyn and flee, because while at the moment they had a small, chancy opportunity to escape, it was not going to get bigger or better with time.

He tried to see her as the enemy—as a woman who had acted with honor toward him, but one to whom he owed no lasting debt. But she had saved his life twice. Once directly, when she'd stepped between him and an angry mob. And once at second hand, when she'd persuaded that Feegash bastard to come get him and Hale.

He'd repaid her for only one of those rescues, and if she stayed close to home or tried to get back in to save her family, she was going to need someone at her side again. That thought didn't depress him anywhere near as much as it should have.

And then he noticed that the fires in the temples were going out.

He crept back to the edge of the shelf and stared at her. Sweat beaded her forehead, and her mouth was set in a silent snarl of pain. Her body had gone rigid; her skin had paled to the gray of ash.

He could still see fighting in the streets, and new fires starting all over. But one and then another and then another of the temples acted exactly as a candle acted with a snuffer held over the flame. All the flames flickered and backed in on themselves and sputtered out, and for a moment smoke rolled from the building—and then the rain began to wash away the smoke.

And the second that happened, the flames started going out in another building. Gair motioned Snow Grell to be silent, and summoned him over to look at Talyn and the fires in Beyltaak.

Snow Grell looked from her to the flames and back to her, and his eyes went wide. He mouthed the word *Her?* and Gair shrugged and nodded at the same time, which he hoped would convey that he thought so, but wasn't sure.

Snow Grell did one of those obeisance gestures he'd brought with him from the Hva Hwa—he had a lot of them, but though he'd tried to teach the meanings of all of them to the other men in the unit, no one, including Gair, had cared enough to learn. Gair wasn't sure, therefore, if Talyn had received the Greeting to a Living Goddess, or the Polite Right to a Warrior of Rank, or the Simple Honorific to a Woman One Wants to Futter.

But he didn't have time to ask. The fire in a yet another building went out, and Talyn collapsed in a heap.

Gair dropped to hands and knees and checked her for breathing. Snow Grell ran to the other side, pressed fingers to her neck, and said, "Her blood still pulses, so her heart still beats."

"She breathes."

"She was putting out those fires," Snow Grell said.

"That appears to be true," Gair agreed. "We can't leave her here. We need her. If she could do that, what else could she do?"

"Faint, maybe," Snow Grell said, and raised an eyebrow at Gair, so that Gair laughed.

Gair scooped Talyn into his arms, telling himself that holding her body close to his affected him not at all, or if it did, it was only that it had been so very long that he'd been with a woman that *any* woman felt good.

She had some sort of magic he'd never seen before; she could do something that could help his people as much as her own. If she was strong enough. He didn't know that she was.

In this day alone, she had suffered torture at the hands of the diplomat bastard and his servants, the loss of her friend the healer to enemy troops, her family's betrayal by the man who had so hurt her, her taak overrun by enemies and set to the torch, and many of her people taken captive.

In spite of everything, she had been able to do *something*— though he could not begin to guess what—that had stopped some of the fires in her taak. In the long run, it had cost her a great deal for nothing, because if the Feegash were determined to burn the temples, one woman wasn't going to stop them. But he could not think of her as weak or helpless. She had survived terrible things. And she'd fought until she fell.

Still, neither could he allow himself to think of her as some goddess, invulnerable to the horrors she had been through, impervious because of that magic she wielded. She feared his touch. She had suffered great physical hurt and surely hurt of the mind and spirit as well. That magic she used was only a tool, and one that had not been able to save her from the bastard's torturers. It wasn't a solution. It couldn't protect her, no matter what it might do for those around her.

Gair held her tighter and carried her to the back of the shelf, where Tonk soldiers or workers had carved well-disguised rooms out of the living rock. He and Snow Grell had put the horses and their few supplies in one such room, though the rooms clearly had not been designed with horses in mind. Snow Grell had his bedroll, and Talyn had her one bag; she must certainly have something useful hidden in that.

"Help me get her onto one of those bunks in there," Gair said. "We'll put her down and check her wounds to make sure she isn't bleeding badly, and then we'll figure out what we do next."

Snow Grell didn't question. They were in the field, and they'd fallen back into the routine of officer and enlisted man. They carried Talyn into one of the rooms carved into the shelf. Snow Grell had discovered supplies in the place—blankets, uniforms, food, and more weapons. Gair put her down on blankets Snow Grell had pulled from the hidden supplies, and covered her with another blanket, and then, lifting just a corner to preserve her modesty should she wake, he rolled her on one side and lifted the back of her shirt.

She was covered with blood, but as far as he could see, all of it was dry. Beneath the blood, her back was an unbroken weave of welts and bruises and barely healed cuts. "Get me water," he said. Snow Grell returned a few minutes later with a good bucket full of clear water.

"Found more supplies," Snow Grell said. "Dried food, another small weapons cache, medicines, healers' supplies, a good well. There are three or four rooms carved into this shelf—maybe more. I haven't had the chance to go exploring, but this isn't the only room that has bunks in it. A team like ours could have stayed holed up here for a month or better without having to leave for anything." Snow Grell looked out the carved door. "She can stay here while she gets better. She won't want for anything."

And we can leave was the implied ending of that sentence.

Gair washed the blood from Talyn's back, saying nothing, and he and Snow Grell both gasped at the scars that remained.

Those sick fucks had carved pictures into her back, onto her arms, her legs, her sides—he would bet that if he rolled her over, he'd find they'd carved her up in front, too. And then they had beaten her with whips until those decorations seemed to peer out from between the close-placed bars of a cage.

She'd done everything she'd done on the same day she got those.

Or at least some of them. As he looked closer, he could see that some of the scars were pale pink instead of bright red. Some had silvered.

The bastard had been working on her for a while, then.

And Gair had almost been too late getting to her.

He and Snow Grell could leave. They could get away from this place and go home. His own people in the Republic would have fared better than the Tonks were faring—they had a centralized government, a strong king, a good Council of Representatives who would make sure that the Feegash did not make the inroads against them that they'd made against the fractious, scattered Tonks and their independent taaks. He could go home, gather up men, and march back here to destroy the Feegash, who had obviously taken the Tonks at the first breath of spring because the Eastils would have slaughtered the Feegash had they tried the same trick in the Republic.

He and his army would be heroes whom the Tonks would have to welcome as saviors. He could end their ancient war for real, simply by demonstrating that the Eastil way was best.

He wanted to stay, though. He wanted to stay and help Talyn save her people. He had grown to like the Tonks, he told himself. Most of them, anyway. They had some good people among them, and those good people might be lost to the Feegash before an Eastil army could reach them.

Too, Talyn had a weapon—or *was* a weapon—unlike anything that Gair had ever seen. She was brave, she was tough . . . but she was one woman alone, and strong as she was, there were things she could not do alone. He told himself that if he left her unprotected, she would die. And his people would never get their hands on what she knew.

He reached out to touch the scars on her back, fighting a lump in his throat, blinking his eyes too fast—smoke in the air from the burning taak below was clearly bothering them. He ran a finger lightly over the closed wounds, then yanked it away as if burned.

Gair made a decision. Based, he promised himself, purely on pragmatism. She was, after all, his enemy. But she was a *good* enemy.

"I'm going to stay here with her," he told Snow Grell. "I want you to go home, gather up some of our people, and lead them back here. We're going to rescue these Tonks and win the war for good, as heroes on both sides of the damned thing." He paused, trying to figure out a way to put his decision in the best light in front of Snow Grell. "I'd go with you, but she won't go with us—her family is here. But she can do something our people can't do. We need to know if she's unique, or if what she can do others could learn to do as well."

Snow Grell raised an eyebrow, and Gair could see that he was not entirely satisfied with Gair's explanation.

Well, in truth, Gair wasn't either, but it was the one he was going to tell himself until he believed it. "Either we'll be here, or if we move on, I'll leave word here in the usual way."

Snow Grell nodded. The unit had its code, and its way of hiding the code. "You want me to stay until you're stronger? Clearly she's going to need help, and you're not fully well yourself."

"We'll manage. Take some of the horses and whatever supplies you need, and find out as quickly as you can how things are back home. And keep safe."

Snow Grell laughed softly. "I'll be safe. But I'll not take anything. If I'm traveling alone, supplies and horses would just slow me down."

Sometimes Gair could forget that Snow Grell was Hva Hwa.

But not when he remembered that Snow Grell had kept to the unit's pace out of a desire to remain part of the unit—and that alone, Snow Grell could run nearly twenty long leagues a day, every day. Over flat, clear ground, he could cover more. That was a pace that would kill a horse on the first day. And a pace neither Gair nor the rest of his men had ever been able to match.

Gair wondered again what had taken Snow Grell from a place where most people were like him to the Eastil Republic, where no one could keep up with him. And why he had been content, in that situation, to follow rather than to lead?

He and Snow Grell clasped hands, and Snow Grell gave the one Hva Hwa salute that Gair could always remember: Friend Taking Leave of Friend. Hands crossed at the wrists, fists clenched, he thumped his chest once. Gair returned the gesture.

"I'll be back. Meantime, watch your backs," Snow Grell said. "You're *both* in enemy territory now."

I woke up in time to hear Snow Grell tell Gair we should watch our backs, that we were both in enemy territory. "My father always told me that," I told Gair after Snow Grell was gone, and Gair jumped.

"You're awake."

I sat up. My head throbbed. I tried to stand, but my legs wouldn't hold me.

"Lie down. I'll get what you need."

I thought about all the many things I needed, the first being to know that my family was safe and the second to know that Skirmig was dead. But the Eastil couldn't give me those. "Water," I told him. "I'm dry as bleached bone." I lay back on one of the bunks, not having the faintest idea how I'd reached it.

He came back with a skin full of good, clear water, and I drank deeply. "Thank you," I told him.

And felt a shock, remembering suddenly the dream I'd had of a choice—and the choice I'd made. Water. I'd chosen water. And had been given a sword.

Where was my sword? The Feegash magic? Yes. That would be it. Ethebet's shield maiden had spoken true.

I finished off the water, and pressed my hands to my temples. My head throbbed.

"Are you sick?" he asked me. "Hurt? Do you need anything else?"

His concern sounded genuine. But Skirmig had been good at pretending, too. I wanted nothing of moriiad, nothing of men, nothing of concern, whether genuine or false. I wanted only to be alone. I was going to have to go back into Beyltaak, find people who would fight with me, and lead them against an army of trained mercs to win a way to my family. I had no Conventional training at all, I had minimal leadership ability, and even though I had a few magic tricks that would be useful in battle, somehow Skirmig—blind to the View—had managed to figure them out almost as soon as I did. And he could walk around and even fight while he did magic, while I had to sit still with my eyes closed, trapped in the helplessness of a trance. I was doomed. But I still had to save my family. And if it could be saved, my taak.

Doomed.

But I said, "I'm fine. You can take off after your friend now. My parents and others within the taak have fallen into collusion with Skirmig and this Feegash treachery, so the tunnels are lost to secrecy. Your knowledge of them will be no greater betrayal than we have already suffered."

He said, "I'm staying with you. Snow Grell is going home to bring us reinforcements to liberate your people from the Feegash."

"Leaving you alone in enemy territory," I said.

He looked at me and shrugged. "I'm not alone. You're here. And we're both in trouble, but less so together than apart."

Which was inarguably true. "I still don't understand why you stayed," I told him. "I asked no debt from you for what I did to help you, and any debt that existed even in your own mind you have since repaid."

He leaned forward, wrapped his arms around his knees, and laughed. "Not true. I've now repaid you for the first time you saved my life. The debt for the second time, which was much larger, remains."

I frowned at him, uncomprehending. "What first time?"

"When the crowd had gathered and was stoning me, you're the soldier who rode between them and me. And my men. You stopped them."

"They wouldn't have killed you," I said. "Someone else would have stopped them, or their own reason would have prevailed."

"Mobs feed on each other, and the more they feed, the uglier they get. You've never been on the wrong end of a mob throwing stones," he said.

"No. I haven't." I sat up and swung my legs over the side of the bunk. "So. You're throwing your lot in with mine. Why?"

"I told you."

"No you haven't. You mentioned what you still owe me. But what I want to know is what you hope to get for yourself."

He had steady eyes gray as the bellies of thunderheads in a building storm, and he didn't smile. Even when he laughed, it was laughter without much humor in it. He looked at me with those gray eyes and nothing inside me twisted. He didn't smile at me, and I felt no sudden urge to do what he wanted, to give him anything he wanted.

He was no golden boy with the powers of a god in his pocket, no lovely, twisted Feegash elite. He was just a man, a wild-haired, wild-bearded soldier from my enemy's army. He couldn't hurt me the way Skirmig had hurt me. But that didn't mean he couldn't hurt me in new ways. Or that I could trust him.

He told me, "Your people held out against mine for three hundred years. Surely you'll find some way to beat the Feegash, especially with my people fighting alongside yours. And your . . . magic weapon . . . that should help. I'm ground troops, but I've worked with Magics for years. I've never seen any one person in Magics pull off what you were doing before you passed out."

Ah. His interest in helping me started to come into focus. "What weapon?"

"Using magic—alone—to put out those fires. We were trained from the earliest that if we had a Magics unit under our care, we had to protect the whole unit. That the loss of even one of you people might be enough to destroy the unit. That you people couldn't operate alone. I was trained to believe that the Tonks had the same restrictions we had, and that if we ever had the chance we should move past Conventional units and go straight for Magics, because that was where your forces were most vulnerable."

"That's all true."

"But you were working alone. You were *effective* alone."

"So you want what I know."

"I want to win against those bastards. And I think you have a way to do it. So I'm staying with you."

"You have no idea what you're trying to involve yourself with. I'm going back into Beyltaak. I'm going to try to find people who still serve Jostfar and convince them to fight against the Feegash mercs—the best mercenary army anyone has ever seen—even though most of the Tonks still in Beyltaak have never been anywhere near Ethebet's shrine, have never held a sword, have never had to stand against an enemy who wanted to kill them. I have to turn such people as I have into a fighting force, and *I've never fought as a Conventional.* You want to throw your lot in with me? I know what must be done—but I have no idea what I should do or how I should do it."

"I do," he said, and those gray eyes studied me without flinching. "I've fought with a sword, and I've trained green men drawn by lot from their homes and their mamas—who had no spine and no fire in their bellies—to stand against enemies and fight. If you can find me men, I can make them warriors."

"You're moriiad."

"I am. I can't help that. But you're not exactly deluged with fighters begging to go into battle with you, and until outside help arrives, you're going to have to work with what you have. And I'm what you have right now. I'm offering you my skills, which you need, just as I want to benefit from skills that you have that I need. That *my* people will need. You be my shield, Talyn, and I'll be your sword."

"Hell of a sword you'll be," I said with a small laugh. "You're still thin and weak and just back from the edge of death yourself."

And then his words slammed me between the eyes, and I was back in that flower-filled meadow again, back with the woman in white and the banquet of the world, and the water. He would be my sword, he said, and I thought, *No, she didn't mean him. I have the magic. That's my sword.*

I stared first at the empty waterskin in my hand, and then at Gair. Beaten, battered, ill-used Gair the Eastil, a plain blade of foreign make if ever there was one, and in need of sharpening. I remembered his scars. His suffering at the hands of my people.

He was Ethebet's gift to me for choosing the warrior's path?

He couldn't be. He wasn't even Tonk. But who could equate elegant magic with a plain blade? Or an ill-used one?

"What's wrong?" he asked me.

I was too shaken to lie. "I suddenly remembered a dream I had. I think . . . I think that in an odd way, you were in it."

He nodded, not looking the least bit disturbed by my confession. "I would laugh at that, never having given much credence to dreams. But it was dreams that told me you were in trouble, and a dream that told me if I did not act this very day, you would die."

"Yesterday, actually," I corrected, and instantly regretted it. I hate it when others do that to me, and do my best not to do it to anyone else.

Gair rose, rubbing his eyes with battered, scarred knuckles. "I haven't had the benefit of sleep in a very long time. To me, this is still the same day." He yawned. "I wish I hadn't thought of that, for now I realize how tired I am. You're quite right—I'm not at my full health." He paced. "So what was your dream?"

I debated my answers, considered my options, and thought of my family in Skirmig's hands, my little brother Rik speaking Skirmig's words. I took a deep breath. "I think my dream was a suggestion that I take such help as was offered to me. But if you're to be . . . my sword"—just saying those two words shook me—"you'll have to make some changes."

"Changes?"

"You'll have to shave, and wear your hair in Ethebet's braid. You'll have to speak only Tonk, and pass for Tonk, because if we can find anyone who will fight with us, they won't fight side by side with an Eastil, or take their orders from an Eastil."

"Fine. The beard was just a way of hiding my improving health from the Feegash bastard's spies. I'll be glad to have it gone. The braid—I'm not sure I can do one of those on my own. It's a complicated-looking thing."

"Nine strands," I said, nodding. "Ethebet's number. And Jostfar's. You learn to do it on your own over time, but to begin with all of us did each other's. I'll braid for you, so long as no one is looking."

"Fair enough. I've had practice living as Tonk"—he winced a bit at that admission, but moved on—"and I never betrayed myself."

"Good." Something about his thinness nagged at me. The back of my brain kept insisting either that he shouldn't be so thin, or that he *needn't* be, but I was too weary and distraught to make much of that right then. Instead, I focused on the look of him, and chased the errant thoughts from my head. "You'll find a few kits in the second room down from this one. They'll be on the lowest shelves off the ground, probably to the right side, wrapped in wax cloth. Each will have a whetstone, all-purpose knife, snare, mirror, and a few other useful tools."

Gair cocked his head to one side. "*Probably* to the right side?"

"We try to keep all the shelves the same so that if we need to find things in a hurry, we can."

"This isn't the only one of these hideouts you people have."

I stared at him, horrified that I had given away so much.

He gave me a tired smile. "And even now you'll not tell me. Naturally. I'll swear my life to doing Ethebet's work if it will make you trust me."

"You can't," I said. "You're not Tonk."

"Of course." He sighed and turned away. "I'm off to shave, then, and find some food among the supplies. You and I will spend enough time up here to rest and make our plans. You have the watch, and the duty of provisioning the horses. I've seen nothing here for them, but knowing Tonks, that was an oversight on my part, not yours."

When he was gone, I stood, testing my legs. The Hagedwar extracted a physical price for its use, I'd discovered. At least as I'd used it. My battle against the merc-set fires of Beyltaak, where I'd put an airless barrier around one temple at a time and then waited for the flames to go out, had taken its energy from me. If I could have, I would have drawn my power from the View through the Fheling Point, but I didn't know how to use the Fheling Point to create and move physical things; as far as I could tell, the Fheling Point touched on spirit only.

Working in the red and drawing from my own power, I'd been able to hold barriers over four temples. Briefly. I could only be sure that three of them had put out the fires. I could not remember the fire going out over the fourth, nor could I remember removing the fourth barrier, though I thought it would probably have dissipated on its own if I wasn't holding it in place.

The red spaces of the Hagedwar offered useful magic, but limited. And I had not yet learned enough to make full use of the areas beyond the red, or to see their full value.

I wobbled, badly. But I had to go out and keep watch. I stepped through the low arch to the main shelf, and faced the midday, and found Beyltaak burning. Or burned. All the temples lay in ruins. So after I fell, the mercs had torched them again. But beyond the temples, the homes of taaksman and Beyl alike had fallen to the torch, as had the businesses of merchants and traders. In the heart of the taak, the market was smoke and rubble, the taverns laid waste, the buildings of government charred ruin. Save only one. The House of Law still stood, and from its tall tower flew the yellow and black of the Feegash flag. I fell to my knees and stared across cleared land—land that had been sheltering forest before the Feegash came—to what had once been the walled jewel of Beyltaak. The yellow and black banner of the Feegash mercs flapped over the harbor, and over the House of Law. In new clearings I could see bodies scattered. Yet those areas in which the Feegash had settled looked untouched, and none of the Feegash-style buildings burned.

I tried to fight back the tears, but they would not be denied. Oh, my taak . . . as much a part of me as my family—it was my life from the moment of my birth to the present. It was my shelter, the holder of my memories, my sacred obligation, my home, my heart.

My family was in there. My neighbors. My friends. The law that guided me, the saint who inspired me. My duty lay there, and all my hopes, and my greatest pride. My people were captives of the Feegash. The Feegash, who used their own little girls for rape and torture, and killed them for amusement once they became bored with them. If the Feegash treated their own people so, how would they treat mine?

But I was one person, weakened by ill use. And my "sword" was in no better shape than I.

I wept for a long time, and then I wiped my tears on a sleeve and clenched my fists against my own impotent fury. My rage alone would solve nothing. Only action would save my people.

I took the horses out through the passageway—well hidden— that led to a little fenced pasture with a spring-fed trough, hidden within a copse of trees. The pouring rain had melted the snow, and the pasture was a mess of dead grass and mud. I wouldn't be able to keep the horses there for long—their hooves would tear up the ground in its current state, and I had an obligation to keep the pasture in good shape against future need. But they could drink and move around for a bit while I climbed the hill above the shelf and tried to get an idea of what was going on elsewhere.

To the northeast, I could see smoke rising from what could only be Halviktaak, a tiny unwalled taak that lay between Beyltaak and sturdy Mattstaak. To the east, smoke. Roovintaak, which lay between us and Injtaak.

To the west, the harbor, filled with ships flying the Feegash flag.

To the south, forest and hills and gray skies and hard rain. I could see no smoke in that direction. Fifteen long leagues to the south lay Chaavtaak, one of the small taaks that had refused all negotiations with the Feegash, and that had closed itself within walls rather than permit entry to anyone wishing to discuss a treaty. Chaavtaak had been a taak of minor import; it had neither riches, nor a strong and powerful army, nor strategic value, and the Feegash had been content to ignore it as a nuisance while they pursued their peace with more important taaks. The nomads traversed the region as well, and had proven troublesome to the moriiad in their lands, and the Feegash had not started any of their roads south. They'd concentrated on the coastline, telling everyone that good roads between the strong taaks close to the sea would improve our commerce and increase our wealth.

And that had been true enough.

They had not added, however, that good roads would make the task of invading us easier.

They had given us their peace whether we wanted it or not, and their peace had been only the first step to their war. But now we would give them *our* war. The nomads would fight. I knew of other taaks like Chaavtaak that lay in the heart of the Confederacy that had not signed the peace treaty. Those taaks would stand against these honorless moriiad, if only I could reach them and tell them what I knew of the Feegash. They would win if I could teach them my new magic. If I could teach them quickly enough, before Skirmig could take the same magic and give it to his people, who were already better armed than us.

I fought despair. Chaavtaak was not burning, but how many taaks had successfully resisted the Feegash call for peace? How many had disarmed in order to give their people all the benefits of new trade that the Feegash had denied to holdouts?

How many of the nomads had taken the Feegash offers to give them land and walls and houses?

How deep did the Feegash betrayal cut us?

And what could two people—two *enemies,* no less—do against a storm that had already flattened us?

I took the horses down into the hollowed-out stable. We had enough space: the stable would hold ten horses in single stalls, and the granary and hayloft had supplies for ten horses for a month.

Food stores were for ten people for one month. Gair and I would hold out longer than the horses, but I did not see us taking more than a few days to put together our plan. I could not see that we dared.

Beyltaak had fallen, taking my family with it. My little brothers. My little sisters. My parents. My sibs and nieces and nephews, too; my cousins and aunts and uncles. Maybe some had fled.

Maybe some had died.

I did not let myself think about that, or about anything. My thoughts were not good places to dwell. Rather, I sought work.

I fed the horses, opened the channel that would run spring water through the troughs in the stalls, cleaned the winter debris, spread straw in the stalls and hay in the mangers, cleaned everything, checked supplies against the standard inventory, and only when I'd exhausted myself did I climb the wide ramp to the doorway back into the main rooms—a doorway well hidden from the other side.

I found Gair asleep on one of the bunks. Clean shaven, he looked younger than I'd expected or remembered. He was no youth; I guessed him to have a decade on me, or maybe the half of one, but he did not look like an old wild man anymore.

But Gair still did not look like the man I needed him to be. I could see the ghosts of frailty yet lingering, the scars of long hunger and abuse. I remembered the first time I had seen him—in a cage, facing a mob with unflinching calm, certain that what he faced was nothing less than his own death. He'd been a sturdy man then, broad of shoulder and deep of chest, built not for speed but for sheer unyielding strength. He'd looked like a man that would have—*could* have—faced an army single-handed and given it pause.

That man might have stood at the head of a rabble army and led it into the teeth of evil. *This* one, though he had big bones and a sort of wiry muscularity, looked like he might fall to his knees in the midst of a charge and start coughing blood like one of the lung-sick. It was not a look that inspired confidence. Not in me, and my life had been the military, and I knew at least something of who Gair was and what he was capable of. If I could not look at him and believe—and belief was much the issue—how much less would shopkeeps and temple keepers and taverners and craftsmen and horse breeders and money-lenders and other civilians who had fallen to the Feegash lie of peace gather under his banner?

How long would I have to wait until he was a leader I could present to my people?

It didn't matter, because however long it took, it was too long.

In the back of my mind, that stray thought caught at me again: that he did not have to be that way. That I might help him.

I had little else I could be doing right then. I might go back out to the edge of the shelf and look down on the ruin of my home. But I could not fight the vast horror that had befallen my taak. And if I dwelt too long on what I feared, I would weaken myself with despair; I dared not let myself chase too hard after the pictures of what my people faced or my fear for them would immobilize me. I dared only acknowledge that they needed help, and that I could bring that help; in that way I might pull myself through the coming hours and days. Thought was not what I needed right then. I needed action.

So I did not go out to weep over my family and my fallen home. I sat on one hard bunk staring across the tiny room at the bottom bunk on the other wall, and at my sleeping sword, my battered gift from Ethebet, and I tried to figure out what I was supposed to do with him.

You sharpen your blade, that little voice in the back of my mind whispered.

I did not see him being grateful should I put him to the whetstone.

I was to sharpen him. How?

I had learned how to use the magic of the Hagedwar to heal myself, but I had not the first inkling of how I might use it to heal someone else. I had the watch for the two of us, but no one had come through the Shields' tunnel. No one moved on the slopes below us. We burned no fire, the horses were hidden, we were well out of sight.

I could, perhaps, use the magic I'd learned to place some sort of warning spell around our hideaway. And then I could slip into a trance and see if I could figure out how to heal someone other than myself.

As soon as possible, though, I had to figure out how to use the Hagedwar without the trance. The helplessness of the trance state was a hobble I could not afford.

The room carved out of the living rock featured two wooden strap-slatted double bunks built on opposite walls, and one stone shelf bed carved into the back wall. Of the bunks, nothing could be said but that they were better than sleeping on the ground. The shelf bed couldn't offer even that small amenity; it *was* the ground, and offered nothing over outdoor sleeping but protection from the rain, ground crawlers, and a lack of lumps.

The room was one of two identical rooms in the hidden shelter; the shelter was one of more than a dozen Shielder retreats that I knew of—and I was quite certain that Senders and Conventionals and perhaps others maintained and stocked such places of their own throughout the hills beyond Beyltaak that I knew nothing about.

These places had been planned as places to fall back and regroup in the most desperate circumstances, as places from which to run operations.

We'd never considered that we would be so stripped of warriors that they would lie unused.

Perhaps . . .

Perhaps the Conventionals had filled some of theirs. The Feegash had seen them disarmed as best they could, but they had not scattered all of our fighters to the four winds as they had Magics. Perhaps a small army of trained men, awaiting only a leader, needing only the support of a Magics unit to give them Shielding, gathered around me, unseen.

I had ways of finding out, but they entailed risks I could not yet afford. And I was not yet ready to know. Later I would see who else of Ethebet's own gathered.

I sat on the uncomfortable lower bunk across from Gair and slipped into the light trance that took me to the Edge, where my still-open Hagedwar awaited me.

I touched its corners, felt the movements of it various energies like different temperatures of water running over my hands. In one of the tograms, well within the red, I felt a nervous power that I could shape into a spiderweb across the ground in all directions, spreading it out in tiny lines that all led back to me. When it rolled out, I could feel the movement of the horses in the stone stall beneath me and, down the slope from the shelf, a small herd of deer picking their way though the undergrowth, browsing on the tender branches and buds of early-leafing shrubs. Along a streambed below them, a Tonk family crept away from Beyltaak.

Nothing that posed a danger to either Gair or me waited within the range of my web.

I turned my attention to the rest of the Hagedwar. I would not be able to heal him from within the red—the manner in which I had reversed the hurts done me had cost me my own energy and some of my strength, and I had done little for myself save emergency repair. I didn't have much strength of my own to spare.

The Fheling Point would not help me. It was a limited link into the View, filtering out everything but power over spirit.

I did not dare try the unchanneled power of the Banjgran—the blue sphere that was the Infinite Eye of God. That was nothing more or less than a raw link into the View, and I could no more use it alone from the Hagedwar than I could have used it while suspended in the View itself.

But the other point lay beyond the red, and it was a point that the Feegash had not conquered. I touched it, slipped my hands through the light of the Hagedwar into it, and felt it touch me.

It sang the song of Man's Will. Spirit again, with the power channeled through me instead of through Jostfar. It wouldn't do what I needed, and with the Hagedwar cast the way it was, what I needed didn't exist.

I studied the flows of power through the different tograms as the Feegash had set it out, and finally decided to reshape the tetrahedrons of Man's Will and God's Will so that each of the three points not cornered would push beyond the red instead of stopping within it. And once I did this, I moved into each of the new tograms in turn, and they sang their different songs to me, and I tried to work within those songs to find something I could understand. I wanted a togram that would let me affect the physical realm.

I found what I thought would work on my fourth try.

For a moment I did nothing else; the beauty of life's melody flowed around and through me. This place was clean and bright and warm—soothing, calming. As its energies moved around me and through me, I was reminded of nothing so much as my mother's kitchen when she was cooking before everyone came to table. I felt better just being there—my thoughts clearer, my goals plainer, my body stronger.

This togram had a different song than that which filled the Fheling Point. It was faster and brighter, but like the music within the Fheling Point, it was a familiar melody.

In the View, I realized, I had been bathed in the whole symphony all at once, with fast and slow and sad and joyous mixed all together into one magnificent composition—ever changing, yet somehow always the same. Each togram let me hear a different voice to the music, separated out from the rest. Somehow, each part was as compelling and lovely as the whole.

I regained my focus after some time. Long or short, I could not say. But I recalled my purpose, and began to work with the power that flowed through me.

I did feel better. It would be helpful, of course, if I had my full strength when I stepped back into the physical world. I could practice healing with other energy than my own, I decided, and when I had figured out how to do it, I could try healing Gair.

So I used the techniques I'd learned within the red— techniques taught to me by Skirmig (Ethebet feed him to starving wolves, balls first, and Jostfar keep him living until they'd crunched each bone for marrow and licked out the last bits of brain)—and from the earth and the air around me I drew the elements that would rebuild muscle and bone and skin to their former health. I again chose to keep my scars, for I had earned them. And I wanted the proof of Skirmig's treachery on my skin so that my people would have a clear picture of who the Feegash were. But I did not want or need the pain of them. I'd had enough of that.

And then I moved to Gair. I found him easily enough, and brushed his sleeping form and touched the waking spirit within. He had no shining aura of calm around him. He was, rather, clear as water. I could see his deep physical pain; his fear of failing his king and country; his anger at his abandonment by his own people and his mistreatment by mine; his shame at being too weak yet to fight; his abiding commitment to honor; his deep desire for his own lands and for a clean victory over my people; his determination to save us as a way of winning us to the path he truly believed was right.

If he had any dark secrets, he had not worried about them in so long that they had fallen from his skin. If he bore any treachery, he bore it so deeply that it never crossed his mind. Every bit of him seemed to be as he had presented himself; I could find in him only a good man and an honorable enemy.

The same things I had found when I located him within the prison.

But there was also something else.

He carried a personal commitment to me, and had worried greatly at the nature of it. He felt himself duty-bound to me because I had fought for him, and he did not resent that binding. He was, as Ethebet's white-clad warrior had described him, my good sword.

But some part of him wanted me as a man wanted a woman, and another part of him held me apart as an enemy of the ideals for which he and his people had fought so long and so hard, and yet another part of him resented me. The resentment was an odd thing; I puzzled over it, teasing out threads of it until at last I decided that he blamed me for not being someone he could serve without lust. That he viewed his desire as a betrayal of honor and duty and a source of shame. That he would have been happier with me if he had not liked me.

Useful information. I would, I decided, give him reason to dislike me. I did not want his desire. I wanted only his loyalty to the cause we both shared for as long as his loyalty served me and my people.

With the shape of him mapped out, my spirit merged into his

flesh—I could think of no other way to find the needs of his body and heal them.

The pain he still bore astonished me, as did the array of sicknesses that had scarred him from within and without. His lungs bore scars, and his bones, his tender organs, his muscles . . . the poisons of disease had ravaged him as cruelly as the whips and pincers and branding iron of his torturers.

The power of life coursed through me, and I channeled it into him, and fed his flesh and blood and bones straight from its stream. With his flesh wrapped around me as if it were my own, I tore matter from everywhere, from air and water and stone and plant, and reshaped it.

I was, for that short time, him. I felt the pain ebb, felt air move freely through lungs once again unscarred, felt bones mend and muscles fill out. I felt physical strength far beyond my own, and I was, briefly, envious. I felt the flow of male passions and hungers, too, and was shocked at their fierceness. Prior to my experience with Skirmig, I had always thought myself a fairly lusty creature.

Clearly, however, I hadn't even dropped beneath the surface of what was possible. I'd often enough bantered with my colleagues in Shields, male and female, about what seemed to me to be a male tendency to try to futter anything that breathed, and when invariably one man or another would joke that breathing wasn't all *that* important, I'd laugh.

I wasn't laughing anymore. In Gair's body, feeling what he felt, consumed by the raw, burning hungers that filled him as his health returned, I would have pogged mud. Did all men feel like this? If so, how often? If often—and more than one of my comrades had told me he thought about women and sex all the time, though until just that moment I thought he exaggerated hugely—how did they ever get anything done? How could they even think?

And Gair was still asleep. Jostfar help me when he woke up. If I made him not like me—even if I made him hate me—I couldn't see that having much effect on his wanting to bed me.

Shaken, I shook off the trance and shed his body and reclaimed my own.

And then I sat there staring at him. He looked better.

He looked a lot better.

I might have gotten carried away in healing him—surely he had not been so well formed, so stocky and strong, when I saw him in the cage. Surely his thighs had not been so muscular, his arms so thick, his wrists so finely tapered. Surely his chest had not been so deep, or so broad. I was tempted to lift the blanket, to lift his shirt for just a moment to see if he was as muscular as his layered clothes suggested. Perhaps I had added . . . things. Had not just sharpened my sword, but enhanced it. Added . . . flourishes. Gair was not beautiful, as Skirmig had been. His face was hard, his nose sharp and long and had been broken at least once, his whole demeanor even in sleep was one of dangerous stillness waiting to explode into fierce action. But he was not such a plain blade anymore.

He had saved me—had fought his way through my enemies and pulled me away from a hell I was helpless to escape, and had given me the opportunity to fight. I had every reason to believe he was a good man. I knew I should trust him. I had seen inside him, seen what he was made of, and I *knew* that whatever he swore to do, he would do or die trying. He had sworn to help me.

But he was morii.

Jostfar help me, Ethebet hurt me, he was morii, and I did not know how I could endure so much as the presence of another morii—or for that matter, another man.

I ached just looking at him. I felt the pain and shame fresh on my skin and burned into my soul. I looked at him and tasted bitter fear—sharper and more awful than the fear I'd known in the days when I was recovering from my wounds following that rogue Eastil attack, when I discovered my barren future. That hell had been at the hands of an enemy, and my mind eventually made its peace with that.

This fresh horror had been the gift of a man who claimed—and believed, I think—that he loved me. And if anything that called itself love could do what Skirmig had done to me, where was I to hope for refuge?

How did I know that Gair's loyalty or oath would not have some hideous trap waiting right in the heart of it, disguised even in his own mind as honor or compassion or friendship or—Jostfar help me—love?

I sat on the bunk, feeling that everything inside me had been burned to ash except for fear and distrust. And even then, some part of me longed to touch the man who lay within my reach, to feel his arms around me offering gentle comfort. Some part of me yearned to be held by someone who would not hurt me, who would protect me and guard me and keep me safe.

But especially, who would not hurt me.

I'd had love and pain and loss with Adjii, and love and pain and betrayal with Skirmig.

Love and pain, love and pain—and I suddenly recalled walking to temple with my father two days after Rik was born, when my mother lay abed, resting from what would be her last child born living and in due time. Da was carrying Rik to consecrate him at Ethebet's shrine, for it is custom to introduce children to their parents' saint on the second day, even though that saint may not be the one the child will choose upon reaching path-choosing. We ask guidance and protection, and show off these fine little people of ours.

And as Da held Rik in his arms and I lit the incense and the papers on which he and Ma and my sibs and I had all written our prayers, Da suddenly started to cry.

I was young enough to find this terrifying, but Da was not full of comfort that day. "Look at him," he told me. "This beautiful, perfect child, my child—he is the whole world to me. You all are. And I touch him, and see his innocence, and know that death is already in him. That someday, whether soon or late, his body will be still and will lay upon a pyre awaiting the fire, and those who love him will mourn him. It's all tragedy, Talyn. Every last bit of it. Because no matter how wonderful it all is, it will one day end in parting, and in pain."

I was nineteen years old when he said that to me, and full of platitudes about meeting again on Jostfar's plain, which I no doubt intended to be comforting, in my know-everything way. When I was nineteen I could not bear to face Da's truth, but sitting on that bunk with the world I had known crumbled to ash, I couldn't hide from it.

I was in the world I was in, and no matter how fine things might be on Jostfar's plain, before I got there, I would lose every single person I loved to death. Maybe theirs, maybe mine, but tragedy would be the single certain end for everyone I loved.

It was all pain. Would all *be* pain.

If I was to have nothing but pain, I would keep it to my flesh and leave my heart out of it. I would not be Gair's friend. I would not trust him, nor seek comfort from him not—even the simplest comfort of reassurance. I was not my parents, who had chosen each other from the start, and had chosen well. I was marked for solitude.

I got up and hurried from the small room. I went out to the shelf to resume my watch.

The rain had stopped and the wind had shifted in our direction but had lessened, too; wisps of the smoke from the burning of Beyltaak now reached the shelf. Mostly we were above it. It overlay the valleys, though, with hilltops peering above gray rivers of low-lying clouds, with bits of Beyltaak rising above it like jagged teeth.

I counted three dozen ships, most of them of Tonk make, many of them with the prow that marked them as the work of Beyltaak shipwrights. All of them flying that yellow-and-black Feegash flag.

I'd felt that momentary yearning for Gair's arms around me because I'd had to put my spirit inside his flesh while I healed him. Because he had felt an attraction to me, and it had echoed inside me for a bit. Because I'd been having a bad time of late, and I was weak, and . . .

Whatever my excuses, they were just that. Excuses. They didn't matter. The desire would wear off. Was already wearing off, I was certain. Sitting on cold, damp rock in cold, wet air that cut through clothes right into the skin would clear my mind of the last echoes of Gair.

Yellow-and-black flags. The Feegash. I could not see any sign of Eastil flags. As I had seen in Skirmig's mind, this betrayal by the Feegash had not included help from our enemies. The Feegash had planned this all along and acted alone, so perhaps Gair's friend would find Eastil troops who *would* fight alongside us, rather than against us, though I would not bet a single rhengi against any odds given that we would stand side by side with Eastils. Gair meant to win us by saving us, but I could not imagine other Eastils sharing his peculiar vision.

Had his thighs really been as chiseled as they had appeared through layers of clothing and blankets?

I stared out at the ruins of Beyltaak, disgusted with myself.

The Hagedwar had given me too much comfort, had cleared away too much of my pain and shame and very necessary fear. It had put Skirmig too far away and had whittled him down to something less terrifying than he should have been, and had at the same time, to all appearances, made me stupid. Stupid. Gair was morii, and my people's enemy, and male. Just like Skirmig, but not so pretty.

And I was actually thinking about his thighs. Clearly, sitting on cold stone was not going to do what I needed it to do. I'd made a mistake in keeping only my scars to remind me of my promise to myself to never let a man hurt me again. I should have kept the pain, too.

Filled with self-loathing, I went through the hidden door and down to the stables to check on the horses.

17

Gair woke from a most astonishing dream, in which he and Talyn had been lying naked together, staring into each other's eyes while they told each other everything about themselves— as if, naked, they would have been talking—to find that for the first time in memory his body was announcing its readiness to go find some women.

He stared down at the tented blanket, looked over quickly to make sure he was alone in the room, and when he was, lay back and laughed. "There you are, eh?" he muttered. "Good to see you back, old friend."

And then he realized that he felt different.

He took a deep breath, expecting to start coughing again, but his lungs filled without pain, fully and easily. His ribs didn't hurt. His knees didn't hurt. His hands didn't hurt. He held both hands up and stared at them. The swollen knuckles and frozen joints the torturers had left behind were gone. He flexed his right hand and watched the muscle between the thumb and first finger bulge. His hand looked exactly as it had when he was in Injtaak, getting ready to carry out his ill-fated mission. He turned his palm toward him so he could look at it. The scar from the branding iron still marked his palm. The torture had really happened.

He studied his right arm. He had good hard muscle in his forearm again, and though his sleeve kept him from seeing much, he felt solid mass in his upper arm. He rolled out of bed with painless ease, and flexed his knees, and rolled forward on the balls of his feet and back on his heels. He jumped once, just a little spring to test everything.

Godsall, but he felt good.

Gair pulled off his shirt. His chest looked like a road map, scarred by whips and knives and irons, and by the tools the healer had used later to nurse him back from death. But the scars lay on the surface, healed and silvered as if they were very old. Beneath them, he no longer wore the body of that frail old man. He was himself again.

Healthy. Whole.

Hungry, in all sorts of ways.

He kicked off the too-tight boots and yanked off his pants, and looked at his knees. He could tell from the scars where the right one had been smashed, but when he felt the kneecap, moving it from side to side with his fingertips, it was whole and round and he could find no sign of the deep damage that had been done.

The dent in the left thigh that he'd had for years, gotten from a sword wound in a fight up in the mountains, was gone, too, though the scar above the muscle wound was still there.

He was back to his fighting weight, in fighting condition, feeling better than he had felt in longer than he could remember. What in the hells had happened to him?

He turned at the sound of a sharp intake of breath, and she was standing there staring at him, wearing an expression on her face that he couldn't have described had he been a poet with a hundred years to do it. Their eyes met, and she turned and fled.

He looked down at his friend, who was still clearly happy to be feeling so good, and shook his head. "Well, she saw *you* at your best, anyway. If not me."

And then he remembered what she had just been through, and swore, and almost punched the bunk. But his knuckles didn't hurt anymore, and he stopped the fist before it could go into wood.

He tugged on clothes, but couldn't bring himself to put those boots back on. He had no pain anywhere in his body for the first time in so very long, and he couldn't bear to cause himself new pain until he absolutely had to.

Dressed, he hurried out to the shelf.

She crouched with her back to him, looking toward Beyltaak.

"Talyn," he said.

"If you touch me, I'll kill you."

He had been naked, hadn't he? With his flag proudly waving? He couldn't blame her for the assumption.

"I'm dressed," he said. "I'm sorry. I just . . . what *happened* to me? I'm well again. Beneath my skin, I can't find a sign that anything was ever wrong. I have my weight back. The pain is gone. My knees bend the way they should again, and I can close both fists all the way."

She still didn't turn around. "I healed us. Me first, then you. We both kept the scars; we earned them, and we are going to need to remember how we got them. *Both* of us need to remember how we got them. We need to remember that above all else, our people are enemies and we're enemies. We'll be fighting together against a common foe. But *we are still enemies.*" Her voice was flat, with an unmissable edge of anger.

He wasn't sure if she was angry at whatever she was looking at, or at him. "I'd ask how, but any explanation would be lost on me. But . . . thank you. I'm myself again."

"You're back to the way you were before, then. I didn't . . . change anything? Make any mistakes?"

"Completely back to normal," he assured her.

"Ah."

He waited for her to say something else, but she didn't.

She was staring at the city. And suddenly he had an image of a kid in his head. A boy. Her youngest brother, whose name was Rik. Short for Riknir. He'd seen the same boy in her house—but how did he now know his name? How did he know that she adored her little brother, that she feared for his life more than all her many other fears.

"We'll save Rik," he assured her. "We won't leave him in Feegash hands."

"We won't," she agreed. "But I don't know that even rescuing him will save him. Skirmig did something to him. To all of them." And then he saw her shoulders stiffen and her back go rigid, and she turned to face him. "How did you know his name? How did you know I worried about him?"

Gair saw fury in her eyes. "I don't know. I just knew it." He paused. "You are one of fourteen children."

"I am."

"Your first horse was named Hroddyn."

"Yes."

"You once loved a soldier who died in battle."

She turned away from him again.

"How do I know these things about you?" he asked her. He closed his eyes, and he could see her with Skirmig, but through her eyes. He knew what she was feeling, knew what she had done, knew all the things that had been done to her. He could chase the memories backward, could pick out images of sitting at table with a huge family, talking and laughing. "How do I know everything about you?"

She was silent for a long time. Then she said, "You have a sister named Elza. She's two years younger than you, and she has a husband and two children. Your father died when you were young, leaving your mother to raise the two of you. You're good at languages; you know the dozen regional Tonk accents and dialects, and half a dozen languages spoken in the Eastil lands. You know codes and ciphers." Her voice grew softer. "You kill without pleasure, and yearn for a true and lasting peace, and are enough of an idealist to think such a thing is possible. Your men loved you, but though you want a wife and a big family, you have not permitted yourself a true love; you have taken your pleasure where you could find it."

She turned and studied him.

"Yes," he told her. "So . . . you and I share each other's secrets."

"Apparently, though I did not know it until you brought it to my attention."

She had pretty eyes, he realized. Light brown flecked with gold. Dark lashes. Thick, glossy brown hair with a red cast to it. In the street, he would never have looked twice at her. He liked short, rounded, golden-haired girls, and Talyn was tall and angular with sharp features—and from what Gair knew of her, he knew that she was no innocent, that she had been with men as he had been with women.

And yet he had dreamed about her, endlessly and desperately. His dreams about her had given him a reason to live, because they had cried out that she would need him, that he would have to save her. She had been a goal and a guiding spirit for him. A destination.

She said she had dreamed of him, too—and suddenly he remembered her dream as if it had been real. As if it had been his own.

In her dream, a spirit had offered her all the world, or a drink of water.

And she had chosen the water. And been given a sword.

What sort of woman would choose the water?

What sort of woman would cherish the gift of a sword?

And she thought he was that sword. He could see why—he had given her water, had offered to be her sword. That memory was sharp and startling.

Gair was not a man of deep faith. He considered service to his country his religion, and spent little time musing over the relative values of all the gods whose paths he had crossed. But had he dreamt Talyn's dream and in the real world been presented with what seemed like such a clear connection between message from a god and actual physical gift, he thought, he might have come to the same conclusion. He *knew* he would have made the same choice.

Was he meant to be her tool, as she believed? Had some god out of all the gods put a finger on him and said, "Here, I'll make this one do what you need him to do?" Was he a puppet who could not see his own strings?

"You've grown quiet," she said, startling him out of his reverie.

"I've discovered I have much to think about."

"As have I. I have discovered, for example, that I know everything you know about the Eastil military, and its actions and plans. You know quite a bit more than I would have imagined."

He narrowed his eyes. "That would mean that I know what you know about the Tonk military."

She nodded, and smiled slightly. "But I was not in a position of command, so what I know will not be terribly useful, I suspect."

"What you know may not be all that interesting, but who you know could certainly answer a few questions our people have had about your chain of command. And on an unrelated note, your taste in men has been execrable and your loose morals are horrifying. No decent woman would behave as you have."

"This is that Eastil 'man's morality' I've heard about, then. Where women must have only ever pogged one man, but men can futter everything that moves. I've only ever taken men I knew and liked." She narrowed her eyes. "Well, except for one when my unit was disbanded. That was stupid. And disheartening. Whereas I remember the face of every woman you have ever bedded, but can recall the names of only a scant handful. *That's* disgusting."

He said softly, "That's all right. I remember the most embarrassing thing you ever did, back when you were fifteen."

He had the pleasure of seeing her go pale, and look away. And then her eyes met his again. "The most embarrassing thing you ever did would be its equal—if you had only done it once. But twice? You don't learn from your mistakes."

"If we're talking about mistakes, I've managed to confine mine mostly to small mistakes," he said, knowing as he said it that he was lying; that his one huge mistake had killed all of his men but Snow Grell and lost his country a chance to defeat the Tonks. But it hadn't actually made the Eastils lose the war. "I didn't let myself fall in love with some foreign pervert who hurt me and humiliated me and used me and what I knew as a weapon against my own people. And my own family."

Talyn grew still, and all the animation and the fury left her face; the fire inside her died as quickly and horribly as if Gair had crushed it out with the heel of his boot. In that instant, he took himself from his own embarrassment at being too well known by someone he suddenly knew too well to remembering what Talyn had just gone through and what she had just lost. And he would have given anything to take those words back.

He didn't see hurt in her eyes when she looked at him, though. He didn't see anything there at all. Wax-pale and wax-stiff, Talyn nodded once, just a tiny little flick of the head. And said, "Thank you. I was missing that pain, and I needed it back. Now it's back." Her voice dropped to a whisper, and she added, "At least when I do something stupid, I don't make the same mistake twice." She didn't look at him again. She said, "I'm going to sleep. It's been a long time since I have had anything like a good sleep. You have the watch."

"I shouldn't have said that," he said. "I'm sorry."

"Don't worry about it. It was true." She walked well around him, avoiding any possible contact between them, and went into the room he'd left.

He almost kicked the stone wall, but again stopped himself. He doubted that she would be any too eager to heal his injuries a second time.

Damnall. He *needed* her. She had magic unlike anything he had ever seen before. She was his connection to the Tonks who could fight against the Feegash. She was his link for saving them and winning the war for the Eastils at the same time.

Of course she knew about that plan now.

Dammit.

She knew everything about him. Oh, gods, everything. Everything he had ever done, every thought he'd ever had . . . every fantasy he'd ever entertained . . .

He closed his eyes and turned his face to the wall and shuddered. He had lived a decent enough life on the surface. Like most of the men in the Eastil army, both lower officers and enlisted, the majority of whom were wifeless, he'd not been a model of chastity. But he had been honorable, he had been truthful, and he had lived his life sincerely and based on tenets he believed were good and just.

His thoughts and fantasies had been less commendable.

Whereas hers . . .

He tried to find examples of things Talyn had thought or fantasized about. He couldn't.

He knew what she had seen, what she had done, what she had heard and smelled and tasted. She shared his determination to be honorable and honest in all things and acted on that determination; she served her taak and her people with great devotion and no resentment; she followed her faith in what she said and in what she did; she bore wounds she'd received in the war—

from his own people and through hellish cruelty—in silence and dignity, in spite of the fact that those wounds had been intended to rob her of her dignity.

But he had no idea what she'd thought about any of it. Did that mean she was equally blind to his thoughts? Could he be that lucky? He didn't have any particular preferred god to pray to, so on a whim he chose hers. At least he knew that god's name and had a lot of practice in pretending to be a believer. "Jostfar," he whispered, "I don't know if you're listening, and I've heard you don't accept foreigners anyway. But this is your territory, so I can't really ask anyone but you. If you can hear me, please don't let her know all the things I've thought about. I don't want her know me for a swine."

I woke feeling healthy and alert; free of pain, strong, clear-headed. And then I remembered where I was, and what had happened to me, and because of me, to my people and my taak. And hard on the heels of that memory, I recalled Gair—my sword from Ethebet, and because of me the man who knew too much—and all that clarity fell into the mire of my fear and regret and bewilderment.

In using the magic of the Hagedwar to heal Gair, I might as well have merged with him in the View. I could not make sense of that—in the View, where we are energy without physical barriers, two bodies can slide into each other easily. And when they separate, each takes the thoughts and memories of the other with him. Which is why those of us who can move through the View content ourselves with "bumping" and gathering surface worries; no one wants to know that much about any other human being.

But I had not merged with Gair in the View. I had made my connection to the physical part of him through a lens of the Hagedwar that filtered out everything nonphysical. I had not healed his spirit or touched it in any way. My only contact had been with his flesh.

Why, then, did I know everything he had ever done in his whole life?

I lay on the bedroll I'd taken from the supply shelves—

coarse, sturdy, heavy blankets that reeked of the oilcloth bag in which they'd been stored—and looked at Gair's life and actions. Everything he had done, every act of heroism and altruism and great honor, every moment of foolishness, each rare instant of laughter and tenderness, lay before me. We are all creatures defined not by what we say but by what we do, and in spite of my taunts, Gair had lived a worthy life.

But when I tried to find out what he thought about it, I could not. His thoughts lay beyond my reach.

My first reaction was utter relief. What I had done in my life held shame enough. What I had thought, though, in dark moments and times of boredom and times of despair . . . well, I would not care to have anyone see my thoughts. I had a hard enough time knowing that they were not secret to Jostfar.

My second reaction, though, was to become curious. I could not find a single actual thought anywhere in the vast collection of memories I'd acquired from Gair. I had rough ideas of what he thought about things because he'd talked to friends and colleagues, and because he had taken actions that were revealing in many ways. I could reach anything he had done or said or experienced. But the secrets he had kept to himself alone were secrets to me.

How did the Hagedwar work to so completely separate thought from deed? What else did it separate—and how might its other filters be useful to the Tonks who would fight the Feegash invaders?

I closed my eyes and found my way back into the Hagedwar, and the soothing solitude of the Edge. I studied only the Will of Soul and the Will of God where they exited the red of the Flesh and Thought of Man. Those were going to be the areas that could work for us as weapons. I had to assume that they would work for the Feegash, too. I could only hope that the general Feegash blindness to magic would give us some advantage considering our new enemies had a ready supply of trained users of the Hagedwar available.

And then a horrible thought struck me.

Skirmig had used magic to turn my family against me, in the same way that he had controlled me. My family included my father, who was a powerful Shielder who I suspected had cross-trained in Sending—something that almost no one succeeded at. If Skirmig could control my father, he could use him against his own people.

I fell out of trance, shuddering, and wrapped my arms tight around myself. Many of our people had been in Feegash lands for several whole seasons. They could all be under Feegash control. The Feegash could very well have full contingents of Shielders and Senders who, with what I had discovered in the Hagedwar, would be able to act independently. And who were not blind to magic as the Feegash were. Who could do exactly what I could do.

I closed my eyes tightly, hugged myself hard. What nightmare had I created? What horror had I unleashed upon my own people and upon the whole of my world? I'd felt so foolish when I saw how easily Skirmig had controlled me, and I had thought, when I broke his chains on me, that I had beaten him.

My eyes flew open, and I leapt from the bed and began pacing. I *had* seen the hooks he had in me, hadn't I? I had broken free from them.

If the Feegash were controlling our people and if they had taught them to use the magic of the Hagedwar, the Tonk slaves would be formidable opponents. But only so long as their slavemasters kept them within the red of the Hunatrumit—the Flesh and Thought of Man. If ever the Feegash gave our Magics folk the key to reaching the tograms outside the red, they would find themselves suddenly facing very angry, very powerful Tonks who had shaken off captivity and had weapons pointed at them that the Feegash would not be able to beat.

"You're awake."

I nearly hit my head on the low stone ceiling, I jumped so high.

I turned and found Gair standing in the doorway.

"How clever of you to notice."

Gair looked down at his hands. Big, solid, scarred hands that had done a lifetime's work already. Skirmig's hands had been smooth as a Keeper's. "I want you to know I'm sorry. I'm sorry for what I said, sorry for the way I behaved. You didn't deserve that. You're a good person, and I'm grateful to you for everything you did for me."

I entertained the temptation to treat him as Pada would have treated a man who had behaved as he had—to look at him scornfully, refuse to speak to him except to tell him how he could grovel if he expected ever to have anything but scorn from me again.

Such vengeance would have been amusing, perhaps.

But not productive. Ethebet had given him to me for a reason.

"I'm sorry for what I said to you, as well," I told him. "Let us agree that we won't do that again. We have too much work to do to fall to squabbling."

He looked up at me, startled.

And I realized that he'd been expecting a Pada response. To be given a set of fences to jump before I would see reason and return to the important work we faced. To be humiliated further. I realized that all the women he'd ever dealt with had been Padas to one degree or another.

Maybe his country was at fault. The Eastils permitted no women in any branch of their military, in any capacity. Women to an Eastil soldier were, on one end of the spectrum, camp followers, tavern wenches, whores, and servants—women who used and were used by men, and who held neither power nor respect; and on the other end of the spectrum of society, "respectable" women whose lives were boxed in by a set of restrictions that would have made Saint Minda gnash her teeth, and whose source of power was manipulation.

He knew how I had lived my life—and better than anyone else ever had—but he still did not know me. He didn't know how to deal with me. I didn't fit in either of his boxes.

"You're . . . ready to get back to work?"

"My people need us. We don't have time for pettiness."

He sighed and shook his head, and the set of his shoulders relaxed. "I'd think you had a cock under those breeches if I hadn't seen otherwise," he said, and then his eyes widened and he looked at me, stricken. "Oh, gods, that came out wrong. I just meant—"

His dismay was almost comical. I interrupted him. "Do not distress yourself. I'm Tonk. And a Shielder. I heard . . . rather worse than that in my time in service."

"I cannot imagine that all Tonk women are like you."

I shrugged. "The Ethebettans are." And then I thought about Pada. "For the most part," I amended.

"Well." He looked out toward Beyltaak, and back to me. "Well. We need to work out a plan, you and I, and put it into action." He sighed. "And we need to be quick about it. More ships have sailed into the harbor while you slept, and if we make haste, we'll have most of this night yet to work. If we plan well, we can accomplish much."

They waited in hiding for three days before Talyn would let herself admit that none of her people would be coming to their hideaway. They kept busy, though, while they were waiting; in that time, she laid out for Gair the Tonk fallback plan, and Gair was torn between admiration for the Tonks for having ever been just so ungodly determined to keep fighting to the last man, and dismay at her trusting naïveté that any people would be able to keep fighting when they'd been crushed as badly as her people had.

He didn't want to break her spirit, but he didn't want to risk the mission that he and his men would be able to put together when Snow Grell brought them in, either. And the Tonk plan looked bad to him.

Gair said, "I don't like the idea of sending up flares. That alerts the enemy that someone is out here, and that something is going on."

"The Feegash are greater fools than they have any business being if they think that the Tonks will not mount a resistance in the face of this betrayal. They already know trouble will be coming."

He kept himself from sighing or rolling his eyes—both temptations. "And if they see your flare, they'll know from where, and can come out and crush you."

"No. We send up the red flare and the code flares from any of several designated launching points, and everyone who sees the flares and who can respond will meet at a second, distant location. You and I will light the flares, then run hell-bent for the meeting place under cover of dark, and then we will wait. The Tonks will show up as they can. If something goes amiss, we send up a second set of flares—all white, and from a different location. It's simple enough."

"It will bring the Feegash mercs down upon all who respond."

"We have no choice, Gair. We need an army. We can't take the Feegash on alone."

"I have an army on the way. Meanwhile, don't you people have some less obvious way of alerting your soldiers that you need help?"

Talyn looked at him with exasperation plain on her face. "Our *soldiers*? Have you any idea who we're trying to reach? We're not just calling for aid from the warriors of Beyltaak who escaped the city walls. We want the nomads who are still wintered close to the taaks around Beyltaak. We want every able-bodied fighter from the little unwalled taaks who pledged loyalty to Beyltaak over the centuries in exchange for Shielder coverage and Sender and Conventional protection. We want the hillmen—"

Gair stopped her. "The hillmen?"

"You think the Tonks come in only two sorts: nomads and taaksmen?" She laughed a little. "Not at all. We have meat hunters and trappers, lake fishermen and miners. They're rough men, most of them, and not much loved by timid Mindan shop-keeps, but we Ethebettans get on well enough with them. They're loyal Tonks. Rogvarans mostly. They'll fight."

Gair shook his head. He could not understand how the Tonks, so scattered and uncontrolled, had not destroyed themselves centuries before. Perhaps fighting the Eastils had given them common purpose that kept them from each other's throats. They were a disaster waiting for just such an event as the Feegash invasion, though.

The Tonks put weapons in the hands of every citizen; left those armed citizens running free and unaccounted for in no-madic clans and as wild men up in the hills; had claimed no control over them save that which the barbarian hordes chose to exercise over themselves; failed entirely to impose any sort of national taxation for national road building and the support of a central government—lacking which, they remained a bewildering rabble; and their military fallback plan actually expected these wild men, to whom the government had given no assistance, to materialize out of the thousand little places where they had been hiding to fight an enemy known everywhere as the best-trained and best-disciplined army in the world.

Gair couldn't accuse the Tonks of any lack of mad-eyed idealism. In all the years he had studied them and immersed himself in their culture and language and religion, however, he had never grasped what complete surrealists they were. And Talyn, for all of her good qualities, was one of them. She *believed*. Gair had learned long ago that faith put in anyone or anything but his king and the fellow soldiers with whom he fought would lead to heartbreak. Broad, blind, trusting faith was for fools.

Talyn was certain help would come. Gair, however, realized that the only sizable force he was going to get was what was going to come marching over the hills when Snow Grell returned with whatever part of the Eastil army he had been able to bring.

However, in the meantime, they would use Talyn's plan. She was putting up a good front of being in control and of having put all that had happened to her behind her. So long as the two of them were on opposite sides of the room, anyway. But he could see her body go rigid anytime he closed the distance between the two of them. He could watch her breathing get rapid and uneven, could see her expressive face freeze and watch her start swallowing frequently. She would fidget, too, and if she'd been sitting down, she would stand up. By the time he stood within arm's reach, he could tell she was ready to bolt, as clearly as if she were one of her horses panicked by a snake.

And the instant he passed that final distance barrier, Talyn would without fail find a reason to flee out of his range. Either the horses would need her attention, or something would catch her eye in Beyltaak below, or she would offer some other excuse. But every time, she would put at least the distance of a room and the barrier of a wall between them.

She gave no sign of being aware that she was doing it. She seemed, in fact, to think she'd handled her ordeal with Skirmig and that it was no longer a problem for her or a legitimate cause for concern from Gair.

Her unexamined terrors, though, would be a problem. She was going to be surrounded by soldiers soon enough—men, all of them, many of them coarse and rough—and was going to have to teach some of them how to work her magic. She was going to have to be still and calm and close to these men just to do what she had to do—what the survival of her people *and* his would demand from her—and he could not see her being effective if any time a man moved within arm's length of her, she panicked and fled. That magic of hers might be a factor that could swing the fate of any resistance from defeat to triumph. That could lessen casualties.

Wars were fought and won on the ground—he knew this, and didn't look for any miracles from her magic. When the time came for battle, he would be leading a solid force of Eastil regulars against a solid force of Feegash mercs, and swords and arrows and strength of will and conviction to cause would carry the day. But Magics, if they could get Magics, would provide support—would offer communication and disruption into enemy lines ahead of the arrival of ground forces, and protection from similar disruption from enemy Magics units.

So they needed Magics, and Talyn would have to provide them, it seemed.

Gair knew that Talyn needed to be able to call out her people. She would end up seeing for herself that the foolish Tonk plans wouldn't work—but that was necessary. How could Gair convince her to offer her magical talents to an Eastil unit if he had refused to help her try to gather a unit of her own people, no matter that he knew before they expended the effort that it would end in failure? He could not refuse to help her and claim to have been protecting her from disappointment and disillusionment— he could not protect her from the truth. He had to let her see for herself.

So he contented himself with raising objections to the riskier elements of the Tonk plan, and otherwise spent hours in her company plotting tactics and strategies, which gave him good excuses to be in the same room with her. He made his attempts to get close enough to touch her look like nothing more than the two of them working together toward a common goal. Had he admitted he was humoring her and passing the time until Snow Grell showed up with his army, she would have had every excuse to stay in the room she'd taken for herself, and he would probably have not seen her at all. And she would have been skittish and panicky when the time came that she needed to do real work.

He was being practical, he told himself. He had no ulterior motives for spending so much time with her, for working so hard to touch her. He gained nothing by the long hours passed in her company. Their common cause benefited—nothing more.

And if his dreams called him a liar, what of that? When Snow Grell arrived with the Eastils, Gair would put his dreams behind him and start fighting the Feegash and winning over the Tonks as best he could. And he and Talyn would go their own ways, and Gair would find a suitable Eastil woman and someday raise a family.

And perhaps Talyn's efforts wouldn't be a complete loss. She might manage to call a few capable fighters, and with even a dozen good men, Gair could run lightning raids against the Feegash and do them some harm. Keep them from getting too settled or expanding their operations outward.

He'd have to focus on sinking ships, destroying Feegash military stores, damaging roads, and other activities of that nature until he got the manpower to meet the enemy head-on. Talyn could stay hidden and add some much-needed magical cover. Maybe they would be lucky enough to get hold of a Communicator or two. Gods knew, they needed communication more than just about anything else.

By the end of the third day of waiting, Talyn conceded that no one was going to come to the shelters. They were going to have to use the flares.

"Let's go," he said. "We might as well get this started as quickly as possible. Every day we let the Feegash dig in and reinforce, we hurt only ourselves."

We passed close to a two-man Feegash patrol on our way to the flare hill we'd chosen. I wanted to stay hidden and let them go on their way, but Gair used a twin-shot crossbow and bolts from the cave's supplies and killed them both before I could even signal him with my preferences.

"Why did you do that? They didn't know we were here . . . and now there will be people out here looking for them."

"Better them dead than us," he said, "and they might have noticed us at any time. Didn't want them to get a free shot."

However, when he started to ride toward the corpses, either to search the bodies or to add their horses to our string, I cut Dakaat in front of Toghedd, which Gair was riding, and blocked him. "Don't go near them," I said. "If the Feegash have turned any of our Shielders or Senders and you touch those bodies, they'll mark you and track us."

"I thought you said the Feegash had lured all your Magics people away to other lands."

"They did. But the harbor is full of ships just back from some of those same lands, no doubt—and maybe full of our people turned against us by Feegash magic."

"Can you check?"

I considered. "Not right here or right now. I think I'll be safe enough to check later, when we're hiding and I can dare trance for a long while."

"Fair enough." He nodded. "Let's go light your flares, then."

He gave the corpses a longing look, though, which I understood. They might be carrying important information, or keys we could use later. And they certainly carried good weapons, and wore decent enough armor, though against a Tonk crossbow and a good Eastil marksman, not decent enough.

I would have liked to get whatever they had, too. But as long as I didn't know what troops the Feegash had to work with, we didn't dare.

Once we sent the flares up, we were going to be able to make a lot more dead Feegash mercs, and we could, perhaps, take the time and the risk to loot them.

We reached the hill without further incident, and while Gair held both strings of horses—my three and his two—I set up the flares on tripods, bound the short secondary flares' wicks to the long main wicks, and put a flint sparker to the wick of the central flare. And then I stood there making sparks that did nothing.

"You can add oil and a wick in a sealed metal case to a sparker like that and get a little flame to start your fires," Gair said. "Much easier to use than a bare sparker. I had an oil-and-flame sparker in the Republic."

"Sounds like a clever idea," I told him, holding the damnable sparker to the fuse and waiting for the fuse to catch.

"Or you could just soak that fuse in oil, and it would catch faster."

"I always carry lighting oil in *my* breeches."

"I thought you might have some in your saddlebags."

The repeated snick, snick, snick of the sparker cast sparks in plenty, but none of them caught the fuse. "No."

"You're in a foul mood."

I considered hitting him over the head with a rock and leaving him where he lay. "Yes," I said.

"What's wrong?"

I stared up at him, furious, but I had no doubt that in the darkness he failed to see the murderous expression on my face. "These fuses are supposed to catch at the first spark," I snapped. "They have powder embedded in the fuses. But this one isn't lighting, and I haven't a second one. There was only one red one in supply."

"Maybe the fuse is damp."

A rock. Where was a good, big rock? "You don't suppose."

"Could you use magic to dry it out?"

I started to snarl at Gair again, because magic simply didn't work that way. And then I recalled *Feegash* magic, something I'd never had the opportunity to use or consider while in the field. I would have to go into trance, of course. I was definitely going to have to learn to use the Hagedwar without the trance. Somehow.

"I can, I think. Or something better. Guard me."

I dropped to the ground, sitting cross-legged next to the flare, and calmed myself to the point that I could find the Edge, and entered the part of the Hagedwar that permitted the transfer of physical objects from place to place. I removed the dampness from not just the wick, but the whole of the flare. And as a backup, I searched through all the places where the Beyltaak Forces stored flares until I found one that still had them. I transferred a small supply—three red, four white, some small greens and blues and yellows—into one of my saddlebags.

And then I shook off the trance, and told Gair, "We should be ready now."

"Still quiet out there," he said. "Light it and lead us out of here."

I snapped the flint against the metal bar one more time, and sparks flew. And this time the main fuse caught, hissing and sputtering.

"Ride!" I said, and ran for Dakaat. "We don't have much time." Gair followed; we leapt into saddles and cantered southward as quickly as we dared. The darkness, made almost absolute by heavy cloud cover, had the horses skittish and jumpy, and I dreaded having one lose footing over the uneven ground or break a leg in a hole I could not see. But we dared not be anywhere near the flare when it went up.

We rode as if the very ground would open up beneath us if we slowed, and when the main flare went off, with its high-pitched scream and its booming roar and its one long moment of turning blackest night to blood-soaked day, followed by the softer booms of the blue and the green, we were far enough away that the horses did not go wild with fright, though one of Skirmig's horses, trailing me as third on the string with no pack, tried to buck and bite, and I needed a moment to get my own string back in order.

We stayed still until the last streamers of light died away and our eyes readjusted to the darkness. Then we started south again, trotting. In spite of the recent rain, the ground was not yet soft. But as we rode over it, we were still leaving a trail that any tracker of even meager competence could follow. We would have to do something about that.

"East," I said, and veered hard to the right, bringing us to the new Feegash-built road to Savistaak and Injtaak in short order.

"Godsall—a road! We have to get away from here," Gair said.

"No. I have an idea." I brought Dakaat as close to Toghedd as I dared and prayed that the horses in Gair's and my strings would behave themselves. I pitched my voice low and murmured, "We'll be too easy to track as we are. If we run along the road for just a bit, we can head toward Injtaak long enough to knock the dirt off our horses' hooves, then double back toward Beyltaak. If we're where I think we are, there are places behind us and closer to Beyltaak that will let us get off the road safely and drop into the tunnel system again. If we don't hide our trail, the Feegash are going to track us down this same day, and anything we might have accomplished will be lost."

He sighed and said, "You're right. I don't like the road, though. We're vulnerable here."

That I could not disagree with at all.

We kicked the horses into a gallop and for a few moments listened to their hooves clattering on the stone. My heart pounded in my throat; we were mad to be riding at such speeds in such conditions, but we had few other choices. And no good ones.

When Gair called, "Far enough," and we reined in, I could only be relieved.

I lay panting along Dakaat's neck for a moment, the low horn of an unfamiliar saddle jammed in my belly. I patted Dakaat and crooned, and after a moment said, "Jostfar, I never want to do that again."

"Bad for the horses," he said by way of agreement. "Nor especially good for us. I don't relish going headfirst into a stone road."

We wheeled around and started back toward Beyltaak, still on the road. I took the lead. I'd never been on the road itself, nor had Gair. But I knew the lay of the land, where we had been and where we were headed. I alone could choose the route that would take us where we needed to go.

Gair dropped behind the last horse in my string. For a while we were quiet save for the clattering of the horses' hooves over stone.

We came to a bridge and I dismounted. Below us lay icy, stony Pathaan Creek. The bridge crossed the shallowest part, a relatively broad, flat stretch of slow water between low banks. This part of the Pathaan flooded every year—the reason, I suppose, for a long Feegash bridge instead of the simple ford that had been there before.

I led our little train down to the water, hugging the foundations of the bridge as closely as I could. And I took us out onto the pebbled shoal and then south, upstream. The Pathaan empties into the Little Hanik, which in turn empties into Beyltaak Bay.

Before long, we reached the end of the wide, slow current and took the horses up the west bank and through old burned forest thick with razorbush and tall cropweed. Even in the dark, I knew where we were. This was my home, my refuge.

I hurried our pace from walk to trot, and marked on my right the hunter's cabin that had stood there far longer than anyone that I knew had been alive. South we went, and my path took us to a scattering of stalls and fenced pastures used by the nomads for their beasts when they settled in for more than a day.

"Into the southmost stable," I told Gair.

We rode in and dismounted, and I led him to the slatted back wall of the building. I felt along it, found the right board, found the latch, and popped open the secret door that led down into the tunnels. The wide, ramped entry would permit anyone using it to take horses and even herds through it. Though I wouldn't have wanted to be the one trying to ride herd on caribou through the darkness.

Once we were safely below, I dismounted, went back and latched the door again, and grabbed torches for myself and Gair. I lit them, having considerably better luck with the sparker than before, and we headed south again, toward the meeting place I'd chosen.

Grief Hill.

The place has a dark history. Shortly after the war between Tonks and Eastils started, a small band of Tonk warriors had snatched the heir to the Eastil throne during a long raid, and fled with him as their prisoner. The Eastils had, understandably, pursued with everything they had. And when they brought their fast cutters and light scouts to bear, they had more forces than the Tonks suspected, and those were better placed than they had any business being.

The Tonks headed overland for Grief Hill, which in those days was Radavan's Hill, and held a post fort called Fort Radavan. My father's namesake, Radavan.

Except some units of the Eastils, namely the cutter-borne Bear's Raiders and a scourge of light scouts, got there first. The light scouts held up a Tonk flag and raced across the open ground to the fort, and the watch, expecting its own raiding party home, swung open the gates and let the enemy inside the lightly populated fort. The Eastils slaughtered everyone, then took the places of the Tonks, and positioned their Bear's Raiders behind the fort.

When the Tonks rode home, the Eastils welcomed them into the fort, then boxed them in with Bear's Raiders and aimed weapons on them. They planned a massacre, but first they wanted their prince back intact.

The Tonks, though, didn't intend to fall without a fight. They held the heir hostage at the center of a ring of warriors, a knife at his throat, and when the Eastils demanded their prince's life in exchange for all of the Tonks'—an exchange no one believed they would honor once the heir was safe—the Tonks refused the trade.

The Tonks demanded instead that the Eastils exit the fort, at which point on their word of honor they would release the prince.

The Eastils did not believe the Tonks would honor *their* word and, certain of holding the upper hand, refused.

The standoff lasted only as long as the fingers of one green Eastil bowman held out. The songs say he was still a boy and his bow was too strong for him, and that, with his bow drawn, his arm began to shake and his fingers to tremble. Those are the songs, of course. He could have just been a bastard looking for a fight, but that would have made the whole of what happened next less tragic, and those who sing for their gold have little use for dull truth when a sweet lie will fill their pockets better. So always the one who shot first was a young lad who had never shot a man, nor thought to.

In any case, the Eastil archer loosed his arrow into the Tonks and killed the clan chief, and when he did the Tonk holding the prince captive saw his chief fall and in a rage of vengeance cut the heir's throat.

Slaughter ensued on both sides.

Best accounts—*not* the bardic ones, clearly—say that no one escaped uninjured, and that only three survived long enough to give accounts: two Eastils and a Tonk who lived with their injuries until a Tonk scout came upon the fort a day later and discovered the horror. All three died shortly thereafter, and considering that those were days long before Eastils and Tonks had agreed upon the mode of treatment for prisoners of war, the two Eastils might have done so with the assistance of the Tonk scout who discovered them. According to the singers' versions of the tale, of course, the Tonk survivor lingered long enough to reach home and kiss his wife and children good-bye and give a sad little speech to all who listened.

Of *course* he did.

The pike-fenced fort is long gone. A memorial sits where the fort once stood—a stone tomb at the top of the hill with an ossuary cut into the hillside, and the name of each fallen Tonk carved into the shelf that holds his bones. At the bottom of the hill, a barrow forms the mass grave of the Eastils, with nothing but a marker noting the number of the dead. No trees are permitted to grow around Grief Hill, nor shrubs taller than a man's knee, nor grass higher than an ankle. A Keeper and his family live in the little temple annexed to the tomb, and the Keeper tends the records at the site as well as the grounds, and writes some of his own as the spirit moves him. He also tends the secret grottos beneath.

As a new Shielder, I made a pilgrimage there; it is one of the places where events show the young Tonks in Magics why their service is essential to their people, and why they alone of all the forces serving taak and Confederacy were drafted.

In the early days of the war, neither the Tonks nor the Eastils had Communicators, or Shielders, or Senders. With only infantry, cavalry, and archers on land and sailors and marines on the sea, casualties ran high. Records suggest 15 percent dead and about the same amount wounded among the armed forces in the first years of the war, with some battles, like Grief Hill, becoming complete massacres for both sides. Nor were conditions good for those who survived the battle but fell into enemy hands. Prisoners of war died of torture, starvation, and hideous forms of execution—but none came home. Both sides targeted civilian populations as well as military forces, and both sides have tales of atrocities that fill long books. In the first years, we hurt each other greatly, and devastated our populations.

Tiriim av Aklintaak changed all that. Tonk warriors distrusted magic and magic users before Tiriim brought his vision of military-trained magic users to the taaklords who served as joint chiefs of the Confederate Forces. They didn't trust him entirely until his small team set up communications between three minor units at the front and the Aklintaak base. The resulting sweep of victories for those three field units, the fall of casualties to a tiny portion of what had been expected, and the utter demoralization of the enemy in those battles where Communicators served, convinced the chiefs.

The capture of a Tonk from one of those units by enemies who tortured him to find out how those tiny units were wiping out much larger forces led to the establishment of Eastil Magic.

Communications was the first branch of magical service, Senders the second, and Shielders the third.

With the advent of the three branches of military Magics on

both sides, the devastation lessened. We could target our enemies better, we could protect ourselves better, and we could both watch and warn. Over the following two centuries, breeding and training programs designed to refine Magics on both sides of the border led to great improvements in our skills, huge leaps in our weaponry, and, though it seems odd, a decrease in death to the point that both populations probably could have sustained war indefinitely and still survived, barring outside interference.

We could hurt each other more. So we hurt each other less. We'd never come close to peace, but except for occasional flare-ups, we had reached an odd balance, and with guarantees of prisoner-of-war exchanges and articles establishing the rules under which we operated, combined military casualties—all wounded plus all dead—stood at just over 2 percent. Civilian casualties were so low they were only some small fraction of 1 percent. We paid a lot of rhengis for our war, but not so many lives.

Until the Feegash returned us to war the old way, first weakening us so that we would be less able to fight their primitive war, and then turning the soldiers they claimed would protect us on us.

And now, because of me, the Feegash not only had their infamous mercs, the best infantry money could buy, and all the weapons they'd stolen from us, but they had magic of a sort they'd never had before. That *no one* had ever had before. And soon enough, one way or another, they were likely going to have the people to use it.

I could hear distant echoes in the tunnel, but I could not be sure if they came from our horses' hooves or from other riders approaching.

"Let's go faster," I told Gair. "It's important we get to the grottoes first. Speculation from those waiting can buy us trouble we don't want."

"Where are we heading?"

"Grief Hill. You'll not have heard of it by that name, I would guess."

"No."

"Publicly, it's a memorial. Tombs of Tonks, a barrow for

Eastils. Your Prince Famrik died there nearly three hundred years ago."

He thought for a long moment. "The Battle of Bear's Raiders?"

"That's the one."

"Ah. And we're meeting there . . . why?"

"A series of large natural caves underlie the site. The Tonks have done a lot of work on those caves in the last couple of centuries."

Gair sighed. "More hidden places. Probably with more hidden weapons. Is there any part of you people that looks the same underneath as it does on the surface?"

I laughed a little at that. "No."

"So even a successful invasion would not have meant an outright win."

"No."

He sighed again. "I'm glad that, for the moment at least, we share the same side."

The Keeper's wife met us at the entrance to the first cave. "You saw the signal?" she asked.

"We sent the signal."

"Ah, good. Some of the nomads have arrived already, but daybreak is upon us, and no more will be coming overland until dark."

"Any by other paths from Beyltaak?"

"Not yet."

Gair looked at me, and though the flickering torchlight in the grotto cast odd shadows across his face, I could see his certainty that none would. That we would be helpless until his Eastil forces marched over the mountain passes to save us. He said, "None yet? We could have gotten here faster. That no one from your taak has arrived seems troublesome to me."

I sighed. He would see soon enough. Meantime, I hadn't any interest in another of his helpful lectures on the superiority of the Eastil system in instilling loyalty into troops and creating a government that could withstand any challenge. He had deep faith in his king and country—so I had to confess the Eastil system had at least instilled loyalty in one warrior. But I still didn't like it. "We were already closest. Our shelf was the southmost of the Shielder hiding places, and we moved closer rather than farther while we were backtracking and leaving false trails. We did not lose as much time as you might guess. Too, those who saw the flare will want to gather supplies, and some will want to bring families with them. And none will come by a direct route."

The Keeper's wife was staring from me to Gair and back, and the look in her eyes made me uneasy. "Why doesn't he know these things? By his braid he's one of Ethebet's, and he wears Beyltaak Shielder marks on his clothes. Yet he does not know what every Beyltaak Shielder knows?"

I didn't falter even an instant. "Let me introduce Garitaas av Lodestaak, who was taken prisoner by the Feegash and escaped from a Feegash-held ship when it made harbor in Beyltaak. He's never been in Beyltaak before. He was a unit captain in the Lodestaak Forces. Apparently they do things . . . differently."

It always pays to have a good lie ready if the truth would kill you.

The Keeper's wife nodded. "We've seen the ships in the harbor, and the smoke. Out of the way as we are, we knew something bad had happened, but we dared not send for word." She unbarred the gate that stood between her and us and let us in. "You can set up where you choose. And when you're ready, come tell us what has happened, for the nomads don't know either. Our oldest daughter does Communications for us, but when the team she worked with vanished, she could not go back in. But you're Shielders. You know that as well."

"I'm infantry," Gair corrected.

I hardly even heard him. My heart stopped in my chest. "You have a Communicator here?"

The Keeper's wife nodded. "Iyalara's had nothing to do since the peace, and is near mad with boredom. Her last orders were to stay at her post, so she has stayed."

The Keeper of Grief Hill was far enough from Beyltaak that he resupplied only once each year, early in the spring. And though he'd had regular visitors from Magics Forces when we *had* Magics Forces, he would have seen few but traveling nomads of late.

He would know of the peace, but clearly he didn't know much of it. And he knew nothing of the war but smoke rising over Beyltaak. And he might not have seen much of that, due to the rain and the hills.

I was going to be the bearer of hard, ugly news.

But I was rejoicing nonetheless. I had a Communicator in hand, and new magic she could use to do her work without her scattered team.

Dawn brought me hope. The resurrection of Magics could be our salvation. I tried to recall other isolated locations in which Magics had maintained secret posts. Might I find forgotten Shielders or Senders or Communicators there?

18

Gair went from huge metal-gated grotto to huge metal-gated grotto, peering through the watch windows, seeing the flickering lights and hearing the soft echoed voices, the dull clopping of horse hooves, that told of approaching help. Talyn had vanished—off to take care of the horses, he thought, or maybe just to hide from the sudden accumulation of men.

So he went looking for her, wandering through the interconnected chambers of the Grief Hill complex, looking as he did at the gathering Tonk.

They had not come in the thousands. They weren't even coming by the dozens. But they had come. Were still arriving in trickles and dribbles. Nomads, some of them, wearing the old-style war garb, swaggering and grinning and head-butting each other as they bragged about the moriiad they would kill. A hillman or three, packing furs and dried meat on sledges, with ash-painted faces and knives on their hips—silent and glowering and wary. City men, too, some alone and some dragging families in tow—clean shaven with close-cropped hair and worry-pinched faces and smooth hands.

Still arriving.

Gair looked at them, and at the place where they had come, and became more bewildered. And in a way, more depressed. The Grief Hill complex was simply magnificent—well stocked, beautifully fortified, completely invisible, big enough to hold the better part of an army. Gair imagined Snow Grell and the men Gair had asked him to assemble passing a place like Grief Hill before the fall of the Tonk. He imagined his own people moving into the trap of the place, and nomads and trained infantrymen suddenly boiling up out of the ground and destroying them.

Why had the nomads come? Or the hillmen? They owed loyalty to no taak. Why did Mindans and Hetterikkans and Cladmussans and Rogvarans and the saintless Keepers of the Words come, when the Ethebettans, who should have protected them, were scattered to the eight winds and their taak already burned? They had already lost everything. They were supposed to be demoralized and crushed and cowering. Their saints hadn't prepared them to fight. Had they?

Gair couldn't make what he was seeing work with what he believed. Why would people who had built so heavily toward the possibility of failure, and who had failed completely at the last, who had been to all appearances abandoned by their government and their god and those who had sworn to protect them, answer a call to fight? Fight for whom? Fight for what?

The Eastils built no such emplacements as Grief Hill. For three hundred years, they had defined their military strategy on the assumption that they would win, that they would invade Tonk lands and triumph because their cause was just, their system was better, and their gods would not let the superior civilization fall to an inferior barbarian rabble. The king had not spent the nation's resources on defense, beyond that powerful defense offered by the Eastil Shielders. Nor had anyone suggested that he should.

The Tonks had not assumed victory. They'd planned, instead, for every eventuality including utter grinding failure.

Gair, thinking on planned but never realized mass campaigns over the borders, could only think that if the Eastils had won their battles as they crossed into Tonk terrain, they would still start to lose, as their supply lines grew thin and an endlessly armed resistance hit them from places they wouldn't suspect, over and over. From the few Tonks that had not accepted the peace, such a thing might still happen.

Gair knew Snow Grell would be as careful with the men he

brought over as he was with himself. But Gair could not know if that would be enough.

Even caution could be of only limited use in a place where any innocent-looking bit of land might hide a full army.

Behind him newcomers arrived, these more nomads from south, and he heard their growling rage as they discovered the deep treachery of the Feegash for the first time. He shook his head.

They were still coming.

Talyn had been right. About her people, about their willingness to put themselves into more danger rather than fleeing. A good lot of these would not fight, Gair would bet, but some would.

The Feegash had stripped Tonk forces to the bone, scattered the military, destroyed the weapons they could find and sold the metals so that no more could be made.

And yet here Gair sat, in the middle of what was a growing army, no matter how much he would have preferred to deny the fact.

He recalled a few lines from the *Song of Salonaya:*

> Will not the trees, the very trees
> reach down and rend you flesh and bone?
> Will not the grasses cut your feet,
> Will not the stones leap from the ground
> And batter you until you die
> To protest your foul treacheries
> If none else live to avenge me?

Salonaya had been an Eastil princess speaking to a lover who cheated on her, and clearly she had been fond of metaphor. Gair had the sick feeling that had she been Talyn, she would have been speaking literally.

Except, of course, that he couldn't find Talyn at all.

Not with the horses. Not with the Keeper or his daughter, who had seen her briefly, not with the nomads or their women, or the hillmen, or the taaksmen and their wives and children.

No one had seen her.

Gair closed his eyes and stood in one dark passageway, feeling that he'd lost her for good—and just for a moment, clear as his nightmares, he could see her in trouble, hanging on to the edge of a cliff by her fingertips. Bile burned his throat, and his heart hammered in his chest.

That way. Deeper into the darkness, far away from everyone. In trouble.

He grabbed a lantern off one wall hook and ran through the darkness, light swinging and stabbing ahead of him, shadows dancing crazily, certain of his direction for no reason that he could explain.

He ran so hard, so scared, that he almost ran right over her. Because she didn't move. She wasn't on a cliff. She lay rolled in a tight ball on the floor, eyes staring off at nothing, and she didn't respond to his voice as he said, "Talyn," or when he screamed, *"Talyn!"*

He put the lantern down and crouched beside her, afraid to touch her but afraid not to. He couldn't see blood anywhere, no sign of injury. She blinked when he waved a hand in front of her face. Her breathing was too fast, and her position—rolled into that tight little ball with her arms locked around her shins and her nose jammed between her knees—scared him. But he could see no sign of physical injury or physical danger.

Gair didn't know what to do. So he did what he would have done with a wild animal in trouble. He started talking to her, keeping his voice low and reassuring, telling her that everything was going to be all right, that she was going to be fine, that he was going to help her.

"You're safe, Talyn. You're with me, and I won't let anything hurt you. I'm with you, Talyn. I'm here, and I'm going to keep you safe." He carefully touched her shoulder.

She hid her face against her legs then, and gave a soft cry.

This business was thanks to the bastard, then, and more of his work. Gair's jaw clenched, and he hooked the lantern over one arm and picked Talyn up, intent on carrying her back to the main part of Grief Hill. He felt her whole body lock up, and she began to keen—a weird, shrill, high-pitched cry that lifted the hair on the back of his neck and set his teeth on edge.

He put her back down, frantic. The cliff was there, all right—in her mind if not in the flesh. And he seemed to be peeling her fingers from the ledge one at a time. He knelt again and pulled her against his chest, unsure what he could do but certain that he could not reach her if he did not touch her. He began to rock her back and forth, stroking her hair back from her forehead. And he started to hum—one of those songs men sang in taverns when the ale was good and the women were willing, because try as he might, he could not at that moment think of any other songs. He hummed until finally he remembered a few of the words, and sang them because they were in Hyerti, not Tonk, and when he sang slowly the song was rather pretty and could have easily passed for a lullaby.

In his arms she began to relax, and the damnable keening stopped. He kept singing, remembering more words, and filling in with meaningless noises when he couldn't recall them—he got the verse about the wench and her skirts, and the one about the rake and his fat purse jingling with gold, the one about the pretty woman who lured the man to her home and sold him to a hideous hag in exchange for the riches of a kingdom.

Gair would have paid good gold for better songs. The ones his mother used to sing him would have served perfectly. But he sang slowly and gently and thanked the gods that Talyn didn't speak Hyerti.

When he finished that song, he recalled the one about the miller and the farmer's daughter, which was, if anything, worse than the one about the rake and the wench—but he sang it anyway. And after the one about the miller, his memory served up the Gretonese priest in the brothel, and that song was by far the worst of the three. Sung slowly and gently, the tale of the celibate's descent into debauchery and wanton excess was bizarre rather than funny, and almost tragic in a way.

Halfway through it, Talyn suddenly said, "I know that tune," and tears of relief started down Gair's cheeks and he choked up and couldn't sing anymore.

She sat up slowly and turned to face him. With one finger, she wiped a tear from his cheek. "For us, it isn't a lullaby, though," she said, and a little smile quirked along her lips—the first he had seen on her face, however short-lived it might be. "Our version is an absolutely filthy thing about a foreign priest and a whorehouse."

Gair sighed and confessed. "So is ours. You had me so scared for you I couldn't think of any but the songs my men and I used to sing when we went wenching."

Her eyes grew enormous, her mouth went round with disbelief. And then she began to laugh, and Gair realized that he'd never heard her laugh before, either. She had a good laugh—strong and open and honest. Nothing tittering or embarrassed or in doubt about it. "You brought me back with that song," she told him when she caught her breath. "It reached me where . . . where I was. I knew the tune, but I couldn't place it; your words were so pretty, but I couldn't understand them, and the tune was so slow and sweet, and yet I knew it, and my mind insisted it was a wicked thing. And then suddenly I could hear it faster, and I *had* to tell you what the song was, because it was clearly a love song or something sweet to your people. And deciding I had to tell you—yes." Her voice broke and she closed her eyes for a moment. "Yes. I managed to find my way back."

"If you want to tell me your version, it probably isn't exactly the same."

"Five whores, a goat, a hot bath, whipped butter, three stout young men . . ."

"It's the same song," Gair conceded.

Talyn was no longer smiling. "How did you find me? Why did you come looking for me?"

"I don't know. Suddenly I was just certain that you needed me. I . . . saw this cliff, and you about to fall." He sighed. "It sounds ridiculous, but it was as if for a moment I was tied to you." And in his mind, an odd line, out of place in context. *Whom the gods have joined together, let no man cast asunder.* That was a line from one of the more common Eastil rites of marriage, and he thought maybe it had come to his mind because Talyn claimed her Saint Ethebet had given him to her as her sword.

The mind made its bizarre connections, Gair thought, and what was he to do with them. Take them seriously?

"What happened?" he asked her rather than pursue the uncomfortable direction of his own thoughts.

"The nomads were there," she said. "And they wanted to talk to me. The men. The soldiers. And all of a sudden, I felt like all the air was gone from the chamber where we were talking, and the walls were squeezing in on me, and I told them . . . something. I don't even know what. And I walked until I was out of their sight, and then I started to run. Away from the light, into the shadows, into the darkness, and finally I fell, and in the darkness I could hear voices. I could hear Skirmig's voice, and I was blind again, and I could feel him touching me, and . . ."

She was shaking, and Gair held her close and wished he had his fingers around the bastard's throat right at that moment.

"I was in the Edge," she said after a moment, her voice so low he almost couldn't hear it. "At the edge of the magic. And I was going to go into the View. Alone. Because Skirmig can't go there."

But Gair still had her years of Magics training and practice in his memory, and he knew about going into the View alone. He knew in his mind, but also in blood and bone and gut, what she was saying when she said that, and fear bled into him like ice water loosed by spring melt.

"You were going to kill yourself," he whispered.

"I wanted to get away from him."

"I won't let him hurt you, Talyn. Ever again. Not ever."

He felt her shudder, and then, carefully, she pulled away from him. Reached out a hand and touched his, once, lightly. "Thank you," she said. "For coming to get me. For saving me. Again. We're truly even this time."

"I have not yet repaid that bastard for what he did to you. I'll not go anywhere until I've done that." He smiled for her benefit, to offer her some reassurance—but he wanted to snarl. He wanted to maim and destroy and slash and burn—that bastard, his men, his people, everything they had built; he wanted to track them back to their little mountain fastness and rain hell down on them until none breathed for what they had done to her, to her people. To his people.

But most of all to her, because she put a face on the enemy's intent for them all.

"I swore it, and I am a man of my word." He saw weariness on her face, saw ghosts of past pain and present dread there, too. "If you have to run again, Talyn, run to me. I'll keep you safe. Death isn't safety. It's . . . it's just death."

And even though he could see she was still afraid, she said, "I will."

They rose and headed back to the main part of the complex, side by side but not touching.

"You won't tell anyone about this."

"No. You and I hold secrets for each other."

She nodded, satisfied with that.

And he was satisfied, too. She seemed calmer walking so close to him. She was alive. Not lost in the View. Not gone.

Finally they reached the main complex again, and through one of the watcher's windows he saw flickering lights, and heard the murmur of voices and the clatter of hooves.

Gair kept his silence. The Tonk were still arriving.

In the first day, we got a good dozen young, strong Conventionals from one of their hideouts to the south of Beyltaak. Some brought families with them, while others had pulled along friends who served saints other than Ethebet. Along with them, a few nearby nomads had already come in, looking for a good fight and an opportunity to add a bit to their clan rank. The hillmen had seen both the flares and the taaks burning and, according to those few who had already arrived, marked shared routes through their territories with the code they used, so that others too far out to have seen the flares would still get word.

We had no great force yet, but we had some good people, and some who at least looked promising.

They settled in, and Gair took the task of organizing them and telling them what we knew and what we planned. To the Keeper's wife I gave the job of gathering any folk from Magics who arrived and sending them back to where I would be working with the Keeper's daughter.

When I left, Gair seemed quiet to me. Not that he had given me any sign that he was much of a talker at the best of times. And these were surely not those. But he seemed to me to carry an air of despair around him like a cloak.

I tried to see his situation through his eyes. I would have hated to be alone, far from home and friends and family, surrounded by enemies that circumstance had forced me to make into allies. I would have stood at the strong gates of these caves, looked at the soldiers and the civilians who were arriving, and I would have seen that they were not beaten or frightened but simply angry and determined. I would have seen that they were armed in spite of all attempts to disarm them, that they were both able and willing to fight, and first I would have compared them to the picture of them I had held in my head.

In my case, I would have compared them to the herds of sheep I assumed the Eastils were—panicky, witless followers who would fold as soon as their head, the king, toppled. Had I been expecting sheep and seen the people before me appearing, I would have been . . . what? Shaken, I think.

Of course, Gair wouldn't be expecting sheep to come through the doors. His people never called mine "sheep." They called us drooling, inbred idiots and god-crazed lunatics and rampaging barbarians.

But not sheep.

Still, as I looked over the trickles of new arrivals, I didn't see a drooling idiots or any leaping wild men.

I saw calm anger, and deep resolve.

Gair knew us better than most moriiad ever would. He knew the language, had studied our beliefs, had lived among us as one of us. But I saw the look in his eyes, and "shaken" would have described it well. Even as much as he thought he knew us, we still weren't what he'd expected.

Which forced me to look at the Eastils with different eyes. Maybe Gair was not a complete exception among his own people. Maybe not all the Eastils were sheep. If I acted on the assumption that Eastils were sheep, something I had taken as fact, I could end up dead.

My father's words echoed up to me from childhood: *Theories are your friends; facts will kill you.*

Iyalara, the daughter of the Grief Hill Keeper and the scribe who was his wife, sat opposite me in a small offshoot of one of the main caves. Iyalara was older than I was by a handful of years, the mother of two sturdy gray-eyed boys and a red-haired imp of a girl. She'd been in the Breeder program for half a dozen years, but then her husband died in the last big Eastil attack. She'd taken her children and returned to her family home to replace the Communicator who had held that post, and who had, by her account, been almost in tears of gratitude at getting out.

The changeover came at about the same time that the Feegash won their first huge victory and got the Beyl to order the Beyltaak military to disband.

"I suppose they forgot me," she said. "On the papers, I was still on Breeder leave; you know how much the paperwork fell apart those last months."

I did.

"I'm praying that you're not the only one they forgot," I told her, "because the ones they remembered they moved beyond our reach."

"But not you." She was watching me with curious eyes.

"Not me."

"They didn't forget you . . . but they didn't think you posed a threat to their plans?"

"One of the Feegash diplomats had . . . something else . . . in mind for me." I lifted my tunic and showed her my back, and turned to see the horror on her face. "I was taken prisoner by the diplomat's use of Feegash magic. That magic was how the Feegash turned the Beyl against Beyltaak and how they used the other taaklords to agree to peace and disarmament. The diplomat wanted me because I was a Shielder, and . . ."

And. He wanted me because he was a sick, twisted bastard, and I had both skills he wanted and a body he wanted to misuse.

I really didn't want to go into it with Iyalara. I didn't want to go into my own complicity in my torture, into the games Skirmig had played inside my head. I thought about where I had been, about how close I had come to breaking, about how somehow I had given the magic that could have been our salvation to our enemies.

I discovered I was shaking, and wrapped my arms around myself, and tried hard to ignore the look of deep pity in Iyalara's eyes. I didn't need pity. I was strong. I had survived, I could take care of myself—*so long as you have Gair at your back,* my mind whispered, but I didn't want to hear that. All I needed was allies with good weapons.

I told her, "The day that the Feegash burned Beyltaak, Gair and Master Idrann—you remember him, don't you?—and a Hva Hwa named Snow Grell rescued me. I was being tortured, was near death . . ." My throat closed up on me and I had to catch my breath. Suddenly I was back in that room, awake, aware, able to hear and feel and understand everything that was happening to me, but not able to move so much as a toe. I couldn't breathe. All the air was gone around me, and I closed my eyes tight and clenched my teeth and made the images go away.

"Talyn? . . . *Talyn?* . . . Shall I get someone?"

Gair had said I should run to him. But he was Eastil. Foreign, morii. The enemy. Male. My gut told me that if I trusted him, when I needed him most, he would betray me.

"I'm fine," I told her. "I haven't talked about what happened until now."

"Not with your rescuers?"

"They *knew* what happened. They saw it happening, and cut down the men who were doing it." I opened my eyes. "But not the man who ordered it. He's still out there. Somewhere. He's looking for me. He wants me back."

"Why?"

"Because I learned Feegash magic, and learned a way to mix it with our magic in the View, and I'm going to teach what I learned to you, and to every other member of Magics I can find. You're going to teach people with little or no magical ability how to use as much of it as they can. We're going to arm our Conventionals with it. We're going to arm our civilians. And we are going to wipe the Feegash mercenaries and the Feegash diplomats and their Feegash 'peace' from the face of the world. We have never done anything more important."

"The Feegash wants to stop you."

I nodded. "Mostly, I think, he wants to own me. He claimed to love me, but the things he did to me in the name of love are unspeakable."

"He . . . ?" She faltered.

"You saw my back."

She nodded.

"The things he did in my head were twice as bad. And he's just one. They're all like him. Depraved monsters, amoral destroyers with gentle words and poisoned hearts. They feed on the death of innocence, on the torture of children. They elevate criminals to their highest ranks and claim that there is no difference between good and evil as a way to excuse their foulness. And they want us to be like them, or if we will not be like them, they want us dead." I sat for a moment. "They burned the temples first, Iyalara. They turned our leaders against us with their magic, and then they burned the temples. All of them. No temple in Beyltaak remains. Jostfar draws a line between what is good and what is evil, so the Feegash decided to get rid of Jostfar."

"Then Jostfar will get rid of the Feegash," Iyalara said.

I nodded. "But we're going to speed the process along, you and I."

She was a true daughter of Ethebet. She grinned at me, eyes narrowed and teeth gleaming in the torchlight. "Teach me."

She was quick. It did not hurt that she could see magic, that she knew it the same way I knew it. It did not hurt at all that I could cut through all my own wasted chases down wrong paths and show her, quickly and clearly, how to find the right paths. But even with the given that she was Magics, and had years of experience, and that I proved a good teacher, she was quick. She had her first workable Hagedwar up between one hour and the next. She had expanded her Hagedwar and created a simple stone ball out of nothing by the second hour. Then we took a break because of exhaustion, and slept for a bit where we sat, curled up on the blankets that had padded our rumps from the hard stone floor of the cave.

She woke me some short while later with steaming stew and fine pan-fried potatoes still sizzling in the griddle, and a big skin of ice-cold spring water, which reminded me of my bargain with Ethebet's messenger.

She had given me a sword in Gair, and the sword had saved my life. But how much did I need him now? He was still morii, and I had good Tonk warriors within my reach now, and the start of a Magics unit the likes of which the world had never seen.

I could give Ethebet more than she had asked of me. I could give her victory; could take my people in to Beyltaak, could save my family and destroy the Feegash monsters. And I would still be able to be true to the Tonks. I would not have to do it with my enemy at my side.

Gair and I were even. I would find a way to release him from his vow and to convince him to return to his home and his family, to his own people. And then I and mine would deal with the Feegash.

"Eat," she said. "And then we'll have to go to the main caves for a bit. Some of the civilians are despairing, and we'll have to show them that there is cause for hope."

I ate, and Iyalara talked. "You said there is a problem with this new magic, but also a solution you have not found?"

I nodded, chewing. I did not know if she'd made the potatoes, or if someone else had and she had only brought them, but they were . . . well, not my mother's potatoes. If we were here long enough, I'd have to make a point of demonstrating my mother's technique with oil, skillet, and spices.

The stew, though, was excellent.

"What sort of problem?"

"Same problem as with the View," I said. "I don't know how to use it except in trance. But the bastard diplomat taunted me with the fact that he could do his magic without the trance. And demonstrated it, so it wasn't just bluster."

"So when you say we can teach this to our fighting men in Conventionals, you're saying we can give them another weapon they can use in combat."

I nodded vigorously, chewing all the while.

"But you don't have any idea how this might be done."

Hard head shake, big gulp of water.

Iyalara frowned and sat still for a very long time. Then she asked me, "Why doesn't your Hagedwar close when you leave the Edge?"

I chewed my way through my current bite, took another swig of water, and said, "I don't know. It did to begin with. It was just like yours . . . right up until I made a little silver figurine that could dance on command. After that, it has stayed open all the time."

Iyalara was thoughtful. "Oh. I was hoping it was something you had done on purpose. Because I was just thinking, if it can be made to stay open all the time, why travel to the Edge to reach it? Why not simply bring a piece of the Edge within yourself and hold it there where you could use it at will?"

I stared at her, dumbstruck.

Why not? Why not build the thing within the body of light

that belonged to me while I was inside the Edge? Then step out of the Edge into the physical world, bringing it with me. I would not be able to slide inside of a single togram to surround myself with its power, but if I knew which togram I needed and could call up its shape and color and energy within my mind, why could I not just reach into it and channel that power?

"Jostfar bless us both, that could work," I told her. "Wait, wait . . . wait right here. No. Into the Edge with me—I think I see how this might be done and better two know it at once than we trust fate that only one of us has the knowledge."

We nearly flew to the Edge, and stood side by side in the darkness, and I waited outside my Hagedwar while Iyalara slowly cast hers, and wiggled the points around until she had everything lined up correctly and it was all glowing like gemstones in bright sun.

I reached out to mine, and compressed it until it was a ball that would fit neatly inside of me, and I pushed it into my chest.

The power vibrated and purred inside me; I felt like I'd swallowed a happy cat.

"Try it," I told Iyalara. "It isn't immediately lethal, anyway."

She took longer—manipulating the Hagedwar at speed is a matter of simple practice, and I thought she would get it soon enough. If she even needed to. Perhaps if they lived within us, the Hagedwars would never have to be cast again.

"Oh, sweet Ethebet, that tickles!" she yelped, and both of us tumbled back into the physical world, where we sat facing each other, both of us with our palms pressed against our chests.

"It's in there still, isn't it?" she asked.

I couldn't feel the purring anymore, but I did feel . . . different. Odd. As if I'd been canted sideways along reality's edges and left leaning up against the wall of the world.

I frowned. "I . . . think so. Maybe."

"Try something," she urged. "You've had much more practice with this thing than I have. See if you can use it to . . . do something."

Making something solid out of nothing would be the clearest test. It had to be something that I could not tell myself I had just imagined. It had to be something others could tell themselves they had truly experienced. My goal with this was to win warriors to the idea of learning this system of magic, and learning to use it.

The best thing you can give a warrior in desperate need is a weapon. And to begin with, you need to give him one he can recognize and use.

I held out my hands, palms up and shoulder-width apart. I felt within myself for the Hagedwar, but I could not actually feel it. Faith, I thought. I knew I'd put it there. I had to have faith that it was there, that when I called on it, I would be able to reach it.

I knew which togram I wanted, so I pulled that one toward me in my mind, expanded it until I could draw from it, and in my mind spun out a pipe that would pour its power from my heart to my hands.

I saw a sword in the eye of my mind—a plain sword, somewhat nicked, of foreign make, a thing of great strength and great utility, and I brought it out from the eye of my mind to my waiting hands. The steel was cold against my skin, suddenly and without warning, and the weight of the blade made my arms drop a bit. I tightened my hands around the weapon to keep it from clattering to the stone, and cut my palm on an edge that was sharper by far than it had looked.

Iyalara gasped. I was shaking again, excited and elated and scared and filled with the rage of righteous fury, and the promise of justice held before me and suddenly within my reach.

"It works," I told her.

Gair had no problem with the military men. Most were young and green—the Feegash had done a good job of scattering the real veterans. He was, so far, not just the ranking officer, but the only officer. But the Ethebettans were military; they knew what would be expected of them, and if they were afraid, they knew that fear was simply the sharp edge of a blade that still cut.

The civilians, however, were driving him mad.

"We cannot fight them," one sturdy shopkeep said. "We have our families to think about. Our homes. Our businesses. We have to find out what the Feegash want, find out why they would behave as they are, and then reason with them. They must have had a reason to turn on us as they did. If we can find out what it was, and give them what they came for, they will just go away."

Another of the men nodded. "We must find our way to the *lesser* of two evils. Either they occupy us and take what they want, or they leave after we give them what they want. Either way, they'll get what they want. But one way, at least we can have some semblance of our lives back. If we fight them, we'll just make them angry. And we can't win. They took our armies, they took our weapons, they took our metals. And they have the Ba'afeegash mercs."

"I don't want to die for nothing," the first man said.

"Really? Then live a slave until you're broken and beaten, and die in your sleep," Gair snapped. "*Then* you will have died for nothing. Your kinsmen lie dead on the ground in Beyltaak, their bodies piled in heaps for burning, and you speak of bowing to these monsters; yet your kinsmen obeyed the Feegash and gave the treacherous bastards what they wanted, and *they're* still dead."

"Some of them fought, there at the end. When the Feegash invaded," the gods-damned shopkeep said.

"Did all of them fight?"

"No."

"Did any of them go up to a Feegash merc before this started and spit in his face or kick his tenders?"

"No."

"So men under attack stood up to defend their families, and you would blame *them* for this treachery?"

"The Feegash had to have a reason," the shopkeep muttered.

Gair looked at the young warriors, who were staring at the civilians with a mixture of disgust and disbelief. The Tonks had that on the Eastils, anyway. The warriors were all followers of Ethebet. They had *chosen* Ethebet and the path of the warrior. They had their god, they had their faith, and they had Ethebet's teachings, which Gair was reading in secret from a book he'd stolen from the healer. Ethebet might have been a woman, but she had been no coward. No frail timid creature murmuring for appeasement and begging free warriors to accept spineless slavery. He read her words and got goosebumps. She was a woman he would have followed into the hells and through them.

The Eastil forces lacked the Ethebettans' uniformity of purpose. Because the Eastils drafted their military, they had within their own ranks people who voiced the same opinions as these craven cowards of civilians. Turning those weaklings and snivelers into men had not been an easy task. Sometimes it couldn't be done.

But Gair, in charge of men he hadn't chosen, had learned to make the best of what he was given.

He drew a deep breath, walked a pace away from all of them, and turned his back on them all for a moment. As long as he was ranking officer, he had the command. When one of the Tonk officers arrived—and surely they would be coming along soon, some of them—he would hand over command. He would attempt to hand over a command that had order to it. He would have given his left tender to have Hale back. Hale had been a hell of a corporal—he would have put the fear of the gods in these shrivel-cocked women before him. But Hale was gone beyond the reach of men, into the halls of heroes.

And Gair remained.

He turned back to face them, and copied the parade-ground voice Hale had used to convey the orders Gair gave him.

"Form up!" he roared, and in the next cave over babies began to cry. Yes, he'd gotten that right. The echoing in the caves didn't hurt, either.

The shopkeep near pissed himself. The bitching moneylender who feared death stood hip-shot, arms crossed over his chest, glaring. The Ethebettans in the bunch formed with a grace and speed that would have brought tears to Hale's eyes, and damned near brought them to Gair's, and they stood at attention in that peculiar stance the Tonks favored—feet apart, knees slightly bent, arms hovering over sword hilts or the place where sword hilts should be.

Gair could see relief in their eyes. They were going to fight, by the gods. By *Jostfar*. The shopkeeps and moneylenders would not hold the day.

The rest of the civilians stood out of line and in odd stances, but Gair could see that they were at least trying.

"What in Jostfar's name do you think—" the shopkeep started to say.

"Silence!" Gair bellowed. And then dropped his voice, and

walked through the ranks until he was nose to nose with the
shopkeep. "You do not speak in ranks unless spoken to, soldier."

"I'm no sol—"

Gair punched him once in the face, hard enough to drop him.
The man went to the floor with his nose pouring blood, and lay
there, unconscious.

Gair kicked him onto his side so he would not drown in his
own blood, then turned without a word and walked back
through the ranks, noticing from the corner of his eye a few of
the civilians starting to head for the man on the ground behind
him. And noticing the soldiers that pulled them back into ranks.

They had the right of it, these Ethebettan Tonks. He could
work with men like them.

He turned and took no further notice of the man on the
ground. He said, "We are at war today against an enemy so
weak and so cowardly that it did not dare try to take us in a fair
fight. Our enemy came wearing smiles and offering peace, and
through his peace stole away army and weapons and in too
many cases will. Then and only then, when he was sure we
could not fight him, much less win against him, did he show his
true face to us."

Gair started walking again, through the ranks, noticing a few
men in the back who had not been there when he faced the
shopkeep—another group must have arrived.

"We are not mere men," he said. "We are Tonks, and we
serve Ethebet and taak and land. Our enemy looks strong, but
inside he is weak, or he would not have needed to try to make
us weak. In his eyes, we look weak, but we are the same warriors we have ever been."

Walking up one of the rows, he had to step over the supine
shopkeep. He heard a snicker at the back, but pretended not to.

"We fight for home and freedom, for those we love, for the
future of everything we hold dear. We may die in the fight, but
death comes at last to all men, whether they have lived for
something . . . or lived for nothing. We will live to win against
these treacherous bastards, these quaking creepers-behind-
masks who hold a child as much of an enemy as a man. We will
live so that when we die we can march head up into Ethebet's
hall of heroes and take our places at that table."

As he was saying it he realized that he couldn't recall Ethebet *having* halls of heroes, nor could he remember any mention of how she rewarded the fallen who had died in her service. The hall of heroes was an Eastil belief. His belief.

Hoping he hadn't put his foot well in it, he turned and saw them looking at him, fierce and proud, ready to fight for God and country. Taak. These units didn't fight for country, because the Tonk lands were a confederacy of city-states with the sovereignty of nations. There *was* no country.

He told them, "Sound off. Name, rank, time of service if you've served."

He listened, looking at this scattered company, pinning last names to faces with pictures in his mind, adding Eastil bars and pips to those pictures so that he could recall rank. He was grateful that for the moment he had only a few more than forty men. He had limits on how many names he could remember, and he would be pushed to get these.

When they were done, he looked at them for a moment.

"Kaadneddu, front and center." Kaadneddu had been a sergeant of the horse with five years' experience. He was a bit green yet for what Gair needed, but he was the best of the lot.

He stepped forward smartly and saluted—fist to heart. Gair, whose body held the Eastil salute of three fingers straight up the gig line to right temple only behind breathing in things he did without thinking, barely got his fist to chest without incident. And the salute hadn't been smooth.

Damn.

"You're ranking enlisted," he said, "and I need a first sergeant. You know the duties of the first sergeant, soldier?"

Kaadneddu, eyes forward, said, "Sir. The first sergeant has daily command of the company, receives his orders from the captain, and conveys those orders to the troops. His duty is the order of the company. He keeps the roster of troops, sees to the maintenance of discipline and the meting out of punishments, ensures that all members of the company are fit to serve, or if they are not, sees that they are trained. He forms the company in rank according to duty, and makes himself available to the captain at call to arms to receive orders. Sir."

Gair raised an eyebrow. This particular sergeant of the horse had been planning a role for himself as first sergeant, apparently. If he matched his ambition with his skill, he would serve well.

"You're brevetted first sergeant of this company, Kaadneddu. You'll report to me until I am replaced by a ranking officer, or you are replaced by a ranking sergeant. If you do well, I'll turn the brevet into a field promotion."

"Sir. Thank you, sir."

Gair nodded. "You may not have cause to thank me later," he said, cutting his eyes quickly to the shopkeep, who had come around and was making his way to his feet. "I'm going to confer with our Magics unit to see how the company support unit is coming together."

"We have . . . Magics support, sir?" the newly made first sergeant asked.

"We do."

The experienced soldiers in the unit sighed their relief in unison. "I'd heard they were all gone," Kaadneddu said.

"No. Most. But the bastard Feegash missed a few, and the few they missed can do the job." He smiled a bit. "And have reason to want to do it well. Meantime, I want you to start putting this company on war readiness." He looked over at the standing men and said, "Carry out such discipline and training as will ready them to fight. Claim every man of size and age to march or ride with arms. Ethebettans will command, but until we have more men than we need from among the Ethebettans, all serve. And find me scouts from their number, or from those still arriving. We need to begin gathering ground intelligence."

With the sound of a voice that had the edge and cadence of an experienced drill sergeant echoing in his ears, he turned to leave the company. And found Talyn and an older woman he didn't know standing in the doorway. Talyn had a look in her eyes that he would bet many a man would give his heart to see. And she was holding a sword.

A familiar sword.

His Eastil sword, the one he'd buried with most of his kit before he and his men rode out of the mountains and into Injtaak.

At first he thought Snow Grell must have brought it back with him. But Snow Grell could not even have reached the Republic yet. He'd had no time to gather warriors and supplies or lead them over the mountains. There was no way he could already be back.

"We need to talk," Talyn said.

Gair nodded, eyes on the sword. "We do. My report could be worse, but it could be better. And I hope *that*"—he nodded at the sword—"does not come with bad news."

Talyn grinned at him. "My news couldn't be better. We have a weapon that is going to destroy the Feegash—and every man you have over there can use it."

Gair leaned over and whispered in her ear, "Where did you get that sword?"

"I made it," she whispered back. "I saw it in a dream, and to-day I made it."

"The hell you say. That's my old sword."

She looked startled. "I made it," she repeated. "Or maybe called it. You can have it if you want."

He took it from her, hefted it, swung it a few times. It was a sweet blade, perfectly balanced, designed by a master sword-maker for him alone. It didn't look like much—that had been by design. He'd wanted perfect movement, a hollow mercury channel in the hilt to let the blade flow with him as he fought, with its weight shifting in unison with his cuts and thrusts. He hadn't wanted a lot of gold or filigree. He'd wanted a sword he could use, and he'd paid as much as some men paid for a trained warhorse to get it.

He had left it behind with tremendous regret; but it was not a Tonk blade, nor would any mistake it as such.

"Thank you," he said. He held it. "I'll need to have someone make me a sheath for it before I can use it."

"Walk to our workroom with us and I'll take care of that for you," Talyn said.

Gair followed her. For all her words, he sensed a darkness about her that had not been there before. He frowned, and looked at Iyalara, who had fallen into step beside him in the narrow passageway, and to her mouthed the words, *What happened?*

Iyalara grabbed his sleeve and slowed her pace a bit, so that they fell a few steps farther behind.

"She talked with me about what happened to her," Iyalara whispered to him. "She showed me what they did to her. Not all of it, I know. I have the feeling that all of what happened to her would be . . . that even speaking of it yet would break her. I'm . . . there are no good words for this. As Talyn told me what they did, she seemed to fade away; her voice fell off and her eyes stared at nothing and she tucked into herself and began to tremble. She put a brave face on this, before and after. But . . . I fear for her."

"As do I," he said. "I know somewhat more of what happened. She healed herself of much of the damage they did. But healing the soul is a chancier thing than mending flesh and bone. And anger remains. After an ordeal such as hers, anger holds close to the bone." In that, he spoke both for Talyn and for himself.

The oppressive dark and damp, the ever-present wood-smoke smell that overlay smells of cave and men, the echoing voices speaking Tonk—these knotted in *his* gut until it was all he could do to keep from fleeing to the surface to fling himself beneath stars or sun and weep. He knew what it was to be close to breaking, to keep going because not to keep going would mean death. He knew.

Talyn knew.

In that, they were kin, no matter how far apart they might be in matters of religion and loyalty to land and people. They both shared quiet fury, close-kept pain, and bone-deep determination to set things right. For a time, those three things put them on the same path and made them allies. And when it all changed—when they could no longer be allies but once again became enemies?

He found himself turning away from that thought. He was not ready yet to face such things.

They came to the little room that Talyn and Iyalara had claimed as their workroom, and Talyn said, "I did not want to show you this within sight of your men. You must see it first. Give me your sword again for but a moment."

Gair handed it to her, reluctant to let it slip from his grasp.

Talyn held it before her with her hands held wide and palm up. For a moment she stared at it, not moving. Gair watched, puzzled, wondering what she was trying to do. Then, in the flickering light, he thought he could see something that almost might have been a swarm of gnats spinning around the blade, just below the crosspiece, but he could not be sure; the movement looked real enough, but the light was so poor—he blinked, and blinked again.

The swarm seemed to thicken rather than clear, and he rubbed his eyes. And then, suddenly, the swarm resolved into a sheath around the sword's blade, a hardened leather, brass-reinforced sheath of Tonk style with a convertible harness that would let him wear the sword comfortably at either hip, or strapped between his shoulder blades.

He stared from the sheath to Talyn, and back to the sheath, and reached out a finger to touch it.

It felt real enough.

"What manner of deviltry is this?" he whispered.

"Feegash magic," she said. "Something the troops could learn for themselves. Something you could learn."

She handed him sword and sheath, and he took a moment to partly draw the blade a few times. It drew smoothly, with just the right amount of resistance. It would not rattle when stealth was called for, would not catch when speed was required. "It's a good sheath," he said, and worked the straps around so that it would ride at his right hip for a clean cross-draw, and strapped the blade on. "It's a good sheath—better than the one I had for the blade before. And I cherish the return of my blade. But what do you mean this is a magic I might learn? I have no skills with magic. I could no more step within the View that Magics holds so dear than I could fling myself off a cliff and hope to fly safely to the bottom."

"Perhaps not. But you could be taught this, and so could most if not all of your men. Not the ones you cannot trust, surely. But those you find worthy—this would be a good weapon for them."

"To summon blades and sheaths from the air? While standing still? That seems to me a trick of limited usefulness—we can use the weapons before we go into battle, certainly, but once our forces have what they need and are engaged against their enemy, I worry that the trick would prove a distraction—that if a man dropped his sword he might hesitate for a moment thinking that he might summon himself a new sword, and that the single instant of hesitation could cost him his life."

"If that were all this could do, I would agree," Talyn said. "It isn't. Each man could cast a shield around himself that would

ward off all attacks by magic. Each man could use this magic to
see the position of his enemies before they are visible to human
eyes. Your men could speak to each other without words, across
the full field of battle. Your scouts could reach you with news
even if they traveled alone. Your men could Send against enemy
positions. A single Communicator is of no value, and we have
only one. But an entire command that consists entirely of men
who can Send and Shield, Communicate and fight, would be a
thing no Feegash mercs could stand against."

Gair shook his head. "It would be a disaster. You have never
fought on the ground at close quarters, nor led such fighting,
and so options seem a fine thing to you. And yet you, who
served in Magics, did not serve as Sender, as Shielder, and as
Communicator. Or as one of those scouts who sat in closed
rooms seeking only those children who would one day be able
to do what you do now. You had one task, and in the thick of
fighting, that one task was all you could do well, and it was
enough. Am I correct?"

Talyn nodded.

"If you can teach men to carry out the tasks of Magics using
this new magic you've brought, then I will separate out some of
the civilians in my command to serve as line Communicators at
the front. I want to keep Senders and Shielders out of the
lines—they're an asset at a distance but a liability when fighters
have to defend them rather than attacking the enemy. And I will
not give up such men as have already been trained to fight on
the ground—there are too few already, and in any battle, they
are the final determinant of who wins and who loses. Those
men who are neither quick nor sturdy—men long in years, and
beardless boys—could fight behind the lines and still do us
good. As could such women as have been civilians. Behind the
fighting, those of courage and resolve could Send and Shield,
and those more timid could yet serve as Communicators."

"Women in Magics have always served in the front lines with
the men."

Gair nodded. "In the past they have. But in the past two equal
armies met who for the most part honored pacts regarding the
treatment of captives and the rules of engagement. And even
then, sometimes men broke those rules." He looked into her
eyes and acknowledged the pain he saw there. But anger, too—

a hunger for vengeance that burned hot in her. "Now we fight an enemy without honor."

"And women cannot die in the service of taak and family?"

"They can. No doubt they will. But we must see that they die in the smallest numbers possible. For if ten men and a thousand women survive, the people might hope to survive. If the women die, no matter how many men remain, everything you cherish is lost."

Talyn said, "And those for whom children are not . . . possible?"

Gair glared at her. Women in the Eastil lands did not push themselves forward this way. Men told them how things would be, and they listened.

"You want to die, Talyn?"

She gave him an odd look, and was silent for an uncomfortably long moment. Then she shook her head. "I want to *kill*. Dying seems such a little thing in comparison."

"You're a Shielder. Even at the front, you would not be killing." He rubbed his forehead, exasperated. He was going in to fight for her. He was going to destroy these Feegash bastards not just because it would win the Tonks over to the way of civilization if he led them and won, but because they had hurt her. She had protected him, and now he was going to protect her, and she wanted to throw herself right in the path of trouble again and chance falling into the hands of those who were looking for her especially—and who when they found her would not be bound by any treaty on the fair treatment of prisoners of war. "They want you more than all the rest of us put together," he said. "Of *all* people, you must stay behind the lines."

Her eyes narrowed and her voice dropped and filled with a chill fury that sent ice down Gair's spine. "I want to rip his skin from his flesh a piece at a time. I want to dice his still-living body into pieces and feed each shred to wild dogs before his eyes. I want the satisfaction of *his* screams in my ears, *his* blood on my hands, *his* futile pleas for mercy." She took a step toward him, and he was tempted to back away, and she said, "For what he did to me himself, and for what he ordered his lackeys to do to me, I earned his life, Gair. And I want it."

He hurt for her. He so wanted to protect Talyn as he would have protected one of the gentle Eastil women of high birth he

had been trained from childhood to revere. He wanted to shield
her from the ugliness of what would come and exact punishment in her name. But she *had* earned vengeance against Skirmig, and if she wanted it, who was he to deny her?

Which did not change in the least the fact that she could not
fight in the front lines, which would not even be lines. With so
few men, he would have to depend on guerrilla strikes supported by such cover shielding and attacks and such communication as Magics could provide.

"I'll bring him to you," Gair said. "I would have killed him
for you and done it well. But I will bring him to you instead, and
you can do what you will with him."

"That will do," she said.

19

Know your enemy.

Is that not the first and best advice every soldier gets? That
our strategies and our tactics must be built around what we
know of the enemy we fight? That one battle plan will not win
all wars?

Know your enemy.

My enemy. Whom did I list first as enemy?

Gair, who would keep me as safe as I could be kept in time
of war?

He was right about my staying behind, and I knew he was
right—I'd be a fool to ride at his side into the reach of the Feegash and those of my people who had become their slaves. He
was right about the place of women in this war as well, where
our enemies were honorless, treacherous bastards; women's
place in this war was not and could not be at the front lines if
we were to make even a pretense of protecting the future of our
people. He was right about the use of Magics in the upcoming
frays. He was right—and I despised him for being right, and
even as I despised him, I found him to be what Ethebet's messenger told me he would be: a good sword.

I could not imagine one better. My enemy, my sword . . . and Ethebet help me, Jostfar forgive me, something more. I found myself listening for the sound of his voice, for his measured footstep echoing nearby. I wanted to look into his gray eyes, wanted to see the brief ghosts of smiles that flickered at the corners of his mouth, that sometimes brightened his face when he looked in my direction. And what manner of foolishness was that, when I could not bear his lightest touch, and when at his actual approach I had to force my feet to stillness lest they launch me into flight to some dark hiding place?

Gair was indeed my enemy. And my ally. And something very like a friend.

I had entrusted him with the rescue of my people and my world—and yet I did not trust him. I probably knew more about him than any human being who had ever lived, including his own mother, and yet he was a mystery to me.

Know your enemy.

What sort of impossible demand is that? It seemed to me that the more we knew of our enemies, the more we would only realize how very much we did not know. For of my other enemies, whom I knew less well, I still knew enough. Of the Feegash, I knew that our war with them would be short, for no treaties would be possible, nor any negotiated peace. We would either destroy them, or they would destroy us. Of Skirmig, who was my template for all the Feegash, I also knew enough. I knew that at the end of this one or the other of us would be dead—and would die badly. I intended it to be him.

I thought that ancient advice might need some revision. Perhaps it should have been *Know your enemy well enough to kill him when you see him, but not so well that you start wondering why he's your enemy.*

But of course that isn't anywhere near pithy enough to be memorable.

Which is why I need to remember to be wary of all those little aphorisms I so love. The wit who can skin a subject worthy of a book down to a handful of words skins off more than just the fat. He rips off muscle and nerve and tendon and blood, too—and bare bones don't run when you need them to.

So I decided that I was not going to be able to unravel the tangle that was Gair anytime soon. My enemy was looking far too much like someone I might want to know even better—so I buried myself in my work.

Iyalara and I had enough of that before us, Ethebet knows.

The Hagedwar would not let us create new Shielders or Senders or Communicators from people who could not see the View. It could give ordinary people extraordinary power, but the direct powers of life, death, and the soul were not among those.

Nor was our only problem the fact that we would have to re-create the three divisions of Magics and the services they offered by using an entirely new form of magic that did not offer direct power over life, death, and the soul—at least not to those who could not already work within the View. We also had no experienced leadership. No officers from Magics appeared in the caves. I knew my father would not be coming. But I had expected at least Yarel or Volann or Heldryn to arrive. They did not. Neither did the six Shielder enlisted who had met those few times in the temple, planning resistance against the wrong enemy.

I had to suppose that Skirmig had known about them all along—that he'd found them through me and marked them, and that when the Feegash were ready to strike, he'd passed on to his superiors their names and locations and the threat they might offer. I could assume that Betraa and Uudmar, Pordrit and Ordran, Matta and Ravii were among the bodies burning in piles around Beyltaak, or dumped into secret graves or the sea just before the actual attack took place. Or perhaps, like my father, they had been hunted down before the Ba'afeegash mercs made their attack and twisted by the Feegash magic until they could not think.

They had no Hagedwar that would let them reach safely into the View alone and pull the Feegash hooks out of their minds. If the Feegash had them, they would hold them until we found a way to break them free.

It meant that we could be attacking against a trained unit of Shielders at the least, and against the full strength of the Tonk Magics if the Feegash had turned all our people against us.

And against this possibly overwhelming force, we were going to send a handful of green ground troops, and we were going to cover them with Magics units staffed by civilians.

At least we had the civilians. But Iyalara and I had no officers to command them. We weren't just ranking members of Magics. We *were* Magics, and our troops' support rested on what Iyalara and I could accomplish with as unlikely-looking a bunch of recruits as any commander ever received.

So, as our recruits began to file into the larger chamber we'd taken for training, Iyalara and I retreated briefly to a grotto at the end of the chamber that had been fitted with a door.

"I'm not an officer," I told her.

She shrugged and looked at me as if I were mad. "Nor am I. And we have no officer to promote us."

"I don't think we're going to. We may be the only two members of Magics in the area that Skirmig missed. And that would be my fault. I found out months ago that Magics had been cut below the level where we could even enter the View. I told my father, and he used every connection he had to round up for us a bare skeleton of a Shielder unit. And I think Skirmig might have let this happen just so he would know where to find everyone when the day of the attack came."

"We're likely to be it?"

"Unless new nomad clans pass by and want to add their numbers to ours, I think we are."

She sagged against the rough stone wall and rubbed her face with both hands. "This is hopeless."

"Probably. But I have family in Beyltaak, so I have no other choice but to try."

"We're Ethebet's. We have no other choice anyway. We didn't take an oath to defend taak and Tonk only if we thought we could win. We swore our lives into her service, and this is where she calls us."

I nodded. And stood there thinking, long and hard. And then I grinned a little. "What's your full name?"

"Iyalara Kethrit av Notrig dryn Aandikandis."

I took a deep breath. "Ethebet forgive me; I mean no disrespect." I put my right hand on her left shoulder and said, "Iyalara Kethrit av Notrig dryn Aandikandis, I award you a command in the newly formed Hagedwar Magics, at the rank of brevet captain—because as Ethebet is my witness, I do not want to overstep my bounds and make you a brevet general— and declare you commander of Communications."

She frowned for just a moment, and then she began to giggle nervously. "Jostfar preserve us. The world is ending and we're playing at war. And Ethebet, send us some real officers to take this from us before we do irrevocable damage. Talyn, give me your full name."

Suddenly my throat felt dry and I found myself offering my own prayer, a silent one, through Ethebet to Jostfar. "Talyn Wyran av Tiirsha dryn Straad," I said in a voice suddenly tight with fear.

She thought for a moment, then said, "Talyn Wyran av Tiirsha dryn Straad, as ranking officer of the Hagedwar Magics, I award you a command in this service at the rank of brevet captain, and declare you commander of the newly formed Combined Combat Magics unit."

"Saints preserve us both," I said.

"Now we act as if we knew what we were doing," Iyalara said, and we went out to face our commands.

To some extent we could guess what we should do. I'd been a sergeant in an active Magics unit, as had Iyalara, though she had both time in service and time in rank over me, and as such would be the one to hand off the command when, or if, real officers ever showed up. We were both veterans, and if we had not studied the tactics and strategies of magic in battle as extensively as had our officers, still we had been required to learn the basics, since of all the branches of service, only our officers could not lead us into battle, but only direct us from behind. Once in the View, we had commanded our teams without officer intervention, and we chose how to carry out the orders we were given.

We knew how to lead. I prayed that would be enough. We ranked our volunteers in two groups. The first comprised Gair's men of fighting age, who would all go into Communications and then into combat. We had seven of those. The others we ranked from oldest to youngest, and after a quick conference in the corner, we decided that for every three troops in that lot whom we assigned to Communications, Iyalara's, we would assign four to Combined Combat, my two units. Once I'd taken my people through basic training, I would further divide them up into Attack and Defense—we agreed that we would not call them Senders or Shielders, since we weren't sure exactly how we would be deploying their Hagedwar magic. But it wouldn't be in Sending and Shielding, because this whole bunch would be View-blind. My two divisions would be smaller, individually, than Iyalara's one. But we both believed that with fighting men in short supply, we could provide the best coverage for them if we emphasized developing a powerful and pervasive Communications division that would give them eyes ahead and to all sides and a way to let us know what we needed. Our Combat specialties would then provide . . . well . . . whatever it was that they would provide. I would have to see what I could teach them before I could figure out how I could deploy them.

Iyalara and I made one other decision jointly before we separated out our troops. We decided that we would modify the Hagedwar so that no portion of either of the two gold josthaddaar would extend beyond the surface of the red cube of the Flesh and Thought of Man. In a way, we would be teaching them a crippled Hagedwar. But we already knew we were dealing exclusively with people who would not be able to see how the energies they were using connected to the View, and we did not want them to experiment with the tograms beyond the red. We could not afford to lose a single person into the seductive madness of the View.

Gair's civilians-turned-soldiers already stood in rank and at warriors' rest—in a short time he and his new first sergeant had made clear to them that bit of military life. And in our ranks, I saw a few of the gray and bent who also held warriors' rest. "Soldier," I said, pointing to one man who looked the same age as my paternal grandfather. "Tell me why you volunteered."

He snapped to attention with a smartness that made my heart glad, and said, "Captain, I served Tonk and taak under Ethebet for twenty-five years, and retired from her service as a sergeant major of the Glorious Ninth Horse. I am too old to serve on the ground, but they told me you would not care what age I was. So I offer myself in whatever capacity you'll take."

I could have kissed him. I could have wept. I turned to Iyalara and she said, "I think we should reinstate him at grade."

"We'd be fools not to. Let him sort them, get us good first sergeants for each of the three units, and make him responsible for seeing that they know the customs and courtesies. That will leave us free to teach them magic and figure out how in Jostfar's name we're going to use them."

Iyalara snapped a salute to the old noncom and said, "Welcome back, Sergeant Major."

When, two or maybe three bells later, Gair appeared to see how things were going, we had first sergeants, sergeants, corporals, and companies. And the size of the companies was growing. Combined Combat Magics had seventy-two people; Communications had fifty-five, not including Gair's men, whose number had increased to ten. The sergeant major, after conferring with us, set companies at twenty-five troops minimum and fifty maximum. He divided Combats into two companies of thirty-six, and Communications into two companies of thirty-three and thirty-two, making sure each of those two companies had an equal portion of fighting men. Each company had one first sergeant, two sergeants, and four corporals. Gair's men he designated scouts. Because we were so short of people, we agreed that Magics would share one quartermaster sergeant among the whole Magics service. We should have had one per company, but only one of our old-timers had served as a quartermaster sergeant, and until he could train others, we decided it was better that we get the job done right than that we have full ranks.

Gair arrived as the sergeant major was leading the whole group through the rite of swearing service to Ethebet—something that was causing a few of our volunteers visible distress. But we had experienced, if very old, veterans in charge of our green-beyond-imagining troops, and the whole process was going as smoothly as anyone could hope.

"I'm surprised you didn't lead them through the Ethebettan vows yourself," Gair whispered to me.

"The man was a sergeant major. Out of respect for his time in service I asked him to take the honor. He's . . . amazing, by the way. He's going to have us formed up and operating on a military footing far faster than I could have imagined. By tomorrow Iyalara and I may very well be able to start these people into actual Magics training."

"It already is tomorrow," Gair said softly. "You need to get some sleep. And I daresay so do many of your people. I've ordered my first sergeant to see to reveille at sunrise; and we've found a piper among our number who lacks only pipes to play us awake. I came to you to see if you might . . . ah . . . create us a good loud set of pipes before you let your people go find beds or bedrolls for a few hours' sleep."

"Bellows pipes?"

"Have you people ever used *anything* else for reveille?"

"Never."

"Then I need bellows pipes." I almost laughed at the misery in his voice.

I love the sound of bellows pipes. But then, I never minded the sound of cats going at each other up on the thatching of the roofs late at night, either. Or of cocks crowing at dawn's breaking. The bellows pipe is a good cross between the least musical elements of cats making amatory advances, sunrise poultry, and a dozen drunks closing down a tavern with a rousing chorus of "She's a Fine, Fine Whore." Tonks have often claimed that a hundred pipers marching down a hill could rout the enemy without aid from foot or cavalry, by simple threat of din and deafness. But the treaties prevented us from torturing the enemy, and common sense kept us from deafening ourselves. So our piper units never fielded more than three pipers to a company, and companies usually had only one playing for anything but pitched battle.

"I can make you a good set of pipes," I told him.

"The only good ones are the ones that won't work," he muttered, but then he looked at the sergeant major, and I saw that Gair was impressed.

I said, "He does that well, doesn't he?"

Gair gave me an odd look. "I was just seeing if he did it the way I did it. He's better. I had a hellish moment when my first sergeant asked me when I was going to administer the Ethebet oaths to the troops. I didn't know the Ethebet oaths. Thank the god—" He shook his head. "Thank Jostfar *you* did. I hunted through your oaths to Ethebet. I found quite a few, both the ones where you pulled out a lock of hair and burned it and the ones where you didn't. I decided we'd best include the braid burning, since I wasn't sure under what circumstances it was required."

"I wondered what the sudden stink in the draft was. Ah, Jostfar, they'll think you the toughest commander that ever lived. I don't know of a commander who *ever* demanded sacrifice of blood and flesh right in the group oath." I noticed the spot of blood at his right temple and said, "You led them by *demonstration*?" I was about to protest the heresy, to snarl at Gair that he had no right to make mockery of the sacred traditions of the Tonk by participating in them. But then I remembered that Ethebet had given me this man as my sword. She had already declared Gair to have great worth in her eyes, and because she had offered him to me, she had already accepted him, even if only as a tool. If her tool wanted to swear himself to her service, who was I to declare that heresy?

The new troops in Magics finished taking their oaths. I saw some tears, but they were tears of people standing resolutely in ranks—men and women, boys and girls—almost all of them forsaking other saints and other ways in the defense of their home. I thought them beautiful, one and all.

I went over and dismissed both Combat companies, giving my two first sergeants orders to get their people to the quartermaster in an orderly fashion to get rations and supplies. I marked out one grotto that we would claim for Combined Combat training and housing, and instructed my two firsts and my sergeant major to get the companies in there and bedded down for the night after they had basic supplies.

Then I went back to Gair. "I'm going to see if I can find a good set of pipes for you rather than try to create one from air and elements," I told him.

He looked as enthused as a man on his way to his own court-martial.

I kept my voice low and said, "It matters. Some of these pipes are old veterans that have been in the wars for hundreds of years. They have their battle decorations, they have their unit badges, and if a piper falls there will be a man to pick up the pipes and carry on."

"You people are insane," Gair told me, whispering.

"You want morale, let me bring in a set of veteran pipes to march before them. Not a lad among them doesn't recognize some of those. And when you get the pipes, fetch your piper, even if you have to wake him, and award him with them. Trust me in this."

Some things are easier to do in trance, and once I'd thought of it, using the Hagedwar to look through the View and search

out the Champions of Black Mountain pipes, the most deco-
rated and most revered set of pipes in Beyltaak, simply made
sense. I sat on the raw rock and slipped into the trance and the
Edge and into the togram that gave me the View with physical
transfer. I looked in the few places where pipes had been stored,
and all were gone. I kept looking—nonliving things don't have
the brightness of living things, but neither do they wax and
wane, shift and slip away. I knew where the Champions should
be, they weren't there, and when I broadened my search, I
found that they weren't anywhere in Beyltaak. *No* pipes were
anywhere in Beyltaak.

But I found the remains of our pipes burned almost to ash in
front of the charred bones of our Great Temple.

Not by chance had the Feegash chosen that place for that act.
I didn't miss either its symbolism or its threat. They did not intend to conquer us. They intended to erase us. To make us no
longer Tonk.

They were not just killing us in battle, or twisting us with
magic—they were aiming to kill our future by destroying our
past. The books in our temples were who we were; they held ar-
guments by hundreds of philosophers over thousands of years
on what made us a people, careful judgments on how we must
live and how we must act to remain a people, reminders that
what we did in the past was a good and worthy foundation upon
which to build a future. Our books were our long conversation
with Jostfar. Our pipes, our badges and flags—those were our
way of carrying our past with us, of remembering that we were
a people found worthy by our God, who both loved us and liked
us, and who wanted us to succeed and prosper.

The Ba'afeegash mercs and the cabal who ran them were at-
tempting nothing less than to destroy Jostfar and erase him
from our memory. If they controlled this generation with their
mind magic, they would succeed, for if they erased all traces of
him and kept this generation from passing him on to the next,
when he spoke to the next generation they would not hear him,
or if they heard him, they would not know his voice from those
of a thousand lesser gods. They might still be his people, but
only he would know it.

I remembered Skirmig and his calm assertion that he would
bring me around to see his reason, his philosophy—that I

would come at last to see the world as he saw it. I saw his certainty that when I saw my world through his eyes, I would welcome the Feegash peace, where all the world would live as the Feegash lived. Without values. Without judgment. Without faith, or hope, or future.

This was not the life my people had chosen, and I would fight with everything in me to keep them from it. I found such little shards of the pipes as I could from the ashes, and remembered everything I could about the Champions of Black Mountain pipes: the weave of the bellows cloth, the placement of the decorations for battles fought and won, the rubbings on the pipes themselves, the harness that kept the thing in the piper's arms but that could be slipped free to let the next man pick it up if the piper fell.

Beyltaak Tonks knew Champions of Black Mountain the way we knew the faces of our great living heroes.

I had traveled with Champions to the front lines on two occasions; he was a veteran who did not age and did not retire.

And he would not die. I re-formed him, pulling matter from the ash that had been him and his brethren. He had no spirit save ours, but we would give him that again. We would lift him up and march to his songs. We would remember Jostfar, we would remember ourselves. And we would prevail.

I opened my eyes to find the heavy pipes sitting across my lap, half over my shoulders, and draped over both arms. It takes a sturdy lad to carry the pipes.

I rose awkwardly, handed the pipes to Gair, and slung the harness over his shoulder. "Hold still a moment," I said.

I looked Champions of Black Mountain over. He looked like he'd had a good cleaning, and perhaps a bit of a buffing along the ivory pipes. His badges and decorations were all in the right places, he had the right number of drones and the right shape of chanter, and those battle scars that I remembered were there. Any I hadn't noticed would be missing, of course, and I could only hope that if anyone knew of other scars, he would think they had been repaired or smoothed away by too-vigorous polishing.

"This is Champions of Black Mountain," I told Gair. "Remember the name, and present the pipes to your piper as follows: 'May his courage be your courage, his steadfastness be yours.' That's all you'll say."

Gair nodded. "Should I present it in front of the men?"

"No. The reaction of a piper getting this particular set of pipes needs to be a private matter between the two of you. And it's *him*, not it. Pipes are never an *it*."

He gave me an odd smile. "Yes. Even I have heard of these particular pipes. These pipes have marched with Beyltaak's people through the whole three hundred years of our war, and a hundred years of other battles before that." He stared down at them, his fingers touching the badges and the decorations. "If I were a good soldier true to my own people, I would burn them."

"That's already been done once this week," I whispered, wishing pain at Gair in a hundred different forms for even daring to mouth the words.

He looked startled. "The Feegash burned this? *Him. Him,* dammit." He was looking at the pipes with a critical eye. "I don't see where."

"They burned all the pipes." My voice broke when I said it, and suddenly my face was hot and my throat was tight. I took a deep breath and got myself under control. "They're burning or twisting everything that we love, everything that we hold sacred. I re-created Champions from the ashes in front of the temple and from my own memory."

Gair looked at me with great sadness. "I'm sorry. Their people will bear the shame of this treachery for a thousand years, Talyn."

"No they won't," I told him. "They don't believe in shame."

He looked dumbfounded. "They . . . *what*?"

"They don't believe in shame. They don't believe in good or bad, or in right or wrong. They think every act is the same as every other act."

Shaking his head like a man who had just walked through cobwebs, he said, "You must have misunderstood. No one could think that. A single day's experience in the world would prove the lie of such a philosophy. No man could claim that . . . that the murder of a child was the same as . . . as . . ." He shrugged and held out a hand, palm up. "As the *defense* of a child." He put a hand on my shoulder and turned his head to one side, as if begging me to tell him that our joint enemy would see clearly the difference between those two things, at least.

"And yet they do."

Gair still seemed to be looking at me, but I realized that he was not—that instead, he was rummaging through my memories looking for the truth. Expressions flitted across his face—disbelief and shock and finally revulsion. His grip on my shoulder tightened—he had big, strong hands, and for just an instant, that grip hurt. "Yes," he said, releasing me. "They *do* believe that, though I would never have thought such evil possible." He hefted the pipes on his hip and said, "I'm going to go give these to my lad now, with Jostfar's blessing."

He turned and walked away, but just as he was about to disappear into the corridor that would take him back to his men, he turned to me and said, "I did not know human beings could hold such lies in their hearts and call them truth. These are not men. They are monsters."

He left then, and I touched my shoulder and whispered, "I know." And found myself wishing that he had not gone.

Training our troops was a hell of wake and work and struggle and fail and struggle some more, of dried rations cooked into soup and more soup and even more soup, sometimes with dried meat thrown in but most times with a few handfuls of rice and dried beans and peas. The scouts were the envy of us all—they got to take the horses up to the surface and ride around and see the sky and feel the sun on their faces, or see the stars.

Tempers flared, fights broke out between those who knew how things should be done because they had done it before and those who thought they knew how things should be done because they'd spent years imagining this world that they had never touched, and arguing the actions of their taak's army in taverns over ale.

For my training, I sat my would-be warriors in a circle holding hands, to the raucous laughter of Gair's men, who happened upon us as we were training and found our unit funnier than they had any business doing. But by connecting all of them to me, I could use the power of the View to take them to the Edge all at once, show them how to build their Hagedwar by building one of my own, let them experience—with their spirits touching mine—the music of the universe that ran through each togram. I could show them what each togram did, and how they could use it.

It took us two long, hard weeks to get a core group of people who could form a Hagedwar on their own and use its energies to do things. We then concentrated on the things that they could do. It was all new territory to us; we had a new weapon, and not a single warrior who could stand before the troops and demonstrate combat-tested uses.

Defense had severe limitations compared to what Shielders could do. My Defense unit could not Shield—that is, it could not prevent massive magical attacks against the very existence of our men as a good group of Shielders could have done. It had no power over life or death, no way to touch the soul. But it developed a decent command of the physical. My Defenders could undo damage caused to people and terrain, prevent damage by creating obstacles for the enemy, and create physical shields against attack.

So I focused them on learning to heal from a distance, learning to create barriers against incoming fire, and learning how to notify commanders of men in trouble.

I came up with a few good specialties for my Attackers, too. I decided that being able to dig holes would be useful. Dropping the very ground out from beneath the feet of the enemy as they charged forward . . . I could envision that being a powerful thing. Also throwing fire—we had a number of people who turned out to be good at that, and one accident that called for quick work from one of our new healers. Balls of fire, walls of fire. And then we had stones—a very nice rain of stones that two of my old veterans developed and practiced until two caverns were filled from top to bottom with rocks and boulders of various sizes and I had to have my hole diggers clear away the debris by expanding their work to include rock dissolving. I had a trio of young women who banded together into a team they called the Sisterhood of Socks and Darts, who spent the little free time they had knitting together and talking about their sibs, and their work hours creating a rain of weighted darts as long as my arm that fell from the sky and that would puncture armor and the skulls beneath it. I kept them as a team.

My people learned to fight standing, with their eyes open, to hold their Hagedwar inside them as I held mine and to reach into it in an instant. Because they could only use the tograms within the red, which meant they had to pull power from themselves and not from the infinite energy of the View, my Attackers and Defenders had hard limits on how much they could do. The youngest of our volunteers required hours to recuperate between efforts. Our old veterans did better. The few men I had who were of fighting age—one legless veteran, one hunchback, one lad who had been born without arms, instead having just stumps with fingers on them—shared the record for shortest recuperation time with women who had given birth to at least one child. These were the people who earned their way into core positions leading teams in the fighting units.

For her part, Iyalara developed a sort of window of air. It was a clever thing—her Communicators within the fighting units sent what they saw and heard to teams on the receiving end, who caught these images and sounds and displayed the results as a glowing picture at life size spread out in the air. I watched them do it, and the blinking and the bouncing made me queasy; I never realized how unsteady was my own view of the world around us until I was forced to see it through someone else's eyes. The sound was flat and chaotic—it was almost impossible to single out important voices or commands unless the Communicator himself spoke to us. But while Gair's forces practiced their mock attacks, I could see how my people could use those views to identify and attack the enemy and protect our men.

It was not as good a system as being able to put ourselves—in spirit—into the heart of the battle and cast Sends against the enemy that could selectively turn every living thing that meant our men harm into dust. Or to stop such attacks against our own men as they approached, turning them back. But it was better than sending our men into battle with no cover of any sort.

Communicators, Attackers, and Defenders spent a handful of days working together, coordinating our units and doing our own practice missions against rats in the upper levels of the caves. Our weakness, which we identified early, was that we became useless as soon as we lost our forward Communicators.

Late that night, Gair, Iyalara, and I sat in conference while Iyalara explained the flaw we'd found.

"You need more Communicators, or Communicator alternates, or *some* way that we can see what is going on even if the Feegash take out the people we have in place. Otherwise, as soon as you lose your Communicators, you lose your cover."

Gair had seen the sort of cover we could provide. They wouldn't have some of their enemies turning to ash in front of them as they had when they were fighting with Senders and Shielders, but they were still bolstered by the fact that they would not be fighting alone. "Figure out something," he said. "As far as they know, they're going to be running raids against the full power of the Feegash military, plus our own Shielders and Senders who have been turned. But whatever you figure, do it quickly, because we're going to be raiding through the South Fourth tunnel tomorrow night. We're going to get as many of the Feegash while they're sleeping as we can."

Iyalara and I exchanged glances. The South Fourth led to a tunnel that branched into Shielders, Senders, and Conventionals bases. It was one of several tunnels that had been designed to allow us to bring units up behind attacking enemies while still defending from the front. Our intent if under attack had always been to crush invaders against our walls, surrounding them and annihilating them.

"Which one are you attacking?"

"All three," Gair said. "They'll only be unwary once, if they are at all. So in this one chance to break them, we must hit all three at the same time. Your people are going to be essential in coordinating the attacks. We're going to hit bunkhouses simultaneously. How much of that raining-darts business can you give me? I like it—it's silent, it's invisible in the dark, and it looks like it's going to be effective as hell."

I took a deep breath and told him and Iyalara, "I can attach one of the girls to each of three Communicators. We'll decide in advance on which three. You split the men off—one to Senders, one to Shielders, and one to Conventionals—and make sure each is going to the biggest bunkhouse. Each of the girls should be able to blanket a full room with darts before exhausting, but once they're exhausted, they're going to be out of the fight for the rest of the sortie. They all three need hours to recuperate."

He nodded.

"Back them up with some of your fire throwers. How many people do you have who can drop rocks and boulders?"

"Two. But they're good for perhaps half an hour of steady attack or longer if we use them in short bursts—we'll be able to move them from Communicator to Communicator, and from location to location. Remember, we aren't tied to any one prong of the attack the way you are."

He sighed. "Right. That's helpful, so long as I'm able to coordinate them where I need them. I should have a Communicator assigned solely to me."

I looked at him and raised my eyebrows. I realized that what had been true for me was true for him as well. "So that if we lose that Communicator, we lose you and the whole of the battle? I think not. You have to be here, so that you can direct all three fronts simultaneously and see what is going on in each place. Captain av Lodestaak, you hold a captain's rank but a commander in chief's position. The commander in chief fights from the rear."

I could see the distaste on his face. He wanted to be in there. He wanted to fight. I could see the hunger in his eyes, and I could understand it, too. He could not see how he could inspire the loyalty he needed if he did not show his men what he was made of. But he was not expendable.

He stared down at the rock floor of the cave, clearly unhappy. "Our needs are clear enough. But why could not someone who outranked me have reached us to direct this battle so that I could fight it?"

"We'll get our officers back," I told him. "Any of them who live, in any case. And then all three of us can demote ourselves." I laughed a little. "What failures we are as despots, though, looking for ways to relieve ourselves of our commands."

The Communicator's voice was tight. "Ready at Shields dormitories, sir, with clear line of sight. We go at your word."

Gair could see through the Communicator's eyes—the darkened hallway, the open doorway into what Talyn claimed was the largest dormitory. She'd pointed out that senior Shielders got their own rooms, and had placed those rooms on a map for him. They would come under the second phase of the attack, which would involve hand-to-hand combat after the Magics Attack forces had finished their work.

"Ready at Senders dormitories, sir. Awaiting your word," a second Communicator said, and Iyalara pointed out the glowing image that was his view. Dark wide corridor, dormitory left, door open, men snoring loudly. A guard walked toward the Communicator, seeming to look directly at him, and moved past him and out of view without so much as a pause. He had a good position then.

They held for what seemed an eternity, but what could have been only a long, silent moment. And then, "Ready at Conventionals dormitories, sir. Main dormitory doors were closed—we had the devil opening them without waking anyone or alerting the guards. At your command, sir." A huge dorm full of sleeping men lay before him, another to his right, a third to his left. This was the layout the men who had served in Conventionals had described, and that Gair had planned for.

Everything looked good.

On his word, they would find out how good it really was.

"Communicators, select targets," he said.

Views steadied up, and in the Conventionals building, two additional Communicators began sending images—one had the left dorm, one the right, and the one who had reported initially took the center.

"Attack Magics ready," Gair said. "On my count, darts drop in full volley. Give it everything you have, girls." He felt his heart racing. Success and a huge blow for the Tonks, or failure and the loss of hope, lay at the end that count. "One," he said. "Two. Three. Drop volley."

In Shields, a rain of huge needle-tipped darts fell from nowhere, skewering men as they slept. A few cried out, but the deadly rain killed most instantly. In Conventionals, the most levelheaded of the three girls studied all three dorms presented to her from three different sets of eyes, and at his count filled all three long, dark rooms with darts.

In Senders . . . nothing.

Gair looked down at the third girl, standing stricken in front of the view her Communicator gave her, with her hands shaking and tears running down her cheeks. "Drop volley, soldier," he said, but she didn't seem to hear him. She stood there and shook.

Damnall. "Rock-man, drop volley now," he said, and his leg-less veteran filled the Senders dorm with boulders in an instant.

"Give us corridors, Communicators," Gair shouted, knowing that they could hear him no matter how loudly he spoke, but caught up in what was happening. "Floors and doors, and hurry."

New images sprang to life as the Communicators who had taken position on the upper floors started sending their images.

"Rock-men, floors! Fire-men, doors. Communicators, hold until my word.

In three buildings, the doors to senior soldiers' quarters burst into flame, the corridors filled with enough boulders to prevent easy escape.

"Down a floor," Gair shouted, and the views bounced and spun crazily for a moment.

"Floors and doors," he demanded, and on the second floors, the views steadied, and doors burned, and boulders fell. In one of the buildings—Shields, Gair thought—some of the men had been wakened by noise from upstairs, and they were shouting and strapping on swords and bucklers and bursting into the corridors, but the boulders brought an end to them.

"Down and hold at the stairwells," Gair shouted, and the views danced and dove again, steadying quickly. "Rock-men, fill the stairwells. Sergeants, your men ready arms now."

He heard the Communicators who were working with the ground troops pass on the "ready arms" and heard the sergeants give the command. Swords unsheathed from scabbards like the ringing of soft bells and Gair thought, We can do this. We can take the bastards tonight. In one blow. In the command cave, the rock-men fell back, depleted, and joined the dart-girls. Gair still had some fire throwers and some hole diggers unused in Magics, but he had to hold them in reserve for defense. The rest of the battle would be won or lost by his Conventionals.

His men cleared the main buildings completely, and the fire throwers set the outside of each of the three alight. Small teams immediately established a clear line of retreat, opening up al-ternate entrances to the tunnels that could be reached from out-side. They set up to hold these exits; the rest of the team started in on the officers' quarters, torching the buildings in the old, less-efficient way, and killing the men who came out.

It was a grim business, and the Feegash tendency to expansion made it grimmer—in each of the three compounds, new dorms unsuspected and unmarked by the people who had once occupied those grounds emptied fighting men into the battle. The Feegash didn't field weaklings or cowards, and these men came forward at a run. Talyn's hole diggers dropped the ground out from the frontrunners, the fire throwers cast walls of flame, but the Feegash went around, or they went through, and they kept coming, with those who caught fire throwing themselves into the midst of thc Tonks and spreading the flames. Swords clanged, bowstrings snapped, arrows rained in both directions, men fell bleeding and screaming.

In the command cave, the healers started working, marking their own people as they fell, fighting to save their lives, getting some up and running, losing others.

The fight at Conventionals was losing ground, and Gair gave his Conventionals Communicators the message to get everyone out of there. Thirty fighting men could not stand against the hundreds that were erupting from everywhere.

The men scattered, moved through shadows, dropped through the hidden door into the tunnel only when they could be sure they were not seen, and gathered below.

His unit in the battle at Senders held its own, doing massive damage, but finally Gair pulled his men out of there, too.

The Shields unit made good progress because it was fighting against fewer men—Shields had been the smallest of the three bases, with the least room for expansion. His team at Shields successfully cleared its ground; Gair's best guess was that his thirty men and the support teams from Magics had killed close to a thousand Feegash there. Finally, though, he pulled the Shields team out, too, because he didn't have enough men to hold the ground he'd won. He hadn't planned to hold territory that night—this attack had been to inflict heavy casualties and demoralize the enemy.

So the Tonks left the Feegash military in flames and mostly leaderless. In Beyltaak, the men and women trapped under Feegash rule would see the burning buildings and know they had not been abandoned. Maybe more of them would join the fight to win back Tonk freedom.

Gair, his head aching, his ears ringing, watched his men

working their way back through the tunnels . . . and for the first time he realized that the noises he heard were no longer the sounds of battle, but of cheering. The people around him were cheering—him, each other, Talyn and Iyalara—and the non-combatants in the bigger grotto had started to sing, "For Taak, for Love, for Jostfar," which Gair had heard before. It was a paean to home and family and God, something men sang to close down the taverns at night, when they were in their cups, and something women sang as they hung out wash to dry on lines, and something warriors sang in deep, booming voices as they galloped across the plains with swords drawn or arrows nocked or spears readied. It had always been his enemies' song before.

Now, somehow, it had become his, and he found himself joining in, and cheering with everyone else.

20

I held myself a bit to the side of the main crowd as our men returned. Counting. It becomes a habit, that counting—the rough mental tally of how many went out, how many came back, how many walked on their own two feet and how many lay on shields, and how many did not come back at all. My people sang the welcomes to the heroes, and the dirges to the fallen, and cheered and passed around cold water in place of the ale that we could not squander. I stood with them, for the time not one of the commanders of the battle but simply a fellow taaksman taking such joy as I could from our victory, which was considerable, while remembering those who had paid for it with their lives.

At final count we had sent out 135 men, to stand against forces that our best estimates numbered at five thousand troops. Our healers had done a remarkable job. Many had been wounded in the fight and healed on the spot, to go on fighting. One hundred twenty-nine came back or were brought back. Of those brought back, three were dead, five hideously wounded—

so damaged that our healers could not draw the strength from themselves to save them, or do anything more than keep them breathing while I reached beyond the red and channeled the life force of the universe itself into saving them.

I shared their pain, moved with them far too close to death, and came back from death with them, one at a time.

When they were well again, I moved against a far wall, out of the noise, deep in the darkness, and pushed the memories of pain and suffering back. All my life the women I had known and loved had talked about childbirth as the pain women had to forget—that it was a bitter, overwhelming anguish, but that at the end of it came children and family and a love that filled the heart and the soul. If you focus on the pain, they said, you'll never have a family.

This horror those men had fought through was like that, strangely. Inside them while I healed them, I could feel them pushing away the memories of the pain even as they mended. I could feel their intentional letting go. They did not forget the pain, but they did not hold it tight against their souls, either. Because to a man they were deciding that it was what they had to go through to have their taak back, their families safe, to regain their freedom to move over the ground instead of beneath it, and win back the kiss of the sun and the bite of the wind—not just for themselves, but for those they loved, and not just for those living, but for those yet unborn.

They felt the fear. They knew that they might yet die. And yet, to a man, they stood as I released them, and embraced their comrades, and cheered their victory, resolved to fight again.

These were my people. I loved them. They were worth any sacrifice. So I, too, shook off fear and pain, and stepped out of the dark places, and beneath the flickering light of the torches, I danced.

We sent up cheers and danced harder some hours later when two we thought dead and left behind helped each other through the gates, injured but alive, and we got their stories. One had been fighting in the Conventionals action, the second at Senders. Both had been injured in the fighting; one had lain senseless beneath a pile of the bodies of our enemies, and the other had taken a wound to the leg and could not run and had somehow been lost by the healers. He'd simply waited until he could crawl to the hidden entrance, and had started the long crawl home. The second had awakened, made *his* way to the entrance, and partway to Grief Hill had overtaken the first, and helped him the rest of the way back.

I wondered briefly how our healers had missed them; anyone alive should have shown up in Magics' images. Something, I decided, that we would have to investigate later.

They were exhausted but joyous—they reported the devastation among our enemies and the confusion we'd left behind. The one who had been unconscious reported that he'd overheard that we killed more than ninety percent of the Feegash officers outright, including the grand general of the Feegash army and both of his adjutants. And that while they were still counting the enlisted dead, he heard the guess to be three-fourths of the entire Feegash force in Beyltaak dead and much of what remained so grievously injured that the two men talking doubted they would survive, much less fight again. This was more by far than we had thought, or dared hope.

The two returning wounded went off to be healed—their injuries were not so severe that they required my help—and Gair and Iyalara and I retired to one of the small grottoes to consider the new and welcome information we'd received.

"We need to strike again, quickly, before they can regroup," Gair said.

I agreed. "How quickly?"

"A day? Two days at most—they will not be able to bring reinforcements in by ship in that time, and we are more than a two-day march from the next of the Great Taaks. Can you have your people ready to go in that length of time?"

"I can," I said. "We didn't suffer losses, other than those who failed to fight."

The Sister of Socks and Darts who could not drop her darts on living men was not the only one of my people to suffer a failure of nerve. Such things are common enough in combat, though less common among forces who volunteer than among those who are drafted. Our Conventionals were forever telling tales of tripping over whole nests of Eastils hiding flat on their bellies beneath shrubs and behind rocks while combat raged all around them.

Some people lack whatever spirit it is that lets a man or

woman face death in the pursuit of something greater. I don't know if this lack is of the mind or of the soul, but all armies have their timid and their weak. But not all who failed to fight when the moment comes are timid or weak. Some have suffered only a failure of resolve—have, in the last instant, lost sight of their goal and their purpose. I could not yet know whether that handful in my two units who had failed to perform their duties were of the former sort, in which case I would have to remove them, or if they were the latter. None of them had faced combat before, and more than one soldier who has frozen in the first advance gets his feet beneath him to make the second.

But I did have to talk with them. Before our next foray, I would have to ask each of the handful who had faltered to tell me of his resolve. To tell me not just why we were fighting, but why *he* was fighting. Sometimes the soldier needs only to remember the names and faces of beloved people who cannot fight for themselves but whose lives and freedom depend on him to regain his resolve.

Each of my people deserved that chance to serve.

Gair had found a way to be alone with Talyn for a while, to sit and talk with her and enjoy the pleasure of her company. He did it by giving the troops a rest day and putting Iyalara in charge of seeing that everyone got a bit of time aboveground—herself included. The troops had celebrated their rest day, for the most part, by sleeping or going off in pairs with civilians to little grottoes within the caves, or to the surface, and coming back some time later, grinning and mussed, to sleep some more.

Gair and Talyn had stayed below. The two of them sat side by side, eating their evening ration and taking advantage of the fact that for a while, at least, they had their little grotto entirely to themselves.

"We have to see if Snow Grell has made his way back," Gair said. "And if he has not, we have to leave him a way to find us. It's still a little too early for him to be back with the Eas—" He caught himself. "With the reinforcements, but we want those men when he brings them. We don't know how many other taaks have fallen to the Feegash, or how many of those have no underground resistance and are therefore going to have to be rescued. But we do know that we haven't the manpower to rid all Hyre of the Feegash. Not yet."

Talyn took a bite of her stew, chewed thoughtfully, and washed the drink down with a sip of her ration of ale. "I think we're borrowing trouble," she told him. "Beyltaak was taken by surprise. But it would be foolish to think that other taaks fell to the same ruse. We can't tell because we haven't managed to get any news from anywhere else."

"The Feegash planned this," Gair said. "From the very beginning, they planned to betray the Tonk."

"Probably the Eastils, too," Talyn said.

"But *we* have a centralized government with good communication, good roads, well-developed trade routes, and a single source from which orders flow. As soon as any one of our cities was clearly under attack, the king would have mobilized the whole country against the would-be invaders. By now, the Republic will be free of the Feegash menace. And though he may have some trouble getting them to see the need, I think Snow Grell will be able to rally forces that will be willing to fight to free the Tonks from the same treachery they faced."

She was smiling at him and shaking her head. "You assume a lot."

He smiled a little, and looked around to be sure they were not overheard. "I know mine is the superior system. A republic is inherently stronger and more stable than this rabble of independent city-states and nomadic herdsmen you have here. This all has its charm. And you people have done . . . well, brilliant things with the handicaps under which you've been operating. When you're part of the Republic, you'll see the advantages—I swear it. And there are no drawbacks."

"No drawbacks? You jest. What about lack of a clear voice in the actions taken by those who govern you? Excessive taxation, and taxes in which you have no say? Laws passed by the whim of a king who does not have to live under them, suggested by a council of men who do not have to live under them? Oh, all the Eastils vote for the members of the council, and they need not own property or have served their country to hold the right to cast their ballot. But what is their vote worth? They elect people who frequently do not speak for them, while they *cannot* speak for themselves. And as for law, how about trials judged not by peers but by men appointed by that same above-the-law council? Armies manned by draft, not by volunteers?" She turned to face him and said, "I can think of a hundred drawbacks, and if you consider your land and my land, so can you. For all that we are imperfect, for all that we are not open to all who would live among us, still I would not welcome your way any more than I welcome the Feegash way. Having served my taak, I could stand in the Faverhend and offer a law or a complaint, or demand a change, and I would be heard. Me. Not someone who might or might not speak for me. If I owned land, and thus could prove myself invested in what I proposed, I could do the same."

Gair looked at her and sighed. "And yet, when not just your family but the families of so many others are free again, and my way has proven itself the better, how will you then defend your list of selfish rights? The greater good will call you then, I think, because you are honorable. I know the depth of your honor as surely as I know my own name."

They finished eating in silence, and left their tiny army resting and sleeping, with watches posted and Iyalara in command of Magics and Talyn's master sergeant brevetted commander of Conventionals until their return.

They rode overland, Gair on Talyn's big gray, Toghedd, and Talyn on her little bay, Dakaat. They rode hard, with Talyn leading and Gair close behind; she insisted that overland they could reach the hideout quickly enough to leave their message for Snow Grell and still get back to Grief Hill before the sun rose.

Gair wanted her to admit that she was relieved help was on the way. But she was stubborn. Honorable, fiercely loyal, kind when kindness was called for, generous with her time and belongings . . . and beautiful in her stern way, though he did not want to think of her in that fashion. But for all her strengths, stubborn as a mired mule.

He had faith in her common sense, though. She would come around when she saw at first hand how the Republic could save her people. She loved her people. That . . . that more than anything, more than *everything,* would be the prize that finally won her. Her people would still be Tonk under the Republic. The Tonks would keep their religion, their beliefs, their language, their history—they would have to make room for other ways, other gods and other laws than their own, of course, but that was a small price to pay for civilization.

They rode a rough path that wove between trees, and had been forced some time back to slow to a trot. And then Talyn held up her hand and stopped completely. "Up and to the left," she said as he came level with her. She pointed to a black hulk against the sky, which could have been any hill anywhere—he could not have identified it as the one that held the shelf on which they had found their first shelter. "Shall I stand watch here while you go up and leave your message, or shall we go up together?"

"I'm not sure I see the path," Gair admitted, after a long moment of peering through the darkness in the direction she'd indicated. They had three quarters of a moon, and when it shone, traveling was not as difficult as it could have been. But scattered clouds blocked it and uncovered it, blocked it and uncovered it again, shifting the shadows on the ground and the look of the land so that he could not see any obvious route up to the top, and when the darkness was deepest, any route at all.

"Come up with me," he told her. "If we have to, we can go back through the tunnels."

He heard her sigh. "I'm tired of the tunnels. I miss the sky."

He laughed softly. "When you got me out of the dungeon, I wanted at first to live just long enough to feel the sun on my face again. And yet I find myself back in darkness and something so akin to captivity that some days it is all I can do to keep myself from running screaming for the stairways, even if doing so killed me."

"Yes," Talyn said. "That's it exactly. I think we all feel it. None of us ever thought *we* would be the people who would have to retreat to the caves. That would be some other generation, or none at all."

"But you had the caves. You had a place to retreat, a place you could defend, supplies, some arms."

Talyn nodded. "We had more than most, I suspect. We were fortunate to occupy land already riddled with caves and passages. Not every taak has such fortunate ground."

"Ahh," he said, and part of him was hugely relieved. He had imagined trying to dig the Tonks across the entire Confederacy out of caves and tunnels, and in his mind it had been like trying to chase moles out of their holes. "Well, shall we—"

"I thought those were your voices," Snow Grell said, seemingly appearing out of nowhere.

Gair jumped and Toghedd reared and snorted. Talyn swore softly, and backed Dakaat away.

"Give us some warning," she snapped. "Else we could end up skewered on the trees when our horses bolt."

"My apologies," Snow Grell said, and bowed.

Gair turned to Snow Grell. "You're back already?" He knew his voice sounded too eager. He knew, but he could not keep the hope from his voice or his heart—that he might be the warrior who could lead his people against the Feegash and save the Tonks from their mutual enemy. That he could be the one who won a three-hundred-year-old war in the process, and the loyalty of the conquered at the same time. "Are the troops with you, or are they bivouacked elsewhere?"

"Neither," Snow Grell said, and Gair heard warning in his voice.

Gair swung his leg over the saddle and dropped to the ground to face Snow Grell. "Neither?"

Snow Grell said, "The Republic fell. There was no resistance, there were no victories, there are no troops. I would have to guess, from the state of things, that it fell some time ago. The Eastils are enslaved, or else they have joined the Feegash slavers. Or else they are dead. Many are. If there is any hope for your people, it lies here."

Gair, facing Snow Grell, felt an irrational urge to punch the Hva Hwa in the face, and to keep punching him until he took it his words back and confessed that they were a lie.

"It isn't so," he said. "The Republic was built to stand for the ages, to withstand all attackers. Hell, it stood for three hundred years against the *Tonks*." A handful of whom had just beaten the Feegash in the most uneven battle he had ever seen, though he did not say that out loud.

Snow Grell said, "It didn't fall to conquest. It fell from the inside. The king made the Feegash his advisors. Even before the Feegash 'peace,' he was working against his own people. He died some time ago, and his son took the throne. The son—the Feegash have his ear, too. The Republic is dead. Its people are slaves. And the sickness of the mind that destroyed them spreads."

"No," Gair said again. But it was true. Snow Grell had made the Republic his home. He had loved it enough to offer his own life in its service. He would not lie about such things.

"The Feegash turned my parents," Talyn said. "If they can turn them, they could turn anyone. It's magic they're using, of a sort not many could resist."

Magic, she thought with a sudden chill, that could have poisoned Snow Grell.

She reached into the Hagedwar ever open within her, and through the lens of the togram of pure spirit, she studied the Hva Hwa, looking for the same deadly hooks that she had found anchored in her own soul.

There were none. He was not an agent of the Feegash.

Gair turned his back to the sympathy he heard in her voice. That sympathy hurt worse than mocking would have, because if she had mocked him for his arrogant certainty that his people would weather the Feegash treachery better than hers had, he could have hated her. As it was, he could only see himself as a deluded fool, with no one to lash out at but himself.

"*You* can resist it?" Snow Grell asked Talyn.

"I can *now*. I can go inside myself and see the hooks and pull them free. But only those who can see into the View can do this."

"Could you pull the . . . *hooks* . . . free from someone else?" Snow Grell asked.

"I think so, though I would have to be inside the other person, and there are other risks in that."

"My lover is lost to them," Snow Grell said, and Gair stared at him.

"I didn't know you had anyone."

"She is highborn," Snow Grell said. "One of the Eastil princesses. We were forbidden each other, but she would not put me aside. I met her when she and one of her uncles came to work out a treaty with my people; my people were simply a stop on the way to Franica, where she was to be offered in marriage to the Franican potentate's second son, but business is business, and the queen's brother wanted to come back with as much as he could—he was currying favor for an ambassador-ship to Sinali."

"And she was not given to the Franican?"

"She had met me, and had hired me into her personal retinue as a guard. She had me find out things about the Franicans that she could use to spare herself the marriage. They were duplici-tous bastards—it wasn't difficult." He laughed a little. "I doubt the Republic of Hyre would ever have had another opportunity to ally with them."

Gair sagged. "Would have. But the Republic is dead."

"Dead," Snow Grell agreed. "The Council is disbanded, the elections are gone, the voting places burned. There is the Fee-gash 'peace,' which is slavery. And nothing more."

Gair's throat tightened. He loved his land. Everything he had done, he had done from that love. And it was gone, destroyed by treachery and magic.

"We have rebels here," Talyn said. "And arms. And the magic to make more arms, though the Feegash hurt us as best they could. We have men who will fight; we've already nearly de-stroyed the Feegash in Beyltaak." She still sat her horse, so she had a huge advantage in height. "We will save ourselves. And then we will save the Eastils."

"And conquer us," Gair said bitterly.

"We'll take the disputed lands in payment, and enforce a treaty that will give us favorable trading status, and will prevent you from making alliances against us. But we don't want you," Talyn said. "We don't want your Republic, or your mess of lan-guages and religions, or your mongrel people who cannot re-member their own histories, much less the history of their land. We know who we are, and all we want is to stay who we are, free from your expansionist zealotry."

"Well, you want that and the High Valleys. And Whayre Harbor."

Talyn said, "Yes. We'll claim the High Valleys, and Whayre Harbor, and the disputed ground from just west of Loree to just west of Safehaven."

Gair snarled. "And yet you have managed to forget that an Eastil led you Tonk to victory against the enemy, and will do so again. That your plans to save my people depend greatly on me.

You conveniently forget how much you owe the Eastils already—and in spite of your debt, you want much."

"*I?* I won't want anything. This the taaklords can work out, after we've rid your people of the Feegash. Or perhaps during—just to make sure you Eastils don't forget to be grateful when we're done and your people are free again." She glared at him. "But you have a point—your services will have value for your people when this is done. I forget when you are fighting who you really are and which side you really serve, but it's clear to me now that I must not let myself forget. Beneath the part of you that looks Tonk and sounds Tonk and acts Tonk lies nothing but another Eastil."

That said with a disdain in her voice that stung him like a whip.

The Tonks wouldn't want the Republic's mongrel people and its mongrel religions. And she wouldn't want anyone like him—he who could not say with certainty who his great-grandparents were, or from whence they had come. He whose faith was little more than a muttered prayer to whichever god might be close by before he charged into battle, and a muttered thanks when he found himself still alive on the other side of it. Though he loved the Republic's celebrations to honor those who had gone on to the halls of heroes, he didn't necessarily believe them. But he did love them.

If she wouldn't want anyone *like* him, then she wouldn't want *him*.

Not that he wanted her, he reminded himself. She was raw-boned and hard-edged and sharp-tongued. And scarred inside and out. And barren. And chaste by no one's definition. And infuriatingly superior. And maddeningly certain of the Divine's favor of the Tonks.

But she had a magnificent set of tits, and beautiful eyes, and a thick fall of auburn hair that he longed to touch. And from her own memories he knew the responses and passions of her body, and her delight in and skill at pleasuring a man, and pleasuring herself in the process. She was intelligent. Sometimes she was funny. She could be kind. And gentle. She was honorable and honest. Her smile broke his heart in the rare moments when it surfaced, and he wanted only to see more of it.

He stared out at the darkness, irritated with himself. He hadn't been getting enough sleep, and he'd been living like a Pethartian monk. He could tell because Talyn was starting to look entirely too good to him, and on this day of loss and despair, he wanted to feel his pain and find its cure—not drug his sorrow with fantasies of some woman's flesh.

"Let's get back," he said. "Before we lose the darkness."

Talyn was quiet for a moment, and when she spoke, hers was the voice of the soldier, not the woman. "Overland."

He put himself on the same distant, professional footing. "Do you think we have enough time to get back before daylight?"

"We can be careful of the horses and get there near daybreak," Talyn said.

"Is there anyplace between here and there to go to ground if we must?"

"Yes."

"Then overland. I don't relish the tunnels any more than you do."

The whole trip back, Gair gave me cold looks and answered anything I said to him with a grunt, or a one-word reply, or sometimes by pulling a bit ahead of me, or dropping a bit behind.

I knew I should feel badly for him—his entire nation had fallen under Feegash command, and all his hopes and plans were shattered. But since my people and the Confederacy had figured heavily in his plans, I couldn't find much pity in me apart from what I felt for his personal loss.

I promised Snow Grell that if I could get to her, I would free his princess from the Feegash magic. And I asked him how he'd discovered that she had fallen under their spell.

At least *he* would talk to me. "I had already discovered how terrible things were in the Republic. I had seen the slave camps, the gallows lining the roads. I was determined that I would get my love out of that hell, no matter what it cost me. So I got past all the guards and found my way at last to her in her apartments in the winter palace. The Feegash have made some pretense of keeping the royalty intact. Lellin and her sisters were doing needlework, sitting in the solarium, quiet and graceful and lovely. Absorbed in their work. The scene before me looked so normal, I thought at first that they had been untouched by the Feegash treachery." He sighed.

"I slid along the wall behind the heavy draperies, and neither she nor her sisters noticed me. I got as close to her as I dared, and whispered, 'Lellin . . . Lellin . . . ' And she looked around for me, and I peeked from behind the curtain, and she saw me. She rose as if to come greet me. And all her sisters looked over and saw me."

I saw him shudder and make a gesture of hand to forehead that spoke eloquently of fear and despair.

"She smiled at me, and in the same instant, and with the same look in their eyes, all her sisters smiled at me, and rose." He looked away from me.

"The same smile? At the same time?" I asked. My mind painted an eerie picture, and I shivered.

Snow Grell nodded. "I could feel the power behind their eyes. I could feel their gazes pulling me forward, and I could see on all their lips that smile—and it was the bastard's smile. On every one of their faces. I could see him in their eyes. I could see him *through* them, as if he wore them."

I thought I might vomit. "The . . . bastard?"

"Your diplomat," Gair snapped. "Skirmig."

Snow Grell nodded, not speaking.

Skirmig.

My hands began to shake. I knew that smile. I knew that look in the eyes, and the power those eyes had to draw in, to compel, to convince. "How did you manage to escape?"

"Fear, I think," Snow Grell said. "Fear, and sudden conviction that I would rather be dead than fall into the Feegash power. I have not forgotten . . ." He looked at me, and looked away. "I would have fallen into the Feegash hands had Lellin been alone, had I not seen the . . . Oh, Great and Merciful Hannak, had I not seen on her face and the faces of her sisters, all at once . . . But I did see. I flung myself out the solarium doors onto the high balcony, threw myself over the edge, dropped to a lower balcony. I escaped. Barely. I slept only as much as I had to so that I did not kill myself; I returned to the shelf. And I could see that you had been there, and that you had abandoned the place, but I could not find a sign of where you had gone. I waited—alone on that shelf, I could sleep and eat and despair. And if there was cause for anything but more despair, I knew you would eventually come back and find me."

As we had.

"How long were you there?"

"Seven days," Snow Grell said.

"How, then, could you be sure all of the Republic has fallen? You were not there long enough to travel through the whole of it."

I heard a sudden note of hope in Gair's voice, and in spite of myself, I pitied him all the more for his loss. I understood only too well that frail, pleading hope buried beneath the rubble of endless loss—I shared it, too.

"If I had been there a year, I could not have traveled through the whole of the Republic," Snow Grell said in a tone of reasonableness. "But I could see what was there, and what was not. The slave camps post guards to keep the slaves in—but they take no precautions against attack from outside. So they do not fear that anyone will attempt a rescue. The guards in cities are also set to prevent anyone from leaving. The people are kept in until they fall prey to the disease of the mind that the Feegash spread. When they no longer try to escape, they begin to infect others, and join in keeping others in. Soon, I think, all will be Feegash in their minds. All of them will be bound by magic. And then what will the Feegash do?"

I considered the picture he painted. Tonk and Eastils faced the same fate, though perhaps at different rates. Not all of our taaks had accepted Feegash diplomats into their walls. Not all of them had succumbed to that first ruse, nor had they bound themselves to the Feegash "peace." Some of my people would still be armed. There is seeming strength in a central government, but depth in many allied governments that fight for the same causes but watch their own backs. And even deeper strength in men and women who are not soldiers but who nonetheless keep their own swords and bows independently, and who will stand when called, whatever their walk of life.

Hyre's last hope lay with Tonk troublemakers, with the small factions of independent taaks and nomadic clans that even the larger taaks had considered uncivilized, with the hillmen who lived alone, with those who had stood apart from the progress

so many had embraced and who had held to old ways. I did not
fail to notice, though, that few of the remaining independent
taaks had harbors. Most, in fact, lay well inland. They had been
less desirable to the Feegash bastards.

Which made them more desirable to me. These were the
taaks from which I hoped to raise an army that would be large
enough to rout the Feegash.

If I could only figure out how to win their trust while still
keeping them from trusting anyone who might have fallen to
the Feegash.

My head hurt. It was all more than I had ever thought to have
to deal with. I'd had officers who could have taken control of
everything, who could have run a war with confidence and ease.
And they were gone, leaving me with far more responsibility
than I wanted, and with an ally who still maintained his status
as my enemy.

I needed to trust him. And yet, I could not, because in the end
he wanted exactly what I did not want, and at every turn, he
would be trying to influence events so that they would come out
to his liking.

And it was such a pity.

He was a powerful, solid creature, and good-hearted. And at
night, when Skirmig and his hell haunted my nightmares and I
ached for comfort and reassurance, of all the people I knew or
had ever known, only Gair understood as well as I did what the
two of us faced, and why what we did mattered so much. In a
better world, he would have been Tonk. Then I could have given
my heart and my trust to him.

We made Grief Hill at sunrise, and exhausted though I was, I
almost could not make myself go back down into the darkness.
I glanced over at Gair and found in the anguished expression
that flickered across his face a mirror to the pain I felt. We went
down into the darkness, though, because we had to. Because we
knew our duty, and because our people needed us.

We set our next foray for sunset that day, gave our orders,
and then, exhausted, Gair and I went to our separate bedrolls
and slept.

I dreamed of the woman in white. She crouched over me as I
lay on the bedroll—no beautiful sun-drenched meadow full of
flowers for me this time. No, I had the cave, and a miserable

stretch of rock in a mostly quiet corner, where I knew I was sleeping and so could not even have a reprieve from my situation while I slept.

"What do *you* want?" I said.

She smiled down at me. "Ethebet gave you only one sword," she said.

I sat up, realizing even as I did that I was still lying there on the bedroll, sleeping. I hate dreams like that. There is no rest in them. "One sword isn't going to be much use against the entire Feegash army, now is it?" I glowered at her. "And he's *Eastil*. Couldn't she have found me a good Tonk sword?"

The messenger laughed. "Ethebet gave you everything you need. But just as she gave him to you, she gave you to him. You are his shield. One sword, one shield."

"All I *need*? How about a bigger army? How about all our Senders and Shielders back from foreign lands? How about weapons and supplies and some officers to command this whole thing? Did she ever consider that we're going up against a force that *cheated*, that was *dishonorable*, that used us and betrayed us and that now owns us?"

"You have everything you need. One sword. One shield. Nothing more. Remember that."

And she was gone, and I was lying in the endless smoke-stinking darkness on a hard, damp bedroll, wide awake and broken out in a cold sweat, with the gut-clenching certainty that something was wrong.

I lay in the darkness listening.

The caves were oddly quiet. No babies crying, no children running, no clank of arms as men trained. I could hear a low murmur of voices that rose and fell at a distance, like waves on the shore on a calm day.

All I could think was, *Hide*. I reached into the Hagedwar, and drew around myself a little blanket of *Don't see me*. And I went out to see what was happening.

The noncombatants were gone from the area of the caves where they were supposed to be. Most of the soldiers were gone. Of those who remained, most sat on the floor, legs crossed, wrists resting on knees, palms upward, eyes closed. They were whispering. Snow Grell stood face-to-face with one of the remainder. They, too, were whispering.

But no one was whispering to each other. Rather, everyone was chanting in unison.

". . . keep them there, but don't convert them . . . I want them both whole . . . I'm coming . . . keep them there but don't convert them . . . I want them both whole . . . I'm coming . . . keep them there—"

I jammed my fist to my mouth and bit down on the meaty part of my thumb, scared nearly witless. The Feegash and their mind magic had infected our rebellion, and in a day everything we had worked for and everything we had done was gone. Gair's comrade, who had came through his own hell to reach us, and who had stood by Gair when everyone else had failed him, was gone. Our army, our victory, our hope—gone.

And the Feegash had a new army, this one an army trained with even more of the weapons I'd given them.

All hope of rescuing my parents, my sibs, Rik . . . I fingered the cloak pin at my throat, and saw the look on his face the day I gave him the Shielder's uniform I'd made for him, and I almost couldn't breathe. My little brother Riknir was gone.

And Skirmig—it had to be Skirmig, because only he would have a reason to want me alive and untouched—was on his way. And who else did he want "unconverted"?

Gair?

Skirmig had much reason to hate Gair, the man who had led my rescue from his hands, and the slaughter of most of the Feegash troops in Beyltaak.

I had to get to Gair.

I made the little *Don't see me* spell around myself stronger, and prayed to Jostfar to keep me safe, and flat-out ran to the place where I knew Gair bedded down.

He was still there, and still sleeping deeply.

I took a slow breath to steady myself, put a finger to his lips, and prayed that he would not make a sound.

His hand clamped around my wrist with the speed of a striking snake, his eyes flew open, and he sat up.

I expanded the "don't see me" spell to cover him, leaned in close enough to feel the stubble on his cheeks against mine, and whispered in his ear, "We have to run. Now."

He rose, graceful as a mountain cat, and cocked his head as he heard the whispering.

He frowned, and then a look of sick realization settled on his face. He wrapped an arm around my waist and pulled me close and whispered in my ear, "Who is left?"

"We're it."

"Snow Grell?"

"They have him."

"I'll kill them all."

"First we have to get out of here. Skirmig is coming for us."

"We can kill him."

"We won't get the chance here and now. He won't let either of us get close enough to him to do him any harm."

"There's no way out of here that doesn't lead right past them."

I nodded. "If we make no sound, we'll be able to move past them. I think. I have a spell around us."

"Pray it's a good one."

I didn't tell him that I already had.

We crept out, keeping to the shadows. We disturbed the drafts with our passing, so that torches flickered. Several of the newly absorbed warriors sniffed the air, and I realized that neither Gair nor I had washed off before dropping into our bedrolls; even competing with the smoke and the dank cave air, we stank enough to be noticed.

I used the magic to add *Don't smell me* and, as an afterthought, *Don't hear me* to our little shield, but it was too late.

"They're gone!" someone shouted, and swords snaked from sheaths, and the warriors scattered in all directions, looking for us. One raced right by us, brushing me with the edge of his blade as he passed.

I yelped as pain flared through my left hand, though I muffled it quickly. But the one who had unknowingly cut me faltered, and stared at his blade, edged suddenly with blood, and looked back toward us.

Gair grabbed me by the uninjured hand and ran with me away from the tunnels that led upward; he pulled me deeper into the caves. "Heal it, fast," he whispered. "You're giving them a blood trail."

Panicked though I was, I managed to steady myself enough to close the wound and stop the bleeding.

Gair took off at a run again, towing me behind him, and led

us into a deep corner within one of the tunnels that led back to Beyltaak. He pointed out a tiny overhang where the natural cave was wider than the part that had been carved out later, and pulled both of us beneath it.

The cold, damp rock chilled us, and we clung together for warmth, and the fact that he held me was enough comfort that I could swallow my fear of his touch and allow myself to stay close.

We lay there, while all around us people shouted, and boots tramped by no more than a hand-span from where we hid.

We barely dared breathe. We did not dare move.

But somehow, exhaustion and fear overtook us, and huddled like rats in a trap, we did find our way into uncomfortable sleep.

21

Gair woke with an aching back, a throbbing head, and a woman in his arms, and with the utter darkness and the silence of a tomb all around him.

No question of where he was. He was in hell again, but with a bit of company this time.

He lay there holding Talyn.

Good company, he realized.

She was softer than he would have guessed, and the curves of her body fit against his as if she'd been made for him. He suffered in frustrated stillness the temptations of running his hands over her as much because he found himself in an awkward position as because of any thoughtfulness about letting her sleep. His body liked the idea of waking her. His body was all in favor of a vigorous campaign to get her out of her clothes, cold stone bed be damned, and this cheerful optimism on the part of his cock was something he wasn't going to be able to hide, and she was not going to be able to overlook.

Damnall. He didn't think of her that way. Well, he did, but he didn't want to. Even if the two of them could get themselves out of this newest disaster and somehow reach safety, and perhaps find a way to counter the Feegash magic that turned friends to enemies—or even if they could only escape to some good place that had no Feegash—and even if he could fully overcome her well-earned dread of men, *still* they had no future together. He and she still stood on opposite sides of a great divide. Should something convince him to join her people, he could not, for only those born Tonk could be Tonk. And she was Tonk to the bone, and *would* not join his.

Sex, his body said. You don't even have to like her to have sex.

But he already did like her. And he admired her. And he did not think that he could futter her and walk away without regrets; aside from the unfortunate fact that she was, beneath everything else, his enemy in all the important ways, she was just the sort of woman he'd been waiting his whole life to find. He did not think she was someone he could be casual about.

Nor did he think he could bear to be put aside whenever she decided he might be good enough for a romp, but not for a husband. He knew himself better than to think he would watch her walk away from him and be able to wish her well.

So he lay in discomfort and tried to ignore her warm, rounded weight against him, and thought about embarrassments in his past until his cock stopped being helpful and he could safely wake her.

"Get up," he said. "We're alone in here now. I haven't heard anyone so much as breathe for a long time—other than you and me."

She sighed and snuggled tighter against him, and her round rump undid all his efforts at saving himself from humiliation.

He poked her in the ribs with an index finger and whispered, "Wake up, damn you! We have to get out of here before they come back."

I was having a good dream. The world was the way it should be, and I was in the Star's Rest with . . . someone . . . naked beneath warm covers, kissing and fondling and sliding together and apart. No pain, no shame, no blood, no despair. Good sex, of a sort that had eluded even my dreams since my first encounter with Skirmig.

And that fine dream ended in a sharp pain in my ribs and an

irritated whisper in my ear that scattered my happiness and brought me back to reality, which was dark and damp and cold and uncomfortable, and which featured my unhappy fellow escapee being rude and irritating and irritated.

I snapped my elbow back, hard, and heard his "Oomph" as I hit his gut.

"You oaf," I said. "You could have woken me nicely. I'll have a bruise on my side from that."

"But not a fractured rib, I'll wager." He groaned and gave me a shove, and I rolled out from under the shelf. I felt around me to be sure I was not going to slam my head into rock, which would have made the whole waking-up process even less pleasant, and cautiously stood.

My stiff muscles protested. I heard him moving beside me, and felt warmth to my left side as he stood up.

"I'm not sure if we slept so long the torches burned down, or if they put them out," Gair muttered. "But it's darker than death's front door in here."

"They put them out," I told him. "Standard tunnel tactics. Leave the enemy blind, and when—or if—he finally makes his way to the surface, you have good odds that the first bit of light will blind him, and give you one clear first shot." I considered our situation. "I can give us a bit of light. But I'm not sure that won't work against us, too, if the Feegash left anyone behind to watch for signs of us."

"We can't just sit here in the dark until we die," he snapped.

"No. We can't. But I don't know what we *can* do."

"Make our way to the coast. Steal a boat. Cross the Brittlebreak Straits and flee through Pindas over the border to Cartajarma on the one side or maybe Banika on the other. Or maybe just run north until we end up in the Hva Hwa territories. They aren't likely to be dealing with the Feegash any time soon."

Running. Considering that we had won our battle and lost our war, running seemed like the sensible thing to do.

But Rik's silver brooch weighed heavy as a millstone at my throat. The Feegash had him. They'd made him into some mind-bound captive, a slave to Feegash thoughts and, perhaps, to Feegash perversions—and with him the rest of my family. My sisters, some of whom were both beautiful and of an age to interest the sick Feegash perverts. My parents, who would both be useful tools for Skirmig and his cronies. My aunts and uncles and cousins, and my friends and neighbors.

"We can't run," I said.

"We can't stay here," he pointed out.

"I don't mean we can't make . . . ah . . . a strategic retreat. But we—or at least I—cannot leave my taak and my people to fend for themselves while I make my escape to safety."

In the darkness, I heard his heavy sigh. "I did not think you could. Nor, I suppose, did I wish you would. But . . . it would have been easier."

It would have. No arguing with that. "And if the easy way were ever the right way, life would be just one merry dance in the meadow."

Silence. Then, "You have any idea how we might get out of here?"

"If I knew where we were—" I'd started to say something cutting. But if it was true that I no more knew where we were than Gair did, I could nevertheless find out where we were. The Hagedwar magic never felt like the obvious solution to me. And I did not know if I would ever get used to having it always at the ready. Thinking of magic without being bound to a team for safety at the same time felt as unnatural to me as thinking about . . . about leaving my taak. But I had the Hagedwar magic. And I could hope to make good use of it. "Hold on," I said, and considered what I needed.

I crouched, and put my fingertips on the floor of the tunnel. In the eye of my mind, I created faint glowing lines that raced out from me in all directions, splitting at each branch in the tunnels, turning bright orange at the points where they came up against doors, marking spots of bright red for each person they passed, and going blue when at last they reached the surface. While I did not permit these bolts to show up in the real tunnels, I spun out a flat image on the floor in front of me that showed their paths.

"That's amazing," Gair said. "That's the tunnel system."

"Yes."

"Where are we in it?"

I saw us as two dots yellow and warm as the summer sun, and those two dots appeared on the map.

"That's you and me," I said.

"Fine. Which way do we go, then? Any suggestions?"

I willed the Feegash to show up as blue dots, and quickly discovered that they had abandoned the tunnels in favor of manning all the exits. I said, "We'll run south."

"*Away* from the coast?"

"*Toward* the inland taaks. A goodly number of them refused to have anything to do with the Feegash, to the point of refusing to admit diplomats or even speak with them. When the Great Taaks fell to the Feegash peace, they shut their gates. Of those, Chaavtaak, which lies due south of here, is nearest."

"They won't welcome us."

"Probably not," I agreed. "Not if they're wise. But we have news they need, though they may not know it. The Feegash will target them when they've subdued the coastal taaks. And we know now what manner of attack the Feegash will use."

"Infiltration."

I said, "I would think so. I think . . . I think the two wounded soldiers who returned late after the fighting . . . they might have been turned. Have been Feegash plants. I've been running this over and over in my head and I cannot think of any others who had the chance."

"Could be." He shrugged, seeming uninterested in the theory.

"I suppose we can't know for sure."

"We can't. And would it matter anyway? It's done now."

Which was true enough.

The map cast enough light that I could make out the faint outlines of Gair's face in the darkness. He stared at the map, frowning. "Concentrations of the enemy all along these routes," he said, pointing westward.

"They think we'll try for Beyltaak again, then," I said, seeing the pattern he pointed out.

"And they're not taking much of a chance of us running north, either."

"Also in the direction of Beyltaak."

"If these people hold their posts, we're going to have to kill one or two in order to get out."

"We dare not," I told him. "That Feegash magic binds them all together. You heard them whispering in unison. You saw them moving out to orders that only they could hear. If we kill one of them, the rest will know that we did it, and know where we were when we did it." I considered for a moment, then added, "Besides, we killed most of the Feegash. The people against us now are likely to be friends and family." I sighed. "Well, *my* friends and family."

"We can die down here, then. In a dark hole where we cannot do any good for anyone. Including your friends and family."

"We'll get by the guards the same way we did before. With magic."

"I don't trust magic," he said.

I nodded, though I doubted he could see me. "Good instincts you have. Magic is a slippery thing. But we have nothing better."

With the map floating in front of us, we took off, heading south and aiming for an exit in a long stretch of forest well behind Grief Hill. We kept quiet and ran as quickly as we could, though most of the time we didn't dare more than a slow trot with our hands in front of our faces. The map cast a bit of light—enough that we could at least see we weren't about to pitch ourselves into an unexpected hole.

There might be holes. Falling boulders. Falling darts. Walls of fire erupting out of nowhere. We had trained a powerful force, but had not been able to keep it from being turned against us. We had, in essence, created the enemy's new army. I couldn't get that out of my mind—that everything I knew that I had given to Iyalara was now in the hands of Skirmig and the rest of the Feegash.

I kept that little cloak of *Don't see us* wrapped around us while we ran, but until a boulder dropped out of nowhere and smashed the two of us flat, I wouldn't know if it failed or if Iyalara or one of the new Magics would figure out a way to go around it.

Then, strangely, while the two of us were running, I remembered Ethebet's messenger, who told me all I needed was my sword. That all my people needed was one sword and one shield.

Which had to be nonsense. Two people could not defeat all of the Feegash, and all of the Eastils who had been turned by the Feegash, and all of the Tonks who had succumbed to the Feegash magic. Against so many, two people would be nothing.

Gair's excited whisper broke through my growing despair. "There's an unguarded one."

I stopped, and he stopped, and we looked at the glowing map. Gair traced a finger from us through the paths to a single tiny exit that lay close to two well-guarded exits. It had to be one the Feegash had somehow overlooked. Perhaps it was in a concealed location, or perhaps it was nothing but a trapdoor flat on the ground that leaves or weeds had covered, so that if we tried to use it we would be stepping right into plain view in the middle of our enemies.

It was the only one, though, that had no one watching it.

"It's probably in an awful location. But I suppose we have to try it," I said. I looked over at him, wishing that I could tell him how I felt about him. Wishing that I *knew* how I felt about him enough to put it into words, because the odds were that we were going to be caught by the enemy, and either swallowed into the magic that had turned the people we loved against us, or executed as being too much trouble. Knowing what I knew about the Feegash magic and the Feegash aims, I was guessing Skirmig and his cronies would opt to see me executed. "This is probably going to be the death of us, you know," I added.

"I know."

We ran together a little longer.

"Talyn?"

"What?"

He didn't say anything for a very long time.

I finally said, "Did you want to ask me something?"

"Yes. But I've decided I'm not going to." He laughed a little. "But . . . thank you for saving my life."

"Thank you for saving mine," I said, but it wasn't what I wanted to say at all. Telling him that—using those words—felt awkward and formal, and a thousand years away from falling asleep on bare stone with his arms around me, feeling the strength and the comfort of his presence as I drifted off. I wanted to feel his arms around me; I didn't know what I would say differently in such circumstances, but I knew it would be better. Not some faltering, stuffy, crippled murmur.

When we finally reached the pathway that led to the unguarded exit, I could see how it had been overlooked. Unlike all the other exits, it was unmarked. It had no gate, no cut stairs. It was nothing but a knee-high crack in the cave wall, barely wide enough for someone to crawl into. Neither Gair nor I had any weapons but the daggers we wore even when sleeping, which was just as well. The space was so narrow I was not sure we'd be able to get into it unburdened. Had we had packs and swords and crossbows or longbows and arrows, we would have had no chance.

"That's not a path," Gair said.

"That's why they aren't guarding it."

He crouched down and studied the darker outline of it in the pale, faint light cast by our map. "It may not even be big enough to get through."

"I know." I shivered. "If no one ever uses it, there are going to be spiders in there. And centipedes, maybe. Snakes just coming out of hibernation. Bats." I got down on hands and knees. "And I'm afraid that if I use any magic to widen it or clear everything out, I'll alert someone on the outside to our presence. So if it is too narrow, we should probably just back ourselves down here again and try to wait them out."

He said, "I have to go first, then."

I frowned. "I'm the only one of us who has weapons we can use to defend ourselves if we end up in the middle of them," I told him.

He said, "True. But I'm the wider of the two of us. It's entirely possible that you'll be able to get through the passage, but that I'll get stuck. If we plan on sticking together, it's better that I go through first."

I sighed, backed away from the opening, and said, "I'll hold your sword in my thoughts as we near the exit, so that if you can get through and you need it, you'll have it."

"Thank you," Gair said, and sprawled on the stone on his belly and started squirming his way into the narrow opening. "If you can think of any way to give me some light in here, I'd appreciate it."

I pushed the map ahead of him. Which left me in the dark. I lay down and started crawling.

I have never liked enclosed spaces, and I liked them a great deal less since my final hours in Skirmig's hands—and I cannot say that I was brave going into this one, or happy about it. I was in absolute darkness, pressed in above and below and to both sides by rock, the floor of the crevice was slimy and a trickle of icy water ran over it, and I kept feeling *things* crawling over my skin in the darkness. I could not tell if they were real or imaginary.

I could move forward only a handbreadth at a time, and sometimes I had to lie on one side to fit through the narrow space between the rocks, and sometimes I had to lie flat on my belly and drag myself forward with my fingertips.

Time slowed, and the world narrowed to just me and the tiny spaces between me and the weight of the world pressed in on all sides, and the air thinned out so that I felt dizzy and gasped just to keep breathing.

It was fear. I knew it was fear, but knowing helped not at all. The air didn't seem any richer because I knew I was afraid, and the crevice didn't seem any less hungry, or the darkness any less heavy.

I scraped my knees and elbows, smacked my head on jutting stone that I could not see, and thought cruel thoughts about Gair, who had a tiny bit of light in front of him and so was not crawling blind. The darkness, the stone, and the closeness all crowded in on me, and I could imagine myself alone, trapped, dying in the darkness unnoticed and unmourned.

I ached. The water trickling under me soaked my clothes, and my belly and my back felt bruised, and my knees and the palms of my hands and my fingertips throbbed. And the back of my skull certainly had lumps on top of lumps from all the times that I had rapped it into the stone.

The crevice had looked short on the map. But it felt like we had been working our way through it for days. Maybe weeks. My mouth was dry, but I didn't dare lick the water from the rocks—I could not escape the feeling of live things in it and on me, and did not want to get any of them on my face or in my mouth.

Inch by weary inch, I moved forward, sometimes hearing a soft grunt ahead of me, sometimes a thump or a rustle. But nothing more. I was grateful when I could tell that Gair was up there, but I could not reach him, and most of the time I could not hear him, and I could not see him—so I was, in essence, alone.

And then I squirmed through one easy stretch that actually gave me a bit of room to get up on elbows and knees, and I moved forward faster.

And because I was in complete darkness, I didn't see Gair ahead of me, and I took a solid kick to the nose, while he fought to get through the narrower next portion.

I yelped.

He said, "Shhh. We're almost out. I can see actual daylight above me. Get rid of the map so that its light doesn't alert anyone."

Then another rustle, and Gair's feet vanished, and I lay in silence and darkness again, clutching my nose and tasting blood.

I banished the map and started forward, making as close to no sound as I could manage, and found myself in a pile of slimy dirt and wet leaves and prickles and burrs and twigs. And things that squirmed and crawled across my hands and over my face and through my hair and skittered across my neck. Things that were most assuredly *not* imaginary.

I wanted to scream, jump up, brush myself off, dance around in circles getting whatever was on me *off* of me—and all I could do was squirm deeper into the mess. Gair had been where I was, in a horribly narrow section worn more or less smooth by eons of dripping water, when he told me he saw light. He'd been right in the middle of the slime and the bugs and whatever else was in there. He hadn't sounded the least upset. I hated him.

I peered forward and didn't see any light.

But then, he hadn't said he saw light in front of him. He said he saw it above him.

I twisted around and looked up.

I didn't see it above me, either. But I did get hit by dirt raining down into my face.

Right. I didn't see light because *he* was plugging up the exit. I shuddered and felt around, dreading touching anything because I could see nothing and had no way of knowing what exactly was down in that hole with me. I'd run out of forward. The exit now went straight up, still narrow, offering some handholds and some footholds, but all of them wet and slimy and cold and covered with moss. I started up.

And heard, suddenly, softly whispered swearing in a steady, miserable stream.

"What are you doing up there?" I whispered.

"I'm stuck. We're going to have to go back."

"You can't be that stuck. We're almost out of here."

"I'm that stuck. I have my head and one shoulder and one arm squeezed through this narrow spot, and the other shoulder won't fit. I'm not even sure I can get back down to where you are without ripping my arm or my head off."

I was wet and filthy and shivering and I could still feel things crawling all over me, whether they were or not, and the only thing that had gotten me through that passage was the promise of fresh air and light and room to breathe and move at the other end of it.

I was *not* going back into the caves.

"Try harder," I whispered. "Here—I'll push you."

I climbed until I could feel his feet, and braced myself, and grabbed one of his ankles and shoved.

I heard his yelp of pain and a hissed, "Stop, stop, stop, *stop*!" And then silence. And then a string of what I guessed would be profanity in his native language, and then, "I can't move forward. I can't move back. At all."

Jostfar, I prayed, let them not be looking for magic. Please. Please, please, please . . .

And I reached into the Hagedwar and with the power there reshaped the rock that pinned Gair just enough that he could get through. I was done in the merest instant, half the blink of an eye, the smallest fraction of a single breath.

But in that instant, I heard voices some distance away begin shouting, "I have a direction! I have a direction. They're that way!"

"Go!" I whispered. "Hurry! We'll never have another chance."

I held the *Don't see us* in place and did not summon a sword for him or any sort of weapon for myself—they clearly *had* been looking for magic use.

Gair's feet moved out of my reach, and I climbed as quickly as I could, and felt him grab me and pull me out of the ground as soon as my head and shoulders were free.

We were in woods. In darkness. Above the bare trees overhead, the stars shone down, and the edge of the moon crept along one horizon. The stars would have cast the light that Gair spoke of, and had it been a cloudy night, he would have seen no light at all. I did not know if we faced east or west—so looking at the moon, I could not even guess whether night was just beginning or nearing its end. I wanted enough time to be still, to see if it rose or set. Just a few moments would tell me. But the voices neared, and we had to flee.

Shadows from the trees, the trees themselves, and the unevenness of the ground around us gave us some cover, but they offered the same cover to those who sought us.

Gair grabbed my arm and pulled me downhill. We moved as quietly as we could over the sodden leaves, knowing that we were leaving a trail a child could follow, but unable to prevent it.

No magic. No weapons. Nothing between us and capture but the tiny single spell I had cast around the two of us that might at any time be broken or fall apart in the face of some other, bigger, stronger, better spell.

Gair had seen a stream or perhaps heard it, and led us down to its banks. It was a fast stream, graveled and with shallow banks and not much mud. He found a fallen tree that lay across it and crawled out onto it, pulling me behind him, and then eased himself into the knee-high water. I heard nothing over the burble of the stream but a single sharp intake of his breath. He turned, scooped me into his arms, whispered, "It's cold," in my ear, and eased my feet into the running water.

I'd had cold showers all my life, drawn from water that came from the same place as this water. I was tougher than those warm-water Eastils.

But he was right. It was cold.

We slogged through the water, going downstream. Crossed a gravel bar. Slipped into rapids that dropped quickly into a deep pool. Ended up neck-deep in ice water with no warm, dry towels waiting for us at the end of our journey, with the cold wicking away our body heat with brutal efficiency.

We had to get out of there. Fast.

I headed toward the far side of the pool, and noticed that Gair wasn't following me. I stepped back, grabbed his hand with numb fingers, and pulled him after me. I could hear his teeth chattering. I could feel mine doing the same.

We climbed up the bank, but the wind hit us, making the water we'd just gotten out of seem warm by comparison.

If we didn't get out of the wind and out of our wet clothes, we were going to die. I was having a hard time thinking, but I knew that was true.

The whole of the woods south of Beyltaak was riddled with caves, but it wasn't a cave that saved us. It was a fallen-down trapper's cabin, of which little remained but a roof that had sagged to the ground on one side, forming a serendipitous lean-to surrounded in all directions by scrub brush and tall grass. One of the things good parents who live in cold climates teach their children is how to preserve body warmth in cases of emergency. And the rules they teach are simple enough. Get dry. Get away from the wind. Make or find the smallest possible shelter, one your own warmth can quickly heat. Share your body warmth with as many other people as you have. In a pinch, hands under armpits can save you from losing fingers, but to save your life, you need warm, dry bodies.

The only way we would get dry fast enough to live would be to get out of our soaked clothes. All of them. And then get close to each other.

Nakedness frightened me. Being naked with a man would be, I thought, something I could never dare again, whatever the reason. Thinking about what I had to do made breathing difficult, and added shudders to my cold-born shivers.

Yet dying frightened me more, and the wet clothes would have killed me. Would have killed both of us. Using magic would kill us, too, and perhaps quicker. I dared not cast some Hagedwar spell to warm us or dry us.

And Gair no longer frightened me as much as he had. I could be close to him without wanting to scream or flee. I could touch him and feel his skin against mine without flinching from anticipated pain.

So naked it was. I took the chance. Under the lean-to, the weeds and ground were dry. With the last of my strength, I fought my way out of my clinging wet clothes and pulled Gair's clothes off of him, trying hard not to think about what I was doing, about the risks I was taking, about my fear. Then I nested both of us in the dry weeds, pulling them in around us, and pressed my body against his and pulled his arms around me so that we could conserve whatever meager warmth we had left.

I boosted the *Don't see us* spell and lay in the darkness, my body nearly convulsing with chills, Gair's the same, and prayed Jostfar would not abandon us.

I did not remember falling asleep, but I awoke to an oven-like warmth, to nakedness and rough grass and soft earth beneath me, to the sleeping embrace of my equally naked fellow survivor.

Sunlight beat down on the roof above us, heating it and everything beneath it. Including us.

I could not believe that we were alive. That we were out of the caves, still uncaptured, gloriously warm and dry. I could not believe our amazing luck, or perhaps the goodness of Jostfar, who had seen us through the hell in which we had been trapped.

I looked at Gair, whose head rested on one of his arms, whose sleeping face was strong-boned, whose dark hair, still braided down his back, had come loose at the front where it tangled in little strands, blowing in the wind. He had a good nose, I noticed. Not pretty, especially not with the scrapes on it, which let me know his trip through the crevice to freedom had been no more pleasant than mine. He had a good mouth, too—it curled a bit at the corners, so that he gave the impression of happiness as he slept. He had a lump on his left temple, streaked with dried blood and bruised to deep purple. His shoulders both bore deep gouges and heavy bruises. His knuckles on his right hand were scraped. . . .

I squirmed just a bit back, and looked harder. He had the same deep, bloody gouges on his chest. But I had not heard him cry out once, except for the time I tried to shove him forward. He'd borne those wounds in silence.

I moved closer to him again and ran the fingers of one hand lightly along his back, finding the old scars, but new injuries, too. I raised up a bit, trying to peek at his back, and felt his body stiffen.

I looked down and found his eyes open, and him studying my face with quiet interest.

"We aren't dead," he whispered, pushing down just a bit with the arm I'd draped over me the night before. I found myself level with him again, my head resting on his forearm as it had while we slept.

"We aren't," I agreed.

"I'd thought sure we were going to die last night."

"It was a near thing."

He touched my face, a finger lightly tracing the line of my

nose, which I discovered hurt a great deal. "What happened there?"

"I got too close to you and your foot hit my face."

He winced. "I'm sorry." He smiled at me a little, and leaned forward, and kissed the bridge of my nose. "To make it better," he said.

My heart, which had been picking up speed since·Gair first opened his eyes, did a wild dance at that touch. I felt fear again—but desire, too.

"It's fine," I said. Then, trying to divert attention from myself, I touched the huge bruised lump on his temple. "How did you do that?"

His grin got bigger. "That was when you tried to *help* me through that tight spot," he said. "When you pushed on my leg, you . . . ah . . . squeezed things that shouldn't be squeezed, and I jerked my head into a little stone outcrop."

"Oh." I winced. "I'm very sorry." I raised up and pulled his head toward me and kissed the bruise as carefully as I could. "To make it better."

He ran a finger from my chin down my throat to the hollow between my collarbones. Paused. Ran it down to the middle of my breastbone. And stopped. "How is it that neither you nor I have any clothes on, and woke up this morning covered in grass and leaves?"

"You don't remember?"

"I remember losing our footing in that creek. And landing in deep water. But I don't remember anything after that."

"We nearly died," I said. "We were soaked, we were freezing, and we managed to get out of the water, but it was even colder in the wind. I found this shelter, got both of us out of our wet clothes, and curled us up together under grass and leaves and out of the wind, and . . ."

"And you saved my life again."

"Whereas you got us to a place where we could lose our pursuers to begin with. Please don't keep count. If we get out of this, we'll both be so deeply in each other's debt we'll need extra lifetimes to repay what's due."

His hand moved from my breastbone to my shoulder, and he lay his head on his other arm and looked at me and smiled. "I could think of worse debts to owe."

Our bodies were warm against each other. I put a hand on his side and ran my palm from his ribs over his hard-muscled waist to his flank. We were both covered in leaves and dirt, wild-haired, but not anywhere near as filthy as we would have been had we not enjoyed our soak in that freezing pool.

We were naked, and alive, and grateful to be alive.

And at that moment, it did not matter to me that he was Eastil and I was Tonk. All I had suffered faded, all that I feared fell away. For the first time in long and longer, I was a woman complete and alive. My flesh and its desires were no longer my enemy. I pressed my body against the length of his and kissed him on the lips.

His arm slid from my shoulder to my back and he pulled me tighter to his chest. I felt his arousal as he kissed me in return, and I tightened in readiness, wanting to feel him enter me, wanting that first plunge as he drove inside me.

He rolled us over so that he was on top of me, his weight balanced on his elbows, his chest brushing my breasts. I slid my legs up the outside of his thighs and rested my calves against the tight cheeks of his rump, excited by the sheer muscular mass of him. I could feel the length of his cock against me, hot and hard, but though I wanted him to, he didn't enter me. He just kissed me until I was breathless, pinning me, and when I hooked my heels against his rump and tried to pull him inside me, he broke off our kiss and smiled down at me and shook his head.

"No?" I said. "What do you mean 'no'?"

He ran one rough thumb over my cheek, and his voice was hoarse. "I could *never* forget your name."

He looked into my eyes, and I stared up at him, bewildered. "What?"

"You're Tonk, and I can never be Tonk. And there are simply some women a man cannot walk away from if he gets in too deep. At least not with his heart and soul intact." He kissed me again, but this time it was a kind kiss, and without passion.

I ached for him, and he was telling me he wouldn't pog me because . . . why? Because he wouldn't be able to walk away from me someday? Because he couldn't have me forever? My legs slid down his thick thighs until my feet rested on the ground and I stared up at him, trying to make sense of his reaction. Could not the moment be sufficient unto itself? Could we not have each other without attachments, in celebration of the fact that we weren't dead yet?

If we could not keep each other—assuming we would want to after—did that mean we could not have each other at all? I was gratified that he would remember me. That he believed I mattered enough that he would regret our parting, for all that when we were together we ofttimes drove each other mad. But I *wanted* him. I wanted his touch. And I had thought I would never want such things again.

He rolled away from me and crawled to where I'd dumped our clothes when I stripped them off us. He rummaged through the still-sodden lumps and found his own things, and started pulling them on. Scarred and battered, he was still a glorious specimen of maleness, and I could taste his lips on mine, the perfection of his kiss, the way his hands had touched me, the heat of his body and the way we fit.

I rolled on my belly and lay with my face buried in the grass, clutching the back of my head with my hands. I felt like a fool, made embarrassed and awkward by his rejection, however polite it might have been.

Gair pulled on the damp clothes, holding in his anger. He wasn't sure, though, whether he was angrier at Talyn or at himself.

She would have taken him into her knowing full well they could not keep each other. She had no doubt at all that when the time came she would be able to cast him aside and walk away.

It was too late to save himself. Lying there holding her in his arms, feeling her body soft and full beside him, and then welcoming and ready beneath him, he'd realized that he loved her. He had spared himself from falling in love with any number of appropriate Eastil women because of his duty, because his first love was to his country, because of any number of other perfectly logical reasons. He'd been intelligent. Rational. Sensible. He'd spared himself endless hurt and heartbreak, and spared the woman, too, who would have had to watch him go off to war and not come back. At least he hadn't made it back so far, so his wife would have had to guess herself a widow by this time.

Sensible. He was a sensible man.

He yanked the damp breeches on, struggling to get them up, pulled on the filthy, wet tunic, yanked up soggy stockings, and forced his feet into wet boots.

None of which either chilled or dampened the ardor he still felt for Talyn.

He would have fought the whole of the Feegash army for her. Alone. Would have lain in a hundred soaking leaf piles patiently squashing with his bare hands as many bugs as he could find before he crawled on, just because he'd heard the quaver in her voice when she mentioned them. Would have made love to her whenever, wherever, however she wanted.

But nothing he did would make him Tonk, and nothing he did would make that not matter to her.

He was not Tonk; therefore she would never return his love.

He should have had the sex, he thought, peering around the edge of the roof to see if any enemies waited nearby. It was already too late to spare himself the broken heart.

22

We ran south toward Chaavtaak, one of the most aggressively independent of the taaks. The Chaav who held the position as taaklord there had never agreed with any of the rest of the taaklords, had never gone along with general trade agreements, had never accepted the offer of troops from outside his taak when his people were having trouble, nor sent any of his own units to help elsewhere when he wasn't. By all accounts he maintained close ties with the area's nomads, however, and if rumor was correct had actually been a nomad in his youth who had chosen taak life for reasons no one had ever sufficiently explained.

We passed patrols out looking for us, but I kept the *Don't see us* spell tight around both of us, and we managed to slip at last past the outer perimeter of the region they were searching.

Of course, Gair was in a foul mood, something I could not begin to understand. He wouldn't start a conversation with me at all, responded to my few attempts to talk to him in grunts or single words, and if he looked at me at all, he glared.

I had no idea what I'd done wrong, but apparently it was big, and it was going to cause a problem between us. Nor did it help either of our moods that we had neither food nor water nor weapons nor horses, and if we were going to successfully approach the nomads who might then be able to get us through the gates into Chaavtaak, we had to have horses even if we had nothing else.

Chaavtaak lay over thirteen long leagues away from Beyltaak. Going at our current pace, we'd need two days to get there.

And I was not sure when I might dare to use magic to bring us the things we needed. Would doing so bring the Tonk Magics units down on us?

Gair decided me on taking the risk, though, when, as we jogged slowly along, he turned to me and said, "We've come through all of this, but with us on foot, we don't stand a chance. Snow Grell might not notice the two of us with that shield you've cast, but we're leaving a trail he could follow while sleeping, and the trail will bring him and those he'll lead right to us. If ever those bastards realize the only direction we can travel is south, we're walking dead."

The Feegash might not realize the limits of our options. But the Tonk would. My own father—assuming he was still alive—would be able to figure out from the simple facts of our situation where I would run. Where we'd been trapped. The method of our escape. Where our closest potential allies lay. If I could get Gair and myself behind the walls in Chaavtaak, we might have a chance even yet to fight against our enemies, however futile that fight might be. But at our current pace our enemies would figure out where we were headed long before we arrived, and with them mounted on good horses and having a talented tracker to lead them, they would have us before we could even get near safety.

I had to chance the thing I didn't want to chance. I had to reach into the Hagedwar again and bring us horses.

I could feel within the Hagedwar the possibility of moving living things. It lay within the outer tograms, beyond the red—it was a magic that touched nothing less than the will of Jostfar, channeled directly through the View. I did not worry overmuch about the risk to myself; I knew my way around the View, and the Hagedwar made the process safe enough. But I'd never tried to move a living thing from one place to another. I wanted my horses back, but I didn't want to kill them in bringing them, and I feared that I might.

"I'm going to try to bring some horses to us," I told Gair.

"Will the Magics units spot the magic?"

"Probably. But if we can get the horses, it shouldn't matter. We have a decent lead."

"And if you can't get the horses, any doubt they might have had about our direction is gone."

"I know."

He shook his head. "We have no good choices here. Go ahead. At worst, it will get us killed a few hours earlier."

I wished he was wrong. But he wasn't.

I closed my eyes for just a moment and slipped into the togram that would let me touch living things. The music of the universe sang to me and soothed me, and I wanted so much to hide in there—to push through the safe walls of the Hagedwar and fall into the View and lose myself forever away from the horrors that existed in my world.

I could have. The togram protected me only so long as I stayed within it. I knew my way into the View, though, and could have crossed into the realm where the universe's beauty and perfection had no filters.

But the brooch my little brother had made for me was a reminder; people needed me to be strong. For a little longer, at least, I needed to keep fighting, because for a little longer, hope remained.

I found my horses—outside with the rest of the herd the Beyltaak Tonk army had taken back to Beyltaak. They were inside the walls, but in the open air, simple to find, simple to catch.

Except that I could not hold on to them. I could not find the way to move them from one place to the other—it was as if they were made of ice and my grip kept slipping over them. I could touch them, I could see them, I could reach into their minds and talk to them. But though I could shape the idea of bringing the horses to me and give it form within the togram, and even though I could feed the power that channeled through the togram into my will, I could not successfully attach my will to them and bring them to me.

"What's wrong?" Gair said.

"Wrong?"

"From the look on your face, I thought something was wrong."

"I can't bring the horses to us. I was going to use magic to move them from where they are to here, but it won't work."

"Too bad," Gair said. "Because once you brought the horses, you could have brought that diplomat bastard, and I could have killed him."

Which would have been, in fact, a tremendously practical solution to at least one of our problems.

"They're alive," I said. "They are constantly changing. I think that I could bring them only if they were dead, because if they aren't . . . well, fixed in place . . . I can't hold on to *them*. I catch an instant of them, but then in the next instant it changes. It's like trying to hold water in your open hand."

Gair studied me, and tipped his head to one side. "To hold water, you freeze it. Can you freeze them?"

I considered that. Could I? I saw a bird flying overhead, and reached out for it with the magic and my will, and willed it to stillness—and it slipped away from me. I could touch its spirit, but I could not still its spirit. I realized I was trying to still the whole of the View, for the life that animated the bird was connected to all of life itself.

I was no Sender, to reach into the View and reshape fragments of life into death. And not even the Senders could reshape life into other life, or death into life.

"No," I said, and realized that Gair was lying flat on the ground, face turned toward me, eyes tightly closed. I cleared my throat. "It's beyond me. Which is good, I suppose. Skirmig might have been able to carry me back to him, otherwise."

Gair opened his eyes, pushed from lying to standing with an athletic grace that made me shiver inside, and said, "Then if you have the magic for it, make us some horses that will run even though they aren't living, because I have had my ear to the ground and the ground rumbles with the approach of enemies, and if you do not, we're walking dead."

For a moment his words made no sense to me at all. Horses that weren't living? Horses that weren't living would be dead.

And then in my mind there flashed a tiny image: the Tonk dancer I'd made out of silver. If a dancer who was not a human could dance, a horse that was not a horse could run. Couldn't it?

Silver would be too heavy, though. Creatures of solid metal that tried to gallop over rough ground would sink.

Something light, then.

Clay? Wood?

I liked the idea of wood. I remembered the magic well enough—I knew my way through the Hagedwar, and the broader paths of my own soul. I could create such creatures, I thought; they would be the silver dancer again, only bigger and useful. I could draw materials from all around me and the spark of life to animate them from myself. So out of magic I spun two wooden horses, perfect in conformation, and gave them comfortable saddles and good bridles, and then I slipped into the togram that allowed me to infuse them with my will, to give them enough of a part of me that they would seem to live, and would respond as if they lived.

They shimmered for just an instant as I watched them, and then they were not simply wooden horses anymore. One tossed its head and the other pranced a bit as it stood there. I leapt into the saddle of the nearest horse, and Gair raised an eyebrow, then vaulted atop the other.

I clicked my tongue and the horse started forward at a trot—it was a well-gaited beast, the trot not in the least jarring.

Gair was right beside me, frowning. "Faster would be good," he said, and dug his heels into the horse's sides.

The forest cleared ahead of us, opening into plains, and we tucked low and urged our horses to quicken their pace.

I clicked and leaned forward, and my horse slid into a canter, and then into an astonishing gallop. Its hooves drummed the dirt with the sweet, familiar cadence that had been my second music as a child—after only my mother's singing as she rocked me to sleep—and the dry grasses made swishing noises very like those I would have heard on a real horse. But the steady deep breathing was gone, and the sound of the wind through mane and tail, and the nickering and snorting and grumbling horses talk with as they run—those were all gone, too. We were as close to silent as riders and horses could get.

I found myself wondering if these odd creatures had the same limitations as regular horses, or if they might go faster. I clicked my tongue again, and urged my beast to a quicker pace.

It extended its stride, and the speed of its legs over the ground quickened.

I heard, "Hold!" behind me as Gair began to drop behind, and then his creature caught up to mine, and passed us.

I had never seen anything move so quickly. At a gallop the ground is a blur anyway, but we were moving so fast the wind hurt my skin and tore at my clothes and I almost couldn't pull air into my lungs. I urged my beast to keep pace with Gair's, and we shot across the ground; anyone pursuing us would quickly fall far behind.

I didn't even dare shout at Gair. I had my jaws clenched and my lips pressed together hard against the fierce wind.

The plain rolled over and between low hills, and we tore across the land with fear falling behind us. No matter who pursued us, they would not catch us. Not in time. Not before we could reach Chaavtaak.

Nor did we have to worry about killing our horses by running them at a gallop until their hearts burst. They had no hearts. They would not die . . . unless I died. My death would break the spell that animated them, I thought. But I was not worried about death at the moment. We had eluded death, and my heart raced with mad joy.

Grouse and ptarmigan and woolly pheasants rocketed out of the tall grasses as we approached, and the horses did not bolt or shy at their thunderous launches. They did not notice.

We weren't going to have to worry about what to feed them or where to water them, either. Weren't going to have to take time to walk them in circles, cooling them down to save them from the gutwrack. Nor would we have to clean their stalls, work pebbles and splinters out of the tender frogs in their feet, brush them, curry them, rub them down, or check their knees and hocks for swelling. They would never sicken with the fevers and coughs and grippes that plague horses. If they broke their legs, I could simply mend the wood.

I tried not to feel disloyal. I owned one of the finest horses I had ever seen and another horse that was superb, if not spectacular. And these wooden things I had cobbled together out of imagination and magic were in all matters of predictability better. Faster.

If I had given them wheels, or perhaps wings, they would have been better yet.

We slowed as we approached another stretch of forest, and went through it at a trot—not for the benefit of the horses, but simply for our own.

"I would have paid a prince's ransom to have mounts like these for my men," Gair said as we trotted forward, pushing branches out of the way when we had the time and getting smacked in the face when we didn't. "Can you imagine the ground an army would cover on horses that never tired?"

"I've been doing just that," I told him. "And feeling like a criminal for creating something that would make the Tonk horses . . . unnecessary."

Gair gave me a strange, twisted little smile. "How would the breeders look at beasts like these?"

"My people have been breeding horses for thousands of years. It is as much who we are as what we do. Tonk horses are unparalleled. And anything that would make Tonk horses irrelevant would deal a crushing blow to my people here and even in Tandinapalis. And if they could trace that blow back to me—" I caught one branch straight across the sore spot on my nose, and tears sprang to my eyes, and I swore. And then, watching the path ahead of me more carefully, I said, "They'll kill me. To destroy these horses and make sure no one ever creates new ones like them, they'll flay me publicly and throw whatever is left to wild dogs."

Gair shook his head, and I could see the amusement in his eyes. "You jest."

"We're talking about *who my people are*. We are talking about me destroying thousands of years of culture and work. I *don't* jest. If they ever see these horses and get any idea of what they can do, they'll kill me."

Gair's smile died. "Then you have to make them look just like real horses before anyone sees them. They can't be wood. They have to look alive."

"Looking alive wouldn't be enough. They would have to

smell like real horses. They'd have to eat and drink and shit. They'd have to blink and breathe, and they would have to be warm and soft and skittish. They would have to respond to other horses. They would have to flick flies away with their tails, and kick at each other when they're annoyed. All of that— and no matter how close to real horses I got them, they would not be perfect, because I cannot make them live. I would miss some tiny detail, and my failure would betray me."

We rode in silence for a time, making our way through the trees, and suddenly he said, "Then make them not horses."

I simply stared at him and held out both hands, palms up, in query.

"*Not* horses," he repeated.

I still failed to express admiration for whatever bit of genius he felt he'd committed, and he sighed.

"The Tonk may be backward, murderous fanatics where their horses are concerned, but as a member of the other army, I can attest that they have never been backward in the adoption of new weapons."

"Right."

"Make these things look like weapons, not horses. Mount crossbows front and back. Stick sword arms all around, and give each arm a sword. Better yet, *make* each arm a sword so that it won't be dropped when fighting. Add tubes on pivots that spray fire, or maybe darts. Make each one bigger, so that a dozen men could ride in a single . . . war carriage . . . running tower . . . protected from the attacks of the enemy. Make them metal instead of wood, so those inside would be proof against the blows that would rain down on them. You and I have both been looking at our approach to the nomadic Tonks outside of Chaavtaak as our key to a friendly voice that would plead our case to the Chaavtaak Tonks. We wanted the nomads to be our friends." He smiled at me. "If you make these things right, we won't need friends. We'll have allies."

I was filled with purest admiration. I'm a Tonk. When I think of going from place to place, I think *horse*. Gair thought of big metal things that would protect and attack and crush enemies beneath their feet while being invulnerable to those same enemies. I wanted to think the way he thought. "You're brilliant," I told him.

"That's all I wanted."

"To be brilliant?"

"To know that *you* think I'm brilliant," he said, and his cheeks flushed bright red and he turned away for a moment.

And I thought, If we make a big metal thing, we don't need to have two of them. We could have one and ride together. If he was still angry at me, perhaps I could get him not to be. Maybe I could get him to put his arms around me again, or kiss me.

I liked the way he'd kissed me.

"Off the horse," I told him.

"You're going to do it?"

"Of course I'm going to do it."

The running tower spun into existence before Gair's eyes, built by the same gnatlike swarm of darkness that had, before his eyes, created his sheath. First the swarm was nothing, and then it was a ghost of something inside a cloud of moving pinpoints, and then suddenly it was *there,* solid and real, and for one long moment the only thought in his head was, Thank the gods she's on *my* side.

The tower stood twice as tall as a man, with four legs bent beneath it and four legs cocked out around it, with a thicket of arms protruding all the way around the circumference of the thing from knee height to shoulder height, all ending in blades longer and thicker than the strongest man could carry or hope to wield. Where the arms joined the body, the metal continued upward to form a domed top of seamless, rivetless metal so shiny and smooth it looked liquid. Eyes looked down at him, countless small flat circles glittering in the sun, and his mind saw the thing into a giant predatory spider, and his mouth went dry looking at it.

Thank the gods she was on his side.

It looked alive to him. It did not breathe, it did not move, but by the gods, by all the merciless gods of war and all the demons who presided over their hells beyond life and hope, it *watched.* His palms sweated and he licked his lips.

"How does it . . . work?" he asked, his voice cracking.

Talyn had not looked away from it. She seemed as chilled and as unnerved by it as he. "Stand," she told it. "Present stairs."

The tree-trunk-thick, big-footed metal legs straightened with the sinuous grace of flesh—lacking both joints and hinges, they nonetheless moved, and the hellish impression of watchful life the thing gave was suddenly complete. Gair clenched his sphincter against the sudden desperate fear-driven need to void.

An opening beneath that forest of legs suddenly appeared, and stairs extruded, and Gair could only think of a tongue dangling from a hungry maw. He swallowed hard, and did not move toward it.

Talyn said, "Stow weapons."

The sword arms, which had suddenly been at neck height and horse-and-rider height instead of knee height, all lifted silently and angled inward, and every blade slid with a metal hiss into slots that had been invisible beneath the readied arms. In an instant, all the blades were hidden and two rows of angled metal handles circled the nightmare tower.

Disarmed, the running tower was no less terrifying, and still Gair did not move toward the waiting steps. Neither, he noticed, did Talyn.

"What manner of man are we that we consider unleashing such a thing into war?" she said softly. "To set that unfeeling, unkillable monster against human flesh and bone?"

Those were his own thoughts given words. "I know not," he said. "Except that we fight an enemy who fights for nothing less than our utter destruction, who outnumbers us, who attacks us from without and from within, and against whom we may not otherwise prevail."

"We had rules," she said softly. "Tonks and Eastils—we had rules of war. No civilian targets, prisoners of war treated humanely and traded regularly, no poisoning of the ground, the water, or the air, magic used only in agreed-upon ways." She turned and looked to him, and he could see the pain and the horror in her eyes. "For three hundred years, we sustained a war by living within our rules, and we forgot that not everyone would fight the same way. And because we fought each other, we weakened ourselves, and we looked inward instead of out. Those outside were not so . . . constrained. We made our weaknesses public, and they used them."

"We were fools," Gair said. "Against this enemy, there are no rules. Except that we must win or we will be wiped from the face of the world, and all mention and all memory of who we once were and what we once cherished will vanish with us."

Talyn looked wistfully at the wooden horses standing still, waiting. She narrowed her eyes, and the same swarm of darkness spun itself around them, making them first into a ghostly haze, and then nothing.

She stared at the open, waiting belly maw of the metal fighting tower, and Gair could see her swallow. "Well, then . . ." she whispered, and took a step forward.

He caught her in a quick hug, and then kissed her. And felt his body go hot all over. He wanted nothing more than to lay her on the grass, pull her clothes off of her, and claim her. But he did not. Instead, he pulled away quickly and said, "We'll go together."

He held her hand as they climbed into the tower.

I had to stop the monster almost as soon as I started it running. The fighting tower ran faster than the horses had—so quickly that the ground seemed to flow like water beneath us. But it swayed as it ran, throwing Gair and me from side to side, and I sickened and had to stop it so that I could flee outside to vomit. I had been aboard a ship, and this was much like that. Only with land instead of water beneath us, somehow worse.

Gair raced down the stairway after me, and I could hear him puking in the bushes behind me. Neither of us had any food in our stomachs; we ended up retching and gagging, and when we at last got through it and confronted each other, we were both pale and sweat-soaked and trembling.

"That won't work," he said.

"No." I looked warily at the monster, which still had its swords stowed, and which stood tall, its stairway dangling beneath its belly. "I thought the eight legs would keep it from tipping over and killing us," I said. "But it just seems to make it—rock."

"Do you suppose we'd get used to it?"

"No. Because I'm never getting in it again unless it doesn't do that. Which would preclude any chance of getting used to it."

He laughed a little, though the color was not yet back in his face.

We had a little time—with the wooden horses, we had pulled well ahead of our pursuers. We could wait for the ground to steady beneath our feet. We could get food and water, since we had been long without either, whether we felt particularly hungry at the moment or not.

"I'm gathering something for us to eat and drink," I told Gair.

He gave no sign of enthusiasm at the prospect of food. And truth be told, I didn't feel any, either. But lately, what I needed and what I wanted rarely seemed to connect to each other, so I ignored my own lack of appetite.

I was uncomfortable with the idea of spinning food out of nothing, so I used the Hagedwar magic to steal some bread for us from Beyltaak—as far out as we were, I did not let myself worry that anyone would be able to track us from the very quick link that I opened and closed. I tore the large loaf, still warm from the oven, in half and handed one half to Gair. "Eat a little. Maybe it will help with the sickness while we get the tower's gait trained to something that won't make us sick."

"Will keep us from puking dry, at least," he said.

We stood for a moment, chewing on our bread. I was hungry. My belly hurt, and the few bites of bread I allowed myself only pointed out how long it had been since I'd had anything but water.

"Don't think about it," Gair said, and I realized that he was watching me closely. "If you think about your hunger, it just gets worse. We'll get a good solid meal when we get where we're going. Or you'll make us some more and we'll eat like kings."

"I stole the bread," I said.

"Either way, we won't starve. So save what's left of this and let's go."

Back in the running tower's belly, I wanted to create saddles that we could sit in to guide the tower, and some form of reins. I didn't like just telling the tower "Left, right, stop, go." Gair argued against reins as being too skittish, and saddles as being silly. "Put chairs in and bolt them to the floor. They'll be easier to sit in, especially if you give them arms. And you'll be able to look out the windows."

But the more I considered it, the more I liked my saddle and reins. Maybe I would make chairs with arms for passengers. But for the tower's rider, I wanted a single saddle, mounted high and on a swivel, that would let me turn to see through any window at any time, and that would respond to leg pressure, shifts of weight and balance, and the guidance of reins, as well as voice commands. I knew how to ride a horse. I had no idea how I might guide such a contrivance as the running tower while sitting in a chair. And the idea of treating the guidance of the tower as riding a horse gave me the idea I needed to smooth out the gait. I spun the guiding saddle and reins out of the Hagedwar, climbed on, and hooked my feet into the stirrups. I tested my weight, and for a moment connected myself through trance with the bit of my spirit that gave the tower its magic. I felt its legs through my skin, and took them into a walk, adjusting their movement until the walking gait didn't pitch or yaw. I moved them into a trot, and that was jarring with eight legs. I could feel a way, though, to smooth that out by rolling the legs forward in pairs. And the canter and the gallop came easily enough once I had the model of riding a horse firmly in mind.

I shed the second skin of the tower and saw Gair sprawled on his belly, arms and legs spread wide to spare himself from injury as he slid wildly over the floor.

"Please make it stop!"

Maybe the gallop needed more work. Or maybe I could just speed that trot up and skip the gallop entirely.

I slowed the tower down with a shift of my weight and a twitch of the reins, and it responded beautifully.

"Chairs won't let you turn to look out any of the windows," I said, "and reins aren't in the least inaccurate if you're a good rider." I watched him stagger to his feet.

"I don't care how you guide it anymore," he told me. "Just give me something that will keep it from killing me while you guide it. A saddle, a seat, something. I don't care. But please don't ever do that to me again."

"It was worse than before?"

"Not so sickening. Much more bruising."

I added seats, then made the dozens of round windows that looked like eyes from the outside a bit bigger. And finally we were ready to take off.

We didn't need a gait faster than the trot. I discovered that the tower could move its many legs so quickly that the rougher gaits would be unnecessary. We sped across the rolling hills, through forests that shuddered and cracked at our passing, and across the ford at the Injvaard River that landed us outside Chaavtaak's outer walls in less than an hour. No need to seek out the nomads any longer. What we had with us, we could present to the Chaav with good assurance of his desire to see more. Gair was, after all, quite right about us. We Tonks love a good weapon.

Which left both of us standing inside our running tower, staring up through the windows at the closed gates and the parapets. Parapets which were filling with Chaavtaak soldiers armed with crossbows.

"What exactly are we supposed to say to them?" I said, turning to Gair.

Bolts hitting the dome over our heads filled the air with a sudden clanging. I couldn't hear myself think, nor the words coming out of Gair's moving mouth. I winced, and clapped my hands over my ears, and willed a field of magic around the running tower that kept the bolts from hitting it at all, and caused them to slide harmlessly off to the ground.

". . . DON'T KNOW WHAT IN THE HELLS WE'RE—," Gair bellowed into the suddenly quiet cabin. He stopped, and his head jerked around so that he could see out the window. "They're still shooting."

"I know. I just made their bolts not hit us."

"You can do that?"

"Yes."

He stared at me, shook his head, and said, "As I was trying to say, I thought you knew them, and would know what to tell them. I don't know what we should say. We're sitting on their doorstep with a monstrous weapon. They'd be fools to let us in if they don't know you."

Which was true enough. And Chaavtaak wasn't known to open its gates for friends. I could not see that it would willingly welcome enemies, or those who looked as much like enemies as seemed possible.

"We could just sit here until the Beyltaak troops catch up with us. And when we attack them, we'll prove that we're not Chaavtaak's enemies."

Gair shook his head. "Not unless the Beyltaak troops fire on Chaavtaak troops. From on top of Chaavtaak's walls, Tonks on horses are going to look like the heroes when they're up against some sword-bearing metal monster. How could they not? In fact, the Chaavtaak Tonks might decide to let the Beyltaak Tonks into their gates to protect them from us."

I felt sick all over again. "And the madness with which the Feegash have turned my people into . . . slaves . . . will spread to Chaavtaak."

"We have to get them to let us in before our pursuers arrive, or else we stand to destroy what we hope to save."

I closed my eyes, and felt Gair's strong hands settle on my shoulders. I looked up and into his face, to find him staring at me as if willing me to know what to do.

"Talyn, think. What magic can you do that will convince them that we are on their side?"

"Magic? Magic will be the thing they trust least, and will have the least reason to trust."

"Do you know if they allowed all their Communicators to leave? Or all their Senders? Or Shielders?"

"They wouldn't have," I said. "They refused even to meet with the Feegash diplomats, so they won't have disarmed, or taken apart their forces. But . . ." I shook my head. "But Chaavtaak is small, and probably has no more than a single crew of Communicators. I know it has only a single crew of Shielders and a single crew of Senders."

I looked out the windows. The rain of crossbow bolts had stopped.

"What are they going to drop on us next?" he asked.

"Magic," I said.

"Can you stop them?"

"No," I admitted. "Hagedwar magic is weaker than magic channeled directly through the View. I can do things by myself, but that's not an advantage if they aren't alone."

"Can you talk to them? Raise a flag of surrender?"

"Maybe. I can at least put us in front of them."

I tried to figure out how I could do that, and ended up creating atop the running tower an image—like those we'd used with Iyalara's thrown-together Communications unit, to show my Attack and Defense squads what they had to hit—that showed

Gair and me and the inside of the tower. This image let the Chavtaaks hear us, too.

"We're here to ask for your help," I said, looking up at the faces that stared down at us. "Beyltaak has fallen to the Feegash, its people are enslaved by Feegash magic, and we have reason to believe that much of the rest of the Confederacy has also fallen. We have weapons with which to fight the Feegash, but no one left to fight."

The soldiers looked down at us. They were Ethebet's still. They were my people in a way that even Beyltaak followers of Minda or Hetterik or Rogvar or Cladmus could never be. My eyes filled with unexpected tears and I had to swallow hard and wipe at my eyes with the back of my hand to fight them back.

I had not seen Tonks in Tonk uniform in far too long.

They looked behind them suddenly, and a few backed away, and another face appeared at the top of the parapet. I could see this newcomer speaking, but could not hear anything.

I had failed to include any way of hearing outside in the running tower.

I said, "Wait—we can't hear you," and reached one more time into the Hagedwar, and used the magic to affix round ears to the mirror that let us hear them. "Speak again," I said. "I think we should be able to hear you now."

"You come in a mighty weapon," the new soldier said. "You could be anyone, intending anything. You could be Feegash."

"I know. But we aren't. Your Shielders can test me if you wish. I'm a Shielder; Sergeant Talyn Wyran av Tiirsha dryn Straad, late of Beyltaak's Ninety-fifth Hawkshanks."

"Did you serve border patrol to enforce the dictates of the treaty signatories against those taaks which were not signatories?"

And how was the treachery of the Beyls in standing Beyltaak's forces against other Tonk forces not going to come back to haunt me? "Yes, sir," I admitted, and cringed inside.

"Then how do you now ask for our help?"

"Sir. I did not sign the treaty, I did not approve of the treaty, and like many others in the Forces, I fought where I could. When the Feegash shed all pretense, Gair and I were the two people in Beyltaak who mounted a rebellion against the Feegash, and had good success against them in our first foray."

Silence. The speaker turned away from us and gestured, and I saw two men take off at a run, their heads bouncing in and out of view over the parapet wall.

"I have runners going to fetch those who might know and vouch for you. Who is the one with you?"

I looked at Gair and started to open my mouth but he put a hand on my arm. "Captain Gair Farhallan of Karvis, late of the Seventy-third Watch of His Majesty's Army of the Eastil Republic." This statement caused such an uproar on the walls above us that Gair could say nothing else for long moments. Finally he held up a hand and shouted, "Please—let me finish." The soldiers atop the wall finally quieted, and Gair said, "I was a prisoner of war when the Feegash made their first invasion, and Talyn saw to my rescue from a dungeon torture chamber. After Beyltaak fell to the Feegash, I had hopes of bringing troops from the Republic to fight beside the Tonks against the Feegash." He looked down, and I turned and saw the pain marked on his face. "But no such help will be coming. I have had word that the Republic has fallen in its entirety and my people are slaves to the Feegash now, too. I have allied myself with Talyn and offered my skills in her quest to save her family and win back her taak from the Feegash. I hope I shall someday find a way of saving my own people."

Once again the soldiers atop the parapet made way, and I saw a face I had thought never to see again. "Pada!" I shouted, and realized from the way everyone atop the parapet covered ears and backed away that I had been too loud. "I thought you were stormwatching in the Path of Stars."

She looked at me without any sign of pleasure. "How much did that horse cost, and who gave it to you?"

Jostfar save me, would I never be free of that? "The horse cost fifty thousand horse cash, and the fool who paid for it, through proxy, was none other than one of the Feegash diplomats that we're fighting today."

"And the man with you? How would I know him?"

"You and I saw him in the View when we were Shielding Injtaak during the peace conference."

Pada turned to the officer who had been speaking with us. "She's Talyn, right enough. Whether or not she's one of the fleshmages I cannot yet say. But if she comes in alone, the

Shielders can examine her. If she has acted as a fleshmage, we should be able to find sign of it."

Some cold wet tongue of dread licked down my spine, and I turned to Gair. "Fleshmages?"

The fleshmages were tales to frighten children—they were mindless creatures controlled by a single master, and whatever he could do, they could do. He could see through their eyes, hear through their ears, speak through their mouths. But they were more than men. In some tales they were walking corpses. In others, they had flesh of stone, and drank blood. Often they could fly, or walk through walls. They were said to steal babies, ravish virgins, suck the souls out of the living.

Fleshmages?

I had never thought there would be any truth to such tales. The nomad Tonks kept the stories alive, and as children we had heard the tales when visiting with our nomadic cousins or the children of friends of our parents who were in the area for a season. But our parents had always rolled their eyes and said such tales were nonsense.

The people who had been enslaved by the Feegash were just people. More than being just people, they were, many of them, *my* people.

Da a fleshmage? Ma? Rik?

My knees went weak on me and my hands started to shake. That could not be.

"Talyn, what's wrong?" Gair asked. "What are fleshmages?"

I told him a quick version of the old Tonk stories. And then I told him the part I didn't want to think about. "The only way to free someone from the fleshmage curse is to kill him," I said.

Gair looked exasperated. "Well, that would kill just about any curse. But it doesn't much help the one who's cursed, does it?"

"You don't understand. The tales always talk about driving a stake through the heart of a fleshmage, and having some healer pull the stake at the instant that the fleshmage dies, so that he can summon the person's true spirit back into his body. The tales vary in a lot of ways, but they always agree that the flesh-mage must be killed by a stake through the heart. And many of them say that the true person can then be revived."

"You're talking child's tales versus very real magic—why

would you, or the Chaavtaaks, think the Feegash are flesh-mages?"

I took a deep breath. "Because those old tales come from somewhere."

Gair laughed. "You jest. We have tales in the Republic of Murdik the Thief, who flew about on a carpet spun of eagle feathers and thistledown, who stole by pointing at men as he flew over and telling their belongings to come to him . . ."

He faltered to a stop. I was holding what remained of my loaf of bread in front of him. "Remember this? Where do you think it came from?" I tapped the cabin wall of our running tower. "And this? It walks, lest you had forgotten." I smiled slowly. "I don't doubt that using the Hagedwar I could find a way to make a carpet fly, too, though I don't think it would have to be made of eagle feathers or thistledown. I suspect any rug would serve."

Outside, the speaker said, "Talyn, if you wish our assistance, you will come alone to the front gate. The Eastil will step out-side of the . . . contrivance . . . and will permit himself to be taken into custody by our soldiers while you are examined. He will then return to prisoner-of-war status."

I looked at Gair. Gair looked at me.

"Know that we honor our prisoner-of-war treaty, and that the Eastil will not be tortured or killed."

I was looking at Gair, who had fought to save my life. Who could have fled, but who risked everything to get me away from Skirmig. Who had stood by my side ever since. I could rejoin the Tonks, and have a chance at winning my people back, ap-parently, but he would have to be the price I paid to get them.

I could have said yes. It would not have been hard—I would know Gair was safe, and these Ethebettan Tonks would come fight with me to save my family and all the other families in Beyltaak. I would, perhaps, be able to see him safely home, if ever the Eastils won their lands and lives back from the Fee-gash. If he stood against me, I could even use the Hagedwar magic to control him; he did not have the strength to fight against me.

But that did not change the fact that I would be betraying him. That I would be demonstrating unimaginable thankless-ness for the sacrifices he had made for me.

I watched him swallow, and take a deep breath. "If you choose to follow that path, I'll understand," he said. "I would do . . . anything . . . to save my family, too. I think. And maybe this is what I have to do to save them."

"No," I said. "There are other taaks. One of them will understand bonds of honor, and that I will not abandon you for my own gain. We'll find one of them." I looked up at the speaker. "We'll find our own way," I said. "I wish you luck against what comes."

I turned away from the windows, trying to recall which other taaks had refused to deal with the Feegash and which might yet be free of the Feegash taint. Of fleshmages. I shuddered in spite of myself.

And I heard a new voice say, "If they were fleshmages, they would have accepted the offer, knowing that they could absorb both the guards and the Shielders into their mind-union, and spread the contagion that way."

"Besides," Pada said, "she still knows honor. She's the friend I knew."

I turned back, stunned. It had been a test?

"We'll help you," the speaker said. "Bring your . . . contrivance and get through the gates quickly; Magics reports that a large armed force is on its way here right now, and will be arriving soon."

I looked at Gair again, and he had tears in the corners of his eyes. I reached out to brush them away, and he caught my wrist and pulled me close. "Thank you," he whispered in my ear.

I kissed his cheek, and moved quickly back to the saddle. I wanted to do more. I *wanted* more. But it was not the time for such things. And if I was honest with myself, it never would be.

23

"Of all the people in Beyltaak, I would never have picked you as the one who would get out intact or lead a rebellion—even if you did lose." Pada had changed in many ways, I was discovering, but she still had her infamous tact. "You know about the

Outside Alliances, of course. I don't understand why you didn't take your people to one of the safe points."

Gair and I exchanged glances. "Outside Alliances?" he asked.

"We've never heard anything about Outside Alliances," I said.

She shook her head, exasperated. "Some time ago a number of Beyltaak military people who had been lured out of the Confederacy by money and work received coded messages sent by someone within Beyltaak. I have heard of these 'blue letters,' but have not seen any. The people who received the letters put together the Outside Alliances, which were sworn to return the betrayed taaks to their free state. Communicators have been setting up posts all over the world to regather all the scattered military and Magics units—the news of the Feegash treachery has been out for some time. A lot of us managed to return; we came to a number of safe taaks, where we have been in the temples researching fleshmagery."

"Why fleshmagery?" Gair asked her.

"One of our people was in a position to watch a Feegash diplomat taking over another person, and because he was nomad-born, he made connections the rest of us wouldn't have. He realized what he was seeing, and put the news out via the Communicators, and we have been trying to figure out what to do ever since. We don't have solutions yet, but all of the nonsignatory taaks have people who are waiting to go up against the Feegash as soon as someone comes up with a weapon against fleshmagery."

"I know about the blue letters," I told her. "My father and I sent them to our family overseas. But Beyltaak hasn't had Communicators since Magics was disbanded. We had no way of knowing any help was out there."

Pada said, "I know of a few messengers who went out to the various signatory taaks to try to locate pockets of resistance."

"They never made it to us," I told her.

"They probably fell to the fleshmages. Which is why the gates have been locked for so long now."

"And if we had brought our whole force to your doorstep?"

Pada grinned up at me. "I'm not sure how they would have tested so many for the contagion of fleshmagery. They might have sent you all away." She shrugged. "We have little in the way of guarantees, you realize. We would have done what we could. This way might be less satisfying, but at least you have some sort of new weapon with you. The lads were warm about that, I swear. Couldn't wait to get their hands on it."

"It won't work for them," I told her.

"No?"

"This one is keyed to my voice, or Gair's. So they'll not be able to trample houses or horses or each other with it. And at least we don't have to worry about it slicing the lot of them to ribbons while we eat."

She led us to a door unmarked by a sign, in front of which stood a man with calm, watchful eyes. Pada, in a new and ill-fitting Shielders uniform lacking her old unit insignia or any of her awards, nodded to the man and said, "Hey, Keben. They're with me."

"Pada," he said, "I'll hold them on your merit. Names?"

"Sergeant Talyn av Tiirsha. Captain Gair . . . ?" She turned to Gair, eyebrow raised.

"Farhallan," he said.

Pada turned back to Keben. "They'll be getting uniforms while they're here. They've been through a bad spot just getting to Chaavtaak."

His stare was concentrated—my face for one long, uncomfortable moment, then Gair's. "I'll remember you both," he said. "Present yourselves in uniform the first few times. And welcome to the White Fox."

And he turned back to watch the streets. We went through the door into a place achingly like the Star's Rest. I heard laughter and loud talking, and saw men and women in uniform sitting at tables, ale and food before them. They were people who still had a place in the world, and knew it. They were my people, all of them. "You vouch for him, right?" Pada said suddenly, stopping and looking from me to Gair and back.

"With my life," I said.

"That's what it'll come to if you're wrong." She looked at Gair. "You'll wear a Tonk uniform if it's offered?"

He nodded. "The Eastil Republic is gone. My king is dead, my country is in ruins, my people are slaves. And the only people left with the backbone to fight the Feegash, and perhaps give me a way to save my people, are yours. I'll wear the uniform if it's offered me, and give it my loyalty."

"He'll do," Pada said. "He's not the first Eastil we've gathered into our fold." She chuckled softly. "On the border, we had a veritable rush of Eastil soldiers and civilians offering themselves to serve against the Feegash. We keep them split up, we keep an eye on them—but they aren't Feegash. They *have* honor."

My mouth was watering from the smell of good Tonk cooking—fresh spit-cooked beef and elk and fried potatoes and pies filled with elderberries and blackberries and apples. At that moment, after weeks of nothing but dried provisions and a couple of days of nothing, or of water and stolen bread, I had no more interest in Eastil soldiers than I had in the magic that sends the sun across the sky once a day. I would take Pada's information as a given and be happy with it, if only someone would put food before me and let me eat.

Pada saw the direction of my glance and said, "You're hungry?"

I nodded, beyond words at the vision of two fine haunches of elk rotating slowly on their spits at the very back of the dining hall.

"We'll do uniforms and oaths and all of that later, then, I suppose."

Pada had changed for the better in at least one way, I reflected as we went in search of a table. She'd learned at least a little bit about how to judge priorities.

Sitting in the White Fox eating a fine, sizzling slab of bloody steak and a pile of potatoes that would have choked a whale, I had a sudden vision of Skirmig. Of his eyes staring into mine. Of his smile. I felt, for just an instant, his touch. It was no faint sensation, either. For just that instant, I could almost have sworn that I was with him.

I pushed the food away, my appetite gone. I was afraid that everything I had already eaten would back up on me. That vision brought back everything—the shame, the pain, the fear, the manipulation.

He was still out there. He was still coming for me. I knew it, though I had somehow managed to get my mind away from that one awful truth.

"Talyn? What's wrong?" Gair said, putting down fork and knife.

"I don't know. A . . . premonition, maybe."

Pada looked interested. "Premonition?"

"About one of the Feegash diplomats. You saw him several times, but you didn't actually meet him. His name is Skirmig." I had a hard time even saying that name. "He's vile. One of those in charge of the fleshmages, I have no doubt."

Pada laughed. "Doubt, dear Talyn. Because there can only be one person in charge of them. It isn't a magic that would work by committee."

I rested my elbows on the table and said, "Why do you say that? I saw the diplomats working together."

"They're pawns. They were all fleshmages, most likely. From everything we've been able to discover, the fleshmages of old could make a decent enough pretense of being normal. At least they could at the beginning of their infection. They would contract the sickness, and in turn infect everyone around them. With time, however, something about the spell began to devour them, so that they weakened and became listless. And finally they simply died."

"The servants Skirmig sent to watch us!" Gair blurted out.

I turned to him. "What servants?"

"He placed two of his servants in the house with us when we were recovering. He said it was to make sure that none of your belongings were stolen or damaged. It was just to keep an eye on us, I'm sure, no matter what he said." Gair took a long draft of his ale, and said, "Before we came to get you, they had grown thin and frail. They were young men—younger than I am, certainly—yet they tottered around the house as if they were walking in their sleep; they almost quit talking; and they slept most of the time. We were certain that they were days away from death, though none of us could guess what disease they might have had."

"You don't know whether they died?" I asked him. I was remembering something I'd forgotten earlier.

"No. Why?"

"Because I saw others of his servants who were also ailing

and weak. But in a single day—on the day that I learned how to use the outer tograms—all of them returned to full health. Somehow Skirmig learned what I had learned and gained the power of those outer tograms that had before eluded him."

Pada looked bewildered. "Tograms? What are you talking about? And you saw fleshmages regain their health and strength?"

It took me a while to explain the magic of the Feegash to her, and to give her the short story of how I had learned it. I skipped the torture and the horror and just described the training Skirmig had given me.

Pada was intrigued. "And that is how you are able to use the power of the View alone?"

I nodded.

"And the Feegash can do this, too?"

"Only some of them. Actually, the only Feegash I've ever seen doing any sort of magic was Skirmig. He said the Feegash kept the training secret, which fits with what I know about them. The people at the top of Feegash society use the rest. They are masters, and the rest are . . . nothing. The Feegash leaders are horrible people."

"Power without accountability will do that," Gair said.

Pada and I both looked at him, startled. "You had a *king*. What did *he* know about accountability?"

"I *liked* our king," Gair said. "I met him once when I was on assignment in Fairpoint. I was sitting in a tavern in a back corner, in uniform, nursing an ale after the man I'd been supposed to contact had left. The tavern had gotten rather crowded, and the last remaining seat was the one across from me. And this man asked me if he could join me. He sat down and we talked a bit—about conditions at the front, about my thoughts on the military, about how I thought we ought to be running the war. He knew a lot of our highest officers and was familiar with a broader scope of our campaigns than I was, and had a nice grasp of broad strategies and little tactics, and I took him for a ranking officer of one of the other branches who was out of uniform and—for whatever reason—scouting for information. I was accordingly careful in my speech.

"And then I noticed that the patrons at the tables around us had changed. We were surrounded by armed men who were not drinking, who were not talking to each other as they sat, and who were surreptitiously watching us.

"I asked him, 'Are you armed? For I think we've fallen into a bad situation.' And he looked at the men at the other tables, and smiled a little. 'My bodyguards,' he said. 'I would leave the castle without them, but then Her Majesty would spend a great deal of time worrying about me. So I let them come. They do a piss-poor job of blending in, don't they?' It was thus that I learned I had been giving my ideas to the king himself. I suspect it was because of that conversation that my men and I were chosen to go to the Injtaak conference to end the war. I still believe he had faith in me personally." Gair stared down into his tankard. "And I failed him. And now he's dead, and his wife and children are Feegash slaves. And the Feegash don't treat their slaves well."

I'd never examined that particular memory of Gair's, but as he talked, I'd seen the king, and watched their easy conversation, and found that I, too, liked the man. I couldn't understand a word out of his mouth, but he seemed ordinary. He did not have the airs of a taaklord, who even in a taaksman's clothes would never be able to pass as a taaksman. I saw no affected gestures from him, no falseness. His smiles looked real, his laughter was clear and hearty, his face was lined by wind and sun, and his hands were large and strong-looking and callused by some sort of work.

Had I not been Tonk, and he the enemy of my people, I would have liked him a great deal, I realized. That discovery shook me. I'd never thought of the Eastil king as a person before, only as the chief symbol of everything that was wrong with the Eastils.

"We can't regret the past," Pada said. "We have too much in the present to worry us."

Gair sighed and took a long drink. "I know," he said.

I turned to Pada. "Why did you say there could be only one master of the fleshmages?"

"Everything we have been able to uncover—and we have not just torn through the temple volumes here, but run our Communicators ragged sending us everything that anyone can find in any of the temples in the other free taaks—has insisted that the spell that creates the fleshmage contagion feeds power from the fleshmages into the caster, and that only one person is ever in control."

"It . . . feeds him? The caster?"

Pada shrugged. "You have to understand that we've been piecing this together from records hundreds of years old, most of which had been second- and thirdhand. We have two records that claim to be firsthand accounts of people who had been fleshmages, but who were then freed. They're . . . odd. None of us have been sure how much to believe of what they say. One is from a criminal nearly seven hundred years ago who claimed that he was a fleshmage when he committed his crimes, but that he managed to kick off the mindsickness and that he was cured. None of us are giving that one a great deal of credibility. The other is an account by a woman who claims that she and her family were swept into a fleshmage group, and that she was only released when she fell through thin ice and drowned. Someone pulled her out and managed to empty her lungs of water and revive her, and her short death broke the fleshmage spell. She claims that she could hear all the other fleshmages thinking, that she could see what they saw and feel what they felt, but that the strongest sensations she had came from the fleshmage master, who could, if he chose, let the fleshmages experience everything he was experiencing. If he ate, they could taste his food. If he drank, they could feel the wetness down their throats. And she was quite certain that he could experience the same information from her or any of the others. She says he could speak directly to any of them, or all of them at once. She says he could make them do things they didn't want to do, and make them think while they were doing it that they wanted to. And she says that the whole time she was a fleshmage, she never forgot who she was, but that it was like she was trapped inside a cage and he was using her body while she ran in circles trying to find a way out."

I had goosebumps on my arms, and the air around me suddenly felt like ice, even though I knew the temperature in the room hadn't changed. "That one was telling the truth," I said.

Gair reached over and rested his hand on mine, and gave a little squeeze. Pada said, "You know this?"

"He used magic on me . . . Skirmig did. Just tiny bits—he twisted me into . . . doing things he wanted. And . . ." I closed my eyes, bit my lip. "It was like that. Being in a cage, seeing what you were doing, knowing that wasn't what you wanted, except at just that moment, you did want it—or something inside you that felt like your darkest thoughts wanted it." I started shaking, remembering the eyes that opened inside me when he and I tore into sex. "True, too, about a master being able to let all the fleshmages see what he sees and feel what he feels." They'd all been watching, all his servants, all his slaves. No. They'd all been *there*. They had all been a part of it, right in it.

The shaking got worse, and my teeth started to chatter, and the room started narrowing in on me.

Pada looked panicked. "What's wrong with her?" she asked Gair.

"She went through a lot she didn't tell you," he said. He caught my wrists in his hands, pulled me out of my seat, and scooped me into his arms. "Where's a bed? She needs to lie down under warm blankets. We have to put her feet up. This is . . . like battleshock."

"What the hell happened to her?" Pada demanded.

Gair said, "Things she made herself not think about. She can tell you if she chooses. I won't."

I lay against his chest, shaking so badly I'm surprised he didn't drop me. My teeth chattered so that I couldn't speak, and I was cold. Cold as I have never been in my life, cold as death. Everything around me faded, faded, faded, and I fought to try to stay with them, but I couldn't. I'd thought with Gair that I was past the worst of everything that had happened, but I wasn't. The truth of it all—of Skirmig and what Skirmig had done to me and what he was doing to others, and how he was doing it, and what it meant—was battering against me, and I couldn't get away from it. I'd felt him with me. Sitting in a taak far away from him, with friends, surrounded by Ethebet's own, he had still managed to reach out and touch me.

Skirmig was still with me. I was blind, and I couldn't move, and all the eyes were watching me, and watching him. While he hurt me.

Gair had seen the same thing before, in men who survived horrible fights while watching their friends die. They would get through it and they would seem, most of the time, to be fine.

And then some sound or some smell or some voice would trigger the memory of what they had been through, and they would fall back into battle, trying to change it, trying to save people who were dead, trying to make it come out differently. Better.

If someone didn't bring them out of it, sometimes they didn't come out of it. Sometimes they just stayed in their mad hells, trying to fix the unfixable.

Talyn didn't need to be in any mad hell. She needed to be safe. With him.

Pada led him up to one of the rooms, and there were people who were throwing open doors and bringing in warmed blankets and setting the foot of the bed up on wooden blocks. The word "battleshock" conjured quick help in a building full of warriors. Someone brought in a steaming mug of some hot drink, and Gair put Talyn in the bed and lifted her head and forced some of the drink between her chattering teeth. She swallowed convulsively, her eyes staring off at nothing. She wasn't hearing him. Wasn't seeing him. She was back in hell with the bastard, her body locked rigid, and he was going to have to fight for her again to get her out.

"She feels like ice," Pada said, touching her hand and then her face.

Gair said, "This is bad. I knew it would be when she finally faced it." He started untying the laces of her tunic. "We have to get her out of her clothes, get her up against the warming blankets without any barriers. The warmth will help her. The drink, too. But mostly she needs to have someone who knows what she went through to talk her through it and bring her back."

One of the soldiers worked on removing her boots. "I'm going to bring in a woman to do this," he said when the second boot came off. "I don't know her."

"Right." Gair knew the Ethebettans were casual about being naked around each other, and generally casual about sex. But apparently they were a little more careful when something was wrong. He was grateful for that.

He pulled her tunic over her head and worked it down her shaking, rigid arms.

Her scarred arms. Pada gasped.

"Oh, my sweet Jostfar and all the Five Saints. What happened to her?"

Gair said, "Someone hurt her."

"The Feegash diplomat she was talking about. The one she said was a master of the fleshmages?"

"That one."

Pada said, "I've never seen anything like this."

Gair had tugged her pants off. Her legs were as heavily scarred as her arms. The cold radiated from her body. Warming blankets would help, but they weren't going to take care of everything. He tugged her underblouse off, and then started removing his own shirt and pants.

"Leave her pantlets and her binder on," he said when Pada started to reach for the binder. "I want her to have some clothes on. I'm going to get into the bed with her and warm her against me."

And then he felt Pada touch his back. A light touch, probably only a finger. "You, too?" she asked.

"I had different problems. No one bothered to play around inside my head." Undressed down to his own undershorts, he climbed into the bed with Talyn and pulled the warming blankets over both of them. She felt like ice against his skin. Her whole body still shook. He wrapped his arms around her and pulled her to his chest, spooning against her. "You're safe, Talyn," he told her. "You're safe. He doesn't have you anymore. He has no hold over you. You're free. You're safe."

He whispered in her ear, oblivious of the people who came in and pulled the cooled blankets off of them and brought in fresh ones from the warmer. He ignored everything but her. He kept talking to her, kept saying her name, promising her that she was safe, that Skirmig would never hurt her again.

And slowly he felt her start to warm. Felt her muscles unlock and relax. He breathed a little easier, and kept talking to her, and the warm blankets kept coming, and warm drinks that he could give to her.

And at last she relaxed completely. Dawn had crept into the east window, and he realized that the night had passed and that he was exhausted. He heard her breathing deepen and grow steady. She was asleep. He waved off the next people who brought in blankets.

"She's through it," he said. "Now she only needs to sleep, and she should be fine when she wakes."

The woman holding the blanket said, "Will we be needing to watch her?"

"I'll stay with her," Gair said. "She knows me. It will be best if I'm here when she wakes."

He heard the door close, and the woman tell someone outside, "Keep it closed. She's sleeping at last."

And with Talyn in his arms, he, too, slept.

I woke remembering shreds and strips and tatters of what had happened, and knowing that Skirmig had not forgotten me. That he was still with me somehow, though I could not find the hooks he had in me. But I woke wrapped in Gair's arms, and in spite of what I knew to be the horrible truth, I felt safe. If I could have simply stayed there until someone else found and killed Skirmig, I would have been happy.

Gair was still asleep. From the angle of the light, I guessed us to be past midday. The room we were in was a typical overnight room in any of Magics' inns—small, plain, and clean, with a wide bed, clothes pegs on the walls, a single window, a washbasin and pitcher, and little else. The mattress seemed to have a bad slope to it; that would have to be the one real oddity of the place. Elsewhere in the inn there would be baths, and water on tap for showers, and other amenities. The rooms were mostly for soldiers who wanted to pog or sleep off too much drink, or who were from other taaks and other units and were traveling through.

I needed to get up, to clean my teeth and empty my bladder if nothing else, but I didn't want to. Being with Gair was safe, and for the first time in my life I discovered that I was afraid to be alone. I was afraid that if I ever let myself be alone, Skirmig would find me. And do things to me. My mind wasn't very specific in dreading particular things, or putting names on them. It didn't need to be. I had Skirmig's face, and that was enough.

Restless and uncomfortable, I lay still anyway, feeling Gair's warm breath on the back of my neck, and the taut muscles of his chest against my back.

"You're awake," he said suddenly, and I realized that the steady breathing that I'd been listening to had stopped.

"Yes."

"How are you?"

I almost said "fine." But I wasn't fine. "Afraid," I said.

"What happened?"

"Skirmig found me. Last night while I was sitting at table eating and talking with you and Pada, suddenly he . . . showed me that he could reach me." My body tensed, and I shivered, remembering the awful intimacy of that ghostly touch.

Gair's arms tightened around me, and he said, "Wait, wait, wait. Hold on. I'm here. Don't drop back into the fear. Don't go back."

I focused on his voice, and Skirmig's face faded. "I'm here," I said.

"Talk to me. Tell me what happened. And just remember that I'm right here with you. I'm not going to leave you."

So I told him about the feeling of Skirmig being with me, and about being able to feel him touching me. I spilled out my dread, and he held me tightly and rubbed my arms when I started to shake, and kept talking to me when I began losing my way.

I got through it.

And he said, "You've found him, Talyn. He might know where you are, but you know what he is, and that is what is going to save us."

"What do you mean?"

"Your friend Pada said all of their research points to there being only one master for all the fleshmages."

I nodded.

"You know he's a master. You've felt what he can do."

"If there can be only one, then he is that one. But he wasn't even the leader of his diplomatic delegation."

"What better way could he find to draw attention away from himself while he built his power base? And how much easier to divert enemies toward the wrong targets. If he can reach any of his fleshmages at any time, and if he has complete control of them whenever he chooses it, what need does he have for uniforms and chains of command? None," Gair said, answering his own question. "He's the whole of his army, and every bit of it knows what every other bit of it is doing when he wants it to.

It's a huge advantage if the enemy is engaging his army. But a disadvantage if the enemy is looking only for him."

I rolled over and looked at Gair. "He's the only target?"

"I don't know. But it makes sense, doesn't it?"

"Maybe. But if we kill him, what happens to everyone who is connected to him?"

"Maybe your friend knows. Maybe her research has told her something useful about this."

"Maybe." A worrisome thought caught at me. "But . . . these aren't normal fleshmages. They all got better on the day that I found the key to the outer tograms. The day that he learned what I knew. They all got better, and if they're weakening and dying now, we haven't seen any proof of it."

Gair pulled me in close and stroked my hair. "We do have to know if they can be broken free from fleshmagery. We're going to have to find a fleshmage, and kill him, and then revive him. We should be able to get information from him."

"Where will we find a fleshmage?"

Gair laughed a little. "They've been chasing us. They're probably already outside the gates now. Finding a fleshmage should be no harder than throwing a rock, though catching one might be tricky." He levered up on one elbow and grinned down at me. "We'll go and do mighty warrior feats and crush fleshmagery for another thousand years. We'll be heroes, shall we?"

"You're mocking me?"

"I'm mocking us." He swung out of bed, and with his back to me, I saw his scars again, carved into his flesh like a relief map of his suffering. Those scars were a reminder that he had every reason not to help me and my people; that he had thrown in his lot with those who had tortured him. Under the same circumstances, I was not sure I would ever consider being so generous of spirit. "I've been in too many battles to think it could be so simple."

I scooted across the bed and stood. Beneath the washbasin were towels of the usual Tonk type—thin and coarse and of a dreary shade of undyed brown. I tossed two to Gair and took two myself. "At least we can face what remains of the day without stinking."

We went first to the showers. They were in the usual open row along one wall of a stone-tiled room. But they were of the new type, with both hot and cold water. The more I had warm showers, the less I was willing to suffer through cold ones, even though the Tonks have long held that a cold shower followed by a steam bath or a hot soak, and then followed by another cold shower, is the path to cleanliness and health. We are overall a healthy people, but our fetish for icy water seems madder to me every time I stand beneath a downpour that doesn't make my teeth clack against each other.

I stripped out of my undergarments, grabbed a scoop of soap powder from the public dish—it's a mix of ground pumice and sand and lye and ash and something that makes bubbles, and it doesn't do to get it in your eyes—and tossed my towels over the towel hook. Gair was looking at the gritty gray soap powder with obvious doubt. "Tonk civilians have bar soap," he said.

"Welcome to Tonk military life. Good food, bad soap."

He sighed, undressed, got his own handful of soap, and took the shower next to mine.

I noticed that he showered with his back to me, almost making a point of not looking at me. I rubbed my soap into the washing towel and scoured myself clean, rinsed the towel, got more of the soap for my hair, worked it through, rinsed again, and all the while I watched him, waiting for him to turn around and look at me.

But he didn't.

Rinsed clean, I took a tooth polisher from the jar supplied for us, rubbed my teeth clean with the sow bristles, and wrapped the polisher in with my belongings. Then I scooted over to Gair's shower, where he was finishing up.

I ran a hand over his back, then turned him around to face me and wrapped my arms around him. "Thank you," I told him.

"For what?"

"For everything you did for me last night. For everything you've done for me since this started. For . . . being willing to stand with my people against a common enemy. I don't know that I could have been so . . . generous." My fingers traced the raised scars on his back. I looked into his eyes and he smiled down at me, and kissed me, and pulled away carefully.

His body was ready for mine. But again he turned away.

"Why not?" I asked him. "Why not now, when the enemy is at the gates and we may not live to see another dawn?"

He had moved to his own pile of clothes. He picked them up, sniffed them, and put them back down. "Would make the whole shower a waste of time," he said, and wrapped the coarse towel around his hips, knotting it at the side.

He was going to ignore me. I could not believe the gall of the man. I wrapped my own dry towel around myself and stomped over to confront him.

"I asked you a question, by Ethebet! And I want an answer. You want me. I want you. So why won't you let us both have what we both want?"

"Because I love you, Talyn, and I want more than just this minute."

When he said it, it stunned me. But only that he had said the words. I think I'd known the truth of it for quite some time.

"I love you, too," I told him, and realized with a sick feeling that it was true. I loved him. Not as I had loved Adjii. That was a love with sweetness but no real substance; it wasn't a love made to withstand tempests. Not, certainly, as I had loved Skirmig; that was a love twisted out of nightmares and sick, hellish fear. I loved Gair in ways I was afraid to examine. I wasn't ready to look at any of those feelings, or what they might mean for me. Or for him. But I shouldn't need to. "You can't know—and probably shouldn't dare to hope—that we'll have more than this minute," I argued.

"I can't. But I want at least the promise of the future. I want your oath and bond. I want to be able to call you my wife, and believe that you'll stand by me now and always. I don't want to love you as much as I do and know the pleasure of your company and then watch you walk away because your damned Ethebet's Law says that you can, to be with some brawny Tonk who will, in turn, cast you off for some woman who can bear him babes." Gair took my shoulders in his hands, and his voice was rough. "I'm no boy looking for an adventure to tell his friends. I know what I want, and who I am. And I cannot say that I don't want the babes in arms myself. I look at you and I can see lovely gray-eyed girls and brown-eyed boys with your smile and my nose. I can see them, Talyn, and I know that they'll never be anyplace but in my dreams. And yet I would accept that, and be true to you."

"But if I marry outside my people—"

"I know what happens if you marry outside your people. You're cast out, and no longer Tonk."

I nodded. "But we can enjoy each other for now. If we do not marry and our arrangement is temporary and relatively circumspect—"

"Circumspect? The public shower?" His laugh was harsh and unhappy. He wrapped his clothes in his wet washing towel and slung the makeshift laundry bag over his shoulders and started back down the hall.

"Wait, damn you." I couldn't believe that he would say he loved me, yet not take whatever time together circumstances might give us. I could not change my people. I could not change our laws, or who I was. Did he expect me to have myself cast out, to be alone in the world except for him? Because that was what would happen. He *did* expect it, and in the meantime we could die on the morrow and I would never know what it was to wrap myself around him and feel him in me, to move with him and touch him and . . .

My eyes blurred with the first haze of tears, and I blinked them back. I would not succumb to self-pity.

Gair looked over at me when I caught up with him and said, "I'm watching out for us both, Talyn. I'm being responsible now because I don't want to watch you walk out of my life later, leaving me wanting to die. It seems a practical solution; when you confront the immovable, unscalable, unbreakable rock wall, you don't set up camp at its base. You don't smash your skull against it hoping it will yield. You just turn around and walk in another direction. And that's all I'm doing."

I glared at him. "Maybe instead of cutting your losses and running, you should figure out how to build a pair of wings."

"I'm not the one with the magic, Talyn. That's you. I'm just a man, and I can only do the things that men can do. You're atop the wall, with wings and the freedom to take to the air and soar down to join me."

I was just realizing that he was leading us to the public rooms of the White Fox when Pada came racing up the stairs and almost collided into us.

"We need you," she said. "Both of you. Did you not find the uniforms left for you?"

"There were no uniforms when we went to shower," Gair said.

"No. They're in there now."

"We didn't go back to the room," I told her.

She looked me up and down. "You're looking better," she said, and her gaze slid from my face to my arms, and then away. She cleared her throat. "The Feegash army is at the gates, and demanding parley or it will destroy us. It has weapons we've never fought against. It demonstrated a rain of stones as a warning. No one is dead yet, but they will be soon. Commander wants to know if you have anything to offer against them."

I thought of the running tower. "I do," I said, and raced back to the room to throw on clothes.

The Shielder's uniform. I had not the time to put it on with the reverence and ceremony that it deserved, but I knew that for the rest of my life I would remember the moment and the circumstances under which I became an active Shielder once again.

I yanked a comb through my wet hair and tugged it into a three-strand braid—not Ethebet's warrior's braid, but it would suffice for the moment. And I turned to find Gair pulling on the black boots, wearing the gray of Conventionals.

Neither of our uniforms had the marks of rank on them. We were in the Forces, but not yet placed.

But for the moment, Gair was a sort of honorary Tonk. And I felt—and crushed—a hard wave of anguish that he was not a true Tonk, that I might claim him proudly and keep him all the rest of my days.

"I'm ready," he said, and we followed Pada at a run, out to the battlements and the Feegash army on the other side of them. An army, I knew, that was comprised almost entirely of Tonk fleshmages.

24

Pada dragged Gair and me in front of the cold-eyed commander of the Chaavtaak Forces, who gave no evidence of being happy to see either of us.

"Feeling better?" he asked me, and the disdain in his voice

made my stomach flip. I caught a glimpse of Gair out of the corner of my eye—Gair looked like he wanted to pound the commander's face into the stone parapet.

I did not wish to focus on my health, or on my inexplicable behavior from the night before. It was done, I was over it, I was fine. So I simply acknowledged the question with the always-useful "Yes, sir," and moved on before he could follow up. "I can give Chaavtaak weapons that can counter the Feegash army," I said, "but most of the people down there are Tonks. Taaksmen from Beyltaak enslaved by the Feegash magic. I don't want to kill the people out there if we can avoid it."

"We're fighting a war, Shieldsergeant—against people who want to kill us," the commander said. "We need to concentrate on winning the war, and not on sparing the enemy."

Considering that most of the enemy spread out on the fields before us were taaksmen of Beyltaak enslaved by the Feegash, I was willing to disagree, vehemently if necessary. I hoped to go back to Beyltaak someday. I wanted to do it knowing that mine had not been the hand that had slaughtered my friends or neighbors. Or family.

"What actions have Senders already taken?" I asked.

The commander glowered at me. "The Feegash forces effectively shut down Senders. We have them at stalemate with our Shielders; they haven't managed to get anything past us yet. Our ground forces outnumber what they have deployed as combat units, but I'm not sending my men out there and throwing them to the fleshmages. Even if they survived, even if they took the enemy and won the day, I would not dare let them through Chaavtaak's gate again, because I could not be sure that they had not become fleshmages themselves. Every single one of the enemy's soldiers is wrapped in a single shield. Our Senders say that it's a simple brute-force shield, but not anything that they have the numbers to overcome."

The only way the Feegash forces could have shields that would stand against Senders would be if they had Shielders of their own. But if they were working through the View, the Shielders would have to take three or four soldiers and wrap them. But if the Shielders—or if even one Shielder—was using the Grandolfitnaj, the togram of the Will of God, then all the dangers the View put on the Shielders would be buffered, and they would be able to power the shields from the endless energy of the View without having to channel that power through their own bodies.

I closed my eyes to shut out distractions and slipped into the Hagedwar I kept within me, and drew the Grandolfitnaj toward me. I looked at the scene before me with eyes closed; at the troops massed, at the shields around each soldier individually, and around each horse and each weapon as well. The shields were identical. Which meant they were the work of only one Shielder. I could not figure out who the Shielder was; he had shielded himself, too. It could be any of the few who'd remained in Beyltaak. It could be Iyalara. It could be my father.

The enemy was setting up for a siege. The Feegash had taken the field with easily two hundred horse troops in front of us and about the same number behind us. More cavalry than Beyltaak had ever fielded, which meant either a lot of untrained civilian fleshmages were in uniform, or the Feegash had gotten reinforcements.

I had no way of telling which. But I could see that ground troops were still coming, and there were a lot of them. I'm not particularly good at estimating large numbers, but I put the ground force on the march at easily a thousand, and passed that on to the commander.

Ground troops were closing on the already-encamped cavalry, which was camped out of range of anything but Magics. The Feegash commander had deployed Feegash-style light ballistae at the front, aimed at the city gate. The light ballistae were fast firing and damned accurate in experienced hands, and would be useful for tearing apart anyone who dared step out of the gate, though they would be useless in any attempts to breach a wall.

They would no doubt be bringing the heavy ballistae for wall work, though those would be difficult to transport and would take at least a few more days to arrive.

The commander did not receive my news with any cheer. "A thousand Conventionals on foot. You're sure?" He sounded desperate.

"Sure as I can be," I said, still watching the scene with my eyes closed.

He swore under his breath, then said, "We have a fifty-rider cavalry and a hundred foot. Even that is a heavy roll for us to carry, considering, with the number of people we have in the taak. We got a few reinforcements through the Outside Alliances, but we could take only as many as we could house. So I can put another thirty or forty on horseback and the same number on the ground, but they'll be untrained boys and old men. My Senders and my Shielders are stymied. My Communicators will let the other taaks know we're under siege, but if the Feegash are already bringing in heavy equipment, that will likely get here before any of the taaks can respond."

I opened my eyes and looked at him. His face was bleak. Chaavtaak was small. From its size and the number of houses within the walls, I guessed that not more that two thousand people would live there, half of them female, many of the boys small children, many of the men old and holding positions as bakers and craftsmen and farmers and herdsmen. The commander was throwing most of his able-bodied men into the Conventionals with those numbers. And they wouldn't be enough.

"I can make more of the running towers," I told him. "Put one of your men in each of those, and set them on the cavalry. Guiding one is the same as riding a horse—your men won't have any trouble."

"We haven't the metal to offer you, nor the craftsmen to do the work, nor the time to create them. We'll be overrun in a day or two."

"I don't need your metal, I don't need craftsmen, and I don't need much time. I'll need some space. You'll have to clear your streets, get your civilians in their houses, move your men up to the parapets. Gair can give your men the commands and get them into the towers while I'm making the towers. The running towers will keep your people out of the reach of the fleshmages and keep them safe."

I saw disbelief in his eyes. I said, "I can do what I say. Move the people you have behind the gate, and I'll show you."

He shouted a command, and in just a moment I had my free space. I took everything I'd learned from making the first running tower, and made a second—a refined one that didn't have sword arms, but that did have capture nets. The new towers would howl like wolves when they ran, too. Their riders would be able to talk to and hear each other as they rode. The towers would terrify the horses, yet would sense people and horses beneath them, and would not trample either. I wanted to rout the forces camped outside of Chaavtaak; I didn't want us to kill them. Those that did not run we could capture. Most, I thought, would run.

We were not going to kill my people. We were not.

The first tower hazed its way into life, and the stair dropped down beneath it.

Gair said, "I'll go down and take your men into the towers and show them what they'll have to do if you'll just send them down."

The commander stared at the gleaming silver monster waiting patiently behind his gate. "Go. Go." The commander shouted his major to get the troops in order to ride the running towers, and told several other officers to clear the streets of civilians.

I got to work, making tower after tower, imbuing each with life, focusing on making sure that each would respond only to my voice and the voice of the man assigned to it. I was careful—I was so careful—to protect the Chaavtaakers, and to protect my people as well. I was focused tightly, all my attention on the Hagedwar and the magic I was doing. . . .

I lost my balance and fell, and lost my focus at the same time.

I felt . . . wrong. I felt torn. Scattered. I looked around me, wondering if the Sender on the Feegash side had attacked me while my attention was elsewhere. But, no, the Chaavtaak shields were in place and holding.

The commander crouched beside me. "You're ill," he said.

"I'm fine," I insisted.

"You're not. Your skin is the color of chalk, and waxy. Your eyes are glassy. You're breathing too quickly. I'm going to have one of my healers look at you."

"I don't need a healer. There's nothing wrong with me that food and sleep won't cure," I told him.

But I was not sure I was telling him the truth. I did feel tired, though not in the least hungry. But more than tired, I felt like I was missing parts of myself.

I leaned forward and rested my face on my knees and heard the commander bellow, "Healer! Up here now!"

"How many did I make for you?" I asked.

"Thirty-seven."

"Will that be enough?"

"It will have to be. Perhaps you can teach my people in Magics to do what you have done, but not now. We're going to get you into a bed and fill you with broth—"

"I have to stay here," I told him. "I have to watch. I have to know how this goes. I have to be able to fix the running towers if they have problems. I'll rest when this is over."

He sighed. The healer ran up, and the commander said, "Get her to a place on the parapets where she can watch the battle. But she's to sit, and she's to be kept warm, and if she faints again, you get her out of here and into the infirmary."

"Yes, sir," the healer said. He was a lean, short young man; when I stood I had a full head's height on him. He wasn't going to be picking me up and carrying me if I lost my balance again. The commander noticed the inequity in our sizes, but just waved me to a tower-top, and had a chair brought for me and set up on boxes so that I could see the field below.

Twilight was already upon us. I thought with regret that I could have added lanterns to the fronts of the running towers so that they could have two advantages in the coming exchange— they would be able to see their enemies and they would be able to blind them. But I had not considered lights, and I did not feel well enough to add them.

Could I be suffering from lack of food? I'd done a bit of eating the night before, but it was almost night again and I'd had nothing since. And I hadn't eaten all that had been placed before me when I'd had the chance, because I'd had that . . . I didn't know what to call it. Fit? Seizure? Attack of hysterics? Case of battleshock? I'd left more than half my meal on the plate.

I wasn't hungry, though. Nor thirsty. I simply felt weak.

Below I heard the rumble as the massive gates pushed open, and the running towers began marching out of Chaavtaak. Suddenly the air was full of the eerie howling of wolves, and everyone stared at me, shocked.

"Wanted to frighten the horses," I said to the healer beside me.

Within Chaavtaak, I could hear panicked whinnies. The running towers without doubt were having the desired effect. I hoped they would prove as frightening to the enemy's mounts. In the bad light, and with the Feegash encampment back as far as it was, I could not see well. But I could see stirrings of panic.

"Yes," the healer beside me said under his breath.

We leaned onto the parapet as the running towers gathered into two staggered rows, roughly twenty towers wide.

Activity in the enemy camp picked up. We could not tell what they were doing, but they were busy as ants in a stick-stirred nest.

I clenched a fist and stared down at the scene, willing the wolf sounds louder and more fierce. The evening air rang with the chilling cries, and I got the goosebumps I always get when I hear wolves singing close by.

The two rows of running towers started forward at a walk, and then moved to a trot, and then to cantering speed. From the outside they were terrifying things to look at—giant dome-topped silver spiders with their legs rising and falling with horrible precision. They bore down on the enemy camp, and someone down the wall from my position screamed, "They broke! They broke!" as the horses lost their nerve and streamed north toward the river and home. Some of the horses had riders, some did not, but none of them were stopping or turning around. Those with riders had taken the bits between their teeth and were fleeing on the same instinct as the rest.

The men on foot held briefly, but as the running towers closed on them, they took off, too. I saw a handful of towers at the fore of the charge deploy their nets, but most of the tower riders were not interested in taking captives.

I felt almost as if I were in the battle. Though in honesty, it could not be called a battle. It was a rout. The thirty-seven giant metal running towers, gleaming still on their domes as they caught the last faint western kiss of the already-set sun, bore down on the men who were readying the ballistae, and the soldiers broke and fled.

I wondered if they were not fleshmages, as I had thought, but free soldiers. But it could be that they were fleshmages, and Skirmig was pulling back his troops in the face of overwhelming assault, hoping to use them later in an action where they might hope to prevail.

At the moment it did not matter. The Feegash camp was

trampled flat and its contents were destroyed, the running towers crushed the light ballistae, and troops and horses had scattered. The running towers swung around in a scythe-blade line and swept toward Chaavtaak's back gate and the remainder of the Feegash forces, and I closed my eyes.

I could hear every bit of what was happening. I could feel it, if faintly. Voices inside my head talked to each other as different parts of me galloped across the cleared fields, and the howling of wolves hung shivering within my skull, as close as my own breath. I could feel the ground shaking beneath my feet—beneath my hundreds of feet. I could feel the whole long blade of the running towers split into two parts and swing around both sides of the Chaavtaak walls toward the Feegash forces holding the back gate.

The feeling got stronger. I *was* the galloping towers—all of them. I could not see, but I could sense the hands guiding me, the voices urging me forward in dozens of different voices, the shape of the earth beneath all my many feet. I could feel the presence of the enemy before me, a glowing wave of life I would not touch. I could feel that wave break and scatter.

"TALYN!" And hands on my shoulders, shaking me. "Get me water!" someone shouted. Someone familiar. And ice-cold water hit me and I sputtered and opened my eyes to find myself on the parapet, lying on the ground, my arms and legs still thrashing and Gair standing over me and staring at me with a scared look in his eyes.

I stilled my arms and legs. Took the hand that Gair offered me, and let him pull me to my feet. The world spun in crazy spirals, and I grabbed on to Gair, trying to steady it.

"What's *wrong*?" he whispered in my ear, a question as angry as it was scared.

Out loud and to everyone, I said, "I need to eat something and I need to sleep. I . . . did too much magic, and it wore me out. But I'll be fine. Let me stay here until the last of the Feegash troops run, and then I'll get some food and a good night's sleep and I'll be fine."

It wasn't true. It wasn't even the smallest bit true. I'd just discovered the price of using the tograms of the Hagedwar that lay outside the red. Of creating living metal.

I'd imbued each piece of living metal with a bit of myself. My soul, my life-essence. And I had just discovered that my soul was not a thing to be diced into uncounted pieces and yet remain unchanged. I was alive, and spread thin—and I wondered if perhaps my being spread over all those living metal creations might make me unkillable. Or if it would simply weaken me so much that I would die faster.

Gair put an arm around me, and when it was over, he helped me walk back to the White Fox. He didn't say anything; he just held me up.

I didn't say anything either, because I had finally made the connection I should have made long before.

I had given Skirmig a working piece of myself. A link, in the form of that damned silver dancer I threw at him to show him what I had that he could not have. And that metal dancer was his key. She was the reason that my Hagedwar had never closed after I created her—the link between us was always there, so the Hagedwar stayed open, and the togram that gave my life to her metal stayed always open, and always had the energy of the View running through it.

The realization hit me so hard I stopped walking. I hadn't the strength to put one foot before the other, Ethebet help me, and Gair muttered something in Hyerti and scooped me into his arms and carried me the rest of the way to the White Fox.

Chaavtaak Conventionals and Magics alike were cheering the two of us when he carried me through the door; those who had not been chosen to ride the running towers and those who were off duty from Shields and Senders had gathered ahead of us, and at sight of us burst into "Swing That Head High," an old Tonk nomad song that hearkens back to the not-so-long-gone days when warrior braids were more than just a symbol.

It could have been one of the finest moments of my life. Instead, I could only look at those elated faces and realize that I alone was the reason the fleshmages were spreading. They did not tire or sicken and die, not because the Feegash had figured out the secrets of the outer tograms at the same time that I had, or that Skirmig had watched me at the Edge and figured out how to use it, but because when he said the dancing figurine was nothing more than a symbol of the mastery of the outer tograms, he'd lied to me. It had been the thing he'd truly desired all along, and I like a fool had believed his lie, and had thrown the very thing he'd wanted right in his face.

His slaves, his new fleshmages, were my people, so I was grateful that they did not sicken and die. But my magic had made it possible for Skirmig to use nothing of himself in enslaving them. So he could take more of them slaves.

He could take all of them as slaves.

Because he didn't need to be able to "see" into the View to use the magic of the outer tograms. He didn't need to do anything except draw the power that I had handed him out of the togram he'd asked me to use, through the clear line straight into it that animated the silver dancer.

I buried my face in Gair's chest. "I'm too sick to eat," I told him.

He shouted, "She's not well," and the singing stopped. The worried men and women of the Chaavtaak Forces cleared a path, and some ran ahead to ready a room for me, and behind me I heard someone calling for broth and beer.

I wanted to die.

Mine was the hand that had enslaved my parents, my brothers and sisters, my friends and neighbors. I had given Skirmig the one thing he did not have to expand his fleshmage empire: the infinite power of the View.

It was my fault. All of it was my fault.

Well, not the Feegash coming to Hyre in the first place. Not their betrayal of their enforced peace. Not the first fleshmages.

But Skirmig's access to the infinite power of the View—that was my fault.

Gair put me into bed with my clothes on, though he pulled off my boots.

He shut the door, and barred it, and said, "You're going to tell me what's really going on."

"I'm tired," I said.

"No. 'Tired' doesn't leave a woman thrashing on the ground, babbling and making wolf noises. Tired doesn't leave that haunted, hunted look in her eyes, or make her hide her face when people whose lives and homes she has just saved applaud her and give her a well-deserved cheer. Don't lie to me. You forget how well I know you."

I turned my face to the wall.

"Talyn, *talk* to me."

"I . . . can't."

"You have to. I'll help you if I know what the problem is. You know that. But you look to me like you're dying, and I'm afraid. I'm afraid for you, and I'm afraid for me because I don't want to lose you, and I have to think there is something you could do that would . . . that would stop whatever is happening to you."

"Soup and beer!" someone shouted outside the door, and Gair rose and unbarred it and said, "I'm going to feed her. And she's going to need quiet for a while."

The bringer of soup and beer vanished with a promise to pass on the word, and outside, sounds of celebration suddenly stopped.

"I don't need quiet," I told him.

"I do," he said. "I need to be able to hear what you're telling me, and I don't want you to be drowned out by all seventeen verses of 'Wild Maids of the South Plains.'" He propped my head on pillows and handed me the mug of beer and said, "Drink it. And then if you won't feed yourself, I'll do it for you."

Nothing about him suggested he was joking. And I did not choose to be force-fed soup. I sipped from the beer—weak stuff, lacking the flavor of a good strong ale, but considered more soothing to the weak and frail—and made a face. "If you've heard only seventeen verses of 'Wild Maids,' you're missing most of the song. The really dirty verses are the last twenty or so."

My weak attempt at humor didn't distract him. "Some better day, you can sing me the whole thing. But right now, I want you to eat your soup and tell me what's the matter with you."

"I made a mistake," I said. "A bad one." I sipped the soup from its mug.

He waited, watching my face.

"I gave Skirmig something that I thought wasn't important. It turns out it was the secret to his new power." I put the mug down, thinking of the damage a man with unlimited power could do. He could have the whole world if he wanted it; he could make everyone breathing into his slaves—into flesh-mages who carried out the duties that he gave them and at his command danced like my little silver dancer on her string.

And wasn't that what he'd talked about with such hope? Bringing the Feegash peace to the whole world?

The Feegash peace was fleshmagery. Enslavement. A living hell that would feed him as it grew, and that would grow ever stronger, until it consumed every man and woman and child.

"The only thing you gave him was that silver dancer you made."

How easy it was to forget how much Gair knew about me. Those borrowed memories faded after a while—I could call up only a few of his anymore, and did not doubt that most of mine were gone, too. But the things I'd considered significant would have lasted longer. I could, for example, still replay moment by moment Gair's attack on the Faverhend of Injtaak, and the subsequent capture of his men and him.

"That was it."

"The dancer? Why was hitting him in the face with the dancer a bad thing? It was just a toy."

"That's what I thought. But it's more. To someone who knows the magic that created it, it is a key into one part of that magic. A key that he didn't have, and could not have had without the dancer."

Gair handed me the beer. "Drink."

I drank.

He handed me the soup. "Now this."

I drank some more.

He sat there frowning. "What can he do with it that he could not do without it? He already had fleshmages. He could already force people to do things they did not want to do. Look at what he did with you."

I considered my words. "Without the link the dancer gives him, he was simply a man. He had to control his fleshmages with his own strength. And I think he's tremendously strong—but there were very real limits to what he could do, how many people he could hold on to. With the link I gave him, I made him a god. The infinite power of the View is now at his command. He can reach into the same well from which I powered the running towers and the dancer and power his command over his slaves."

Gair's eyes narrowed. "But the running towers are what's the matter with you, aren't they? Keeping them up and moving is tearing you apart."

I nodded. "The difference is simple. I have to give each of them a piece of my soul to give them life. Once I have done that, they will run as long as I live. But Skirmig does not need to give the people he enslaves anything. They already have souls. They're already capable of moving, of making decisions. They're alive. So all he has to do is take."

"Break the links between you and the dancer. That will destroy his power over the fleshmages—or at least over most of them."

I handed him the empty soup mug and lay back. "I can't even find it. The noise of the running towers is so great when I close my eyes that I could not even hope to find something so small and delicate as that connection between me and the silver dancer."

"Then cut *all* the links. Break them all."

"Is anyone still in one of the running towers?"

"I'm sure there are patrols out rounding up stray fleshmages. But the commander can call them in."

"They haven't brought any of the fleshmages into the taak, have they?"

"I don't know. I can find out."

I closed my eyes. "I'm going to sleep for a while. I truly am tired. When you are sure no one is inside any of the running towers, I'll disable them. And then I'll be able to hear the silver dancer and disable that."

Gair's thoughts were with Talyn asleep in their room, but at the request of the Chaavtaak commander, he was stuck in a tall, smoky, stone-walled meeting hall with a handful of Chaavtaak officers and specialists from the different branches. He was along as the man who had encountered the fleshmages in person. All of them stood watching the two Beyltaak prisoners in their separate cages in the opposite corners of the same wall.

"You're taking too many chances just having them in here," Gair said. "You haven't seen what they can do. You need to kill them now and be done with them."

"If they can turn the taaklords of the major taaks into Feegash slaves, we *know* what they can do. We don't actually need to see it. What we do need to do is figure out whether they can be released from the fleshmage spell."

Gair looked at the commander. "You're talking about the myth Talyn relayed to me?"

He nodded. "A knife in the heart, and then one of the Magics healers to revive the fleshmage at the moment of death." He sighed. "We've read that this is the only manner by which a fleshmage can be cured. Of course, the records note that many times the victim does not survive the cure."

Gair watched the two men in their cages. Both of them were sitting on the floor, legs crossed, hands resting with palms up on thighs, eyes wide open. They were staring forward, seemingly unaware of everything that was going on around them.

But Gair didn't believe it. He was certain that they were watching and listening. That the odd pose was an act, an attempt to lure any of the men in the room into their reach. "Do the records note that sometimes the fleshmage converts his would-be rescuer?" Gair asked. "Because if just one of you is converted, Chaavtaak is done."

"That's why we're all here," a man in healer garb said quietly. "Because the risk that the fleshmage will take the one of us who moves within range is huge. And we understand what that would mean."

"What's the range?" Gair asked.

"We don't know that."

"Nothing in the old stories?"

"The old stories claim that a fleshmage need only look into the eyes of his victim to steal his soul," the commander said softly.

Gair turned to face the man and gave him a level look. "Then why don't those bastards have blindfolds on? And barring that, why are we standing here facing *toward* them?"

All the officers stared at Gair, and several blushed. They turned their faces away from the two sitting fleshmages.

"Putting a blindfold on one of them would solve the problem, then," the healer said. "Though even that is not without its risks."

"You cannot be sure even that will protect you." Gair heard Talyn's voice behind him, and spun to face her.

She was still ashy gray, and her eyes seemed too big for her face.

"What in all the hells are you doing out of bed?" Gair asked.

"I dreamed that you were in danger," she told him. "I saw you dancing on the blade of a knife, and I heard terrible voices, and there was . . . blood."

She looked like she was about to fall over. Like she might simply collapse on the floor at any moment. Gair's heart constricted, and he ached to save her from the thing that destroyed her. But he could not. He might help, though. He turned to the commander. "Are all the men out of the running towers yet?"

The commander said, "I had the last two brought in when you told me there was a problem."

"Talyn, all the soldiers are safe," Gair said. "Destroy the towers now. They're killing you."

With a tremulous smile, she nodded. "Yes, that will help." She sagged to the floor, boneless as a rag doll, and he ran to her side. "I'm fine," she said, looking up at him. "I just needed to sit down. I'm . . . a little weak."

He wanted to scream. He wanted to smash things. "Get rid of the towers. Quickly, Talyn. They're devouring you."

He crouched beside her, and she leaned against him and closed her eyes. And sat there. He hoped she was doing something—that she hadn't collapsed again. Her skin felt too cool, and he turned to the men who had gathered around the two of them. "Can someone bring her a blanket? And her boots? She didn't even wear her boots when she came in here."

"What's wrong with her?" the healer asked. "It has something to do with the towers?"

Gair nodded. "She told me she put too much of herself into them."

The healer stared at him with an uncomprehending face. Gair shrugged. "I don't know anything about magic. I only know what she told me—that too much of her is in them, and that they're weakening her."

The healer shook his head. "I cannot imagine what sort of

magic she's done. That she could create the towers in the first place is beyond anything I have ever seen, and that she could do it alone is outside of my understanding of the way magic works. I'm not sure I can help her if anything goes wrong—"

"I don't imagine that you can," Talyn said quietly. And then she said words that froze Gair. "I can't destroy them."

"What do you mean, you can't destroy them? You made them."

Talyn shook her head. "I can't. I don't know what is wrong. They're . . . resisting me . . . somehow." She glanced past the officers to the two men in the cages and she froze. "Get me out of here," she whispered, and the last vestiges of color drained from her face. "Get everyone out of here."

Gair dragged her to her feet and half ran with her to the door. "She says everyone needs to get out of here," he shouted over his shoulder.

The Chaavtaakers followed him, though all of them looked uncertain. "We were none of us within physical reach," one said, "and we were not looking in their eyes."

"*Close the door,*" Talyn snapped, and only when she heard it click did she say, "They were listening to you. *He* heard everything you said to them."

Gair stared at her. "Listening."

"They used to sit like that in his house. When they weren't doing anything, they would just sit there. Staring. Or they would stop in the midst of working and stare off at nothing, and then drop what they were doing and go off as if they'd just received orders. I always thought it was just that they were flitterminded. But when I look back at them and understand that they were fleshmages—"

The commander crouched down beside Talyn, a look of terror in his face. "You lived in the house with fleshmages. And . . . you know who the fleshmage master is? How did you not become a fleshmage?"

Talyn said, "I've asked myself that over and over. I don't know. I think . . . I think that for some reason he doesn't want me to be one of them. That he has at least some control over the process, and that he has kept me aside."

"Why?"

Gair felt her shudder, and tightened his arms around her. "He says he loves me," she whispered.

"The master of the fleshmages."

She nodded.

The commander said, "Loves you?"

She pulled away from Gair and tugged up the back of her tunic. "That's what he calls it. But this is what his love looks like." Gair heard the shock of the men around her. He winced and pulled her tunic back down again. One of the commander's aides came running up with boots and a blanket.

"We're out here? What has happened?"

"A . . . security problem," the commander said.

Gair took the blanket and wrapped it around her, and helped her put the boots on. "Talyn, you have to figure out a way to destroy those towers. I can see them killing you."

"Not killing me," she said. "Stretching me thin." She smiled at him. "But either way, no good being me right now. Yes, I have to destroy them." She laid her head against his chest again, and he hugged her close. "Take me to them. Maybe something will come to me when I'm near them."

He started to pick her up to carry her, but she shook her head. "I can walk. I'll lean on you, but you needn't carry me. I'm strong enough to do this, and I'm not some delicate little creature. I don't want you to hurt yourself hauling me about."

He kissed her cheek and whispered in her ear, "I'd carry you to the top of a mountain if it would make you whole and well again."

And she gave him a smile that nearly melted him. "Just a boost to the towers."

Gods, he wanted her. He wanted to break his promise to himself. He wanted her to get better, and then he wanted to take her to bed and show her how a man who knew what love was could love her.

And he couldn't.

No, that wasn't true. He could. But if he did, she would eventually leave him because he was not Tonk and keeping him would cost her everything she was and everyone she loved, and if he let himself love her and then he had to give her up, he would die.

At least he would want to die.

He helped her to her feet, wishing that touching her didn't feel so good. He draped her arm over his shoulder and tucked his arm around her waist, and she wobbled a bit, then steadied. "We're going to the running towers," he said.

The commander said, "I'll come with you." He turned to the rest of those gathered. "No one is to enter that room until I return, on pain of death."

The three of them set off, out of the corridor, through the huge metal doors of the building that housed the command center for Conventional and Magics in Chaavtaak as well as most of the officers' quarters. Gair could see the sign for the White Fox just down the street.

And in the other direction, the lines of running towers gleaming in torchlight.

Talyn moved slowly toward the first tower. She stared up at it, and said, "I'm going to try again. Maybe seeing it will work."

He held her up, and she grew very still. And nothing happened.

"No. It might be that I've created things I don't have the power to destroy. And that . . ." She sagged against him. "That will be the destruction of us all."

"The silver dancer," he said.

She nodded.

"You have to try something else, love," he said. "There must be something you can do. I cannot bear seeing you this weak. And if you can find the key to destroying these, you can destroy the dancer, too. And the bastard's power with it."

"I know," she said, and leaned against the nearest of the running towers.

He felt her back stiffen. He heard her whisper, "Oh, please tell me it isn't this."

And then a deeper darkness swirled around the tower, and it faded, and faded. And vanished.

"Futtering damn," she said softly.

I had my answer. I could destroy the towers I'd made. I had to touch them to do it. I had to be in physical contact with that bit of my soul, myself, that I had thrown into the magic. And that would be fine for destroying the towers. For getting me back to strength again. But it was not going to help much in breaking Skirmig's hold on his fleshmages.

"You did it," Gair said, and hugged me. "That's wonderful!"

So I explained to him why it wasn't.

"We're going to have to hunt Skirmig down and take the dancer away from him," Gair said when I finished.

"Yes."

His grin showed a lot of teeth, and very little humor. "I can rejoice in that hunt."

I hugged him. "I love that about you. You see the best side of problems."

"Only the ones I really want to solve."

I spent a long hour destroying the towers that I'd made, while Gair held my hand and the Chaavtaak commander walked behind me, making pitiful little noises in the back of his throat when he thought I wasn't paying attention. I left three—one to guard the front gate of Chaavtaak, one to guard the back gate, and one that Gair and I could take when we went after Skirmig. With the destruction of each one, I got stronger. My thinking got clearer, the world became steadier, and I regained more of my confidence.

When only the last three remained, I turned to Gair. "Do we go after him now?"

Both Gair and the commander asked me, "Do you know where he is?"

"No."

Gair sighed. "Can you feel him with the three running towers still in existence?"

I looked up at the sleek, powerful towers standing still in the starlight, with the lamp-cast lights around them burnishing them golden. I had taken far too much pride in my own creations, and was much too unwilling to let them go. "No." Apparently, too, my thinking was not yet as clear as it needed to be.

"We'll have to see if we can get horses," I said, heading for the last of the towers.

"No we won't. On horses we'll be vulnerable in ways I don't want to be. We cannot go cross-country back to Beyltaak—or to wherever he might have gone in the meantime—when the Beyltaak forces can rain darts and stones and fire on us at their convenience."

I nodded and turned to Gair. "You have another plan, then?"

"Of course." He grinned at me and said, "We'll simply get one of the fleshmages to talk."

I heard the false note of cheer in his voice and realized he was putting a brave face on something that scared him.

It scared me, too. "We can't make either of them talk without breaking the fleshmage spell. Skirmig will be able to completely silence either one of them, no matter what steps we might take." I was thinking of my own experiences with Skirmig's magic. And fighting hard not to panic again.

"I know that."

I turned to the commander. "That's what your people were in there talking about, wasn't it? Killing one of the captives to free him from the spell, then healing him."

"Yes," the commander said. "We have a team of good healers in Magics. If we can do what we have to do without risking the fleshmages turning my people, I'm sure we can save them both. But, again, the risk is so great I'm not sure we dare take it."

He was right. I was not sure how easily the fleshmage contagion could be passed on, but with anything that could consume the whole of Chaavtaak if it got loose, any risk was too great.

But as I considered the problem, I realized that there was a way to do what had to be done without risk. I was the only person in Chaavtaak who knew the Hagedwar. While no one who did not know the Hagedwar would be able to see the bonds cast by Skirmig's magic, I already knew that I could see them, and that I could cast them off. Of all the people in Chaavtaak, I was the one person who would be immune to the contagion of fleshmagery.

But even more than that, now that I had some idea of what was wrong with the people whom the Feegash—no, just Skirming, I reminded myself—had turned, I realized that I might be able to use a combination of the Feegash and Tonk magics to free both of our captive fleshmages without killing them. If I could use the View to see the bonds fleshmagery had on them, I might be able to break them as I had broken the bonds with which Skirmig had held me captive.

We started back to the Chaavtaak Forces headquarters. "I have to be the one to deal with the fleshmages," I told Gair and the commander. "I think I can heal both captives without having to kill them. Even if I can't, I know that they cannot use fleshmagery against me."

Gair stepped in front of me and stopped me. "How do you know that?"

"I already broke free of Skirmig's magic once. I know how and where it sets its hooks. I know how it works. I can *see* magic across its full range—something that not even Skirmig can do." I took Gair's hands in mine. "I can *do* this, Gair. And I need to. I need to be the one to set this thing right."

"You didn't cause it."

"I made it worse."

"But you didn't *cause* it, Talyn, and I think the guilt you're feeling—guilt that you have no business feeling—is pushing you to take foolish chances."

I turned to the commander. "I can do this, sir. I know what I can do."

He nodded. "I've seen what you can do. I can easily believe that there is nothing my people match you in. If you cannot handle the fleshmages safely, no one can." He said softly, "I'll give you permission to be the person who works with the fleshmages. But I'm going to require some safety precautions."

"Of course."

"Don't do this, Talyn," Gair said.

I made a point of ignoring him. "What sort of precautions, sir?"

"You'll have to deal with the fleshmages from inside their cages, and I'll insist that the cage doors are locked behind you."

"Those are both big men," Gair said. "Trained soldiers— Conventionals fighters. She doesn't have the strength or the fighting skill to control either one of them, no matter how much magic she knows. Either one of them will know a dozen ways to take the knife away from her and kill her with it."

"I'm not going to be stupid," I said. "I'll manacle both of them."

"How?"

I reached into the space inside me, and drew a single heavy manacle and two thick links of chain in my mind, and cast it around Gair's left wrist. I heard him gasp, and saw him raise his left arm to his face so that he could see the manacle in the almost nonexistent light. I said, "That's how."

"I could use a hundred like you," the commander said. "That was brilliantly done."

Gair had no such encouraging words, though. "You'll have them bound and blindfolded. And then what?"

I dissolved the manacle. "And then I will connect to them through the View and break the bonds that tie them to fleshmagery. And if I cannot do that, I will run a knife into each of them and heal them when the fleshmagery leaves them."

"And what if for some reason you cannot do that? What if your plan fails? What if they can control you and infect you?" He took my hand in his and held it so tightly my fingers throbbed. "What if you become one of them? What shall we do then? What shall I do?"

"You'll do what I suspect you're wanting to do right now," I said, and laughed. "You'll kill me, and set me free, and the healers will heal me, and that will be the end of it."

He didn't laugh. He said nothing else. He let my hand drop, and stepped a few steps away from me. I did not think for an instant that I had convinced him. I would never convince him, because he feared for me. I could only prove to him that I could succeed at this. And in the process of succeeding, I could crush some of the demons that still tormented me—my own helplessness under Skirmig's spell, the way that I had tossed into his face the key that let him hurt me and my people so deeply, my own stupidity at ever loving him. If I walked through the fire, I thought, it would burn me clean.

And so I went into the meeting hall in headquarters with an image in my head of what I had to do and how I would have to do it.

I would not carry a knife into the cage. I told the commander that I wanted crossbowmen with steel bolts standing at the ready to kill the fleshmage should I signal it, and that he should have the key in hand so that should I be unable to heal the fallen fleshmage on my own for some reason, there would be someone at hand who could cast the healing spells at the appropriate moment.

I had him bring the one man who had seen the making of a

fleshmage, and I had him tell me and everyone who gathered in the room the tale of what he had seen.

"If they get you, we'll know," he assured me. "The one what's taken fights something terrible before the spell goes all the way over him. Thrashing, screaming . . ." He stared at his shoes and bit his lip, and his hands clenched into knotted fists. "It was like watching my sister drown," he said. "She came up a couple times, screaming, but I couldn't reach her fast enough." And tears glinted on his cheeks. He brushed them away and breathed in and out a few times until he was steady again, and said, "That's why they have to get their victims in private, I reckon. So we'll know if they get you."

"They won't get me," I said. "But we'll have healers standing by for that, too, just in case." I turned to the commander. "Won't we?"

"They're already here. They're our best combat team—skilled with battle wounds, and not a one of them that hasn't done the spells they'll need for this at least ten times while under fire. All five have worked together at distance—and the rest of our on-duty Magics are in the View already and standing by."

The healers and I clasped hands, and the last of them said, "Good luck, and go with Ethebet's guidance and Jostfar's blessing."

"Thank you." I walked over to Gair, who wouldn't look at me. "Can you think of any other precaution I should take?" I asked.

He said, "Yes. Don't do this. How many other precautions could you need?"

I leaned in close and whispered, "I have to do this. I will never be whole again until I do. Until I beat Skirmig for what he has done—to them, to my people, to your people, and to me. We have to have this."

He looked at me at last, and all I could see in his eyes was pain. "And if I lose you?"

"You won't."

"You can't promise that."

"If you lose me, you'll bring me back."

"Only to lose you again someday." He breathed the words out again so softly I nearly missed them.

I turned away from him so that he could not see that I ached, too.

I could not help but feel the awful irony of it. At that moment, my people were nearly destroyed, my family was gone, the world that I had inhabited all of my life existed only in my memory and in a few little taaks that would sooner or later be overrun. If Gair and I fled out of Skirmig's reach, I could marry Gair and I would be losing nothing that I had not already lost. But I was fighting to restore the things that would keep me apart from Gair; my family, my people, my way of life. I was risking everything to re-create the world that would keep me from him, and he had been at my side all along, fighting and taking the risks with me.

If we were successful, our reward would be to lose each other.

"Have your own crossbow ready," I told him, my back to him. "If for some reason I fail and fleshmagery takes me, I trust you to send the bolt true and give the healers the best chance of bringing me back." I turned and faced him again.

He was shaking his head. "You cannot ask me to kill you."

"I'm not. I'm asking you to make sure that the bolt goes only through my heart, so that the healers will be able to bring me back. A gut shot, a head shot—there are things they cannot fix, or cannot fix well enough. If you have to, send it true, Gair."

I turned away again, because he did not need to see the shine of tears in my eyes, and I did not need to see whatever crossed his face.

I went to the commander. "I'm ready," I said.

I knew both men in the cages. Baaret had a fine, fat little wife and five young children; Tomis was a much-scarred veteran whose wife had died, but whose children loved him dearly and were not far from giving him his first grandbabes the last I had heard. Both had been Conventionals, both were good men, both were people that deserved freedom. And neither deserved to die.

I could not choose one to free and one to keep enslaved, and I would eventually have to risk both their lives. Tomis had the higher rank, so after agonizing, I chose him as the one I would free first. I cast the manacles around his wrists and ankles, attaching them so that he was forced to a standing position with his hands over his head and his feet spread wide. I wanted to give the crossbowmen the clearest shot should they have to step in.

I made sure the blindfold I cast affixed itself well over Tomis's eyes. Then the commander unlocked the gate and let me inside, and I heard the gate close again behind me, and heard the solid, heavy click of the lock sliding into place.

I did not want to be where I was. Who would? I knew that no matter what I had told Gair and the commander, I faced some risk. I thought it was small. I thought I had addressed it. But the unforeseen is part of every battle, from the largest to the smallest, and I had to wonder which part of this battle I had not foreseen.

I move over to Tomis's side, and touched him, and felt a little shiver run through his body. "Touch me some more," he said. "Why don't you bite me? Why don't you claw me?"

His voice was Skirmig's voice. Skirmig. I pulled my hand away, and he laughed. "You can still have me, my queen. I have saved a place for you at the head of my table, and have created the start of a kingdom that is worthy of you. Come and be with me."

Bile burned at the back of my throat, and Gair said, "Get out of there. Don't let him anywhere near you."

But I couldn't turn tail. No matter how frightened I was—and suddenly I was terrified—I was the best person to do what had to be done. If I could do it without risking Tomis's life, so much the better.

"You already have the knack of it," Tomis said in Skirmig's voice. "You've got the spells of fleshmagery. You controlled all those lovely metal creatures; you can make some of those for me someday, by the way. I thought them quite clever, and clearly useful."

"I'm getting rid of you, Skirmig," I said.

"You think so, do you? I'll be interested to see you try."

I put a hand on Tomis's arm again, and he licked his lips and laughed and said, "Oh, hurt me, beautiful. Make me scream. Make me squeal. You know you want to."

And Gair raised his crossbow and shot Tomis once through the heart. The bolt ripped through Tomis and out the other side and clattered into the stone wall behind the cage and bounced away and down to the floor.

"Damn you, Gair! I *had* this," I shouted, and put both hands on Tomis, who was still chuckling, and as the blood bubbled from his mouth, I moved into the togram of healing and watched Tomis's spirit through the lens of the Hagedwar. I did not let myself see the blood. Did not let myself be led astray by his physical appearance. I watched his spirit, and just before the moment that it separated from his flesh, I saw a gray cloud flee him.

I rejoiced. Skirmig cast him free when death was inevitable, but not when death had actually taken him. Knowing that, I could save any fleshmage we brought in, I thought. I healed the hole in his heart, and set it beating, and filled his veins with blood again.

I stepped away from Tomis, and he whipped his head back and forth, and for a moment he babbled like a madman until he finally slowed down enough that I could hear the individual words. "—he's gone, he's gone, that filth is out of my head, oh, Jostfar, I'm saved, I'm free, I'm blind but I don't care I'm free—"

Blind. I pulled the blindfold off of him, and his eyes went wide. "I'M NOT BLIND!" he shrieked so loudly that my ears rang.

I crouched and touched his ankles, and the leg irons dissolved in haze. I rose and stretched a hand up to the manacles above, and with a twist through the Hagedwar, willed the manacles away.

Tomis's legs sagged beneath him and his arms barely caught him as he dropped to the floor. He gripped the bars of the cage and wept, huge racking sobs.

I knelt beside him and put a hand on his shoulder, and made the same sort of crooning, wordless noises of comfort I would make with a panicked horse, and after a while he calmed down. Raised his head. Looked at me. "I'm safe now. But that perversion has my family," he said softly. "My friends. Your family. And he has your sister Nedris, though he's not made her one of the greddscharf. He keeps her as his concubine, and he calls her Talyn, and he locks her in a tower room away from the greddscharf and pretends she's you. Often he . . . makes the greddscharf watch what he . . . does to her."

All the air seemed to vanish from the room, and I fought to draw breath.

"No."

His eyes were angry. "The greddscharf-master is evil, Talyn.

Foul and filthy and soulless. He feeds on the greddscharf, and it has made him a demon, with the powers of a god in his hand." He looked down at the bloody hole in his padded tunic. "You cannot kill all the greddscharf and save them. There are too many, and faster than you can kill them, he can make more."

I stopped him. "What is the greddscharf?"

"One of his filthy Feegash words. It's the shared mind that he commands. On which he feeds. The chains in which he holds the thoughts of his prey."

I considered that and said, "It isn't our intent to kill all the fleshmages. We plan to kill Skirmig, and stop this disease at its source. You're to tell the Chaavtaaks everything you know about Skirmig, and about the fleshmages. And I'm going to see if there's a way to save the fleshmages without killing them first."

His gaze locked with mine. "I owe you thanks for saving me. Let me repay you by telling you—stop now. That monster wants you, Talyn, and he intends to have you back."

I knew this. I had known it all along.

The commander opened the cage door, and Tomis and I stepped out.

I stalked over to Gair, seething, and said, "Next time, no matter what Skirmig might say, don't shoot the fleshmage without my signal. I need to see if some manner exists by which we can save them without the risk of them dying, and we have only this last one on which to practice."

"We could have more," he said under his breath. "Do you *want* more, Talyn? Shall I go climb in the cage with the one that remains and let him infect me? Then you could practice on two of us. And maybe I'd get lucky and one of the bowmen could just shoot a hole through my heart. Because that's what it's like for me, listening to that bastard talking to you. And it doesn't matter if he's doing it by proxy, or if he is doing it in person."

"If you cannot help me, why don't you leave?" I snapped.

"If you cannot accept that I *was* helping you, maybe I should."

My cheeks burned and I couldn't think of anything to say that I wouldn't regret later, and model of prudence that I am, Saints know, I somehow nevertheless managed to keep my tongue in my head and turned back to the cage and stretched

Baaret in irons and covered his eyes with a blindfold and at the last minute put a gag in his mouth so that he would not say something to enrage Gair.

The commander was at my side, I realized, unlocking the door, and my hands were shaking.

Anger? Fear?

Maybe some of both.

"Watch for my signal," I said loudly, and showed them the hand gesture one more time.

The commander opened the door and I stepped into the cage.

I walked up to Baaret's side, making sure that I left a clear shot for the archers should I need one, and rested the palm of my hand on his rib cage.

I stood with eyes open, but I was looking inward, sliding into the togram of God's Will, and I pulled his spirit-self from the Edge into the togram with me. I could not see anything wrong with him; the clear hooks Skirmig had driven into me were not present in Baaret. He was no different to look at than he would have been in untouched form. The fleshmage spell didn't leave the same outer marks from the Edge, then, as whatever Skirmig had done to me.

I peered into the View, and quickly found him there, too—the physical connection between us made finding the spirit form simpler.

His spirit-form was neither particularly bright nor very active, but I would not have been able to tell it from the form of someone who was not a fleshmage. Baaret's spirit-self was quiet and withdrawn, round-edged and pulled in; I would have thought him simply sad if I hadn't known better.

He had no hooks that I could pull to free him. No lines that I could cut. The fleshmage contagion lay completely within him, self-contained, hidden. I could back out, signal to the bowmen to shoot him, and I could simply admit defeat—that there was no way other than killing a fleshmage to cure one.

But killing Skirmig might not end the fleshmage contagion in those who already had it. It would stop it from spreading, I was almost certain, but I had no reason to think that his death would set those already infected free. And I did not want to have to kill my parents, or my sisters, or my brothers to save them. I did not want to shoot a bolt into Rik's heart and watch him bleed his life away while I waited for the evil to let loose its grip on him.

So I steeled myself against whatever might await me: Skirmig's touch, some clutching madness, or maybe the emptiness of a house left to dust and echoes while the owner is away. And within the relative protection of the togram, I merged my spirit-form with Baaret's.

For a moment nothing was there. I thought I had perhaps failed to connect with him, though I could not imagine how. But then, gradually, I could feel my wrists in manacles, my ankles in leg irons, the taste of the gag in my mouth—unpleasantly soggy already, but coarse and vaguely sulfurish.

I did not relax. I knew I was in enemy territory, and the ambush could be waiting in any direction, and come at any time. I was disturbed, though, that Skirmig could so completely hide all signs of his presence, and erase all signs of Baaret, too. I did not understand fleshmagery, but even in hiding it left tracks that terrified me.

Then, however, I caught a little flash of conflict, something that felt like Baaret struggling to free himself. I had a direction. I had something I might be able to use, and I pursued it deeper, reaching out to give him something to hang on to. I was careful. I kept my exit clearly marked in my mind, and was ready to jump.

The struggling spark of light that was Baaret burst suddenly free of the calm, false surface of nothingness that held him and screamed, "Get *out*! HURRY!"

And an invisible dam broke, and from all sides incredible power poured in on me, battering me, calling to me to embrace, to give in, to become part of something greater than myself. The power that I could become caressed my skin and burrowed beneath it, and the pleasure and the pain and the delight and the horror all came at once, so thick and fast and overwhelming that all I could do was hold my breath and fight for the surface that I was sure still had to be there.

Greddscharf. It was not one man. It was one man-made ocean, deeper and broader than could be known, seeing and knowing everything that touched its borders or moved within its waters all at once, and in the instant that I comprehended how someone could give in to such complete power and lose self in the embrace of the vast deep, I also realized that it had me. That I was beneath the waters, and that I had just exhaled with no surface in sight.

I struggled to find my way out. I remember that well enough. I fought like a trapped wildcat for my freedom.

But the sea was too vast, and I was too small.

Talyn was standing there staring at nothing with a glassy expression that scared Gair nearly pissless. She breathed, and the fleshmage beside her breathed, but nothing else changed.

Beside him a man cleared his throat. Another scratched absently. He heard a woman cough, and the sound of people shifting from foot to foot, readjusting clothes, repositioning weapons.

She was in there with the bastard. With Skirmig, even though Skirmig's wasn't the body on which her hand rested. The bastard was there, waiting for his chance to grab her and hurt her again, and Gair's finger tightened instinctively on the trigger of his crossbow.

He forced his hand to relax. He forced himself to trust that a woman who could do with magic the things that Talyn could do was not some poor lamb in a pen waiting for the slaughter. She had weapons at her disposal—more weapons than her enemy. She was hampered in some ways; he knew there were things she could do but simply would not. And things she might do under extreme duress that would haunt her for the rest of her life.

But she was not helpless, he reminded himself. She was capable.

Still, sweat dripped from his forehead and down the tip of his nose, and beaded on his upper lip, and crawled like some live thing between his shoulder blades and down the small of his back.

And still she stood. She blinked occasionally. She breathed.

The people around him fidgeted, and he wondered if somehow there had been no warning, and the bastard had her in his grip already and he and everyone around him was watching her die.

And then her breath caught—a tiny gasp that locked everyone into position. Her eyes snapped shut, and her mouth closed tight, and he realized that she was holding her breath. She was . . . somewhere else. Somewhere that he couldn't go. He sighted down the barrel of the crossbow on the heart of the fleshmage, and put as much pressure on the trigger as he could without actually shooting the bolt.

His knees felt weak. His gut knotted as if he'd had a bad meal.

Suddenly Talyn screamed and pushed away from the fleshmage, clawing at something invisible. Gair did not hesitate; he put a hole in the fleshmage, praying that if he did so he would break the connection between Talyn and whatever she fought.

The healers ran for the gate, but the commander stopped them. Talyn was still fighting. The fleshmage was slumped in his shackles, gouting blood, but she was still fighting.

And the commander said, "Her, too. It has her."

And no one pulled a trigger.

She was a hero. She had saved them, and they could not kill her knowing they might not get her back.

Gair said, "Don't you let her die."

And as she stilled, and turned, and smiled at him, and said in a voice that ripped his heart out, "Too late. She belongs to me, and I have taken what's mine," and as she lifted a hand to point at him, he loaded a second bolt. And as she said, "I'm sending you to your warrior's table today," he sighted on her chest, and she sent fire shooting at him, and he pulled the trigger and the bolt ripped through her heart and her eyes went wide and she fell.

The fire singed him as it dissipated, took his knees out from under him, sent him crashing to the floor. The bastard had missed him. But not by much.

Gair scrambled to his feet and ran for the cage; the commander was unlocking the gate and throwing open the lock, and two healers rushed to the man in the shackles, and the other three dragged Talyn out of the cage and crowded around her as she lay on the floor.

She twitched, and then breathed out and did not breathe in again; her eyes stared up sightlessly.

Gair threw the crossbow to the stone floor of the great hall in helpless rage, and the wood shattered and the bowstring whipped out and lashed across his leg, cutting through boots and pants and skin. It hurt like the devil, but he barely noticed. He hung on to the bars of the cage she'd been in, watching the healers touching her, listening to them fighting to save her— "Fixing the hole in the heart," one said, and a moment later, "Restarting the beating," the next said, and at the same time the other two said, "Replacing lost blood."

And Gair waited for Talyn to open her eyes and smile at him and tell him that she was back.

But she did not.

"We've lost the man," one of the two healers working on the shackled fleshmage said suddenly. "We were too late getting to him."

"Then get over here and help us," one of Talyn's healers snapped, "because we're losing her, and we shouldn't be. We've done everything right, but she won't . . . come back."

The other two healers ran over and dropped to the ground beside her.

"Checking the heart for leaks or damage."

"The amount of blood in the veins seems too small."

"You need to be forcing air into her lungs. Don't waste magic on that—just hold her nose and breath into her mouth."

"I'm having a hard time holding on to the link with the healers' ring," one of the healers said suddenly. "It's almost like . . . she's interfering."

"Like she doesn't want to live and is fighting us."

Gair shoved his way to a place by her head, and leaned down and whispered in her ear, "Live, damn you. You're going to marry me and we're going to spend the rest of our lives together, and we didn't come this far so that you could die."

He was swallowing tears, forcing words past a burning lump in his throat, trying to will her to want to live.

"I love you," he said. "I love you, Talyn." He closed his eyes, searching her fading memories for the thing that would bring her back. "Rik needs you," he said. "Without you, we aren't going to beat Skirmig. And . . . whatever happened to you, and wherever you were, he's still there."

* * *

I stood on the broad, flowered plain that I had seen before. I was alone. No horses, no children playing, no woman in white. The sky was so blue it almost hurt my eyes, and the sound of the wind rushing by me felt almost like the lullaby my mother sang to me when I was just a babe in arms. I could remember that—remember her holding me close while she fed me, stroking my head, singing to me. I was safe. I was safe.

And now I was safe again. The pain was gone, the horror was gone, the desperation was gone.

I had shed it and it did not hurt me anymore.

I could remember hurting, though.

"You have suffered greatly," a voice said behind me, and I turned and faced a nomad woman, taller even than I, with hair red as fire and eyes green as deep winter ice.

I knew her, and dropped to my knees and pressed my face to the ground. "Ethebet."

She reached down and took my hand and pulled me back to my feet.

"You have suffered much, my daughter. But I still need you."

"There are so many others, Ethebet. And I am so weary. The horrors of the place in which I was trapped reach out for me even here, and I am too afraid to face them again. I'm not big enough, or strong enough."

"I gave you my sword," Ethebet said. "I did not give him to you so that you could throw him away."

"He's not Tonk," I said, and immediately wished that somewhere between life and death I'd learned to be a bit more careful with my words.

Ethebet raised an eyebrow and a tiny smile touched her lips. She answered my thought, though, not my words. "This is not death, daughter. This is simply a place where you and I can talk for a moment without interruption. I'll let you see death. But not yet."

"Ignore what I say," I told her. "Pretend I was a sane woman with manners, and just don't hear the words that come out of my mouth."

But she laughed and shook her head. "He isn't Tonk. He isn't even the best sword I have. But he is the best sword for you, and for all that you have yet to face. Realize that right now he is with allies, but they are his allies because of you. Without you, they will once again be his enemies, and there is no one else who will see in him what you saw, or who will fight to save him. Without you, he will be lost. And without the two of you, the war will be lost. The foul disease that touched you will swallow the whole of the world, and the power the monster at its head wields will be so great that no one will ever be free of it again. Everything you love will die, not just in this age, but until all of mankind is erased. And that will happen not at the end of eons, but in a span of days you yourself might expect to see."

I stared at her. "There will be no more people?"

"We were not born to be slaves," she said. "Jostfar did not create us to be bound hand and foot and thoughts. In the cage that monster has cast, there is no room for breath or life. If he prevails, this generation of mankind will be the last."

I sagged. "I don't have the courage to go back."

She looked sad.

"I'll let you taste of death, and wait a little while you drink," she said. "Be quick, though, and careful that you do not drink too deep."

And the field of flowers vanished, and the warm breeze went away.

I had no form. I hung in nothingness, twisting against forces that pulled at me from all sides. Pain ripped at me; I was not whole, I could not move, and though I could see before me the light of eternity, and feel behind me the weight of mortality, yet I could not reach either. I hung all alone in a place of great fear and agony. I wanted to name my formless, placeless, companionless suffering one of the many hells of the moriiad, but I could feel familiar threads in the pain, and as I followed them back, I discovered that my hell was one of my own making. I had shredded my own soul, and parts of it waited in three running towers, and part of it hung around the neck of a beast.

I tried to call those bits to myself, to break them out of my handiwork. But they were where they were, and if I died, I was where I would be until that handiwork was no more.

I would not walk in Jostfar's fields, or see the magnificent horses running in his many pastures. I would never meet again with those I loved who had gone on into death. My eternity would be nothingness and tearing pain.

"Ethebet!" I screamed, but nothingness swallowed me up.
Had I waited too long?
"ETHEBET! JOSTFAR!"

The healers stared at each other. "No good," one said, and Gair turned on her in a fury: "You cannot give up. You cannot. We will not beat Skirmig without Talyn; she alone knows both his magic and hers and can destroy the key that gives him his power."

The healer said, "And what would you have us do? Pound on Jostfar's door and demand that he set her free?"

Gair rested his forehead against Talyn's, and despair filled him. "You tell me where Jostfar's door is, and I'll go break the thing down to get her, if that's what I must do."

No one said anything, and Gair grabbed her hand and begged her, "Live, Talyn. Don't give up."

He closed his eyes as the tears built up, and felt them leaking from the corners anyway.

Everything was lost. And she was lost. And for nothing. He couldn't even be angry at her for the senselessness of it; he could understand why she'd done what she did. But he had feared for her life, and now when he least wanted to be, he was proven right.

He felt a hand on his back, and realized that he was sobbing, and remembered that other people were present; he didn't care.

Gone. She was gone.

"There is nothing else we can do," one of the healers said. "Let them take her away."

"I can mourn her," he said, and did not move.

And heard a gasp.

Felt the fingers he clasped in his hand suddenly clasp back.

He sat upright as Talyn reached up and grabbed his shirt and clung to him.

She screamed, "Ethebet!" once, and he pulled her into his arms, unable to believe she was with him, and heard her whispering, "I'm back, I'm back, I have another chance."

"You're back," he said.

Around them, pandemonium broke out.

The Tonks cheered and screamed and hugged each other and pounded Gair on the back and crowded around the two of them. Gair pulled Talyn closer. He could say nothing to her; he could not have shouted loud enough for her to hear him over the noise in the room.

She was not lost. Hope was not lost.

But he wished he could be with her alone, just the two of them. He had things he needed to tell her.

One instant I was in a hell of my own making, the next, in pain of a different sort. I had no transition, no easing into change. I was screaming Ethebet's name and no one was listening, and then I screamed once more with everything in me and felt the words tear at my throat, and heard them hit my ears.

Fingers twined through mine, squeezing my hand so hard the bones hurt; I opened my eyes and Gair was there.

And I was back.

I clung to him while around us the Chaavtaak warriors cheered my return, but Gair and I had things to talk about, and when I was finally steady enough on my feet and the noise had died down, I told the commander I was exhausted, and asked that I be dismissed to quarters with Gair to accompany me— that I needed to sleep and get something to eat before I would be of much further use to him.

He dismissed both of us, and we walked in silence the short distance back to the White Fox, and made our way upstairs with no one paying us the least attention—so news of what had happened, and almost happened, in the great hall across the way had not yet spread.

"I'll take the quiet when we can get it," Gair said. He stopped long enough to give one of the serving girls orders for two hefty meals to be brought to our room, and we made our way up the stairs.

My uniform was blood-soaked and had a hole in it. I grabbed another from supplies, and took a quick shower, and by the time I was done, with Gair standing by, braced as if he expected to have to catch me at any moment, our food had arrived.

We had said almost nothing through this, and we ate in awkward silence, too.

I knew for myself that I had so many things I wanted to tell him, but I did not know where to begin. The silence that grew longer and more uncomfortable with every instant did not help me start, though.

Our meal was roast fowl off the bone—I would have guessed pheasant by the flavor, but the spices and sauces the Chaavtaakers used were different than Beyltaakers used for fowl, and without the bones, I was hard-put to guess with confidence. The cook had mashed and spiced and gravied the potatoes, and they weren't unpalatable. He'd boiled the greens though, until they lay limp and raglike on the plate.

I didn't waste much time on the greens.

I pushed my plate back when I was done with it, and turned to Gair.

He'd already finished.

We sat there staring at each other like two fools, until he blurted out, "We need to talk," and I said, "I have to tell you something," at the same time.

He laughed a little. "You first."

"I'll wait," I said. "I could use another moment or two to organize my thoughts."

"You were right," he told me. "We have no assurance that either of us will survive this, and I love you, and you love me. You do love me, don't you?"

"Yes."

"I discovered that I'll hurt no more when eventually you have to leave me than I hurt today when I thought I had already lost you."

I watched him, suspecting that I knew where he was going, lacking the courage to tell him to stop.

He said, "If the only way I can have you is for a while, I'll take that."

I rested a hand on his thigh and did not allow myself to think about what I would be losing, but only about what I would be gaining. "I'm not going to be able to give you up. Not in a year, not in a hundred. Not ever." I leaned forward and kissed him lightly on the nose. "You were right, too."

"You're saying . . . that you'll marry me?"

"Yes."

He pulled me into his arms and kissed me, and said, "But I

can't ask you to. I cannot let you give up your family and your people."

He was going to make this difficult. Of course. Making things difficult defined the man.

I kissed him. "Just agree with me. It will go easier this way."

He laughed. His smile was stubborn, but he kissed me back, and shoved the meal cart away from the bed.

I would not let myself be afraid. He was not Skirmig. He was not looking to see fear in my eyes, nor was he excited by visions of pain or blood. I could trust him, I told myself. I could trust him.

He slid my tunic and underblouse up and touched my breasts, and I sighed. He kissed my lips, my eyelids, my cheeks, my neck; I squirmed gracelessly out of both shirts, and he laughed a little.

"I wanted to do that."

At his words, at his laugh, I had a hard, cold flash of Skirmig ripping clothes off of me, and the memory must have sparked fear in my eyes.

Instantly, Gair stopped. "I won't hurt you," he said. "I won't hurt you." He held me close and swore softly. I couldn't make out most of what he said, but I could hear him promising to have Skirmig's hide.

I gathered my courage, such as it was, and began to undress him, kissing and touching. I was more determined than excited; honestly, at first all I could think was that I had to get through this. I was trying desperately to find that ardor and hunger I'd felt that day beneath the wrecked cabin, lying in the tall grass.

But Skirmig had been inside my mind so recently, and all the horrors he'd committed burned fresh in my soul and my memory, and I had walked with Death, and in truth, I had more need than passion in me at that moment.

Gair was careful after my brief show of panic. He kept himself in tight check, however eager he might have been. He took his time with me, touching me gently, caressing me, stroking me, stopping any time he sensed panic in me. Nothing he did hurt. I could feel his strength—in his arms, his thighs, his muscled back and hard belly—and he could have been too much for me, had he not been so cautious, so willing to let me lead.

I had thought myself over the worst of what Skirmig had

done to me until those long, anxious, tentative moments with Gair; I had thought I'd handled what had happened to me far better than I'd handled my battle injuries that had taken from me any chance of motherhood or a normal life.

I was wrong. I trembled at each new touch, and several times had to fight back tears of rage at my own cowardice. I was safe with Gair, and I knew it, and still I feared.

When at last he entered me—at my urging—and we began the slow dance of ages, a dam broke within me and I had to pull his chest down hard on mine and hide my face in the curve of his neck so that he could not see the tears that streamed from my eyes. My fear nearly swallowed me. Gair was pleasure I could not have imagined—we were a perfect fit. Still, all my guilt for having fallen for Skirmig's lies, for having been fooled by him, all my dread that the monster would yet find me and catch me and take me back as he intended to do, clung to me so tightly that it was all I could do to focus on where I was, on who held me.

Gair whispered comfort, murmured reassurances, waited when it got to be too much for me. At last I managed to relax enough to let go.

Gair and I, connected to each other in our dreams for so long, connected in the flesh at last, and we were clear, pure, cleansing water. I felt his touch, body and soul. Knew that he was with me completely, as I was with him—that between us we were life itself—storm and thunder and rain and the washing away of poison and hatred and pain, and the renewal of the earth.

I knew love. Real love. In Gair's hands, in his eyes, in his lips, in the strength of his arms that held me and in the controlled power with which he filled me, I came home at last to the one place in the world I could not live without. The scars on my heart and soul might still be there, and might never completely leave me, but I wouldn't have to fight them alone. Gair was with me. He was where my heart belonged.

Finally I understood how my mother could leave her taak forever and live in a place where she was not a citizen, where she had no voice except through my father. How she could leave her parents and sibs and the world she had known. Finally I could see and understand, rather than envy, the magic she had found with my father, and I could no longer think her half mad for having done what she had done.

For each of us, I think, one person exists for whom we would change our whole world, though we never believe this until we discover ourselves ready to make that previously unthinkable change. Someone for whom we would leave everything we own, for whom we would travel to foreign lands and suffer foreign ways and foreign climes willingly, because when we discover that one someone, our home is no longer a thing with walls of stone and windows of glass. That one person becomes our home, and where he goes, there too is everything we value. Ma told me this, and I never believed her, thinking it a fancy she held to so that she did not have to ache for all she had lost and left behind.

But as usual, she was right.

Afterward, as we lay in each other's arms, Gair was solicitous, anxious that he had hurt me, seeking reassurance that I was all right; I could not quite convince him that my tears were not because he had done something wrong. I fumbled to explain—the fear and the storm and home being in the heart—but I hadn't the words to do justice to the light that glowed inside me. But he caught the gist of it, and kissed my forehead and swore that he would never let Skirmig hurt me again.

We curled together in the bed, spooned close, and twice woke from sleep to find pleasure in each other's touch. Each time was better than the time before; each time I was less afraid, though I could not say in truth that the fear left me completely. Each time I drifted into sleep, Skirmig watched me, smiling through nightmares that haunted me, but I kept the nightmares to myself.

25

Gair and I spent all of the next morning and as much of the afternoon as we could spare together in seclusion. Our story was that we were resting, but in truth we got little enough rest. Neither of us mentioned the possibility of death, but it hung above us constantly, a cold, watchful specter that lent increasing desperation to our embraces as the day wore on. I loved him, and he loved me, and all I could think was that we should have had whole lives ahead of us, filled with children and grandchildren and aunts and uncles and cousins who lived in the busy, noisy movable feast that is Tonk life.

And instead we had a future that would never have anyone in it but the two of us and that might well stretch out before us no further than a day.

I had just found him—or at least I had finally found what an amazing gift Ethebet had given me when she gave him to me. And the two of us might not have another day.

Desperation.

Magic exists for lovers beyond pogging for amusement and beyond raw animal sex, and far beyond the twisted, sick pursuit of pleasure through pain. A single moment births it not in the flesh but in the soul, with a flash of recognition exchanged in glances between two strangers. The moment creeps into dreams, and the dreams touch waking, and the strangers, if they meet again, might grow slowly toward friendship, and to the love born of friendship, nurtured over time, rooted deep and grown strong against the storms that will come. I had known a pale promise of that love with Adjii, who died before we could become what we might have been. It had never come near me with anyone else. I had found it at last with Gair. I, who had believed that because of my barrenness it was my lot to be a moment of interesting memory for a long line of men on their way to the women they could love and keep.

I held Gair—I clung to him. I had found the love that would weather a lifetime of storms just in time to face the storm that could end our lives, and I wanted forever with him.

I wanted so much to run away—to flee north past Beyltaak to the Brittlebreak Straits, to sail away to Pindas or Cartajarma—or maybe even along the Path of Stars to the Islands of Fallen Sun. I had never yearned for the sights of distant lands, for lovely names and exotic places. I had always been content with my taak, my people, my world. And I cannot say that I yearned for strange lands and strangers at that moment, either. I hungered more for a safe hiding place far from Skirmig and his spreading poison.

I discovered that I had within me the makings of a committed coward, and that if I did not move forward quickly to do what I knew I had to do, that coward was going to give me even more reasons to hide myself and my love away.

Ethebet had said that without me the world would fall. That without *both* Gair and me, this generation of humanity would be the last. That Skirmig's poison would spread beyond Hyre, across all the seas, that it would devour all of mankind in this age.

There was no place to hide, and no time to hesitate.

We would be heading back into Skirmig's reach, into his domain, and we had no guarantees. Everything could end badly. We could lose—and I was under no illusions; if we lost, everyone lost. That damned silver dancer that I had thought so unimportant would survive even if I died, and would bind me forever in hell, and would give Skirmig the whole world.

Meanwhile, Gair and I could fail in a thousand different ways, but we could succeed in only one. We had so little chance of success, so great a chance of dying or falling into Skirmig's hellish greddscharf.

It could all end. But if this was my last living day—if the rest of my eternity would be spent in hell, forever within sight of the heaven I could not have—I had one thing I had to do. I had one promise I had to keep.

"We need to go to temple," I told Gair.

"I'm not Tonk. I can't go in there."

"You can. The Keepers hold Ethebet's doors open to all who would enter, and offer her wisdom and her courage and her teachings to any who would accept them. You cannot be Tonk, and you cannot belong to Jostfar, but you can still go to temple. Hurry, though—the hour grows late, and you and I have much to do before nightfall."

We showered and dressed, and I helped Gair get his warrior's braid right. "And in the front, a sacrifice braid," I told him.

"I'm not Tonk. What kind of heresy would it be for me to sacrifice at Ethebet's shrine?"

"No less than sacrificing before your army," I told him, and grinned, and watched him blush. "You've already been a bad boy, and Ethebet still seems to think quite highly of you. She chose you," I said, braiding my own hair. "She calls you my sword. If she chose you, she will hear your prayers and promises and bless your sacrifice."

We went without eating—we had daylight left yet, and would not move toward Beyltaak until we could do so under cover of night, and I did not want to break the tradition of fasting before prayer. Chaavtaak had a number of temples, of course, but Ethebet's was nearest—had it not been, I would have hunted it down. Still, I was grateful that it was close at hand.

Warriors sat at tables throughout the temple, reading and studying. Ethebet's shrine had three permanent altars set up, suggesting she had been doing a steady business since the arrival of the Feegash to the shores of Hyre. One station was in use.

The two of us bought prayer supplies from one of the Keepers, and we went to one of the stations together.

I described to Gair how I would do the offering, and how he would do it if he chose to; then, facing Ethebet's ikrii, seeing the woman I'd met in the realm of death overlaid on the stylized painting, I said my prayer.

"Ethebet, through your gift and blessing I have my sword, Gair Farhallan, and with him I ride into battle this night. Jostfar, I offer myself as your tool, for the preservation of my people, and ask your hand in our victory, and such protection and guidance as you will give over both of us. And in what I next must do, I swear that I will never renounce either you or Ethebet, though all I cherish may be stripped from me."

I took a deep breath and tried to steady my hands, which were suddenly shaking.

"By my oath and bond, before Jostfar and Ethebet and in both of their names, I swear my life to Gair Farhallan, forsaking all others, from this moment until my death. Nor do I take this oath lightly; I understand in full its meaning and its consequences. Jostfar, I ask your blessing on this my oath, and Ethebet, I ask your blessing on this my oath—and if my actions have angered you, I ask your forgiveness."

I yanked out my sacrifice braid, hissing at the pain, and threw it into the bowl, but did not yet light the fire.

I turned to Gair, from whose face all color had drained. "You just . . . married me?" he asked.

"I gave you my word that I would. And we may not have another chance. We could both be dead by morning."

He stood there staring at me. "Is that it, then? We're married?"

"No. I'm married to you, in the most binding fashion." I smiled a little. "If you change your mind, I have just sworn myself to celibacy for the rest of my life." I shrugged. "Without you, I'd as soon do that anyway."

He hugged me, and his voice was gruff as he said, "I'm not going to change my mind. You're mad, I think. But I can't see why that should stop me marrying you."

He took his place before the bowl. "Are there words I have to say?"

"No. Say only what you mean. Then make your offering, and when you're done, we'll light the fire together."

"We don't have to have witnesses?"

"Jostfar and Ethebet are our witnesses. If they cannot be trusted to hold us to our oaths, what purpose would a human witness serve?"

He nodded, and one eyebrow arched. "Truly," he said. And took a slow breath, and began his prayer.

"Jostfar, Ethebet . . . I'm not one of yours, and I'm sorry for that. Nevertheless, I swear my life to Talyn Wyran av Tiirsha dryn Straad, body and soul, forsaking all others now and forever, knowing I have found in her the one woman I have spent my life seeking."

He stilled, and yanked his sacrifice braid out, making not the slightest sound as he did so, and tossed his braid into the bowl.

"And if you would, give into my hand the monster Skirmig, that I might honor both of you, and Talyn as well, by slaying him. And forgive my presumption for being here and not being Tonk."

I had never heard vows like Gair's, nor, clearly, had the warriors who had stopped their reading to listen to us. I felt them watching as we lit two incense sticks from our altar's flame, and lit our sacrifices with them. The acrid smoke of burning hair and the sweet smoke of incense coiled around us, and we stepped into a close embrace, and kissed. And heard around us a smattering of applause, which considering our circumstance I would not have thought to hear—these were Ethebet's own around us, not just Tonks but warriors who had fought against the Eastils. And they knew Gair was Eastil.

And they did not wish me ill?

But they could afford to be broad about it, couldn't they? I wasn't bringing shame to their taak, after all. I was someone else's embarrassment.

Gair seemed neither surprised nor bothered by the applause. He grinned at the warriors present, gave me a second kiss—with flourishes—and then whispered in my ear, "The Eastils—well, *some* of the Eastils—have a tradition for the wedding night . . . bedding the bride. Might I hope the Tonks have the same tradition?"

I looked at him sidelong. "You already bedded the bride. Quite a few times," I whispered back, and started tugging him toward the door. "For our wedding night we get to go hunting monsters. But we've only a little light left, and we have much to do if we're to start off at first dark."

We did not waste time getting what we needed to travel back to Beyltaak. Most of it we already had.

We ate to keep our strength up. We took such weapons as we thought might be useful. I did not want to use the Hagedwar again until I could be sure Skirmig was dead, though I knew I might have to; it was a link we shared and one he would surely try to use against me. I had planned to get information on Skirmig from either of his two fleshmages, but my own brief journey through fleshmagery to death and back had given me everything they knew. The greddscharf—the shared mind of fleshmagery—was a twisted hell of insatiable hunger for pain, perversion, torture, and shame, driven and guided by Skirmig's lusts and obsessions. In the short time I'd spent as part of it, I'd seen myself as the greddscharf had seen me. And I'd seen my sister as she was at that moment.

And I had seen Skirmig through the countless eyes of his slaves, sharing in that brief moment everything every other one of the fleshmages had experienced and were experiencing up to the instant that Gair killed me and the healers brought me back. The greddscharf didn't know what Skirmig knew; he could hide his thoughts quite well from his slaves. But his actions took place in full view of all.

Skirmig had stayed in Beyltaak, and had taken up residence in the Beyl's fortress. He was keeping my sister Nedris in the concubine quarters, which were reachable by the secret concubine's gate; concubinage had long fallen out of favor with all but nomadic clanlords, and with a handful of taaklords, but *they* had ever acted as if they had their own version of Preference Law, one which far exceeds Ethebet's. So long as the lords represented their taaks and clans well and did not actually cause anyone physical harm, most pretended not to notice.

Their secrets were secrets only in the politest sense. The greddscharf knew the location of the concubine gate. They simply could not pass through it, since Skirmig had barred it with barriers both physical and magical. We would have no problem with either.

From my time within the greddscharf, I'd discovered something else as well. Skirmig, who had been able to keep iron control over his fleshmages when he used only a few of them and used none of the limitless power of the outer tograms to control them, had discovered long teeth on his new horse, as the saying goes. As his empire of slaves expanded, his control over individual slaves was lessening. He drew power from the greddscharf in proportion to its numbers—so as the greddscharf expanded, he grew steadily more powerful. But the fleshmages also drew power from those they recruited. This I had to guess was something that he had not known would happen, since before I foolishly tossed him the magic that gave him unlimited power, he'd had to recruit all of his fleshmages on his own, and control them even as he drained their life-energy from them. With the energy of the View flowing through the whole of the greddscharf, his use of the fleshmages no longer sucked the life out of them, so they did not weaken and die. Instead, the hunger of the greddscharf compelled them to search for fresh meat— untainted life among the unrecruited. The fleshmages who recruited slaves of their own were developing a degree of independence as those they had recruited began to recruit; they were gathering power that let them act against Skirmig at times, and though they could not break away from him, neither could he destroy them without breaking the bonds that tied all their recruits to him. He could not stop his fleshmages from recruiting, either—their hungers drove them to hunt for new sources of the life-energy that fed them. They hunted, they grew stronger, and they moved to some degree beyond his reach.

Skirmig was both horrifically powerful and trapped by the source of his power. In some ways he was like a queen ant fed and pampered by her hordes of devoted slaves, kept too bloated to escape to freedom.

Were it not my people on whom he fed, I could almost have found his situation funny.

But they *were* my people. And Skirmig had used them to grow powerful beyond all reason since he and I had last crossed paths, and Gair and I were going to have to fight him. And win. I'd not been able to win against him when he was weaker. I *might* have grown stronger since that last awful encounter. But he certainly had.

I couldn't find my way to laughter from any part of that.

The fact that he kept his fleshmages out of the concubine wing with both magic and physical barriers meant only that we were heading into a situation where our enemy could not control his own army anymore, and where it worked against him at times, but would never work for us. We could not hope for the aid of sympathizers—the poison with which he had infected the fleshmages drove them only to more frenzied feeding, and though he did not want them "converting" my sister, his rogue fleshmages would not benefit us.

Our one advantage as I saw it was that Skirmig's growing fear of his rogue fleshmages meant Gair and I would have a clear path to Nedris once we got inside the concubine gates. We would have to go through the tunnels beneath the taak and run to the Beyl House entrances, and that I did not expect to be an easy path. From there, we would have to uncover the hidden, locked, and spelled concubine gate, but I had faith that I would find it, and that Gair and I would be able to open it.

I would figure out how as I went, if necessary.

Then the run through the concubine passage, which I hoped would be simple enough. We would rescue Nedris. Skirmig would come to us then, I guessed, either to protect his property or to reclaim me as property; we could then fight him, if only we could figure out how.

We took our leave of the commander, and Pada, who offered a hug to each of us and whispered, "How could you of all people have married? But I suppose that you're damaged doesn't count if you marry an Eastil. Still, congratulations, and good luck to both of you," in my ear.

We refused offers of allies to travel with us—Gair and I already knew we had to go alone; we could watch each other's backs, but the more people who came with us, the more risk we faced of at least one of us falling to the fleshmages and destroying the rest.

Gair and I were confident that we could keep each other safe. We had only two goals. Get Nedris away from Skirmig so that he could not use her as a hostage, and then kill Skirmig. It was a simple enough plan. It required not massive force, but stealth and guile. More people, for us, would be less.

I studied the two spare running towers. I wanted to leave them behind, to leave the people of Chaavtaak with something solid that they could depend on. But I dreaded irony. I could imagine Gair and me winning our way through to Skirmig, and beating him, and me destroying the little silver dancer—and then me dying from some unexpected complication in the process. And being tied in hell not by the silver dancer I had so foolishly tossed away, but by the running towers I had left behind out of an excess of good intentions.

I had meant to leave them. I had told the commander that I would leave them. But I was too afraid, finally, to do what I had said I would do. My cowardice shamed me, but I had been in the hell between life and death, and my fear was far stronger than my shame. I had a second, deeper fear. If I did not destroy them, the Hagedwar I carried inside of me would not—*could* not—close. And I dreaded that Skirmig might find a way to make use of it, even without the silver dancer. That, having learned the path to my soul, he would be able to find it even if I took his map, and would still be able to hang on. He'd had his hooks in me for far, far too long.

I walked to the nearest of the running towers, touched it, and willed it to dissolve into nothing. Behind me, the commander cried out and came running toward me.

"Why?" he shouted.

I turned to face him. "I have to," I told him. "Their existence could be the difference between us winning this and losing it. They're a part of the magic that binds me to the monster. I can't leave them." I walked to the other one I had planned to leave behind, and destroyed it, too. "Don't let anyone in or out," I told him. "If we win this, we'll . . . send up a signal. Something you won't miss."

"If you win this, we'll have our own ways of knowing," he said. "Likewise if you lose."

I accepted that. No doubt we had our own spies within Chaavtaak—currently damned glad they'd been in Chaavtaak when all of this happened rather than back home. Chaavtaak would assuredly have a few spies within Beyltaak. If they had lived, if we won, if winning freed the fleshmages rather than killing them . . . So many ifs. But *if*, then they would find a way to get word back to Chaavtaak.

And *if* was the question we all faced. The answer to that question was *probably not*.

Darkness came too quickly.

Gair and Talyn stood at the base of the remaining running tower. Many of Chaavtaak's soldiers had come out to see them off. The crowd kept mostly silent, except for pats on the back and encouraging words as he and Talyn passed among them; no one could see the two of them going off to face Skirmig and everything that Skirmig could bring to bear against the two of them and make much of a brave face of it. The Chaavtaakers tried. Gods knew, they tried. And if anyone had been able to suggest a way of getting to Skirmig and crushing him that had taken the whole of the Chaavtaak Forces, Gair believed the Chaavtaakers would have taken it without hesitation.

But Ethebet had melded Gair and Talyn into a single unit, bound together by magic and dream and a thousand not-yet-faded memories; she had given them each other and the tools to protect each other, and had set them a task that no one else could do. They might yet fail. But no one else could hope to succeed.

All men had such tasks, Gair realized—to each human born, the gods gave a destiny, and free will either to fulfill it or turn away. No man could live another man's life—or at least, could not live it as it was meant to be lived. No man could embrace another man's destiny. Each man could only take up the burden of his own, and seek it with all his courage and hope.

For the defense of this single truth Gair and Talyn were going to war. For the bastard—the monster—fought to subsume all destinies and all free will and to live every man's life, and every woman's, and every child's as his own. All the world his slave, all eyes his eyes, all voices his voice.

Gair took Talyn's hand as they moved toward the last running tower. He squeezed it, and she squeezed back. Theirs was a war worth fighting, and theirs a cause worth dying for. Better to live if they could, better to win if they could. Better to triumph. But if all they could do was give their all against the darkness, at least they had not watched the darkness devour their world as cowards, hiding in a corner to preserve their own worthless skins.

Gair watched the soldiers swarming around them, clapping them on the back and wishing them luck and sending them off with the blessings of Jostfar and Ethebet, and the soldiers stood out to his eyes in sharp relief; Gair felt suddenly as if he stood in a pool of silence in their midst. Torchlight cast hard shadows along the planes and projections of their faces, making them seem not men at all, but fantastic creatures of fancy and nightmare. Destiny. Theirs still waited, but if he and Talyn failed, they would never have the chance to reach them.

Gair felt the bond that tied him to Talyn pulling the two of them toward *their* destiny.

The stairway dropped down from the center of the running tower, and Talyn climbed up into the gleaming silver beast first, and Gair paused, feeling destiny heavy on his shoulders, tasting the first step of this last fray against the enemy they would conquer either now, or never.

He took the step, and the next one after it. Climbed into the running tower. Talyn crouched on the floor, hands splayed flat against it, eyes closed, whispering. Gair did not disturb her. He just waited, thinking that she was beautiful, and that she was his, and that she had deserved so much better than what life had given her. And that the two of them could run away someplace far, far away, where no one would ever find them, and live out their lives together in solitude.

And guilt.

A man of honor faced his destiny; he didn't run away from it.

She opened her eyes and looked up at him. " 'Don't see me' spell," she said. "I took a chance on the Hagedwar just this once. It covers you and me and the running tower."

He offered her a hand and pulled her to her feet. And kissed her. "Good idea. I suppose we cannot delay this any longer then."

Her smile was tiny, mischievous, there for just the blink of an eye and then gone. "I've thought of all sorts of ways we can delay this. Just none that we should." She gave him a hard squeeze. "Are you riding first or am I?"

"I'll take the first run. Sleep a bit, and when you wake, you can take us in as far as the outermost tunnels. From there we'll have to go on foot."

"I wish we didn't. I don't like the idea of being exposed."

"Nor do I," he agreed. "We'll be careful."

26

"Wake up," Gair said, and I opened my eyes. My head was on a bedroll, the floor of the running tower was hard and cold beneath me, and I did not feel I'd had any rest at all.

"How long was I asleep?" I asked him.

He shrugged. "Perhaps half an hour."

"Problems?" I sat up, rubbing my eyes. I'd hoped to get a couple of hours of sleep at least, and to be able to give Gair the same.

"Not really. We're there."

I couldn't believe my ears. "There . . . where?"

"Not too far from the Magics cave we can use as our entrance. Providing the bastard has left no traps for us there."

"How is that possible?" I stood and peered through the windows out into the darkness, thinking that certainly Gair has mistaken one roll of ground for another. But we were perched just behind a ridge with enough clearance that the front windows of the running tower looked down on Beyltaak. I could see the bay. I could see the walls of the taak outlined in the darkness. And in the center, I could see the lights of Beyl House.

No other lights at all.

Because the fleshmages did not have lives. Did not have reason to see if Skirmig didn't want to see through their eyes.

No other sight had so chilled me as Beyltaak dark. No other sight had so clearly shown me the true shape and nature of the world that Skirmig was creating. Or how alone he was in the midst of his own creations.

In that instant, at last, finally, I understood why he needed me. Why when I was not there, he took my sister and pretended she was me.

He had to have someone outside of what he had made to see and understand the thing he had created. He had to have someone else who needed light—someone who was not his own reflection. Someone who could fear him.

He needed that fear. He needed to cause hurt, and like a man admiring himself in the cascade of reflections cast by angled mirrors, he needed to be able to watch himself doing that hurting, feeding the pain through all of his fleshmages and making the horror and the anguish and the shame stronger by means of endless repetition.

And he needed someone strong—strong enough to survive everything he had in mind for a very long time indeed. Strong enough to fight him, because he found the fight exciting.

But not strong enough to win.

That was the future he had planned for me. I was to be his captured warrior, his durable torture-toy for as long as he could keep me alive, the sole source of the agony and humiliation and terror with which he entertained himself and fed his fleshmages. I guessed that, powerful as he was, I would live a very long time.

So if I died . . . hell. And if I lived but Gair and I failed to kill Skirmig . . . hell again.

Yet how could we hope to succeed?

I turned away from Beyltaak, shaken, and moved into Gair's waiting arms. "I love you."

"I know. I love you, too."

"I'm afraid."

"You'd be a fool if you weren't."

We held each other, me with my face buried in the curve of his neck, him with one arm around me and one hand stroking my hair. I wanted never to move. Never to leave that embrace, that moment when I knew I truly loved and was truly loved in return, when we had each other and were safe and warm and touching. I wanted that to be my forever—it could have been as much a heaven to me as Jostfar's meadows where the horses ran free and the flowers grew tall.

I had my heaven in Gair, and when I lost him, whenever that might be, in that instant would my heaven end.

Forever, Gair had said. Body and soul.

I didn't say anything out loud, but I prayed to Jostfar then, and through Ethebet, *Let death not be our parting. Let us share this life and whatever comes after.*

I heard Gair sigh, and I knew what he was about to say, what he *had* to say. Just as I knew I didn't want to hear it.

But I forced myself to stand straight, to pull out of his embrace, to look in his eyes and not let any tears fall from mine.

"Time," I said before he could beat me to it.

"Time," he agreed.

We'd brought more with us than we needed. Food, a multitude of weapons, bedrolls. We were used to thinking of a distance such as that between Chaavtaak and Beyltaak as one that could be traversed only in days, not in an hour. The running towers could have changed the world, the way wars were fought, and beyond that, the way men lived in peacetime. They could have been wondrous . . . if their cost had not been higher than their makers could bear.

Before we set out through the tunnels, I would destroy the last one. And then the only thing that would tie me in that cold, dark middle place between life and Jostfar's meadows would be the silver dancer.

Gair and I crouched over the weapons.

"We don't know how to fight him," I said.

"We fight him with everything you have and everything I have. Just as we've been fighting him."

"We've been losing."

"Well, those were battles. This is the war."

"So we can lose the battles and win the war?"

He laughed a little. "We have to win *this* battle. Somehow."

"If we could win it by losing, we'd be golden."

Gair grew very still. He turned slowly to stare at me. His eyes measured, calculated. The look unnerved me just a little. I loved him. He loved me. But that moment when he studied me the way I'd study a horse I thought I might want to buy gave my heart a little skitter.

Then he leaned over and kissed me. "Have faith. You have Jostfar and Ethebet behind you, and me beside you. Stay ready, don't despair, and we'll be fine."

We took swords and daggers. Gair insisted that the weapons were optional—that we were counting on stealth and my magic. But we took them anyway. I destroyed the last running tower, feeling our safe exit ripping itself into nothing beneath my fingertips. I would never bind my soul to metal again; for better or for worse, we were committed to our path.

We ran through the tunnels, avoiding Skirmig's guards. The *Don't see me* spell worked, and though we were navigating by our fingertips because of the darkness, our ears warned us of danger. Even fleshmages have to breathe, and they were not particularly stealthy. They didn't talk. They didn't move around, either. But we had a better warning even than the sound of their breathing. I have to guess that when Skirmig was sure he had everyone in Beyltaak under his control, he stopped worrying about whether his fleshmages bathed regularly or not. Because most of the time we could smell them long before we could see them.

We had to traverse through at least two long furlongs of tunnels to get to the core of Beyltaak, sometimes at a good steady jog but more often at a creep. The waiting fleshmages got more plentiful as we got closer to our target.

The darkness got to me. The walls wore on my fingertips, and I had the constant feeling that something could see me that I could not see. Gair's hand in mine became my only link to the world beyond the awful unending blackness of the tunnels, darkness that we dared to break only in rare instances to check signs.

The feeling of being watched grew stronger, and the voice in my mind, quiet for some time, started talking again.

Do you really trust him? it asked. *You love him, but as you want to save the Tonks, so he wants to save the Eastils. Your people are enemies—have been for hundreds of years. And he is as loyal to his people as you are to yours. Why is he helping you . . . really?*

Doubt is a vile thing. It gnaws in invisible places, weakening from the inside out. I did not think the doubt was mine—Gair and I had saved each other's lives so often I could not see how I could not trust him. I suspected Skirmig's touch in the whispers, in the tightness in my throat.

And yet, I could not be sure. After all this time, after all my suspicions, I did not know if Skirmig could do that, if he could push doubts into my head, or if all of them, all along, had come from me. I wanted to believe that Skirmig was trying to manipulate me, trying to trick me into doubting Gair and betraying him somehow. I wanted to think that my love would brook no doubt. But I didn't know.

The doubts might be my own.

They had no basis. I knew that. But if they were coming from me, I didn't like what that said about me.

My fingers dragged across yet another marker in the tunnels, and we stopped, and I cast the single speck of light that would make the marker readable for an instant.

It had the Beyl marks on it. We were close.

Somewhere in one of the nest of tunnels that ran beneath Beyl House, there would be one well-hidden entrance, barred and locked and warded. That entrance would lead to the concubine chambers.

Gair gave my hand a squeeze, and I knelt on the tunnel floor and dared one last time to cast the map spell, focusing it on finding blocked passages and places guarded by magic. I had to use the Hagedwar to cast the spell, and I knew doing so might give Skirmig more information about us than we wanted him to have. We might end up racing him to get to my sister first. But I did not see any other way for us to do what we needed to do.

The map this time did not light up; even with the *Don't see me* spell we were not confident that we would be able to remain unnoticed if we were casting light. Instead, the spell tugged at us like tiny hands, pulling at skin and clothing and hair, drawing us forward, taking us around obstacles, pulling us both past steady breathing and warm places in the cool air and ripe stinks that overrode the damp, fungal odor of the tunnels.

We traveled on faith. By that time, I didn't have much else left. I could not say what Gair was thinking, but he clung tightly to my hand as we inched forward.

We walked into a wooden wall. For me, it was literally; I took one step too many and my face hit wood and I stopped.

Gair was right behind me, but his reflexes were good. He missed hitting the wall, which meant only one soft thud disturbed the near-perfect silence of the tunnels, not two.

One, however, was all it took. Fleshmage guards started moving toward us from a number of directions.

Gair let go of my hand and I heard the faint metal-on-leather hiss as he drew his sword.

I rested my hands against the wood wall, trusting that this was the place, and hating to use the Hagedwar that was my only solution, my only way through. I willed the wood out of the way, and felt the buzzing beneath my fingertips that would have looked like a swarm of gnats if only I could have seen it.

Beneath the wood lay a metal door. Barred, locked, padlocked.

I willed my way through that, too. Smelled stale air blow toward me. Grabbed Gair and dragged him into the darkness.

And because the fleshmages were after us, I willed the wooden wall back into place, though I didn't waste time re-creating the door.

"If you've been using that magic, does that mean he knows we're here?"

"Maybe," I said, and cast a map that we could actually see, and traced the path up to the concubine chambers. "Nothing between us and her, if we hurry."

"That dot is her?"

"That dot is the one person in the chambers. No way of knowing if it's her, but if we suddenly see two people in there, we can be pretty sure one of them is her, and the other is him."

We ran through the narrow, exitless corridor, and I could feel how easy it would be for Skirmig to trap us in it. Not to keep us, perhaps, but to slow us down. We kept expecting him to . . . do things.

He didn't. He tried nothing that would keep us from getting to Nedris.

"This isn't good," Gair said as we ran. "He had to know we'd go for her when we came. This corridor should have been littered with traps. That he isn't trying to keep us from getting to her only means we're going where he wants us to go."

"I know that," I said. "But what are we supposed to do? Not rescue her?"

"We're doing what we have to do. But . . ." He stopped.

I stopped, too. I waited for him to say something else, but he didn't. "But what?"

"No," he said. "Doesn't matter. We'll do this. Either we'll win or else we'll lose. No sense chewing the what-ifs."

I turned and put a hand on his shoulder. I couldn't see him—by Jostfar, I was heartily sick of the dark. I needed to touch him to try to convey my seriousness. "If you've thought of something I haven't, you need to tell me."

"No," he said. "I don't. I need to let both of us focus on our missions. I have doubts and worries. You do, too. But they don't change what we have to do, whom we have to fight, what's at stake. They don't change anything. So I need to keep them to myself and we need to hurry."

He started off again, and I lagged for only an instant, and quickly caught up with him. And I thought, Missions? Getting my sister, killing Skirmig. One mission to my way of thinking—and yet he had said "missions," and all I had thought when that word came out of his mouth was, *He's Eastil, I'm Tonk. Of course we have separate missions.*

And then I hated myself for being so vile that I could think such a thing. That I could betray his life and his trust with such a thought. He said he had doubts. Were they doubts that concerned me? I wanted him to confide in me. I wanted us to have the same doubts, and for none of them to concern each other.

We came to heavy metal doors. Barred on the other side, of course, and on this side as well. So no one could get in, so no one could get out. The bars were bolted into place.

"He wasn't so incautious after all," Gair said.

I laid a hand on the doors. Looked at them through the lens of the Hagedwar. "Yes, he was." I reached into the doors with my will, and they began to dissolve into nothing. "He put no guard against magic upon them at all."

It was too easy. All of it—getting past the fleshmages below, running through the secret passage, removing the door that stood between us and the concubine chambers—it had been nerve-racking, but only because I'd kept expecting Skirmig to do any of the things that he could do. Falling darts. Falling stones. Pits and fire. Not because we'd had to fight real obstacles.

Before us lay a maze of rooms, but we had a map, and the dot of light that represented Nedris waited three doors away from us, all alone. No one waited with her. No one waited near her. Not a guard, not a fleshmage, not Skirmig. The three of us had the dozen connected rooms all to ourselves.

"We could just yell for her, tell her to get out here and hurry up about it," I said.

"With what he's put her through, would you go running to a call like that?"

I considered it only an instant. "No."

"I'm concerned that she hasn't moved this whole time," Gair said.

I realized that he was right. The dot of light that represented her on the map had been fixed the whole time we'd been in the Beyl House passageway. It wouldn't have been there at all had she been dead. But it was morning, and had been for a while. Perhaps she was asleep yet.

But perhaps not.

"He might have her in a cage. He has probably placed a trap between us and her," he said. "We open a door, or step on a trigger, and set off whatever it is the bastard has set. He knows we're coming. He simply cannot tell when."

I shook my head. "The map would have showed me any physical traps he'd laid."

"It would have? Why?"

"Because when I created it, that was part of what I created it to do."

"Then why isn't she moving?"

"That I don't know."

"He cannot have intended to let us walk out of here with her."

I did not know what to think. I'd expected us to have to fight most of the way to Nedris, not to just run up to her. "He knows we'll be coming for him. Perhaps she simply isn't a factor in . . . whatever he plans."

Gair was scanning the sunlit anteroom in which we found ourselves, looking at everything with narrowed eyes, crouching to peer under the few furnishings and leaning as far over as he dared without touching anything to look behind the tapestries. "He's a bastard, Talyn . . . but he's not a fool. Your sister is the perfect bait. He has a thousand ways to use her against you. We just haven't figured out which one he's chosen yet."

My stomach knotted. "Oh, Jostfar. He's turned her into a fleshmage."

He studied me. "That would at least explain why she's been so still. If that's what he's done, Talyn, we can fix it. We can still save her. Don't panic."

"He knows we're coming for her. And that we know he's protected her from the fleshmages. So he thinks we'll . . . trust her." My hands knotted into fists.

"He doesn't need her anymore. You're on the way. And all he wants is you."

"We shouldn't go to her, then. We should find him."

Gair sighed. "I was hoping he would come to us. I'm thinking he is not going to be the easiest man to find."

And that was true. When we'd made our plans, we'd made them thinking that Skirmig would try to stop us from rescuing Nedris. I'd not considered that he would infect her with fleshmagery in preparation for our coming. I should have.

"I don't like playing this the way he wants," Gair said. "But I think we should go to Nedris. We may not have a second chance to rescue her."

I had to agree with that.

We were still careful moving through the next two rooms, but there were no traps. We walked up to the ornate double doors behind which Nedris waited, and looked at each other, and Gair and I drew daggers. If she was a fleshmage, things were going to get worse before they got better.

My mouth was dry. My heart was thumping.

"Stay close," Gair said.

We kicked open the door.

The room was weirdly dark except for a light that poured down from the ceiling to center on an altar upon which Nedris was chained. She was naked, and I could see that Skirmig had been working on her for quite some time. His style was unmistakable. She was gagged, but she could see, and her eyes, when she turned her head to stare at us, were wild with fear.

"Oh, Jostfar," I whispered. I started for her, and Gair's hand shot out and dragged me back.

"Why is the rest of the room dark?" he asked.

"The light comes from a magical source. The spell keeps it focused on Nedris and keeps it from illuminating anything else. What does it matter?"

"Why did he do it?"

"For shock value?"

"I don't think so. Cast a light around the rest of the room."

I did.

And found Skirmig standing just behind the altar and holding a dagger, which he moved forward to press against Nedris's throat. Against the walls stood perhaps forty soldiers, all well armed, all staring at us, expressionless.

Skirmig smiled at me with the smile I had once found beautiful—until I discovered the monster that lay behind its disarming charm. "That little hiding spell of yours is quite good, isn't it? I finally figured out how to cast it, though I cannot yet make my own silver dancer." Neither Gair nor I said anything. I was stunned. But our lack of response didn't seem to bother Skirmig. "Welcome home, beloved," he said. "Your sister was a bore. I've missed you terribly."

There we were. The doors slammed behind us, and outside the doors, I heard other doors slamming.

"I made it as easy for you as I could . . . without being too obvious about it, of course." Skirmig sighed and nodded at the soldiers, who still stood along all the walls. "They don't get impatient, of course. But I do."

My throat had closed up. My knees went weak, my hands trembled, and the dagger fell from my fingers. I hadn't realized how very afraid of Skirmig I was until we were in the same room again, until I heard his voice and saw his smile and all the memories were not just memories anymore—they were all real. All happening again. I froze. I knew I had planned to fight him. I had planned to attack. There had been magic I was going to do—that I could do. Something to disable the soldiers all around us, surely; something to stay Skirmig's hand so that he could not hurt my sister anymore.

But I was lost in my fear.

And Skirmig knew it. I could see his triumph in his eyes. He grinned. "So I'll just get rid of that baggage you've been dragging along with you all this time. And then you and I can be together again."

He turned his gaze on Gair, and the smile died. "I should have killed you in the carriage that first day. Or left you in the cell. What a nuisance you've turned out to be."

"I'm only just getting started," Gair said, his voice rough and hard. He yanked me in front of him, locked an arm around me, and jammed his dagger to my throat. I felt it cut me, felt swift, sharp pain, and I cried out as warmth and wetness dripped down the side of my neck. Skirmig's eyes went huge with disbelief.

"You can't think I . . ." Skirmig faltered. "You can't think I take this threat of yours seriously. You love her."

Gair's laugh cut deeper than the knife by far. "No. She loves me. She has a knack for trusting the wrong men, doesn't she?" Gravel-voiced, he snarled, "I value her because you value her, and because you are going to give me what I want in exchange for her, or I am going to gut her like a fish and watch you watch all your sick little fantasies die a quick, ugly death."

"But you *love* her," Skirmig said again. "I know you love her."

"I *love* the Republic of Hyre. I love my land and my people. I've been fighting for their triumph since I was a boy—have been risking my life for my cause since I was old enough to take up arms against my people's enemy. And this"—he shook me—"this foolish girl is a powerful weapon for her people. And my enemy. She forgot that somewhere along the way." He laughed a little. "But I never did."

My world fell to pieces in that moment.

If I had any consolation at all, it was that Skirmig looked even more stunned than I was.

"She has the power to turn you into cinders," Skirmig said.

Gair laughed. "She doesn't. And neither do you. She was afraid that you might control her again, so she put a shield around me that she cannot remove without destroying herself. You can't touch it without utterly destroying her."

"And if you kill her, the shield will fall."

"It will," Gair agreed. "But you're the one who wants her to live. She made it possible for me to get exactly what I want and walk out of here, protected from both you and her for the rest of my life. No vengeance from either of you. Sweet of her, wasn't it?"

Skirmig looked at Gair, and then at me, and then back at Gair. "You're . . . vile," he said, but he didn't say it with the loathing and the hatred that those words deserved. Instead, he sounded almost admiring.

"You would know," Gair said. I felt him nod at Nedris. "Put that thing out of its misery, why don't you? Surely you've hurt it enough by now, and I don't like the way it's looking at me. And then you and I and your favorite plaything are going to walk out to a room where we aren't surrounded by soldiers, and we're going to make our exchange."

I shrieked, "No!"

Skirmig glanced down at Nedris, and for one horrible moment I knew he was going to kill her right then. He'd planned to—I could see it in his eyes. But his voice turned shrill with annoyance and he glared at Gair. "You haven't any refinement at all, have you? No sense of style, no idea of how to get the most out of your . . . resources. Killing her—that's what *you* would do. *I'll* save her for later. I can think of a few interesting games yet to play with her and her sister."

Gair's arm tightened around my chest, knocking the breath from me. "Your choice, then. But your people are going to let me out of this room with Talyn, and they're going to stay here while you and I talk in the next room. Either we both get what we want, Skirmig, or neither of us does."

Skirmig walked around the altar that held Nedris, and came toward us.

"I don't think I believe your story about you being proof against my magic," he said. Lightning slammed down from the ceiling and poured around us and shot into some of the soldiers standing along the walls. They crackled and crumbled to the ground. The others didn't even twitch. Fleshmages, all of them.

"Not worth my time to lie," Gair said softly as Skirmig looked furiously at the dead soldiers. "Not worth yours to play games with me." He jammed a knuckle from his free hand into my ribs, and at the same time tightened his grip on my neck. The sudden sharp pain in my ribs got a whimper out of me. At the same instant, I felt the trickle of blood down my neck speed up.

But Gair hadn't cut me a second time.

I closed my eyes to avoid letting my expression give anything away, because I suddenly realized that the blood running down my neck was his.

Trust. Doubt. Love.

Either Gair had been lying to me all along, and I was twice the fool I'd thought I was. Or he was lying right then, and Skirmig was walking into Gair's trap.

Did I love Gair? Yes.

Did he love me? I thought so. I'd believed so; I'd believed it so much that I had forsaken my own people to swear myself to him as his wife with a bond that offered no out except death.

Did I trust him? That was a harder question, and the last few minutes hadn't made the answer any easier. He had fought for me in my dreams, but dreams are only dreams, and in the end we can never prove to ourselves that they hold the truth within them, or if they hold only the lies with which we would deceive ourselves. He had fought for me in reality, too. Yet I could make the case that he had done so because only I could break the curse of fleshmagery and restore his people's freedom, and not out of any love for me.

Did I trust him?

He was Eastil. He was my people's enemy, had been captured trying to destroy much of the governing body of the Confederacy, had spent most of his life in the pursuit of the Tonks' downfall.

I could list reasons not to trust him that would convince his own mother.

And yet.

He had proven himself over and over again a man of honor—and though honor was something Skirmig could not comprehend, because it was alien to him, it was something that I understood. We are not what we say, but what we do. In his every action since I had taken Gair into my home, he had lived by his word, and his actions had proven him time and again my sturdy champion. My sword.

If I had dreamed Ethebet, if I had dreamed the woman in

white, if in the moments of my dying I had dreamed the hell that I had created for myself between earth and Jostfar's fair fields, I had not dreamed that Gair had fought for me and with me, that he had protected me, that he had been kind to me. That in his every action, he had been a man of honor.

"I want what I want," Gair said, "and I want it now."

I opened my eyes. I trusted him, and most of the fear drained out of me. Not just the fear I'd felt of Gair, but the fear of Skirmig that had paralyzed me. Gair was up to something. He had thought of a way that we might yet beat Skirmig. He'd already gotten the bastard away from my sister. He'd managed to get Skirmig to kill a good half of the soldiers with which he'd surrounded us. I needed to look afraid so that Skirmig wouldn't realize he was stepping into a trap. But I needed to be ready, to trust that I would understand what Gair was doing when the time came for us to fight.

Gair took a step back, dragging me with him.

Skirmig took a step forward, and another, and he looked truly afraid. "Don't kill her," he said. "She's . . . she's to be my queen. If what you want is within my power, you can have it." He reached out a hand toward me, and Gair yanked me back and I shrieked and felt fresh gouts of hot blood coursing down my neck. Gair grunted a little—he'd hurt himself badly that time. I would have healed his hand, but I dared not use any magic that would betray Gair's trap, or my own complicity.

"I know how this fleshmagery of yours works, Skirmig," Gair said, and dragged me back another step. "Have your people open the doors behind me now." Skirmig stared at the blood pouring down my neck, and didn't say anything, but I heard the doors open. "Good," Gair said. "Now have your soldiers back off, clear to the other side of this room. If so much as one of their fingers touches me, she dies, and all your future plans for her magic die, and she and I and maybe you can go to merry hell together. So don't try to be clever."

Skirmig nodded, mute, following Gair's retreat with measured steps.

"You have some trinket she created and gave to you. You use that to connect to a . . . a sort of house of magic that she built inside herself. You're using her magic to power your world. Is that correct?"

"Yes."

"Fine. I want you to pull that thing out, and make it set my people free."

Something shifty flickered in Skirmig's eyes. "Your people. In the Eastil Republic."

"Those are the only people I have."

Skirmig laughed a little. "Have you considered how you'll verify that I've done what you ask?"

We were out of the altar room, standing in a sort of gathering room, its fine old Tonk furniture perverted by the addition of some of Skirmig's devices. I'd not let myself look at those devices on the way in, nor had I let myself think about what they meant.

I didn't let my attention drift this time, either. The important information I could get from what I could see was that, at least in my limited range of vision, Skirmig had no soldiers waiting.

"I've considered that if you want your toy back, you'll figure out a way to prove to me that you've done what I want you to do. To my satisfaction. Proof is your problem, Skirmig, not mine."

"You would have made a good diplomat," Skirmig said.

"Don't insult me again, and be quick. She's already losing blood. As it is, you'll have to hurry if you want to save her. I have pressure on the cut now, but I think I sliced a bit too deep."

Skirmig sighed and stared at me. "This, my beloved, is why you should never have left me. Your punishment for causing me this problem is going to be . . . severe."

"Worry about her future later. Right now, free my people."

Skirmig reached beneath the collar of his elegant black shirt and pulled out the dancer. He took another step closer. He was only a few short steps away from us now, and I saw the hand that was not holding the dancer sliding toward his sword.

I felt Gair's muscles bunch. It was the only warning I got. He shoved me into Skirmig, hard, and I heard Gair's sword snick out of its sheath as I fell into Skirmig's arms, and Skirmig staggered back a half step.

And my hand wrapped around the dancer.

And I willed her out of existence, pouring everything within me into the act of dissolving her. She purred and buzzed beneath my fingers, getting smaller, thinner, and then she was nothing, and the last strand that had stretched me thin snapped back into place; my soul coiled whole and strong within me once again. I had only the blink of an eye to appreciate my wholeness, though, because within me, the Hagedwar closed for the first time since I'd created the dancer.

And a massive band of power, vaster than any sane man would dare try to control, stretched tight and then tighter, and then it snapped with a flash inside me that threw me to my knees. I heard Skirmig scream—a horrible anguished animal noise that made my flesh crawl. I stared up at him, saw him start to burn from within as that vast energy whipped into him the way a snapped rope would whip back toward the post that anchored it. Skirmig's flesh began to bulge, to lump, to billow and glow and stretch, and his keening grew sharper, higher, more terrible. In the altar room, I heard other cries of pain, but they were nothing like the slaughterhouse wail that poured from Skirmig's throat.

The light got yellower, brighter, then whiter, and with a sudden blinding flash it ripped him into pieces so small they felt like a sandstorm blast against my skin.

My head ached, and the screaming in the other room got louder, and I thought, oh, Jostfar, I've killed them all.

My little brother Rik's sweet smile was in my mind as I slammed face-first into the floor and oblivion claimed me.

Gair, who had been keeping pressure on that sliced artery in his wrist, dove toward Talyn as she crashed to the floor, shouting, "Talyn!" and almost getting to her in time. But not quite. Her face hit the woven rug nose first, and he winced—when he turned her face toward him, her nose and mouth were bleeding profusely, but at least she was alive, which was fine. He ripped his shirt off and stood on it and with his good hand tore a sleeve free, and used that as a tourniquet. Because Skirmig was gone, the silver dancer was gone, but the sounds of hell were all around the two of them, and hell was not going to claim his Talyn.

Gair drew his sword and crouched over her, and watched the door from which enemies were going to pour forth in just a moment, or perhaps the pieces of enemies.

Screaming filled the air; it poured out from the altar room, and up from the streets below, and from the rooms outside the concubine chambers. Gair had never heard anything like it, and he could not help but see the next moments in his mind's eye, when everyone he had ever known, when everyone Talyn had ever known, blew apart from the inside out and the screaming stopped and Hyre lay empty, save for a few taaks and a handful of nomadic clans.

Gair had reached the end of everything as he had known it, and as no one burst through the doors—telling him all the rest of them were dying, too—he knelt and stroked Talyn's hair and wept, unashamed, for the mother and sister he would never again see, for the friends who would die hideous, ignominious deaths. He wept for his home, for his people, for her people, for the stupidity of the Tonks and the Eastils that they had failed to find their common ground in time to save everyone they loved from the greater enemy. Rage swept over him, and the fingernails of his good hand dug into his palm until it bled, and he wept for the sacrifice of three hundred years to stubbornness and foolish pride and avarice and whatever else had kept them apart, for three hundred years of Tonks and Eastils failing to understand that they held more in common than they had differences. That had they stood together, they could have withstood any enemy.

It all lay before him, so clear, so obvious. Hindsight had a hawk's eyes, didn't it?

He took deep, shuddering breaths, and looked down at Talyn. She was stirring.

"Talyn? Can you hear me?"

She groaned and opened her eyes and looked up at him. "Oh, Jostfar, my nose . . ." She sat up, clutching her nose. Then she looked around and the color drained from her face, and he grabbed her, fearing she would faint again. But she said, "Your hand. It's still hurt."

"I stanched the bleeding as best I could," he told her, and held out the arm. The hand was deathly white, the nail beds almost gray, and the rag he'd knotted around the wrist was blood-soaked in spite of how tightly he'd tied it.

He felt light-headed, too, he realized. He'd lost a good deal of blood.

"Give me," she said, and held out her hand. After an instant she ripped off his tourniquet, and life and color flowed back into his fingers as the darkness swarmed over and around and through them, her magic closing the hole he'd sliced in his palm, and the second one where the blade had slipped and slashed deep into his wrist.

She touched the places where the cuts had been, where unblemished skin replaced the gashes, with no sign that he'd ever been injured.

"No scar?"

"We both have enough of those."

She reached up and kissed him, and he could have lost himself in that kiss and wished the world away.

But then she broke it off and looked toward the closed doors behind which her sister was chained.

"The screaming," she whispered. "It's stopped. They're all dead and we killed them. We couldn't save them after all." Tears started down her cheeks.

He hadn't heard the end. He'd been too lost in his grief to notice when the screaming stopped. He hadn't seen any flashes of light, hadn't felt anything that would suggest explosions.

Gair frowned and leaned toward the altar room. Nedris was in there of course, and now that he listened, he thought he could hear her trying to cry out—the gag would be hindering that. They needed to get her out of there, poor girl, and find her some clothes. But . . . what else was he hearing? He could not attribute all the noises he thought he was hearing in there to Nedris.

He looked at Talyn, who was also staring toward the closed double doors. He stood and reached down and pulled her to her feet. Clutching each other's hands like they were keeping each other from falling off a cliff, they walked together to the doorway.

I didn't know what to expect as we opened the doors to go back into the altar room. Something terrible, certainly. Bodies and bits of bodies. A sea of blood. A nightmare.

Neither Gair nor I said anything about it, but we knew that whatever lay behind those doors also lay behind every other door in the Confederacy, every other door in the Republic. Our future and the future of our two peoples lay—in miniature—behind that door. We didn't let go of each other's hands. I don't know if Gair was breathing right then, but I know for certain that I wasn't. I didn't dare. I heard . . . shuffling? Little odd thumps? Certainly the sound of my sister rattling the chains that bound her to the altar. But what else? Did my imagination conjure noise out of deathly silence? Or did I hear real noise?

Clinging to each other, we opened the doors together, Gair and I, and a bit of light from the outer room bled into the windowless altar room. Skirmig's magic no longer illuminated my sister on the altar, but it no longer hid everything else in absolute darkness, either.

Around the walls, the soldiers curled into balls, or clutched their heads and rocked back and forth, or sat with their faces buried in their hands. Most wore their full armor. A handful had shed helmets, the better to grip their skulls as if they feared they might fly off. Some of them looked up as we stepped into the room, but most seemed far too lost in private anguish to notice us.

Still, they were alive, and my heart took a leap upward. If those soldiers were not dead, then I could not think that everyone else would be dead. Rik might yet live. Ma and Da. My other sibs. Gair's family. Our comrades in arms. Our friends.

The men on the floor gave no impression that their minds had been shattered by what had happened. Their eyes were not vacant—only full of pain. But they got stronger as I watched them—a few who had been rolled knees-to-belly unrolled, and one who was further toward recovery than the man beside him reached out and put a hand on the sufferer's shoulder in a silent gesture of comfort.

Of those who looked our way, none tried to stop us or even move toward us.

One man began muttering as he rocked back and forth, but it was in the Ba'afeegash tongue—I couldn't make out a word of what he was saying.

These, then, were actual Ba'afeegash soldiers. Not my friends and neighbors hidden behind helmets and armor. I wondered if I should kill them all—but Skirmig was dead, and without him, the Ba'afeegash were nothing but mercenaries. The sons of distant mothers—for hire, without work, and a long way from home. If any moved to hurt us, I would use the Hagedwar magic to destroy them. But if they did not, I thought we had seen enough of death for a time.

So I stayed my hand, and instead went to Nedris, and cut the gag and used the Hagedwar magic to dissolve the chains that bound her, and to spin good Tonk clothes out of the elements and air, and I helped her dress while Gair looked away, while the men on the floor, in a show of decency, looked away. Some of them had glanced at her, and with tears filling their eyes, had turned their faces to the wall.

These men were not like Skirmig, then.

Nedris could stand, though she was weak. I healed her injuries as best I could, and while I was about it, healed my nose, which had been feeling like someone had strapped a smashed melon to my face and kept hitting it with a hammer. I erased the scars on my skin that I had kept to remind myself what my enemy had done to me. He was dead, and from that point on, the only person who could hurt me with what he had done was me.

I could do nothing to heal Nedris's mind—time might help that, or it might not. I had few words of comfort for her that I could have faith in; I was not yet whole, and I did not know if I would ever be free of the scars my soul bore from Skirmig. How could I presume that *she* would be well someday, when I could not even guess that for myself?

I wanted out of Beyl House. Quickly. I wanted to find the rest of my family if I could, if they still lived. I wanted to know what was left of my world. I started toward the door, and Gair moved when I did, but Nedris hung back.

"You came for me," she said. "You beat him. He told me when you came he was going to kill me. He . . . promised. All I wanted was to die. But then he didn't keep his promise." She turned and looked doubtfully at Gair. "You . . . told him to kill me, just as he was going to anyway. That stopped him. Why did you say . . . anything?"

Gair looked hard at Nedris, judging her, weighing his response. He sighed. "I wanted you to live. Your sister wanted you to live. And I know men. Their eyes. Their faces. I've fought for my life, have seen my death in my enemy's eyes more than once. I know the look. He was going to kill you right then. But he was a stubborn bastard, and as soon as I suggested that death would be a release for you, something you might want, he stopped himself."

"But if I was dead, I would have been safe from him. Safe from hurting. What if he finds his way back to me?"

"He's dead," Gair said. "I watched him die. It was bad, and he suffered for what he did, even if he didn't suffer enough—"

"Yes, he did," said one of the men on the floor. "You don't know, but we were there. *All* of us were there. Every chain that chained us to him broke at the same time. All our pain, all our hate, all our rage, it was in there with the chains. Half the chain whipped back on us, smashed us hard—but that half spread out among all his slaves. A little piece to each. No one shared his half. We hurt. I hurt so bad I wanted to die right then. But nobody in all the world has ever hurt like . . ." Words failed him, and he spat on the floor. "Like that *dog* hurt when he died." He tugged his helmet off and clutched his head. "Good, I say."

Nedris leaned against me, and I hugged her, and she started to cry. "I *wanted* him to kill me," she said softly. "How can I walk down the street ever again? How can I ever let anyone see my face? Everyone knows what he did to me. To you, too. Everyone saw it. Everyone *felt* it. They were all *there*."

"They didn't want to be there," I told her.

She pulled back and stared at me. "Some of them did. Some of them were glad to be there. They liked it. I could feel it."

"Them, I'll find and kill," Gair said with a quiet ferocity that made me shiver.

Nedris heard the truth behind that threat, too, and turned to me with frightened eyes. "Who *is* he?" she asked me.

"My husband. His name is Gair Farhallan." I sighed. "He's Eastil."

Her face wore disbelief and then dismay, and for a moment she was thinking about my problems rather than hers. "Eastil. And you . . . married him?"

"Ethebet ceremony. In Ethebet's temple in Chaavtaak."

"Oh, Jostfar! Ma and Da—if they're still alive—what will they say when they find out they got you back just in time to see you banished?"

I'd managed to forget about my eventual banishment in the midst of everything else. I'd been too frightened that I'd killed everyone I'd ever known, and then too worried about Nedris and Ma and Da and Rik and the rest of them, and I'd pushed my own future completely out of my mind.

It was back, though.

I took Gair's hand. "We have to find them. We have to tell them," I said, and he wrapped an arm around me, and I put my other arm around Nedris. "Come on. It's time for you to go home."

The taak smelled like death. We walked through the streets and saw men dragging the carcasses of horses out of barns into pastures to be burned. The horses . . . Skirmig had cared nothing for horses. Had been afraid of them. When he had the whole of Beyltaak clenched in his fist—and other taaks, too, I reminded myself, and most if not all of the Eastil Republic—he had prevented his slaves from tending to the horses.

And, trapped in stalls and barns, hundreds of them had died.

I had felt this in the short time that I had been lost in the greddscharf, and I had known it was not the worst of what he had done.

He hadn't liked babies, either, or small children. He had not permitted any care to be given to those too small to care for themselves.

I knew, then, the meaning of the weeping I heard behind some of the doors of neighbors' houses. There would be other fires soon. Pyres lit as grieving parents burned their hopes and dreams and lives and love. Ethebet had been right when she told me that this generation would be the last if Skirmig was not stopped.

Eyes watering, we made our way through the smoke and the stench of decay and the thick clots of flies and the sorrow, up the cobblestone streets of Beyltaak to my parents' house.

I prayed every step, and died a coward's death with every step, imagining the worst.

We walked faster as we got closer, and by the time we reached home Nedris and I were running—we burst through the front door screaming "Ma!" and "Da!" and sounding frantic as lambs pastured away from their mothers at weaning time.

Rik was holding Ma in a tight embrace. Both of them jumped at the noise we made, and Rik came racing to us shouting,

"Tally! Neddie!" He was stick-thin, bruised, beaten. His eyes were too big for his face. But he was alive, alive, alive. And Ma . . . she got to her feet with an old woman's caution, and I could see that her hands were shattered, that both her arms were broken. Fresh breaks. She'd been tortured. She could barely stand, and I gave Rik a final squeeze and ran to her and pulled her into my arms and put as much power as I could gather into healing her.

I took her pain into myself, and felt it, and I changed it. Made it go away, filled her with warmth and comfort, made her bones strong and whole again. When I backed away, she was well.

Rik ran back to her and wrapped his arms around her, and they rocked back and forth like that while she and I exchanged glances.

The rest of the house was silent.

"Ma, where is everyone else?"

"He wanted to hurt you, Tally. That monster wanted to destroy you. Toward the end, he started to be afraid of what he had done, because it got away from him and he couldn't control it. It was beyond him. He knew he might lose—but he wanted you to hurt even if he couldn't hurt you himself anymore."

I leaned against a wall, trying to hold on to the image of Skirmig ripped to pieces by the magic he had worked. I was trying to make it enough.

"He put me in a dungeon," she said. "Pulled me out of the greddscharf a few days ago and threw me in there and told me it was fitting. He came by and tortured me, but he didn't stay very long. I . . . knew . . . that I wasn't the only one. Sometimes he would come to me, and hold up his hand to show me the fresh blood on it, and he would just smile. I knew."

"But if you weren't in the greddscharf . . ."

"I don't know what he did to any of the rest of us. He left that for you to discover. Rik was in a box. That monster forced one of the fleshmages to put him in there—but Rik remembered my fight training."

"I kicked the box apart as soon as he was gone," Rik said, looking a little pleased with himself. "And then I came here and hid until Ma got here."

Gair said, "That bastard didn't suffer enough."

"He is dead then?" my mother asked.

Gair just nodded.

I had hoped that others of my brothers and sisters and cousins and aunts and uncles would start showing up, but we couldn't count on everyone Skirmig had locked away being found or released. It was just chance that a recently freed flesh-mage had heard Ma's cries and set her free. Gair and I pinned a note to the door, and left Nedris with Ma, and took Rik. And the three of us begged help from every living soul in Beyltaak, and we tore the taak apart.

In ones and twos we found my family, hidden away, hurt, sometimes near death. Gair was relentless, and proved to have a knack for thinking of possible hiding places the rest of us might have overlooked. On his own, he found two of my brothers and one of my sisters and three little nieces dumped in one cage together, left with a steady supply of water and a knife, in the hopes, I realized, that they would start killing and eating each other when they began to starve. Skirmig had found my horror of cannibalism particularly amusing.

My family owed Gair more than it would ever be able to repay just for finding them.

Da we found last of all, and we found him the worst hurt. Skirmig had put everything he had into breaking Da, and it took everything *I* could do to put my father back together again.

I wanted us to come through unscathed, but like others in Beyltaak, my brothers and sisters and cousins mourned lost babies, and I mourned with them.

We, too, would burn our dead and rebuild our taak and our lives, and find such comfort as we could from the living.

I kept the secret of my marriage to myself, Gair, and Nedris for four days. As best I could, I found old friends, wished them well, said my good-byes without ever saying good-bye in so many words.

I memorized the faces of those of my family who were near, and tried to recall those still absent. I tried to make those days as full as I could.

When we gathered at table on Jostfarday, we were a somber bunch crowded tightly together for comfort. I knew I would never hear any of my family laugh again, and would never see them get past their grief, would never even see them again after that day. I felt sick. I'd known this would be difficult if the day ever came; I could not have imagined, though, how difficult. When my family finished eating, and I quit moving food around on my plate, I rose and said, "This has waited as long as it can, but you need to know now."

The dread in their faces broke my heart.

"Gair and I are married," I said, and when they started to smile, I almost let it go, simply because I had not seen any of them smile in so long. But would it be easier to leave them all in a month, or in a year, knowing I could never come home again? No. The pain of it was already unbearable.

I held up my hand. "We married in Ethebet's temple in Chaavtaak, before Jostfar and Ethebet, with lifelong vows."

"That's wonderful, Tally," Da said, and started to stand.

I waved him back to his seat. "Gair is Eastil."

Their faces were an education. Confusion, disbelief, uncertainty, and then, at differing speeds, realization. And dismay.

"Eastil?" Ma said, and looked to Gair for confirmation. "You don't look Eastil. You don't sound Eastil."

"I'm Eastil," he said. "The cell the bastard threw you in was the cell I was in when I was a prisoner of war—the reason Skirmig put you in there was because he took me out of there at Talyn's request, and I later took Talyn away from him." He folded his hands together on the table. "I was in the Eastil Secret Forces." He looked at my da. "You stopped me and my men in Injtaak."

I saw the recognition flash in my father's eyes, and heard the despair in his voice as he asked, "Why, Talyn?"

"Because he is the man I want to spend the rest of my life with," I told him. "When she found you, Ma gave up her taak. I never understood how she could do that until I found him. I knew what the price would be when I married him. I knew, Da. And I *chose* him."

I had the man I loved—we were sworn to each other for the rest of our lives.

And I was to be banished from my taak and my family and my people, set apart from Tonk lands for the rest of my life, never to be mentioned again.

My older sisters wept and embraced me, and my younger sisters hugged me and wished me well, and my brothers, after some uncertainty, clasped hands with Gair and congratulated him, though they did not—could not—welcome him into the family. And my mother and father . . . left.

None of us noticed until in a pause in the general confusion looked around to say something to Ma and realized that she was not there, and looked to Da's place and found him gone as well.

None of us had seen them leave except for Rik. "They went outside," he said. "Out the front door."

Edrig ran to the front door and looked out. "They aren' there," he said.

We tried to guess where they had gone, but between the lot of us all talking at once, we could come up with not a single sensible guess.

The bells outside rang the hour of the Dog, and all of us rose and turned to the west and said, "Gitaada," to the setting sun and the front door opened and Ma and Da came back in, and with them the newly established Beyl, who had been Ratir av Damekiis, one of the taak's surviving veteran warriors, before our world fell apart.

He beckoned to me and to Gair, and we rose. My parents were grim-faced, and the only thing I could think was that they had decided to get the banishment over with quickly so that they did not have to think about the daughter they would never see again.

The five of us went into the workroom, and the new Beyl closed the door, and turned to face Gair and me with my parents behind flanking him on either side.

"You knew the price of your actions would be banishment when you married this man?" he said to me without preamble.

"I did."

"Yet you made vows before Jostfar and Ethebet. Were they temporary vows?"

"I swore to be faithful to him for the rest of my life."

"Not temporary, then, as judged by Jostfar's law." He turned to Gair. "And you—what vows did you make?"

"I swore before Jostfar and Ethebet to be faithful to Talyn through this life and all that might follow, forever after."

Three sets of eyebrows performed the identical comical upward charge; had the situation not been so awful, I would not have been able to keep myself from laughing.

But the situation was so awful.

"You're Eastil. Do you then consider the judgment of Jostfar and the guidance of Ethebet binding?"

"I do," Gair said.

He turned to my parents. "I cannot sever this union. Jostfar has joined them; I am but a man and cannot part them. So we are faced with your solution or none at all but banishment."

The new Beyl turned back to Gair. "There is not a one of us in this taak, nor are there many folk in all of Hyre on either side of the border, who do not know what you two did for us. When she became briefly one of the monster's greddscharf, our minds and hers became one. We saw everything you both did and risked and fought for to save us, and at the end when the two of you faced the monster himself and destroyed him, we saw all of that, too. We would be worthless, ungrateful bastards if, knowing you had saved all of Hyre and likely all the world as well—for it would have fallen to him—we banished you." He sighed. "Yet Jostfar's law is Jostfar's law, set down thousands of years before any of us were born. Jostfar's law is clear—if any Tonk marries any who is not Tonk, the couple and all their offspring are banished from Tonk lands, from taak and family, and the banished's name is erased from the records as if he or she had never been born." The new Beyl looked at the two of us. "I cannot change that, not even for you."

Which we had already known. So why were we standing in my father's workroom acting like this was a big surprise?

"I have some say over man's law, though," the Beyl said. "And men, not Jostfar, define who is and who is not Tonk. For the most part, our definition has been that any child of two Tonk parents is Tonk. But in special cases, we can . . . give the definition some bend. Gair, you have stated that you accept Jostfar's authority over you. Your actions have proven you willing to defend Tonk lands under Ethebet's guiding hand. You have done this taak and the Confederacy great service, for which all of us owe you our lives and our freedom, in equal part with what we owe Talyn here. I will, this instant, declare you Tonk, and a citizen of this taak, if you will relinquish your citizenship in the Eastil Republic."

Gair looked at me. "You were willing to give up everything for me. How can I not give up everything for you? For us?" He turned to my parents and Ratir—now Ratir Beyl—and said, "I

don't think there is an Eastil Republic anymore. The king, from
what I have heard, is dead, and with him, no doubt, the rest of
the royal family. I don't know that I relinquish anything that
still exists. Nevertheless, I relinquish my citizenship from
whatever new government arises in the Eastil lands."

My parents hugged each other. Gair turned to hug me. And
my many sibs, their ears no doubt to the door in the same manner with which we had ever kept abreast of family news when
we were small, poured into the room shouting and cheering,
and Jostfar as my witness, even laughing. And crying, too, of
course.

Gair and I had to catch up later.

We had our wonderful moments, Gair and I. And our miracles.
I had healed my scars . . . but Ethebet replaced what I could
never have healed, and graced us with a daughter, whom we
named Ethebetta Avrii, which means Ethebet's Gift. In such
fashion, Gair and I joined my family's Roster of grandbabes
and new horses.

A year later, we added a son. Havaad.

We greeted the start of each day and thanked it at day's end
at temple. I taught the new magic to the Ethebettans old and
new who volunteered to learn—Shielders and Senders, Communicators and civilians alike. Those who chose to follow Ethebet in these new days were plentiful. Among us, we created new
magical weapons and defenses where the old had fallen. Gair
and the other Tonk warriors trained a new generation of boys to
fight—to attack and to defend. We rebuilt out taak. We rebuilt
our temples. We healed as best we could. And life went on.

Yet at odd moments, I could see Gair looking east, and I
could not miss the pain in his eyes. He was teaching me Hyerti
because he said Hyerti had much better dirty words than Tonk,
and that I should know them—but that was not his true reason.
I knew he simply yearned to hear his own language spoken
from time to time. He was one of us, but part of him still lingered, aching, in the places and the people he'd left behind.

Then, one morning, as I watched Ethebetta balancing precar-
iously on the back of her first pony, riding in a little circle
around our pasture, and while Havaad lay in his basket beside

me, discovering his toes, a great carriage preceded by one contingent of riders in fine foreign garb, and followed by a second, clattered down the road and stopped before our home.

I did not hesitate. I gathered the children and ran them inside and tucked them into the safe room. Bade them be still. Checked the location of Gair's sword and saw that Gair had already taken it with him. I readied magic that would destroy every man in the foreign parade with one blow, then followed Gair to the front door to see what the strangers wanted.

Gair had already greeted them, and the man inside the carriage had stepped to the ground. All the riders had dismounted; they knelt facing Gair and the man he spoke with while their horses, ground-tied, stood patiently in neat rows in the street.

Gair and the lavishly dressed stranger—a skinny, pale-haired man with pimpled skin and no chin—walked toward the house. I watched them, a sick feeling in my gut. This was nothing good.

Gair introduced me to the stranger. "Talyn, this is Agbyrt Fairhaired, sole surviving male cousin of the queen of the Eastil Republic and First Envoy of the Realm. Agbyrt, my wife, Talyn Wyran av Tiirsha dryn Straad."

The Fairhaired waited for me to bow, but I just nodded. Tonks do not bow to Jostfar—by no means will we bow to mere men. I raised my left hand, and showed the mark of my clan on my palm, for so we greet foreigners in these days. "Agbyrt Fairhaired, if you come intending good, you may pass safely through these doors. If you honor your intent, you will live to pass through them twice."

He flushed red and glanced uncertainly at Gair, who offered no reassurance. "Do you come intending good?"

"I bring word from the King of the Republic of Hyre, our Liege and Swordbearer—"

Gair held up a hand. "*Your* king, but no longer mine. I've been made Tonk and have relinquished my Republic citizenship." In Hyerti, he added, "Be quick, man—if you intend good, say so before she roasts the lot of you where you stand."

The Fairhaired's face went deeper red, and for a moment he sputtered and murmured in Hyerti—but said nothing intelligible, at least not to me. Then he turned to face me, and bowed, and said, "I come intending good. I bring . . . brought . . . *bring* an offer of great honor to your husband."

"Then enter," I said, and let him pass within. He and Gair sat at table, and I put bread and cold water before them, and sliced cold roast, and got out pan and potatoes and bacon fat. I was finally learning my mother's art with a skillet.

While I cooked, I listened.

"My . . . *our* king has named you the Republic Permanent Envoy to the Tonks," the envoy said. "You're to be put in post for a salary of a thousand stadams a year."

"Stadams?"

"Our new gold standard," the Fairhaired said. "To celebrate the marriage of the king and queen, and the birth of the heir. Figuring in the local currency, a stadam is worth about . . ." He closed his eyes, and I could see his fingers and lips both moving. ". . . about ten gold rhengis. I think."

"Right." And I heard Gair laugh. "And I cannot be commanded to a post, for I'm no longer Eastil. Hell, man, I don't even know who your new king is. I've heard that you had one— nothing more. We here have had little time to worry about your goings on. You know this; you're rebuilding as well."

And the envoy's head bobbed up and down as if a puppeteer was yanking his string. "Precisely. We are. It is because both Republic and Confederacy are rebuilding that the king commands you to his service. He says we and the Tonks must work together because we cannot forget our common ground, or the threats that surround Hyre from the outside."

The envoy lowered his voice. "As for why he chose you, I cannot say. I don't know how the king knows you; I cannot even say how he became king. He's a foreigner, from one of those heathen tribes in the far north, and all we know is that he rescued the queen and her sisters. Freed them from captivity and certain death. She fell in love with him, so it's said, and they married quickly. But as to who he was before he broke down the cell doors and freed Her Majesty . . . well, there are rumors that he was some soldier of low rank. But those are only rumors."

I pulled the potatoes off the stove's surface and put them on the set-aside. I turned.

Gair stared at me.

I stared at him.

"Snow Grell?" Gair asked. "Snow Grell Warrior Born of the Hell Hill Woman?"

And the envoy nodded. "Then you do know him as well."

Gair looked at me. "I have to go talk to him."

"We'll go together," I said. Finished the potatoes. Considered how our people could do what needed to be done without Gair becoming Eastil again and me relinquishing being Tonk.

It turned out not to be such a difficult thing. Gair, after all, was Gair, and Tonks across the Confederacy remembered the role he had played in freeing them. Gair, our children, and I traveled east with the blessing of the Beyl, with Gair made the official Beyltaak envoy, but carrying with him the tacit approval of many of the Confederacy's taaks as well. He did not speak for all the Tonks—none but Jostfar could hope to do that. But he spoke for many.

And Snow Grell and his wife were glad to see us when we arrived. Snow Grell congratulated us on our marriage, and gifted us with two exquisite pedigreed Tand studs. We did not ask how he had acquired proscribed horses, nor did he offer to tell us.

We brought to him an alliance agreement, signed by all seven of the core taaks and two dozen of the minor taaks, offering aid and the sharing of resources across our borders in the event of outside attack, and offering the High Valleys and Whayre Harbor as shared ground to seal the deal. Since the Confederacy had claimed both of them as its own in the confusion following Skirmig's death, this was no small gift.

Gair also brought the offer of free trade between the taaks and the Republic. A handful of other offers beneficial to them and to us. Gair and I would be back and forth between Beyltaak and the Republic regularly in service of our alliance—and in his eyes I saw at last what I had been seeking there since he gave up his nation for mine.

Contentment. He would see his family again. Would share in the future of *his* land as well as mine. And because he was content, I could be content as well.

I cannot say I love the Republic, yet. Their ways are not ours, and I think many of their ways are foolish. But if we learned one thing from our ordeal with the Feegash, it is that we and the Eastils are more alike than different. We share a common ground that will let us be friends and allies in spite of our differences, and that will make us strong against those who would be our true enemies.

As Gair and I sat at the table with a king and queen, sipping ale and telling tales not fit for the ears of children—and it was well both theirs and ours were sleeping in trundles by our sides—Gair leaned back and laughed. "All men have their destinies, but I would not have thought that I was slogging through the muck and rain with the Republic's future king, or giving him orders."

All men have their destinies, as do all women. I have lived mine, served in war and peace, in fear and pain, and finally, in love. And I have asked Ethebet, if she has any more destiny to pour on my head, to let it be watching my daughter—now barely walking—learn to ride her pony well while her little brother chases after her. While I bring her other brothers and sisters into the world, as Jostfar and Ethebet see fit to gift us with them. While I teach the next generation of Magics how to fight. While I hold my husband's hand and help rebuild my taak and feel the seasons change around me in a peace earned on both sides—a good, clean peace between old enemies who have at last become allies, who have at last found in honor the common ground that eluded them for so long. Honor is a thing to be cherished and a worthy foundation for two peoples destined to share a future and a land.

I once wished that I might find a lover more faithful than guilt.

Destiny has given me something even better—a lover as faithful as honor, in this life and in whatever may follow.